KU-287-515

Fay Weldon was born in England, reared in New Zealand and educated in Scotland where she took a degree in Economics and Psychology. After a decade of odd jobs and hard times she started writing and now is well known as a novelist and screenwriter. Her novels include *Female Friends*, *The Shrapnel Academy*, *The Life and Loves of a She-devil* and *The Hearts and Lives of Men*. She is married with four children and divides her time between London and Somerset.

FAY WELDON

The Cloning of
Joanna May

FONTANA/Collins

First published in Great Britain by William Collins May 1989
A continental edition first issued in Fontana Paperbacks December 1989
This edition first issued in Fontana Paperbacks 1990

Printed and bound in Great Britain by
William Collins Sons & Co. Ltd, Glasgow

The Cloning of
Joanna May

1

This has been a year of strange events: some wonderful, some terrible.

In the autumn a great wind swept through my garden one night, and toppled two oaks, three maples and a chestnut tree, all top-heavy with wet leaves, rooted in sodden earth. Had the gale come a week later the leaves would have been gone and the trees no doubt survived: a week earlier and the earth would have been dry and the roots steadier, and all would have been well. As it was, the chestnut crashed through the conservatory and set off all the alarms, which joined with the sound of the gale to frighten me out of my wits, so that I would have telephoned Carl, my ex-husband, and forthwith begged for his forgiveness and the restoration of his protection, but as the chestnut had brought down the wires I couldn't. By the morning the wind had died down and I, Joanna May, was my proper self again, or thought I was.

I went out into the garden and studied the sorry fallen giants, their earthy boles pointing unnaturally skyward, their scuttling insect population stricken by sudden cold and light: and wondered if there was any way of yanking them to their feet again, resettling them in the soil, making good what had been spoiled, but Oliver, my gardener and lover, told me there was not. The truth had to be faced – the trees were finished. That was the end of them: now all they could do was slowly die. I found myself weeping and that was very strange, and wonderful.

And that evening when preparing for bed I looked into my mirror and saw the face of an old woman looking back at me, and that was very strange and terrible. I attended to this apparition at once with astringent masks, moisturizing creams and make-up, and by the time Oliver padded into my bedroom on bare young feet with earthy nails, I, Joanna May, looked almost myself again; but there is no avoiding this truth either – that the task of rehabilitation will get more difficult year by year. Most things get easier the more they are done – but not this. The passage of time makes fools of us all.

I said as much to Oliver and he replied, 'Well, you're sixty, and should be used to it by now,' which is easy enough to say when you are twenty-eight, as he was. Personally I had expected to live for ever, frozen in time at the age of, say, thirty. 'I don't mind how old you are,' said Oliver that night, 'let alone how old you look. It's you I love.'

'Love' I could understand, but what did he mean by this 'you'? Small children (so I'm told) start out by confusing 'me' with 'you'. Addressed so frequently as 'you', their clever little minds work out that this must be their name. 'You cold,' they say, shivering, as the wind blows through the window. 'Not you,' comes the response, 'me.' 'Me cold,' says the child, obligingly. Presently the little thing progresses to the gracious 'I

8

am cold.' But is the 'me', the 'I', really the same as that initial 'you' with which we all begin; the sudden bright consciousness of the self as something defined by others? Perhaps we did better in our initial belief, that the shivering cold is jointly experienced, something shared. I wonder.

Well, well, we will see. And as so often happens, the events that ensued ensured that I did see. Any enquiry, however primitive, this 'you' of ours manages to formulate in its mind as to the nature of reality, is met at once by such an eager response from that reality, such a convulsion of events, as to suggest that its only function is to provide us with examples, illustrations, of propositions that occur to the mind. Like Directory Enquiries, existing only to be asked, there to be consulted.

By the end of that year of strange events, I can tell you, when I looked in a mirror, I saw a face that would need a great deal more than a jar of wrinkle-cream and some exfoliator to bring it back to order. I was indeed old. Having children makes you old. It is the price we pay for immortality. God's last laugh, imposing this extra penalty on mankind before he flew off, leaving time the murderer behind, just waiting.

2

The great October wind frightened Jane Jarvis, aged thirty. It howled and raged outside her attic window, and quivered the panes until one of them actually cracked and shattered; then it swept in and around the room, bringing wet and cold with it. Rain spattered the TV screenplay she was sitting up late to read for Home Box-Office, and the wind somehow pried the sheets loose from their binder and swept them into the air and fluttered them round the room. Jane Jarvis thought the wind was alive: that it was some kind of vengeful spirit: that it whined and whinnied like the ghost of her aborted baby, long ago. She went into her bedroom and shut the door on the wind and the manuscript – not one she would recommend, in any case – and tried to sleep, but could not. She considered the temporary nature of all things, including her own life, and panicked, and rang her live-out lover Tom when she heard the clock strike three to say she'd changed her mind, he could be a live-in lover, they'd have a baby, but no one answered and by the morning prudence and courage had re-established themselves in her head and heart. She tacked strong polythene over the broken window; there would be a long wait for a glazier. The streets of London glittered with slivers of broken glass.

'You don't need me at all,' said Tom. 'You're self-sufficient.'

'I need you for some things,' she said, in the lingering sensuous voice that came so oddly from her rather thin, ladylike lips, 'of course I do. It's just I'd be mad to give all this up.' By which she meant freedom, independence, control over her own life.

'You're cold,' he said. 'Cold and over-educated and selfish.'

'Just rational,' she said, but Jane Jarvis was hurt. She took care not to show it. She had her pride. She did not want him; she did not want to lose him. She did not know what she wanted – except her career. Soon, if she played her cards right, she would be head of the London office of HBO.

'Where were you last night at three in the morning?' she asked.

'That has nothing to do with you,' he said. 'How can it?'

———•◦•———

The wind lobbed someone else's chimney through the neat suburban roof of the home of Julie Rainer, aged thirty, and spoiled its perfection in many ways, and broke the round fishbowl in which Samson the goldfish spent his timeless, circling days, and Samson died on the wet thick pile of the carpet. Julie was frightened and wept and in the morning rang the vet and asked him, in her lingering bedroom voice, why she brought death to so many small lives and he said they died in the glare of her perfection; and she

11

puzzled over the answer for days. When he rang her the following week and asked her out to dinner she accepted the invitation. She liked the smell of antiseptic on his fingernails and her husband was away.

———◆◆◆———

The wind not only frightened Gina Herriot and Gina's three children Ben, Sue and Anthony (ages twelve, nine and two) but crashed an oak tree through the bonnet of the car in which they were sleeping. None was hurt, but the frame was bent and the doors were jammed and had to be opened up by the iron claws of the emergency services, as if it were a can of beans and they the can-opener. The car was parked in the road outside the house where the Herriots lived. The children's father, Cliff Herriot, had been drinking, and it was sometimes easier, as Gina explained to the social worker in her gentle, sexy voice and using language of a violence which issued oddly from her rather thin, ladylike lips, to lock him in than lock him out. Gina seldom confided so much of the detail of her situation to anyone, having her pride, indeed too much of it, but the violence of the wind had frightened her, more than her husband ever did. Fortunately the report went missing, since it was made out at the time the contents of all Social Service file cards were being transferred to disc: or perhaps because fate has a propensity to behave in the same way to people of similar nature. Events fall out, this way or that, beyond our apparent control, yet in keeping with our expectations.

Gina was thirty, but born seven weeks prematurely, and this initial misfortune, this first hard, grating sharpening of the knives of fate, echoed like a sound, a siren song, through her life. 'Trust Gina', her neighbours said to each other, 'to be in the car when the tree fell,' but they didn't say it to her face. They feared her calm, quick look of disapproval: she did not like personal comments or appreciate advice. Her nose was broken but she remained chilly in her beauty: like Grace Kelly, they said, in that old film. 'Why doesn't she leave Cliff?' they asked. 'The brute!' But they didn't ask her to her face. Anyway, they knew the answer. She loved him.

As for Alice Morthampton, aged thirty, in the womb a week longer than her mother-apparent had expected, the great wind bypassed her: of course it did. Alice was smiled upon by different stars than were Jane, Julie and Gina. The storm cut a swathe through southern England, passing from east to west, taking in London on its way, but Alice was not in London at the time, but in Liverpool, where she was engaged in a photo session: smart clothes against demolished warehouses.

'Smile, damn you, smile!' Angus the photographer had implored her during the day, but Alice Morthampton would not, saying in her languid, croaking voice that she knew better than he; she had surely been employed to actively not-smile, since that was her speciality. She spent the night in bed with him, however. 'You don't care about me,' he complained.

'You only do this for the sake of your career.' And she sighed and said she wasn't sure why she did it, she certainly didn't enjoy it: her career would get on well enough without him, probably better – and as she felt his assault upon her, as it were, weaken and tremble within her at least had the decency to apologize for her habit of speaking the truth, even when least welcomed, so he felt man enough to continue.

'I love you,' he said.

'Whatever that means,' she said, apparently un-moved by either desire or emotion, or perhaps too proud to show either. The storm caused a short delay on landing at Heathrow the following morning, true: aircraft were slewed across the runways and took time to move: but on the whole the fates were on Alice's side.

Jane, Julie, Gina, Alice: these were the clones of Joanna May.

3

After Carl May divorced his much-loved wife, Joanna May, for infidelity and had her lover killed, he lived celibate for several years (as did she) concentrating upon his business interests, which were many and various. But nature abhors a vacuum, in particular one to do with sex, and presently a Mr Hughie Scotland, aged forty-five, a TV and newspaper magnate, fleshy, vigorous and wilful, reached for his address book and ran his finger down the M's. Then he called Carl May on his personal number, not even leaving it to his secretary to do. She was crying anyway. His staff often did: tears dropped into the word processors, doing them no good at all. But Hughie Scotland was rich enough not to worry.

'Let me be blunt and to the point,' he said.

'You always are,' said Carl.

'I'm in a fix,' said Scotland. 'My wife is screaming at me all hours of the day and night –'

'I thought she was in Iceland,' said Carl. Susan Scotland, born in Alabama, had recently been appointed US Lady Ambassador to that chilly, prosperous country.

'She is,' said Scotland. 'I don't mind her screaming in person, but she screams over the international telephone system, and causes me embarrassment, for nothing is private to a man in communications who has enemies; you have no idea the language she uses. I don't want it to get about, for her sake.'

'I have to be at a meeting in ten minutes,' said Carl, 'or I'll have enemies.'

'I'll be brief,' said Scotland. 'I want you to take this bimbo of mine off my hands. These girls topple presidents and bishops, and I don't want this one toppling me; she could be on the phone to the gutter press day and night; she'd upset my wife.'

'Hughie,' said Carl, 'you *are* the gutter press,' but Hughie took no notice. Susan Scotland's recent distress had been caused by press photographs of her husband and a young woman named Bethany bathing and sporting naked in the waters of a trout farm: they had been published not only in rival newspapers but throughout his own extensive syndicate. 'You'll shit in your own nest for a profit,' she'd wept down the line from Reykjavik, thus shocking and alarming her husband.

'Hughie,' said Carl, 'I don't need a bimbo. I am a serious person. I am not like you: I am not in the habit of splashing about naked in trout tanks.'

Hughie said, 'Carl, those were free-range trout, it was a pool, not a tank, and a hot day, and a man can surely do as he wishes on his own property. You know I've diversified into fish farms? If my wife wants to see more of me let her come back from Iceland.'

'I'm sorry,' said Carl, 'but no. Pay the girl off. Isn't that what people do? What's the worry?'

'You're a dry old stick,' said Hughie, 'and getting worse since your wife left.'

And Carl went to his meeting. But presently he was tempted out to lunch by Hughie: few people can resist the lure of an inside story. Even Carl May could be affected in this way. Hughie, rather disappointingly, chose an obscure restaurant.

'I can cope with governments,' said Hughie, 'and monstrous taxes and creeping socialism but I cannot cope with women. Take this bimbo off my hands. She keeps crying. Why do women spend so much time in tears?'

'Why me?' asked Carl, picking at a lemon sole. He ate little, and drank less. He preferred his fish unfilleted.

'These girls have to move upwards,' said Hughie, 'or they get offended, and that's when the trouble starts. And you have class. I have style but you have class.'

'Me?' asked Carl, surprised. 'Me? Class?'

'How many women have you slept with in your life?' asked Hughie.

'One,' said Carl. 'My wife.'

'That's class,' said Hughie. 'Why don't you leave that fish alone? It comes from the North Sea; it will have died of pollution, caused by your outfall.' Carl May was Chief Executive of Britnuc, a corporation which had become involved with the rehabilitation of the old Magnox nuclear power stations, two of them sited on North Sea shores. 'Freshwater fish are the meat of the future. Do me a favour, I'll do you a favour.'

'What?' asked Carl.

'I'll hold the story on the plutonium leak last March at Britnuc A. No one else has got it.'

17

'They haven't got it,' said Carl, 'because there wasn't one.'

'The public's too sanguine about nuclear power,' said Hughie. (How was he to know Chernobyl was to blow?) 'They need stirring up. So do you. Bethany's the girl to do it. Those press photos didn't do her justice.'

'I only read the financial papers,' said Carl.

'Out of touch,' said Hughie. 'You don't want to lose your touch. What you need, mate, is a bit of pain to stir things up again. You're slipping.'

It seemed to Carl that he would use less energy obliging Hughie Scotland than disobliging him, and so he agreed to take the girl Bethany on to his personal staff, Scotland paying her wages. The rich stay rich by staying mean. Fish with the bones in cost less than fish with the bones removed.

4

'I dreamt that I dwelt in marble halls,' Carl May whispered to himself and sang,

'With vassals and serfs by my si-i-de,
And of all the assembly gathered there
You were the joy and the pri-i-de.'

And well might he sing, and thus, as some months later he stepped from the back of a limousine and his sneakered foot touched conquered ground, while the Thames ran by as busy and significant as the ancient Euphrates.

Bethany Turner stepped out from the other side of the limousine and a different tune ran through her head. 'Shoo fly,' she whispered and hummed, 'shoo fly don't bother me, for I belong to somebody.' And she thought, of course, if she belonged to somebody, that somebody must be Carl May, her rich grey man, but she was wrong. Bethany loved, like a million million other women, someone who existed only in her head, who would never, in all her life, materialize. She loved a phantom, in whose image Carl May stood.

'What are you singing?' she asked Carl.

'Tunes from the dog-house,' he said. 'Tunes from the dog-house, that's all.'

It was a joke. For Carl's mother had kept him much of the time, when he was little and hungry and stole, chained up in the dog's kennel in the yard, to teach him a lesson. His father was a dead dog: his mother was a bitch. That much he learned. 'Marble Halls' would drift over the neighbouring fence, from next door's wind-up gramophone, and sustain his assaulted spirit. The child Carl shivered, he wept, he slept, he dreamed, and later he made the dream come true, as a few, just a few children, can.

'And you?' he asked. 'What are you singing?' For Carl heard everything, however soft, especially soft.

'Tunes from a childhood,' she said. 'That's all.' As for her, she'd been brought up in a whorehouse. Thrust people down when young and most stay down. A few rise up, like Carl and Bethany, and then if they're lucky they find each other.

He took her arm in his and they walked off to inspect this especially poignant part of his empire, there beside the Thames, and were happy for at least this one hour: he had found someone he truly desired, whom he could mould to his will, and she had found someone she truly admired, who would do as she wanted; the past, they thought, was now well and truly over. None so dangerous as those who believe they are happy, and are not. They flail around them, laying waste.

How at home they felt, young Bethany, old Carl, in this wasteland of razed warehouses and mean streets. Her high crocodile heels caught in crevices where weeds and grasses still found temporary hold, just enough dusty soil to live. His spongy-soled sneakers made light work of cracked, uneven surfaces. Soon builders and container-gardeners would move in and a new People's Park spring up all around: fast-food concessions in ferny precincts; disco dancing in leafy glades; Goofy and Peanuts and Garfield fighting it out in flowery pastures. Miniature sheep would graze on new enriched turf for the delight and wonder of young and old; there would be fireworks by night, TV stars by day, entrance £5 per head and few extras, and all thanks to the ingenuity and enterprising thrust of Riverside Gardens plc, the funding of the DTI, the involvement of local government, and Riverside Developments Inc.

Carl May was on the board of both Riverside Gardens and Developments. Six months after its no-doubt-royal opening, Riverside Gardens was destined to pack up its container plants, crate its miniature sheep, fill whole lorries with stacks of well-watered turf and move on to the next inner-city waterside site. Then Riverside Developments would move in, all planning permission and social grants agreed by the local housing authority, to erect high-price housing for those young professionals who wanted a river view and easy access to the City, and who were prepared to pay for it.

In this way everyone would benefit: not only the people who flocked to the part Disneyland, part Garden Centre of the People's Park – in particular a thousand thousand dispossessed fathers who needed somewhere to take their children on access weekends – but those who would obtain a minimum of six months' employment in its running: that is to say craftsfolk, fast-food concessionaires, builders, painters, waitresses, gatekeepers, security men, artists and artistes, cleaners, hedgers and ditchers, occupational therapists and so on. And after they were gone there would be permanent employment for the servicing agents of the young property-owning incomers – janitors, hairdressers, manicurists, dress designers, drivers, dentists and so forth. Yes indeed, all would benefit, and not least the profit and status of Carl May himself: Carl May of Riverside Parks plc, Riverside Developments Inc., and many other interlinking business concerns beside, including the one of which he was Chairman – British Nuclear Agents, Britnuc for short.

Bethany was twenty-four. She wore high crocodile shoes, ginger stockings, suspendered beneath ginger woollen jodhpurs held by leather bands at calf and waist, a not very clean white cotton shirt, highwayman's style and well unbuttoned, chains of gold butterflies round neck, waist and ankle. Her red hair had been untidily pinned up with a Spanish amber comb: she wore emerald-green contact lenses in her eyes. The look of the wanton was intentional, and as fake as her orgasms: she could do student, or executive wife, or lady doctor just as well. The only school exam she'd ever taken was Drama and she'd got a credit for that. But she could think of easier and livelier ways

22

of making a living than being an actress, and recognized it as folly to waste her father's training in being what men wanted.

Carl stood 5 foot 10 inches in his shoes, or had done last time he was measured, thirty years ago, in the days when he still needed life insurance to set against mortgages. Suspecting that time might have shrunk him, thinning the discs in his spine, as time does, he now wore elevated shoes. He knew the value of height when dealing with other men: but also that height is in the mind of the observer, it is a matter of bearing rather than actuality. He saw no deceit in the elevated shoes: he would have reached at least 6 foot 3 inches had it not been for severe malnutrition in early childhood, or so he had been told: he knew he was in essence a tall man. He wore carefully casual clothes for this outing with Bethany: he had a natural tendency to be dapper, to wear carnations in buttonholes, which he was at pains to overcome. To dress too carefully was to display nervousness. He had the well-developed chin of those accustomed to telling others what to do. His hair remained thick, though white.

The gap in their ages, the gulf in their manners, their way of dressing, the sense of his wealth in proportion to that wiliness born of helplessness in her, the very place in which they walked – exploiter and exploited (but which was which?) – made their perambulation altogether disreputable. People looked after them puzzled and not altogether pleased, as if expecting something sudden and terrible to happen any minute – as if a bulldog and a kitten, not a man and a woman, were out walking together. But Carl and Bethany saw in their looks only admiration and envy.

Carl and Bethany returned to their limousine to drive over rough ground to a site of special interest, where a brass plaque was to be set into the ground: a place of pilgrimage for future generations.

'Perhaps,' said Carl, modestly.

'How can you doubt it!' said Bethany, as expected of her.

The mythology of Carl's past had become familiar to the public, and even to himself: his childhood had indeed, by constant reference, been all but sucked dry of pain, drained of poison. Yet this pain, this poison, he knew well enough was the source of his energy, his power.

'Let there be buildings!' Carl May had only to cry, pointing to an arid landscape, and lo, so there would be. In the beginning, it is true, unlovely stubby concrete profitable blocks arose, but then, confidence breeding confidence, came the glassed towers and steel pinnacles of the finest architectural imagination. And all at Carl May's command – he, who until he was ten had lived in a shed down here by the river, chained with the dogs.

'Let there be beauty!' Carl May had only to murmur, he whose stepfather had battered and abused him, and lesser men would scurry forward with trees and flowers – albeit grown in container pots with soil substitute, well sterilized against all insect pests – and yes, there would be beauty, of a sort.

'Let there be light!' Carl May ordained, and nuclear power stations sprung up at his command and pumped their power into the National Grid. He, who was rescued by a teacher at the age of ten, half-dead, passed into council care, thence to foster parents and public school, Cambridge, business school and the Institute of Directors. He, who had everything except what he wanted – that is to say that which was not to be bought with money, that cluster of blessings which trip off the tongue as faith, hope and charity.

'See,' said the world, 'anyone can do it. It is perfectly possible to rise above circumstances, however dire those circumstances may have been. An unhappy past can be no excuse for the actions of murderers, sadists, child abusers, wife batterers, criminals of any kind. Carl May did it – so can you!'

It was to revive the pain and thus maintain the level of his achievement that Carl May took green-eyed Bethany down to the banks of the Thames. So, on this very pilgrimage, he had on occasion taken his blue-eyed wife Joanna. But that had been in the days when the mean and horrid streets still stood, before Carl May had conceived the idea of Riverside Parks plc, and Riverside Developments, and the main area of his fame and accomplishment (apart from his notable capacity to overcome the rigours of the past) was seen to be in the new world of nuclear power, the harnessing of the atom for mankind's advancement, that peace, happiness and prosperity might reign henceforth, and so forth.

'Without my wife,' Carl May had said for all the world to hear on radio and TV, 'I am nothing.' He was brave enough to bare his soul in public, or at any rate such part of it as he wished the public to know. 'The love of a good woman', he had joked, 'behind any great man!' only half-joking, and popular psychologists at once put pen to paper. 'You see,' they said, 'the wife can do for a man what the mother did not. No one should give up hope: no personality is irredeemably lost, destroyed. The narrow eyes of the tormented, anxious child, the thin mouth of the frightened child – they need not be permanent. With time, and love, those eyes will open wide, the mouth fill out. Fear not.' Carl May believed it too.

5

A couple of days before Chernobyl went up, making a large world into a small one, by reason of our common fear of radiation – the invisible enemy, the silent murderer, that which, like age, creeps in the dark – in this case consisting of a myriad, all-but-immortal particles, too small for the eye to see, of one man-made radioactive isotope or another (selenium, caesium, strontium – you name it, we invented it) flying through the air and causing death and decay wherever it fell, at any rate in the popular imagination – I, Joanna May, read of another strange event.

A girl in Holloway, doing three years for cheque offences, plucked out her eye. The technical term for this is 'orbisecto de se', and very nasty it is, for those who have to clear up afterwards and put flesh and head back together. The human eye, if you regard it without emotion, is a glob of light-sensitive jelly attached by strings of nerves and muscles to the convoluted tissue mass of the brain, in itself a fine ferment of electrical discharges. But it works, it works. The 'you', the 'me', the 'I' – behold, it sees! The soul in the dark prison that is the flesh looks out through the senses at the world: the senses are the windows to

27

that dark prison. And what the soul longs to see is beauty; smiles, grace, balance — both physical and spiritual — love in the maternal eye. It longs to see evening light over summer landscapes: crimson roses in green grass: birds flying, fish leaping, happy children playing — all that stuff. Yes, all that stuff.

What the contemporary eye gets to see on a good day is Mickey Mouse: it can just about put up with that, some joke is intended in the ugliness. The white lacy Terylene of a wedding dress makes up for a lot. A nice strong erect penis, viewed, can reconcile a lustful girl to some grimy back alley. But three years in Holloway! What is the eye, the I, to make of that!

Three years in Holloway, three years of grey concrete, the stuff of anti-life, the stuff that keeps radioactivity in (at least temporarily) or out: three years of looking at old Tampaxes in corners and cigarette stubs and grime and grey tins holding the brown slime of institution stew, and any sane person would be tempted to pluck their eye out, let alone the mad, who more than anyone proceed by punning. The word in action. The deranged pursue their sanity down the only alley known to them: giving language more meaning, more significance, than it was ever meant to have.

If thine eye offend thee, pluck it out. And quite right too. Broadmoor's a handsome place, set grandly in the wild hills: a great sweep of dramatic sky; old bricks not new concrete. One eye in rural Broadmoor's better than two in suburban Holloway, any day. She plucked her eye out and got transferred to Broadmoor. That's where one-eyed girls go.

I wanted to write to Carl to say, 'Carl, Carl, did you read about the girl in Broadmoor who plucked out her eye?' but how could I? I had betrayed Carl, spoiled the achievement which was his life, made of him a murderer (how could one doubt Carl's hand in Isaac's death: as well believe that Kennedy's assassin – and his assassin's assassin, and his assassin's assassin's assassin – all died of random acts) and Carl May had divorced my mind as well as my body – of course he had. And that was the hardest thing of all to bear.

Instead I rang for Trevor and asked him to fetch me the *Yellow Pages*. I turned to 'I' and there found Investigation Agencies, and ran my finger down the list, passing by the Acme and Advance and Artemis (they cluster their names in the A's, these places, and advisedly) all of whom I had used in the past and from whom I had sucked all possible juice of entertainment, and presently came to Maverick Enquiries, an agreeably innocent name, I thought – and dialled their number. It is my experience that the cool appearance of any Investigative Report, the comings and goings, contacts and activities of the investigatee neatly and impersonally described, acts like antihistamine ointment on a wasp sting to soothe the obsessional and tumultuous mind, if only – like the ointment – for a time.

I did not report to Oliver what I had done. Oliver thought I should just forget Carl. Oliver thought such a thing was possible – of course he did. Oliver was a nice guy, and young with it. But I had been married to Carl for over thirty years, and Carl was intertwined in my mind and body like the strands of dry rot fungi in the damp bricks of an empty house.

Let Oliver say as often as he liked, 'Forget him, Joanna, as he's forgotten you,' the simple fact was that Oliver had not been alive as many years as Carl and I had been married. But I liked to hear him say it. The young find everything so simple. That is why their company is refreshing. The young, moreover, see it as their duty to be happy and do their best to be so. I was brought up to be happy to do my duty, and so tend to equate happiness with boredom.

I would say to Oliver (or words to this effect), 'If Carl May has forgotten me why hasn't he found himself a wife, or even a girlfriend; why does he stay celibate?' and Oliver would reply (or words to this effect), 'Because he's so busy making money.' Oliver was kind. He could have said, 'Because he's in his sixties; too old to get it together,' but he didn't, in case I was reminded of my own age, and suffered. Isaac was kind, in the same way as Oliver. He too tried to smooth the path that ran before my thoughts. Too kind, when it came to it, to live in the same world as Carl May. My fault.

If thine eye offend thee, pluck it out! I wait for the arrival of the soothing ointment, the person from Maverick Enquiries. I want to be told, as I have been told so often in the past, that Carl still lives as a celibate, in memory of me.

30

6

How had it come about that Joanna Parsons, that English rose, had married Carl May, this upstart from a kennel? Why, because she fell in love with him, of course, and he with her, and her father was too busy and her mother too complacent to interfere with the course of true love. Nor were Carl's natural parents in any position to object to the match, being dead, and his foster parents were only too happy at this sudden uxorious turn of events: proof that the trouble they had taken with the boy, and the love and money they had expended upon him, were to be rewarded as they had hoped. He had joined the ranks of the achieving middle classes.

Little Joanna – for this is the way fate often works; sealing in our memories what is yet to come – had, when she was a child, read about the strange case of Carl May in a daily newspaper. The image of the abused and abandoned boy stayed in her mind, waiting, as it were, to pounce. The one to whom she, who had so much, could give so much!

How was it possible, thought little Joanna at the age of ten, weeping (unusually for her) into her porridge and cream, served by a maid, the plate so prettily laid on the white linen cloth, how was it possible that a world that contained so much excellence, pleasure and refinement should be the same world in which a boy could be kept in a kennel, beaten and abused, all but starved to death, have to teach himself to read from scraps of newspaper; a boy whose mother would then kill herself and whose stepfather be battered to death in prison at the hands of a vengeful mob? What, all this, and porridge and cream and dab your mouth as well? What a strange and upsetting world it was turning out to be!

'That child should not be allowed to read the newspapers,' her father said, observing her tears. The Parsons lived in Harley Street, above the shop: that is to say his consulting rooms. It was Dr Parsons' joke. Joanna's father was a physician: his speciality ear, nose and throat; two windows from the soul's prison on to the outside world, one organ of communication. The doctor's function was to keep all three bright, clean and properly receptive. Dr Parsons smoked a good deal, and coughed quite often, and presently was to die of lung cancer, but never made the connection between cigarette smoke and his ill health.

'The newspapers should print only what is happy and good,' said her mother, 'not upset people the way they do.'

Dr Parsons had disappointed a family of generals and majors to go into medicine. He was a man of moderate height with regular features, fair hair and bright blue eyes – the latter a recessive gene. He came from the North East – he was of Scandinavian stock.

Mrs Parsons, daughter of a West Country solicitor, had pleased her family by marrying a man a notch or so above her in the social scale, three inches taller, four years her senior, and well able to support her. She was slightly built and reckoned beautiful, with high cheekbones, wide green eyes, and the red hair sometimes inherited from two black-haired parents. She was of mixed Norman and Celtic stock. The strands of the different races met in their child, Joanna: she was beautiful, strong, healthy and bright, as if to encourage just such a blending.

'Do stop that child snivelling,' said Dr Parsons. 'Take away that newspaper.' The maid did so.

Mrs Parsons dabbed Joanna's eyes tenderly while rebuking her crossly. 'You have no business crying,' she said. 'Remember there are others far worse off than you!'

It is the custom of intelligent and competent men to marry women less intelligent and less competent than themselves. So mothers often have daughters brighter than they, and fathers have sons more stupid. It does not make for happiness. Nature looks after the race, not the individual.

Joanna stopped crying the better to puzzle it all out. But she did not forget Carl May. She saved him up, as it were, till later: stored him in her mind. One day she would make it all up to him. In the meantime she learned her letters and presently Latin and Greek, at an all-girls' school, and amazingly nobody stopped her, for the more a girl knows the more trouble she has finding a husband who knows more. But then prudence prevailed and she went on not to university but to a finishing school in Switzerland, where, in the interests of a future marriage, she was taught the mastery of flower arrangements, the organizing of dinner parties, the proper control of drunks (speak firmly but politely), servants (likewise), and the finer points of deportment. She 'came out' gracefully, being presented at Court, in the traditional way, when the ceremony was revived at the end of the war, and at her very first dance just so happened to meet Carl May, a pale, intense, not very tall but good-looking young man who worked at the Medical Research Council in Hampstead. He had not been on Active Service: his was a reserved occupation.

Carl May was famous already as the young man who'd started life in a kennel. Joanna Parsons' heart went out to him at once: she saw him as the solution to a puzzle which had worried her all her life. His body went out to her, in trust and confidence; and though his head regretted she was not of the titled, moneyed classes, he thought he could put up with that. He needed a wife to look after him and he needed one now. He did not need children, but he did not tell her that, not at once.

'I love him so much, Mummy,' said Joanna. 'I do so want to marry him. I want to make the past up to him. I want to make him happy.'

'If you love him you should marry him,' said Mummy. 'After all, I loved your father.' It was 1949, the nation was three years into socialism, everything was upside down. The young man had fought through heavy odds to end up well educated and well spoken: what were a few years in a kennel? They would make him appreciate her daughter the more. It was time the girl was out of the house: she made her mother feel faded, dusty and stupid. Mrs Parsons wanted Dr Parsons to herself again.

'I want to marry him, Daddy,' said Joanna, waiting for opposition. But none, to her disappointment, came.

'Why not?' was all her father said. He'd rather she'd married a doctor and perpetuated a race of physicians; he'd rather the young man had faced up to Hitler directly, but those few hard early years should at least help keep the young man's feet on the ground, and besides, Dr Parsons was busy. Men had brought back odd diseases from the African deserts and the jungles of the Far East; ears heard wrongly, noses smelt falsely and words came strangely from tortured throats. And it was time the girl was out of the house. The vivid presence of the daughter made him discontented with the mother.

Only Joanna's Aunt Anne was against the match: she said, 'the child who's beaten grows up to beat,' but she was years ahead of her time and regarded as

35

an hysteric. What a hopeless doctrine it would be, if true! That we never recovered from our past! What price progress then? For what applied to individuals applied to nations, and societies too. So much the world was beginning to see.

Now Joanna was sixty, and disgraced: she had failed, in the end, to make the past up to her husband, failed to make him happy. And Carl was sixty-three. Age wears out the resolution of youth: or look at it another way – the past seeps through into the present, as the garish colour of underlying old wallpaper, left unstripped for one reason or another, but usually financial, will eventually show through to the pale expensive layer on top and spoil everything.

7

'She should be thoroughly punished for making you so unhappy,' said Bethany to Carl, when he ran through his life for her, the way new lovers do.

'My mother is dead,' he said, surprised.

'I didn't mean your mother,' she said. 'I meant your wife.'

'Oh that old woman, that Joanna May,' said Carl, 'who cares about her?'

Bethany had heard that kind of thing before, for all she was so young. On the night she met Carl, she turned over in bed and said, 'I'm twenty-four going on forty-two and you're sixty-three going on thirty-six, so who's counting?' And Carl stopped counting there and then, though of course the world did not.

That first night he said to her, 'You're the second woman I've slept with in all my life,' and she said, 'I don't believe you,' and he did not care if she believed or not: he just got out of bed to make some calls to Australia, and so she believed him.

'I was totally faithful to Joanna all my married life,' he said, when he had finished his calls and got back into bed. He had skinny white hairless shins but she did not care. 'That was my folly.'

'What happened?' asked Bethany, though she knew pretty well; these things do not go unnoticed, even in circles of power, where policemen seldom enter in.

'I found her with another man,' said Carl, easily, though this was the first time for several years he had found words for the event. Well, who had there been to speak to? And in so saying, he bound Bethany to himself, or so she thought. She was safe with him now, she told herself: he would not, could not, surely, pass her on to some subordinate.

'What did you do?' asked Bethany audaciously, and audacity was rewarded, as it so often is.

'I killed him,' said Carl, even more easily. 'That is to say, I had him killed. But it amounts to the same thing.'

Bethany wondered how the deed had been done, but did not like to ask. Screams in the soft suburban night had many a time disturbed her childish sleep; she had never liked to ask. Once she did and her mother slapped her. 'What you don't know can't hurt you,' Mother said, and Bethany had believed her.

'Why him not her?' Bethany enquired further, now, of Carl. 'Most men kill the woman and leave the man.' Twenty-four going on forty-two, no doubt about it, reared in a whorehouse! The things she knew for all she never asked.

'I left her alive,' said Carl dreamily, 'to suffer from the loss of me.'

'Most women left alone for that reason,' said Bethany, 'just find someone else.'

'Not when they're old,' said Carl. 'Don't you want me to tell you how I disposed of her lover?'

'No, I don't,' she said, so he didn't. Confidences are dangerous. Witnesses get killed. Those who know too much disappear. The world is not a safe place, even for the well intentioned; especially the well intentioned.

'Why did Joanna betray me?' asked Carl May, that first night, he who so seldom displayed ignorance or doubt, thus suddenly loquacious. 'I don't know much about women. What did my wife need that she didn't have? I still can't understand it. We'd been married nearly thirty years. She was never much interested in sex; what did she want with another man? She had more than enough to do – the house to look after and so forth; I was good to her: attentive when I had the time: generous – she could spend as much money as she liked on clothes, though she never would: ask Joanna to choose between Dior and Marks & Spencer and she'd choose Marks & Spencer. It was her background – middle of middle. Revenge of some kind? Insanity? She liked animals more than people: she said so: it hurt me. She had a little grey cat which died. That upset her. And then of course the dogs – it's true I got rid of the dogs. But she never found out about that. It can't have had anything to do with that. No, it was just in her female nature, buried deep, but there it was. The need to betray, to spoil, to turn what is good bad. The bitch goddess, at it again.'

'How do you mean, Carl? Got rid of the dogs?'

He was not in the habit of explaining himself, and

she knew it. But still she asked, and he replied, as she knew he would. As he trusted her body, so he began to trust her mind.

'I was jealous,' said Carl May to Bethany. 'I didn't like the way she stroked the dogs. I didn't like the way they nuzzled her, as if they'd been there many a time before. Or how she'd talk to them instead of me. It upset me – a kind of spasm attacked my throat: such a lump in it I couldn't swallow. Once, looking at her with them, I almost fainted. A lot of people depend upon me. I have to keep myself steady for their sake. I had the animals stolen: I was going to sell them; then I realized I'd have to have them poisoned. You know how dogs will find their way back home. But enough of all that.'

'You did the right thing,' said Bethany, who felt quite safe, having no dogs to poison, no lover (so far) for Carl May to destroy.

Bethany knew well enough the value of the benefits she offered her new lover; how hard, once enjoyed, they were to do without: the sheer surprise, the sudden joyful restoration of self-esteem, as conferred by the sexual act when performed with the right (even though unlikely – especially the unlikely) person. Moreover, Bethany surprised even herself: she had never known the magic work so well before: not in the many sometimes profitable, sometimes distressing couplings of her adolescent days; not even when she moved away from home and the suburbs to the nightclubs of the fashionable world, not even then had she and whoever come even near it; no, not even with Hughie Scotland, Carl's predecessor, not for all his fame as a media stud. Those others had not seemed to notice any lack of anything.

Those others had given her money, cars, racing tips, sexual satisfaction, all kinds of things – but what Carl May gave Bethany, in return for his pleasure, was confidence. And what she felt he felt too. Oh yes, she was safe enough. He wouldn't want to do without her. So Bethany believed. So Joanna had believed.

'You be careful,' said Patsy, Bethany's mother, when Bethany reported back to her that she was moving on from Hughie Scotland to Carl, and rather liked the new arrangement. 'Don't go falling in love. Love's all misery and muddle and never any profit.'

'Don't talk like that!' said Bill, Bethany's father, to his wife. 'You and I are in love, always have been, and look at the profit we've made! Look at the child we made! Our Bethany, child of love. No wonder she's sought after; and fate is on her side, it's obvious. Carl May! That really is the big time.'

Patsy and Bill, ex-flower-folk, kept a house of moderate ill fame in an outer-London suburb, halfway down a very long quiet street. They went together to local pubs: he brought home lonely men, she brought home lonely women. They brought them together in the upstairs bedrooms of the large suburban house, charging an agency fee. Bill mowed lawns for the neighbours; Patsy would meet their children out of school if they were ever in a fix: they were an obliging pair, they took care to be, no one ever complained. Where did altruism stop, self-interest begin? Hard to tell. Whoever can, of other people or themselves?

41

Patsy and Bill met in the fifties, at the cinema. *Gigi* was showing: Leslie Caron of the wide brown eyes as the girl reared in the brothel who found true love, Maurice Chevalier as her protector. 'Thank heaven for little girls,' he sang, with all the faux-innocence of that sickly decade. There at the cinema, to that tune, Patsy and Bill fell in love, and reaffirmed that love at a rerun in the sixties, at a half-empty local cinema, while they were trawling for custom amongst the dispossessed and empty-lifers at a Tuesday matinée, and there, in the back row, Bethany was conceived in a fit of wholesome life-trust. How else should they rear her but as Gigi was reared? So the beauty advice came from women's magazines, and the style was suburban not *fin-de-siècle* Parisian, but never mind, never mind! Bethany was created.

And Patsy and Bill, proud in their achievement, while valuing the joy of sex, all sex, and perhaps overvaluing Bethany their daughter, for a time all but priced her out of the market; many was the boring night she spent alone: lying empty, as a house may lie empty while its value increases. That was when she was fifteen. Noticing what was happening, they brought the price down.

All things are chance, thought Bethany, who bore no malice against her parents, no resentment for the manner of her upbringing, or thought she did not. I might have been born in Africa in time of drought, she thought, and had stick arms and legs, and a stomach which stuck out: I might have been born an Eskimo, and hardly seen my legs and arms at all, so

42

cold would it be to undress: as it was I was born to Patsy and Bill, and if they had not been so foolish, so trusting, and so adored Leslie Caron, would I have been born at all? And now here I am with Carl, and happy and safe, so what's the point of complaining? But he still hasn't got his wife out of his system. Something must be done about that.

'Well,' said Bethany, 'it seems to me your wife lived an empty life and was a shallow woman and you're well rid of her. But perhaps her life was boring. Perhaps she was just bored. Some women will do anything not to be bored.'

'She could have gone to classes,' said Carl. 'She had no reason to be bored. She had me. Boredom is no excuse for infidelity.'

'She should have had babies,' said Bethany, 'with all that time to spare. Why didn't she?' Not that she wanted or anticipated children herself, belonging to a younger generation, one which did not define women as people who had babies.

'She did,' said Carl, cunningly, 'but she never knew it.'

'That's impossible,' said Bethany. 'How can you have a baby and not know it?'

'In the same way,' said Carl, 'as you can have an hysterical pregnancy and be convinced you're growing a baby when you're not. That's what Joanna did to me when she was thirty. She got morning sickness: her belly swelled up. She looked terrible. I took her to this doctor friend of mine, Dr Holly; a very clever man. He just looked her over and sent her out of the room and said to me, "Your wife and Mary Queen

43

of Scots! There's no baby there, only air and wind."
"What's the cure?" I asked. "Love and kisses," he
said, "or failing that, a mock abortion, a ceremony of
death." Almost nothing he didn't know about women.
So that's what we did. Told her she was to have a
termination, anaesthetized her, and whee-e-ee, like a
balloon going down, went Joanna's belly. When she
woke up she was cured. My lovely wife, slim and fresh
and all for me again!'

'But that's not having babies and not knowing it,'
said Bethany, 'that's not having a non-baby.'

'Oh so clever she'll cut herself,' said Carl May, his
old finger running sharply down the skin between
Bethany's breasts, where she should have buttoned
her blouse, lifting the white nylon rosebud in the
centre of her bra and snapping it back so she jumped.
'Wait! Joanna knew well enough I didn't want children: I told her the day before our wedding: she
accepted that when she married me. I took that phantom pregnancy of hers badly, an imagined one seemed
to me worse than the real thing; let her conscious
mind be loyal and loving, in her unconscious, in the
depths of her being, Joanna May betrayed me, went
against me.'

'You were to be all in all to each other! Just you,
just her! I think that's sweet – my mother and father
were like that, in the beginning. Then they had me,
and felt differently.'

'How could Joanna and I have had children? Do
you understand just what sort of inheritance I have?
What do you think it's been like for me, knowing
what kind of parents I had, what sort of bestial blood
flows in my veins?'

44

'Your parents were mentally ill, Carl, that's all. They must have been.'

'That's all? Insanity? All?'

How white he suddenly was. She ran her finger over his lips. They were dry and trembling. He calmed. She had not known he could be upset. She felt privileged, and powerful. Carl May, Chairman of Britnuc, power in the land, TV personality, calmed by Bethany's young finger.

'I had myself sterilized when I was eighteen,' he said. 'A vasectomy. I would be the end of the line: that particular experiment of nature's. I chopped down the family tree.'

'Joanna didn't mind?'

'Joanna didn't know,' he said. 'Why should she? What difference did it make? She understood my mind when we were married; we would have no children. There'd be just the two of us.'

'Tea for two,' said Bethany dreamily. 'Just me and you. Two for tea and baby makes three.'

'Baby makes five,' said Carl sharply, and nipped her finger suddenly with teeth made sharp and fine by the passage of sixty-three years. 'While she was opened up we took away a nice ripe egg; whisked it down to the lab: shook it up and irritated it in amniotic fluid till the nucleus split, and split again, and then there were four. Holly thought we could have got it to eight, but I said no. Growth begins so quickly: there wasn't time. A truly vigorous egg, that one. We kept the embryos in culture for four whole weeks, had four nice healthy waiting wombs at hand and on tap, for implantation. All four took like a dream: there they grew until they popped into the world, alive and kicking and well. Four nice assorted ladies, desperate for babies, got four very pretty little girls: little Joanna clones. Not cloning in the modern sense, but partheno-genesis plus implantation, and a good time had by all. We kept it quiet. So quiet one of the mothers didn't even know we'd done it. What passive creatures women are: they just lie there, trusting, and let the medical profession do what it wants.'

'That's two for tea and four babies make six, Carl, not five.'

Carl bit Bethany again. 'Wrong!' This time she yelped, and quite reminded him of his younger days. 'There wasn't anyone to tea. There ain't a father in the whole wide world,' crooned Carl May, 'that gave help to my poor old dutch. All on her lonesome ownsome. Her DNA and hers alone. She was thirty. She was growing little hairlines round her eyes: so I gave time itself a kick in the teeth. It seemed a pity to let it all go to waste, when you could save it so easily.'

'Like an old Magnox power station,' said Bethany; he looked at her sharply.

'Don't be so cutesy,' he said, not even bothering to bite, so she desisted.

'Well,' said Bethany, 'all I know is if it was me I'd have told her. I'd never have managed to keep it to myself. I can't keep the smallest secret, let alone clon-ing someone and not telling them!'

'It's sensible to keep things in reserve,' said Carl May. 'Information may not be wisdom, let no one tell you it is: but knowledge – ah, when it's secret knowledge is power.' And Carl May looked at

46

Bethany hard, until she wondered which of her secrets he knew and wasn't saying.

'No,' said Carl May, 'she'll never get it out of me. Let her go to her grave not knowing. She chose loneliness: let her be forever lonely.'

'But now I know,' Bethany said, 'what about me?' and wished at once she hadn't opened her mouth.

'You'll keep it to yourself,' Carl May said, and she thought, yes, I will: on the whole I better had. I can see I better had.

'One day you might tell her,' she said. 'You never know what's going to happen next. One day you might, to punish her. To take away her singularity.'

'A long word for such a little girl,' he said, and pinched her with sharp-filed fingernails – she'd given him a manicure: he enjoyed that: he on the chair, she crouched on the floor, red hair falling – better, she could see, in future, to file his nails less sharp or use words that were less long, or both.

'What can happen next,' asked Carl May, 'that I don't know about: what can surprise a man like me? I win. I always win. I need to win, as other people need sex, or food, and that's all there is to it.'

Bethany shivered, and hoped Carl May hadn't noticed, but of course he had. So she looked and spoke as bright as could be. 'I wouldn't like to have a lot of little me's walking about,' she observed. 'One of me is quite enough,' and the jabbing nail turned into a stroking hand, a pressing mouth, and she felt safe: yes, she felt safe enough. One of her, she told herself, was more than enough for him. Besides, she wasn't perfect, not like Joanna: on the contrary, she was flawed; she knew it: people had told her so often enough. Now she was glad, not sorry, Carl May had noticed. If the penalty of perfection was reproduction she could do without it. Her bone structure was not good: she was pretty rather than beautiful – she had her mother's chin: it would droop and double by the time she was thirty: she was all artifice: she inspired lust not love: she was cunning not wise: bright not clever: could memorize well but not categorize easily: was a good guest but an over-effusive hostess: affec- tionate but not constant – being able, at will, to switch that affection in the direction which most suited her, and often tempted to do so. These things Bethany knew about herself. She was in fact too vulnerable to the passage of time. She was the kind who went off early. Never mind, when she lost her capacity to charm she would start a business: an employment agency: a chain of them perhaps: Carl May would help her, pension her off: she would be powerful through money, that safe and snazzy stand-in for sexual pleasure. She liked to be safe. She didn't like to be bored. It was difficult to keep a balance between the two.

'What a pity you can't have babies,' she said, quite forgetting to whom she was speaking. 'I'd like to have your babies. Then I'd always have something of you to love!' Men liked to hear that kind of junk, but Carl merely shook his head impatiently, as if some gnat had bitten him, so she shut up and let him get on with it.

8

The day they went down to the river, Carl May returned to the subject of his ex-wife, and his secret knowledge. He and Bethany sat side by side in the back of the limousine. Perhaps he thought she was too confident: he liked to have her a little frightened. He knew how to frighten her. It's always pleasant to do what you're good at doing: hard to refrain from doing it. Anyway, Carl May had said, 'You could always give birth to one of my clones. I could use your womb to implant me.'

'What a lovely idea!' said Bethany, in her best and politest voice. 'They can't really do that, can they?'

'Oh yes they can,' said Carl May. 'I'll take you down to my friend Holly. There's an advance on freezing now: the rage is all for drying: keeps the nuclei intact. It used to be just frogs and below: now it's sows and upwards. Shall I take you down to Holly? Prickly Holly?' He pinched the tip of her little finger, and they watched it turn blue between the bloodless nails of his thumb and third finger.

'He must be rather old by now,' said Bethany, and wished she hadn't.

'No older than me,' said Carl May, but added kindly, 'Lost his nerve, lost his bottle, you're quite right,' and he let her finger go. She sucked it. He liked that.

'One of you,' said Bethany, 'is more than enough for me. I'd be exhausted. I want you, not your clone. What would be the point of a clone?'

He nipped her neck. She was covered with little bruises in tender places: mementoes of Carl, he called them. She loved them.

'It would come in handy,' he said. 'It could stand in for me here and there – at banquets, for example, when all anyone needs is my presence; when my opinion counts for nothing. It would save my digestion.'

'But what would you do while you stayed home?' asked Bethany, whose idea of pleasure it was to be out, not in.

'Learn not to need to win,' he said and, as if to make up for a lifetime of over-controlled Joanna May, flung himself upon Bethany, digging his teeth vampire-like into her neck, tearing her blouse, his hand approaching her crotch from the top, not the bottom, down between her clothing and her skin, forcing her belt to give and break, without any thought at all for the presence of Philip the chauffeur in the front seat. Philip was indeed embarrassed by their moans and groans, but Carl May paid well: it was a privilege to work for such an employer, who had led a lonely and prudent life far too long, and the girl was not reluctant, on the contrary, so he put up with the embarrassment easily enough. He had faced worse in the course of his job – the poisoning of Joanna's dogs for one thing, the backing his car into and over Joanna's lover Isaac for another, as required of him by Carl May. Who was he to object to anything? What kind of moral stance could he take? What outrage would now be justified? Once a servant, an employee, has decided that loyalty to the one who pays him supersedes all other moral obligations, and has acted upon that decision, to change the mind becomes impractical, not to say dangerous. Reason and self-interest must be called upon to counteract the pangs of sensibility.

Philip kept his eyes on the road and drove slowly beside razed warehouses, over broken tarmac, where the weeds kept bursting through.

'You know far more about me than you should,' said Carl to Bethany, after his final climactic gasp.

'It was all just a story anyway,' said Bethany prudently. 'All that about clones. Just to frighten me.'

'Of course,' he said. Then he added, 'But just think, if there were more of me, and more of you, how much pleasure we would bring into the world!' and he actually smiled, and she remembered that she loved him and was pleased to give him pleasure.

He slept a little. Bethany stared out of the window on to a broken landscape. Philip parked the car. His employer woke up with an old man's start: a shiver: where was he? The river air was in his nostrils: the air of his childhood: a flowing tide of soot and despair mixed: there in his mind for ever, lying low but always there. He got out of the car. Bethany followed. The sun went in and a cold wind blew across the river.

'I brought you down here,' said Carl to Bethany, 'so you could see for yourself how I began. Of course it's all gone now — but where we stand used to be the corner of Jubilee Road and Bosnia Street. This is where the brass plaque is to be.'

And Bethany said, 'If it was all so nasty, why do you want to come back? Or is it like a loose tooth? You want to jiggle it even though it hurts?'

And Carl knew he had been deceived in her: she was not after all what he hoped. He was disappointed in her, hurt; he had forgotten what it was to be disappointed, hurt. Bethany did not begin to understand the significance of his achievement. She belonged to the TV age: nothing surprised, nothing impressed: real life rolled off a scriptwriter's pen. To have started here, yet come to this! Magnificent, but she could not see it.

The chauffeur buttoned his coat and straightened his cap, feeling the alteration in his master's mood: though if you'd asked him he'd have said, 'Just something in the air, that's all: just something in the air that chilled me, reminded me of this and that. I wouldn't work for anyone else: not for twice the wages and half the hours. It's an honour.' He'd been in tanks in the war and killed men for less reason than he killed for Carl, which was from loyalty, obedience and self-interest mixed.

'But it's all such a long time ago,' said Bethany, compounding her error. She felt the cold wind in her hair and round her chin and cutting down against the white and tender skin of her still partly unbuttoned bosom; harsh against the grazed skin where he had sucked and bitten her neck. Had he told her where they were going she would have worn boots and brought a scarf. With almost every step over the uneven ground she caught the leather on her high heels; they would be badly snagged: she would have to have them rewrapped. He was thoughtless.

'If you're not interested we can go home,' said Carl. She understood then, too late, too late, that the cold wind was somehow his doing, and said, 'Of course I'm interested,' and then, 'They say one's childhood is never over. Do you think that's true?' But it was no use: the cold wind whipped and zapped through her red hair, and that was the only answer she got.

'You are not sufficiently interested,' Carl May said, 'for me to waste any more of my day on you.'

They rode home in silence, to the big boring house at 20 Eton Square, Belgravia, where the May collection of Egyptian art and artefacts was housed in what used to be the stable block, open to the public on the first Wednesday of every month. Very few of the public in fact took the trouble to attend. The windows had been blocked up to save specimens from the dangers of direct natural light; the ceiling rose to a central peak: the single door was arched: the room, though vast, was for all the world like a kennel. It was a dismal place. But Carl liked it, which was all that mattered.

As the chauffeur pulled up outside 20 Eton Square, a small group of reporters rushed to meet the car. Microphones were pushed under Carl's nose and flashbulbs popped. News was coming through that the power station at Chernobyl had blown, and in the light of the fact that two of Britnuc's plants, like Chernobyl, were WCRs, water-cooled reactors, could he make a statement? Was the public in any danger?

'Making electricity is not like making a sponge cake,' he said kindly in his soft gravelly voice. 'It is dangerous and things go wrong. When I know exactly what has happened at Chernobyl, if anything, I will be in a position to make a statement. Not before.'

'But, Mr May, the public is worried.'

'The public is right to be worried,' he said, smiling, and closed the front door, swiftly, and upon Bethany's right foot. The picture of the snagged and torn leather upon the six-inch heel of her shoe was upon the front cover of a tabloid newspaper the next day. 'May Faces Snags,' it said, going on to speak of the unseen killer which now stalked Eastern Europe. Other newspapers relegated the item to the middle pages. It was one of those stories which was to grow and grow, as wind patterns in the upper atmosphere made nonsense of national boundaries.

Carl went straight to his study to make telephone calls, his face still set cold against Bethany.

Bethany was a practical young woman. She dumped her shoes in the bin, feeling that since they brought her no luck they might as well be discarded, changed into more restrained clothes, dabbed ointment on her neck and, in the cold light of the bathroom, brought her hair under better control. She did not like the bathroom. It was too large, too full of marble, too brightly lit, and the washbasins were antique and their porcelain, being finely crazed, never looked quite clean. She did not like the house; Joanna's house. She did not like the servants; Joanna's servants – who did not like her, with her tiny knickers left everywhere and her strewn junk jewellery and hairpins, and her waterproof make-up smeared on sheets and cushions: but that was her role; how Carl liked it; they would just have to get used to it. In fact Bethany came to the conclusion she did not like Joanna, whose ladylike presence in the house was still too clearly felt for comfort.

The woman had no natural taste, that was apparent. She had re-created her father's consulting rooms in her husband's house: dark, highly polished mahogany furniture, dusty pale-green velvet curtains, over-plump greeny chintzy sofas and blue-and-white en-crusted Chinese jars of arguable value standing on every available ledge. Twice a week the housekeeper would arrange fresh flowers – unnaturally large blooms – in the bleak white fluted floor-standing Italian vases which stood boringly in each corner of the room.

Bethany assumed, and rightly, that the twice weekly arrival of the peculiar flowers was an expression of gratitude from whatever container-gardener firm had been granted the contract to supply the Thameside Garden Park – a gift, of course, not a bribe. Bethany well understood the difference. Many a gift had she received in her life, before or after a favour. But she could not be bribed – that would be an indignity.

Bethany bent to smell the flowers, which seemed to occupy some point between gladioli and chrysan-themum and withdrew her face at once. They had been sprayed with a strong flower perfume somewhere between violet and rose. It was not her place to comment or improve. She thought longingly of her parents' suburban garden, filled with nothing more exotic than pansies and roses, and settled down to read *The Layman's Guide to Nuclear Power*. It was one thing to appear ignorant; quite another to be so.

9

Carl was on the phone to a certain Gerald Coustain. This is how their conversation went:

Gerald Coustain said, 'What you're telling me is that there is no indication of additional radioactivity from any outside source at either Britnuc A or B?'

Carl May said, 'That is correct. I would add that this is hardly surprising since our instrumentation is not designed to pick any up.'

There was a short silence from Gerald Coustain, who worked for the Department of Energy.

'You're being remarkably frank with me,' he said.

'Why not?' enquired Carl, who was still in what Joanna had learned to call 'a mood'. Bethany had failed him. It was not his time he feared to waste, so much as his emotion – and what were referred to in a booklet he had recently received through the post on the subject of AIDS as 'bodily fluids'. He was aggrieved. He had made himself vulnerable. It was dangerous. If, as he felt, the experiences of his childhood energized his present, a fire to be fanned and nurtured back to life, that fire was as like as not to go out altogether under the thwack of cold water delivered by Bethany. There was a lot at stake here. A long time ago! What had that to do with it?

'I have done everything the inspectorate required,' said Carl May. 'I have followed its instructions to the letter, no matter how absurd those instructions were. Nowhere could I find regulations appertaining to the upper limits of instrumentation.'

Again there was a pause.

'Nuclear power is a new industry,' said Coustain, his voice receding as if he held the receiver further and yet further away. 'It is essential that the spirit of the law rather than the letter be followed.'

'Come off it,' said Carl May. 'You don't want Britnuc A and B off line every time instrumentation shows a rise in local activity any more than I do. You fellows have your own information-gathering network. Don't come bleating to me every time the shit hits the fan.'

Coustain, thinking he should perhaps make a virtue out of necessity, asked Carl May if he would make some reassuring statement on TV the next day: along the lines he had sketched out: and so Carl May did, in the programme seen by his ex-wife, Joanna May.

10

'God's last laugh,' I said, 'before he flew off,' I, the original of the clones of Joanna May. I said it, of course, more for the sake of a neat phrase than anything else: my way of vaguely invoking the name of God whilst yet dismissing him. God was there once, I safely maintain, thus explaining away some intimation of immortality, some general notion we all have of 'more to this than meets the eye' whilst disposing of him, whoever he may be, for all practical purposes.

'Joanna, define your terms!' – Miss Watson, 1942. A certain Miss Watson taught me English language when I was a schoolgirl. She was in her eighties. Young women were at the time busy making explosives in factories to blow young men up: they had no time to teach their juniors anything. The old were brought out of retirement to be of some use, while the young finished each other off. No wonder the war was so popular with everyone. A long, violent, riotous, disgraceful party! Miss Watson died of a stroke on VE day; and quite right too – the party was over.

If I'm forced into a corner by the ghost of Miss Watson, who returns to me often in dreams, I would define God as the source of all identity: the one true, the only 'I' from which flow the myriad, myriad 'you's'. We acknowledge him in every 'I' we so presumptuously utter. Now what could be more all-pervasive than that?

Carl once told me God flew off the day Fat Boy was exploded in the Nevada Desert, when man entered the atomic age (though of course man — and woman — had in fact entered it long before, when Pierre and Marie Curie first started sieving and filtering their dusty mounds of pitchblende), leaving the field to the likes of my husband. But I prefer to think He flew off when the first flicker of television appeared upon the screen. He knew he was beaten. For Lucifer read John Logie Baird, inventor of TV, toppling the Ultimate Identity from his seat of power: spoiling the currency of 'I' forever. The 'you' that is the real 'I', the one perceived by others, the one understood by the child in that initial bright vision, now watches the 'you' that that you perceives. There is no end to it. Our little shard, our little divine shred of identity, so precariously held, is altogether lost as we join the oneness that is audience. My clones and I. After I found out about the clones I began to worry a lot about 'I'.

As for evil — which everyone knows is the absence of God — what could it do when God took off but take up residence in the source of its trouble. The minute parents, those stoical folk, look away, evil creeps out of the TV set and settles in the wallpaper.

The children ask for sneakers now, not proper shoes. Why? Because sneakers have long laces, long enough to hang a person by. And every year the laces get longer and tougher, the better to do it; to hang, to dangle yourself or others. Why bother to preserve the 'I'? It's seen too much of sights not fit for human eyes, it is not fit to live. It no longer believes in life: all it gets to see is corruption, seared, torn and melting flesh. There is no 'I' left for any of us. The great 'I' has fled, say the eyes in the wallpaper: only the clones remain, staring.

If the I offend thee pluck it out. Idopectomy.

My children who are myself pun too. Bloody clones. That was Carl's doing.

On hearing the first news from Chernobyl, I sent Trevor the butler to the Post Office with a telegram to Carl May my ex-husband saying, 'Yah boo sucks, signed Milly Molly Mandy', but Trevor came back saying the Post Office now sent only greetings telegrams – Happy Birthday, Congratulations on your Wedding, and so forth – and I decided silence was the better policy. One must go with the flow of events. If waves slap against your face, turn back to shore.

The next day Carl made a statement to the press saying (or words to this effect), 'It can't happen here. Our reactors are constructed on a different principle from theirs. Children may safely drink milk though sheep may no longer safely graze on the uplands.' His lies were soft and persuasive, as ever: and his face calm and handsome. It had the tranquillity of a death mask: as if someone had placed a waxed cloth over his corpse's face – after it had been composed by the undertaker, of course – and moulded it into shape and propped body and mask up before the cameras and used puppet strings to work the mouth and eyelids. Carl was dead, pretending to be living. That is what a diet of lies does for you – and now I am no longer with him what else will Carl choose to eat but lies? There is no nourishment in them, the spongy junk food of the mind. The soul dies from malnutrition.

I longed to tell him so – yah, boo, told you so – to ease the itch of spited, spiteful love, watch the pale dead face suffuse with the living pink of rage, but I didn't. Let him stay dead. It was what he chose when he threw me out: it is why he lived without a woman after I was gone.

I dedicated my life to Carl: I threw away the children I could have had, for his sake, to keep him happy. Isaac was nothing; a side-show, a weak man: he died and I scarcely noticed. Oliver is nothing either, when it comes to it: a pet which curls up alongside, by a warm fire, or on a forbidden bed, to be indulged. Better than nothing, that's all, poor Oliver. Of course Carl is dead, dying: so am I, without him. But Carl is at least able to blow up the world while he waits. I'm not.

11

The clones of Joanna May also blamed their nearest and dearest for the accident at Chernobyl, with rather less reason than did their original.

In their case, of course, near did not necessarily or permanently mean dear, and this was either an affliction ironed into their genes, or the common cross of humanity, as may be decided by events. Nor was the tendency to blame irrationally peculiar to these four women, of course: it afflicts all mankind. When the weather is fine on polling day, the sitting government is returned. If the weather is wet, it gets thrown out. And that's that.

Jane Jarvis listened to the news on the radio and slammed her attic windows shut to keep the radioactivity out. A pity, because it was such a fine spring day, but to keep out the bad you had to keep out the good. Then she returned to the brass bed where her lover lay. It was Saturday, and lunchtime. Presently they'd get out of bed and walk into Soho for something to eat. Her flat was in Central London: she had the whole attic floor of a big house in Harley Street. She could afford it. Such was the reward of beauty, intelligence, education, and the capacity for making decisions others feared to – saying, simply and firmly, 'this is good but not profitable' or, 'this is bad but commercial', or 'this is neither good nor profitable', or, just occasionally, 'this is both good and commercial' and having the results bear her out. Tom designed book jackets and lived in half a house in Fulham, and earned a quarter of what she did, for eight times as much work. He would take her out to lunch, so she would have to eat spaghetti, not oysters.

Jane Jarvis was 5 foot 7 inches tall; precise and orderly in mind and body. She measured 36 inches around her chest, 24 inches at the waist and 36 round her hips, as had her original at the same age. Her nose was straight and perfect; her eyes widely spaced: her cheekbones high, her top lip a little short, the bottom lip a little thin: her gaze was direct. To wash her hair she dunked it in a basin of soapy water, rinsed it and towelled it dry. It frizzed out round her head. She belonged to some new, insouciant age. She walked like someone who knew herself to be free. She lived at the top of No. 30 Harley Street. Her original had spent her childhood in No. 34.

'I want the windows open,' said Tom, when she got back into bed. 'I can't sleep with the windows shut.'

'I didn't realize you had come here to sleep,' she said.

'Besides which, why bother?' he asked. 'If there is radioactivity out there glass isn't going to stop it.'

'It will stop alpha rays,' she said.

'Smarty pants,' he said.

'You can't bear it if I know things you don't,' she said.

A row was approaching through the window: no glass could stop it: the hideous black cloud of the spirit: tumulus and cumulus fighting it out: lightning flashes of dire perception, thunderclaps of rage, hail storms of battering distress; every passion and woe of the past returned to plague the present, bent on turning love to hate. They knew it, Jane and Tom: both looked uneasily out of the window: they could see rooftops and sky: no sign yet of the storm they expected to see, but they knew it was coming, in spite of there, in the real world, a blue sky, a few white clouds. On the bed the grey cat Hattie sensed their unease and stopped purring. Tom put his hand on Jane's thigh, the better to forget what was going on out there, seen or unseen.

'I thought you wanted to sleep,' she said.

'This is crazy,' he said. 'Why don't I live here? Then we could use beds the way other people use them. We wouldn't have to be in bed in the middle of the day.'

'I like it like this,' she said.

'You don't love me,' he said. 'It's obvious.' He removed his hand. 'You don't know the meaning of the word love,' he said. 'You're over-educated. What do you think I am, some kind of stud?'

It really made no difference what they were arguing about. Her reluctance to marry, settle, wash socks, have children — which he saw as just a habit of thought, a pattern of belief, an ongoing fear of change, something more to do with the ascendancy her mind had somehow gained over her body than anything to do with her essential nature; his failure to match his sexual desires to hers, which she registered as a hostile act; his intention to punish and humiliate her for earning more than he did; his fear of giving voice to his feelings; his inability to offer reassurance and comfort; his failure to acknowledge her equal status; her lack of taste, as he saw it; his lack of understanding, as she did. One way or another accusations and insults began to crackle in the air, feelings no longer contained but given voice to. You did this and you said that. Wimp and harpy, bastard, bitch. Unfaithful! Gutter slut and macho pig and the simple, friendly, curing pleasures of desire fulfilled denied – and just as well, perhaps, lest sex itself become the weapon, and then indeed there'd be an end to everything, and neither in their heart wants that. But spite and rage preferred – preferred, that's the shocking thing, the self-revelation that hurts and wounds – chosen above love and kindness not just by the other but by the self. Not so much the other hurt, humiliated by the other, as the self by the self. The row is with the self, the other stands witness, accepting the bruises: it is some kind of horrid, magic, contrapuntal duet: variations on a theme; how can the unloveable, my self, be loved by you; your fault that it cannot. Projection. Simple! He accuses her of his own deficiencies: he hands them over. She does the same to him. Outrageous! How can I be expected to put up with this? And what is more, and have you forgotten; accept this evidence, accept it or I'll kill you, that you do not love unloveable me! Unforgivable!

The row is vaporous: it circles blackly, out this window, into that: it never stops; when you make up others begin: their turn next; always someone's. It feeds on itself, it feeds on you, the more you give in to it, the bigger it grows, the more powerfully it affects your neighbours, down here in the shameful gutter world, up there in the reeling attic sky, breeding every ill that flesh is heir to.

Keep your mouth shut, keep it shut, take a pill to knock you out. How gently, silently, this ire crept, the first cold wet breath through slammed shut windows. *You* shut the window: *I* want it open: Why? Because *you* want it shut. *I* shut it, knowing *you* didn't want it. Why don't *you* love *me*? Why, because *I'm* unloveable, but not as unloveable as *you*. And what is radiation compared to this virus already in the bloodstream?

Oh yes, a virus. The row comes like a virus. Unseen, unheard, unknown. It comes in a droplet, through a break in the skin, the brushing of flesh, a flavour in the air, a particle inhaled. Once in the blood it's there for ever, an infection; a lingering, debilitating disease, flaring up from time to time. Once you're sensitized, the first time you succumb, there it is, yes, for ever; a spiritual TB, before the development of antibiotics; sometimes it kills, sometimes it doesn't: it just doesn't go away; it merely hides to wait its triggering. Can't wait! AIDS of the spirit.

In the end Jane Jarvis scratched and clawed Tom Jeffrey and he left the house saying he'd rather die than return to face the virago, and they didn't make it up till Sunday, when they went out to supper and she ordered oysters and he let her pay. He was growing a beard. Lemon juice trickled amongst the black bristle. He had a square jaw and even teeth. He was a good-looking man, a sensitive man, a talented man. One day the world would recognize him. He would make a good father. He wanted to be a father.

Oh yes, indeed a virus, caught somewhere along the way by Jane Jarvis, at Oxford perhaps. He certainly thought that was where she'd picked it up.

It could not be in the genes, could not be in the nature, must be culturally induced, caught. Joanna May suffered a severe attack at the age of sixty, but had not been previously afflicted. Her relationship with Carl had ended with the murder of a third party, true, but that was Carl's doing and coolly done; no one had ever shouted, screamed or clawed. No, there was this to be said for Joanna and Carl – they never descended hand in hand, step by step, into that shocking desert landscape where the air is rent with whining and spiteful complaint, and the self stands isolated and terrified in all its snarling, scratching fury.

Jane Jarvis said to her Tom as he left, in the rain, 'With people like you in the world, how can it be anything but doomed. I hope you inhale beta particles and die.'

And this was the man she loved, or tried to love, or hoped to love, and knew if she didn't love, who else would there be?

Julie Rainer heard on the news that a radioactive cloud hovered over the country, and blamed the Russians, since her husband was away on business as he so often was, and there was no one else to blame. She closed the windows and poured away the milk. She stalked her lonely, perfect, tasteless house and filled in yet another form for yet another adoption agency: checking her lies against a note of previous lies in a booklet kept solely for this purpose. Her husband could not have children: he was infertile. She had spent hours, hours of intensive life with doctors' fingers and spatulas inside her, investigating, before they turned their attention to him: it was her fate, her destiny, she felt, to have these prying feelers there. She despised herself. She lacked the courage to be artificially inseminated, she lacked the courage to leave her husband, though she did not love him, whatever that meant. She felt she would gain courage in the end: but by then it would be too late to have babies.

Time was against Julie, as it is against all women, in such gynaecological matters. In the meantime, she loved her animals, who gave her work in the way that babies do: removing dog hairs from a sofa, replacing chewed seat belts, nursing aged cats, cleaning up after kittens, discouraging algae in the fishbowl – these things gave her pleasure, a sense of achievement . . .

'You love those animals more than me,' said Alec,

closing his leather briefcase, off again, mini-computer in hand.

'I expect I do,' was all she said. She only told lies on forms.

She called up the vet to ask him what to do with the animals in view of the radioactive cloud and he said he doubted they would come to much harm, no one seemed to know how much radiation was about, or indeed what radiation actually was, but it would also do no damage to keep them in, and even perhaps to bath the dogs.

'But supposing the water's radioactive?'

He thought she was the most beautiful woman he'd ever met, but over-anxious. He thought her husband neglected her. He had the sense that she waited for her life to take its proper direction, and that also, if she was not careful, she would wait for ever. She was lost: in the wrong place: with the wrong fate: making herself neutral.

'Shall I come over?' he asked.

'No,' she said sadly.

'It's a pity your husband's away at such a time,' he said. 'Chernobyl has made everyone nervous, probably more nervous than they need to be.'

'You can't see it but it's always there,' she said, 'like my husband. I'll just call the animals in, shall I?'

'Good idea,' he said, and went to deliver a calf which had two heads. These things happen, with or without radiation. The farmer was inclined to blame Chernobyl, all the same, and however irrationally.

Gently, Julie Rainer, aged thirty, 5 foot 7 inches, 36–24–36, wiped the paws of Hilda her grey cat with a damp cloth, but Hilda took offence and scratched her. Julie watched a line of blood ooze along her white inner arm and threw the poor creature – the one she loved – across the room.

'Bloody animal,' she shrieked, 'bloody animal! It's all Alec's fault.' Later of course she stroked and cosseted the cat, who fortunately had not seemed to take deep offence, and then she went out into the night and breathed deeply, to punish herself.

———— ◦◦◦ ————

Cliff came home on time and Gina did not realize he'd been drinking until too late.

'Isn't it terrible about this thing at Chernobyl?' she said, when he came in. She was 5 foot 4 inches, 38 around the chest, 28 around the waist and 40 around the hips. Well, she had been seven weeks premature and reared in a less fortunate environment than Joanna May, her original.

'Don't give me any of that fancy stuff,' he said. 'Where's dinner?'

'Not quite ready,' said Gina. 'I had to get the kids back home from the park. It was raining; supposing what they say is right: the rain's radioactive?'

'I want some straight talking round here,' he said. 'Dinner is either ready or is not ready, and if it is not this is what happens,' and he hit her.

Now, the kind of row that occurred between Gina and Clifford was of a rather different genus than the one that slowly developed between Jane and Tom. It was not a black cloud that little by little took over a clear sky: not a virus sent to blight the life of the potentially happy. No, this was the kind of domestic discontent that runs like gutter sludge through the houses of the depressed and desperate, be they smart new bungalow, palace or slum – and once your children get their feet wet there's no drying them out. Mothers' noses get broken, eyes blacked, kidneys damaged, unborn babies killed; the little witnesses have a hard time of it; thwarted in their desire, their passion, to love someone, anyone, who is worthy of their love, they grow up to lay about them likewise. It is never over. Parents must be worthy of their children's love, and that's all there is to it. And whoever grows up, properly, finally? Not *you*, not *me*, not *him*, not *her*.

'Where's my dinner?' he says. He might be four. 'Not ready,' she says. She might be six. Wham he goes: he's all of fourteen. 'How can you?' she wails; fifteen if she's a day; and to the neighbours, grown-up at last, 'I walked into a lamp-post,' denying truth, so what sort of grown-up is that? And not so different in essence perhaps, just more swift, more desperate, more dangerous than Jane and Tom. Where's my dinner means did you care for me in my absence, did you notice I was gone, Mum oh Mum, how can I trust you? Not ready means no actually I didn't, I don't care about you one bit; wham means I can't express this sorrow, this grief, this disappointment, in words, you self-righteous bitch, you cow: the wham arrives reinforced by a great communal strength, the sudden surge of the male's hatred of the female who will not be possessed, will not be owned, will not be all body but will have a soul, and who in the refusing suggests some unattainable, other ideal. And then her tears, her silly tears of resentment mean see I knew you were like this, you've proved it again; her loyalty acknowledges that if I am punished it must be my fault, things will get better, you my neighbour can't possibly understand the complexity, not his fault, mine, I have failed, I have failed – the whole thing's impossible . . .

If there's no one around for Gina, and no one around for Cliff, either will kick the cat. There! Told you after all that I was unloveable. See what you've done?

In the next room the children turn up the TV – they'd have done better to stay in the park, in a different kind of fallout. Presently Gina comes in to say, 'Sorry about the explosion. It's all over now.' Except her nose is bleeding, so it clearly isn't. Why does she tell such lies? Why doesn't she leave? She doesn't leave because how can she leave, where can she go, she hasn't got the courage: one day perhaps she will, she says, leave. But leave what? Who? Herself – that's what she fails to understand, late with his dinner because Chernobyl exploded. How does she leave herself behind?

He is the product of her imagination taken flesh: she married him to make him flesh, he is what she deserves. She stood there and said, 'I will, I will!',

73

knowing his nature, the strength of his backhand, the cheap wine reddy-brown upon his teeth.

Those who have rows are more alive than those who don't: make better friends, more interesting companions. They may wreak havoc but they understand their imperfections – witness how they project them upon others – they cry to heaven for justice. They believe in it.

––––⋅•⋅––––

Alice had a row with her agent. He was her nearest and dearest. Other men came and went, but he was the voice on the phone, unsweaty, unsmelly, a man firm and strong upon a letterhead.

He rang her to say Kiev was cancelled. She'd been going to do a show there.

'I don't believe it,' she said. 'You're doing it on purpose.'

'Alice, be reasonable,' he said. 'How could I make a nuclear power station explode?'

'You're using it as an excuse. You didn't want me to do this show. You don't want me to represent my country abroad. You want me to do some cheap swimsuit for some cheap mag because there's more in it for you.'

Alice was 5 foot 8 inches tall, 33 inches around the chest, 22 round the waist and 32 around the hips. She'd spent a week longer in the womb than Jane or Julie, and eight weeks longer than Gina. She exercised and dieted. She was in love with herself: she would stand naked in front of a mirror and run her hands across her body: she would do anything for herself.

'There's never anything in it for me,' he said. 'Ten per cent! A tip. That's all it ever is, a tip.'

'Perhaps it's time I got a new agent,' she said.

'Perhaps it is,' he said.

There she went again. Prove *you* love *me*, before *I* prove *you* don't. Later *he* called to apologize. *She* knew *he* would. *He* needed *her* more than *she* needed *him*.

Sometimes Alice felt alone in the world. She wished she'd had a sister: all she had for company was her little grey cat, and that was often left for neighbours to feed and so was cantankerous. Nevertheless the penalties of continual companionship, that is to say marriage, seemed too onerous to contemplate. What did she need with a husband in the flesh when her agent on the phone cared so much about her – how she looked, how she felt, where she'd been, what she earned – and all in exchange for a tip. Sex she could take or leave – and often left, for the sake of her looks. Not just because of the necessity of early nights if her eyes were to stay bright and large, but because sex made her screw up her face and that encouraged wrinkles.

One day she might marry, one day. Not yet. One day she might find the courage to marry.

So thought and felt the clones of Joanna May, before they discovered each other and themselves.

12

After his conversation with Carl May, Gerald Coustain put down his cordless telephone and said to his wife Angela, 'The man's a monster.' They sat in the garden. She was setting examination papers in A-level European history: she had lean academic fingers. He was potting out delphiniums: he had plump and clumsy ones: he was a civil servant of the stout complacent kind. She did not reply: what was the point: she knew Carl May was a monster. The sun went behind clouds; the wind was suddenly cold: there was rain in it.

'I think perhaps we should go indoors,' he said.

'Why's that?' she asked, absently, lost somewhere in the Boer War. 'It will stop in a minute: it's only spitting.'

'There is a possibility the rain is radioactive,' he said.

'Don't be absurd,' she said. 'Things like that don't happen.'

But she gathered up her papers and they went inside. He left the delphiniums to take their chances.

'Perhaps we should change our clothes and shower?' he said.

'I would rather die than do anything so extreme,' she said.

'Death itself is extreme,' he said.

'If you envisage this alleged radiation as life-threatening,' she said, 'shouldn't you be measuring it to find out? Or something?'

'Our organization is a little sketchy,' he said, 'and I am not getting much cooperation where I had hoped to find it. I can't get through to the Department. The lines are jammed.'

'Perhaps you should go in to the office,' she suggested.

'On a Sunday? I spend Sundays with my family.'

'All the same,' she said.

'Besides which,' he said, 'it's safer indoors. Bricks and mortar offer some small protection. No one would expect it of me, to go in to the office through radioactive streets on a Sunday.'

He felt her disapproval and stood out against it. He must be allowed to make his own decision, surely.

'How is poor Joanna?' he asked, to change the subject. Angela had been Joanna's best friend, until the divorce. After that, of course, the relationship had become difficult.

'Joanna was never poor,' said Angela. 'Nothing poor about Joanna. Her house would make two of this, she has a park rather than a garden, her month's alimony is my year's housekeeping.'

'In the circumstances, Carl May was generous. I would not be so generous, if I caught you at it.'

She laughed. It was hardly likely that he would. She was plain as a pikestaff, warts and moles all over the place and hairy legs. People were amazed at the match.

77

He'd been a good-looking man when young: he could have done better for himself. But he hadn't wanted to: he'd wanted her: and as for her, she didn't give two figs for her looks. Their children, surprisingly, were all handsome, in a tall, strong-jawed way, and being male, their facial hair was not a matter for concern.

'That way he can control her,' said Angela. 'If she accepts his generosity.'

'I suppose it is better to be controlled than ignored,' he said. 'Poor thing.'

'She has a young friend,' said Angela. 'The gardener: the man who pots out her delphiniums.'

'You're making it up.' Gerald Coustain did not want to know this.

'But I saw him when I went round the other day. She was looking wonderful. Not quite so perfect and clear-cut as she usually is – a little blurred around the edges. Swollen-mouthed. Sex, I suppose.'

'What were you doing round there, in any case? I'd rather you didn't call on her. Meet for lunch, of course, in town, if you insist. But not too close, Angela. No home visits: especially not if what you say is true. Carl May might see you as an accomplice. Be prudent.'

'If your promotion depends on my prudence, you've had it anyway,' said Angela. 'Hadn't you better be getting along to the office?'

'There are no trains to speak of, not on Sundays.'

'Then get a taxi.'

'Certainly not. It is not a question of my promotion, Angela, but of your safety. God knows what Carl May might do next. He had his wife's lover written

78

off, blanked out, knocked off the perch, however you want to express it –'

'Murdered. But there were special circumstances. One can't condone it, of course.'

'It has hardly reached "condone", Angela. One doesn't even know about it! Just don't get involved, that's all. I hope she has the sense not to boast about her lover to you ladies, or this one won't last two minutes either.'

'You ladies!' she scorned him. 'You ladies! Where has your courage gone? Can't say boo to Carl May, can't get to the office in case the rain's radioactive –'

In the end he went, as she knew he would. Angela served as her husband's conscience. Women who play this role are often as plain as pikestaffs – indeed, the plainer the better: Angela had a grey skin, a double chin, short grey greasy hair and wore belted navy blue around a waist almost larger than her hips, and her husband was never rude to her, or tried to make her unhappy.

13

The next day Angela called Joanna.

'How are you, darling?' she asked.

'Do you really want to know?' asked Joanna.

'Yes,' said Angela, settling in to listen. Angela had undertaken to see Joanna through her divorce: so much one woman will often do for another, although with luck the service may never have to be reciprocated. But you never know, you never know! The burden of guilt, indignation, upset, and general sense of injustice must be handed round, communally shouldered: it is too much for one person, one 'I', to bear. The 'you' must take a hand. At first the phone calls come at any time of day or night: the woman wronged, the 'I', has no idea of time, place or pertinence: then the notion of the otherness of the recipient, the sharer of distress, the *you* reasserts itself: the calls are at least prefaced by 'is the milk boiling over? the toast burning? is Hollywood on the other line? have you a minute?' and it's clear the healing process is under way. Joanna was by now far down the road to recovery: whole conversations could be held without mention of Carl. But of course Chernobyl and his face on the television screen that morning had stirred up what Angela saw as a good deal of muddy sediment:

nasty little insects crawled again in and out of slime: they had only been playing dead: they were back again, spreading disease and discomfort.

'When I think how Carl has behaved to me!' said Joanna, and it was clear to Angela she had had quite a relapse. 'When I think how I wasted my life, simply threw it away! Why did my parents allow it? Carl May was a completely unsuitable match: it was unforgivable of them. They just wanted me out of the house. I was born to have children, but no, Carl May wouldn't have that: the day before we were married he told me he didn't want any. What could I do? Everything arranged: all the guests: the presents: I had to agree. You know what he's like. I was so young I thought it didn't matter. Infatuated! His unhappiness had to be loaded on to me; that was what it was. He denied life, made me deny it too. He turned me into some sort of snow queen and when I made just one small attempt to thaw myself out he used it as an excuse to throw me out of his life – he set it all up, I swear he did. He was just waiting for the opportunity to be rid of me.'

'Yes, but Joanna –' said Angela, cautiously.

'I'm sorry, am I boring you? You do agree, don't you? I am right?'

'Carl may look at it a little differently. Carl came into his art gallery one day and found you and that Egyptologist together.'

'For heaven's sake, Angela, I was over fifty.'

'What has that got to do with it?' Angela sounded really interested: she really wanted to know.

'Obviously I was desperate and Carl should have understood that.'

'But Joanna, I'm over fifty and I'm not desperate.'

'But you're happily married!' Joanna's normally quiet voice was suddenly quite loud.

'And now you're not married at all,' replied Angela. Joanna was silent. She sniffed a little.

'I don't know what's the matter with me today. Why did Carl choose to come into the gallery at that particular time? He never went in, normally. Besides, I thought he was away: he usually was.'

'Perhaps he suspected something. Perhaps you seemed unusually happy.'

'Oh, I was. Isaac was so much the opposite of Carl. But he had to put paid to that, didn't he? And then that accident – if accident it was.'

'Of course it was, Joanna.' Though nobody believed that for one minute – Isaac, crossing the road outside the Eton Square house, in too much of a hurry, knocked down and killed by Philip the chauffeur, reversing into the garage. Oh yes!

'Carl was so hard and cold about it all: not an ounce of sympathy for me.'

'Could you expect it?'

'Yes I could! We'd been married for thirty years and it was always me looking after him, worrying about him, listening to tales of his dreadful childhood; didn't I deserve anything in return? We were supposed to love each other.'

'I think that's what Carl believed, Joanna. And then you went and had an affair with another man; not even someone more important, or younger, or richer than him, but some penniless librarian with straggly hair. What an insult! Of course he reacted. I know you think he over-reacted, but men are like that,

82

especially men like Carl, who are used to having their own way.'

'Whose side are you on, Angela?'

'Yours, Joanna, you know I am. But Carl did have a point of view.'

'Well, I don't see it. I suppose you're busy.'

'I am a bit.'

'Your children are about to visit you, I suppose.'

'Yes.'

'And the grandchildren?'

'Yes.'

'You see, you have everything and I have nothing.'

'Joanna,' said Angela briskly, 'you have a house worth two million pounds –'

'It's falling down, and Carl won't pay a penny for repairs.'

'You have a butler –'

'He's gay. Carl will only let me have gay servants. I'm surprised he doesn't have them castrated as well, just to be on the safe side.'

'And a gardener who shares your bed. Perhaps Carl is right. You are simply not to be trusted.'

'How do you know about Oliver?' asked Joanna, after a short silence.

'It's obvious.'

'Don't tell Carl,' said Joanna, 'or he'll kill me.'

'Or the young man, judging from past form,' said Angela, quite bleakly, and quite seriously.

'I'd thought of that,' said Joanna.

'And you let him take the risk?'

'If I do,' said Joanna, 'so can he. It's worth it. I don't care any more. I don't mind being dead. What have I got to live for? Next year's crocuses?'

Angela said, 'All I can say is, Joanna, keep your young man out of the garden for the time being. His parts might begin to glow in the dark, and you wouldn't like that. Gerald seems to think we're getting quite a lot of radioactivity over here.'

'How lucky you are,' was all Joanna said, 'to have Gerald.'

14

Angela is a good friend. She is a Doctor of European History, but she pretends to be less than Gerald in all matters because thus she preserves the domestic and marital peace, and she reckons those are of all things the most important to preserve, above dignity, truth and honour, and who is to say she is not right? She is married and I am not, and I am sufficiently a child of my generation to believe a woman who has neither husband nor children is scarcely a woman at all.

I, who revealed the truth one day, and lost everything, including dignity and honour, should be the last to suggest that she is wrong. Isaac of course lost more in a similar revelation; that is to say his life. But he had often told me he'd die for me if he had to. Fate listened, that was all: happened to be passing by, as he spoke, with its ear-muffs off. Alas, by dying, Isaac did me no good. He stepped without looking into the path of a reversing car just outside the May Gallery. There were no witnesses, and it was known that Isaac had left the gallery early with a migraine, and a man who has a migraine does not look carefully where he is going, so who was to doubt the driver's word – he being chauffeur to Carl May, and with a clean driving licence, and doing nothing more sinister at the time than backing into his own garage, albeit across the public pavement? And Isaac King had no family to dig away at the matter, to fling up dirt and dust until some nasty scandal was revealed, some bleached bone of unfleshed-out truth discovered.

Isaac was one of those rare and valuable people who are, or appear to be, totally innocent in their life's work: who, by pursuing their own interests, do no apparent harm to anyone. An academic, an antiquarian, an Egyptologist, his imagination fired by Rider Haggard's Cleopatra when he was a boy, his fervour fanned in various university departments; and then, discovering the civilization of Ancient Egypt to be a culture of the wholly benign, the unmalicious, thereafter lived by sifting the desert sands for scraps and shards yet undetected, nodding politicly at museum curators, with impossible care and patience deciphering the all but indecipherable, piecing together fragments, writing up, collating, publishing papers only a handful of people anywhere in the world would understand. He wanted to bring the past to life. A benign and beautiful past, like no other.

'Is there any money in it, this Egyptology of yours?' asked Carl, at the interview. He was looking for a curator first and a collection second. He had a gallery: he wanted to put something in it: he wanted to be known as a cultured man. An enviable opportunity for the right person. I was there at the interview. I was to be involved. I was to be cultured too. I rather fancied Meissen, but Egyptology turned up.

Isaac smiled at Carl's question. He had a kindly but melancholy air. His smile was somehow forgiving. I understood then for the first time that Carl needed to be forgiven: the understanding cracked wide my wifely love and admiration, and through the crack all kinds of emotions and sensations came rushing unannounced.

'Twelve chairs of Egyptology in all the world?' Isaac King enquired. 'Six hundred devotees at most, turning up to the occasional conference, to compare notions and theories? Of course there's no money in it.'

And Carl, I knew, was both impressed and horrified by such selfless dedication. And as for me, I thought this Isaac King was just wonderful. A good man. So kindly was this man, so generous, so trusting, that coming across the embalmed mummy of a newborn baby, and discovering no body inside, but only sawdust, he concluded not that the embalming priests had cheated the grieving parents but, being too enthusiastic with their fluids, had disintegrated the body by accident, and decided to go ahead with the funeral without telling the parents for fear of upsetting them.

Carl May would never have reached such a conclusion. Nor would my father. Nor indeed did I. But I loved Isaac for believing the best, and not the worst. We were in each other's company from time to time, in that musty vaulted room, the May Gallery, and the pleasures of ideas exchanged became the pleasure of emotion shared, and eventually touch as well. We were as close as we could get.

Carl had me locked in my room so I couldn't go to Isaac's funeral. It would not perhaps have been proper: in giving evidence at the inquest it was I who told the world Isaac had complained of a migraine. He had complained of no such thing – merely that I would not leave Carl there and then, discovered in flagrante delicto as we were, and go off and live with him in his bedsitting room in Ealing, which smelled of gas fire and tooth powder, for all his goodness and generosity. But I was guilty and afraid. I had betrayed Carl and been discovered. Yet I still hoped for Carl's forgiveness. Indeed, I expected it. I had made my demonstration of discontent: now I wanted things to be as before. But how could they be?

And so I moaned and groaned about the unfairness of it all to Angela, while trying not to acknowledge that, of the two of us, Isaac had had by far the worst deal. And she, to her credit, kept pointing it out, waiting for the day when I would have ears to hear. How *good* she is. This practising of so prudent a doctrine, of course, that of female subservience, does have some drawbacks. It renders Angela catty in her conversation: occasionally, one feels, out of sheer desperation, giddy in her behaviour and desperate in her undertakings. The unplucked whiskers on her chin, the straggly hair and wrinkled stockings, suggest some kind of revenge upon the world in general and on her husband in particular. But Gerald, dear Gerald, the amiable fool, seems not to notice, or care: they enfold each other happily enough at night, she tells me, her bulges against his paunch; her feet, untreated bunions and all, tangling with his softer, whiter, smoother ones. Gerald is a civil servant, he drives a car, his shoes are softest leather – his feet are in good shape. I saw his feet once, when the couple kindly asked me, the sorry divorcée, out to the local lido one weekend, to share with them the pleasures of an unexpectedly warm summer day: on littered grass crowded with suburban folk and children eating hot-dogs. Gerald and Angela are not smart at all: Carl couldn't abide them: once I too looked down on them; now I am grateful for them.

(Now Angela knows I am not so alone, of course; that Oliver leaves his nettle-pulling and rose pruning to slip into my bed, I may not get asked to the lido again. Pity may give way to envy – or so I pride myself.)

Something is going to happen. I can feel it. It is so quiet and orderly here in the house, it is unnatural. It is the lull before the storm. Even Oliver feels it. He makes love silently, as if afraid of disturbing someone, something. I am in the habit of being quiet in any case: Carl required very little sexual response from me, and seldom got it. Well, that suited me. Sex between us was a kind of formal dance: a ritual performed in the presence of my beauty, his power: confirmation that the one could be owned by the other. There was little sweaty enjoyment here, little ecstasy of the flesh – but it had its compulsion; like any rewarding habit it had become necessary – as going to church on Sunday might be for a religious-minded person. Or so it had seemed to me. Perhaps I was wrong? Perhaps it was central to his very existence

– in which case I had indeed provoked him. How could I, when it came to it, feel on Carl's behalf, any more than I could think for him? I should have allowed him, even after thirty years or so of marriage, some independence of emotion.

Oliver has dirt under his nails, both finger and toe: his broad working hands assist me in altogether new pleasures: I daresay I should be too old for these responses but I find I am not. Does he love me? I don't know. Why should he? I think he likes the thought of screwing the rich older woman who employs him: kicking off his muddy boots at the door and walking barefoot (he seldom wears socks, finding them constricting) along thick carpets on his way to my room. I don't think he laughs at me or reports on me to his friends.

I am fairly sure Oliver likes me. Carl never liked me. But then I didn't like him. I loved him. I admired him and was awed by him: Lord of the dark domains, as he was, and myself the Ice Queen, having dominion over many secret things.

A woman may go out to work, earn her independence, spurn suitors, decline marriage, and be in every way her own mistress. But she will never wake in the morning with this particular gratification – she will never open her eyes to tranquillity and luxury, as I so often did, with the agreeable thought, 'Good Lord! Little me! All this, and just because I look the way I do, am the person I was born.' Enough for this woman just to *be*; not like the other to be forever proving, convincing, striving, placating, buying the comforts and respect of the world. Let someone else, for this fortunate, idle woman, do all that: let he who loves her, maintain her.

Of course it may all come to an abrupt end: the husband's, the lover's, favour may suddenly and dramatically be withdrawn. All the same, the flavour of that confidence remains: it is not forgotten ... See how I crook my finger and young Oliver comes to my bed. The Ice Queen may be deposed, but she still knows who she is, and so does her subject. She who rules with the divine right of the old-fashioned female, she-who-must-be-obeyed, whose bag must be fetched, lawn mowed, glass kept filled. Someone has to do it.

I like Oliver. I like him for his implausibility, his trust in the future. He means to be a rock singer. He is getting it together. He has been doing this since he left college ten years ago. He lives by odd jobs; he can dry-stone-wall, dig ditches, lop trees, wire houses, clear blocked drains; he can paper and plaster, tell a comfrey from a borage leaf – the kind of things snow queens are not so hot at. Oliver looks like a young Elvis Presley and like him might presently run to fat. When things don't turn out right – the drummer loses his drums (how can anyone *lose* drums; they are so plentiful and bulky: still it's done) so the one gig of the year can't be set up – his girlfriend sends the engagement ring (such a *little* diamond!) back. She lives in Scotland: he only sees her at Christmas and Easter: of course she sends it back! Oliver simply smokes a joint or two, and ceases to worry. I join him. We pass the magic weed from hand to hand, enjoying

– as no doubt they will presently say in the ads – a special languid intimacy. I find simple things move me. When Oliver rolls a joint for us both, unwraps a boiled sweet for me, my heart turns over. Such kindness! I am unused to it. Carl would mix me a gin and tonic before our dinner guests arrived and hand it to me, smiling with his lips, but barking in his heart, a high-pitched non-stop frantic bark: the gesture did not really register as love, or kindness. Poor Carl. Poor me.

I try to forgive Carl: try not to burden my friends with these sudden spasms of anger, misery and resentment. It is my experience that a quiet mind is gained only by forgiveness: when you cease to see the other as enemy, as merely yourself in another guise, see the 'you' as perceived by the other, forget the notion of 'I' – *I* shiver, *I* suffer, *I* bleed; *I* hate, *my* head will burst with *my* resentments; *you* whom *I* hate for not acknowledging this *I* – then peace descends. Our lives are our own again.

Until the next storm bursts.

15

Those who fear a storm breaking have it in their hearts to whip one up. So Joanna did, forthwith. She too had seen the press photograph of her own front door (or so she regarded it) closing upon the high heel of young Bethany, but shut her conscious mind to its significance, putting aside the yellow press with conventional murmurings of 'rubbish' and taking up *The Times*, who contented themselves with a ten-year-old library shot of her ex-husband at the opening of the May Gallery, the bearded face of Isaac in the background, just discernible. These things combined – the conscious, the barely conscious, the unconscious – to send winds both hot and cold, feverish and chill, through her mind to brew up a veritable hurricane. Well might she fear the lull before the storm.

Joanna paced her marble floor and then went out to find Oliver pruning and digging out rhododendron bushes.

'I mean to sell this house,' she said. 'I hate it.' The King's House stood on the edge of the Thames, near Maidenhead. The river divided around it, to form an island.

'It's a very special house,' he said.

'Oh yes,' she said, 'I know. Some king kept it for his mistresses. Now it does for discarded wives.'

'George the Third,' he said, 'had it renovated for Priscilla Evans. Part of the kitchens dates back to the sixteenth century.'

'Oh, you would know,' she said.

'Yes I would,' he said, 'because I am interested in what goes on around me, not just what happens in my head.'

'Does that make you better than me?'

'No. Just different.'

Clip, clip went the secateurs, firmly and sharply. He took care not to bruise the wood he cut. She found his concern for the bush insulting.

'I think it's a very vulgar house,' she said, 'but you wouldn't understand that. You think because it is old that justifies everything.'

It was true that the house was an uneasy mixture of the cosy and the elegant: much balconied, pink-washed outside, a nook-and-cranny effect inside, suggestive of weighty lovers chirruping at one another, peeking round corners. Successive purchasers had added marble floors and gold taps, and green watered-silk ruffled curtains of such expense Joanna had been reluctant to take them down, though only ever truly at home with crimson velvet curtains, round shiny mahogany tables and sideboards, patterned carpets and Chinese vases.

Oliver put down the secateurs and carefully brushed each small wound with bitumen paint.

'All that trouble for a bush,' she said. 'I mean to put this house on the market, I'm not joking.'

'I don't think you'd be wise,' he said. 'It would be a lot of trouble for nothing. If you're not happy here where would you be happy?'

'Somewhere far far away,' she said, 'and don't tell me wherever I go I'd have to take myself with me or I'll scream.'

He laughed, and took up the spade and began to drive it into the stony ground beneath the largest of the bushes. His arms were bare; the muscles moved beneath brown skin.

'I'm sorry about this,' he said.

'About what?'

'I was talking to the bush,' he said. 'I'm digging it up. I'm apologizing.'

She fretted and tapped her foot.

'Why are you digging it up anyway?' she asked.

'Because it's old and keeping out the light from the others,' he said, 'and because purple rhododendrons very easily become a pest.'

'Well anyway,' she said, 'I'm going down to the estate agents now.'

'Look,' he said, 'this is a perfectly good house with a fine garden which had been allowed to go to rack and ruin and I'm just about getting it into shape again. I like it here very much.'

'Well, I'm bored and lonely here,' she said, 'and since I pay, what I say counts.'

He raised his eyebrows.

'You're just in a bad mood,' he said.

'Of course I am,' she said, scornfully. 'And I'll do

what I want, when I want, with my own house, my own garden.'

'Joanna,' he said, 'the garden can't be yours. Gardens are like children, they belong to whoever takes care of them.'

'Then stay round here and weed it for some other employer,' she said. 'Because it won't be me.'

'You need me, Joanna,' he said, and put down his spade. 'You have a very jealous nature. You're even jealous of rhododendrons. Why don't you help me dig them up? You'd feel much better.'

She looked at her long idle nails, her well-kept hands: she looked at his grimy and hardworking ones, no longer gardening, and felt better . . .

'It isn't in my nature,' she said, 'and besides, the air is full of radiation. Angela says it isn't wise to be out.'

'Perhaps I'd better come in then,' he said, 'or perhaps you'd better come under the bushes.'

And he would have pulled her under them there and then, and she would not have objected, or minded sharp stones against her back, her front, or twigs in her hair, or dirtying her purple dress, only the postman chose to come up the path at that moment, with a packet from the Maverick Enquiry Agency, which she could not ignore.

She left Oliver digging in the drifting outfall from Chernobyl and went inside, to read the report.

Fifteen minutes later she came out and said, 'I'm going to see Carl right now.'

'Why?' he asked.

'Because it's all too much to be endured,' she said.

'Don't go,' he said, and had she been listening, had she really cared about him, she would have heard that tone in his voice which is used by bit-part film actors who know that a sudden fatal blow is about to fall, in the next few frames, and try not to show it. But she wasn't listening; she didn't care; she was going to see Carl.

16

'Yet each man kills the thing he loves,' murmured Carl May, as he paced his elegant office in the tower block in Reading which was the hub of Britnuc's empire. The building had been designed to dominate the city skyscape, and so it had, but not for long. No sooner had the foundations settled, no sooner the first window cleaner toppled to his death – always the mark of a properly finished office building – than all around arose the thrusting towers of usurping empires – leaner, taller, glassier – but doomed to crumble and collapse, built on the hot and shifting sands of finance, not the rock of industry, the cold power of the atom. Carl May was neither shaken nor dismayed, though the arch of sky he loved was now the merest tent of blue, so high and near the false towers crowded. He knew they would not last.

'What is that you said, my dear?' enquired Bethany, looking up from her VDU, upon which she played computer games. He'd had the contraption carried up from a lower floor. In this calm and spacious room all was grey and pink and empty surfaces: uncluttered: all that was needed here was mind: no tools of trade, no paper, pens, or telephones: he was too grand for that. But Bethany must have her toys.

'I was quoting,' he said, 'from *The Ballad of Reading Gaol*.' It was Carl May's joke. His empire, his prison! Oscar Wilde, once imprisoned for imprudence in Reading Gaol – still there, that gaunt grey building, still used, not a quarter of a mile away from where Carl May now had his throne – had through that imprisonment received his immortality.

'Do you think,' asked Carl May of Bethany, 'anyone would have taken any notice of Oscar Wilde if he hadn't gone to prison?'

But how was Bethany to answer a thing like that? She shrugged, and went on playing. He sighed. Carl May was restless. In the outer offices phones rang and minions ran; press officers dealt with queries concerning outfall and infall, becquerels and water-tables, cladding and coolants, leukaemia and bone cancer, prevailing winds and drifting particles. Head Office personnel took calls from Britnucs A and D where staff threatened action over the recent tightening of various safety regulations, and from B and C where there was some anxiety that the tightening had not been sufficiently extreme. PR withdrew distribution to better facilitate the instant re-editing of an entire series of linked film for internal, external and educational purposes: no one could say Britnuc was not on its toes since Chernobyl went up; and the External Services division within the day had liaised with Concrete Casings – of which Carl May was also a director – to tender to the Soviet Union so many tonnes of special-grade radiation-resistant (though so far untested in the field) concrete for immediate shipment to Kiev.

Carl, confident in the efficiency and dedication of his staff, reserved his energies for the highest level – that is to say ministerial dealings; but the Government was, on the whole, wisely quiet, until such time as ignorance, panic and bad judgement in the lower levels were either cured, or covered up.

One female journalist did get through to Carl May that day by impersonating the Prime Minister's voice, but that was the only entertainment in an otherwise boring morning for Carl May. Those who have perfected the art of delegation tend to suffer, in emergencies, from too much peace.

In Carl May's childhood kennel, there had been a lot to do. Not only had he soothed the savage heart of Harry the bull-terrier but trained him to fetch him scraps of newsprint from the streets around: Carl May himself, being chained by a collar, was in no position to do so. Those were the worst days. But they had not been boring.

'I never saw a man who looked
With such a wistful eye
Upon that little tent of blue
Which prisoners call the sky'

said Carl May to Bethany, but her hand was upon the control stick, her eyes upon the screen, and she seemed not to hear. In theory she worked upon a special personal project of his, an Open Day for Britnuc two years hence, thus avoiding bad feeling amongst his other secretarial staff; it was an arrangement which he could safely cancel nearer the time. He liked to have her close. He realized he had been lonely, and resented his ex-wife Joanna for having by her behaviour rendered him thus, so sadly and for so long. With what great effort had he, Carl May, brought himself to trust a cruel world, and how she had destroyed that trust, completing what his mother had begun.

He wondered, as he sometimes did, whether to trace the clones of Joanna May, and see how they had turned out, and whether one of them might not do instead of Joanna, but he could see the folly of it. The capacity for infidelity, Carl May suspected, ran in the genes; it could not be in the rearing—for surely Joanna had had a calm, tranquil and orderly rearing; she had seemed neither too fond of her father nor too antagonistic to her mother, and yet she had succumbed − and all he would do was set himself up again for the same shock and sorrow. Joanna at half her age would still be Joanna.

Bethany, thought Carl May; now Bethany was a different matter. She knew where her bread and butter lay. She had been bought. She acknowledged the transaction. He had taken, as it were, an option out on Bethany, body and soul. When it ran out, he would either renew on his terms, if he so chose, or let it lapse, and she would be free to go. He felt well disposed towards her. She gave him pleasure. He told her things he never told anyone. It would not last.

He did not want it to last. He felt humiliated as well as pleased, lessened as much as augmented. She was less than him in everything but youth.

'It is sweet to dance to violins,
When love and life are fair,
To dance to flutes, to dance to lutes,
Is delicate and rare:
But it is not sweet with nimble feet
To dance upon the air –'

said Carl May aloud.

Bethany hummed a little song as she worked upon her game: little trills and tweets rose round her, as if flocks of tiny birds flowed from her machine: her red hair fell enchantingly upon her face.

'Do you understand that?' asked Carl May.

'Understand what?' she asked. Carl May felt a stab of displeasure: it cut between his ribs like a knife.

'To dance upon the air is to hang,' he said. 'Love is a hanging offence.'

'Why's that?' she said, not caring.

'Because each man kills the thing he loves,' he said, 'which was where we began.'

'You didn't kill Joanna,' said Bethany, 'only her boyfriend, so what are you going on about?' On her screen, in search of paradise, she dodged monsters and beheaded and delimbed her enemies with a sword which flailed every time she pressed the space key.

Carl May thought if he had Bethany cloned, he could perhaps undo the effects of her upbringing. If he got Holly to remove one of Bethany's eggs, fertilized it *in vitro* with any old semen, removed the resultant nuclei and reinserted the nuclei of any one of Bethany's DNA-bearing cells (which the new dehydrating technique had made just about possible), and then had the egg implanted in a womb as stable and orderly as that of Joanna's mother – and such wombs could be found, now as then; their owners crying out for implantation – why then Carl May might create a perfect woman, one who looked, listened, understood and was faithful. If he reimplanted the egg in Bethany herself – but no, that would be hopeless; she was spoiled, sullied, somehow she would reinfect herself.

'Shoo fly,' murmured Bethany. 'Shoo fly, don't bother me,' and ping, ping, wimble, doodle, cheep cheep, splat went the little fluttering doves and ravens, the electronic sounds of victory and defeat – he'd made her turn the volume right down but still the small inanities, the false excitements, trembled and hovered in the air, insistent. He decided the cloning of Bethany would be more trouble than it was worth: it would require more time and energy than he had available. She made him feel tired, and that was the truth of it. Old King David's maidservant may have warmed his bed but she sure as hell carried him off quicker. He would be too old by the time Bethany was reissued, as it were, to get the benefit of it.

Now, if he had himself cloned, as he'd threatened Bethany – then the two younger versions of themselves could indeed pair off. But what use would that be to Carl May? Another body would feel the pleasure: another mind register it. Odd how the notion kept reasserting itself – that what one clone knew, would be known by all: what one felt, the others would feel; that to make clones was to create automatons, men without souls – soldiers, servants, deprived of will, decision. How could it be so? Did the common mis-conception suggest that the soul, whatever that was, would be split, divided out fairly amongst the repetitions — as if nature and God were indeed in some kind of partnership? For every new exercise in human diversity — a quarter of a million of them every day — God would dole out only one soul? They were in short supply? Nonsense! He wanted to talk to Joanna about it. Joanna the faithless, the betrayer: Joanna who mocked him, whispered about him behind his back, trapped and tortured him. Joanna Eve.

'Shoo fly,' murmured Bethany. 'Shoo fly, don't bother me!'

'What are you singing?' he asked.

'Just something that goes through my head,' she said.

'What's that?' he asked.

'It has no words,' said Bethany, but she lied. The words were clear in her head. If you went on from 'Shoo fly, don't bother me, For I belong to somebody,' you got to:

For an old man he is old,
And an old man he is grey,
But a young man's heart is full of love,
Get away, old man, get away.

Bethany stopped singing. She felt sad, to be so young and yet so old, twenty-four going on forty-two.

17

The clones of Joanna May would have been faithful if they could, but fate was against them. Like their master copy, Jane, Julie, Gina and Alice, for good or bad, were of a nature which preferred to have the itch of desire soothed, settled and out of the way rather than seeing in its gratification a source of energy and renewal. Here comes sex, they said in their hearts, here comes trouble! But trouble came. There was no stopping it, for them or anyone.

———◆◆◆———

Of the four, Jane Jarvis made the best and closest approach to monogamy. Her chosen parents, Madge and Jeremy, were academics – chosen by Dr Holly of the Bulstrode Clinic in conjunction with Carl May, of course, rather than herself, but when did any infant have the choice of its environment? No, the child is landed with what it gets, albeit sharing with its natural parents a characteristic or so – his brown eyes and her crooked little finger and a tendency to sniff, not to mention the bad temper of a maternal great-grandmother, the musical ability of a paternal great-uncle – which may or may not make the family placing easier when the baby erupts into it. But little Jane, long awaited, painfully implanted, was eagerly received into the world by parents who knew she was nothing to do with them, and didn't care, and never said: she was cherished, taught, instructed, cosseted, pressured and expected to pass exams, which she obligingly did. At sixteen she appointed – or so her manner suggested – an unkempt and unsuitable lad as her permanent boyfriend, much to his surprise and gratification and her parents' initial dismay. While other girls moaned, giggled, sighed, heaved, chopped, changed, got pregnant, gang-banged, gossiped and groped themselves out of any hope of further education, pretty little Jane Jarvis sat studying, her faithful and besotted Tom beside her, making coffee and replenishing pens and paper as required.

When she was seventeen, her quasi-father Jeremy the economist, the most steady and rational of monetarists, owl-eyed, unimpassioned, kindly and distant, startled his family and the campus by making one of his junior lecturers pregnant. He seemed sorrowful that the event had caused distress and concern; he announced the news at breakfast the day after Jane sat her English A-level and the day before her Sociology exam, thus greatly compounding his offence. 'Surely it could have waited,' wept Madge the Eng. Lit. structuralist. 'Are you trying to destroy her as well as me?' Jeremy seemed puzzled: he said he was going with Laura to the antenatal clinic so he would be late home for tea. Laura had been a frequent visitor to the house and had coached Jane in Economics, since Jane somehow cut off when offered instruction by her father.

Jane got a B in English and A's in Economics and Sociology. The results arrived the day Laura gave birth to a boy. 'You see,' said Jane to Tom, 'adversity just makes me concentrate the more.' Oxford let her in: she'd done the three A-levels in one year.

Madge wept and said to her husband at breakfast, the day the letter came from Oxford, 'I don't want you, I don't need you, go to her if that's what you want.'

'Look here –' he said.

'Go, go!' she screamed, so he went. Perhaps that was when Jane caught the row virus: her quasi-mother, rushing out of the room, beside herself, brushed one bare ageing arm against Jane's young one.

'It was their timing that was so awful,' Jane lamented to Tom later. When she went up to Oxford, leaving her mother alone in the big house, with its many bookshelves and bicycles and good prints, she found she was pregnant. Madge offered to have the baby; she needed something, anything, and Jane almost consented, but in the end she couldn't, she didn't, she had her future to think about. She had a termination at twelve weeks: a boy. A couple of years later Jeremy returned home: so that was just as well. It had been a kind of convulsion in all their lives, that was all. Everything smoothed out again. Laura married someone her own age and went to Sweden with the child. Madge became Professor of American Studies. Jeremy just seemed somehow older, and more tired, as if he'd tried something terribly important, and had failed at the last hurdle.

At the degree ceremony – she got a First in Eng. Lit. – he kissed the back of her neck with dry tired lips and said, 'I'm proud of you. I wish you were mine,' and she did not understand that, or pursue it, as she would have had it been some puzzling line in *Beowulf* or *Sir Gawain*. Some things are safer thought about than others.

And she'd ditched Tom by then. She had to. He was off at Art College in London, making a mess of things, quarrelling with his tutor, refusing to train for a career in advertising, too proud for this, too good for that, scratched and sore about the abortion, no matter that he understood the necessity, approved in theory, knew her body was her own, and so forth, knew there was lots of time for both of them – it had just been *that* baby, at *that* time – but he would keep reminding her, would keep upsetting her, and she needed a boyfriend on the spot, to save trouble and tantrums all around. Tom had to go.

Men pursued her, waylaid her, entreated her favours; yet when and if she looked in a mirror she could see only an ordinary, expected face, nothing special. Madge had never noticed how she looked, only what went on in her head. No one at home had told her she was pretty: Jeremy had seemed to notice her exam results more than herself, though responsive enough, it had seemed, to Laura. It was all a bother; too much to think about. She took up with a young man, a certain Stephen, a mathematician, good-looking, undemanding, as quiet and steady as Tom was noisy and wayward.

'You faithless bitch,' yelled Tom down the phone. 'You're never *here*,' she moaned, 'and when you are you're horrid.' 'I have to get my degree,' he shrieked, 'how can I be there?' 'I don't see why you can't be here,' she murmured. 'What do artists need with degrees?' 'You're cold, manipulative, selfish,' he said. 'You want to own me, control me. You treat me halfway between a little boy and a stud.' 'Then you're well rid of me,' she said. And he said, 'It's education has done this to you. It's changed you. Everything's in your head: there's nothing left in your heart. You don't know how to be natural any more: last time I was with you, you actually poured my coffee into a dirty mug. You've even forgotten how to wash up.'

'Good,' she said, and put the phone down. She stayed with Stephen for six years but wouldn't marry him, as he had hoped and expected, because of the problem of her needing to be in London – she had a good first job as a reader for MGM – and him having to begin his life as a chartered accountant in Newcastle, which was the only place he could get a job, so, coolly, she did without him. Well, fate was against her. If he'd been offered a job in London she would have stayed with him.

Madge and Jeremy were disappointed. When it came to it, it seemed they wanted her to be settled and ordinary, not independent and special. So much of it had been all talk.

And then Tom came back into her life, as they say in the magazines and, although it hardly seemed what she wanted, it was familiar, and would do. He filled her bed and sat opposite her in restaurants and they shared the bill, but he always had the feeling, did Tom, that she was looking over his naked shoulder –

109

him on top of her, no variations considered – to see who was there, who had come to the party more important, more interesting, than he. And she would croon and stroke her little grey cat, sadly, even directly after they'd made love, as if it was his fault, as if he were the gatekeeper to some other, more richly sensuous world than this, but would not let her in. When actually it was the other way round.

———◦◦◦———

Julie Rainer's chosen parents were not academics and did not believe in girls taking examinations: on the contrary: they had a feeling, vague though it was, that too much thinking made girls undomesticated and argumentative. If Julie was seen with a book, her mother Katie would say, 'Don't mope about reading: why don't you go for a nice walk?' or 'Look, there's some washing-up to do,' and Julie would obligingly put the book away. Her father, Harold, worked in Sheffield for a firm of stockbrokers: Kate did voluntary work around and about: they lived in a pleasant house with a large garden.

Harold and Katie had tried to have children for eight years, unsuccessfully, before they agreed on the new and risky method suggested by Dr Holly, and Katie had the little female foetus implanted: but being pregnant, swelling up, did not bring the ease she'd hoped for, the sense of fulfilment she'd been promised. The fact that the baby was so close did not, when it came to it, make it feel less of a little foreigner, on the contrary: and Harold would not be present at the birth, which was just beginning to be fashionable, and in the end she'd have preferred to have adopted a baby in the usual way, actually *seeing* what she was going to have to live with for years and years, making much the same kind of choice as she had when she married Harry. 'Like that, want it.' Not a bad way, when it came to it. She was happy enough with Harry: they'd wanted a baby badly, so badly, because they wanted it, couldn't have it.

Nothing wrong with little Julie, on the contrary: the brightest, prettiest, easiest little thing, Harry's pet, too much Harry's pet at first, perhaps that was the trouble, always sitting on his knee, him fondling perhaps overmuch, but how could one say a thing like that, except the baby wasn't Harry's flesh and blood, was it, and he knew it. Dr Holly might have been right when he suggested Katie didn't tell Harry about the implantation, simply went home and said, 'We're pregnant! A miracle!' but she hadn't taken Dr Holly's advice though, had she? Then the miracle did happen; when Julie was five (and playing Mary in the school Nativity play, of course) Katie did become pregnant, in the ordinary marital way, with a boy, a son, a firstborn no matter what Harry said, a wonderfully easy, natural birth, and Harry was there to hold her hand, and they called him Adam, and after that, really, though she was always perfectly kind to Julie, of course, that went without question, Adam was her real child, her only child, and when Julie, by then trained as a secretary and working in a local estate agent's office, came home one day and said, 'Mummy, I've met this wonderful man, Alec: he's my boss, actually: I want to marry him,' Katie said, 'Of course, darling, if you really and truly love him' and Julie said, 'I love him with all my heart and soul,' and who knew enough about her to disbelieve her, and Harry, who was having a secret affair with his own secretary, a girl Julie's age, a serious affair, true love, and wondering whether he had the courage to leave Kate, and if he did would Julie and Adam ever forgive him, said, 'Her life, her choice: pity about his wall-eye, but I suppose it makes the one that works the more acute, and the fellow's got a good business future, that's the main thing. When the chips are down it's income that counts.'

And Julie married Alec, dressed appropriately in virginal white. (Neither believed in sex-before-marriage:
Julie: '*What would Daddy think of me? He'd die.*'
Alec: '*I think marriage should be a sacrament: should really mean something.*')

The wedding took place in the village church, and it was written up in the *Daily Telegraph*, and their first house was on an executive estate. And after Alec had had his wall-eye fixed, thanks to new laser surgical techniques, there was no stopping him: they moved to bigger and grander estates, and he was away most of the time, developing holiday resorts, flying the world Club Class British Airways with his computer on his knee: and she never worried about other women: Alec really wasn't interested, she knew that and she didn't think she was or why would she have married him? She would have loved children but Alec couldn't have them: and her father had left her mother and gone off with his secretary which had thoroughly upset Julie, but she had the cats and the dogs and the fish, and loved them, especially her little grey cat; she could run her hand over its soft fur and watch the light catch the grey and turn it into a hundred different changing shades and now suddenly she found herself in love with the vet, or rather he was in love with her, and it hadn't been sex, really, just closeness – but who in the world was there to talk to about these things? Not Alec. For Alec the past was over. Like his wall-eye, better not remembered. And how could you talk to someone who wasn't there, but flying about the skies all the time? How could you talk to your husband about your lover?

There was no talking to her mother. Her mother had gone downhill since her father left. She ranted and raved and said odd things, which hurt. Julie thought she drank too much. 'You're no flesh of mine,' she'd say to Julie, and in the same breath complain that Harry hadn't been there at Julie's birth, and Julie had bitten her on the way out: she'd been born with one tooth already cut. So how could she talk to a mother who wanted only to hurt and confuse her? And how could she not go to bed with the vet, because it was bed first and talking after, with him. She'd have been faithful if she could, but fate was against her. If she'd had friends, it might not have happened. She could have talked to them. But friends where she lived came in couples, talked in couples; you could go out to dinner and talk non-stop and say noth- ing: and disloyalty over morning coffee was not allowed: and besides, the others had children, and she did not. She was an outsider, alone and lonely. Of course she went to bed with the vet. But she didn't want to. She would rather have been happily married.

———◦◦◦———

And Gina? Ah well, Gina. Gina lifted her skirt to show the boys her knickers when she was nine, and took off her knickers to show them more when she was ten, and at twelve was deflowered in the back seat of a cinema, and at thirteen was hitchhiking down the A1 for the fun of it, and at fourteen was declared beyond parental control, and by sixteen was back home again and quite reformed and at eighteen was pregnant and married to Cliff, a would-be pop singer, and garage mechanic, and by twenty-eight had three children by two different fathers, but she'd still have been monogamous if she could. She'd had sexual encounters with some thirty men by the time she was married, fate being against her, and had felt altogether happy and at ease for perhaps ninety minutes of her life till then: the minutes in which she exercised proper sexual power over men, became the magnet to which they were drawn which could never fail; the minutes, however brief, just before actual penetration. From then on the man's energies took over, she was neither here nor there, and it was no fun: sometimes, depending on circumstance, it was even horrific. The more of them, the less of her. She felt it.

Perhaps the seven-day-old Joanna-foetus that was to become Gina lacked some vital energy, or, if you look at it another way, perhaps some segment of the double helix of the DNA which so strongly and happily composed Joanna, Jane, Julie and Alice had

114

become fused and blurred in Gina. These things do happen, chance intervenes, being no respecter of the wishes and intentions of geneticists, let alone microbiologists. Gina was implanted in the womb of an impetuous young woman, by name Annette, who'd come south from Scotland to start her life afresh, and had been swept off her feet by an earnest and intellectual bookseller named Douglas with exotic tastes and a wen on his almost bald head.

They were married within the week. She was a good cook and a fine bookkeeper and he needed both. She worked in the shop, typed the bills, learned the book trade, charmed the customers – and then she wanted a baby. Douglas didn't. Later, later, he said, standing over her every morning to make sure she took her contraceptive pill. He didn't trust her and was right not to. 'I'll do it another way,' thought Annette, and went to visit Dr Holly at the Bulstrode Clinic, whose fame had spread throughout London in the late fifties as the maker or taker away of babies, depending on which you wanted. She told Dr Holly what she hadn't told Douglas – that to date she'd had one stillborn baby, Down's Syndrome, and four abortions. And Dr Holly said, since her husband's sperm was unavailable, and her eggs not reliable, he could give her a baby of her own without either. And under local anaesthetic, there and then, he implanted little Gina.

Dr Holly wasn't sure how long he could keep the processes of cell division going outside the womb; he said time was running out for this particular foetus; he could feel it. Carl May said he saw no reason for

115

or evidence of any such deterioration, but Carl May, Dr Holly said, thus offending his benefactor, had a layman's view of the material world – that is to say he thought there had to be a reason for things to go wrong. Things just happened, as any scientist could affirm. You knew by the pricking of your thumbs. Had Dr Holly not been in such a hurry, he might well have rejected Annette as a suitable birth parent: as it was, he trusted to luck. There were more than enough wombs to choose from; he had little excuse; they thronged the waiting room of the Bulstrode Clinic, brought there by rumour. There were women who wanted babies, and couldn't have them, or had babies and didn't want them, women trying to save babies, women trying to lose babies, and most of them weeping or on the verge of weeping. Dr Holly felt, and Carl felt with him, that an evolutionary process which caused so much grief could surely be improved upon by man: genetic engineering would hardly add to the sum of human misery, so great a sum that was, and might just possibly make matters a good deal better. No doubt in time the techniques of artificial reproduction would be further advanced and manipulation of DNA itself made possible so that improved and disease-resistant human beings could in the end be produced. In the meantime, Holly and May did what they could; May providing money and inspiration and Dr Holly surgical deftness and experience. It was just he was perhaps, this time, in rather too much of a hurry.

So there Annette was, pregnant with a diminutive Joanna, who seemed less and less likely to reach her potential as the pregnancy proceeded. Annette's husband, discovering her pregnant, threw her out of the house, claiming the baby was not his. She told him the truth, which made matters worse. (He'd tried to sue Dr Holly but lawyers would not take on his case: he was excitable and it sounded like sheer fantasy to them, a tale told by a guilty wife. In the end he gave up.) Annette, distressed, drank too much, smoked too much, went home to Scotland, had the baby six weeks early, failed to love it, left it with her parents, who, the more they feared their granddaughter would go the same way as their daughter, brought this fate upon her.

'Mum,' Annette would say, at the beginning, over the phone from as far away as possible, 'she can't inherit anything from me, because she isn't anything to do with me. Her genes are different. I know what you're going to say next. "We don't let her wear jeans. She always wears a dress." Christ, I could almost feel sorry for her.' Then Annette drifted away altogether. Grandfather had a stroke, grandmother's vision was impaired. Grandmother drank too much, mostly sherry. There were no books in the house. Gina learned to read from the back of the cornflake packet and the fronts of buses. She had a weak bladder and wet her knickers a lot which made her unpopular at school – a graffitied, run-down place – with both teacher and pupils. She was classified as disturbed, she was unhappy with herself, unhappy at home, beaten by teachers for answering back, frequently locked in her bedroom by her grandmother as a punishment for 'being dirty', frequently climbed out of the bedroom window, and on one occasion was helped by a passing alcoholic; as a result of which, being observed, she was taken to the police station as being out of control and put in a children's home from which Annette reluctantly rescued her.

Annette who by now kept a junk stall on the Portobello Road and lived with a Rastafarian drug dealer.

'You're not mine,' she'd keep telling Gina, 'but no one deserves my mum and dad,' and Gina would look down her straight disdainful nose and lower the lids of her bright blue eyes, in the sexy way she'd lately acquired, and wonder where she'd come from, if not out of Annette, and ate another chocolate bar to keep her somehow rooted, tied to the earth. The world outside kept changing, without apparent cause or reason, out of her control. She had a weight problem. If she didn't keep herself heavy she'd fly off and be lost, like a piece of scrap paper. She went round with boiled sweets in her pocket, and boys knew by just looking at her she was anyone's, which these days she wasn't: her stepdad Bilbo belted her if she was, though Annette jumped up and down and told him he was a savage.

Gina liked Bilbo: he seemed to care what happened to her, and actually stir himself to do something about it, however painful. They ate good food, hot and rich with chillies; they watched a lot of TV; the cat had kittens: Gina begged and pleaded to keep the fluffy grey one for herself, and was allowed. Life was almost good. She did OK in school, too: caught up, quickly: would have passed exams and even gone to college (she wanted to be a doctor: how her mother laughed) except she met Cliff, got pregnant, wouldn't have the abortion Annette suggested – 'But it's murder, Mum' – and married him, and there was young Cliff, son of a Portobello repairer of clocks, who wanted to be a pop singer, obliged to be a garage mechanic the better to support her and baby Ben. And Cliff drank too much, though he went into car sales and ended up selling second-hand old Rolls-Royces, which you can buy for a couple of hundred in the trade and sell for a couple of thousand to fools, so they lived OK, except Cliff began hitting her, and she knew somewhere she deserved it, and she could no longer look down her nose so well, if only because it had been broken a couple of times. He was always sorry afterwards, and she was sorry for him and bound to him, and loved him in a kind of way; but she was never quite sure Sue was his, though she hoped so – it had been an accident, a one-night stand when she was really miserable, between a black eye and an apology, right at the beginning – and Cliff certainly had no idea, he would *really* have killed her, and in a way she was killing herself, she knew it, but how did you stop, once you had begun? But she would have been faithful, if she could. One life, one man. But fate was against her.

———◆———

And Alice? Alice was implanted in the womb of Honeybell Lee Morthampton, a mother of four boys so anxious to have a girl she would not take the chance of another boy.

'Let's see,' said Dr Holly, 'we've only had frustrated wombs to date, eager and waiting. If we can make this one stick in an elderly multigravida with a history of rejecting females, we've really got it right.'

'I don't see,' said Carl May, 'why the womb history should make any difference; if hormone levels are sound, how can it? It's like believing that a pedigree bitch, once it's had pups by a mongrel, never breeds true again.'

'But it doesn't,' said Dr Holly. 'I have one and I know. The fleeting flavour of the brat about her last litter, purebred labrador though they are. Pure in theory, not in practice. There's more goes on inside the womb than meets the eye. Flavours are caught. Call it propensity, synchronicity, call it God, what you like: at the last fractional moment balances are tipped, this way and that. Interesting.'

'You mean we ought to *pray* this one sticks,' said Carl May derisively.

'I do,' said Dr Holly, and though neither of them prayed, little Alice stuck, and grew up, pretty little sister to four big brothers, alternately bullying and protective, resentful and admiring, lecherous and rejecting, mother's little helper, sweeping, cooking, wiping, serving, flirting, sulking, weeping, giggling, absurdly tender-hearted or else cruel beyond belief, valued for the sheer femaleness of her being, brought up with an amiable father and four big brothers no real kin to her.

Alice entered a beauty contest when she was fifteen, was 'discovered', won a holiday in Florida, kept the company of long-legged beach girls with millionaire boyfriends, came back, went to charm school, discovered the value of disdain, the power of active nonpleasing, failing to placate; she looked at her perfect self in a mirror one day and decided not to have children, not to get married. Who could she ever find to love better than she? Who better to be faithful to, than herself? Men were useful as admirers: sex kept them quiet: love was for suckers: when she felt the first pangs of love, lust, she went home to Honeybell Lee, the dogs, the cats, the nieces and nephews, love, muddle and mess abounding, and was cured.

'She's not like the rest of us,' said Honeybell Lee, puzzled. Honeybell Lee believed Alice to be her natural child: so far as she was aware the Bulstrode Clinic had carried out a simple investigation under local anaesthetic to change the acid/alkaline balance of her internal secretions in favour of the survival of sperm carrying female chromosomes when next it arrived. And it had worked to the great pleasure and satisfaction of all concerned.

And Alice would have been truly faithful to herself, if only fate had so allowed, and not pushed men into her bed, photographers and clients and so forth. Her infidelity brought her no pleasure. She really preferred to sleep alone, being of a nature that saw sex as a drain on her personal resources, not something that enriched them.

Jane, Julie, Gina and Alice.

18

So it was that the four clones, Jane, Julie, Gina and Alice, produced by the irritation of a single egg, were successfully implanted in waiting wombs. Beyond confirming that growth was normal and the infants were successfully born, Holly and May made no attempt to follow the fortunes of the children, or to do the personality studies that would, both agreed, be interesting, if only to make some contribution to the nature/nurture debate. But the complications of setting up such studies would be immense; their research would come under an ethical and legal scrutiny it could not for the time being afford; and it would, they told themselves, be difficult for the four little girls to live normal lives under scrutiny. Nor did they see any good reason to tell Joanna May herself what they had done. Joanna May, the calm, normal, healthy, beautiful and apparently well-balanced woman whom they had, out of love, respect and admiration so successfully reproduced, was still a woman, and therefore liable to extreme, hysterical and unhelpful reaction: she was a creature of the emotions, rather than reason. That was the female lot. And look at it this way: if the population of, say, Egypt increased by a million every nine months, why then, were four more

Joannas dropped into the pool — rather than one each of a female Madge/Jeremy, Harold/Katie, Douglas/Annette, Honeybell/Patrick (unlikely in any case to come into existence because of nature's own inefficiency) — to be in any way abhorred? Holly and May had done no harm to anyone, so far as they could see, or anything: though Holly sometimes, when reviewing the past, did wonder a little about Carl May's motives: could a man brought up in a kennel, barking in his heart, baying at the moon, really ever know himself? Did anyone?

The Bulstrode Clinic experiments in parthenogenesis had long since ceased, becoming irrelevant as the whole field of genetic engineering and microbiology opened up. Dr Holly had moved on to run an enterprising and well-funded Research and Development unit at Martins Pharmaceuticals, an international conglomerate of which Carl May presently became a director. Here his field was at first the decoding of DNA; at which time the visits and special requests of Carl May became less frequent, rather to Dr Holly's relief. But later Holly moved on to the development of dehydration techniques in relation to egg-cell nuclei; there was much excitement and talk of Nobel Prizes — and all of a sudden Carl May was back again, having met up with Isaac King, requiring that Holly drop everything and search the gut of an ancient Egyptian body, dehydrated rather than mummified, which he just so happened to have in his possession, for cells with sufficient intact and living DNA for nuclei transference to be possible. Holly hinted, rather than protested, that he had better things to do than bring the past to life, since the present was surely difficult enough to cope with. He tried to keep the matter light in the interest of his funding, and in the attempt made matters worse than he had thought possible.

'If our motives are impure,' said Dr Holly blithely, 'we will suffer for it: we will be caught like birds in a trap.' The Curse of the Pharaohs was in his mind: Tutankhamen's curse which, according to Isaac King, pursued leading Egyptologists all over the world – tumours and heart attacks killing at an unusually early age, cancers and road accidents striking others down – so that the quality, forget the number, of professors in the subject fell as the best and brightest of them were removed from the human race. Dr Holly half-believed it, half did not, could joke about it.

Carl May did not consider it a joking matter. Carl May dismissed the matter of the Curse of the Pharaohs as the merest, most vulgar of superstitions; how could any scientist even half-believe such junk? Handling a lot of dusty, ancient, possibly carcinogenic material could well result in early death. Road accidents? Well, Egyptologists were by their nature impractical and vague. The myth of the absent-minded professor had its roots in truth. They just didn't look where they were going. They got killed. Dr Holly, rashly, disagreed. He was a professor himself, he reminded Carl May. He was not absent-minded, not in the least.

The Curse of the Pharaohs, Carl May then pointed out, was no more than a warning, albeit engraved in stringent stone and in a prominent position. It was the Ancient Egyptian equivalent of a burglar alarm: 'If anyone enters my tomb with unworthy intentions, be warned. I will catch him like a bird in a trap and

124

stand witness against him by the throne of the Lord of Eternity.' The Ancient Egyptians, Isaac King had explained to Carl May, who now took the trouble – and he was a busy man – to explain it to Dr Holly, caught their birds in clapnets, the two wooden sides of a net coming smartly and suddenly together, and that for the bird was that: kept trapped until it was time to be killed and eaten, or killed and embalmed by some patron who would gain credit in the afterlife for so doing. Absurd!

'You never know,' laughed Dr Holly, 'just when the past will catch up with you! You should always be prepared. Embalm a bird or two!'

Carl May did not laugh. Carl May took irrational offence. 'Gobbledygook!' he cried, and Dr Holly found his department's grant cut presently by many millions. For once too piqued to apologize or oblige, Dr Holly allowed his department to limp on as best it could, left the pursuit of Nobel Prizes to others, and diversified into the safe, cheap and interesting study of brain-cell activity in identical twins. Carl May did not take this side-stepping sitting down: no, he fretted, threatened and fumed – but shortly afterwards came the unfortunate matter of Isaac King's death, and the divorce of his wife, and he was quiet. Something seemed to have knocked the spirit out of him, at least for a time.

19

I, Joanna May.

Isaac King taught me many important things. Carl May taught me many boring things, mostly about how to keep him happy.

Isaac taught me that there need never be an end to seeing. Isaac insisted that I could look at the stubbed-out cigarettes in an ashtray and see beyond it to the meaning behind – know that everything has significance, even if it comes, for a time, to this trash. Those who grew the leaf and waited and prayed for the rain to come: those who profited by its processing and selling: those who smoked it, and defied death: those who stubbed it out, envisaging life – all are part of it. Even in that detritus of ash and grime was something to be marvelled at, something to make you quite giddy with delight. Isaac smoked, of course, and had no intention of stopping, and as it turned out, he was justified, his death by misadventure preceding any major damage to lungs or circulatory system. Carl did not smoke. Carl meant to live for ever in perfect health in a world he hated.

Isaac King taught me that patterns are being woven around us every minute of the day: if we have eyes to see them, they are there to see. When the stray cat miaowing on the doorstep one morning turns out to be the illegitimate grandchild of the grey Persian owned by your father's favourite patient, long deceased, there is no need for surprise. All things are interrelated: the cat was lost and found just to make sure all the cogs were locking properly; or some loose overlap, perhaps, needed to be sealed. The Egyptians knew how cats, who have their own strong familial links, interweave with ours, and our friendships and ventures. Fate offers us hints: shrugs if we don't take notice. No skin off its nose. Isaac taught me to accept mystery. Carl May believed in cause and effect, action and consequence, and nothing much else, except the laws of probability. He thought it was so obvious it didn't need teaching, or no doubt he would have. Brides get taught.

I once tried to explain to Carl what I meant by 'fate' but he didn't listen: he went on reading the *Financial Times*, fidgeting slightly to demonstrate his irritation. That was after Isaac and I had started sorting out exhibits together, but before our further intimacy.

The word 'fate', of course, did not help me, being inadequate to describe the sense of a multifarious, infinitely complex, dreamy yet purposeful universe which I had in mind – being altogether too singular a word, too single-purposed, like a chisel driven hard into the delicacy of experience. A single brain cell, one amongst millions, millions, were it self-conscious, might I suppose have just such an inkling of what was going on around it. The 'Fates' had it better, being at least plural, something capable of consensus, though separately driven.

Miss Watson taught me, I remember, that the concept of One God, Jehovah, was a great step forward for mankind – an end to all those piddly little Gods with brazen feet it thereafter became a capital offence to worship. I had done my best to believe her, but as Isaac and I unpacked and recorded from straw and sand the little artefacts, the various little deities of Ancient Egypt, our eyes melting from time to time and hastily looking away, I began to see the concept of a single God as a narrowing of our perception, not an expansion: the beginning of the long slow end of civilization and not its dawn at all – this cowardly insistence of ours on leaders, fuehrers, the someone who knows exactly what's going on and what's best for everyone; the One above All who demands our loyalty, our obeisance. Undemocratic. The truth is many, not one. Carl May was my Jehovah: it did me no good. I preferred Isaac. Now there's Oliver. More, more! More and more Gods, each to be worshipped in a different way before lightning strikes us to death.

Isaac King nudged and nurtured my body into a capacity for orgasm, that stretching of the body until it meets the soul, with its astonishing shudder of recognition, elation. Proof, proof, cries the body, proof of my purpose, sinking back into languor, all passion spent: I knew it was there if only I looked hard enough. I perceived it, stretched for it, touched it, just with my fingertips encountered the infinite for an instant! I told you so! We're all in this together — we share it, one day we'll know this joy for ever, out of body. Those of us who can — which does not include those faithfully married to Carl May — must pass the message on to those who can't. It's OK. I told Carl May that day in the gallery just what pleasure Isaac gave me, and he seemed not to understand what I was talking about. Well, he wouldn't want to, would he?

Isaac King taught me about the Tarot pack and how it was possible to contain the world in just seventy-eight cards — shuffle the pack, deal them, and observe the pattern of the times: the Ancient Egyptians were great diviners. That there was a Major Arcana of twenty-two cards, which represented the great guiding passions of mankind; intellectual, moral, material. That there were four suits, Wands, Pentacles, Swords and Cups, from which our ordinary Diamonds, Clubs, Spades and Hearts derive. How, broadly, Wands stand for the power of the intellect, Pentacles the strength of the material world, Swords the capacity for endurance, Cups for aesthetic and sensual perception. Or so Isaac interpreted the cards; the power to interpret hieroglyphics at the tips of his fingers. Isaac was so *clever*: I was so proud of him: I felt I caught intelligence from him: and also, I daresay, something of his impracticality. It is wonderful to be taught: it is almost worth the years of ignorance to have it so suddenly, wonderfully stop. But I wanted my fortune told: I wanted to know the future. His future, my future. The cards are not for telling fortunes, Isaac said. They're for focusing the mind on the patterns which the world around you makes. But I wouldn't have it.

That was before we'd been to bed. Sex was in the air: it was inevitable: it was the best, the most powerful of times.

'Tell my fortune,' I repeated.

'What do you want to know?' he asked.

Will we go to bed, I wanted to know. When, where, how, what will happen next? Will you be the fulfilment of my life, will you take the cup of my emptiness and fill it to the brim, and so forth. But I didn't tell Isaac any of that. I wasn't quite such a fool.

'I just want to know,' I said, 'what's going to happen next.'

Isaac acquiesced. Isaac shuffled the pack, picked out the four queens: Wands, Pentacles, Swords and Cups. 'Pick the one that most represents you,' he said, but none seemed quite right to me. I reached for the Empress instead: a card from the Major Arcana. She held the world in her hands: it was what I felt like at that moment. 'Work with that,' I said.

So Isaac took out the Empress, put back the Queens. I shuffled the cards. He laid them face down:

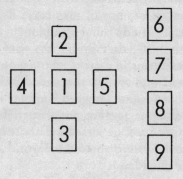

The Empress in the middle was at number one. Above me, two was what ruled me: beneath me, three was what underlay me. Four was what I was leaving. Five was what I was approaching. The significance of the positions of six, seven and eight I can't remember — it scarcely seemed important at the time. Nine was the final outcome: that was what I waited for.

Isaac King turned over the cards.

The four Queens surrounded me. Wands, Pentacles, Swords and Cups: above, below, to left and right. I cannot remember what stood at six and seven; but at eight there was the Hierophant; at nine, Death, a skeleton riding on horseback.

Isaac looked at the Hierophant and laughed.
'There's Carl,' he said.
I, Joanna May, looked at Death and moaned.
'Death means nothing,' said Isaac. 'The card's reversed. It means rebirth, new life; not what you think at all.'
'That's your story,' I said.
'But those four Queens,' said Isaac King, 'that's really something. I don't understand it.'
'I do,' I said. 'I didn't shuffle the pack properly, that's all that means.'
He laughed and swept the cards together and wouldn't say any more. I begged him to tell me more. I touched him in the begging, and though he wouldn't tell the cards for me, he kissed me and that was the beginning, and I forgot about the Tarot.

Except I told Carl that Isaac was teaching me about the Tarot pack: I couldn't resist it. I told Carl about the hand the Fates had dealt me, I tried to suggest to my husband that perhaps there was more to life than here and now, birth and death, that 'because' was a more complex word than he dreamt of – but he wouldn't have it, of course he wouldn't.

'I thought he was some kind of academic,' said Carl May, 'and he turns out to be a charlatan. Is the fellow weak-minded? Is his brain as limp as his shirt collar? Will I get a proper PR return on the gallery? Who does this fellow think he is?'

It did not occur to Carl May to be sexually jealous. How could the servant be preferred to the master? I was affronted. Pique made me guiltless. The more he spoke, poor blinkered Carl May, the more I lost my respect for him, my fear of him. I felt justified in infidelity: it was a wonderful feeling: my spirit soared like a bird, circling, dancing, dizzy with sunlight: I was allowed to be happy. I was born to be happy. I remember sitting on my hands to weigh myself down, as though the very discovery would somehow waft me away. We were sitting, as I remember, in some riverside restaurant. It was night. Lights flickered over running water, and made patterns on the deep red silk of the dress I was wearing. There were only the two of us. It must have been our wedding anniversary, or we'd have been in company – some politician, or magnate, accompanied by boring wife. I've no doubt but that I appeared equally boring. Who is she? Oh, Carl May's wife. What does she do? Nothing. She is Carl May's wife. What does she think? Nothing. She is Carl May's wife. What does she feel? Nothing. She is Carl May's wife. My mother died on the fourth anniversary of my wedding to Carl May. I felt nothing. Carl May had somehow made my feelings for my own mother illicit – as if my life began with my marriage, and that nothing that went before was of any significance: not even the root of my very being, my mother. I went to the funeral alone. Carl May was in China. He did send a telegram and flowers: a wreath, too enormous for the coffin. My poor mother. Everyone should be mourned: remembered: somehow sustained in their journey through the afterlife, until the need for it is gone. Isaac taught me that as well: but I had never until that moment connected it to my mother.

'Superstitious nonsense,' Carl was saying. 'And by God I'll prove it nonsense.'

'How will you do that, Carl?' I asked, politely. 'People have been trying to prove or disprove magic, prophecy, ESP, since the beginning of time, and haven't succeeded.'

'I'll prove it,' he said, 'if it kills me.' And he started the Divination Department. I was glad to think the conversation had at least had some effect upon him. And in that original hand of cards – the first time the cards are dealt for someone the reading is always clear, always significant – was indeed my future. It was just that Isaac was to die, not me. No wonder he swept the cards up and reshuffled as quick as he could.

And I remember now what the cards at six and seven were. Six was the Star, kneeling by her pool beneath a sliver of moon; seven was the Fool, reversed.

133

Treachery, one would imagine: self-delusion. I talked too much. I betrayed Carl, by finding sexual fulfilment with Isaac; and Isaac, because I couldn't resist telling Carl.

I, Joanna May. No longer 'Eye'. Acting; not observing. Doing, not looking. Dangerous, murderous, and not even knowing it.

20

Joanna May, impassioned at last by virtue of the blue-foldered report from the Maverick Enquiry Agency, which told of Bethany's existence, went straight to the heart of Carl May's evil empire, his glassy prison. She meant to tell him a thing or two. She rose by means of a pink and white escalator from the fountains and greenery, marble and glass of the reception levels, and smoothly ascended through layer upon layer of noise and tumult, panic and excitement, bells and clatter, of messengers running, girl clerks checking and pot plants wilting unattended. Then, audacious, was whisked up unchecked in a cage of green glass studded with yellow lights, right into the still centre of the storm, the quiet nexus of energy, the Executive Floor. She walked straight past secretaries on her expensive sensible heels and right into Carl May's office suite where all was silent, sparse and aesthetically correct. The nerve of it! There she found her husband, her ex-husband, flesh of her flesh, heart of her heart, with that tragic ruined girl, that Bethany, that almost beauty, with her sad brightness and her ersatz emerald eyes, his long pale tampering fingers tangled in her hennaed hair. And some might think it served Joanna May right, but she did not.

No. Joanna May spoke the truth to Carl May, or the only truth she knew: that once long ago she'd handed her life to him for keeps, as she was expected by all and sundry to do, being nothing but a girl, in truth, love, and hope, and what had Carl May done? Why, he had not only rendered these things sour for her forever, but drained her being dry as if it were an orange; with powerful lips sucked up the juice and the flesh through a hole in the skin the size of a sixpence, and then thrown the poor flabby thing away. And now look, now look, now look, Joanna May wept, self-pity overcoming rage. Look at me!

An orange, Carl May laughed, an orange. I thought women got thrown away like old gloves, not old oranges, and Joanna May screamed and shouted and banged her fists against his chest, and he didn't even catch hold of them to stop them, so distasteful did he find her flesh, or pretended to. And Bethany thought at last, at last, boredom is ending here, at last something's happening, not this quiet, this still, this nothingness, from which all things emanate but yet is nothing. So bored, she thought, I've been so bored. Ex-wives are better than nothing.

You have destroyed me, Joanna May said to her husband, in essence, used up my youth, my best years and thrown me out.

Carl May said to Joanna, men do not destroy women, some women destroy themselves, that's all; if Joanna May is indeed destroyed, why then he's glad for her sake since that was clearly what she wanted.

Women choose the man they want, said Carl May, the man their calculating eye first falls upon; then, lacking the capacity and the will to stick by that decision, must chew away at their own loyalty – self-devourers all, rapacious of grievance, noisy in complaint – gossiping to neighbours and friends over fences and tables, round fires and out shopping, the yackety yak of the female affronted: first he did this and then he did that, can you imagine, and can you believe it, after all that she does for him how much she loves him the bastard, the brute! And how after all that complaint how can a woman expect to find in her own heart constancy, loyalty, truth or affection? Split a plain and single path into a thousand tracks of conversational interest and how can you expect to find yourself ever back upon the right one? In other words, Joanna May, in the course of our marriage, you talked about me to your friends, committed disloyalty with your mind and after that with your body which was how it was bound to end up. Your fault not mine, said Carl May, your fault, your fault, your fault, not mine. What's more, I just behaved as any man would behave, said Carl May.

What, murder? enquired Joanna May and Carl May said you're mad, you're insolent, my chauffeur knocked him down, that's all. An absent-minded Egyptologist, how could he ever bring the dead to life, and you were dead enough yourself by then. Old. A weak man, a *nebbitch*, a nothing, a better-dead, dead already so far as anyone had ever seen. Trust you to pick a zombie, Joanna May. Your fault for not finding a better man: how could you find a better man, a zombie the best that you could do, your fault that now he's dead, as dead as you, and you're alone. Lost him and lost me, lost us both, silly old you.

Oh phooey, she said, it's all men's fault, everyone knows it's all men's fault. Ask anyone.

Just a woman, only a woman, he said next. You should have died twenty years ago, what use to the world are you? A woman without youth, without children, without interest, a woman without a husband; old women have husbands by the skin of their teeth and there is no skin left to your teeth, Joanna May, your yellow discoloured teeth.

My teeth are not so yellow, said Joanna May, they're perfectly pearly white as ever. You're talking about your own miserable molars. And Carl May gnashed them and said he was a man, he was immortal, his immortality lay here in this building, this achievement — by his name on a hundred powerful letterheads he would outrun his death; but what was a woman such as Joanna May, a woman without children, here and now and gone with a puff, blown away like a withered leaf, just for an instant a stretch of limb, a flash of thigh, and gone, a flower that never left a seed, the merest annual, passing thing, a nothing. Here today, gone tomorrow.

I am so something, said Joanna May. Ask my lover, he'll tell you what a thing I am, how far from nothing, here today and here tomorrow. I have my lover, my young lover, I have a man a thousand times better than you, who makes me happy and satisfied, which is what you never did. Never, never, never, never.

Carl May was silent.

Oh ouch – thought Bethany, better she hadn't said that, better she'd kept quiet.

Then the fat was in the fire, oh yes it was. How it spat, how it sizzled and spat.

Carl May's eyes seemed to turn a kind of yellow red, as false a colour as Bethany's own emerald eyes, but the pupil went to slits through which a blackness showed, as her own would never do, or so Bethany hoped.

Then Carl May said in a voice as cold and clear as ice made from bottled water, let your poor old flabby legs be parted by whom you choose, it will be for money not love – Not true, not true, Joanna May began to say, but of course it was, it was perfectly true – so why then, she said, it's true for you too you poor old man; and he said no it's not, you poor Joanna May, you female, the music stops for women long before it stops for men, and pitiful and degraded are the ones who dance on when the silence falls; your dance is over, Joanna May, you thoroughly useless lonely person, and mine is not, why don't you go away and die?

Oh flesh of my flesh, love of my soul, husband of my heart, she weeps, to speak to me like this. How can you!

Because I am Lord of the Dance, he says, and I am man and you are only woman, and I am something indeed and you are nothing at all, in spite of your young lover. If he exists, which I take leave to doubt.

I am so something, she wept, I am, I am, and he does exist and I love him, but already she felt herself vanishing, though she still beat her hands against his neatly suited breast and Bethany yawned to hide her nerves and looked around for a door to leave by, but there seemed to be none, so perfectly, architecturally flush were they with the wall. You have to have good eyesight to detect those very expensive doors and Bethany's contact lenses had slipped and chafed and her eyes were watering and she couldn't see a way out at all.

You are nothing, said Carl May, quite bright and glittery all of a sudden as if the sun had come out to shine on a world of icebergs, hot in pursuit but chilly with it, and what's more I proved you nothing thirty years ago and I've known it ever since, and I swore I'd never tell you, but now I will. I proved then you were nothing so particular after all, and that, to be frank, is when I lost interest in you. I proved it by making more of you, and the more I made of you the less of you there was, so it hardly mattered when you betrayed me, because how can what does not exist betray. One a penny, two a penny, hot cross buns; more buns came out of that oven than ever went in.

What do you mean, she asked, quite soft and quiet all of a sudden, and listening hard, of course she did, so he told her – I cloned you, Carl May said, I cloned you, added another four of you to the world, and he told her how he did it, and Bethany put her oar in and said Carl only did it because he loved you really, did it as a compliment, take no notice of what he says today, he's bitter and twisted and furious because you've got a boyfriend, that's all, at which Carl May gave Bethany a push and a shove and would have sent her right through the window and windmilling to her death thirty floors below but the windows didn't open (and just as well, or how the bodies would have piled below, from hatred and self-hatred) so he didn't bother, just forgot.

Joanna May, shocked into calmness, paced and thought and considered herself split into five and her gorge rose into her throat.

Carl May smiled and it seemed to Bethany that his teeth were fangs and growing as long as the wolf's ever were in 'Red Riding Hood'.

There are many of you and many of you gloated Carl May and that means there are none of you because you amounted to so little in the first place. Now see how you like that.

Joanna May thought a little. All the more of us to hate and despise you, she said, flickering into defiance, and make wax models of you and stick pins into you. See how you like that!

Superstitious junk, he shouted, and I'm proving it, I'm proving it. Do you know who I am? I am master of mortality.

Bethany sighed: the children were squabbling again, that was all, perhaps that was all, perhaps it was nothing, could be sighed away, would vanish away

141

like a thirties film disintegrating, unseen in its vault –
the mad male cloning scientist crumbling into the dust
of fantasy, Frankenstein dissolved, the monster only
a dream, a fright, and the world return to normal. But
no. It was real. It was true. It was the present – not
the future. And it was all Carl May's fault. It was his
fault.

You're the devil, said Joanna May, you're the devil.
Your mother was right to chain you up with the
beasts, she knew the truth about you. I wish they'd
gnawed you to death, eaten you up, why have you
done this terrible thing to me, imprisoned me forever
in a bad bad dream?

You did a terrible thing to me, he said, you made
your bed and didn't lie on it, chose a man and wouldn't
stick with him; you're a piece of drifting slime in a
murky female pool. You're all alike, you women.

Carl May, said Joanna May, I'm sorry for you. You
look out of the dark prison of your soul which is your
body, and the only windows you have are your eyes,
your ears, your nose, your touch, and what can you
know but what those windows look upon and it isn't
up to much, never has been: a little tent of sky outside
a kennel. What a pity you slipped your leash, you
should have stayed forever, baying at the moon. I see
a different world, said Joanna May, I see one which
is perfectible without your tampering.

I don't, said Carl May, and my view is the true one,
however disagreeable. I see a world of accident and
not design, never perfectible left to itself. Besides, I
want to amuse myself. I can make a thousand thousand of you if I choose, fragment all living things and

re-create them. I can splice a gene or two, can make you walk with a monkey's head or run on a bitch's legs or see through the eyes of a newt: I can entertain myself by making you whatever I feel like, and as I feel like so shall I do. Whatever I choose from now on for ever.

I don't believe you, said Joanna May.

Believe what you like, said Carl May. Chernobyl has exploded and now all things impossible are possible, from now on in.

And then Joanna May just laughed and said do what you like but you can't catch me, you'll never catch me, I am myself. Nail me and alter me, fix me and distort me, I'll still have windows on the world to make of it what I decide. I'll be myself. Multiply me and multiply my soul: divide me, split me; you just make more of me, not less. I will look out from more and different windows, that's all you will have done, and I will watch the world go by in all its multifarious forms, and there will be no end to my seeing. I will lift up my heart to the hills, that's all, to glorify a maker who is not you. I should carry on if I were you, cloning and meddling, you might end up doing more good than harm, in spite of yourself, if only by mistake.

Carl May snarled and his eyes grew redder still for this was the heart of the evil empire and he was its lord, or so it seemed to Bethany, and he dug his yellow fangs into Joanna's neck just above her genteel string of pearls and he scraped up a piece of her skin with those disgusting teeth and went to the little designer fridge where he kept his whisky (for guests) and his

Perrier (for him) and he took out a little box and with a spatula scraped the flesh, the living tissue, of Joanna May off the teeth and shook it into the box with a short sharp shake and put it back in the fridge and said now I'll grow you into what I want, he said, I can and will, see how you like that, I'll make you live in pain and shame for ever more, I have brought hell to earth.

Joanna May just laughed and said Carl May you've really flipped, wait till I tell Oliver about this, Oliver loves my soul not my body he loves my mind, my hope, my courage, me: he loves about me what you loved, Carl May, and still do, you silly spiteful thing, judging from how you behave. I was made in heaven not hell, as you were. You're not king of the Dark Domains, that's all in your mind, you're just head of Britnuc and in a state because of Chernobyl and the guilt and responsibility you feel and the whole world nagging on.

Carl May said if you'd loved me properly, Joanna May, if you had kept your word, I would make roses without thorns, I would make dogs who didn't want to bite, I would make all men kind and good and wonderful, and women too, I would create a sinless race, I would perfect nature's universe, because nature is blind, and obsessive, and absurd – consider the ostrich – and has no judgement, only insists on our survival, somehow, any old how: nature is only chance, not good or bad. All I want is the any old how properly under control, directed, working better: I, man, want to teach nature a thing or two, in

144

particular the difference between good and bad; for who else is there to do it? But how can I, because woman makes man bad, I know it, I feel it. Joanna May, you nearly saved me once, you nearly made me good, and then you failed me, that is why I can't forgive you. You have made me bad, Joanna May: if I'm the devil that's your fault: if I create monsters, you've no one to blame but yourself.

Oh phooey, she said. So I'm Eve to your Adam, am I, that old thing. Take your own apple, bite its flesh, give me a break. All I wanted was a little conversation, for once: all I was doing was discussing the apple: if you chose to see that as temptation, God help you.

And Bethany saw them both standing in the Garden of Eden, Carl and Joanna May, or thought that was what she saw – Carl May long-limbed, tall, ruddy and eager, as he ought to have been, if everything had gone right, and Joanna May young again and looking down her perfect nose, as ever, just a sniff of disdain about her and in the sniff of that disdain the root of much trouble to come, perhaps even all of it, and between them they stared at the apple, red one side, green the other. Carl May bit first, choosing the red half, the better half, the riper half, and that made Joanna really spiteful. But Bethany had taken pills that morning, to get her through the day, as people will these days, and the pills were tiny and the pillbox in a muddle and as her lenses had scraped her eyes were blurred and she could easily mistake the yellow and the red, so who knows what she saw.

Thank you, Carl, for the gift you have given me, said Joanna May, cheerfully, and now I'm off to find my sisters, and I bet I find them different every one, different as sin and yet the same.

And with no apparent trouble at all she found a door in the perfect wall and was out of it and gone but on her way down in the lift she wept, and she nearly stumbled getting off the escalator, she trembled so. What woman of sixty would want to meet herself at thirty: rerun of some dreary old film, in which she gave a bad performance, like as not, and split-screen technique at that.

21

Bethany said to Carl May, 'That was a perfectly horrid thing to do, scraping her neck like that. You're nothing but a Dracula.'

And he said, still in a bad mood, 'Be careful or I'll do it to you too. You might be helped by a little sorting and a proper upbringing, so I should shut up if I were you, or you'll have a very sore neck indeed.'

So she did shut up, for a time. But unlike Joanna she could see the advantage of being more than one: the thought did not horrify her at all, not one bit. The more of her the better. She would sit back while the other clones did the shopping, yes she would; after all she could rely on them bringing back what she wanted, choosing what she would choose – until, thinking about it, she realized that was like believing you were Marie Antoinette in another incarnation, and not one of her maids, which was more likely statistically (one of Carl May's favourite words) there being so many more ordinary people than queens in the world. One of the other clones might seize command, and Bethany would be doing the shopping while the Queen clone was the one just sitting – and Bethany wouldn't know what was going on in the Queen's head, really, except

147

she'd know it was pretty much what was going on in her own, which might or might not be a help. But somehow Bethany felt she would indeed have the benefit of extra strawberries and cream upon the tongue, not to mention all the lovemaking multiplied, because she'd know what the others would be tasting, feeling, doing, not just having to guess.

And, then again, though Bethany loved her parents, she could see they had not brought her up in a safe or sensible kind of way. Reared in another fashion, encouraged in different directions, Bethany might be a fashion designer, or fly an aircraft, not be just a girl who lived by her looks. Or would she? How could one tell? Except by trying.

Bethany said to Carl May later that evening, when he had calmed down and lost his satanic overtones, and she and he were in the bath – it was too small for their cavortings (she knocked her elbow quite painfully) and white, which she thought boring and old-fashioned – 'What happened to Joanna's clones? Didn't you want to find out?' and he said, 'Good heavens, you didn't really believe that tale did you? I was annoyed with Joanna, that's all.'

This time Bethany didn't believe him. Bethany said, 'You did so do it. You just frightened yourself with what you'd done. You realized, and stopped, the way people do. You set things marching you couldn't control, so you just shut your eyes, and left it to the other people to clear up the mess! Like the waste from your power plants. What's going to happen to that?'

Twenty-four going on forty-two. He got out of the bath. Either she annoyed him with her perspicacity, or irritated him with her stupidity. She confused him. He would be filled with tenderness and gratitude towards her, when she had rendered him some peculiar sexual favour – though in theory that was when he should most despise her – and yet wish to push her out of the window if she failed to read his mind properly, or was insensitive to his feelings. Carl May did not like being confused.

'Oh,' said Bethany, 'now what have I said? Why did you get out of the bath?'

'Because I banged my knee,' he said, wrapping himself in a towel, which smelt of Bethany, sweet and warm and agreeably cheap, 'and bed is more comfortable. Let's go to bed.'

In bed she said, 'If you were making it up about the clones – and you told me about them yourself once before; did you forget? – why did you take that piece from her neck?'

And he said, 'To frighten her off. Who wants ex-wives dropping in at any time of day or night, making scenes?'

'Well,' said Bethany, 'if you ask me, it was a bit drastic. Most men don't behave like that when they find their ex-wife has a lover. And after all, it's only natural that she should. You have me, after all. And there can't be one law for men and another for women.'

'Oh yes, there can,' said he.

'Well, don't have him run over too,' said Bethany, 'or there'll be more talk. Punish him some other way.

149

Have a thousand of him made, each one with a high sex drive but impotent. That should pay him out.'

'I'll pay him out the simple old-fashioned way,' he said, and looked at his watch and laughed aloud.

'Why are you looking at your watch?' she asked.

'Because it's the most expensive watch in the world,' he said.

He wondered how Dr Holly was doing; how long he would hold out, when he would give in and return to the fold. Men within a whisper of a Nobel Prize do not easily turn their backs on glory, renown and the plaudits of their peers. If Holly didn't, there were younger, smarter, more ambitious men in Holly's own department upon whom Carl May had his eye, more than ready to do a favour or two. But Holly was the best, the most creative, the most imaginative: the younger generation of scientists were more concerned with their careers than the marvels of the universe. You had to pay them to get them to think. He would confront Holly with hard evidence on the absent-mindedness of professors of Egyptology: how they did indeed step out in front of cars: how they died young for reasons which were nothing to do with the Curse of the Pharaohs. Dr Holly would admit Carl May was right, would agree to put at least a section of his department to searching the gut cells of the ancients for living DNA, and get his grant back, and off they'd go again, Holly and May, May and Holly!

Unless of course Joanna was herself the Curse of the Pharaohs. The thought made Carl May laugh aloud.

'Why are you laughing?' Bethany asked.

'Because you're such an idiot,' said Carl May, 'and that's the way I like it. I want you bright, I don't want you clever.'

'I may be cleverer than you suppose,' said Bethany.

'What great big teeth you have, Grandmama,' he said, which was silly, she thought, because she had very little white even teeth of which she was very proud, having spent many years wearing a brace, about which her parents had been very particular, allowing her to take it off only when being kind to their lame ducks, their lonely sea-captains, their newly widowed majors. 'One day you'll be pleased,' her father would say, when she moaned and groaned about the brace, and so she was.

Carl May looked at his watch again, and this time she didn't ask him why. He had the bright eyes and flushed cheeks of a delinquent child; he was up to something; she knew it, and she thought it might be better, safer, not to know exactly what it was, and she was right.

The next day Carl May took part in a TV programme about the Chernobyl disaster and the question of the threat or otherwise of radiation, which seemed to so absorb the nation. He took an aggressive and positive line, as suited both his whim, his business interests and the future of the nuclear industry; all of these being pretty much the same.

He said he doubted very much the story of 2000 dead and large areas laid waste and desolate, never to grow a blade of grass again. He deplored the scare stories in the media that death was raining down from skies all over the world. He drank a glass of milk front of camera, and said there was more to fear from cholesterol than radioactivity. He said he thought the death toll would be more like thirty-five – very modest for a major industrial accident (though of course tragic for those concerned: families, etc.) and naturally there would be a statistically calculable increase in cancers in those countries subject to fallout but certainly no more than would be produced by atmospheric pollution consequent upon the continued burning off of fossil fuels. These things had to be balanced.

Look, Carl May said, this argument that we should all live as long as we possibly can is barmy: who wants to live an extra five years in a walking frame anyway? Better an earlier death, be it cancer or heart attack, than a later one. It was an old-fashioned sentiment which favoured length of life over way of life, quantity over quality. You found it the other end of the spectrum, when it came to how societies regarded birth: the old school, emotional, religious, said no contraception, no abortions, let the disabled live: the more life the better, regardless of quality of life. A younger, more reasonable, generation said no, let's have quality not quantity. Freely available birth control, worldwide family planning, sterilizations, vasectomies on demand, terminations all but compulsory for those diagnosed before birth as handicapped, every child a wanted child – and so forth, Carl May said, while Friends of the Earth, a Bishop and the Minister of Energy tried to get a word in edgeways.

Friends of the Earth managed 'What about childhood cancer? Leukaemia?' and Carl May replied briskly if this nation really cares about the lives of its children it will stop driving about in cars – how many get killed a year on the roads! – and increase family allowances: if it cares about cancers in the old it will ban cigarette smoking and free hospitals for the potentially healthy and those who have not brought their troubles on themselves.

Now look, said Carl May, people will work themselves up into a state about anything, especially if it's new. They thought the building of railway lines would destroy the nation, they thought TV would destroy its culture, they thought vaccination killed. ('They were right, they were right,' muttered the Bishop.) Nothing much to fear from radiation, compared to other dangers, compared to crossing the road, compared to smoking. A burst of intense radiation could kill you, sure. So could an overdose of aspirin. Nuclear power stations were, if you asked him, even more crippled by safety regulations than they were by the unions, and that was saying something. The unthinking and uninformed always fear an unseen enemy. From reds under the bed to radiation in the head, the public gets the wrong end of the stick, is ignorant and hysterical and impossible.

He stopped. Everyone in the studio was startled; even the camera crews were listening.

Next day Gerald Coustain called from the Department and said he thought Carl May had gone a little far in insulting the public so; it might not be a wise move considering the state of near-panic it appeared to be in. Let him at least appear to take the Chernobyl fallout seriously.

'OK, OK,' said Carl May. 'I'll bleat away in public if that's what you want.'

'We've now pulled together some very fine and modern instrumentation,' said Gerald, 'so we won't be calling on Britnuc any more. I have to tell you that in some parts of Cumbria, it now seems, the needles had been going once round the dials and back again, and our technicians simply hadn't noticed: they weren't expecting it. Human error's the real problem.'

'It certainly is,' said Carl May.

'Still, we've got the problem solved now, I think. We may have to take lamb off the market, though.'

'That'll just panic people more,' said Carl May. 'If Cumbrian lamb is twice as radioactive as Sussex lamb, why don't you ask people just to eat one Cumbrian lamb chop instead of their usual two? Or if they're *really* hungry, buy Sussex.'

'Because people's minds don't work like that,' said Gerald.

'I know,' said Carl May. 'That's the trouble with them.'

22

The world turned upside down. I went to Carl's office to have it out with him, but he had it out with me, and took some living cells from my neck, what's more: the kind of good fresh bloodless tissue that's rich in DNA: he could grow all kinds of me from that – he's right. Ugly, headless, always miserable, always in pain: five-legged, three-headed, double-spined: every leg with perpetual cramp, all heads schizophrenic, and spina bifida twice over. If he wanted, if he could persuade them to do it, that is – and he is a Director of Martins Pharmaceuticals, isn't he, and benefactor of this and that: an interesting experiment, he'd say, a favour. You do this for me and I'll do that for you. Would they? Snip and snap, create a monster? Not if Carl May put it like that, probably not, but if he said, humbly, in the cause of knowledge, just let's see if we *can*, just let's see. Only the once, then never again. (For once is ethical, twice is not.) Then you never know. They might. But what should I care; what is it to do with me? 'I' wouldn't suffer. The 'you's' might. Poor distorted things.

I saw my husband run his hands through her hennaed hair, that's what I remember, that's what makes the 'I' suffer, become well and truly me, with a shock which got to my solar plexus. I know he despises her. I could tell. Yet still he ran his fingers through her hair. Patronizing little bitch, little whore: in my home, bathing in my bath, her hairs blocking my plughole. I know. It was all in the blue-foldered report of the Maverick Enquiry Agency: there it stuck, a hennaed hair, long and silky, catching soap scum. Disgusting. Bethany! To be supplanted by a slut called Bethany: me, Joanna May. It would be easier if she was called Doris, or Betty, a name so ordinary it was deprived of resonance: became what I wanted it to be.

The world turned upside down: inside out, round and about; fire burn and cauldron bubble: bubbling vats of human cells, recombinant DNA surging and swelling, pulsing and heaving, multiplying by the million, the more the merrier: all the better, the more efficiently for biologists and their computers to work upon the structure of the living cell, the blueprints of our lives, decoding the DNA which is our inheritance. A snip here, a section there, excise this, insert that, slice and shuffle, find a marker, see what happens, what it grows: record it, collate it, work back and try again. Link up by computer to labs all over the world. Bang, goes Mr Nobel's gun, and off they go, false starts and fouling, panting and straining, proud hearts bursting, to understand and so control, to know what marks what and which – and better it. This DNA, this double helix, this bare substance of our chromosomal being, source of our sameness, root of our difference – this section gives us eyes, that segment of this section blue eyes, take it away and presto, no eyes – laid bare the better to cure us and heal us, change us and help us, deliver us from AIDS and give us two heads. And all of it glugging and growing in a culture of E.Coli – the bacteria of the human colon, tough, fecund, welcoming, just waiting around all that time to do its stuff at our behest – toss it, turn it, warm it, start it; nothing stops it. Well why not? Let the brave new world be based upon E.Coli – the stuff that gives us healthy shit. If our purpose on this earth is to salvage goodness from a material universe gone somehow wrong (which was what Oliver maintained) how more appropriately should it be done than by starting with shit and building up: creating not out of nothing, where's the glory in that, but forging miracles from debris, detritus. Now there's an accomplishment!

The vats are filled with pale, thin, milky translucent fluid, life itself, remarkably reflective of colour; slip, slop, plop. If the lab ceiling's green, then the culture shines green. Change the colour at will. Violet most impresses the visitors, but who wants a violet ceiling?

If you've got a good cow, don't breed from it, just repeat it: two by two, out of the ark. Take out the nucleus, cow-and-bull, mix in a newly fertilized cell, reintroduce an all-cow nucleus and what do you get, with any luck? Little twin clones, cow plus repetitions! I, Joanna May, beautiful and intelligent in my prime, now past it, am a woman plus repetitions, taken at my prime. Carl's fault, Carl's doing.

I am horrified, I am terrified, I don't know what to do with myself at all, whatever myself means now. I

157

don't want to meet myself, I'm sure. I would look at myself with critical eyes, confound myself. I would see what I don't want to see, myself when young. I would see not immortality, but the inevitability of age and death. As I am, so they will become. Why bother? Why bother with them, why bother with me? What's the point? I can't bear it. I have to bear it. I can't even kill myself — they will go on. Now night will never fall.

I have never felt so old: I am all but paralysed. The back of my neck hurts where the vampire bit it. My heart aches where he struck at it.

I should have stayed home, as Oliver suggested.

23

Gerald Coustain said to his wife Angela, 'I don't know what's got into that fellow Carl May.'

Angela said, 'Is he any worse than he usually is?' They were eating fish and chips in a Chinese chippie with an eat-here section. With the meal, which included slices of white bread and butter, they drank sweet tea. This was their favourite food. They resented spending good money on food they liked less at expensive restaurants.

'Yes he is,' said Gerald. 'He's saying what he thinks on television. He's usually much too discreet for that. There'll be a public outcry. People can hear the sound of jackboots marching, the minute he opens his mouth.'

'I expect it's his new girlfriend,' said Angela. 'People who're foolish in one direction become foolish in them all.'

'What makes you think he has one?'

'Joanna rang me up in a state. Something had set her off.'

'That's not very reasonable of her,' he said, 'if what you say is true, that she's having it off with the gardener. What's sauce for the goose is sauce for the gander.'

'Yes,' said Angela, 'but neither likes the other having any.'

'Is he a good gardener?' asked Gerald, when he had absorbed this.

'She didn't say. I expect so. She's very fussy about that kind of thing. Always having her curtains cleaned and her wallpaper changed, and her kitchen units brought up to date.'

'I'm a good gardener,' said Gerald.

'I know you are, my dear,' she said. They each took a chip from the other's plate, in a gesture of continuing love and trust.

'Now she has a lover,' said Gerald, hopefully, 'we won't have to ask her to the lido again, will we? We won't have to be sorry for her.'

'I rather liked her coming to the lido with us. I think she enjoyed it. She looks very good in a cossie, I must say. Didn't you think so?'

'I didn't notice. She looked down her nose at me,' said Gerald. 'I had to stay wrapped in my towel. I didn't want her to see my paunch. There was nothing I could do about my varicose leg. She stared at that. No wonder Carl May got rid of her.'

'It would be a better idea,' said Angela, 'if you got rid of your paunch and your varicose veins. Eating here won't help. If only something healthier was our favourite food. Do you think the fish is radioactive?'

'Pretty well everything is,' said Gerald, sadly, 'if we're to go by our new monitoring equipment. But I'm not sure if it's been calibrated correctly. We'll just have to hope for the best. You don't mean to go round and see Joanna, I hope? You know my feelings about getting too close. All of us at the lido is obviously a good deed: you and her together smacks of a conspiracy.'

'She's my friend,' said Angela. 'I really do like her. She keeps saying things I don't expect!'

'If being her friend makes him your enemy, it isn't safe. I've told you that. I always take care to be very polite to him.'

'I think,' said Angela, 'they ought to get back together again. I think they still love each other in their hearts.'

He was pleased she thought so; a professor of Modern History both so wrong-headed and so romantic at heart; his wife, sharer of his chips.

24

Joanna May did not get back for many hours to her house on the banks of the Thames, where once a monarch had kept his vulgar mistress, and when she did she found Oliver dead. She'd wasted time talking to Angela, and then walking around Richmond Park to calm down. She found Oliver hanging by a rope around his ankles from a beam in the barn which was now a garage, swinging gently first this way, then that, his arms fastened gently across his chest as if he were an Egyptian mummy. His face was calm and not distressed, his eyes were open and everything he saw, if only the dead could see, was upside down. His bare young feet were smooth on top and rough-skinned underneath, but that was no surprise to Joanna May: she'd felt them often enough, and the nails were tough and horny and had earth beneath them as usual – the boots he liked the most to wear were not watertight. They stood neatly together in a corner of the garage, placed as if on guard. Who in the world would want them now, poor battered useless things? This way, that way, he swung. She sat down to adapt to a world deprived of this especial goodness, to recover from the shock. She grieved for his mother, and his friends, and the girl in Scotland he would never marry and the seedlings in the greenhouse which no one now would get round to planting out. She grieved for herself, of course she did. Who now would fill her bed? She was old. She was old: surely the old could be spared the shock of losing a lover, of understanding that the body that inspires you, fills you, is frail, mortal, corruptible, as liable to stop on the instant as anything else. This way that way. Through the grief and shock ran a thread of relief: it was over, finished: sharply, quickly: now he would never decide it wouldn't work: wouldn't one day see her wrinkling skin in a clear light, or some aspect of her nature she could no longer hide and decide she wasn't the one for him, and be off (in the fallow season, of course) to some other garden in need, some other divorced lady with excellent alimony and a waiting bed. The back of her neck hurt when she moved it. The graze smarted.

Her fault, of course, her fault: she wailed aloud, and a bird fluttered down from the eaves and out the open door. (She thought it carried Oliver's soul with it, and now she was truly alone and he was truly gone.) His eyes had shut now, the lower eyelids drooping, as the flesh gave up its residual resilience. She was glad of that: he had seen more than enough upside down.

On the floor, beneath the hanging body, brushed by Oliver's hair, lay a single card from the Tarot pack. It was the Hanged Man, from the Minor Arcana, that benign and peaceful fellow suspended by his feet. Above, below, to right and left were four more cards, the Queens of Wands, Pentacles, Swords and Cups.

163

She should never, as a wife, have tried to discuss the nature of reality with Carl: her fault. She should never have told him about the Fates, about there being more gods than one God, about the Tarot pack: fidget as he might over the *Financial Times*, he heard, he heard: he did not forgive and he did not forget. As an ex-wife she should have faded away, ceased to exist: not quite murdered, not quite unmurdered. Her fault. She should never have told Carl May about Oliver, boasting, denying the inevitability of her desolation, her non-existence; her fault: she should never have answered back: her fault. She should never have gone in the first place, but listened to Oliver. She should have come straight home to warn him: her fault: she should never have allowed him into her bed: her fault. She had, she had, and now Oliver was dead. Her fault. A little niggle of anger arose, swelled; she screamed and screamed. Not her fault, not her fault at all. Carl May's fault. Carl May the murderer.

She went into the kitchen and found Trevor the butler, with his soft hands and soft round face, sitting at the scrubbed-elm table shaking and weeping; and the expensive wall-to-ceiling kitchen units, which he so loved and Oliver found claustrophobic, rising like the walls of a mausoleum around him, and a dozen hanging copper pans caught the reflection of his shock and grief and threw it back and forth across the room, one to another. Well, it was his world: it was fitting.

'What happened?' asked Joanna, and Trevor told her.

164

25

Why was Joanna so late home? Should not her instinct have been, having betrayed Oliver, to go straight back home and warn him? Of course, but her neck hurt, she was confused and upset; she was not convinced, even if she tried to persuade him of it, that Oliver would appreciate the danger he was in. He would say she was imagining it, and go on shaking off dahlia tubers, or whatever he was doing. It was difficult to convey the extraordinary and drastic nature of Carl's world to a young man whose concerns were so very horticultural, with a dash of rock guitar thrown in. He would be positive about the matter of the clones, which she was not sure she wanted him to be. He would say, 'Well, you always wanted a family: now you have them. Sisters and daughters both,' and if she complained that it was altogether too sudden, and done against her will besides, and Carl May's behaviour outrageous, he would have told her not to be so negative, or the peas wouldn't swell in the pods or the bees wouldn't fertilize the pears – some threat, at any rate, to hold over her head – and remind her that the reason she was no longer married to Carl May was because he was outrageous, so why act so surprised?

In the end she called Angela from a phone box and confided in her, and Angela was gratifyingly startled.

'You mean you didn't even know, Joanna?'

'No.'

'Cloned, and not known it?'

'That's right.'

'Well, I wouldn't like that.'

'Neither do I, Angela. That's why I'm calling.'

'Poor Joanna.'

'Because you know how all this time I've been complaining about having nothing – no children, no career, no family, no husband, nothing I've earned or worked for myself: a whole life wasted –'

'Yes, I do, Joanna –'

'Well, there was a kind of pride in that, Angela. It was my singularity. He has taken away my singularity. He has shovelled all these bits and pieces at me, and I hate it.'

'It would make me feel better, I think.'

'It made me feel like just nothing, Angela; and this makes me feel perfectly dreadful, I can tell you. All I can do is just wander about. I'm calling from a phone box, I'm not even home.'

'Why did he save it till now, do you think?'

'Because he was angry, I suppose.'

'I expect he was. Men don't much like their ex-wives bursting into their offices. Good old Carl, always has to be in the forefront of everything, even test-tube babies. Tinker tinker with the universe.'

'I don't know how you can say that: "Good old Carl."'

'I was being ironic, Joanna.'

'Oh. I see.'

'Joanna, would you say Carl was mad? Answer frankly.'

'No,' said Joanna, 'I'm afraid he isn't. I think he just likes to have his own way, and get his own back. He's childish.'

'I see,' said Angela. 'Can I tell Gerald about the clones?'

'If you feel you have to,' said Joanna, a little tearfully.

'Are you going to try and find these creatures?'

'I don't think so. I don't suppose they know. It might be an even worse shock for them than it has been for me.'

'I can see that. A kind of extra mother, dreadfully like oneself. Seeing what one would grow into. Thirty years ago, you say.'

'Yes.'

'What it amounts to is you've got four identical twins half your age walking round unclaimed.'

'I suppose so, yes.'

'Well, don't tell your Oliver or he might go after them.'

'You mean to kill them? Because they upset me? Like slugs, snails and greenfly?'

'No I don't mean that, Joanna. I mean he might fancy them.'

'Why should he?'

'Because they're half your age. You, but more so, Joanna.'

And Angela thought, but was too kind to say, even though she was jealous – how could she not be jealous with Joanna still beautiful, still pulling them in, at sixty – 'You'd be the first taste of a drug on his tongue,

167

Joanna, and they the real stuff, the full flavour.' Instead, she said, 'I hope you didn't tell Carl about your gardener lover. I hope that wasn't why he was so angry?'

'Well yes, I did.'

'Oh dear,' said Angela. 'Wasn't that rather stupid?'

'Yes,' said Joanna.

'I hope your clones are more prudent than you,' said Angela, 'or their nearest and dearest will be having a terrible time. I think you should go straight back home and warn this gardener of yours. Gerald takes Carl quite seriously, you know.'

'I should hope so,' said Joanna.

Joanna went and walked about Richmond Park, in totally impractical shoes. When she was thirty she had imagined all her troubles would be over by forty, there would be nothing left to go wrong: at forty she had imagined the same about fifty, and at fifty she had given up: she still found herself walking about distracted and alone, carefully refraining from crying, just as she had when she was a child.

She remembered coming home from the Bulstrode Clinic and that time she had really wept, from physical weakness more than anything else, or so she had supposed. She remembered that the doctor's name had been Dr Holly. Holly and May, she'd thought at the time, berries and flowers. Red berries, white flowers, and nothing coming out of either.

Well, she'd been wrong about that. Too much had come out of it. She would go back to Oliver and tell him everything, everything, no matter what Angela said; they would go off for six months to some secret destination. New Zealand, perhaps. The soil was good, she believed, and the gardens were wonderful. If he loved her, he would believe her; they would go. Or she would apologize to Carl; tell him she'd been making it all up. Something. Her head ached, her neck hurt: she had to sleep.

26

Angela went straight up to Gerald's office after she'd talked to Joanna; she took the car to the station, the train up to London, a taxi to the Department, and Gerald came straight out of a meeting to see her. She hadn't been to his office for eight years, he reminded her, not since the time their eldest son had made a passing girlfriend pregnant and she'd been upset.

It was Joanna May, she told him. Joanna had phoned her from a callbox on Reading station to tell her the most extraordinary story. Gerald said perhaps he'd better get back to his meeting, since it wasn't family, and the less he knew about the Mays the better and the same went for Angela, and the news from Chernobyl was not good, it was still belching peculiar things into the atmosphere, and there was more trouble with the monitoring equipment. He might have to go back to Britnuc for help. But he didn't return to the meeting, of course. They went to the canteen instead, for tea. Not liking the look of the pastries, he had the steak and kidney pie: she took the braised beef and mushrooms. Both had roast potatoes, boiled potatoes and buttered parsnips as well. It would keep them going until supper-time.

'It probably isn't the equipment's fault; it's just the

technicians don't know how to use it,' said Angela, which hadn't occurred to Gerald. He admitted they were barely trained. The truth was, the nation was totally unprepared for such an emergency. If emergency it was – radiation was still pretty much an unknown quantity. The danger was not critical or immediate – damage would show up in the morbidity statistics of the future when a different government altogether would be in power.

'I hope you were careful,' said Gerald. 'I wouldn't put it past Carl May to have our phone tapped.'

'Neither would I,' said Angela. 'Is cloning someone without their knowledge illegal?'

'I have no idea,' said Gerald. 'I hope so.'

'The other thing that bothers me,' said Angela, 'is will Carl try and get rid of the gardener?'

'You mean fire him?'

'I mean kill him, like he did the professor. What Joanna calls "that thing with Isaac".'

'I shouldn't think so,' said Gerald. 'There was more to that than met the eye. I nipped over to the Home Office and had a look at the files.'

'Why did you do that?'

'Always useful to have a hold over a fellow like Carl May,' said Gerald, and there was a gleam in his eye she seldom saw but liked to see. Not for nothing had he risen through the ranks of public service; she used to know the reason well: these days, as his face grew softer and pudgier, she tended to forget. All round them people drank herbal tisanes and ate muesli bars. No one took tea seriously any more. She cleared their plates, and went to fetch spotted dick. Custard was off.

'I hope you like foam cream,' she said when she came back. 'There's no custard and it's kind of stiff without any lubrication at all. What did the files say?'

'Just that prosecution was against the public interest,' said Gerald. 'That fellow King had a pretty dicey record, anyway. He was collecting brain tissue from Egyptian mummies and taking it to some lab somewhere and trying to grow an ancient Egyptian. Garden Enterprises was funding the lab.'

'What a peculiar thing to want to do,' said Angela, 'considering how the population of Egypt grows of its own accord. By a million every nine months, I believe.'

'I don't know about peculiar,' said Gerald. 'It might have been rather interesting, if it had worked. Anyway the Home Office didn't seem too upset the professor was out of the way. So I don't reckon he was got rid of just because Carl was jealous. Something else was going on.'

'Poor Joanna,' said Angela, 'she won't like that at all. But at least it means the gardener is safe. Well, safe-ish.'

'So long as he keeps out of the rain,' said Gerald. 'That seems to be the main danger, these days. Personally, I hope he stays out in it, and his balls fall off. Are you sure there's no custard?'

'One wonders a little,' said Angela, 'about the wisdom of having a man such as Carl May in charge of quite so many nuclear power stations.'

'They're very old ones,' said Gerald.

'I should have thought that made matters worse.'

'Not really,' said Gerald. 'They're like old cars. You can patch them and repair them and keep them on the road; and they give you due warning when something bad is going to happen. They knock and clank a bit: in time for you to do something about it. It's the new ones that are the problem: all built-in, fail-safe factors, and non-labour-intensive, because human error is always the non-calculable hiccough, ergonomically speaking: nothing at all to go wrong in the new ones, but if it does, pow!'

'All the same,' said Angela.

'We'd never have him in charge of the new ones,' said Gerald, reassuringly. 'Don't you worry. As it is, he's a popular fellow and a public hero and good for the image of the nuclear power industry.'

'But he's a murderer,' said Angela.

'Hush,' said Gerald, 'that's a very strong way of putting it. All these fellows tend to dispose of their enemies one way or another: if governments can do it, they think, why can't they, quite ignoring the electoral mandate. One can't condone it but it does happen. At least Carl May confines his activities to the personal sphere.'

'Think about it, Gerald,' said Angela.

'He isn't mad,' said Gerald. 'One draws the line at people who're mad, in charge of anything.'

'I'm not so sure about that,' said Angela. 'I'm not so sure about him being sane.'

'We'll see what transpires,' said Gerald. 'We'll keep a careful eye on things. Are you really sure there's no proper custard?'

'Quite sure,' said Angela, brushing away a flake of suet pudding which stuck to her hairy chin.

'Pity,' said Gerald. 'This cream is rather much.'

27

Had Joanna bitten back her anger, jealousy and resentment, and not visited Carl, her life would have gone calmly on: as it was, she was saved. Without the assault of these passionate saving graces she would have aged slowly and gracefully, developed a touch of arthritis here, a backache there: Oliver would have drifted off — men with guitars seldom stay, as she knew in her heart; a few languorous, heart-strumming chords, and they're off — and her fate would have indeed been that of the elderly woman who has never been employed, has no husband, no children, no former colleagues or particular interests, a handful of friends still around, with any luck (though their particular loyalties stretched by distance, exhaustion, their own problems) but who is fortunate enough to have a lot of money.

She would have given up the King's House in time. It would have come to seem, as her body shrunk, too big, too echoey, too frightening, too empty. Most women end their lives in bedsitting rooms, one way or another; possessions exhaust; they get discarded. Even pets become too much of a responsibility. The walls close in as the years pass: rooms get smaller.

Joanna might have joined, for a time, those groups of women who go from good hotel to good hotel, up and down the coasts in winter – in to the cathedral cities in summer – filling up the vacant rooms of hoteliers, who smile to see their income coming through the door, but whose hearts sink at the very sight of them, boredom and grievance incarnate. And how can these old ladies, these outlivers of men, not be boring, being so bored themselves? And how can they not complain, whose very life is a reproach to the young and vigorous? Joanna May's mind would have narrowed with her life: she would have stopped contemplating the nature of existence, stopped worrying about the constituents of identity, thought only of whether Tuesday's lamb chop and mint sauce was any more or less digestible than Wednesday's escalope and mushrooms. These terrible things she knew in her head: they lurked on the edge of her consciousness. And with that instinct for the preservation not just of life but of aliveness, not just the body but the soul, Joanna acted; driven by indignation, whipped-up emotion, frothed up to twice its proper size like a dollop of cream in a fast-food restaurant, she was moved to confront Carl in his lair, knowing perfectly well that he'd snarl and scratch, that his snarls and scratches were dangerous, and she was glad of it.

Why else had she married Carl May, in the first place, but to be saved from boredom? The boredom, the depression, of childhood, of home? Why had she brought about the divorce, but because boredom hadn't been routed, no: it had been creeping behind

175

her for thirty years, waiting to pounce, and it had almost caught up with her again, peering out from behind soup tureens at official dinners, perching on the white ties of elderly gents at functions, waving; nothing to talk to Carl about any more: or anything he was prepared to listen to, his life so divorced from hers, yet she so used to him, he to her, they could hardly tell each other apart.

Something had to *happen*.

Isaac happened. Isaac talked, talked, everything interested him; more, he listened. Illicit excitement sent boredom running, far far away, over distant hills: but excitement, danger, was like a drug, you got used to it, you needed more. At first, sex in his bedsitting room was enough, more than enough, mad enough, with the strange smells of toothpowder, and undone laundry, and disorder, books and papers everywhere, bits of old pottery, half a mummy's head; dead flowers in a vase, from 4000 BC for all she knew, the old sometimes looked so new, the colours so bright, the shapes so distinct. And Isaac's voice wonderfully on and on, including her in his universe, and the universe seemed to have a history, a purpose, a meaning, which started in the past, collecting as it went, arriving at *now*. Carl's universe started in the future and came back to today – it collected nothing. Well, that was understandable. Carl May's experience of the past was not pleasant, so he looked to the future, of course he did. But then Isaac's bedsitting room was not enough: she got used to it: it seemed too ordinary for something as extraordinary as Isaac and Joanna May, wife of Carl: boredom crept back, nearer, began to wave, sitting on mummy cases, on the edge of the chipped bath, sooty from an ancient gas-fired geyser, which puffed out black dust if you wanted hot water to wash. In the end the gallery was the only place he wouldn't come, this ghost of her own past, outdone at its own game by the half-haunted gloom, the watching eyes of history, which seemed to approve – or Isaac said they did; sex was just fine with the Ancient Egyptians, according to him – and of course in the gallery it was perfectly possible for Carl to come in at any time. They must have been mad. She must have been. But again, she was angry. A woman without children, now wanting children, too late to have children. Carl's fault. She loved Isaac, let Carl know it. He deserved it. Something had to happen. And one day it did: Carl pushed the door open.

And that stopped Carl being bored, for a time. He'd got too cosy anyway: he was the media's darling, the Government's blue-eyed boy. Garden Enterprises was under way. Britnuc was belching clean air into a threatened atmosphere – with only the occasional release of unscheduled radioactivity, which was in any case the least of many polluting evils. Something had to *happen*.

Carl May, before his wife's infidelity, was beginning to get pains in his chest. His was the kind of boredom which destroys life, like a slowly creeping fungus on a pear tree, causing leaves to wither and fruit to fall, unripened. Let him lose his wife, then, thought Joanna: that'll cure him: a swift blast of fungicide in the form of jealousy, outrage, anger. She'd been right.

177

Carl shook himself and thrived. Only in the shaking he'd shaken her off too. She hadn't done it for his sake, had she, but for her own.

28

If thine eye offend thee, pluck it out! Now there's a desperate doctrine, a right dollop of lateral thinking, a fine biblical recipe for preserving thy view of thyself as a fine and upright person. Kill the bearer of the bad news, would you; much good may it do you. The enemy still advances over the hill. If thine eye lusts, sever the optical nerves; chop off your hand if it strays where it shouldn't: destroy your ears to keep out the seducing voice: eyeless, earless, legless, armless, roll around in the mire: you will still be in the valley of desire. Just unable to function. After the inquest, after I, Joanna May, had perjured myself and betrayed the memory and love of Isaac King, the better to protect the interests of my husband Carl, I walked back to Eton Square, to the big pillared house which was Carl's and my home. I walked up the steps, put my key in the lock, and found it would not turn. The key was the right key — it was the lock that had changed. I banged the knocker and rattled the handle but no one came. Yet I'd seen Anna's pudgy face at the window, just a glimpse of it, or thought I had.

I believed that by perjuring myself I would win Carl's forgiveness, that it would be over: it could be forgotten. That Isaac's death was sufficient punishment for me. I stamped and shouted and banged upon the step, and I expect I screamed and cried, I can't remember. The solid door stood between me and my marriage, my home, my friends, my clothes, my possessions, my past, my future, my life. Those strong upright houses of Pimlico are built to keep the poor out; to keep the rich secure, the noise of riot at a distance. Carl had cast me out of his life; I had become a supplicant: I belonged the wrong side of the door. I knew it was no accident. It bore the hallmark of Carl's vengeance. The sudden shock of horrid surprise which he knew so well how to deliver, the lightning stroke out of an apparently clear sky. First he lured you into complacency; then, clap, snap, he got you.

I went to the phone box on the corner and rang my own number but no one answered. I wondered what Anna was thinking as it rang and rang, and she knew it was me: poor Anna, straight from the Philippines, witnessing this cruelty, obliged to be part of it. Carl paid her wages. Would she be horrified, or would she just think this is what happens, always happens, always will happen, to women when they cease to please or, worse, step out of line. A plain girl herself, stocky and puffy-eyed, bad-complexioned, hesitant in English, used and abused, fleeing one set of harshnesses to run into another, still thinking herself lucky, allowed to pick up the crumbs of Carl's and my life. Poor Anna. She'd know whose side she was on: whichever hand had the power, held the food, would be the one she licked. I went back and stood on the step: it began to rain a little: I didn't know what to do: to go to friends would be to start a scandal: I was still Carl's wife.

And then the garage door whirred and opened, and the big Volvo backed out, black and shiny and somehow ordinary, with the dent still in the wing which had been the death of Isaac, and in the back was Poudry the solicitor, and in the front was Philip the murderer. And Poudry held the door open for me, and I got inside, because I didn't know what else to do. And while we drove to a small and rather grimy hotel in Paddington – where someone or other who needed their wages no doubt, and knew which side their bread was buttered, and that it wasn't my side, had unkindly booked me a room – Poudry told me Carl was divorcing me, that I would be bought a house and given an income, that I was not to set foot in Eton Square again, that I was to think myself lucky.

That my clothes had been destroyed, my papers and my books and my family photographs shredded, and my parents' marriage certificate and my father's death certificate too; and no sign of me was to be left in the house, all trace of me was to be destroyed. I was free to begin life again as he would be, without evidence of the past, and I should think myself lucky.

'Do you think I'm lucky?' I asked Mr Poudry.

'Yes, I do,' he said, after thinking about it for a little. We were, I think, both very conscious of the dent in the Volvo's back wing, and of Philip the chauffeur in the front. Mr Poudry hummed a little in a nonchalant way that reminded me of Pooh, in *The House at Pooh Corner*, singing a little song the better to sound at ease: 'How nice to be a cloud, floating in the blue. It makes me very proud, to be a little cloud.'

As it happened my husband was generous. Not that 'as it happened' is a phrase that was much bandied about in Carl May's life. It suited him, for reasons of his own not immediately plain to others, to be generous, or appear to be.

I moved out of the Suffolk Ease hotel only when the decorators finished in the King's House. I could have left at any time, but the hotel was a desperate place and suited me. I had a room to myself: others, immigrants, lived twenty-five to a room, in a stench of urine and cooking, refugees from one horror or another – flood, famine, persecution, torture, war. Carl, booking me in here, meant to tell me something. So I sat it out, recovering from my own desolation, my own sudden loss of home. I had no one. The other lodgers had each other. Night after night I sat alone in a room, sitting on a bed – damp stains on the wall, the murmur of human grief around, crying children – staring at television: a woman of more than fifty, whom even money couldn't save. And I wanted to see Carl, and he wouldn't: I wanted to talk to Carl, and he wouldn't. How could he do it? How could he wrench us apart? If it hurt me, surely it hurt him? I mourned Isaac but I mourned for my marriage more.

And all Mr Poudry would say, when I visited him in his office, was, 'You are very lucky, Mrs May,' and one day he added, 'It might be a good idea to move out of the Suffolk Ease: you'll forgive me for saying so, but there is beginning to be about you the pong of the underprivileged.' And I looked at him closely for the first time and saw he was not more than thirty: it was the weight of authority had aged him in my eyes. I wouldn't go. The hotel was where Carl wanted me to be. I was obedient. Only when I moved into the King's House did I begin to find my will again, or some of it. I washed, I dressed, I looked after myself: I became accustomed to life without Carl. Sometimes I even enjoyed it. I began to like the vision of myself, the drama of a woman lonely and alone, living in isolation, rejecting the world which rejected her.

Then I employed Oliver as a gardener: and one day he took out his guitar and sang some folk song to me, some wispy song of lust and longing, and asked me if I'd like to play the guitar, and I said yes, and he put the guitar in my arms, and stood behind me and put his arms round my arms, and that was that. I no longer thought about Carl. I was cured. I assumed he was cured too. I thought I was safe from Carl.

I thought all would be well if I did not love Oliver: I could not let myself love him. I knew quite well what would happen if I did. That if I cared when it ended – and it must, it must, I knew in my heart it must though my head pretended otherwise – the pain this time would kill me. A lump in my breast, a swollen lymph gland under the arm and that would be that. And who would there be to come to my funeral? Gerald (reluctantly) and Angela (weeping: if only for the loss of a good gossip) and Mr Poudry and the accountant, and a nurse from the hospital if I'd re- membered to smile while dying; and Carl would not come, or if he did, it would be so the press didn't pick up the fact that he had not. The funeral was not worth the dying for: let Oliver be a nightly visitor to my bed, let him return me, little by little, to the fullness of the world, but that must be all. It should not be difficult. I had loved Carl May: having loved Carl May, I could not easily fall in love with, become emotionally dependent upon, sexually infatuated with, addicted to, a gardener who played rock guitar.

Oliver died and I found it was true. I had not loved him. You only know what you've got once it's gone, and it wasn't much. Trevor the butler gave an account of Oliver's death, his murder – and how could it be anything but murder: a man doesn't easily hang himself by his feet – and I heard the account with equanimity. I winced, for it was a horrid thought that a life which could bring me to life, purply-red, strong and pulsing, had changed suddenly and permanently into limp white rotting tissue. I wept a little, because Oliver had been cut down in the spring of his life, and of the year, with the whole blossoming, blooming, fruiting season yet to go. I was saddened because now my evenings would have to be spent alone, the forbidden pleasure, the companionable calming marijuana joints no more. I was shocked, pale and shaking – a physical reaction, I imagined – but the roots of my being were untouched, steady, compacted in dry earth. I surprised even myself.

If thy love offend thee, pluck it out.

29

The gardens of the King's House ran down to the river Thames, gently sloping, occasionally terraced. The river split to form an island, shared by a little group of houses, of which Joanna's was the biggest and best. The jetty, however, was seldom used. Oliver did not like the water, and Joanna mistrusted it. The garden was old; first established in the eighteenth century, used originally as an overflow for Kew Gardens, neglected and cosseted by turns. 'What a pity you don't like gardening,' Oliver would say to Joanna. 'Looking after a garden is like looking after children. Feed plants and they grow, neglect them and they suffer. It's all rewards and punishments – with more than a dash of chance thrown in, in the form of weather. I'm sure you'd be good at it.'

But what Joanna liked was to sit out on a sunny morning, and breakfast at leisure, dressed in white as often as not, watching Oliver work: the garden and herself presently drifting into one: she the prize lily, a little past peak flowering perhaps, but still what the garden was all about: the culture and cultivation of beauty.

She liked to sit in the spring and summer and watch the pleasure boats go by, music approaching, passing, fading – while those who had the gift of life, the understanding of enjoyment, the privilege of friendship, went sailing by. Or so it seemed. Joanna did not doubt that on closer acquaintance the crews and guests aboard the yachts, steamers and launches were as vulgar and foolish as anyone else, as prone to anxiety, misery and jealousies as she: that the music masked a thousand discontents, and that the champagne moved to mock exhilaration, not necessarily the real thing: nevertheless the illusion was pleasant, there was no need to get too near. She did not grudge these river people the possibility of happiness, at least, and certainly admired their ambition to achieve it. 'Such a lovely day! Let's go on the river . . .' Still, she had managed the lido, with Gerald and Angela: that was water and outing enough.

On the afternoon of that day, the day Joanna, her own resentments finally focused, had gone to Reading to have it out with Carl, Oliver, having finished with the rhododendrons, was weeding out the herbaceous borders. He worked with a hoe, standing to unsettle the shallow roots of the clover which crept up from the river bank in spite of all efforts to prevent it; or, occasionally, kneeling, with fork and trowel, to dig out plantains, patiently easing out the long, stubborn root, loosening soil and levering back and forth until they gave up, apologizing as he did so for thus putting paid to their best endeavours. His habit of talking to plants of all sorts, including weeds, and especially weeds he meant to destroy, quite irritated Joanna.

'If you're going to kill them, kill them,' she'd say. Oliver would droop his lids over his soft brown eyes to mask his displeasure, giving him what she called his 'I meant to please but now look' spaniel look; his hippy look, of reverence to all things, gentle, kind and understanding; his Age of Aquarius look. Then she'd say, 'I don't know why you don't just use weedkiller, like anyone else,' just to incense him, to watch the pallor of determined sweetness give way to the pink of indignation, and then she'd laugh and he'd know she was teasing.

But these pleasures were over now. An expensive-looking pleasure launch of the kind Oliver least liked, being moulded in some kind of new fashion to give it rounded, bulbous lines, and in a colour Oliver knew to be called Whisper Pink, trimmed with Whisper Cream, its CD playing Elgar's 'Pomp and Circumstance', cut its engine, its music, on the stretch of river which ran by the King's House, slid slowly into the jetty and tied up. There were five young men on board, strangely dressed.

Oliver straightened up, and watched the five young men disembark and come towards him, up the garden path where the tiger tulips bloomed on either side. They smiled, but he knew they were not friendly: something about the tense way they held their necks; he knew at once that retreat would be more dangerous than standing ground, that to placate would be safer than to challenge. They were, he thought, in their mid-twenties. They talked and joked amongst themselves, halfway between yobbo and yuppy: yobbo down below, layers of ragged and chain-strewn trouser; up above, collar, tie and suit jacket. Their heads were apparently shaven, and they wore bowler hats.

'Nice place you've got here,' the leader said. His name was Jacko. He was blond and beautiful. 'You the gardener?'

'Yes,' said Oliver, 'that's my trade.'

'Got quite a bit of age to it,' said the second in command. His name was Petie. He was dark and sulky. 'This garden has.'

'That is certainly so,' said Oliver. 'It was old when George Three bought it and renovated it for his mistress.'

'Did he now?' said Elwood, who was black and beautiful. 'Those old geezers weren't half naughty boys.'

And Haggie and Dougie, who were pale, thin and spotty, and didn't fill their trousers or their suit jackets nearly as well as the other three, kicked a tulip or two out of the ground.

'Pity to do that,' said Oliver, mildly. 'That's quite a rare flower. A black tulip. Not my favourite, as flowers go, a black flower being unnatural, if you ask me, but some people like them.'

In answer, Dougie and Haggie tore up handfuls of daffodils, and Oliver didn't mind that so much. They were more or less over and he'd been going to move them, in any case, to some less-overlooked patch of ground where they could deteriorate in peace and wait for their replanting in the autumn. But he pretended dismay, since that was what they wanted.

'Can I help you fellows?' he asked, wondering where Trevor was. Trevor would sometimes come out in the mornings with a cup of coffee, and sit on a stone wall in the sunshine and talk about the minutiae of his life with his lover – he was having an up-and-down relationship with a masseur at a nearby health farm – and Oliver would listen patiently and respond constructively. If Trevor looked out of the window and saw the young men he might, with any luck, call the police.

'Is the missus out?' asked Jacko.

'The missus is out,' said Oliver, 'but the master's in,' half a truth being in his book better than no truth at all, albeit in the circumstances any lie might have been justifiable. Those capable of knocking off the heads of black tulips, in passing, were in Oliver's eyes quite capable of knocking off human heads.

'That's a lie and a half,' said Jacko. 'The mistress is out as we very well know – and what a naughty boy you are, Oliver, young enough to be the lady's son – and the master ain't here neither.'

'If you know,' said Oliver, brightly, 'then why ask me?' and was quite pleased with his own courage. He'd said the same thing, at the age of four – according to his proud mother – to his teacher when asked what three and two made. 'If you know, why ask me?'

Jacko took out his fob watch and looked at it, and took off his hat to reveal a topknot of golden curls, and nodded to Elwood, who opened his briefcase and took out a length of bamboo pipe. Petie took out a dart from the yellow child's lunch box he carried, and Petie carefully handed the dart to Elwood who put it in the hollow tube and blew the other end, hard and sharp, and it landed in the back of Oliver's hand, the one that was carrying the trowel.

'Ouch!' he said, and dropped it, and Jacko, Petie, Elwood, Dougie and Haggie counted to five in unison and Oliver felt numbness running up his arm and down to his heart. He noticed the sudden quietness of his whole body, as it stopped beating. He thought, this is what it must be like for a fuchsia killed by frost; when water turns to ice, and that was all he thought.

Trevor was coming out to meet the lads. He had seen the gleam of yellow hair when Jacko took off his hat, and the flash of handsome male profiles, and wanted to know what was going on. He feared no evil on his own home ground.

But they were bending over Oliver, whoever they were, and turned their smiling faces towards him, and one said, 'It can only be Trevor, the man's man,' and he detected in their smiles something which made him shiver. 'Better get in the house, Trevor, before it's you as well,' so he did. He walked smartly back into the house and locked the back door and slammed shut the stainless steel mesh shutters on the windows from the security console. He watched through the mesh but they did not come after him, and he was affronted, as well as relieved. It seemed he was no business of theirs. Instead, they picked up Oliver and carried him shoulder high into the garage, which had once been a barn. Trevor thought they were singing something.

He did not call the police. He had enough trouble with the police. They followed him when he went out shopping, just waiting for him to go where they assumed he was going, to the public convenience that is, the better to pounce and get him for some disgusting act or other, which he would never perform, but they quite happily invent.

After five minutes Haggie reappeared and looked

over the garden in a puzzled kind of way. He called to his friends, 'What's a shitty rose look like anyway?' and Petie came out and wrenched a branch off a rose bush, and went back into the garage, Haggie following.

After ten minutes or so all five men appeared again, without Oliver; marched down to the launch moored at the jetty, boarded it, and left in the direction of Reading. Trevor went out to the garage and found Oliver hanging as Joanna was later to find him. The back of his hand had been scratched by, presumably, thorns from the rose branch. A few petals lay on the floor. Oliver's boots had been pulled off and tossed aside. Out of custom, Trevor put them neatly together. On the floor, beneath the hanging body, brushed by Oliver's hair, lay a single card from the Tarot pack. Trevor recognized it as the Hanged Man. Trevor had had his fortune told often enough to know that the card was supposed to signify innocence and the over-coming of difficulties by sheer good luck, but he had always taken leave to doubt it; the Tarot pack in his opinion was more sinister than its diviners would often allow. In this case he could see the card signified what he had always suspected: death by hanging because you didn't look out. And above, below, and to the left and right of the signifier, the Hanged Man in person, were the four Queens. Oh, kinky, thought Trevor: what is going on?

He said goodbye to Oliver in the same spirit as Oliver would say goodbye to doomed weeds and went to sit in the kitchen. He opened the shutters. There seemed no point in keeping them closed. He would wait until Joanna came home and let her decide whether or not to call the police. If she did, he could explain the delay as the general inefficiency and stupidity of the man they insulted him by supposing him to be. He tried to call his friend Jamie but the line was dead. That did not surprise him.

He assumed Joanna would understand the significance of the four cards, and he was right.

30

'On either side the river lie,' quoted Carl May, from Tennyson,

'Long fields of clover and of rye –'

'Barley,' said Bethany, and Carl May chose to ignore her. Once.

'That clothe the wold
And meet the sky
And through the fields
The road runs by
To many-towered Camelot.'

'That's where my ex-wife lives,' said Carl May, 'in Camelot.'

'I thought she lived at the King's House, Maidenhead,' said Bethany. They lay in bed together. The sheets were white. There were blankets, not a quilt. How quaint, had thought Bethany once, how like him, how pure, but now she thought, how old-fashioned, how uncomfortable, how like death. He ignored her. Twice.

'And up and down
The people go
Gazing where the lilies blow

Round an island there below
The island of Shalott –'

'Shallots, onions,' said Bethany.
Thrice.

'Four grey walls
And four grey towers
Overlook a space of flowers,
And the silent isle embowers
The Lady of Shalott.'

'Yes, I know,' said Bethany, '"She left the web, she left the loom, she made three paces through the room" – we did it for diction – "the mirror cracked from side to side, the curse is come upon me, cried the Lady of Shalott." Then she mooned about for a bit and topped herself from sheer boredom. Which reminds me that the curse has not come upon me. What are we to do, Carl?'

Carl was silent.

'I know you said you had a vasectomy, Carl, but it can't have worked because I'm pregnant and I've been with no one but you, Carl.'

Still Carl was silent.

'There, I've said it,' she said. 'I'd been getting really nervous.'

Carl sat up in bed, looked down at her bare breasts, her smooth narrow arms, her blue eyes – she took out her contact lenses at night – and rested his hand upon her throat. Then he moved it down over her body, on the whole quite gently, though tweaking her nipples rather sharply, to which she was not averse.

'You be careful,' said Carl, 'or you'll end up like

Squirrel Nutkin,' but she didn't understand the reference. Nor did she have time to puzzle it out, as the whole of Carl May advanced upon her.

'You were only joking about being pregnant, I suppose,' he said, presently, disentangling his legs from hers reluctantly, but he felt the first twinge of cramp, to which he was prone.

'Of course,' said Bethany. 'Twice in one night. Wow! What a man!' She was tired. She used the language of porno films. She did not have the energy for finesse. He did not seem to notice. There was no real reason for her to be tired. She thought it might well be the effect of boredom.

'I had a man killed today,' said Carl, pleased with himself. 'Perhaps that's it.'

Bethany blinked, but was careful not to let her body tauten against Carl's. She no longer felt tired. Then she thought, well, one pregnancy joke deserves a murder joke. A death for a life. Silly old you.

'He didn't suffer,' said Carl.

'If you're going to kill a man,' said Bethany, 'why bother if he suffers or not?'

'One does bother,' he said. 'For some reason. I don't wish to inflict pain, or terror. Some lives simply need to stop. Have you ever had a termination, my dear?'

'Once.'

'Well, there you are. You understand.'

Bethany put on her contact lenses and turned her eyes green, and fluffed out her red hair, and pranced about the room. It could do no harm.

'Who was Squirrel Nutkin?' she asked.

'Squirrel Nutkin danced about in front of a wise old owl,' he said from the bed, 'taunting him and teasing him, asking riddles and telling jokes.'

'What sort of riddles?'

'Riddle me, riddle me, riddle me, ree,
 How many strawberries swim in the sea?
 I answered him as I thought good,
 As many red herrings as grow in the wood,'

said Carl May, 'for example.'

'What happened?'

'Nothing happened.'

'Then what was the point?'

'Nothing happened and nothing happened.'

'Then what?'

'Something happened. The old owl pounced and ate Squirrel Nutkin up and there was peace in the wood again.'

'Oh,' said Bethany, and put on her clothes rather quickly. Sometimes he did give her the creeps. But presently her spirits were restored, for she was indeed young and she found herself singing her favourite song:

'For a young man he is young
 And an old man he is grey,
 And a young man's back is good and strong,
 Get away, old man, get away.'

'I haven't finished yet,' said Carl May. 'Indeed I have only just started,' so she had to get back into bed again, but that was not really what he was talking about.

31

Thus thought Joanna May, missing Isaac King badly (for he *knew* what the cards meant, and she could only guess): now, if the four Queens of the Tarot pack, or, as some would have it, the long-lost Egyptian Book of Toth, are seen together, they denote nothing worse than arguments. If reversed, however, the argument might become excessive; fatal, even. In conjunction with the Hanged Man, a card from the Major Arcana, which when reversed denotes selfishness and sacrifice, rootlessness and riot, things don't look too good. If you laid all at the head of an actual hanging man, murdered, they might begin to look very bad indeed. And, as the Queens of Wands, Pentacles, Swords and Cups could be seen to represent all the women in the world – excepting only the few from the Major Arcana, the High Priestess and the Empress (positions Joanna May and Angela might contend for) or the female half of the Lovers (which might well suit Bethany), these great cards having in their own peculiar way dominion over all the humble folk of the four suits – why then, things might be looking quite appalling for all the women in the world.

Prudently, Joanna spoke none of this aloud. She merely said to Trevor, 'Gobbledygook. The police will not be interested in what they say is gobbledygook: they will not understand the insult and the threat involved: go and fetch those cards and put them in the kitchen drawer, and don't even mention them.'

Joanna May called the police. Of course she did. What else could she do? The duty sergeant she spoke to said they would send a police car the moment one was available. He was soothing and competent. He said if she was certain her gardener was dead, leave him where he was and touch nothing. It sounded, from her description, like some kind of inadvertent death by way of sexual perversion, and was at least less messy than a crucifixion. They'd had quite a lot of those lately: a lot of nuts in the homosexual community: they were sending an ambulance, but that might take even longer than the police car. Emergency services were stretched.

'I don't think he was gay,' said Joanna May.

'Gay, bi, hetero,' said the duty officer, 'makes no difference to us. We are not prejudiced. Where did you say? The King's House? The big place on the island? Wait, that's come up on the computer recently ... yes, here we are ... knew I'd seen it. Trevor Hopkins, occupation butler: indecent behaviour. And this one was the gardener, you say?'

'The charge against Mr Hopkins was not proven,' said Joanna May. 'In fact the charge was dropped. What's it doing on your computer?'

'You're quite right,' said the duty officer amiably. 'It shouldn't be there. No doubt it's on its way to wiping.'

198

It was an hour before they arrived, and an hour and a half before the ambulance came to take the body to a morgue. The police doctor said there'd be an autopsy but it looked to him as if the young man had had a heart attack while engaging in some kind of kinky sexual activity – there was no evidence of foul play. No end to the things that people got up to: a pity: from the look of his garden he was good at his job. The world was short of gardeners.

'And of police officers, too,' said the plainclothes man, hurrying him on. They had another suspicious death waiting. Four men had arrived. They questioned Trevor, but kindly, to his surprise. He told them nothing about the boat, about the bully boys: just that he'd gone out to the barn to take Oliver his coffee: had found him swinging, dead and upside down, and gone inside and just sat, till Joanna came home. If they thought there was more to it, they didn't say. It would only take everyone into the complex and miserable area of sexual deviance, and Mrs May's butler had, from the look of him, suffered enough.

'What we don't want', said the police officer, by way of explanation, 'is copycatting. If it gets into the papers, before we know it everyone's hanging from their ankles trying to get heart attacks. We have enough to do –' and they left. The body had already gone, by ambulance.

Joanna May called Angela and told her all about it. Angela offered to come over but Joanna said she was OK. Only quite some time later did she begin to weep.

32

God flew off in three stages, if you ask me, Joanna May, the childless and the cloned, and none of them anything, I have now decided, to do with nuclear bombs or Logie Baird.

God the Father flew off on the day mankind first interfered with his plans for the procreation of the species: that was the day the first woman made a connection between semen and pregnancy and took pains to stop the passage by shoving some pounded, mud-steeped, leaf up inside her. He flew off in a pet. 'But this is *contraception*,' he cried, 'this is not what I meant. How can I work out my plan for your perfection and ultimate union with me if you start doing this kind of thing?'

God the Son flew off the day the first pregnant woman made the next connection and shoved a sharpened stick up inside her to put an end to morning sickness and whatever else was happening inside. 'But this is *abortion*,' he cried, 'it's revolting, and no place for a pro-lifer like me to be.'

And God the Holy Ghost flew off the day Dr Holly of the Bulstrode Clinic, back in the fifties, took one of my ripe eggs out and warmed it, and jiggled it, and irritated it in an amniotic brew until the nucleus split, and split again, and split again, and then started growing, each with matching chromosomes, with identical DNA, that is to say faults and propensities, physical and social, all included, blueprint for four more individuals, and only one soul between them.

Call me egocentric if you like, but that's when the Holy Ghost flew off, muttering, 'Christ, where is this going to end?' for it's been trouble ever since, hasn't it, all downhill; war, and riots, and crime, and drugs, and decadence, and dereliction, and delinquency, because there's no God. Well, there's no bringing him back; it's up to man to step in and take over. (I say 'man' advisedly; I don't think women will have the heart, the courage.) He gave us minds, didn't he, and the aspiration to do things right, as well as the tendency to do them wrong.

Carl may be wicked, but Carl's right. Takes a wicked man to be prepared to think like Carl, that's the trouble. I know how Carl May thinks: though not always what he thinks. I know what he was doing; I know why his teeth did not draw blood. Carl is not interested in my blood: blood cells do not contain DNA. A good place for obtaining DNA, from the tissue at the back of the neck. What Carl does with it depends upon what he feels like. So many things are possible. He could take a fertilized egg from, say, Bethany, give it the blueprint for my growth, put it back inside her, and she'd give birth to a little me. Would she like that? Perhaps she would. Perhaps mothering a man's first wife might make you feel altogether better about her. All these relationships are about incorporation, if you ask me, everyone in one big bed together – me, Carl, Oliver, Bethany, Isaac – all rolling around, warm and safe and companionable: we only get upset when we're left out in the cold. If I had a cell from Isaac I would ask Bethany to re-create him, in penance for taking Carl from me. And death would not divide us any more. If he were dug up from his grave, there'd still be enough residual DNA there, even now, to do it. But I won't do that: it seems forbidden, as forbidden as abortion ever was. I don't think Carl will do it: to impersonate God is a terrifying thing. Even for Carl, who as a child bayed at the moon. Microbiologists get so far, then lay down their tools, put aside their electron microscopes: take up gardening instead: they frighten even themselves. These days scientists talk a great deal more about God than does the rest of the world: they acknowledge magic – though they call it 'propensity', or 'something intervenes'. 'Something intervenes,' they say – as they break matter down to its smallest definable particles, the merest flicker in and out of existence of the most fragmented electric charge – 'or else our observation alters it.' What is that but obeisance to the shadow of the God who ran off, the God they drove off, when bold and young and frightened of nothing!

What Carl could do, what Carl might well do, for Carl controls the scientists, since Carl has the money, is mix up some of my chromosomes with those of some other creature and set it growing, and know more or less what would get born, forget a fingernail or two. He could snip out the section that decrees I will have long and elegant legs, and snip in a section from someone else's DNA, someone with short piano legs, the kind without ankles. He could give me a dog's back legs. If he wanted, he could do horrible things. He could do good things: sometimes he wants to do good things. Just as man can use nuclear weapons to make war or keep peace, to destroy or build, Carl could make me live with arthritis for ever or keep me disease free, never to catch cold again. He could interfere with my mind: make me nicer, more gregarious, kinder, happier, more socially conscious: he couldn't control the environment I grew up in, not in the short term, but if everyone was kinder, happier, loved their children better, didn't shut them in kennels – why then presently the environment of the growing child would indeed change, improve, step by step, little by little. Look at it this way, Carl would say, every time a woman uses contraception or has an abortion, she interferes with natural selection. Not this baby, the next baby, says the mother, bold as brass, standing in nature's way. Let's go for a better father, or a better environment: let's hang on a bit. That's what it's about: that's what's important. Not the first baby that comes along but the best baby, the one that'll have a decent chance in life. And let's do better by the ones we have, stop at two, not six. Quality, not quantity. Choice, not randomness, and there being no God, why not? That's what Carl thinks.

In the meantime, being unreconstructed himself, and cured of the notion that death is final – for it isn't, not if he can keep the genetic line running – Carl May has killed Oliver, and now he means to kill the clones. He has told me so, by way of the cards. He thinks this will hurt me. He offered me a family: now he snatches it away again. But I'm not at all sure that I recognize their right to life, these thefts from me, these depletings of my 'I', these early symptoms of the way the world is going. I might myself be rather in favour of termination. I must think about it.

Time to consult the Maverick Agency once again. I like the Maverick Agency. They make me feel the world is real, that the boats on the river, the cars on the road, are truly there. That a debt could affect you, a bullet kill you. Everything in this house is so still and quiet. The weather is warm. The windows are open. The watered-silk curtains, palest green, stir just a little. In the garden the weeds are growing, that's all, with no Oliver to clear them. And the caesium falls, and the strontium, and God knows what, silent, minute, invisible, as Carl makes his deadening presence felt.

33

Jane, Julie, Gina, Alice.

In the lives of the clones of Joanna May something stirred, some instinct of self-preservation was awakened, and not in that fact itself (for what woman does not wake in the morning once or twice in her life saying 'this can't go on a moment longer') but in the timing of that fact, lay whatever strangeness there might be to find. As Joanna May, Empress of inner space, fought for once to control her life, so too did the four Queens – Wands, Pentacles, Swords and Cups (rulers of the provinces, as it were), fight to control theirs, not quite sure what had moved them to action, groping for understanding of their own behaviour, and not quite finding it, so looking for justification instead.

———◆◆◆———

Jane received three letters by the same post. One was from her employers to announce the appointment of the new head of the London office: and it was not Jane but a snip of a girl of twenty-three, without a degree to her name, who got it. Too old at thirty! If you hadn't made it by thirty in the film world, you'd had it. The next was from someone she'd never heard of, a woman called Anne, written on thin blue paper in what looked like a drunken scrawl, saying she, Jane, should take her claws out of Tom and let him get on with his life, or she, Anne, would come round and personally strangle her, and the third was from the ground rent landlords, asking her for her £8000 contribution towards repairing the roof, a matter she'd never heard of until that moment.

She rang HBO and offered her resignation, which was accepted with an alacrity she found humiliating. She rang Tom and asked him who Anne was, or rather screamed at him about her, and Tom said she was just a friend: he'd come round. She rang the landlords and said it was monstrous, and they agreed, but nevertheless, there it was. If she did not hand over £8000 forthwith they could, if it came to it, foreclose on her mortgage and resell to raise the necessary funds. She rang her father, Jeremy, who said he feared she hadn't read the small print of her tenancy, and she said, 'Why couldn't you read it for me? Why have you never helped me?' and he said, 'Jane, you were always so self-sufficient, even from a baby: it came more easily to admire you than help you,' and for some reason this made her weep and weep more than did any of the other sudden and unexpected blows from fate.

Tom came round and showed her photographs of Anne, who was blowsy and uneducated and had a daughter called Roma, aged eleven. Anne was his landlady. Yes, he spent nights with Anne sometimes.

Why not? Why had he never told her? It didn't seem anything to do with her, that was why: Jane only wanted half of him, so she could have half. She couldn't own him: they didn't have a child. Jane knew he wanted a child. Little Roma needed him. She didn't have a father of her own.

'You're not fair, you're not fair,' wept Jane. Once men, according to Madge, said if you don't sleep with me I'll find someone who will. Now the threat had changed, gotten worse: now it was if you don't have my baby other women will be only too glad.

Anne didn't have a degree: she worked down the council baths: she had a council house: she acted as his model: yes, he was painting nudes. No, he didn't want Jane as a model, she was too twitchy. She couldn't relax. He thought he would have an exhibition soon. He was sorry about her job, her roof, her father. But her job made her hard and smart and cynical; it was a good thing she'd lost it: if she sold her car she could pay for the roof: and she'd always been hopelessly in love with her father and how could he, Tom, compete: and yes of course he loved her, what was all this talk about love all of a sudden; if he moved in with her and she settled down and they had a baby he would finish with Anne though of course he'd have to go on seeing Roma, she was only a child.

'You go back to Anne,' said Jane. 'That's the end, I don't need you, I don't want you, I don't want to see you ever again.'

So he went, and she wondered why it all felt so familiar. She began talking to friends and colleagues about possible openings not just in films, but in journalism, put her solicitors on to the matter of the roof, went round to the doctor and demanded a sterilization, which was refused. She did not argue, however.

For it seemed to her, as she advanced reasons, both laudable and derisory, in favour of her sterilization – her career, her freedom, her revulsion, her dislike of baby mess and smells, her figure, her need of sleep – that there was another one she was only just now beginning to put her finger on. She didn't want a boy; but who would understand that? If she had a boy it would be homosexual. It would have to be. Because how could she, being female, give birth to something male? Her little twelve-week foetus, which they'd said was male, had looked a real mess to her, and she wasn't surprised. She could understand how her body could somehow spit out a daughter, a replica: but the female was less than the male: how could the lesser give birth to the greater? How could she tell Tom a thing like that? Better forget the whole thing: just not have babies: just be in some other more rational arena, where life was for living not passing on. Nevertheless, when refused, she was remotely, somewhere, somehow, pleased. She had a coil put in, instead.

So much for the Queen of Wands.

———◦◦◦———

As for the Queen of Pentacles, Julie, well, her husband Alec flew in, ate supper without tasting it, went to bed without noticing her new provocative nightgown, let alone her determined serious sweetness – she had parted for ever (or so she really and truly believed)

208

with her lover, for the sake of the marriage – was too tired to make love, rose in the morning, grumbled at the state of his shirts – though they were perfect – and flew straight off to West Berlin.

'This can't go on,' she said, and made an appointment to see a solicitor. Yet Alec had flown in and out, just so, a hundred times before.

Julie, Queen of Pentacles.

———◦◦◦———

Gina, Queen of Swords, woke up to a usual kind of day and limped to the doctor's, as she often did. But while she was sitting in his waiting room – and she had to wait for a full hour with coughing young women and spluttering old ones all around, trying to reassure Ben (who had stayed off school to help her) and pacify little Anthony, who sat grizzling on the floor dealing harshly with the few old toys brought in by passing benefactors – she said something strange, to no one in particular. 'This can't go on,' she said.

'What, Mum?' asked Ben. 'What did you say?'

Ben always listened out anxiously as if his life's duty was to be on guard, waiting for something he could do nothing about, except watch for its coming.

'Never you mind,' she said. 'But don't worry. Things will get better,' and she'd said that to him a hundred times before, and it hadn't got better. But this time when she limped into the surgery – her knee stiffened and swelled with every hour that passed – and the doctor said grimly, 'I suppose you fell downstairs again,' she actually said, 'No, I was pushed. Will you write it down, please. I'll need some kind of record.'

The doctor wrote it down, with alacrity. The clones of Joanna May always found protectors: though it must be said that this particular clone seldom looked her best.

Gina, Queen of Swords.

———◦◦◦———

And as for Alice, Queen of Cups, that morning Alice woke from a terrible dream in which she had been split into five from the waist up and four of them were eating alive, with fanged teeth, the one which was her, and when only one of her eyes was left and half her mouth, Alice woke screaming. She told the essence of her dream to the photographer who happened to be with her and he said well that's you struggling for survival with your four big brothers, and having understood it, or thought she understood it, she felt better. Except that the one-eyed image continued to bother her, and instead of going back to sleep, she thought about it. One eyed, cock-eyed; something was wrong. She, usually so restrained, too controlled even to smile if she could possibly help it, suddenly kicked the sleeping photographer (his name was Radish; an absurd name) with a smooth, round muscular foot and shrieked, 'I can't stand it a moment longer. Go back to your wife' – for of course Radish was married: her relationships usually were with married men, who could be relied upon to go away – so he did go back to her, poor man, startled, surprised and upset. That is to say, he walked the streets until ten the next morning, when he was due back home, believing Alice had thrown him out because he was married, and had the evening before explained how he couldn't leave his wife, she being pregnant and relying upon him, and so forth. He could see it was all for the best: but it hurt, it hurt.

Alice had to take four sleeping pills before she could get back to sleep and as a consequence failed, for the first time in her life, to turn up for a 7.00 a.m. call. The studio had to send a taxi for her, and she arrived without her make-up box, and was, in fact, so thoroughly unprofessional all round they decided not to use her again. She was clearly paranoic. She claimed she was being followed by a young man carrying a child's lunch box, that he was standing outside the studio even now, and if they looked out they'd see him – and they looked to placate her – but there was nothing unusual to be seen, just people standing about on street corners waiting for taxis, and workmen waiting for other workmen and so forth, but no one looking out for Alice. Who did she think she was? Really beautiful women are admired and loved but seldom liked. She could not afford to step out of line, and she had. Alice, Queen of Cups.

34

Carl May did not believe in divinatory magic, of course he did not. To tell the cards, the stars, the lines of the palm, tea-leaves and so forth was to divine what was in the fortune-teller's heart, and that was all. How could it be otherwise, the clues to interpretation being so numerous and to reach that interpretation so many contradictory clues having to be taking into account? Moreover, the wisdom behind that interpretation – that is to say the sum of the experience of long-dead seers and necromancers – had always been so sloppily recorded and translated from one language to another, one culture to another, as to add up in the end to sheer gobbledygook.

Gobbledygook, and he would prove it.

To this end Carl May had started Britnuc's Divination Department, housed on the eighth floor, a floor which had heating and ventilation problems. Divination was made up of cartomancers, astrologers, crystal gazers and so on, and the greater part of its work involved participation in research, funded jointly by Britnuc and the University of Edinburgh, into the comparative validity or otherwise of the various occult disciplines. So far, as Carl May had expected, the balance was tipping otherwise. To justify the existence of the department in the eyes of his fellow directors and the shareholders its reports and prophecies were registered along with those of other sections: forward planning now included propitiousness of time in relation to event in its computerized forecasts. All other things being equal, which seldom happened, recommendations from the eighth floor would be allowed to tip the balance on minor decisions this way or that. Carl May reckoned it would be no worse than tossing a coin, which on occasion he had been known to do – though sitting alone at the head of the great board table as he did who was to say whether he reported its fall correctly?

Carl May was interested and displeased to observe how quickly the staff came to take the existence of the department for granted: how it had become common practice for Garden Developments to plant according to phases of the moon in spite of the virtual impossibility of controlled testing – variables in the rearing of plants being almost as numerous as they were for humans; how at lunchtimes the lifts to the eighth floor would be busy with not only female clerical staff (which he would have expected) on their way to have their fortunes told, but with middle and senior management as well. He wondered if there were a marker gene for gullibility: he waited impatiently for Holly to repent and come back on line. He would not wait for ever.

Since the Chernobyl event Carl May had had Divination, in conjunction with the University, working

213

on maps of the British Isles, predicting regional variations of wind patterns and subsequent fallout. Now came a phone call through to his office from Edinburgh. A former music-hall entertainer, Wee Willie Bradley, who had the apparent gift, or talent, or capacity – call it what you like – of shutting his eyes and projecting imagined pictures on to ordinary black and white film, was proving successful in producing accurate maps two days in advance.

'How successful?' demanded Carl May, who was putting on his shirt.

'One hundred per cent,' said Edinburgh, smugly.

'Impossible,' said Carl May, 'because no one's maps are accurate. As well say today's instrumentation readings are influenced by Wee Willie's maps two days ago.' Which stumped Edinburgh, for a time.

'What's your star sign?' Carl May asked Bethany, who, dreamy and languid, still lay on the palely carpeted office floor, since she found the designer chairs too uncomfortable to sit upon. Since bits of carpet came off on her yellow cashmere sweater she hadn't bothered to put that back on. It was an idle kind of day.

'I can't remember,' said Bethany, prudently, for all Carl May was in a good mood. 'I don't really believe in all that junk.'

He wondered whether there might be a gene for the propensity to tell lies, and whether it would be desirable or undesirable to shuffle it out. Would Bethany honest be less or more desirable? He tickled her chest with his bare toes. The red light on the telephone blinked.

'What a busy day,' said Bethany.

It was Gerald Coustain. He had come back to Carl May, reluctantly, to ask if Britnuc could possibly make available to the Government one or two technicians properly trained in radiation diagnostic techniques, in the urgent national interest. Carl May was pleased to put at his disposal Britnuc's entire Divination Department.

'I don't quite understand,' said Gerald. 'What use are astrologers and palm-readers in this particular situation?'

'Our research shows,' said Carl May merrily, 'that they're as good at anticipating fallout as our technicians and they certainly cost less.'

'That may be,' said Gerald cautiously, 'because your diagnostic equipment is out of date. You have the technicians, the Department has the equipment; couldn't we just get them together?'

'I'll think about it,' said Carl May cheerfully. 'How's the family?'

'Just fine, thank you.'

'I hear you've been seeing something of my ex-wife.'

'We all had a jaunt to the lido, one day,' said Gerald, after only a second's pause.

'Joanna must have really liked that,' said Carl May. 'I'm glad to hear she's taken up swimming. Women need to look after themselves as they get older. Poor old thing, did you hear about her gardener?'

'I think she called Angela, just to say. Quite a shock.'

'Good domestic staff is always hard to find,' said Carl May, 'even more difficult than trained technicians and accurate, up-to-the-minute equipment in this ever-changing field of ours. Perhaps the Department of Energy will see its way to some form of co-funding when this Chernobyl lark has calmed down. That way we could ensure Britnuc was always in a position to help you lot out.'

'I'll put it to my Department,' said Gerald.

'And I'll put your requirements to mine,' said Carl May. 'You're quite sure you can't make use of my Divination Department?'

'No thank you,' said Gerald.

'Pity,' said Carl May. 'What a lot of old stick-in-the-muds you civil servants are!' He was in a talkative mood. 'Reminds me of someone I used to have working for me. What was his name? King? That's it. Curator of the gallery – you know my gallery? The May Gallery? Egyptologist fellow. Well, never mind, it's a long story – he was interested in the Tarot pack. Hieroglyphics, and so forth. Poor fellow, he got knocked down in a road accident, killed.'

'I seem to remember that,' said Gerald, cautiously.

'That's the problem for stick-in-the-muds,' said Carl May. 'So stuck they can't even look where they're going!'

'Well,' said Gerald, 'it's been an interesting conversation, Carl. I'll come back to you when I've spoken to my Department.'

As Gerald Coustain put the phone down he heard Carl May laughing, and the sound of agreeable female giggles. He wondered if it were mad laughter and decided probably not: just that Carl May had discovered the answer to executive stress. You murdered the people who angered you, tormented those you despised, teased those who depended upon you, and

216

kept bimbos in the office. He was about to pick up the phone and discuss these suppositions with Angela, but thought better of it. If Carl May knew about the trip to the lido, someone's phone was probably tapped: possibly even his own. It could wait till he got home.

35

The Queen of Swords and the Queen of Pentacles.

————◦○◦————

The Queen of Swords left the doctor's surgery with one child in a pushchair and the other walking just a little behind her, as was his practice, and had been for years. She walked away from home, not towards it, she wasn't sure why.

'Where are we going?' Ben asked.

'I don't know,' she said, 'but I don't want to go home.'

'Where else is there to go?' he asked, which was of course the point. But he moved up to keep pace with her, and actually took charge of the pushchair, since she was limping, and it was the first time he'd done that – as if admitting their common interest, mother and son, in what was going on in the family, and encouraging this new train of thought in her: namely that things could not go on as they were, but would, unless she did something. At least for once she was walking away from home, away from Cliff, and not back towards him. They kept walking in the wrong direction until it was lunchtime – although Ben should have gone straight to school, and she would have been more prudent to have just sat down and rested her leg, as the doctor had instructed. Then they went to McDonald's, which was a luxury, and bad for them, but she had lost faith in a future in which care taken meant benefit returned. Ben ordered at the counter while she, her whole leg now painful and throbbing, unstrapped Anthony and heaved him out of the pushchair and into the high chair provided by McDonald's. He enjoyed sitting in it, which was something. She should never have had him, of course.

'These children that we should never have had,' she said aloud, 'still have to eat.'

The Queen of Pentacles heard. Julie was sitting at the table next to Gina's. She had gone to visit her solicitor: he had not given her good news: she had no children and the house was in her husband's name: she was young and able-bodied: if she divorced she would be expected to shift for herself. At the same time she did not, as her solicitor pointed out, have the capacity, let alone the training, to earn a decent living. His advice, offered to her unasked, was to stay home and make the best of things. And so she had driven not home but in the wrong direction, not sure why or where, alone and lonely, childless and more than ever conscious of it, but also let it be said without the exhausting responsibilities that went with the company, the pleasure of children. This Julie recognized, and now tried not to stare curiously at Gina; this messy, overweight, distracted, sloppy woman of too many responsibilities who had said aloud something so remarkable. 'I might have been like that,' she thought, 'if I'd had too many children too young,' and envied the other woman but at the same time pitied her, and felt, if not grateful for her own lot, at least a little more reconciled to it. Her heart was breaking, but she would not, would not, see the vet again. He was married, so was she. Supposing Alec found out? A woman could lose everything, so easily.

Gina saw Julie watching and thought who does that woman think she is, staring, and why is she so familiar: do I know her from somewhere? And what was a woman like that doing, sitting in a McDonald's, in a pale cashmere jumper, trying to get her pearly teeth into a Big Mac when everyone knew you didn't bite but somehow drew the layered substance into your mouth. Prettier than me, thought Gina; taller, thinner, younger, certainly richer: dressed so you hardly noticed, but you could tell expensively, and looking miserable but down her nose. If things had gone differently for me, thought Gina, if I'd been given a chance in life, if I hadn't had these bloody children, if someone, anyone, had had the heart to stop me, got me to school, let alone college – but they hadn't, had they. No one had cared. She felt herself beginning to cry. She was stuck here in McDonald's, marooned. Now she'd stopped walking and taken her foot off the ground she didn't think she could put it back down again. It would hurt too much. Moreover, she had set things in motion at the doctor's she could not control, and wished she hadn't: there would be more violence ahead: how was she going to collect Sue at four o'clock: she could send Ben, she supposed, but Ben would resent it, Ben had never wanted Sue to be born any more than Sue had wanted Ben to exist; and worse, she, Gina, wouldn't be there to stand between the two children and their father when they got home: and they were as likely to be met by blows, insult and humiliation, as chips and a video: you could never be sure with Cliff. Sue could walk home on her own, and would if no one turned up, but she would sulk for days and that would feed back tension into the whole family and make matters worse. Ben always wanted things to get better: Sue somehow wanted them to get worse, so whatever awful thing it was would be over quicker. Only, one row was just like another. When Cliff was sorry, and making amends, he was the best person in the world, but these days his being sorry was turning into a memory: a hope. She had failed her marriage, herself, her children.

Gina caught sight of her face in a mirror, and the tears running down it, and thought she didn't look so bad after all, almost glamorous, and then realized she wasn't looking at a reflection of herself but at the woman opposite, who was also in tears.

'Well,' said Gina, startled into friendliness, 'I suppose all women look the same when they're crying.'

'I don't cry,' said Julie, 'I never cry,' stopping on the instant, though the same thought had crossed her own mind: that looking at Gina she was looking at a reflection of herself. What a terrible thought! She gave up battling with the Big Mac and sipped a little black coffee and dabbed her eyes with a lace handkerchief. ('A lace handkerchief!' thought Gina, astounded, blowing her own nose on a McDonald's serviette.)

When Ben came back with the two Big Macs, one Chicken McNuggets, three large fries and two milk shakes, Julie gave up altogether and joined Gina at her table. Julie said, 'You're so lucky to have children; we can't have any,' and began to cry again. Gina wished she wouldn't cry in front of the children, but Ben seemed impervious to this extra distress, just stared stoically into space over his hamburger. He was a handsome child; but he did, she acknowledged, look pale and nervous. How would he grow up? 'You could have mine,' said Gina, joking, but Julie said, quite seriously, 'It's not the same. And I have this great house with no one to fill it, and somehow it makes things worse to have so much of what you don't want. I am never going back into that house again. I'm not. I don't care what anyone says.' Even as she spoke she realized she was, in her own mind, peopling her world with concerned observers, who of course in reality didn't exist. Lonely so lonely!

'Aren't you lucky,' said Gina. 'I have a house with too much to fill it, and I reckon I've got to go back into mine, I've no option.'

Gina looked across at Julie and again had a sense of familiarity. Had they known each other as children? At school? She couldn't put her finger on it. Julie looked at Gina and thought this woman is like the sister I never had, and doesn't she just need cheering up, cleaning up, and taking over. I could do some good here, for once in my life.

Ben said, 'Mum, there's a man following us. He was behind us when we left the doctor's and there he is, sitting over there –' and he pointed to where a

222

young man in a suit sat behind a copy of the *Sun*, hiding his face. He had chosen a coffee and an apple tart. There was a briefcase on the empty chair beside him.

Gina said, 'Well, I haven't lost all my charms, then,' and Ben, who didn't seem to take to Julie but kept looking at her curiously all the same, went into a real sulk at being made, as he felt, to look a fool. Sometimes, when in a mood, he was so like his father, Gina quite disliked him. One of the problems about bringing yourself to divorce point, deciding this was the man you hated and not the man you loved, as you had rashly thought at the beginning, was not just the practical one of how you went and where you went, or the emotional one of how you lived on your own, coped on your own and put up with loneliness, but how, if you hated the man, you went on loving the children, who were after all half his. You saw the father looking out of the eyes of the son. The whole business of it taking two to make one, Gina had long ago decided, made being a mother and doing it right all but impossible. She found her daughter easier. She just told her what to do and she did it. But that irritated her, too. Where was the girl's spirit? And she would snuggle up to Cliff, too, as if she was taking Cliff's side, as if she'd just move in with him the moment Cliff had battered her mother to death, and that drove Gina mad. It was all horrible; everything all went right or it all went wrong.

Julie said to Gina, 'Why don't you come home with me until you sort things out?'

Gina said to Julie, 'What about your husband? What would he say? He wouldn't like it.'

Julie said, 'He's never there, and if he does turn up, so what? The house may be in his name legally but it's mine morally, and it needs filling up with people. I do what I want with my own house.'

'Well,' said Gina, 'in that case, yes, OK,' and that took Julie aback, but she was not the kind of person to go back on her word.

'What a day of surprises,' Julie said, as she helped Gina limp to the car. Ben pushed Anthony.

'Yes, isn't it,' said Gina. 'But my motto is, something always turns up at the last moment!'

This had not been Julie's experience but she supposed that if you were consistently afflicted by misfortune, as Gina appeared to be, you would develop, as antidote to it, the art of optimism. Julie had never had the opportunity of so doing. The misfortunes that afflicted Julie masqueraded as good fortune, and so were the more difficult to locate, comprehend and deal with. If your husband blacked your eye and threw you downstairs, you at least knew there was something wrong. If your husband was away most of the time, but paid large cheques into your bank account, how could you tell what was going on?

'There is another child,' said Gina. 'A girl. We have to collect her from school.'

'Oh Good Lord,' said Julie, startled. 'Well, never mind. The more the merrier.'

If that husband came home to a house suddenly full of women and sticky, sulky, noisy children, none of them his own, it might force things to some kind of issue.

As the two women left the restaurant, two young men got up from separate tables and followed them. They met at the door, engaged in a brief conversation, and strolled down the street together. They got into the car parked behind Julie's, and when Julie pulled out, so did they. All this Ben noticed but did not say. His mother had laughed at him, now she would have to take the consequences. It was the same kind of drastic, horrid, nourishing feeling his father often had about his mother, and Ben knew it, and though he didn't like it there wasn't much he could do about it. You could stop how you acted, but hardly how you felt. This new friend of his mother's, picked up at random in a McDonald's, seemed to have something of the same quality. He didn't like it. And where were they all going? It seemed that their lives were about to change, and no one had the courtesy to explain it to him, let alone consult him. But he could see that simply to be away from home for a time, without the fear of bangs, crashes and screams in the night, not having to put up his own defences against his mother's terror or hurt, not to have to watch anxiously for the turns and changes in his father's mood, not to have to listen out for his mother's putting of her foot in it, which he sometimes thought she did on purpose, not to feel so confused about Sue, whom he felt obliged to protect but didn't want to, would be a great relief.

'You OK, darling?' asked Gina.

'I'm fine,' he said. He'd missed another day at school, and no one seemed to bother about that, either.

'Do you often go to McDonald's?' Gina asked Julie.

'No,' said Julie. 'Hardly ever. Only when I'm upset;

225

then I like it. It's as if you were more like other people than you thought, and you might as well accept it. We're all in the same boat together.'

'That's what I feel too,' said Gina, feeling quite uneasy, that there was more to all this than met the eye. She wished there wasn't. In better times, she would have got out of the car there and then. But like so much else, once you had children, it became a matter of necessity, not choice. Where you were was where you stayed.

The car that followed them was white, all white, from its white-painted hubcaps to its white-coated aerial; a vehicle fit for angels from some phantasmagorical heaven and on the front seats, grey-suited, prosperous and clean, two young men who might have been God's accountants. The boot of the car was slightly open: part of a bicycle stuck out of it. People stared at them and forgot them.

Petie said to Elwood, 'Well, fancy you.'

Elwood said to Petie, 'Fancy you. Wheels within wheels. Just as well, my calves are aching.'

Petie said, 'That wasn't a coincidence, was it, that was drugs. That was the McDonald's connection.'

Elwood said, 'It was, and was I glad to see it. I'd begun to think that was no lady but a wild goose set up by Carl May to get his money's worth out of us.'

Petie said Carl May knows what he's doing and Elwood said you mean Jacko says Carl May knows what he's doing and Petie said it's the kids I'm sorry for and Elwood said we were all kids once even Carl May, especially Carl May, and Petie tuned the radio to rock but Elwood wanted classical so they had an argument about that, and Elwood drove rather hard around a corner just as Petie was feeling the sharpness of a knife against his thumb, so they ended up outside Julie's house with rather a lot of blood on the white upholstery. 'Serve you right,' said Petie, child at heart.

36

The Queen of Wands and the Queen of Cups.

———◦◦◦———

The Queen of Wands tossed and turned in her penthouse bed and the moon shone in. 'I want, I want,' she said aloud, but she wasn't sure what it was she wanted, except perhaps what she couldn't have, that is to say Tom. And him she could have, if she would, which she wouldn't. Some barrier stood in her way: some wall of glass. She could not allow herself to be happy.

The attic was now a penthouse. Thus the landlords advertised it, threatening to call in her mortgage if she didn't cough up for the roof: they had put it on the market just to frighten her: they didn't have a legal leg to stand on: she'd put her solicitors on to them. It would be all right in the end, it would, it would, if only the moon didn't seem to rock so in the sky, if only her limbs didn't twitch with longing, the feel of Tom's body beside her so lacking, if only her savings would last for ever, if only she had the energy and will to go out and find another, better, less blackmailing lover than Tom, but she didn't, she couldn't.

All you had to do, she supposed, if you wanted sex, was to get dressed and go out in the night street and walk about, and see what happened next, and something would. Only such an act was unthinkable. Why? What did other people do? Did they have possible partners lined up, waiting? The longer she lived in the world the less she knew about it. It baffled her.

Other people had the gift of peopling their lives with friends and colleagues; went to outings, parties, reunions, but she remained solitary, distant, voices sounded from the other side of the glass wall, muffled: people's smiles were distorted. She waited for some kind of matching private intimacy to happen, but it didn't. She'd known Tom for so long he'd gotten through the wall, but perhaps he was the wrong one: how could the only one be the right one? Was that the trouble? Perhaps she just couldn't believe her luck?

She would go home for the weekend: she would retreat and lick her wounds a little: she would try and feel close to her parents. Difficult to look her father in the face since his strange adventure with Laura: difficult to feel close to her mother since she'd been so wounded: no matter how unaffected Madge seemed to be, how bright her intelligent eyes still shone behind her pebble glasses, she now sapped the energy of Jane's youth: she no longer fed it, nourished it. Madge had been mortally wounded, and that was the truth of it and there was no strength left in her.

'I'm depressed, that's all,' thought Jane, no longer wanting anything, and remembered standing as a small child in the hall of the big, pleasant house, and seeing through the glass door of the study her father working at his desk: and the other side of the study window the dim stumpy form of her mother, working in the garden. She'd begun to cry, for a reason she didn't then understand, from the sense of not-belonging, sense of having herself received some mortal wound, and knowing, with the clear prescience of a child, that she would thereafter limp through life: there was no healing this. Yet nothing had happened – just the sight of an ungainly woman through glass, and the understanding that beauty of spirit and beauty of body were not the same, and that the knowledge itself could maim for life.

She was grown-up now: she had controlled her life: she had remained free of emotional and domestic commitments for just such an eventuality as had now happened – she was free to move to Los Angeles where the obvious career opportunities were: the English were popular: their special talents appreciated. And now she didn't want to go. Nor did she want to lie where she was, in an empty bed, staring at a moon tossed by clouds. Where did clouds come from? She scarcely knew what clouds were, let alone why they were. It was all intolerable. The thing to do, obviously, was to let 'I want' get the better of 'I don't want'. Desire must triumph over reluctance. But how?

The Queen of Wands felt like the kitchen maid. She gave up sleep, got out of bed and switched on the light, and a sensor peeped gently in a van parked outside, and Haggie, who had been sleeping therein, woke and yawned and took out his notebook.

Jane got on with her work, her diversionary activity. She went through files and cuttings. She was writing a series of articles for *Film International* on 'Images of women: the changing generations'. She could not get excited about it, but it was work, it would keep her name up there in front of those who mattered. In the morning she could try and contact Alice Morthampton, who had the reputation of being a smart-arsed bitch. A year back she'd turned down a film part – typecasting, playing the lead, a model. She'd turned it down on moral grounds, the screen view of the model's life being so far from reality, she said, it was intolerable, and the producers refusing to change the script. Well, you were as moral as you could afford to be, supposed Jane. Alice Morthampton must be pretty rich. Pretty rich. She could not understand why Alice Morthampton was considered so beautiful. A face was just a face. The features were regular, it was true. There were two kinds of women, Jane supposed, the ones who looked like herself, and this Alice, and the others, the majority, who looked like Madge. Jane took out a ruler and measured the proportion of eyes to nose, to ears, to jaw on a fashion shot of Alice, and then did the same for herself, in the mirror. As she thought, pretty much the same. It proved something, she wasn't sure what. She was suddenly very tired.

Morthampton – house of death. She hoped not. Jane went back to bed and fell promptly asleep, forgetting to turn off the light, so Haggie was up pretty much all night.

The Queen of Cups.

Alice lay in bed with eyepads over her eyes and considered the emptiness of her life, and wondered why nobody liked her and decided it was because she didn't like them. She could see the justice in it. She thought if she called her agent and instructed him to double her fees she would then halve her work and be just as rich. If she priced herself out of the market altogether, why then she would have forced an issue: she would have no option but to change her life. She might have to anyway. She had a feeling sour looks were going out of fashion and smiles were coming back and she wasn't going to start smiling for anyone; before you knew where you were they'd have you doing idiot shots, up telegraph wires and under water on your head.

The phone rang. It was some woman journalist without an appointment; freelance, too, not even an assignment. Alice thought perhaps she'd better try to be pleasant. When it came to it, self-destruction was a frightening thing.

'So long as there's none of that crappy feminist junk about sexism in fashion,' said Alice, 'you can come on round now. This minute, before I change my mind.'

Jane came, within five minutes. She only lived around the corner it seemed, in Harley Street. Alice lived in Wigmore Street. Alice opened the door. Jane and Alice stared at each other. Alice's eyebrows were plucked and her hairline had been taken back to give her a high medieval forehead. Jane's frizzy hair fell down to her eyebrows and beyond. Alice thought she might be looking at herself on a bad day, when she was feeling particularly short and squat. Jane thought, 'I could look like that if I wanted to. Which I don't.'

Jane went inside and sat on a sofa covered in the same Liberty fabric as covered her own sofa, only hers was green and this was brown. Still, it was a fairly common fabric. But there was the same Picasso print on the wall. She said as much.

'Someone gave it to me,' said Alice. 'I don't know anything about art. But there's a damp stain on the wall so I put it up – the roof's leaking. What's it meant to be?'

'Children playing,' said Jane.

'What, those splashes and dots? Well, write down I know nothing about art, and hate children. That should be a start. Who's it for?'

'*Film International*,' said Jane.

'Add I hate films too,' said Alice. 'I know nothing about them and don't want to.'

'But you did once turn down a part. It was that I wanted to talk to you about.'

'That old thing,' said Alice. 'I'm not an actress. I'm a model. I couldn't remember the lines.'

'I thought you turned the part down for moral reasons.'

'That's what my agent said. I was fired.'

Jane's pen stayed poised.

'People aren't going to want to hear that,' she said.

'You talk like me too,' said Alice. 'Only I try not

to. This is going to be a crappy interview. So let's forget it.'

A little grey cat jumped up on to Jane's lap. Jane squealed.

'Don't tell me,' said Alice, 'you have a little grey cat just like that one and *Candid Camera* is hiding somewhere in the room. I warn you, I'll sue.'

'Would it be watching you or watching me?' asked Jane.

'Me, of course,' said Alice.

'Bloody egocentric,' said Jane, but both looked for signs of *Candid Camera*. There was no sign of hoax or hoaxer. They looked at each other.

'You should do something about your hair,' said Alice. 'It's an insult.'

'I like it as it is,' said Jane. 'I don't believe in artifice.'

'Then you're a fool,' said Alice, and both fell silent.

Presently Alice asked Jane when her birthday was and Jane replied September first, and Alice said, well, I was born on September thirteenth, so that's something, but Jane said not enough. Twins could be born as much as three weeks apart, even identical twins.

'Who's talking about twins?' said Alice.

'I am,' said Jane. Then she said, 'But I'm sure if I'd been a twin, someone would have told me. Besides, it's not in my parents' nature to give children away. If my mother Madge had had twins she'd have reared them both, and made a good job of it, at least in her terms.'

Alice said, 'You might have been the one given away. You're the one who's egocentric. My mother never did anything she didn't want. She'd have given away anyone.'

Jane said, 'I'm certainly not adopted, if that's what you're suggesting.'

Though when she came to think about it, she could see that not to be Madge's natural daughter would relieve her of a great deal of guilt. The wonder had always been that so pretty a child as she had come from a pair so rigorously plain as Jeremy and Madge: friends, both hers and theirs, had remarked on it: she'd hated it: she saw herself as the source of her parents' discomfiture. If you had no friends, you didn't have to put up with the pain they caused: she'd learned that early.

'My mind's going so fast,' she complained, 'I think I'm going to be sick.'

She was, in Alice's mirror-lined bathroom, so full of creams, unguents, oils and lotions she could only marvel. She kept books in hers. When she came out she said, 'I can't possibly be your twin; we're completely different,' but Alice was standing in front of yet another mirror and had combed her hair down over her eyes and there was no doubting it.

'My experience is,' said Alice, 'it's not that people tell you lies, so much as they forget to tell you the truth. Personally, I trust no one. But then I was brought up with four brothers. All the same, I can see we're going to have to face up to this. Who's going to see whose parents first?'

In the street outside, Haggie found himself double parked next to a manhole in which none other than Dougie was working on telephone wires, yanking them out and then plugging them in. Dougie wore bright-yellow Telecom overalls.

'Well, fancy that,' said Dougie. 'Looks like yours has gone to visit mine. What's the connection?'

'Drugs?' said Haggie. 'Do you reckon?'

'More than likely,' said Dougie. 'Or prostitution. Women living alone.'

'It's too bad,' said Haggie, 'what goes on these days.'

'The world would be a cleaner place without their likes,' said Dougie, as Haggie joined him in the snugness of the manhole. 'Spreading disease with needles and sex.'

'This isn't a snuff mission,' said Haggie. 'It's a sniff mission.'

'One drifts into another, in my experience,' said Dougie.

'Mine's a tough cookie: no doubt about it,' said Haggie. 'No husband, no boyfriend, no children. Send a scrap of foreskin, or more, through the post, but if it's a stranger's what does she care?'

'You could slash my girl's face,' said Dougie, 'and all she'd do is call round the photographers, and there'd be even more of them in and out of her bed. Oh yes, they're tough. You have to admire them.'

'You don't,' said Haggie. 'You just have to stop them before they spoil the world for everyone else,' and Dougie said, 'I'm sure that yellow lead matched up to that yellow socket a moment ago,' and Haggie

236

said, 'What the hell, Dougie, what the hell. At least Carl May knows what he's doing.'

'I suppose,' said Haggie.

37

'This Holly fellow has got nothing to hide,' Mavis of Maverick told Joanna, seeming disappointed, 'or if he has, he knows how to act innocent. Easy-peasy to trace.' Young Mavis strode into the house with muddy boots, reminding Joanna of Oliver, bringing the world with her.

The Bulstrode Clinic, according to Mavis, who – or so it said in the Maverick prospectus – had a First Class Honours Degree in Classics from Cambridge, was one of the first fertility clinics in the country, part NHS funded, part private, properly registered, licensed and inspected: it did legitimate terminations, blew fallopian tubes and stuff (said Mavis, with distaste) and carried out a few properly authorized tests on artificial insemination and ex-utero fertilization (makes you puke, doesn't it, said Mavis. Why do women *want* babies?). They also did vasectomies (more like it, said Mavis). When it closed there were letters to the papers saying what were women to do now? (What they did, said Mavis, was to come out as lesbians and sod the men.)

Holly had moved on to the Genetics Research Department of Martins Pharmaceuticals, where he'd been ever since: some files he left, a few he took with him: a common enough practice, in research. He was married, had grown children, lived within a comfortable income, contributed to the odd learned paper: apart from dabbling about in women's insides, said Mavis, he seemed OK. He wasn't making an illegal fortune, so far as anyone could see. Of course your ex is a director of Martins, said Mavis, but then he's on the board of most things, isn't he, so it probably doesn't mean much.

Martins Pharmaceuticals, said Mavis, specialized in the manufacture of synthetic hormones and made a particularly popular brand of birth-control pill with good sales in Third World countries, and drugs for hormone-replacement therapy in the West for, said Mavis, spoilt old women who wouldn't give in. Martins had a good reputation, compared to other pharmaceutical companies, for responsibility and reliability — which wasn't difficult. They had been known to take drugs off the market as soon as dangerous side effects were notified, and not fight through the courts for years to keep them on: they had been known to pay damages voluntarily to people whom their products had blinded and maimed, and their gifts to the medical profession could not be said to amount to bribes. Martins maintained large biotechnology departments in their various divisions, and their latest claim to reputation was the development of a certain Factor 10, which almost amounted to altruism, inasmuch as it offered hope of treatment to sufferers from sickle cell anaemia and everyone knew genetic engineering would eventually breed the disease out of the human race so Factor 10 was not even a long-term money spinner. They've cost-accounted integrity, said Mavis, and found it pays.

'Why do you want to know all this?' Mavis asked Joanna May.

Joanna May told her.

'Bloody men,' said Mavis, 'so competitive, always muscling in on women's wombs. I hope you're not going to barge into the lives of these wretched young women and stir everything up.'

'I don't know,' said Joanna.

'Well, think about it,' said Mavis. 'Thirty years on! How would you like it if your ninety-year-old self came walking through the door?'

'I wouldn't mind,' said Joanna, but she wasn't sure.

'Unless you have another reason,' said Mavis, booted feet up on the sofa, 'you're not being straight with me. What else is your ex-husband up to?'

Joanna May told her.

'I don't know anything about Tarot cards,' said Mavis, 'or all that gobbledygook, but that's a nasty wound you have there on the back of your neck, and you should get it seen to. A man who can do that to a woman, forget what he can do to other men – which is really of no interest to me, murder-schmurder, call it what you like, it's a man's gotta do what a man's gotta do affair, and boring with it – but I don't think he should be let loose on your young versions. God knows what he'll do, vindictive bastard, since no doubt he thinks he owns them, typical male, taking claim for their creation.'

'He had a very hard childhood,' said Joanna May. 'Childhood-schmildhood,' said Mavis, 'reclaim your sisters! I speak both in the political and the family sense.' She sat on the sofa where Oliver had been accustomed to sit, and, like him, she smoked; and like him she coughed. Her skin was tough, her hair was frizzy, her T-shirt none too clean, but she brought with her energy, common sense and determination. The world was not too much for her: it was for action, not contemplation.

'Well,' said Joanna. 'Perhaps.'

'Perhaps is not enough,' said Mavis. 'You must go to Dr Holly straight away. You must insist that he opens his records to you, the ones he took with him.'

'Can't you see him for me?'

'No,' said Mavis, crossly. 'There isn't time. You do it. What are you frightened of? What did men do to you that has made your generation so timid? I accept that Carl May is a special case, he scares even me, but an old fruit like Dr Holly?'

'He wore such a white coat,' said Joanna, remembering. 'He was so kind, he was so clever; and I, I was doing something so very wrong, something I didn't want to do. I was getting rid of a baby; I was having my husband's abortion, not his child. I put the Bulstrode Clinic out of my mind and tried not to think about it again. What I did was so very wrong.'

'It wasn't,' said Mavis. 'You weren't pregnant. Two psychiatrists certified it as an hysterical pregnancy.'

Joanna May's hands moved to her small waist, her flat belly, no longer young; she felt her belly swell – she knew it could still. She understood her body's desire to do just that – its capacity to think wilfully, to deceive itself. She felt herself widen and grow, and then she felt herself shrink again, defeated. Tumescence and detumescence.

'Oh,' said Joanna May, cheated all her life.

'Your husband had a vasectomy early on,' said Mavis.

'I see,' said Joanna May.

Joanna May saw. Joanna May saw back into the pattern of her life, black and white, greys and duns. There are no colours in the inner landscape. She saw a dull web of non-response, picked out by miseries and misconceptions, disappointments and remorse, sparkling away with courage where no courage was needed, glittering with hope where no hope was; of trials overcome where no trials were; a false web, not her own, woven by Carl May: and she was the wretched fly and he the whimsical, scuttling spider.

'I'm pregnant,' she had said to Carl May. Where had they been? The States. Boston. She remembered a hotel suite, and a big white boxed-in bath, and taps out of which water gushed with terrifying power. She had been afraid to say it: fear where no fear should be. He did not want children. The day before the wedding he'd told her so – a walk in the park, a moon, a lake, romance, as the world knew it – he'd said, 'Just you and me, forever, no one else, no children, I don't want children, to be a child is to suffer . . .'

'Not my child, my child wouldn't suffer, I'd protect it.'

'Yes, your child too, anyone's child – to be helpless is to suffer: there's no escape. Let the human race end here, with us, its triumph, love complete and final,

242

whole.' And in that understanding she had agreed — only you, Carl, you and me: our no-children and our perfect love thus linked: and the stars, the treacherous messengers of fate, looked down and smiled. Carl and Joanna May, hand in hand.

Yet there she was in New York, ten, eleven years later, with her breasts heavy and sore, like the breasts of her friend Nancy, and feeling sick, as her friend Helen had been, and all her being focused in on this one wonderful fact: a baby, a baby! Treachery to Carl, but he'd understand, he'd forgive; surely their meshing was not so tight now, not so complete, as to forbid a little budding-off to come between; his past must seem a little further off, the remembrance of it not so desperate. Surely! What was her love worth if it hadn't healed him, hadn't undone the past sufficiently to make the future possible? Carl May had been kind. But he had said no.

And now, see! The kindness a lie: the no unnecessary. No living baby there: a notional baby in the head, not a real one in the womb. She'd had a spaniel once, whose nipples grew, whose sides heaved — nothing there, said the vet: an hysterical pregnancy. Animals do it a lot, said the vet, if you stand between them and their purposes. The bitch, Carl May had said; I've half a mind to have the thing put down. He'd laughed. A joke. Kick it and that will cure it. Later the animal had simply disappeared: it and its labrador companion. Dog thieves, people said. Now she wondered. A lifetime believing Carl May was sane, seeing black where white was, white where black was; if you practised too long you could no longer tell. You just

243

saw what was convenient, what sounded best, what kept you out of trouble. Perhaps he'd envied even her dogs.

'Just you and me,' Carl May had said. 'Just you and me.' So back from Boston to England, off to the Bulstrode, to meet charming Dr Holly. Really nice, when it came to it, understanding so much, interested in everything. After the termination she'd felt he owned her body. She would have run off with him if she could, if she'd known how to go about it. But she never knew how; she'd had no practice. It was a trick you learned: as a kitten learns to scratch earth to cover its mess. If there's no one to teach it, it never learns. Tales of Joanna May, the deceived, the self-deceiver.

No baby, no abortion. No pleasure in the sadness, no delight in the grief, no soaring knowledge of I can, I can, I have, I am real, a woman, a grown woman, here's proof of it at last — likewise no regret, no shame, no sense of courage failed, of having thrown a child away, because that child's life was not worth hers. Selective breeding, Carl May had said. Come now, Joanna, if you make a fuss, if you weep and wail, I'll think you don't love me wholly, totally, as you promised you would, for ever and ever, in the park, with the moon, the most perfect moment of my life. Was it yours? Oh yes, Carl, yes. A sacrifice on the altar of Joanna's love for Carl, Carl's love for Joanna.

All lies, all lies. What was a mountain was in fact a chasm: what looked a chasm had been a mountain. Falling when you thought you were climbing. What a fool she'd been. What fools women were: they didn't need mothers to teach them folly.

Lonely and alone these last few years; used to it: liking it. I alone, Joanna May, in the perfection of my childlessness, the tragedy of this single drama: content here in the centre of the web of my life, what's left of it, repairing it as Carl May tears it: only not my web, it now turns out, a borrowed web, too late now, to build my own.

These clones, these sisters, these daughters, what are they to me? I know nothing about them. Let them die. Carl was perfectly right: to live is to suffer. And not just the child, but the adult too. It never stops. The clones, like their original, are better dead. I don't have the courage to die, to kill myself, to put an end to the shame, the rage, the desire, the fear that is Joanna May. But let them die, those other versions. No action is required by me. Leave it to Carl May to act. That at least is familiar, true, comforting.

'It must be upsetting,' said Mavis. 'All this kind of lovey-dovey complication.'
'It is a little,' said Joanna May, politely, vaguely.

Joanna May saw herself at the centre of a web: what did it matter who built it? It was no one's responsibility but her own. She perceived that she was held suspended, harmless and impotent, by the equal forces of the passions which stretched the web, one at each corner. Shame, outrage, fear and desire, the four saving and refining passions of the universe, holding

245

her suspended, centring in her in exactly equal proportions, cancelled themselves, nullified Joanna May. The shame which should purify, the outrage which should move to action, the fear which should quieten, the desire which should sanctify, brought to nothing.

'Are you all right?' asked Mavis.
'I'm just fine,' said Joanna May.

And the greatest of these is desire, and the second greatest outrage, through which we recognize evil and sweep it away because it has no business hanging around, spoiling things. Joanna May willed: it was like using a muscle forgotten for years: you searched, focused, used – it hurt, but it worked. Enough.

'I want my life back,' said Joanna May, petulant and passionate as a child of five. 'The murdering bastard! He took Isaac, he took Oliver, but he shan't have the clones. I want them. I need them. They're *mine*.'
'That's better,' said Mavis.

38

'Hey ho, the holly,' said Carl May, bouncing into Dr Holly's office, 'this life is so jolly.'

Perhaps he's been taking rejuvenating hormones, thought Dr Holly, or is it just those old things, amphetamines, or perhaps youth is indeed in some measure infectious and he's caught a rather hefty dose of it from the young woman who keeps him company, but this is the third time in a week he's been to see me, and I wish he wouldn't. I don't like it. What does he want?

'Hey ho, the holly,' corrected Dr Holly, 'this life is most jolly.' Carl May is a powerful and wealthy man, why doesn't he get his secretary to call me on the phone, why doesn't he send his chauffeur, what is going on that he needs to see me in person? Does he have nobody to talk to? Or does he just want to show off his young companion? That was most likely.

'He's always getting things wrong,' said the young companion, and then, rather quickly, 'don't you, darling?' and she moved over to plant a kiss just above Carl May's eyes where the white hairs grew sparsely in stretched skin.

She seemed nervous. Just a two-a-penny scrubber, thought Dr Holly; an old man's toy, equivalent of a young man's Porsche, and then thought, no, that's just defensive, if she were mine I'd take her everywhere too, for all the world to see – could you breed from the emerald eyes? She wouldn't age well: the bone structure of the face was blurred – she had a look about the mouth: how was it you could tell the whore from other women, just by looking? Psychosomatic damage affected growth, as surely as did hunger: the failure to reach emotional potential left its evidence in the face: the outcome of the psycho-genetic battle was there for all to read. Poor thing. Poor damaged thing. As for Carl May, it was pathetic: a humiliation. Dr Holly did not like to see it. The girl was so clearly bought. He wondered if there would be any point in trying to find the marker for the propensity to use younger members of the opposite sex as symbols of status – it might not be too difficult; some variant in the reproductive organs might well prove to have just such a behavioural link – but decided there were far more urgent matters to attend to. Future generations might locate and shuffle the marker out, if it existed. If they had a mind to. Certainly his own department, after his disagreement with Carl May over the absent-mindedness or otherwise of university professors, could not even begin to take it on board.

'Did you hear what I was saying, Holly?'
Dr Holly hadn't. Bad mark, Holly.
'When do they make you retire, Holly? Got to make way for the young ones, isn't that so, Bethany?'
'Young men are boring,' said Bethany. Then quickly, 'Anyway, Carl, you're not old.' Whew!
'I'm ageing better than he is,' said Carl May. 'I've

pickled my bones in radioactivity, that's what it is!'
He poked Bethany's young flesh with a bony finger.
'Isn't that so, Squirrel Nutkin?'

'Martins don't enforce a retirement age in their R
& D departments,' said Dr Holly, whose beard was
white but whose eyes were bright, alert, even kind.
'Good men are hard to find. There's a surplus of
competence in the young, but not much imagination.'

'Is that so?' said Carl May. 'No fixed retirement
age! I must have a word about that with my friend
Henry.' Henry White, chief executive, Martins International, subsidiary of Britnuc. And Dr Holly wondered exactly what kind of task Carl May had in store
for him and how he would get out of it. Certainly
Carl May was building up to something.

Dr Holly had read about Carl May's divorce in the
newspapers and had appreciated the silence which
followed it. The man, he had hoped, was permanently
subdued. But then he had turned up again, Bethany
on his arm, bouncing about like a newly-inflated
balloon.

On the first visit Carl May, on his way to a board
meeting, had talked amiably about the possibility of
injecting more funds into Martins R & D. He had
then left two specimens for dry-storage, which Dr
Holly could see no reason to refuse. Carl May did
not volunteer information about the nature of the
specimens. Dr Holly did not ask. Bethany had worn
white boots, black stockings, a scarlet miniskirt and
an old grey-white torn T-shirt.

On the second visit they'd talked about the quest
for the new non-addictive painkiller the world was

looking for, and how after the expense of Factor 10 Martins deserved to be the ones to find it. Bethany had worn a grey suit, a white blouse and pearls and would have looked like a businesswoman only her hair kept falling out of its combs. On that occasion Carl May had been called away abruptly, back to Britnuc. Chernobyl was causing an uproar, apologized Carl May; the world had gone mad; and the thought came into Dr Holly's head that Carl May believed he was the world and was trying to tell him something. Carl May certainly had delusions of omnipotence.

On this occasion Bethany wore a long flowered skirt and an ethnic blouse, which kept falling open at the front where a buttonhole was too large for its button, and Carl May said, 'Tell me more about what you're doing,' and Dr Holly, who thought Carl May knew very well, told him more. He was studying brain-cell function in addiction, said Dr Holly, using identical twins as subject and control, stimulating the pleasure centres of the inner brain, rather than the pain centres – which would hardly be ethical –

'Impractical, shall we say,' said Carl May, 'since I daresay you're dependent upon volunteers, and only masochists would turn up, and then you'd have a biased sample.'

'Quite so,' said Dr Holly, calmly. 'How well you put it. Fortunately, you get much the same kind of hormonal excretion from the brain cells whether they're excited by pain or pleasure.'

'Much the same!' scorned Carl May. 'Time was when you wouldn't be satisfied with "much the same". Time was when you could have got a Nobel Prize, if only you'd pressed ahead, not backed out, sold out, let me down.'

'Well,' said Dr Holly, 'chance would have been a fine thing. It just so happened that Martins halved my funding one fine day for no reason that I could see.'

'Perhaps they halved it,' said Carl May, 'because you, being a professor, were such an absent-minded old fart and only half there most of the time.'

Bethany stirred uneasily. Language! Another button popped open.

'Perhaps they did,' said Dr Holly, 'perhaps I am,' and Carl May smiled. He always won, in the end.

'Time was,' said Carl May, 'when you'd have bubbled the vats and brewed the broth and grown a million million brain cells and not have had the bother of asking in living twins and parking electrodes into their brains, and perhaps the time will come again, sooner than you think.'

'Do you think so?' asked Dr Holly. 'At least stimulating the pleasure centres of consenting twins, triplets, quads if we're very lucky, is ethical.'

'Ethical smethical,' said Carl May. 'What do you think Martins are doing in the other labs, or don't you ask? Pushing ahead with what you began but didn't have the guts to see through. The transfer of nuclei, perfect and whole, dried not frozen, from the frog right up to the mammal – and by mammal I mean human, you bet I do.'

'So much is interesting,' said Dr Holly. 'There is more to science than genetic engineering. Perhaps, as you say, the field should be left to younger men.'

'Potter on, potter on,' sang Carl May sweetly, which meant he was taken aback, 'to the end of the road, and you'll never walk again,' and he pinched Bethany so that she squealed and leant forward and the next button came undone.

'Walk on, walk on,' corrected Dr Holly, 'to the end of the road, and you'll never walk alone.'

'How's the wife?' asked Carl May kindly. 'She must be getting on.'

'She's very well,' said Dr Holly.

'No arthritis, no spondylitis? A fluttering of Alzheimer's in the brain?'

'A little,' admitted Dr Holly.

'Pottering on to the end of the road,' said Carl May. 'I really must take young Bethany home. Look at her! I'll be back for your answer within the week. A plague on your living twins, I say. I need you back in the field. Money no object.'

Dr Holly nodded and smiled vaguely as if he hadn't quite understood, but Carl May seemed satisfied and left with a cheery 'Hey ho, the holly', and when he was gone, in spite of the relief that he was gone, Dr Holly's office seemed oddly dull and quiet, as if Carl May had sucked out all the energy through the door, like juice from a hole in the skin of an orange, leaving nothing but pith and fibre behind. He wondered what would happen next and he hadn't wondered that for quite a while.

39

Dr Isadore Holly looked up from his desk and said, as Joanna May came into his office, 'Why, Mrs May,' he said, 'you've hardly changed at all.'

'Don't begin by telling lies,' she said. 'You haven't seen me for thirty years. You can't possibly remember me.'

'I'm not telling lies,' he protested. 'It's not in my habit to tell lies. I remember you very well. Naturally, you look older; time has passed: I merely remarked that you hadn't changed, and you may think of that as a compliment, or otherwise. You were the most beautiful of all my patients; your husband claimed you were perfection itself, and I had to agree. The mixture of Scandinavian, Celtic and Norman stock we call typically English sometimes turns out very well indeed. And you have aged well. That too is in the genes; of course. Like mother, like daughter, we find.'

'And you could say the same of identical twins, I daresay. Like this one, that one. No credit in it.'

'Truly identical twins are rare in nature,' he said. 'When the single fertilized ovum splits, it seems the division of the chromosomes is not necessarily exact. It is possible to get identical twins with different-coloured eyes, did you know that? And eye colour is known to influence behaviour, and therefore personality. But I don't suppose you've come here for idle chitchat. One must not suppose that one's life's passion is even remotely interesting to other folk.'

'Your life's passion, Dr Holly,' said Joanna May, 'has had quite an effect on me. Tell me, if someone came to you and asked you to grow a human with frog's legs, would you do it?'

'It wouldn't be a very practical proposition, Mrs May,' said Dr Holly, his shrewd eyes crinkling with artificial mirth. 'We have to respect the laws of physics. Such a creature wouldn't jump – it would be top heavy. And it wouldn't look very nice.'

'I was not talking about practicalities, Dr Holly, nor aesthetics.'

'You mean the ethical considerations? Rest assured we would not. We are not in the business, Mrs May, of creating monstrosities, but of removing disease and, in the fullness of time, and with all possible ethical and legal safeguards, mental illness – a tricky area, mind you, because what is defined as mental illness differs, as we know, from society to society, culture to culture: what seems insane to one nation is mere dissent in another – but no doubt we'll come to terms with it. And eventually we will have to tackle the genetic basis of behavioural problems, and that too will be ethically and politically tricky. But nowhere does anyone wish to create monstrosities, Mrs May. Do I look like a mad scientist to you? No, of course not! Don't you go believing what you read in the gutter press.'

Dr Holly smiled benignly. Joanna May did not smile back.

'But you *could* do it.'

'Of course.'

'And no one would do it just for money, say.'

'Good lord, no.' Dr Holly looked quite shocked.

'People do all kinds of things for money,' remarked Joanna May, 'they make instruments of torture and poison gas, for example. Why not me with frog's legs, for money: or worse, just for fun, to see just how far I jumped, or couldn't jump? Fun is a great incentive. There's always a shortage of it.'

'Mrs May,' said Dr Holly, 'this is very interesting, but I'm a busy man. Can I help you in any way?'

'I just wanted to know what kind of person I was dealing with,' said Joanna May. 'What kind of person you'd turned into since, under cover of performing an illegal abortion thirty years ago, you stole what was rightfully mine, one of my eggs, you and my husband between you. A lot can happen in thirty years. I have come for the names and addresses of the women in whose wombs you implanted my babies.'

Dr Holly was silent for a second or so.

'I think "my babies" is an unfortunate misnomer, Mrs May. I don't think ownership comes into it. Does a woman's egg, once fertilized, belong to her, or to the next generation?'

'Mine wasn't fertilized,' said Joanna May, 'that was the point. It was jiggled into life. So, yes, I reckon it was mine.'

'I should point out,' said Dr Holly, 'that there was no question of illegality, since as I remember there was no actual pregnancy. But these are interesting points; for lawyers to decide, not us. And, as I say, I am no longer personally engaged in genetic engineering. It's a young man's field, these days.'

He felt discouraged and resolved that he would stay with the study of brain cells. They at least would not turn up years later to pester and reproach him.

'The files,' said Joanna May. Mavis waited in the car outside, to make sure she persisted. 'Or has my husband been to see you already? Is that it?'

'Your husband?' Dr Holly seemed surprised. 'I haven't seen him for a couple of years, since he had this idea about cloning a mummy.'

'Cloning a mummy? An Egyptian mummy?'

'The idea was, if we could get enough tissue with at least some segments of DNA intact, we could shuffle it together, insert what we had into a growing egg cell, and the resulting child would have the same genetic make-up as an ancient Egyptian. What a lot we'd learn! Of course, the child's privacy would have to be respected. Just because someone dates from the past doesn't mean they don't have present rights.'

'How far did you get?' asked Joanna May. If Dr Holly was playing for time, she had enough of that and more to spare. This was the advantage of being useless. He was a busy man, she was not a busy woman.

'Well,' said Dr Holly, 'not very far, as it happened. Dead's dead, so far as I'm concerned, and in nature this turns out to be pretty much the case, though your husband finds it difficult to accept. On the whole such scraps of DNA as we managed to retrieve weren't sufficient for our purposes. We had such a deal of patching and joining to do, whatever we grew might well have had the odd toenail missing. Of course these days we can dehydrate the cell before freezing; every year brings new developments, and indeed, more promising ancient bodies to light. We reckon, eventually, to find a few gut cells inadvertently dehydrated. There's one fungus which will do it – before death – which would help a lot. Your husband doesn't give in easily, does he?'

'No,' said Joanna.

'Unhappy childhood; to the point of trauma. Your husband represents the victory of nurture over nature: he is a great encouragement to us all. A source of inspiration. Interesting to reproduce him, wouldn't it be, and rear him in more benign circumstances, see just how it turned out.'

'It must have been fun,' said Joanna May, 'to clone me and see how that turned out.'

'Our major concern at the time,' said Dr Holly benignly, 'was in the successful implanting of fertilized eggs in stranger wombs, and testing the efficacy of certain immuno-suppressive drugs, rather than in personality studies, or making any contribution to the nurture-nature debate.'

'The records, Dr Holly.'

'I must say here and now, Mrs May, I would be happier if the request for information came from the child, rather than the natural parent.'

'I am not a parent, I am a twin.'

'You could look at it like that,' said Dr Holly. 'These personal and ethical ramifications do keep emerging – one hardly thought about them at the time. But, as I say, in ordinary adoption cases, the natural mother and child are brought together by the relevant agency only at the request of the child. The mother gave up certain rights, knowingly and willingly, when she gave up the child to adoption.'

'I neither knowingly nor willingly consented to anything at all,' said Joanna May, 'wriggle as you want, and I want those records now or I'll blow the whole disgraceful thing wide open.' She felt the pressure of Mavis waiting, filling the car with cigarette smoke, thicker and thicker as the minutes passed. She felt the dependence of the Queens of Wands, Pentacles, Swords and Cups: her sisters, her children, her family. They needed her.

'There is nothing to blow open,' said Dr Holly. 'Nothing that was not approved by the district medical ethics council at the time.' But he allowed her access to his records just the same.

40

I, Joanna May; not so young as I was, not so strong as I was, but braver: finding courage. My bed is empty again, but I dream it is filled, with lovers real and unreal, lovers I remember and men I never knew I wanted. I wake to find Joanna May sleeps alone, to face a day now peopled with the ghosts of the past: they throng around me, reminding me, instructing me. This, they say, relates to that. How simple! Why did you never see it before? But still the nights are stronger than the days. When the days triumph, I will act.

How the feelings of childhood haunt us. We think we forget, but we don't. Those initial pains grow stronger with the years: instead of fading, as one might expect, they merely afflict the present more and more. One image now torments me. I remember standing on the wide polished staircase in the big house in Harley Street. A scarlet carpet runner ran down the centre of the stairs. The pattern was both boring and complicated. I must have been very small. The front door bell rang and the receptionist walked through the hall. She wore a white coat, and was not friendly to me, or anyone. She opened the door to the patient. On the step stood an old woman. She had on a black coat with a fur collar and brought with her an air of what I can now see was genteel despair mingled with anxiety: the sense of a life misspent, of opportunities missed, of knights in white armour who never came, of husbands, children who were never grateful. So many of the patients were defeated women. Women, I perceived at that moment, were by their very nature supplicants. The outside world knocked on our front door and yielded up its goodies, and its goodies were nothing but female desolation, decay and disappointment. My father's voice sounded from behind closed doors in one direction: my mother's from another. My mama played bridge, and I was not supposed to disturb her. I ate in the kitchen, with the receptionist: rationing was in force. There was a war on. Food was simple and boring: so was conversation. My mother and I were not evacuated from London: she said we must defy Mr Hitler but I thought it was because she did not want to miss her bridge. My father said the same about Hitler and I thought that was because he did not want to miss his patients. Even fear was a deceit. Sometimes bombs fell and the outside world trembled and crashed and the door knocker banged of its own volition, but the house didn't fall down, which was what I wanted to happen.

I remember standing on the stair as my father's patient was let into the house, and voices sounded, muffled by closed doors, and I knew I was cut off from the real world; that I was alone: that other people would never quite touch me, or me them: that I was only acting this child upon the stair: there was no real and undeceitful me: therefore the voices that came would always be muffled. The prescience was true: children fall into uncontrollable grief when they realize, small as they are, certain truths about the world, and about themselves. 'I just feel like crying,' the small child will explain. Don't believe it. The future is seen: the grief is real and profound.

Only Carl could I hear loud and clear; his voice came through to me not muted, but somehow at first hand. I didn't like what he said or did: that didn't matter, it wasn't the point. When I met him I thought he was rude and plain and rather short, but his edges were somehow defined; quivery, like a real person superimposed against a fake background in an old film. And that was that. I don't suppose it was love I felt; I think I just recognized an opportunity for being healed, for becoming real, breaking through the shrouding veils and mists, and that for me was all, at the time, I needed. I somehow knew what Carl knew, though I had come to the knowledge in a different way than he. Carl had suffered cruelty and hardship and I had not. Carl's early world had been small, black, wretched, terrified, until suddenly the clouds had parted and revealed a new bright world, full of privilege, animation, possibility: and with the last drop of strength he had leapt out of the one world into the other. And myself, female, given everything yet nothing, in my grey, muffled, lonely world, bred to serve, to be a supplicant, knew a different kind of cruelty, but the same kind of terror – the inevitability of illness, age, death: the impotence of love. When I lifted my eyes to Carl's I thought how peculiar, how bright and naked they are – and then realized that was how eyes ought to be. It was other people's which were out of order, clouded by wishful thinking and self-deception. There were just the two of us, in all the world, who knew what the truth was, and how terrible it is. 'You have my kind of eyes,' he said.

It took little to persuade me that I didn't want children. How had it happened to me that I knew what Carl knew? The thought frightened me. How could you protect your own children from that one dreadful moment on the stair, the prescience of defeat and death? You could feed your children, love them, nurture them, act the good mother, do all you could to be close to them, and still it might happen. On that one occasion when I thought I was pregnant I was afraid. When I had what at the time I thought was a termination I was relieved, as well as angry. Let me not deny it.

When Isaac said of the card 'Death' that it meant rebirth too, I took leave to doubt it. But then Isaac's eyes did not have the naked brightness of Carl's. I liked Isaac because he talked to me. Even good wives get bored. What are stay-at-home wives, executive wives, determinedly childless, supposed to do, even if, like me, they are wives of captains of industry not the mere foot soldiers? It is all performance in the real executive estate. She must be like the others, or he will know the reason why, and so will they. She must act, in the first few years, as if she waited for a child: she must hold the babies of other women, and sigh with longing, although the little wriggling thing appals and upsets her. Is this the sum of woman then – to be the instrument of reproduction, a walking womb; the pulsing, gurgling, bloody redness inside the whole point of her being? Never, but let her dissemble! Later she must act out the emptiness of not having children; lament her inability to conceive: it is expected of her: though she glories in the leisure of her mornings, the flatness of her belly, her peace of mind in a world where the lot of women appears to be worry, grief, toil and anxiety, as their children, their hostages to fortune, sap their cheerfulness, will and energy. Only later, when it's too late to change her mind, when the cyclical messiness has stopped, does a kind of truthful desolation set in, as the world around her empties; and she understands that of her own volition she has become one of nature's dead ends: an experiment set aside, because it didn't work. Then she may well blame whoever's around (as I do Carl), whoever, however unreasonably, she holds responsible for her initial decision, the tying of the knot that severs her from the future. She curses fate, instead of herself. Her executive husband has not got quite where he wanted, what he wanted: whoever does? She has seen him through an affair or so: smiled bravely and grimly through this or the other dinner party, when his mistress picked at her avocado and crab salad; worried through his threatened heart attack, put up with the bad temper and depression of his mid-life crisis; and at last she says what about me, me? Where is this promised life, this happiness, this fulfilment? It must be somewhere!

Perhaps, she says, she could be of service to the community. But how? She has learned something about the world, for all the comfort and security of her life: enough to know there's nothing she could tell the poor and oppressed that they didn't know already. That what the poor want is not advice but money. She knows above all the value of money: how it keeps people quiet and good. Put a hundred thousand pounds in the hands of a child abuser and he'd stop abusing. She can't even give all she has to the needy, because she has nothing of her own to give. It is his. The outside world knocks upon her door: she goes to open it, softly on deep carpets, and outside in the storm, begging for shelter, stands a crone, a beggar woman, and it is her future self. She slams the door, she closes her ears: calls up her bridge partner. If it's not too late, if she's kept her looks – and why shouldn't she? – she 'takes' a lover. Well, one just happens to come along, even if she's married to Carl May. Forget takes. A woman gets taken.

I, Joanna May! See how easily it comes to me to turn from 'I' to 'she' – joining my lot with other women, universalizing an experience, as if the better to justify myself. As if I, a woman who never gave birth but has four daughters, an only child with four sisters, could ever be quite like anyone else. Perhaps what Dr Holly took away from me at the Bulstrode Clinic was not so much my identity, as my universality. He made me particular, different from other women: he turned me into someone of scientific interest. Worse, he stole my soul, the thing that threads me through and back to the human race, and never mind that in my heart I'd tied a knot in it, it wasn't too late at thirty to change my mind, give it a sharp

264

tug, untie it, take my chances along with everyone else, not let the moment on the stair last a whole life, but send my children and my children's children on down through the centuries, mingling and mixing with the others, sharing and partaking, into the future. I think when they took that part of me, the singular me, away, and interfered, they stopped me in my tracks. It isn't reasonable to think so, but when Dr Holly says to me, 'You haven't changed,' I think he's right, and I think it's his fault I haven't changed. He has stolen thirty years of life from me. And now it's too late. For me, but not for them. I have my four more chances, and that's how I must see it.

How had it been for the Queens of Wands, Pentacles, Swords and Cups? If Dr Holly was not interested, I was. I would ask them. I wondered if they lived their lives, or acted them. I wondered if they had their equivalent for the moment on the stairs, and if they had overcome it, as I, their master copy, had not. I felt what it was to be Dr Holly, to want to *find out*: I felt the pleasure of it. I felt what it was to be Carl, and want to change the world: I felt the power of it. But most of all, I wanted to see what I would be, born into a newer, more understanding world: one which allowed women choice, freedom and success. Perhaps I had merely been born thirty years too early and that was the only trouble. The young Queens of Wands, Pentacles, Swords and Cups: myself the ageing Empress: not devastating, frightening, shocking any more – just how very *interesting* to see how it all turned out. What fun it would be – that rare commodity.

It was with pleasure, animation and excitement that I waited impatiently for Mavis to come to me with the names and whereabouts of my sisters, my daughters, my twins, myself.

41

Angela called Joanna May.

'Darling, how are you?' asked Angela. 'I wondered if you had any clues as to your ex-husband's current mental health.'

'One or two,' said Joanna. 'Why?'

'Well,' said Angela, 'Gerald is getting quite alarmed. I tell him there's no need. I tell him that for a man to wipe out his wife's lovers may not be legal, or nice, but it doesn't mean he's insane.'

'Angela, I know you're only joking but I think this telephone may be tapped.'

'Ah. Well, listeners hear no good of themselves. My husband says your husband wants him to employ the entire staff of the Divination Department over this fallout business.'

'Then perhaps he should, Angela. I'm very fond of Gerald.'

'But then everyone will think *my* husband is insane.'

'He will at least be around to refute the view, Angela.'

'I see. You mean, on the whole, it's best to do what Carl May wants.'

'For the moment,' said Joanna May, 'yes.'

'In that case,' said Angela, 'Gerald is right. Gerald

says it's quite alarming that this man should be in charge of such large sections of the nation's wealth and property.'

'These large companies more or less run themselves,' said Joanna. 'The man at the very top is so often a figurehead. Part of Carl's trouble is that he gets bored.'

'Gerald thinks something should be done about it.'

'Listeners may hear no good about themselves,' said Joanna, 'but they sometimes hear very useful things. Shall we meet and talk you know where?'

'Where's that?'

'Where I saw and admired Gerald's nice soft feet,' said Joanna.

'Ah, so that's what you were looking at,' said Angela. 'He thought it was his varicose veins. You sound much better.'

'Oh yes,' said Joanna, 'I'm better. I'm sorry about going on so the other day.'

'That's OK,' said Angela, of the hairy chin and thick legs, and the waist as broad as her hips, salt of a world fresh sown with salt. 'That's OK.'

42

'I'll be waiting at the corner
 Of the bottom of the street,
 In case a certain little lady goes by.
 Oh me, oh my,
 In case a certain little lady goes by'

sang Carl May. 'I wish I'd learned the ukelele,' he
said, 'but in the circles in which I moved when a child
it wasn't done!'

He and Bethany were in the May Gallery. The
morning sun shone in the east window and made the
place almost cheerful. Workmen – they wore glasses
and were elderly – gently inched in from outside
a large earthenware vat dating from the sixteenth
dynasty, the great days of Egypt. The hieroglyphics
were worn: it seemed to the untrained eye a rough-
hewn if workmanlike artefact.

'Why's it so special?' asked Bethany. She wondered
how many questions she'd asked in the last few weeks,
in order to make Carl feel good by supplying her with
answers. She wondered how she was going to get out
of this. She wondered if Hughie Scotland could help.
She was frightened of Carl May, who seemed to get
happier and jollier with every day that passed. She

didn't even correct him, saying, 'I'm leaning on a lamp post on the corner of the street,' and just as well, as it happened.

'This jar contains the dust of ancient liver,' said Carl May. 'Liver cells are rich in DNA. The ancient Egyptians mummified their dead to keep them in good shape for their journey to the next world. Nothing died unless you wanted it to in that fair land, under the wide Mesopotamian sky: everything went on for ever: so there was nothing to fear. The God Osiris died only as the sun set: he rose again. The priestess aroused the God and gave birth to the King and all was well in the world of men. And because there was no fear of death, no terror, simply a passing on, agreeable or disagreeable as it might be, all men were good, and all women too, and kind. Sometimes a bit stupid, of course. But they didn't shut their children up in kennels, or beat them, or torture them, or rape them, to express their disapproval of life, because life simply *was*, infinitely variable, infinitely long-lasting, and there was happiness upon earth. And the secret of it all lies there in the dust of all those livers, which are so very rich in DNA.'

'How do you know it's people's livers? Couldn't it just be dust?'

'Imperial Caesar, dead and turned to clay,' said Carl May, 'could stop a hole to keep the dust away. Dear little Bethany, we know it's liver because the hieroglyphics say so. Embalmers sucked the brains of the dead out through the nostrils, and the entrails out through I've forgotten where, including the liver, and saved them all in case of need in great big separate labelled jars like this one. This is a liver jar.'

Bethany felt quite dizzy and blackness made clouds around her. She'd never fainted in all her life, not even when her father had suggested she made a one-armed man happier than he ever had been in his life before – a service the complete in body must always surely be happy to render the incomplete – and she'd seen her father's choice for her had a hook instead of a hand, and she was only fourteen, but she thought she might faint now.

'I knew this existed,' said Carl May. 'That moony fellow Isaac King tried to say it didn't, but I knew he was lying. They had it at Liverpool University all the time. The pool of livers! I think we must get old Holly over and show him what we've found. Would you like that?'

Bethany hadn't liked the way Dr Holly had looked at her. She didn't much like the way anyone looked at her. At first she had thought the looks were admiration and envy; but now everyone seemed to think she was somehow cheating. She didn't know what she was supposed to have done. Carl May was being good to her. She was being good to him. Yet somehow she seemed to have stepped out of line. At home, there had never been this particular feeling of *unrightness*. Things at home were sometimes sleazy and sordid; here they never were: servants cleaned the bath and changed sheets: cats never passed worms on the table: but luxury seemed to make things worse, not better. Nothing was real. Perhaps she was just homesick.

'I liked Dr Holly very much,' said Bethany. 'It would be good to see him.'

And Carl May wondered, now what is the matter

271

with this fragrant girl, this Scotland hand-on, this product of the outer suburbs, this despoiler of my celibacy, this firm-fleshed luxury, this stirrer to pleasure, this brightness which flickers on and off like the sun behind a yew tree on a windy day, this little liar – what is the matter with her? I know what it is, she has a lover. She can't be bothered to turn the brightness on for me. She's thinking of him and anything will do for me.

'Is something the matter, Bethany?'

'It was the thought of all those livers mixed up, that's all; it made me feel quite faint.'

'I hope they're not too mixed up, Bethany, or we'll have a hard task in front of us. I hope they're still nicely layered so we can tell one individual from the next. Are you sure that's all that the matter is?'

'Well, Uncle Carl . . .'

'Don't call me uncle, Bethany.'

'Sorry. It's what I used to call my father's friends, back home. And talking about my dad, I had a phone call from him yesterday. He's not too well.'

Then he knew she was lying. She'd had no such phone call. Every morning at Britnuc Carl May was handed a private pink folder, in which were reported the substance of all phone calls made and received at Eton Square, the King's House, the Coustain residence, and many another household besides, not to mention industrial firms and government departments. Knowledge is power, as Carl May had been told at school: '*Scientas est potentas*'. Carl May the sceptical, Carl May the shrewd, looking up the original text, found '*scientas est potestas*' instead.

Knowing is to be empowered. More like it. But, understanding why the misprint was preferred, he told no one; just hugged the empowering truth to himself. Truth was power. Truth was so disagreeable you could, if you had the stomach for it, keep it pretty much to yourself. Joanna his wife was one of the very few who understood these things; in her bones, in her blood, for no good reason: in her genes: Joanna May, Carl May's ex-wife, to whom he had trusted his being; here in this very room: this place, no longer young, no longer his, no good to him; but empowering him, proving yet again the world was what he knew it was, the empire of despair, beneath the little tent of blue that men call sky.

'She must die, or she'll go on to ruin other men,' said Carl May aloud, or just about. The removal men from Carling Antique and Rarities Specialist Transport let slip the giant jar – they felt it had a life of its own, sometimes, but hoped they were wrong – only a couple of inches, but it made quite a bang on the cold marble floor. Carl May seemed not to notice. They breathed again. Carling Transport was a subsidiary of Garden Developments. They specialized also in the moving of rare trees and plants.

'I'm sorry, darling, I didn't quite catch that,' said Bethany.

'Just something from *Othello*, my dear.'

'Oh. We didn't do *Othello* in diction.'

'No,' said Carl May. 'I daresay it's not often done in girls' schools.'

'Can I go home to see my dad, since he's poorly?'

'*Beauty and the Beast*,' Carl May said. 'Of course you can, my dear. But be back by five thirty this

273

evening. Such a pity you can't come with me to the lido. I rather thought of going there this afternoon.'

'The lido?'

'The Brent Cross Lido. A charming place, prettily landscaped; though I'm afraid the chlorine fumes don't do the shrubs and flowers much good. Joanna's favourite place, it seems.'

'You be careful, my darling,' said Bethany, 'don't be outdoors too long. They say the fallout's dreadful: worse than Windscale. And to be frank with you, I'm not a lido sort of person. Now the south of France . . .'

Oh yes, she had a lover. She laid her hand on his arm, a pretty hand, long-fingered, each finger slightly trembling, promising pleasure, but promiscuous.

'I'll be back this evening,' she said and, suddenly giddy and happy again, whirled round the musky gallery, yellow skirt flaring, white shirt gleaming, gold shoes glittering, murmuring fond farewells to the embalmed remains of Gods and kings, waving goodbye to the stolid wooden funereal peasants, even dropping a quick brave appalled kiss on the crown of the liver jar, and then back once again to Carl.

'I don't think you got the *Othello* quote quite right,' said Bethany. 'But a good try, Carl-O-Carl! We didn't do it at diction, but my dad did take me to the theatre a lot. He said there was no need not to be cultured, just because I was kind.'

'Four,' said Carl, but Bethany did not even notice. Bethany said, 'And I may be the Beauty but you are not the Beast. You are not even a fiend in human form, you are just a little boy in a right old state, you silly thing!' And he was about to say 'five' – he'd given her to five – but Bethany was gone, emerald eyes and all, in a flash of yellow white and gold, and in strolled Jacko, Petie, Elwood, Dougie and Haggie so he let her go. The lads claimed to be a pop group. Theirs, they maintained, was a new close-harmony rock sound. They called themselves Barbers of the Bath. Carl backed them with recording studios, equipment, venues, wheels, even though they took little advantage musically of what was offered. Some people will do anything for money, the better to maintain the illusion that they have some purpose in life; and this failing, this conceit, suited Carl very well.

43

Jane, Julie, Gina and Alice.

————◆◇◆————

Gina left Julie in charge of her three children and went to visit her mum.

'You have let yourself go,' said Annette, kindly. Her hair was tight permed and blonde and her black plastic belt broad and close around a dieted waist. Bilbo had gone, Annette said. She was now with Nigel, an ex-policeman, something of a racist, but only thirty-five. It was over a bit of trouble with Bilbo, in fact, that Nigel had had to resign the Force. Bilbo was in hospital, more of a cabbage, said Annette, than a man. He'd suffered brain damage. A tragedy. She and Nigel were going to move to the country and open a pub. Start afresh. Nigel had quite a few enemies, Annette said, not without pride. She'd be sorry to sell up their little flat: could Gina take the cat, she'd always liked cats, hadn't she? How were the kids? How many did Gina have? She'd forgotten. She smelt strongly of sherry; a warm sweet smell which reminded Gina of her childhood.

'It was never your flat,' said Gina, 'it was Bilbo's flat.'

'Well, Bilbo's a cabbage, and what good's a fortune to a cabbage, and that's what this place is worth, a fortune. We can buy two pubs and still have some over.'

'Can we talk about me, Mum?' asked Gina.

'Little Miss self, self, self,' said Annette. 'Some people never change.' She looked closely at Gina. 'I told you not to marry what's-his-name,' she said, 'but you wouldn't listen. You never used to have a bust like that!'

'His name is Cliff,' said Gina, 'and you were all for my marrying him. In fact you talked me out of a termination just to get me married and this place to yourself.'

'It was always just right for two, never for three,' said Annette. She kept budgerigars now, and the living room, with its view over the market, was warm and musty with the smell of birds, and birdseed, and the air stirred with the soft brush of feathers. 'And you mustn't be bitter. I'm sure you don't regret that little baby now! Mothers never do.'

Annette offered Gina tea and biscuits and when Gina accepted a biscuit raised her eyebrows.

'Mum,' began Gina, and Annette said, 'I'm sure I'm not old enough to be your mum, Gina. If you ask me I look more like your younger sister than your mother. I certainly weigh a lot less.'

'Don't worry, Mum,' said Gina. 'I'll be gone before your Nigel gets home,' and after that Annette was a little kinder.

'Mum,' said Gina. 'I met a woman who's exactly like me in all sorts of ways and we went to a clinic to

277

be tissue-typed and it turns out we're identical twins.'

'What a peculiar thing to want to do,' said Annette. 'I expect all kinds of people are twins and don't know it. They certainly don't go rushing off to clinics to find out. It's rather like squeezing your breasts to see if you've got lumps: better not start or you'll only find them. A hit and miss kind of thing, I imagine, tissue-typing, whatever it is when it's at home, but you know what these clinics are, They told a friend of mine she had cancer and they'd got the slides mixed. She got the radium treatment and the worry while the other one stayed home happy and died. They'll tell you anything that suits them, these doctors.'

'Mum,' said Gina, 'I'm going to sit here until you tell me.'

Annette's mouth clamped shut, to demonstrate that she did not respond well to threats, but opened again soon enough.

'Don't you try and blackmail me, young lady.'

'I'm not blaming you, Mum,' said Gina. 'I can see twins are a real handful and my dad had thrown you out and you were very young and you couldn't be expected to cope. But I want to know. I have a right to know: was I twins?'

'No such thing as rights,' said Annette, acutely. 'Just such a thing as it would be nice if only, only it usually isn't. All I can say is the doctor never said anything about twins to me. Mind you, I was under anaesthetic at the time. Anything could have happened. Anything. A girlfriend of mine was raped under anaesthetic, but would anyone believe her? No.'

She had some more sherry. She drank it by the teacup full. As she filled and refilled Gina's cup – and she proffered little thin china cups with saucers, flowered and gold-rimmed – with tea, she filled and refilled her own with sherry.

Gina wondered what Nigel was after: cosiness, or daftness, or pneumatic sex, or budgerigars, or just the money for two pubs and some over, or to have what Bilbo had, poor Bilbo, or perhaps it was true love, who could tell?

'You aren't telling fibs, are you?' she asked presently, hoping against hope for maternal reassurance, comfort. 'You didn't adopt me, by any chance? I wasn't some other mother's cast off twin?' to which Annette replied, 'No such luck. Split me coming out, you did; God knows why I did any of it. I must have been mad. All that fuss and trouble and pain and you not even my own child, from what I could make out, though I never could make out much. They talked so fast, the pair of them, and one of them not even a doctor. It was the end of my marriage, not the beginning of it, contrary to all their fine promises. If they were wrong in that what else were they wrong in, that's what I want to know. A twin! They should have told me that. If it was a boy you might have grown up to marry him. You'd have had to be warned. To tell you the truth I was glad when you got pregnant – at least it showed you were normal. I always had a feeling you mightn't be. Like a mule, that's the one, isn't it, or do I mean a donkey, the one that's a cross between a horse and a something else? At any rate, it's sterile. That's what I thought you might be. Sterile. Unnatural. I thought you ought to have that poor

279

little baby. It might be your only chance. And Cliff wasn't so bad. You have to forgive me, Gina. I did the best I could.'

Gina sighed, amazed that she had once taken this woman so seriously, longed to please her, hoped to impress her, and with the worldly competence that enveloped her like some cloud of embracing, protective mist the minute she was out of the children's company, soon had the details of her birth, and an old appointment card for Annette to see Dr Holly at the Bulstrode Clinic.

'I know you think I haven't a heart, dear,' said Annette, 'and sometimes I think you're right, but I kept that card as a memento. Time and time again, when the occasion arose to throw it out, I refrained. I knew it would come in handy. I've always done right by you. Didn't I come and rescue you from Granny and Gramps that time? Say what you like, when you needed me I was there.'

'Yes, Mum,' said Gina, 'you certainly were!' and was off to the Bulstrode Clinic by the next available Underground train. She went to Acton Central and took a bus down Acton Lane and found the Bulstrode Clinic. But it was now a lending library. A white car stood outside, all white, startlingly white. She noticed it. There were a lot of them about, these days. They must, she thought, be very hard to keep clean. Only very particular people would own them.

The librarian was of the old school, motherly, dustily dressed; she stood at the noticeboards and pinned up leaflets on rate support, rent rebate, family allowances and Citizens Advice.

'What do you want?' she said. 'We're about to close.'

'I want to know where the Bulstrode Clinic is,' Gina said. 'Where it went, if anywhere. Where Dr Holly can be found.'

'I've told you once,' said Mrs Avril Love, sub-librarian, for so her badge proclaimed her.

'No you didn't,' said Gina. 'I only just came in.'

Mrs Love looked at Gina more closely.

'I'm so sorry,' she said. 'I thought you were someone else. My eyesight is going, and then what use am I going to be to anyone? Mind you, all you young things look alike to me.'

She shut the library door, switched off the library computer; she offered Gina a cup of tea. She wanted company. She was in no hurry to get home: the later she got home the more likely someone else was to make the tea. Gina was the third young woman in a week to ask about the Bulstrode, after years and years of nothing. What was going on? Something finally come home to roost, the way things did? Birth would out, like murder. Funny things had happened up the Bulstrode, she'd always said so. They'd been fiddling around with women's eggs all that time ago, doing God knows what, the field even less regulated then than it was today. More people walking round who came out of a test-tube than anyone realized, said Mrs Love. She served tea in wholesome mugs, with biscuits. In the end the past caught up with you, said Mrs Love. No use running. She'd had an abortion there herself: she often wondered what they did with the poor dead foetus – and if it was dead. How could a woman know? They knocked you unconscious and did what they wanted: you couldn't object; what you were doing was wrong, illegal. She was sorry to have to speak like this, it sounded unhinged, but she'd never recovered from the experience, for all it was thirty-five years ago. She'd never married: the Mrs was a courtesy title. If Miss was on the library badge, the young mocked her and the old patronized. Ms didn't ring true, not for her. She never had more children: that had been her only chance, she'd blown it. Odd though, that she'd come to work in the very building where it had happened. Sometimes she thought life was just a pattern of spoiled expectations which you weren't allowed to forget. Was Gina a Catholic?

'No,' said Gina. Mrs Love said she nearly was. She'd taken a diet pill. It made her talkative. She was sorry. How old was Gina? Thirty? No. Too young to be her child grown-up. Because Mrs Love always had this notion that at the Bulstrode they'd take your baby away and just implant it in someone else's womb, like moving a fish from one tank to another. She hadn't killed her baby – somewhere it lived. Did Gina think that was possible?

Gina said she really didn't know. She thought it was more complicated, more difficult than that. She had begun to feel very tired. First her mother, then this.

'And to think,' said Mrs Love, 'I lost my baby here – well, gave it away, what kind of mother is that, to give her child away, hand it over to death, and now you lot come along, three of you, and say you were born here, and there's nothing here but books, books.

282

Doesn't it make you feel funny? It did the other ones who were in here asking. They were twins if you ask me, though they said they weren't.'

'Yes, it does,' said Gina, 'it makes me feel really very funny,' and went home feeling hunted and haunted, and told Julie she thought there might be more than just the two of them, and that she wasn't going to see Dr Holly on her own – Julie would have to come with her.

'In the meantime,' said Gina to Julie, 'it looks as if my mother's the one who had us. Yours just bought you in.'

———◦◦◦———

But Julie was in the honeymoon stage with the children: there were fish fingers and wet towels everywhere and she didn't mind one bit. She'd bought a tropical fish tank and set it up and called the vet to ask his advice, and he'd said he'd come round to see if it was fit for fish and she'd said OK but only to see the fish and he'd said of course and both knew different. She told everyone Gina was her sister. Her sister and her children had come to stay. Now when the neighbours talked about the price of children's shoes, so could she. Cliff called round, of course he did, and Julie wouldn't let him see Gina; Julie was cold and reasonable and said a cooling-off time was required, that was all, and he agreed but both knew differently. Cliff was intimidated by the cleanliness, the orderliness, the ordinariness of the house, the net curtains, the glimpse of parquet and framed prints when the front door was opened: this was how people

283

were supposed to live, he could only imagine. He'd never somehow achieved it himself, or rather Gina had failed to achieve it for him. Weeds grew round his and Gina's door. What could he say, what could he offer? Cliff did not want to be a bad husband, he said so: it distressed him to be one: he was just too young to be a father of three: the wrong person to be Gina's husband, or else she was the wrong person to be his wife. 'Quite so,' said Julie, crisply, closing the door. 'Come back on Wednesday week and we'll see how things are. Who's right for who, if anyone.' He'd banged once or twice upon the door to prove a point and then left, apparently satisfied. No one had asked him for money.

'The more of us the better,' said Julie. 'There could be a hundred of us and I'd be glad.' As Gina had got thinner, she'd got plumper. They could wear each other's clothes.

When Alec rang from the airport she said, 'Look, why bother to come home? It's a long way. You'd rather be in an hotel.'

He said, 'There isn't an overnight laundry service.' After a short pause he said, rather pathetically, 'I'm sorry, Julie. I hadn't realized things had got so bad. I don't know what this is all about.'

She said, 'I do. If there aren't any children, there isn't any point.'

He said, over the noise of the airport, 'If only you *did* something: had a job. It's like coming home to a stage set. You hardly seem to exist.'

She said, 'But you didn't want me to work, you wouldn't let me. You wanted me there when you came home: you wanted proper home-cooked meals, you said you had enough plastic hotel food, airline food.'

He said, 'Did I say that? I can't remember.'

She said, 'I can hardly hear you. Why don't you check in at the Sheraton or the Holiday Inn –'

'– the Hilton,' he said.

'– and call me from there.'

'OK,' he said and he hung up, but he didn't call back.

'There could be a thousand of us and it'd be OK,' said Julie. 'The thing is, I'm not my mother's daughter. I thought I had to be like her, but I don't. I'm free to be me. Now everything can change.'

'You've still got to share,' said Gina. 'You got rid of her but now you've got me. You can still see your limits, your outline. And instead of your mother, you now have to put up with mine.'

'But it doesn't defeat me,' said Julie. 'How can I explain it to you? I don't know your mother, and since she didn't bring me up she doesn't count as my mother, and she's nowhere near as boring as the one who did. Boring, boring, boring. I thought I had to be boring, and I don't.' She danced about the house, elated.

Sue was wetting the bed; Julie didn't like that at all: it was smelly. She wanted to make Sue wash the sheets, but Gina said no, that made things worse. The children were upset. They'd lost their father. They were grieving.

'It can't be true,' said Julie. How could they miss a man like that!

285

'They were born loving him,' said Gina. 'And it's not so long since they were born.'

'There's such a thing as contraception,' said Julie. Women without children are smarter, tougher and more decisive than women who have children. Women with children are torn in so many directions they become kind, nice and hopeless in their own interests in the effort to understand themselves, let alone their children. Gina tried to be like Julie, and Julie like Gina.

The two grey cats slept next to each other on one or other of the children's beds, and Julie thought they ought to be in the kitchen.

'No,' said Gina, 'they need all the comfort they can get. Everyone does.' She missed Cliff; of course she did. Perhaps he'd change. If she went back now it might be different.

'No, it won't,' said Julie. 'You're just addicted, that's all. You've got pain and pleasure mixed.'

Little Anthony turned up the thermostat on the fish tank and one of the angelfish died. Julie slapped: the vet wouldn't like it one bit.

'Don't do that,' said Gina.

'What those children need is discipline,' said Julie.

'Don't you use that word to me,' said Gina. 'It was Cliff's favourite word. When are we going to see Dr Holly? We can't keep putting it off. It's getting on our nerves.'

And Ben said, 'Look Mum, look Auntie Julie, there's a man working on the gas main outside and there isn't gas down this street, only electricity.'

Ben had just started at a new school. They were hopeless at football which meant he was the best and to be the best player in a losing team is easier than being the worst player in a winning one.

Ben said, 'He has a notebook and he writes things in it.'

Julie said, 'By the pricking of my thumbs, Something evil this way comes. There's more going on than meets the eye. We'll go to Dr Holly tomorrow. Ben, you'll have to stay off school and look after the little ones.'

'Oh, sh—' Ben began to say, and then, out of deference to his twin Aunt Julie, whom he had begun to quite like – he admired her toughness – 'Oh botheration. I don't want to miss too much school. I want to be a doctor. Or perhaps a vet.' He would be quite happy here if it wasn't for Sue, who kept getting on his nerves, so he'd start hitting her. He didn't want to, but he was sure she wet the bed on purpose, just to put everyone to trouble.

44

Jane, Julie, Gina and Alice.

———◦◦———

Jane went home and announced: 'I've lost my job and I've lost my boyfriend and it looks as if I'm going to lose my home. That's the good news. The bad news is I've found a twin. Which means, Madge, either I'm adopted or you had twins and gave one away. I need to know which.'

They were having Friday supper. Jeremy had met Jane off the train, and been late. She'd had to stand about waiting for him in the outfall from Chernobyl for a full twenty minutes. The waiting room had been too full of cigarette smokers to afford acceptable shelter. When her father did arrive, she scarcely recognized him. She was used to a tall, albeit gangling, man. This one seemed shrivelled and shrunk, old. She didn't like it at all. She liked it even less when he said, 'I'm sorry I'm late. We have little Tobias staying. Not so little, of course. He's thirteen.'

'Who in God's name is Tobias?'

'Laura's little boy,' said Jeremy. 'He's over from Toronto to stay with us. I'm sorry, he's in your old room. We didn't know you'd be visiting. You so seldom do.'

'What a Godawful name,' said Jane. 'Tobias!' She had learned the power of bad temper from Alice, and the value of non-smiling. She practised them assiduously.

'He always was called Tobias,' said her father serenely, 'but you weren't listening.'

'I was too busy trying to pass my exams,' said Jane.

'Well, it's a wise child knows its own father.'

But her father did not rise to the bait. She found Madge shuffling round the kitchen, wearing slippers. Madge had a bunion, Madge said. The glass in her pebble lenses was thicker than ever, but not so thick that Jane couldn't see love for Tobias shining out from behind them. How could she! Madge's eyes had always shone with emotions that shouldn't be there: good emotion, noble emotion, masochism triumphant. They streamed out from her in a bright trail of kindly confusion. Now Madge loved Tobias, her rival's child, because he was there, because he was her husband's, because she should. How could she be like this and still teach grown people? Didn't she understand the value of the negative emotions? Have I, Jane, ever understood them, come to that? Would she ever let me? It was my mother made me what I am, and what I am is what I'm not. So thought Jane, as she looked for forks clean enough to lay the table with.

It was the better to annoy and upset, no doubt, that Jane kept her announcement until Jeremy, Madge,

Tobias and herself were sitting round the table eating shepherd's pie – a typical English dish, Jane explained to Tobias, who was a beastly clear-skinned, thick-skinned Canadian lad, very plain, with his father's shortsighted eyes (no doubt there, alas). By a typical English dish, Jane implied, though did not say, she meant improperly cooked, fatty, stringy, English mince, hopelessly old-fashioned, unhealthy, and awful: even Canada could do better: sometimes Jane felt Madge did it on purpose to persecute Jeremy. After the mince she went on to her parentage.

'Well,' said Madge, 'I'm glad you've raised the matter but I hardly think this is the time.'

'Why not?' asked Jane.

'We don't want to upset the child,' said Madge.

'Either he's my brother or he's not,' said Jane. 'And he doesn't look like it to me. My belief is I'm adopted. Do I look like either of you two? No I do not.'

'You're upset,' observed Jeremy. 'You'll get indigestion.'

'If I'm upset it's Madge's cooking,' said Jane. 'Tough old shepherds, these, Tobias. Tough and greasy. A great mistake to cook them, if you ask me.' Her parents were shocked into silence. Jane felt terrible and began to cry. There was a kind of noise in her ears, as of breaking glass.

'Dear, dear, dear,' said Madge, 'it's as if she was six again.'

'She was like this at fifteen,' said Jeremy.

'But worse at six,' said Madge. And Jane had always had a vision of herself as a placid, easy, perfectly well-behaved child!

290

Madge made Jane go to bed in the spare room with a hot water bottle and sat on the edge of the bed, spare leg flesh swelling over the tops of her slippers, wispy hair awry – shouldn't she have hormone treatment, thought Jane, but she wouldn't, would she: she'd say she didn't want to interfere with nature; what she herself would have said, as little as a week ago, come to think of it. Since she'd met Alice she'd become a great deal less pious, but also a great deal more critical and, she began to see, really rather nasty. Alice had lent her a photographer for a bed companion and she'd found him so boring she'd asked him to go and buy a bottle of wine and then locked the door and pretended to be out when he came charging up the stairs again. She enjoyed that far more than she would the night in bed with him.

Madge said, 'Well, dear, to tell you the truth you're not quite adopted: I most certainly gave birth to you: your father isn't Jeremy: you weren't quite a test-tube baby: it wasn't quite artificial insemination by donor . . .'

'Stop it, stop it,' shrieked Jane. 'This is disgusting.'

'I don't think it's nearly as disgusting as sex,' said Madge.

'You always told me sex was wonderful,' said Jane.

'A child should think that,' said Madge. 'Just because it never went right for me didn't mean it would be the same for you.'

Jane opened and shut her mouth like a goldfish in a bowl hoping for sustenance, reassurance, information, nourishment, anything.

'So I must tell you that although Jeremy isn't technically your father – I was told he was a Harley Street surgeon – he really is your father in essence. What was it Brecht said in *Mother Courage*? "The child belongs to the one who looks after it."'

'Brecht is a man,' said Jane.

'I don't see what that's got to do with it,' said Madge, a little peevishly, Jane thought, in the circumstances. Surely she, Jane, was central to this drama. All the emotions should be hers.

'You mean you've never had sex with my father?' said Jane.

'No,' said Madge, 'and he isn't your father. It's all a long time ago and I think the best thing to do is go and see the Dr Holly who helped us to achieve you. He made a very good impression. I imagine that what's happened is that you and this other young woman share the same father. They may have used the same semen more than once.'

'Taken semen from the same batch, you mean,' said Jane.

'Well of course,' said Madge.

Jane was sick in the washhandbasin: she could not even get into the bathroom; Tobias was having a bath. The rest of the weekend went well enough. She got used to her father looking so old and her mother looking so soppy. She thought perhaps Brecht was right. These were the ones who had looked after her: these were her parents. She felt quite pleased, however, not to have to repress those qualities in herself she had always disliked in her father – the apathy, the sitting about, the slow movements, the grunts as his mind worked, as if some infinitely complicated inner machinery ground incessantly on. She could take of him what she wanted, and simply leave the rest. And the same went for her mother. She need take only what she fancied. She had been so amply served with a helping, she could well afford to be fussy.

She even took down Tobias's address in Canada and promised to write to him. But she didn't ask after his mother. She wouldn't go that far.

45

Jane, Julie, Gina and Alice.

———◆◆◆———

At 10.30 a.m. on the third Tuesday in May, Jane and Alice sat in Dr Holly's outer office, by appointment, and waited for Dr Holly to return from, or so his secretary said, an important meeting. They sat as far from one another as they could. Just because they were sisters or half-sisters, they did not see why they should like one another, let alone resemble one another: in fact, the more they thought about it, the less they felt they did either. For the occasion Jane wore a tweed skirt and jacket; Alice wore jeans and a pink sweatshirt. Jane's hair was now cut remarkably short; Alice's was pulled back from her yet higher forehead by a sweatband but cascaded down her back. They came in separate cars. When Dr Holly's secretary Sarah said, 'Identical twins?' and neither replied, she said, 'You both turn your heads at the same time at the same angle. It's quite funny really.'

She went back to her word processor and Jane tapped with her fingers on the side of the chair until she noticed Alice was doing the same, so she stopped.

'Have you come in for the study?' asked Sarah. 'Is

that what you want to see him about? Because they're not starting till next month. He is very busy.'

Neither replied.

'Oh well,' said Sarah, 'no skin off my nose. It may not even get off the ground, I warn you. I get these letters from the Biomedical Ethics people. He leaves me to answer them. Never a dull moment.'

Alice and Jane stared into space; four pure-blue eyes staring at nothing, giving nothing away if they could help it. Jane had lost some weight since she had discovered her twin, confronted her mother, and gone, as Tom put it, finally barmy. He kept out of the way. Alice had put on a little, since she'd begun losing so much work, and slept alone.

'Most of the twins are babes in arms,' said Sarah, filling in the reproachful silence. 'Lots more twins being born these days. Mothers have their babies later, when twinning's more likely; and they're healthier, so they carry both babies to term. One used to just get lost, before the mothers even knew. We get triplets and quads quite often, and nothing to do with fertility drugs. So it's not as if you two are a rarity. They might not even take you on.'

The blue eyes turned slowly towards her.

'At least it's just brain cells, these days. He's stopped doing all that egg-cell stuff: he got frightened. I wouldn't do it, I wouldn't have my eggs taken away in the cause of science, no matter how much money they paid. I don't want to even *have* eggs, it makes me feel like a hen. I'd rather not know about them.'

She thought she'd better shut up and get on with the mail. She was being disloyal to her employer. She had hoped for a decent conversation but seldom got it. Perhaps there was something wrong with her. People didn't like her. She did say sharp things, she supposed. She couldn't help it. She wished she could: was there a pill which would make you likeable? If not, no doubt Martins was working on it. Would she take it if there was? Probably.

Two more of them came down the corridor: the eleven o'clock appointments, no doubt. Sarah could see them through the glass door. She worked out the number of eyes that were now going to stare at her in disbelief, dislike and reproach: eight. These two did seem jollier, however, than the two already in the room. Both wore pink sweaters and jeans. She was glad to see they were at least not quite the same height. Too much similarity gave her the creeps. Reared separately, no doubt, though they'd end up much the same in the end. The impact of the rearing environment wore away with time. In old age genes triumphed. Mind you, all old people seemed pretty much the same to her: as did small babies. People started out true to the broad human type, and ended the same way. Variation peaked in the child-bearing years.

'Oh, quads,' said Sarah, when the next two came in. 'That is a bit more interesting. But why didn't you all come in together? I'll see if Dr Holly can be brought out of his meeting.'

'You do just that,' said Gina, mother of three, accustomed to telling others what to do for their own good. 'And fast. We have a right to some kind of explanation.'

Like so many who have dealings with a beneficent

296

but controlling state, she had a clearer view of her rights than many another, and was quicker to voice them. The others seemed stunned into silence. Not just two, but four. So far.

46

Gerald called Hamish Tovey of NBI – News Broadcast International – and said, 'The public are getting hysterical. They won't go out in the rain: they won't have picnics; I went to the lido with my wife and there was almost no one there, just us and a couple of friends. The farmers are complaining; the horticulturists are complaining; the fashion trade's complaining; and the Electric Power Authority are having kittens because the future of nuclear power is in jeopardy. Not only that, the vets are complaining of litters having two heads; I'm even getting tales of budgerigars exploding.'

'Budgerigars can explode if you feed them the wrong grain,' said the NBI man. 'We've just done a feature on it, nothing to do with Chernobyl.'

'Tell that to the public,' said Gerald, bitterly.

'That's what we are doing,' the NBI man pointed out, 'as best we can. But the public can't tell a roentgen from a rad, and to tell you the truth neither can anyone at NBI. If you could put some of your experts at our disposal to help our graphics team out, I'd be grateful. We've a world opportunity here and it's going to waste. It's sickening.'

Gerald said he thought Britnuc had some spare

experts in the divinatory area, tested and proven in the field, and Hamish Tovey seemed as interested and grateful as a TV newsman can get: that is to say, he said, 'There just might be an interesting wind-up item there, I suppose. A light closing laugh. I could look into it. Now what can I do for you?'

Gerald said his Department could see the value of some kind of prize-winning news feature, fronted by someone from the commercial rather than the governmental sector – inasmuch as official announcements had lost credibility in this particular area. A popular yet authoritative figure, if such a person existed.

'Carl May?' suggested Hamish Tovey.

'Brilliant idea!' said Gerald Coustain.

'Did you see him drink that glass of milk on TV?' said Hamish Tovey, suddenly animated, 'defying the roentgens! Brilliant PR! How's he been since?'

'Fit as a fiddle, top of the world,' said Gerald. 'Perhaps we could get him to do something just as dramatic.'

'Or even more so,' said Hamish.

'So long as it's safe,' said Gerald. 'We don't want to lose him!'

'So long as the roentgens and the rads are as harmless as you lot make out,' said Hamish Tovey. 'I have my crew to think about, not to mention the union.'

'Back in 1957,' said Gerald, 'when Windscale caught fire and the instrumentation failed – twice round the clock and back again and no one noticed – the duty engineer lifted the lid of the pile to see what was going on. He stared right into the burning heart of the dragon. He's still alive to tell the tale. Head of the Nuclear Safety Inspectorate, as it happens.'

'Is that so!' said Hamish Tovey. 'Now that would be really something by way of a visual fix. Radiation's something we're all going to have to learn to live with, I guess.'

'I guess so,' said Gerald Coustain.

'Do you think Carl May would do it?' asked Hamish, wistful and dependent all of a sudden, like a greedy child lusting after a cream cake it knows its mother's purse can't afford.

'You can only ask him,' said Gerald. 'I have his personal number here, as it happens. He's not averse to publicity, of the right kind. If you took his astrologers and tea-leafers off his hands, he'd certainly feel obliged. I think his board aren't too happy about them.'

'I'll have to ask the boss about that,' said Hamish Tovey.

'I didn't know you had one,' said Gerald.

'When it suits me,' said Hamish.

'Mind you, these old Magnox stations of Britnuc's aren't the same as Windscale, or Sellafield as we call it now,' said Gerald, 'but I suppose they could raise a fuel rod from the pile and Mr May could clasp it to his bosom. How would that do? Or he could jump into the cooling ponds with his young companion: something like that might not go amiss.'

'Oh yes, the young companion,' said Hamish Tovey. 'I filmed her jumping into a trout pond with someone or other, once. Quite a looker. Amazing eyes. Now that's really interesting. It would have to be a zoom lens of course, this time. I don't see my crew with an underwater camera in a cooling pond.'

'Depends if they're running scared or not,' said Gerald, and left him to it.

Gerald was using the public phone at the lido. He knew better than to call from the office. He made a further call or so to contacts in Britnuc too low down the ranks of command to be directly under Carl May's eye, but men of action and responsibility, like himself. Then he went back to his family and friends.

The lido was almost deserted, in spite of the warm weather. Angela, Joanna and a brusque young woman with boots, who seemed a security risk of one kind or another, sat in the tearoom, under shelter. He didn't like them sitting out in the open: he'd asked them not to and they'd obliged. Angela had ordered the full tea for everyone — sandwiches, scones, cream, jam, muffins, cake. He went to join them.

Dr Isadore Holly beamed his goodwill towards the four Queens but they weren't having any of it. Interesting.

'Life,' said Dr Holly piously, 'is the only wealth, and I gave you life.'

'You did not,' snapped Cups.

'You just fiddled around in a test tube,' scorned Wands.

'Who do you think you are?' sneered Pentacles.

'God?' jeered Swords.

They had rapidly acquired the habit, now they were together, of dividing up a sentence amongst them and handing it out, with fourfold emphasis. So long, that is, as their emotions coincided, which fortunately was not always the case. They produced, or so thought Dr Holly, a kind of wave motion of feeling and thought, a trough in one giving way to a surge in the next. Alice had the sharpest peaks, the lowest troughs; Jane and Gina flowed more moderately in between: Julie was the smoothest, the most languid. He thought she was the most successful, or was this merely a sexist reaction in himself, what the man liked in the woman, a kind of acquiescence? More research, more research!

But how could research into personality ever avoid the bias, the conditioning, of the observer? Interesting.

So God must have thought when the first sea creature grew a fin sufficiently strong to be called a leg and put his weight upon it – how much it hurt but how interesting!

Dr Holly sat on a swivel chair, and moved it gently to and fro in time with his thoughts; his short legs did not quite reach the ground; he had to use the muscles of his buttocks to provide the impetus for movement. He wished the women would go away and leave him alone with his thoughts, but they wouldn't. They came to ask questions, and stayed to nag. How much easier theory was than practice: how much more convenient the idea than the reality. And where was May, Carl May, whose theory, whose idea these women were, this multiplication of perfection out of technical ingenuity? He had thought to breed passivity and had manufactured its opposite. May should be here to witness this turn up for the books.

How they tapped their feet, how they drummed their fingers, these four handsome creatures, the clones of Joanna May; each one amounting to more than the original, by virtue – by virtue of what? What was it that gave the illusion that there was somehow more room in them than in their original, some sort of inner space not altogether taken up by flesh and bone, nerve, muscle, brain, blood; which gave them an energy, a freedom, a distinctiveness which Joanna May had never had? The life force skipped about in their bodies, toeing no particular line, if only because that line had opened out, widened, become fuzzy. These women were less the sum of their genes than was Joanna May, that was what it was, by virtue of being born into a later decade — as if time itself was a factor in the making of a personality, and ought to be included along with diet and education, and social expectation as a complementary building block. Each year its special character, as with wine, and due to something more than weather: rather some complex, so far undefined, pattern at work. Interesting. Except that it smacked of that insult to the civilized and rational mind, astrology.

'We're waiting,' said Alice.

'We've come a long way,' said Jane.

'We won't be put off,' said Gina.

'We have a right to know,' said Julie.

'Who our parents are.'

'What our relationship is.'

'Why this has been kept secret.'

'And are there more of us?' asked Julie, and a little breath of air stirred the air of the perfectly air-conditioned, even-temperatured room, as the other three drew their breath in surprise and alarm. More? It was intolerable.

'There is one more of you,' said Dr Holly, consolingly. 'But only one.'

Five of us!

They would not sit down. They moved about the room, their energy focused upon him. He had the feeling their energy bisected him. He expected their gratitude, but they had none to offer. Well, this was the fate of the prophet, the searcher after knowledge,

the reformer, the artist, the innovator: he should not
be surprised.

The room was acoustic-tiled, palest green: the light
came from gently humming fluorescent tubes, the
carpet was neutral oatmeal, the furniture pale ersatz
oak veneer, the files a dingy yellow, computers, VDUs
and faxes creamy white. No money had been spared:
equally, none wasted. The room was male, male;
straight-lined, hard-edged: he saw now what was
wrong with it. No pot plants, no family photographs,
no cushions – not an ashtray, not a coffee cup –
nothing to bear witness to human frailty, everything
to further unimpassioned thought, that divine inspiration, that necessary trigger if Utopia was ever to be
achieved. And how else but by logical means, since
all other ways had been tried, and had failed? Poet
priests, and painter kings, all failed; empires crumbling as art and nonsense prevails: aspiration and
practicalities always so little in accord: no, this was
the way forward, through the digital clicking of information, the intricate matching of fact with fact,
through memory forever retained, patching together
the parts of wisdom to get at the wider vision: as
DNA is logged and booked and coded and patched.
Working up from minutiae rather than in from the
macrocosm, for that could never be grasped in its
entirety, only guessed at intuitively, and how much
time and money you would waste if you got it wrong.
Obviously, you had to start with the little bits and
make them up into the whole. No wonder computers
wrote such bad poetry.

'We're waiting,' or rather 'w—we—we'r—we're wait, waiti, waitin, waiting.' Odd, that; the ripple effect when they all said the same thing at much the same time, just fractions of a second apart. Did it follow the same sequence as the initial cell division? Well, he would never know. He longed to know. How uppity they were, how irritating, these grown children of his invention. 'Which of our mothers had quins, then,' they demanded, 'was it a fertility drug, and who was our father? You?'

'Good God no,' said Dr Holly, shocked. 'You seem to be labouring under considerable misapprehensions.'

And Dr Holly explained to them the detail of their birth. ('Not birth,' snapped Alice, 'say genesis.') Afterwards they were silent for a little. He was glad he had shaken them.

'It isn't nice to be so unusual,' said Julie presently. 'To be implanted, not conceived.'

'We were so conceived,' said Gina. 'We were conceived in Harley Street sixty years ago. We are orphans. Our parents are dead.'

'Well if they're not,' said Alice, 'they needn't think I'm visiting them.'

Jane said, 'We were postponed for thirty years. We should sue.'

'I gave you life,' repeated Dr Holly. 'You should be grateful.'

They were not. Why only four, they demanded. Why not a hundred?

'We couldn't get more than four, in those days,' he apologized. 'We weren't in the business of swapping

306

nuclei, shuffling genes, just parthenogenesis, and ex-utero conception.'

Then they despised him for a failure in ambition. He felt bad about it. He wished them out of existence, but they failed to dematerialize.

The clones turned their mind to Joanna May. They needed someone more exotic than Dr Holly to blame. She should never have let it happen. What sort of person could she be? How could you be cloned and simply not notice? Jane wanted to know.

'Easily enough,' said Gina, sadly, who had more experience of hospitals and doctors than her sisters.

'I don't want to meet her,' said Alice. 'She's so old we'd have nothing in common.'

But Julie said, 'You might learn something from yourself grown old,' and they pondered that.

Dr Holly rashly said sixty was not old, it was positively young, and they turned the energy of their attention back to him. They jeered.

'You have made orphans of us,' they said. 'Snatched away the ground from beneath our feet. We are un-natural, and all you can do is talk about yourself.'

Gina began to snivel at the notion of being un-natural. Alice slapped Gina: Julie comforted Gina; Jane restrained Alice's hand. They swirled around a little, touching, hugging, patting, settled down again.

'And now,' said Alice to Dr Holly, 'I suppose you think you're God and we should worship you. Well, we don't. We are much more likely to sue you.'

'The general opinion is,' said Dr Holly, kicking his

feet against the central pillar of his chair, as if he were a little boy, 'that God is dead.'

He felt himself grow tall: his legs extended to the floor and below; his head to the ceiling and beyond. He floated. He felt himself swell, he thought he would burst. It was a most unpleasant feeling. Still his mind worked, computer racing, information pitted against wisdom. Interesting! The Gods were dead, starved to death by lack of belief, and when the Gods died the Titans returned, and he was a Titan untrammelled. Dr Isadore Titan Holly, suffering from gigantism of the head: outside the laboratory windows were the chimneys, the puffers, the suckers, the spitters and nibblers of Martins Worldwide Pharmacopoeia, patents taken throughout the universe, through all eternity, nothing too small, nothing too short, just everything, everything buzzing and whirring and blinding, swifter, faster, cleaner, neater, smarter, richer, glossier exploding markets, expanding universe, stretching time, smash, crack, ecstasy, smack, the cocaine culture, a faster mile, bigger muscles, sweeter smiles, shorter skirts, up their own arse and out again, he was part of it, feet through mud and head through clouds – and splat, he'd fallen flat on his face. The breath was knocked out of him. He was having a fit: a bad one: perhaps this was the one which would carry him off?

Not one of them helped him up, these, the women of his creation. Not one of them loosened his collar or made his tongue safe. They stared down at him, watching him froth and twitch, waiting for him to die, or not, as the case might be.

'He can't die now,' said Alice eventually, brutally. 'There's more we need to know.'

He felt better, as if having been given permission to survive. He tried to speak. He couldn't. But his limbs moved now of his own volition, not of his brain's convulsion. That was something. Perhaps he should crawl out to Sarah? But they closed in on him. He thought they might kick him, even to death. Supposing they felt as entitled to end him as he had been to begin them? What would happen to his research? Had he remembered to put away his own dehydrated DNA? Yes, of course he had. A loss to humanity, otherwise. A multiplicity of ingenuity was what he had, and others had not. So much to be done, so very much it had frightened him off: nothing to do with Carl May. He had wanted the grant cut: he had wasted time unforgivably. Brain transplants: memory transfer: personality shuffling: all waiting for his attention. He of all people needed to be cloned, properly. Effective genetic engineering; not a hopeless dream: just a great deal of money and international cooperation. Another fifty years would do it. It would not be personal immortality for him, even so. It couldn't be. Just look at these four to know; to know what? Not one soul to go round, but a soul apiece and more to spare, and man, woman, was more than the animals, and God was there, and to find out that was enough for a lifetime.

But had he told Sarah where his DNA was? Where he'd put himself? Would she remember? Oh fallible, fallible! So much industrial security in a scientific arena; records always so secret: things got lost. Death was something you never expected. Four straight noses bending down. Perfect noses. Beautiful eyes. It couldn't be bad to have achieved this. He was proud of them. At least he was down to proper size. Little size, almost child size. Four short upper lips, four rather thin lower lips. Better breed clones than rely on finding twins: why had he doubted it! He would do what Carl May wanted: it was what he wanted. He was decided. He would take all the money and get going again. If they let him live. They did.

'What did you say?' asked Alice.

'Interesting,' managed Dr Holly, and they fetched Sarah.

'He had some kind of fit,' said Jane.

'Epileptic,' said Sarah. 'He must have forgotten his tablets. He'll be OK now. I expect you exhausted him. He's not as young as he was.'

The clones left, still angry: they blamed the bearer of bad news for the news: and the bad news was they were not who they thought they were, and that is always difficult to accept, no matter how little you may like being who you thought you were. Dr Holly had given them life and they'd drained the life out of him to the point of death, exhausted him, to punish him for every unpleasantness received and recorded during that life. Children do it to parents every day of their lives, to pay them out for not providing a perfect world to live in. They felt their own unreasonableness and it made them irritable rather than guilty. They felt the inherent guilt of the female, but not powerfully; being four that guilt was quartered. The

310

soul was multiplied, the guilt divided. That was a great advance.

The realization cheered them up. They thought they should celebrate. The clones went back to Julie's house as soon as they could because Ben couldn't be left alone with the little ones for too long. A mild obligation, when divided by four. Alice said, at first, she wouldn't come, she wasn't interested, but in fact she did, she was. The others understood quickly that though Alice needed persuading, she was not difficult to persuade.

Julie and Gina went in Julie's small automatic Volvo, Jane followed in her Citroen Deux Chevaux, Alice in her Porsche. They were glad not to have chosen the same car.

'Alec likes Volvos,' said Julie.

'Tom only believes in Citroens,' said Jane.

'Mine's just more expensive than my brothers' cars,' said Alice, cheering up. 'At least they're not really my brothers. Thank God, it wasn't incest, that on top of everything.'

'I never had time to learn to drive,' said Gina.

48

Carl May sent for Jacko, Petie, Elwood, Dougie and Haggie.

'Tell me about the clones,' he said. It was Thursday evening.

Carl May looked at his watch as he spoke, unusually conscious of the tyranny of time. So much to do, and so few years to do it in! The skin on his right calf itched; his circulation was bad. Would Bethany return of her own free will, and by five thirty, as she had promised, or would she have to be fetched? The hands of the watch blurred: the most expensive watch in the world, sleek, unobtrusive, infallible, but still the hands blurred. It was bitter. The fault lay in his eyes. They had tears in them. He wanted Bethany to return to him of her own free will. If she had to be fetched, he would feel discouraged and end up removing her from his scale of reference: that is to say from the material and current world. She would not die, or only so far as friends and relatives were concerned, and up to a point herself – though what that death experience was, who was to say? No, she would merely be put off to some other time, as Joanna's gardener had been. A pity for the genes of that particular talent, greenfingers, to be lost to the human race. The experience of Garden Developments plc was this, that — forget science, nutrients, temperature, humidity, and so forth — plants simply grew better in the care of certain individuals than in others. Greenfingers. He thought perhaps Bethany had pink fingers. See what happened to his circulation when she went away. He had been happier, calmer, of course, when married to Joanna. White fingers. But white fingers betrayed, strayed. If Bethany did not return, if Bethany removed herself from Carl May and the world — for were not the world and Carl May the same thing? — then perhaps one of the younger versions of Joanna May would do: white fingers he himself had made tolerable by tingeing them with youthful pink: redipping the faded stuff in stronger dye.

But Jacko was delivering the report on the clones. He was dyslexic. He held folders but spoke from memory. They were in Carl's penthouse office suite at the top of Britnuc's tower. Carl May sat in his architectural chair, and tried to find it comfortable. He thought for the first time that it was a young man's chair: it was uncushioned: it demanded resilient young flesh for its proper occupancy. The Barbers of the Bath did not sit, however, no matter how resilient their flesh. Their layered trousers were too bulky, or the chairs too narrow, to make it possible. He stared at Jacko's trousers: a ragged hole in dusty black cotton gave way to ripped green wool tartan, which showed slit red satin beneath, and that was patched and pinned. Three of them smoked: ash fell unnoticed on their clothes and on the pale floor. He would be glad when he was finished with them. He would not use a rock group again: they were easy to buy, easy to bribe, so unnecessarily cynical were they about the ways of the world – citing 'everyone does it' as cause and justification of their actions when of course the truth was everyone did *not* do it – and they were certainly stylish, but he felt more at ease with professional villains, who could make a proper distinction between criminal and ordinary citizenship, and stood their toddlers in a corner if they swore.

Jacko recited the qualities and lifestyles of the clones, rather as a nervous waiter recites a memorized menu, babbling a little, eyes to heaven. Carl May was accustomed to nervous waiters.

Carl May looked at his watch. He still could not make sense of it. Haggie took out his Victorian pocket timepiece 'Five thirty-five, sir,' Haggie said, rounding to the nearest figure, as people always used to, in the old world. Carl May was surprised that the lad could tell the time from a handed watch. So many of the younger generation could not. In the four Magnox stations under Britnuc's control, all clocks had of necessity been converted to digital display, at considerable expense. A wave of despair made Carl May catch his breath. All to no avail, all efforts on behalf of the human race; how could science hold back this tide of stupidity, flesh and blood rioting, breeding uncontrollably, surplus upon surplus, so excess a quantity that quality went out the window, more and more and more, this plague of unthinking, all-feeling humans, no better than a plague of locusts, chattering, devouring, destructive, monstrous. To no avail, this latest heaven-sent breakthrough of the geneticists: the happenstance in nature of a dehydrating fungus, so that henceforth the nuclei of mammals could be treated and transferred unharmed, the building blocks complete. And not just transferred, but multiplied a million times in the E.Coli vats, so the shuffling of DNA, the improvement of physique and personality, could now be done at will. Jacko, Dougie, Haggie, Elwood, Petie. What could you do to them? Require the skill, refine the spirit, make *good* not bad. Too late, too late! Too many now. The random creations of nature would overwhelm the desires and designs of thinking man. Five thirty-six.

Carl tried to listen to Jacko's report. For the hors d'oeuvre, Alice, light and astringent (but too much lemon). For the fish, Julie, tentative and delicate (but a little stale, a little flat, too long out of the water). For the entrée, Gina, full-blooded but overcooked. Jane, a delectable dessert except salt not sugar had been put in the topping.

Faithful, monogamous? The Barbers of the Bath allowed themselves sounds of derision, close-harmonied snorts. Promiscuous at best, lesbians at worst. Carl May said perhaps it was because they had never met the right man, and the four young men shuffled their great Doc Martens eighteen-hole boots and looked uneasy: they had not expected words for the defence spoken by the prosecutor. They had understood their task to be to report adversely.

'So what's the message, sir? What's the next step?' Jacko asked.

Gina and Jane, meat and dessert. Too rich and indigestible. He had an old man's gut, it had to be faced. Those two would have to go. Alice and Julie would replace Bethany, one or the other. Which would he choose? Hors d'oeuvre or fish? One too lemony, one a little stale. Why not both together? They'd consent. They'd do as he asked, as Joanna always had. They'd love him, as Joanna had. Of course they would: they were Joanna. When he multiplied her he had not so much tried to multiply perfection – that was a tale for Holly – he had done it to multiply her love for him, Joanna May's love for Carl May, multiply it fourfold: to make up for what he'd never had: Carl May, the bitch's son. But love was strong, when it came to it: you couldn't stand too much of it: Joanna had been more than enough. It took Bethany, a sorbet between courses, tasted, relished, to restore a jaded palate, a tired appetite. Alice and Julie it would be. Five thirty-seven.

He tried to speak. His voice shook: he stopped.
'Instructions, sir?' asked Jacko. They sang the word, in inefficient close harmony. Inst-instr-instruct-instruction-instructions. He wished they wouldn't. His leg began to itch badly. There was a whining and whuffling in the air: it was the snuffling harmony of a bitch and her litter of pups. He'd lived amongst the excrement and the noisy, messy warmth of the litter and got quite fond of it. The need to love, for a child, is stronger than the need to be loved. When he was hungry, he'd sucked from her. But that had been when he was very small; he'd been told that: he didn't know if it was true. Five thirty-eight.

'Oh yes, instructions,' said Carl May. His voice came back, and his will. He told them Jane and Gina would have to go. Julie and Alice would be fetched. Their ten eighteen-hole Doc Martens boots marched out, blurred by a flurry of dangling fabrics.

49

When Bethany went home to Putney she found her father weeping and alone.

'I knew there was something wrong,' she said. 'I knew I wasn't lying. What's the matter?' Patsy had gone, torn the flowers from her greying hair, been born again as a Christian, and given up her life of sin, said her Dad. Now Patsy was living in an hotel for born-againers, going from door to door, converting as she went.

'But, Daddy, it wasn't sin,' said Bethany. Empty coffee cups stood around, and biscuit crumbs, and sugar bowls with mice droppings in them, and piles of stained sheets on the floor. He needed her. Upstairs there was the sound of revelry. 'It was never sin. Sometimes I'd wish I'd been brought up differently, sometimes I thought that you didn't know what you were doing, the pair of you. Sometimes I was so scared – you and Mum never knew quite what was going on, you thought what they did was just ordinary sex, but sometimes it wasn't, you have no idea. I tried to be kind, I tried to be loving, I tried to bring happiness into other people's lives, especially the disabled, but, Dad, they sometimes sure as hell weren't bringing happiness into mine.'

'Don't you start,' said Dad. 'I've had a bellyful. We had good times, didn't we? Don't take that away from me along with everything else. Your mum will be round here before long, trying to make me believe in Jesus Christ, and I can't, I just can't. Remember how he cursed the fig tree?'

'Well, I can't either,' said Bethany, sadly. 'I can't believe. We went to the theatre too often. You made me read too many books.'

'I suppose you hold that against me too,' he said.

'Of course I don't,' said Bethany. 'Let me help you get this place cleaned up before Mum comes back. She'll just die if she sees it like this.'

'You will stay, won't you?' said Dad. 'This is where you belong, your proper home.'

'I don't know,' said Bethany. 'I really don't know.'

It was three o'clock.

'Who's upstairs?' Bethany asked.

'That's another thing,' said Dad. 'I think I'm getting old. People don't seem to go. Once I used to tell them, quite quietly, it was time to get dressed and go, and they went.'

'You always were a big man,' said Bethany.

'I don't register that way any more,' said Dad. 'It's got worse since your mother moved out. Now I tell them to go and they don't: or worse, they turn up and walk in and use the bedrooms without so much as a by your leave, any time of day and night, as if this was Liberty Hall, and don't even put money in the box. I don't know who's up there, Bethany. You've got to help. I need you here.'

'But, Dad,' said Bethany. 'Carl May needs me too.

I'm only on leave of absence, as it were.' And she cooked him a meal. Only omelette and beansprout salad, because of course he didn't eat meat, but better than boiled eggs and toast, on which he lived. It was four o'clock.

'Beauty and the Beast,' Bethany's father remarked, watching her clear and wash up. 'I must say you're looking good. Why bother with a beast? I'm proud of you. We were right about sex, weren't we, your mother and me? We grew you proud and true.'

Bethany's father had a cavernous, grizzled face. His thick hair had turned greyish since last she saw him. He reminded her of Father Christmas, the kind she'd been taken to in stores when little and on whose knee she most hated to sit; agony shone out from behind the joviality. You had to not notice, for fear of hurting feelings. To hurt feelings was the real sin. It was four thirty.

'We'd better put locks on the doors,' she said. 'And the front door, and the back door, and get a dog.'

'I don't believe in locks,' her father said. 'Lock the door and get robbed. The only time I ever locked my car was once in an underground car park and when I got back someone had broken into it and I had to get a new door.'

She'd heard the tale a hundred times, and taken many a lesson from it. If you kept the door unlocked, as it were, you didn't get raped. Some personal doors, alas, were on permanent lock; she sighed. Her father, for all his experience, for all his principles, was an innocent. She'd had stitches twice, and neither she nor her mother had liked to tell him. She was glad her mother was born-again. She hoped she was happy.

'We can't have strangers coming and going,' Bethany said. 'Things have got to change.'

'I don't like it,' he said. 'The world goes round on love and trust. I've always believed that. Besides, we have nothing to steal.' He made a concession. It was his principle to make concessions, save face wherever possible. 'But a dog, now . . . your mother always wanted a poodle.'

'I'll get you an Alsatian pup,' she said, and ran down the market and did so once she'd cleared up the rest of the house. The bedrooms were disgusting. It was five thirty-five. She'd said she'd be back at Britnuc at five thirty. She could feel Carl thinking about her. She didn't want to feel it. He spooked her. 'For a young man he is young, And an old man he is grey,' she sang as she cleaned, as much to dull the puppy's lamentations as anything else: it had been torn too young from its mother. But where was the young man? Where were they all? They so seldom travelled First Class and she so seldom Standard Fare. They never met.

'Don't lose your trust, Bethany,' her father said, petting the puppy in a way which once would have made her jealous, but which no longer did now her father was old. 'My little girl. Don't ever forget how to love. Keep the flag of faith flying.'

She said she'd try. Somehow there seemed no place between the two of them, Carl May and her father, where she could properly dwell. It had to be one or the other, and she didn't like cleaning, so that settled

321

it. It was five forty-six. She called Carl May, and said she'd be late back, but she would be back. She was on her way.

50

How desperately I, Joanna May, tried to be myself, not Carl May's wife. Even in exile, even divorced, I was married to him, linked to him. She married to him is so different from he married to her. She occupies a little space in his head; he surrounds her, encloses her, as a white leucocyte surrounds some invading cell: if he puts his penis in her it's just to test the breeding warmth: he's really there already. He can escape, she can't. She is squeezed in there, in his head, without room to manoeuvre. Even in Isaac's bed, his uncomfortable, lumpy-mattressed bed, his comfortable arms, I was Carl May's wife, his employer's wife, source of his funding: he was my illicit lover. Therein lay the excitement, the pleasure. I could understand Carl's rage, I could understand my guilt, but not his jealousy. How could he be jealous when what I was doing could hardly be acting, could only be reacting? When Carl divorced me and Oliver climbed into my smooth, firm, clean and luxurious bed, Oliver was my comfort, my consolation, because Carl May had eased me out of his life, as the head's squeezed out, eased out, of a pimple. If Carl May did it painlessly, it was for his own sake, not mine:

he didn't want any nasty, unsightly inflammation left behind.

When I acknowledged my sisters, my twins, my clones, my children, when I stood out against Carl May, I found myself: pop! I was out. He thought he would diminish me: he couldn't: he made me. I acknowledged fear – what would they think of me? I recognized shame – I am old, so old. I faced my rage – how dare they exist. I felt desire, and a great swelling energy, a surging pleasure, the joy of being one of a million million, part of the life of the universe, in all its absurdity, its tremulous glory: I was part of a living landscape, and the function of that life was to worship and laud its maker, and the maker was not Carl May: he had not made me: wife I might be, but only part of me, for all of a sudden there was more of me left. The bugles had sounded, reinforcements came racing over the hill; Joanna May was now Alice, Julie, Gina, Jane as well. Absurd but wonderful!

Carl May could not go on. I let Angela know, who let Gerald know; a man may murder his wife's lovers, but cannot be mad in charge of four nuclear power stations. I was no longer just a wife; I was a human being: I could see clearly now.

If thine eye offend me take a good look at yourself. If thine I offend thee, change it.

It's not lies that kill the soul, it's the effort to believe the lies, especially your own. Carl's dead, white face on the TV screen alarmed me, and should have alarmed the world sooner than it did. The walking dead can't be in charge. There is no room for zombies.

That day at the lido Gerald had a word with someone, who had a word with someone, who had a worker in the field, of course he did.

Sometimes accidents, or events as they are called, do occur without prompting in relation to the fuel rods of the old Magnox stations. Are bound to. The spent fuel rods – fissile uranium wrapped in magnesium – are removed from the pile when they've worn out their usefulness, are no longer capable, poor tired things, of sustaining a reaction. They're taken out, in sequence, en bloc, as they went in – some thirty at a time. But sometimes rods which are not quite spent, may even have quite a vigour to them, get in with the others: they too get dumped in the cooling ponds – square concrete-sided pools, open to the air. Such events do happen – it hardly seems to matter much. No one's going to swim in the pools, are they! What does it matter, if the dials do go round a second time, a third time, a tenth time, and no one notices – or in this particular case, cares to notice, gets paid not to notice, who's to say what goes on, no skin off anyone's nose, unless, that is, the owner of the nose is vain enough, proud enough, sufficient of a scorpion to sting himself to death. When it would be the scorpion's fault, no one else's. The old-fashioned dial readouts should have been converted to digital display long ago, but if management is mean, mean, whose fault is that? Management baying at the moon –

snapping, howling: how dare you shine so bright! It doesn't stop the moon.

Accidents will happen. No such thing as an accident.

I, Joanna May. Or perhaps now, just Joanna.

51

Joanna, at the age of sixty, chaired the first meeting of her life. Her clones appointed her chairperson. The meeting took place in Julie's house, where Mavis had led her. On arrival they found a Volvo, a Citroen and a Porsche in the drive. They could hear the sound of children playing, or squabbling, not to mention TV-set, radio and hi-fi all turned up loud.

'How very peculiar,' said Mavis, who wore for the occasion a long brown woollen coat of amazing plainness. 'My report says this one, Julie, lives very quietly, and has no children. Isolated, rather the way you are. An "executive wife" is what they call this particular brand of woman.'

'Perhaps she's had no choice,' said Joanna. 'Or perhaps she lacked the courage to have friends. Look how brave I have to be to have Angela!' Joanna wore a nice little black suit and high heels to give herself confidence, or perhaps to annoy Mavis.

'Perhaps they've found each other already,' said Mavis.

'Yes, perhaps that's it. All of a sudden, like you, she has a family. And noise and drunkenness breaks out!'

Mavis rang the bell, because Joanna hung back,

and knocked, and tapped upon the window, and finally was heard. The door was flung open.

'Mother!' cried the clones, elated and irreverent, 'it must be Mother!', as Joanna May stood in the doorway, startled. They crowded round, inspecting, touching, laughing. Even Joanna, accustomed to sobriety, could see they'd been drinking. But she was relieved they had recognized her with so little difficulty: had no doubt at all but that she was theirs.

'Mother!' she said. 'Oh, I see. I'm to be mother, am I!' She looked them up and down: she hushed them and tutted them. She felt like her own mother, disapproving; she felt a flicker of forgiveness for the poor dead woman. Mother! The girls would have to take the consequences, the general brisk comment and interference for their own good. Joanna May, mother, refused champagne, fearing alcoholism; she accepted tea. (Mavis took what remained of Alec's whisky from the mahogany-and-glass cabinet.) Wildly, the clones asked Joanna for her opinion of them: they insisted, insisted. They wanted a proper mother's report – at last, they would have what every daughter wants, a mother to wholly appreciate them.

'I see,' said Joanna May. 'You want my true opinion, do you? My maternal view? Then here it is.'

She, Joanna, didn't like one bit the way Alice had taken back her hairline; it was vulgar; she felt Julie's sweatshirt was too informal considering this was her house and she had guests, and what is more she didn't care for the patterned drink coasters, they were common; she thought Jane should comb her hair properly – and it was much too short – and Gina

328

should lose some weight and stop smoking. She couldn't help saying these things. They were true: she was right about them: they must listen to her. It was for their own good. She had been around longer than them: she *knew*.

Joanna felt resentment rising in her daughters; they were oppressed: they wanted her to go away, and yet she'd hardly said a word to them, had she, nothing that wasn't necessary. Just she didn't like this and she didn't like that. Which was true. And for their own good. And look how they drank – alcoholics, every one! They drummed and tapped with their fingers: they were one split into four: they defended each other: to attack one was to attack all. Joanna May stopped as suddenly as she began. She had shocked herself as well as them.

'I'm sorry,' said Joanna May, 'but this is the penalty of daughterhood. I remember it well. The mother must make the daughter as much like her as possible, unthread, unknit, the father in her. In this case, as it happens, my father is your father: you *are* me, so there's no point in me doing it, but still I can't help it.'

'I do it to Sue,' said Gina. 'I can't help that either. I don't do it to the boys: I let them be themselves, I could never work out why. I suppose that's what it is: you try and unravel the father out of the daughter. How else can she be properly female?'

'Worm and the sperm!' said Jane.

'Disgusting,' said Julie and Alice together.

'I will not be your mother,' said Joanna May. 'I hereby renounce the role. If this is motherhood, save

329

me from it. I always wanted it, but this is all it is! Nag, nag, nag!'

'She can't be our sister,' said Alice scornfully. 'She's much too old.'

'She'll only get jealous,' said Jane, 'of the way we are.'

'She does age well,' said Gina. 'I suppose that's something to look forward to.'

'I don't want to look forward,' said Julie. 'I want to live now.'

They allowed Joanna May no authority: she had disclaimed mother, she must take the consequences: they would not even accept her status as originator. They looked her up and down, inspected her, now their equal, their equivalent, but somehow dusty with it. So that was what the passage of the years did – it made you dusty. They resolved never to wear black. It did not suit them. They were in a manic state. As for Joanna, she wanted their pity, all of a sudden, their acknowledgement of her wrongs, but they'd allow her none of that. An easy life, a quiet life! Married for thirty years! To Carl May, the famous Carl! They had all been wronged, more than she, each one claimed. Joanna of all of them had her proper place in the world; she'd been born at the right time. They were a generation out. No wonder they'd been lonely: their lives had been in a mess. They could see now that was the trouble – they'd been lonely. They used men to stop them being lonely. No wonder it all went wrong. Now they had each other, nothing need be the same. They were delirious, giddy. It was absurd, wonderful. Joanna thought they were far too young, far too noisy, far too energetic. She wanted to be alone. She said so. They wouldn't have it.

'We'll make her chairman,' said Julie. 'That's what we'll do. That should keep her happy.'

'Chairperson,' said Jane. So that was what Joanna May consented to be: someone who controlled an agenda but couldn't vote. Mavis watched, and said nothing, but every now and then looked out the window, uneasily.

Ben came into the room and said 'Mum', and Julie and Gina both looked up. 'Those men are back,' he said. 'There are five of them this time, and if you don't do something about it I'm going to take Anthony somewhere safe. And Sue too, I suppose.'

Jane said, 'You let him watch TV, Gina, you shouldn't,' but Joanna said, 'No, we have to be careful. You don't know Carl.'

'I'd rather like to meet this Carl,' said Julie. 'Can it be managed?'

'At last,' said Alice, 'a man worth loving.'

'What everyone wants,' said Jane.

'If you did, Joanna,' said Gina, 'so could we.'

'To be able to love!' said Julie. 'Truly love.'

'He's a demon, a monster,' protested Joanna. 'It wasn't love I felt. Something else! He doesn't deserve to live. He is wicked, he is mad. It took me a lifetime to see it.'

'All that happened,' said Alice, 'is that you grew old.'

'Lost energy,' said Gina.

'Got the worst out of him, not the best,' said Julie.

'Any of us could manage him better,' said Jane.

331

'How would you do that?' asked Joanna.

'By not taking him seriously!' said Jane, and they all crowed with delight, and poured more champagne, and Joanna turned to Mavis in alarm.

All Mavis said was, 'I didn't think about the back,' and tried the telephone but there was no dialling tone when she lifted up the receiver.

Ben said, 'It's OK, I've already called the police. All the times I wanted to call the police, Mum, and never dared, because it made it worse for you.'

Jane, Julie, Alice and Joanna were shocked. They turned and looked hard at Gina and Gina said, 'I know, I know, I can't cope, I'm an awful mother, I don't want to be a mother, please help me.'

Mavis and Ben seemed to understand each other, to comprehend that the world was a desperate and dangerous place. Police sirens sounded. Joanna said, 'Why did they come so quickly?' and Mavis said, 'It depends what Ben said,' and Ben said, 'Well, I'd better get it over,' and went out, and Mavis followed.

Alice said to Gina, 'Why don't you go after him, he's your son?' and Gina said, helplessly, 'Well, he's a boy,' and Alice said, 'This can't go on; personally I hate children but after all he is my nephew. Something has to be done about this.'

'About Gina, you mean,' said Jane.

'I'd like to help,' said Julie.

Mavis came back and said Ben's wonderful; he told them this tale of child assault, sex assault, five men in the car, and they believed him, and they took the men

332

away; now they're going to have to talk themselves out of that. Ben's got to go down to the station. Someone ought to go with him.

Gina didn't stir. It was Julie who said, 'I'll go,' so that decided that.

Joanna, Jane, Julie, Gina, Alice.

52

A memo reached Carl May from the Divination Department: his PA thought it advisable to let this one through. The department was becoming an expensive joke, rumours of its existence having reached the media. The memo took it upon itself to warn Mr May fairly and squarely that the auspices for the day of the projected PR event in Wales were bad indeed. The common pack had produced the Ace of Spades 40 per cent above probability: the Tarot pack the Tower 90 per cent likewise; the *I Ching*, the Chinese Book of Oracles, that normally sedate and encouraging book, had come up with No.23 (Splitting Apart) four times running with mention of Tears of Blood; the prophetic dreamer had wakened screaming, the encephalic discs popping off of their own accord; so far undiagnosed telekinetic forces in the office had shredded the Welsh map, and the teacups came up repeatedly with coffins on the rim.

Carl May laughed aloud. 'Gobbledygook,' he said, and to the gratification of his PA dictated a memo back to Divination: 'If you have foretold anything it is the death of your own department: the end of your payslips,' and told his PA the Welsh PR event was now on and he himself would graciously participate.

A couple of days later, Hughie Scotland ran his finger down the M's in his private address book, and once again got straight through to Carl May.

'I take that back about you being a dry old stick,' said Hughie Scotland. 'I understand you mean to jump into a cooling pond to prove radiation's safe. Young Bethany has certainly brought you back to life. I hope you're grateful.'

'Moderately,' said Carl May, who sounded buoyant, almost happy. 'It's the TV producer's idea. I must make a fool of myself, it seems, to bring the country to its senses.'

'I jumped into a trout pond for the same reason,' said Hughie Scotland, 'to popularize freshwater fish. These days we men of power must make sacrifices.'

'I thought you were drunk,' said Carl May. 'Bethany told me you did it because you were drunk.'

'Bethany tells lies,' said Scotland. 'How is Bethany? You know my wife's in Nigeria? Is Bethany jumping in the cooling pond, too?'

'The TV man says yes,' said Carl May. 'We're in his hands. And Bethany is looking forward to it.'

'What is a cooling pond exactly?' asked Scotland. 'Is it safe?'

'I wouldn't be jumping into it if it weren't,' said Carl May. 'It's where they put the old spent fuel rods to cool off, lose any short-term radioactivity they might have picked up in the pile, before they're carted off to Sellafield. No harm in them at all. The water's

335

filtered and purified, monitored daily, just to be on the safe side, to keep the local populace happy.'

'I'd rather Bethany didn't jump in it,' said Hughie Scotland, 'all the same. I find I'm very fond of Bethany. Does she ever talk about me?'

'No,' said Carl May, 'and she is indeed jumping into the cooling pond with me. It can hardly be worse than into a trout pool with you. Personally I find freshwater fish unnatural. Our streams and rivers are a great deal more polluted than our seas, even the North Sea, and that's saying something. Well, good to speak to you, Hughie. I take it your men will be there in force, cameras and all. If one's going to do something like this, one might as well make as big a splash as possible.'

A joke too. Hughie Scotland winced.

'As it happens,' added Carl May, 'Bethany and I are getting married.' And he put the phone down. That last would stir up Scotland and his media troops.

Carl May told his secretary to confirm detailed arrangements with the NBI. He did not think he would marry Bethany, when it came to it, not even to annoy and upset Joanna. What he did not want, what he did not like, what upset him, was Bethany staying away of her own accord. But when she was there, he could do without her. He could never win in his own head, only in the outside world.

Bethany looked up briefly from her computer game.

'I have the highest score ever,' she said. 'There's this little figure you have to guide through rooms full

336

of demons and ghosts. I'm really good at it. What was that about you marrying me?'

'Only for the press,' said Carl May. 'We want them all there, not just the science boys. Why, do you want to marry me?'

'Of course I do,' said Bethany, but she wasn't sure. It would take her too much out of circulation. You could never divorce Carl May, and if he divorced you you'd be lucky to be alive to collect your decree absolute. The Barbers of the Bath might sing you to death.

'It was Hughie Scotland on the line,' said Carl May, waiting to see how she'd respond.

'That's nothing to me,' said Bethany, and for once she didn't lie. She had a short emotional memory which, considering her life, was just as well.

53

The journey to Britnuc B, in the heart of the Welsh hill country, impressed and awed as many of the journalists and newsmen who travelled down, by car, by train, by helicopter, to cover the media event of the year (for that, according to Britnuc's PR, was what it was) as it troubled and depressed others. The wild beauty of the hills, their sheer scale, the overwhelming presence of nature unorganized and unconfirmed, the indifference of the shaggy cattle, the unkempt quiet roads, the general dwarfing and rendering risible of mankind, inspired as much deference to nature as resentment of it.

Britnuc B had been carefully landscaped so as to offend the aesthetic sensibilities of landscape lovers as little as possible. Some – on the whole those with country cottages – shuddered as they approached the power-station complex, and their radios crackled and faded beneath the marching pylons. Others were thankful that something sensible, profitable and organized had at last, thanks to Britnuc, enlivened the rural torpor of the area.

Green grass grew wherever possible inside the security fence: the massive containment unit was so placed that it was all but dwarfed by the flat rock face that reached up to the sky behind it. Birds wheeled unconcerned above it, delighting in updraughts and downdraughts, the low, interesting, steady thunder of the heavy steam-driven turbines. As Carl May loved to say, 'What is a nuclear power station but a gigantic kettle? All we do here is boil water!'

Only the security gates themselves, the high fences, the handing out of security badges, the requiring of passes, the writing down and checking of names, made matters appear the least unusual: that here was the focus of a nation's terror, the very fount of paranoia.

Britnuc's PR teams made coffee, poured drinks, handed out booklets. Chernobyl could not happen here, the Russian designs were *other*, all *other*, hopelessly old-fashioned, and even if it did, would be no worse than a coal-mine explosion – less horrible, in fact, less likely to be a lethal accident. Nuclear power plants were the opposite of labour intensive! Carl May himself wished to make this very point. And if this proved too technical for the mass-circulation papers, middle rather than front page stuff, why, Carl May was engaged to be married – yes, he was free to marry – yes, he was divorced: a matter of mutual consent many years back: there would be a press handout presently. In the meantime, international TV was present on this wonderful day: a cinema film was being made, not just TV – though we're glad so many TV stations are represented here today: we really do have to get this message across to the general public. Yes, the film was to be part-funded by Britnuc: of course, why not? Part of the PR job – and look here, mementoes for everyone, on this splendid occasion.

Choose from a genuine leather-bound Filofax or this genuine Barbour – if the rain should just possibly fall no one must get wet – and of course there'd be a buffet lunch after the event. Telephones, telex and fax facilities all available in the press office – and out, everyone out into the beautiful fresh air of Wales! The show's beginning. Carl May, nuclear magnate, and Bethany his bride – well soon to be his bride: no, the date wasn't quite fixed, but the press would, of course, be informed the minute it was – would ceremoniously jump into the cooling pond to prove low-level waste was no threat to anyone, and the future of nuclear power, clean, efficient, safe, would be assured.

And all trooped out into the clean, bright, windy air: a good day! A long way to come but at least Britnuc knew how to organize things.

'Do I have to jump?' asked Bethany. She stood on the edge of the concrete bunker looking down at the clean bluish water below. She'd felt the water with her long, nervy, trembly fingers. Pink fingers, as Carl kept saying. Pink fingers. It made her uneasy. The water was just nicely warm. Bethany wore a yellow bikini, with polka dots; it was cut high up the thigh to make her long legs longer. Her red hair flowed out in the wind. Her bosom was only just encased in yellow, polka-dotted fabric.

'This is really something,' murmured Hamish Tovey. 'Get a look of that!'

'This'll travel round the world,' said someone from a newspaper not in the Scotland chain. 'This'll really hit headlines.'

The Scotland chain were concentrating on the copycatting angle. They were rerunning the Scotland/Bethany trout-farm pics, to go out side by side with this one, inviting the reader to decide whether Bethany was going up or down in the world.

'Focus on the girl,' said Hamish, as Carl May joined Bethany on the concrete ramp. He wore black swimming trunks and was in good trim condition for a man of his age. But he was shorter than she was. 'Forget him.'

Carl looked Bethany up and down: he was elated.

'She wore a teeny weeny ultra-teeny
Yellow polka-dot bikini –'

he chanted.

'No, Carl,' said Bethany. 'I'm sure it's not ultra-teeny.'

He pushed her in.

'Oh Christ,' shouted Hamish. 'What are you playing at? We'll have to do that again!' Though most of the press had got it, he wasn't yet rolling.

'We'll do it without the girl,' said Carl May. 'She's irrelevant,' and so they had to, because Carl May said so. The mood of the day changed. The media became bored and sour: what a waste of time: all the way to the Welsh mountains to get one old man, who had to hold in his paunch, jumping into a pond, top executive or not. Carl was in and out of the water six times before NBI was satisfied. They did not make it easy for him. As for Bethany, she'd scrambled to the side at once and had a really good hot shower straight away, and washed and dried her hair, and then sat gently crying. Carl May had finally really upset her. She hadn't wanted to do it in the first place: she had only said she would for the sake of the nation, for their moral health, as Carl put it: to keep the flag of faith flying, as her father did: doing the kind thing which was the right thing. And now Carl was angry, swimming around in the water, doing stupid things for a camera, not himself – where was his pride? Where was his integrity? She had more than he had when it came to it, and now she was frightened again: Carl had taken the name of marriage in vain and would be punished for it: yet he knew no better. She found she was sorry for Carl, which was almost worse than being bored and she hated the countryside: green hills closed in around her. She wanted to be back in the city.

A man came up to her and said he was Hughie Scotland's PA: Hughie had said if she wanted a lift home, he could give her one. Bethany was doubtful. Then she looked over to where Carl May still thrashed about in the water of the cooling pond, white head bobbing.

'Hughie says not to worry,' said the PA, who was young, broad-shouldered, good-looking and interested. 'Hughie says he'll look after you. If you know what I mean.'

'OK,' said Bethany. 'I seem to remember what he means.'

She sat next to the PA in the car on the way back to London, not in the back as he'd expected. She felt shivery and a little sick presently, but it soon passed. She took out her contact lenses.

'I like your eyes grey,' he said, his own eyes off the road.

'Do watch where you're going,' she said, 'or you'll kill us both,' but she was pleased. Presently she started humming to herself:

'I do, I do, I do,
    And I ain't going to tell you who.
    But I belong to somebody,
    Yes indeed I do!'

and felt positively brave and cheerful, and as if her life had begun anew, which indeed it had.

54

Carl May sat amongst the Pharaohs and wept. 'I am a stranger in my own land,' he thought. He shivered and felt sick. Painted eyes stared at him, oval, beautiful and calm: the carved and soulful eyes of strange beasts, but there was no one to talk to. His impatience had driven them away. His own easy irritation, his flashing anger, his unreasonable demands, had seared a burnt and blasted space around and no one came near him. Why should they? He wouldn't if he were them. He lived in a kennel, and barked. If he'd been his own mother, he'd have put himself there.

He was dying. He did not care. Only that none of it had been what he wanted, none of it what he meant. He hoped Bethany would be all right. Death, he could see, was too great a punishment for the habit of correcting someone out of turn. Nausea made him feel kind: as if you needed strength to be cruel and kindness was just the easiest, most natural thing. There was no more time to investigate the notion. The mind had to die, that was the dreadful thing: bodies were two a penny, but that all the buzzing speculation of the individual mind had to go – therein lay the tragedy. He should never have got involved with the Barbers of the Bath. That had been insanity. He wished to apologize to the clones of Joanna May. But he didn't have the strength. Too late.

After he'd got out of the pond, towelled and walked back to the VIP room, the meters — the ones put in to reassure the visitors — had started to chatter. The area had been cleared, more or less. Media men will risk anything for a story, even stay round chattering meters. What a fuss! They'd wanted to put him in the isolation room and start emergency treatments, but he knew already it was no good. It had been foretold. Let them suck out as much bone marrow as they wanted, he was finished. Philip drove him back to Eton Square. Good for Philip. He'd make the alarms chatter now, too. He wondered if it had been an accident. Probably not. Who had fixed it? Coustain? His own Divination Department? Joanna? He wouldn't blame her. He wished she was with him. In spite of everything, he wished she was there. He thought Isaac was in the room; he hoped he was: it would be somebody to talk to. But there was no one, nothing animate. No sound at all, unless he was deaf. He would have to take his own journey through death, so alone, without servants, without friends; stand at the Throne of the Most High, and make his explanation there, without support, without witnesses. What could he say? I wanted to know what would happen next? Was that enough? There had not been time: he had been clapped like a bird in full flight, soaring. Fate was unkind, but just.

It wasn't Isaac. It was Joanna. He saw her blue eyes. He shivered so much he could hardly speak. He said, 'No, don't come too near.'

She said, 'I never did, I never dared. I should have been more brave.'

He said, 'I know all that. I know. My fault.'

She just stared at him, but at least her eyes moved. They weren't dead. He had, after all, spared her, saved her. Now he had his reward.

'Joanna,' Carl May said, 'take me, remake me. For God's sake, remake me.'

'All right,' said Joanna May.

55

That was a year of strange events, some wonderful, some terrible: and there are stranger years ahead, no doubt. They don't frighten me; even death has lost its sting. The future shouldn't alarm us: how could it possibly be worse than what's gone before? Little by little, wisdom replaces ignorance, self-knowledge overcomes stupidity, awareness gets the upper hand of cruelty. It is the past which is so terrifying, with its capacity to spoil and destroy the present. That can't get better.

Little Carl runs round my feet. He's three years old, an energetic, noisy little boy, with thick pale hair and bright red cheeks, interested in everything, bored by nothing. He can read and write already, and even recite nursery rhymes, which he loves to do, never getting them quite right. If I correct him he has a temper tantrum: he is beside himself with upset and indignation – I have failed to recognize the difficulties he has overcome, the achievement; so great a task for one so small – and his small frame cannot contain such passion. His whole body turns as red as his cheeks, he flails and kicks and beats the ground, the door, me, anything; and then I, hurt in mind and body, have to carry him, as best I can, to his room and shut him in until we both calm down and can begin again. I could beat him black and blue, and am still sometimes tempted to, to punish him for what he did to me, for the unlived life he gave me, so many years of it, the guilt he made me feel, the loss he made me endure, for the deaths of Isaac and of Oliver. Except this innocent has done nothing: I know he could, that's all, and knowing what he could do also know what I could do, sufficiently provoked; and so I have to forgive him, both in retrospect and in advance.

Easier not to correct him, one way or another, to avoid the confrontation, to let the error go unchecked. 'Spoiling,' Gina calls it. Now she has given her children away, how quickly she has taken on Julie's former role, and become censorious. But I'm older, I know better, I no longer fight for fairness, truth and justice. I just say, 'That's wonderful, Carl, how clever you are!' We christened him Rex, Alice and I. King. Why not? But Julie was against it – a dog's name, she said – and it soon drifted back to being Carl, little Carl.

Alice, of all of them, Queen of Cups, was the one who volunteered to give birth to little Carl, on condition she didn't have to rear him. Dr Holly, back in the business, used his own tried and tested techniques of nuclei transfer to bring it about. Alice proved a good and dutiful birth mother: didn't smoke,

348

didn't drink, watched her health and her moods – trained as she was in keeping her body well under control. She relinquished the baby to me at six weeks, without protest – glad of a decent night's sleep, I daresay, and happy enough to let the simple pleasures of narcissism prevail over the more complicated snakes-and-ladders game of motherhood; anxious to get back to work; and knowing I'd bring up the child pretty much as she would. How could I not?

Julie, Queen of Pentacles, is happy bringing up Ben, and little Anthony too; Alec, their adoptive father, comes and goes. He is resigned to the noise, the mess, the constant upheaval; consoled by the sense of present and future, so long as he can fly off from time to time, leave it all behind and tread the clean and flattering corridors of world class hotels until such time as his strength returns and his self-esteem is restored.

Jane, Queen of Wands, no longer toys with the idea of working in film: she has settled happily and quite profitably as a journalist – the work suits her better, being more about facts, less about fantasy. She felt obliged to take Sue in because three was too much for Julie, and Alice had done her bit by actually giving birth to little Carl, and Gina wasn't fit, and a child will take any clone, it seems, for a mother. The essential nature is the same, after all: only the frills are different. Sue then felt the lack of a resident father, so Jane, running comfortably on only a quarter guilt, finally consented to allow Tom to move in. Jane is always out and about so Tom does much of the childminding and cooking, grumbling the while, but the three of them, Jane, Tom, Sue, seem happy enough. Sue sees her birth mother from time to time, of course, but prefers the Jane rather than the Gina version, or at any rate, she'd rather have Tom for a father than Cliff.

Gina, Queen of Swords, now childless, is at medical school but back with Cliff. He still drinks, he still hits her, but not so much or so hard. Pain is indeed addictive, and perhaps the effort of curing it is hardly worth it, if there are no children about. If it's pleasurable, why not? We've had so many oughts and shoulds, all of us, we've all but given up being critical of one another. Good for her, say we.

We would have been perfect people if we could, but our genes were against us. We would have been faithful, kind and true, but fate was against us. We are one woman split five ways, a hundred ways, a million million ways.

It's autumn. I, Joanna May, am out in the garden, raking leaves. I keep things tidy, and growing, in memory of Oliver, and besides, I like to do it. Little Carl runs round my feet and all but trips me up, and falls headlong into a pile of leaves. 'Careful,' I say, 'I'm not as young as I was,' and I pick him up and set him straight, and he laughs cheerfully and rushes off to set to flight a flock of seagulls, rashly gathered on the lawn: and when the wicked deed is done, and the birds have risen crossly and unwillingly into the air, where they hang around to wheel and squawk their reproach, he stands stock still, amazed at what he's done. I do love him. Never stopped.

(1903-1961) was born Eileen Arbuthnot Robertson in Surrey, the daughter of a doctor. Her family moved to Notting Hill, London, when she was fourteen. She was educated at Sherborne, and in Paris and Switzerland. In 1927 she married H. E. Turner, general secretary of the Empire and Commonwealth Press Unions, later to become Sir Henry Turner, CBE. Her first novel *Cullum* was published in 1928, followed by *Three Came Unarmed* (1929), *Four Frightened People* (1931), *Ordinary Families* (1933), *Summer's Lease* (1940), *The Signpost* (1943), *Devices and Desires* (1954), *Justice of the Heart* (1958) and *The Strangers on My Roof*, published posthumously in 1964. She also wrote *Thames Portrait* (1937) and *The Spanish Town Papers* (1959), both with photographs by Henry Turner, and a children's book, *Mr Cobbett and the Indians* (1942).

E. Arnot Robertson was a broadcaster, lecturer and film critic; she was at the centre of a famous lawsuit when she sued MGM who had tried to stop her attending screenings as a result of her 'hostile' reviews. She lived with her husband and son in Heath Street, Hampstead: ardent sailors, they would frequently cruise to France, Belgium and Holland on their yacht. After 34 years of marriage, Henry Turner was killed in a boating accident on the river, a loss from which E. Arnot Robertson never recovered. She committed suicide in 1961.

Virago also publishes *Four Frightened People* and will publish *Cullum* in 1987.

ORDINARY FAMILIES

A novel by
E. ARNOT ROBERTSON

With a new introduction by
POLLY DEVLIN

Published by VIRAGO PRESS Limited 1982
41 William IV Street, London WC2N 4DB

Reprinted 1986

First published in Great Britain by Jonathan Cape Ltd 1933

Copyright © 1933 Gordon Turner

Introduction copyright © Polly Devlin 1982

British Library Cataloguing in Publication Data
Robertson, E. Arnot
    Ordinary families.-(Virago modern classics)
    I. Title
    823'.912 (F)   PR6035.0548
    0 86068 281 1

Printed in Finland by Werner Söderström Oy

CONTENTS

THE GREEN THINGS

If I had made this earth, I'd be too proud
Of all things green to leave mankind in doubt
Of My existence. 'Love My grass!' I'd shout,
Flinging a fierce green shadow from a cloud,
While, 'Mercy, Lord of leaves –!' implored aloud
The trembling priests instructed in My praise.
Seas, and the after-glow of summer days
Should be My sacred symbols to the crowd
– And scum on ponds, gratuitously green! –
Oh, I'd be merciful, and men be sure
Of immortality, absorbed in Me;
But not for love My godhead should be seen;
Rather, divine conceit – I would secure
Homage for all the green *I* caused to be.

To the best of my knowledge no one in any way resembling a figure in this book lives or has lived in Pin Mill, Suffolk, where the story is set (except in so far as all ordinary families anywhere have certain similarities). These characters lived elsewhere, and are in most cases composite portraits: only the localities described and the newspaper extracts given in the book are entirely 'real'.

E. ARNOT ROBERTSON

INTRODUCTION

By the time *Ordinary Families*, her fourth novel, was published in 1933 when E. Arnot Robertson was twenty-nine, she had built up such a devoted and mass readership in the USA as well as in Britain that it was one of the literary events of the season, book club choice of the year, and greeted with almost unanimously good reviews – 'eloquent', 'exhilarating', 'brilliant' were the words most often used, although 'hardhearted' and 'ruthless' crept in too.

In *Ordinary Families* she seemed to find her own true voice. In her earlier novels she had placed her characters in a baleful jungle and observed their behaviour in the ensuing chaos with the eye and ear of an *enfant terrible* but without its artlessness; or had put jungle characters into her frenchwindowed rooms and caused them to wreak havoc with astonishing verisimilitude. Here she left her creatures where she appeared to find them, in a terrain she knew by heart rather than by imagination, a sailing village called Pin Mill on the Suffolk coast in the 1930s. And although 'here there Be no Tygers', there is lots of burning bright human life going on among three middle-class families, the Cottrells, the Rushes and The Guests observed through the eyes, ears and voice of her young heroine Lalage Rush. Lalage reports on their doings with a naturalist's passionate accuracy for habitat, habits and plumage, an anthropologist's curiosity for tribal rituals, initiations and ceremonies and the novelist's rapacious greed for happenings, emotions and the cruelty of circumstance.

Until this book, there had been something curiously unreconciled about E. Arnot Robertson's writing: it pulsated with an energy which was never quite released by the detonations in her stories. But here her energy found its outlet, although there are far less overtly dramatic moments and fewer stunning stage effects and volcanic explosions than in earlier books.

Ordinary Families is full of lovely things: extraordinary minute observations of nature in the wild; enchanting and accurate and microscopically detailed descriptions of animal behaviour, told with such felicity and grace and humour that they sidestep gracefully the terrible traps of nature writing best parodied by Evelyn Waugh – 'feather-footed through the plashy fen passes the questing vole'. Indeed she parodied herself, taking enormous pleasure in keeping her tongue in her cheek, both by making Lalage have some success writing bogus letters to *The Times* about extraordinary and fictitious incidents in the animal world, all of which were published as gospel truth, or by having Lalage pass comment herself. (She compares her mother's attitude towards her appetite as somewhat like that of the adult wasp, which, when kept under observation without food with which to feed its grub, bit off the grub's hind leg, offering it solicitously to what remained.)

Throughout *Ordinary Families* her writing about the land, the sea, bird-life, nature in elemental or tranquil mood has a certitude and a generous accommodation that makes one think of Hudson or Hardy. She was a woman who noticed things, with gratitude, and she limited her scale of vision as though in thanksgiving, eschewing the grand, the picturesque, determined never to compete with or pre-empt nature's own effects. When finally she couldn't resist, or needed a great dramatic moment and engaged with the tempestuous, she did so by concentrating on its effect on man and his little effects – especially his leaking unseaworthy boats.

'The finest yachtsman's novelist now writing in the

English language,' one critic wrote, in perfect seriousness, and many of those people who were the targets of her proper passionate criticisms read her books with fondest pleasure because she wrote with such functionary grace and accuracy about the classic English way of life and living and country-side, and the classic English passions – sailing, bird-watching, adolescent love, and the tremblings of stiff upper lips.

The implications in many reviews – and in assessments of her art and writing – is that she appealed only to the middle-brow and the middle classes, and certainly she did, if only because she was such a marvellous delineator of their lives. She was a cartographer of their territory, always working on an ordnance scale, closing in on her chosen terrain, stalking and observing the tribes therein with rapt interest as though from behind an invisible hide, and with such close and passionate attention to geography, weather, vegetation, animal life and means of survival that these accounts of thirties life in Suffolk have an anthropological exploratory quality.

But it was perhaps her very popularity that made her extraordinary talent for catching life on and off the wing and setting it down, as translucently, precisely and economically as a water-colourist, remain for so long under-rated. That, and the fact that she wrote such cracking good yarns.

But she had her champions, her parfait knights: Edmund Blunden and James Agate wrote of the artistic brilliance of *Ordinary Families*, and Harold Nicholson, influential in the *Daily Telegraph*, saw himself as its champion and with infinite patronage placed her in the first rank of modern British novelists. Until then, in the curious Form Book of 'points, placings and Earlier Outings' which underpinned much of the literary criticism of the thirties, she had remained in the second rank wherein most women-writers were made to lurk awaiting starter's orders from the predominantly male reviewing staff of newspapers and journals.

Nicholson expressed profound regret that his estimation of her rank and placement in the world of letters was not shared by a sufficient number of his contemporaries

Miss Arnot Robertson is too interested in bird-life, too contemptuous of aesthetics, too brisk and bouncing to please the high-brow; and the low-brow finds her saying sharp and horrid things about the public-school tradition of romance and what-not.

Miss Arnot Robertson had quite a few biting things to say on brow-levels as well as aesthetics – especially about 'thin-brows who only admire what is fashionable'.

She was perhaps sharpest of all about artistic pretension for although she was profoundly interested in the Keatsian concept of beauty and truth and the possibility of their divergence and separation, as far as she was concerned 'there is one subject of conversation past all bearing – "my art" – when a semi-artist of any kind gets worked up about it. But like most of my generation, I can be made uneasy by any-body's romanticising about the things for which I care.'

So intent was she on being straightforward, in showing things as they were, so determinedly did she set her face against sentimentality that she was sometimes abrasive. 'I wanted to stick a pen nib hard and often into their smug mental dishonesty,' she said: but in stripping away manifold illusion to get to the hoops underneath she occasionally stripped away the softer fibre of sentiment which lies flatter and closer to the bone. And she was sometimes guilty of mental dishonesty herself. Whilst idealising men extravagantly, she scoffed at the very idea of anyone idealising women: 'women are physically, mentally and morally (in the widest sense) inferior to men and always will be ... in the rare case where a woman is a man's equal in anything let her be treated as such...'

Her lovely gawky heroine Lalage is one such rarity.

xiv

Daughter of a breezy sailing father, a girl with commonsense, a fine pervious sensibility and an irritating habit of being an underdog, she links the story together; in her ceaseless puzzled intelligent hunt to get to the bottom of the mystery of ordinary people Lalage sees the falseness in family relations, the cracks in the glaze of unity.

She is, as are all of E. Arnot Robertson's main female characters, a heroine – women of exalted spirit and achievement who must needs leave the rest of womanhood behind, lurking in some devious shrubbery of deceit, snobbery and illusion.

Miss Arnot Robertson was herself a heroic creature and looked it. Long limbed, needle thin with red-gold hair, anonymously famous as the model for a much reproduced painting 'The Red Haired Girl' by James MacBey long before she was famous as an author, she cared passionately about a great many things – her husband, her writing, the countryside, liberty, freedom of speech, the right to express opinions. When she was working as a film critic and broadcaster, she brought a lawsuit against MGM who had forbidden her to attend any more screenings, because of what they called her 'hostile' reviews.

Although £8,000 was raised to help her continue the case after the decision in her favour given in the first hearing had been reversed in the Court of Appeal, she lost £7,000 of her own money, and thought it well spent. Reading her autobiographical words it is hard not to think of her as the original for all her heroines and it was generally assumed that she based many of her characters on her family.

'No author wants to do an act of spontaneous generation over any characters,' she said. 'The creatures of imagination must have some close relation to real existence or they would be completely uninteresting. Personally, I think only the normal is interesting…'

Much of her writing is permeated with an amazing energy

and a kind of anger about women. It is as though she were fighting an inward battle for a space for herself, for her sense of herself as a woman, fighting to resolve the ambivalence that emerges in her writing: that heroines are outside the common run of women, and that most women are condemned to second-class citizenry by virtue, as it were, of their natures. She herself at some profound level could never reconcile her awareness of herself as a first-class citizen with this ranking.

There is always a sense of pain, of gaps in her psyche, of acute tenderness. She is a progressive, battling against the conservative stamp that has been placed on her by her background, and always there is an impatient quality running through her work, her spiriting intelligence, her fleetness that makes her suddenly be done with something before it has quite come to its proper end.

She had that in her life too. She committed suicide and that knowledge throws an eerie light on her writing, gives it a different balance. The authenticity of her convictions is there in the evidence; the indomitableness, the pride in her own strength, a kind of stubbornness that runs through her writing like a twisted muscle.

'She had always talked openly of suicide,' her son said, 'and when my father died she simply felt that life wasn't worth living. It was a peculiar partnership, successful very largely by his efforts. Emotionally she liked an audience and he provided it unstintingly. She was one of those women who needed to be admired. He did not wish to be free, he was her mate in every sense and he was very happy. He was not reflected in her glory but in helping her do what she wanted to do.

Blake once advised Samuel Palmer to stare at a knot in a piece of wood until it frightened him. E. Arnot Robertson stared at it until it had ceased to do so and showed it to her readers. Her view of *Ordinary Families* might be summed up thus: ordinary families are all alike, every ordinary family is extraordinary in its own way; and she made of her theme and her vision a novel that is real as life and abstract as history.

POLLY DEVLIN, Gloucestershire 1982

CHAPTER I

AN OBSESSION WITH TIME

MARGARET and I quarrelled because she would not let me sink her makeshift boat in the marsh pool, in which a fine steep sea could be worked up by hand in a few seconds. More exactly, I quarrelled with Margaret about it, for my sister always remained passive in the many disagreements we had when I was getting on for eleven and she was nine. It is hard, as it always is with vivid childish memories, to know how much of the incident is recollected from the time of its happening, and how many suitable details the mind has added afterwards in reconstruction. The whole trivial occurrence seems clear in retrospect, but so objectively seen that it might be happening to any two other damp and dirty shrill-voiced children, playing on a strip of marsh ground much bigger than I now know it to be. The Lallie in the picture, who is myself, is as visible as the Margaret, so that probably most of my memory of what followed hangs on my mother's re-telling of the story she heard from Margaret two days afterwards.

I do definitely remember, though, stretching my ankles ecstatically to straining point as I knelt, resting back on my heels, so that the spongy ground should make long black stripes of dampness, like those on the beech-boles just behind us, all the way down the front of my brown stockings, and not only patches on the knees and toes. This was luxury: no other children, we had gathered, were encouraged to get as wet as we were – who else would have been allowed to play in February on the marsh by the river? – Certainly none of our friends.

I loved wrecks when the boats were only old cardboard picnic plates, like these. The whole family was taken sailing by father so often, in such filthy weather, that I found much delight in watching an unseaworthy craft get a bucketing and eventually founder when there was no personal anxiety attached to the performance.

But Margaret was naturally more of a sailor than I was: she had my father's liking for unsound craft. Her boat must stay afloat as long as possible.

I pressed my suggestion, pointing out that we could not spend all day messing about with a rotten old plate. I had already in me the seeds of the obsession with time which developed later: I can remember no period when I was not uneasily aware of time as something that slipped by too quickly unless I thought about it at intervals, when its passage would slow up a little. A heron was just settling in one of the trees on the edge of the marsh, landing clumsily for once with back-tilted wings flapping awkwardly, and legs feeling forwards for the unaccustomed touch of a branch. I am certain that the heron really did appear just then; I can still see it and no one but myself would have thought it important enough to notice particularly. If one of these birds alighted in a tree in February it was looking for a place to build, I knew, and I wanted to keep watch on it, but I was not going to be baulked of my light-hearted wreck, first.

Margaret went on playing with her greasy plate, and I might not have been there, for all the notice she took. I was already resentfully aware that she was lovely; even a ten-year-old sisterly eye could see that as she squatted there, engrossed in her own game. In her place Ronald, my brother, or my other sister, Dru, who were both out sailing with father, would have argued hotly that having sunk my own plate I had no right to wreck theirs, but Margaret went on her own way imperturbably as usual, and, as

16

usual, this exasperated me. For years I had heard enough about Margaret's looks from the Cottrells, our neighbours, who occasionally broke into French about her to my parents, to realize dimly that in any battle of selfishness between us she would always win with honour. I did not understand French, but like any other child, I generally knew, with contempt, what was being said when they spoke a foreign language in front of us, particularly as Margaret's name was nearly always mentioned. I knew, also, that Margaret could take larger spoonfuls of home-made jam at the Cottrells' house than I could without being reproved; the two things being somehow connected.

At no period of her life could one say fairly of Margaret that she deliberately disregarded other people's wishes; she seemed to remain unaware that there were such things, as a flower is superbly unaware of all but sunshine and warmth and the secret elements in the soil which minister to its well-being.

I insisted that she should let me have the plate to sink, adding that 'She'd better,' because the repetition of the order was having no effect.

Margaret lifted wonderful dark eyes to me indifferently, and asked why.

'Because you just had!' was the inevitable answer to that question in our family. This gave the threatener a second or two in which to cast about in his or her mind for a reason.

The heron looked all wrong, jumping from branch to branch with short flurried movements of its great wings. I was almost ashamed that its need of a nest should make it unstately for once, and hoped that Margaret would not see, because she might laugh and imitate its hopping, and I loved herons with the touchy protectiveness of a child – loved, without thinking much about such things, the impressiveness of their slow flight and the exquisite precision of their return to earth. I might wave my arms and shout to scare it, laughing at it myself – that would be all right as long as no one guessed what I really felt about herons. But I did want it to nest in the park.

'Why, Lallie?'

'*Ah!*' If she would not do what I wanted I could, of course, push her into the pool, as Ronald had done with me. It was only about six inches deep, a brown graze in the thick reddish skin of young samphire which grew over the marsh at this time of the year. But it was part of our family tradition that none of us objected to getting wet, and actually I was the least willing to be soaked through at any time: the aggressor was nearly always as damp as the victim at the end of one of these struggles. Margaret would not mind being sopped very much, and I should. Still, it was the sort of thing that the Rush children were expected to do, and I fancy this weighed with me for a minute or two.

'Why'd I better?'

I said, on the inspiration of the moment, that I must not tell her that. The heron lifted one leisurely wing to a sudden puff of wind, allowing itself to be blown sideways from the tree with its legs trailing behind it, and then swung effortlessly in a grand, heart-quickening curve towards another group of beeches. Such a display of lazy skill, as the bird lay still and steeply tilted, at rest on the uncertain air, made amends to me for the indignity of its hops among the branches. Now I could forget it altogether. A light breeze of fancy was stirring in my mind: would it hold and freshen, or die away? – Well, if I did tell her, would she keep a secret?

She promised. I told her that she was not really my sister; she did not belong to us at all. I was amazed at the unaccustomed speed with which my thoughts were gathering way and fairly scudding along before the breeze of fancy. It was strengthening nicely.

'Lallie!'

What else was I going to tell her? I should have preferred more time in which to think this out. But at least she was properly conscious of my existence now. I see her, either as she was or as my imagination afterwards painted her, staring across the narrow pool at me, one hand fingering her mouth apprehensively: there must have been something triumphantly ominous in my tone, even though I was uncertain what was to come next. Vague resentment against Margaret, who secured all the attention that I coveted, may have sharpened my powers of invention, but mainly I think I was carried away by the conscienceless joy of creation as bit by bit I adopted circumstantial evidence into the story I was evolving.

The details are beyond recall, but the main theme on which I harped was that she had been taken out of an orphan home for me to play with. Had she never thought it funny that she should be dark when the rest of us were not? The pleasing arrogance of the notion was wasted on her. I followed it up by saying carelessly that I had only to say the word at home and she would go back. She began to gulp. To both of us that mysterious thing, an orphan home, was a place of unimaginable horror.

The two older ones, Ronald and Dru, had each other for company, I pointed out, and she knew that the baby between me and Ronald had died. So naturally my parents felt I ought to have someone too. But not if I preferred it otherwise. (If only that were true! I thought.)

In order to prolong this savoury moment to the utmost I loaded it with as much repetition as Margaret would stand. Credulity grew in me as it did in her while I added subsidiary details. One of them, of which I was proud enough for it to stick in my mind, was that I myself had picked her out from the other babies in the home and begged my kindly parents to let me keep this one as against a rival choice of their own: a good touch, that. I saw the orphan home; a long and dismal row of iron beds, like those in the Ipswich hospital where my tonsils had been removed. The wind of imagination was blowing great guns by this time, and it was the frail barque of fair play (so deeply venerated in the Rush family) that was properly pooped and sunk, leaving the sodden plate still floating almost forgotten on the pool In decency Margaret ought to do everything I wanted, I gave her to understand, because if I had not chosen her, where would she be now? And who? Certainly not a Rush!

I gave this time to sink in.

'Now you let me have that plate!' I said, and the moment stands out sweetly in memory. 'Shove her right over. There! Look! Look, Margaret, she's going.' But Margaret was crying too hard to watch the jolly swamping. The noise she made did not matter: mother never came down to the water in the mornings and the rest of the family was almost out of sight down the estuary. There was even an advantage in her weeping: it left her in no condition to question my next statement, for which I could think of no support. If they discovered at home that she knew about this, they would send her back at once; she had better not let them guess!

The unhappy child nodded and made an effort at self-control, but it was not successful for some time. I was afraid that she would not cheer up in time for lunch, but fear helped her here; and afterwards, as a propitiatory offering, she let me have the water-proof sand-paper that father gave her for the hulls of Ronald's and Dru's dinghies, which were to be raced the next day, though really it was only my turn to scrub the insides, a dull business.

In the evening I began to feel slightly guilty about my invention after mother had said good night. Remorse, I had discovered, was in some way related to the prone position, because I was only sorry about things when I was in bed, and when, for a week or so after I came home without my tonsils, they made me lie down in a darkened room in the afternoons, I found my conscience pricked by numbers of things which would not have otherwise stayed in my mind until night and repentance overtook me. So for a while I sat up in bed in order to keep an unbiased view while I worried as to whether I had better mention this matter of Margaret and the orphan home in my prayers. We were allowed to say these kneeling humped up between the sheets in cold weather. But I was always chary of drawing the Lord's attention to small lapses from grace which, but for my stressing, He might have been willing to overlook.

Perched up on my pillow, I stayed awake longer than usual, and heard a commotion starting in the house, doors opening and footsteps passing along the passage. Twice, the slight tinkle of the telephone bell sounded outside my door as someone took off the receiver in the hall. Later a car came, and woke me up afterwards by its going. I listened as long as I could, and inadvertently dropped off to sleep without saying my prayers at all.

In the morning I heard that my grandfather, who lived with us, had died of heart failure in the night. I had not seen him for weeks, but about ten days ago we had been told to pray for him, by mother, who was still in her Roman Catholic phase, which ended soon afterwards. Mother (mistakenly, I thought) was very fond of the old man, who had said, 'Well, Lallie, what have you got to say for yourself, eh?' – an impossible conversational opening – at our last meeting. But mother had been so earnest about it that I had prayed dutifully until this occasion. She had read us something from the Bible: 'Whatsoever ye shall ask in My name . . . .' And now he had died because I had forgotten on account of Margaret and an imaginary orphan home. How could I have given a thought to anything so insignificant and thus virtually killed my grandfather?

No one knew that it was in any way my fault. I dared not

tell them, to ease my growing sense of responsibility. I'll feel better in time, I thought wretchedly. I always had felt better about sins a few days after their commission, but I disliked the idea of trying to get through time for any reason: time went too fast and always in one direction: it was continually taking further and further out of reach things that I had liked – a guinea pig which died, and my first venture alone in a dinghy, and the day on which I saw a sheldrake fighting׳ a skua gull away from its nest. Now if I thought hard of it, '. . . . Time . . . Time . . .' so as to brake its disconcerting passage, I was left the closer to my unbearable knowledge of what I had done that night in forgetting to save my grandfather. Occasionally a happy doubt of my responsibility lightened the gloom, but not for long. 'Whatsoever ye shall ask –' I had asked and he had gone on living. I had not asked and he had died. The coincidence was too great.

For different reasons Margaret and I both went about depressed and silent for two days, but no one noticed this in the disturbance of the household. Both of us, from motives of self-interest, made heroic efforts to keep our preoccupations from becoming noticeable. I, with my greater burden to bear, grew annoyed at times at the sight of Margaret's pale apprehensive face, more appealing than ever, I suppose, in its aloof childish sadness, for my father, whom I adored, took her sailing alone, a huge treat. As the two youngest we were nearly always taken together. He said he would take me separately too, but forgot because an Italian steamer came up the river to unload at Ipswich, and he found two noisy and alarming old friends of his among the crew.

Believing my story as she did, I felt that Margaret should have shown me more gratitude for being the instrument of her removal from the orphan home. After that one occasion when she let me rub instead of wash, as my share of our regular Friday dinghy-chores, she behaved to me in her usual way, as though I existed only vaguely, on the outskirts of an inviolable world where she lived alone in the immense secrecy of her childhood. One consolation came to me in the dreadful days after my grandfather's death. On the following Sunday we were taken to the Catholic church at Ipswich, and Jeremiah's gorgeous exaggeration – 'Is it nothing to you, all ye that pass by, behold if there be any sorrow like unto my sorrow?' was quoted during the sermon. I shot a triumphant glance of misery round my bereaved but fairly complacent family: Jeremiah and I, we knew. I stared particularly hard at Margaret, pettily worrying about her possible return to the home, while I was bearing up under my load of guilt so well that it actually *was* nothing to those who passed by – But Margaret did not see: however, there was subtle comfort in the quoted words, when I recalled them from time to time during the day.

All that Margaret did when the Cottrells made a fuss of her in the afternoon, when we went to our customary weekly tea with their children, was to shoot covert glances at me, and these I met stonily. This was the first occasion on which she had ever shown that she was aware of the preferential treatment she received. She took it for granted at other times: I doubt that she had really noticed it herself until then. At least I had made her conscious of her present well-being; she should have been yet more grateful to me.

We and the two Cottrell children were brought up as fast friends for the convenience of our parents, who gained by dumping us all together in one house or the other, an occasional respite from family life. It was years before we realized how much we had always disliked Marnie Cottrell, a studious little girl with adenoids and a habit of saying 'Oh, don't you know *that!*' and particularly Lester Cottrell, who talked, at thirteen, like an affable middle-aged gentleman. They were about the same age as Dru and Ronald. Trained

23

from earliest years to the highest standards of intellectual honesty, they already knew that they did not like us, and dimly realizing this, we thought it rather horrid of them, considering what close friends we were.

Talk at the Cottrells', starting on common ground, had a way of wandering off to planes beyond our reach, but especially fast when anyone threw nice, spaniel-like Mr. Cottrell a conversational bone in the form of a reference to music. As a composer, he was appreciated only in highly musical circles, his work being of the kind that people like ourselves could rarely recognize even after several hearings, because of its total lack of those useful landmarks for the uncultured — tunes. He would play to anyone on quite small provocation, and the slightest excuse was enough to set him off on discussion of the theory of music. Time after time he would pounce upon a chance-thrown remark, his mournful dog's-eyes lighting up eagerly, and drag it away to some spiritual lair where we could not possibly follow. There, worrying it excitedly, he would suddenly recollect his audience, and returning to our level with a few vague words of explanation, relapse into mortified silence.

This happened at the beginning of tea, and mother, in her kindly way, at once talked servant with Mrs. Cottrell (we shared the services of a local girl with them) to cover the abruptness with which Mr. Cottrell had relinquished the bone. Mother's kindness was a byword. No one could be more devastating in her way of making allowances. 'Such an *unfortunate* hat,' was all she could ever be induced to say of the sort of thing worn by the Cottrells' musical women friends; or, 'Perhaps rather a *distracting* accent; need he come to stay, dear?' would dispose of one of father's boon companions. As condemnation, the Cottrells' æsthetic and articulate dislike of almost everything was far less effective than mother's irrelevant charity. When mother started being indulgent towards anything one felt that there was absolutely nothing to be said in its favour. Poor Mr. Cottrell always seemed more than usually annoyed with himself after he had given tongue to enthusiasm in her presence: as though the casting of pearls became doubly embarrassing to the caster when the well-bred swine were nice about it, pretending not to notice. 'You see, Eleanor,' she said, 'when the lower classes are a bit – well – unimaginative, like Olive' (the joint maid), 'I always try to think of them as if they were animals. I suppose that sounds silly to you. But it does help. Because then instead of feeling, "Oh, *why* must Olive bring the soup in a vegetable-dish again instead of a tureen!" I feel, "Really, how clever of her to know that soup goes with a soup plate, and wants a ladle, and so on!" Just as one would, dear, if she wasn't human, don't you see?'

They saw, but we could not understand why they laughed so much, and said that if in their day England achieved the peaceful revolution for which they hoped, as good socialists, they would see to it that mother's end was the one unpeaceful incident: she was not fit to live in a decent social state. However, we were used to not seeing their jokes; and they rarely appreciated ours. Their disapproval became more puzzling when mother protested, 'But I like the lower classes, Eleanor, on the whole!' their attitude being that with her views she had no business to like anything of the kind. They seemed to take the matter seriously. That, I thought, was the worst of having tea with enlightened people; one never knew when they would suddenly become earnest and almost insulting in argument over some everyday subject, after dismissing flippantly half a dozen graver topics. They seemed merely amused, a few minutes later, by mother's attitude to the furniture which my grandfather had left her, though I felt uneasily that there was something wrong somewhere, but I could not tell where. Having no room for his things in the house, she was giving them all to the

25

Roman Catholic training college at Dovercourt. A keen convert, mother always flushed when she mentioned anything connected with religion in the Cottrell house, and became as nearly truculent as she could: they were so heavily agnostic. 'But, Phyllis, wouldn't he have hated that more than anything?' asked Mrs. Cottrell, who knew that he had never left the Church of England. 'Oh, we-ell,' said mother, looking quite lovely as she coloured up, 'he knows better now.'

I soon gave up trying to puzzle out why the Cottrells should be so delighted about that, for father was there, and it was really too jolly a tea to spoil by worrying – the pleasantest meal, in fact, since my grandfather's death. It was always lovely to be with father, and we had home-made cherry jam, as I had hoped all the afternoon that we should – Mrs. Cottrell's invariably perfect cherry jam, runny, not too sweet, with large cherries floating in it which tasted like cherries and not only like jam-fruit. Mrs. Cottrell was superbly the domesticated woman, the modern mother, the musician's intellectual wife, and an artist herself in wall-paper designing, all in one. Everything that she undertook was carried out successfully with a triumphant effortlessness which sometimes suggested, to a perverse mind, that none of it could be really worth doing if this were all there was to it.

Father, as the interesting man from everywhere, talked down to the insignificant-looking Mr. Cottrell; who as an artist of some importance in his own sphere, also talked down to father, and so both enjoyed themselves as usual, until mother inadvertently threw Mr. Cottrell another bone, in the shape of a question about the date of the Norwich Festival, where some of his work was to be performed, and he was away after it at once, wearing that endearing spaniel-like expression of reproach – 'I-know-you're-making-me-make-a-fool-of-myself-again-but-I-can't-help-it.'

For once we were to stay on to supper after father and

mother had gone home: the hilarious friends of father's bachelor days, whom he had found again in the Italian ship, were expected to turn up at our house some time during the evening. – 'Whenever you're free, just drop in. Meals at our place are movable,' father had said. Father always issued invitations like that, even when there was no reason why he should not specify the hour. Like many lavishly hospitable poor men, he was generous with other people's trouble as well as his own in entertaining all comers. The only servants we were ever able to keep for more than a month or so were those whom he fascinated as much as he fascinated his friends, but they were few. Olive, alone, stuck to us for years, but then, as mother's gentle evasion of the truth only emphasized, she was little more than half-witted. Mother did not share the keen delight he took in his own delight in odd acquaintances, and we were protestingly bustled out of the way whenever his reminiscences threatened to become really interesting, in the course of conversation with the stokers and actors and big game hunters whom he picked up in trains and clubs, and the exotic foreigners who occasionally descended on us, as souvenirs of his world-wide wanderings.

Mr. Cottrell began playing to us. I decided that I must get away before it came to my turn to choose something special, because though his trickly music was dreadfully dull to us, I thought politeness prescribed that I should ask for something of his own and, in spite of countless Sunday teas at his house, the only thing I could remember by name was what his own children called 'Air in Gurk Major' on account of its explosive ascending chords. I could not say 'Gurk' in front of grown-up people (privately we all thought that the Cottrells were awful: they talked about stomach noises and lavatories just as freely as if they were hiccoughs and bathrooms) so I went out and Margaret came too. We were free to do as we pleased in that house. Margaret, I supposed, wanted

27

to be alone with her unhappiness; I did not ask her. I told Mrs. Cottrell I wanted to catch our deck-hand, Sootie Mawley, on the way down to the water, and go out with him in the dinghy to put up the riding lights on our three bigger boats: he was teaching me to scull over the stern, in the way that fishermen do, and it was much easier to learn in a heavy smack's boat like his than in one of our light dinghies. I only explained this in order to hear Mrs. Cottrell protest that it would be bitterly cold and uninviting on the river now, adding with some amusement that she supposed it was useless to try to keep any of us away from the water from one meal to the next. This made my desire to go so Rush-sounding, and in those days I was growing uncomfortably aware of not being, inside, anything like as Rush as I should have chosen to be if I could. We spent most of our time on the Orwell because father, nominally an engineer in Ipswich, made more than half the little money we had through buying, reconditioning and selling small yachts; it was understood that we were all equally keen on sailing.

Actually what I wanted at the moment (apart from escaping my turn to choose the music) was to see if it were true, as mother had said carelessly, that the stars shone all the time, unnoticeable in the daylight, instead of springing suddenly to life at nights as I had hitherto believed, and still half believed. It was preposterous to think of their carrying on during the day. Appealed to incredulously, father had backed up mother's statement in an equally off-hand way, as though there were nothing surprising about this. Fortunately it would be easy to check by personal observation, I thought. One had only to watch the sky at dusk. If the stars appeared gradually, their theory was right, but if they lit up suddenly, as I rather feared they would, there was nothing in it. It would be appalling to find that father was wrong about anything so important. It would not have mattered so much if mother's word alone had been in question.

28

I had already passed the first of the three main stages in a child's relationship with its parents – the stage when they are automatically believed to be right – and was now labouring through the difficult middle period, when I had already caught them out once or twice, and hated the discovery of their fallibility. It was years before I finally emerged into the easier third stage, when I knew that they were both as likely to be wrong as right on almost any subject, but that this need not affect my feelings for them. Now I was really worried. Sitting in the dinghy while Sootie went aboard our yachts I stared hard at a small patch of sky, hoping for the vindication of my parents. But out of the corner of my eye I half saw stars leaping into faint light in every part of the sky, save in the chosen area over distant Harwich. When I took my eyes off it for a few seconds, to glance at them resentfully, I found, on looking back, that another star had meanly taken the opportunity to shoot into sight unobserved in the place which I should have been watching. I could almost have cried with distress, had this not been too dreadfully un-Rush; it seemed practically certain that father was wrong. Then Sootie would speak to me, asking me to pass up the paraffin can, or let out the painter because the dinghy was rubbing against the topsides, and when I looked again towards Harwich, several more stars would have come out unseen. Wings passed over us, a pulse in the night that grew and died, and stare as I would, I could not see the solitary sea-bird which flew so near that I could hear, through the beat of its flight for a second or two, the dry, soft rustling of its feathers. One never could see birds passing at night, I knew, however bright the sky, however startlingly close in one's ears sounded their mournful crying. The liquid, aching call of a curlew came now, from almost within arm's reach it seemed, and something old and half forgotten, or not yet apprehended, either painful or happy, stirred in me for a second, and my attention

29

fled back for safety to the stars. They made a fairly calm anchorage for the mind, I knew already, as long as I was making them useful in some way – forcing them to solve a troublesome problem like this doubt of father, or keeping some special one on a line between the shrouds and the forestay when steering at night, so that I did not have to stand up to look at the compass after father had set the course. They were only disturbing, I had found, in the way that a bird's call was disturbing, if I looked at them idly, as in the long hours of the night passages we did every year when we went over to Holland and back in one of the yachts. Throughout my spells at the tiller at those times (and each of us, even Margaret, was expected to take two hours of it if we were sailing all night) I was always careful to find some slightly practical job for the stars, even if it were only forming letters or odd saucepans or new-shaped beasts in the sky, knowing that then they could not get at me as they would if they caught my mind while it was empty. If they pounced on unoccupied thoughts, they could do something to them which left one feeling small and alone and strangely pressed down into the unfriendly night.

Finally, I decided with an effort of loyalty that probably some weak stars shone all day invisibly, and the others lit up suddenly in my way, but unless the subject were mentioned again I need not tell them about it at home: it would only be awkward for them after what they had said, and uncomfortable for me.

It seemed a little hard that while I was considering their feelings like this my people were not, at the moment, considering mine in a kindly way at all in return. When I landed I found that there had been an ill-natured hue and cry after me for some time. Dru gave me the details with ghoulish satisfaction when she met me on the Hard (the low causeway that ran out through the mud flats into the river). Margaret had unexpectedly been discovered crouching in the coal-cellar, the one place, she had felt, where she might safely go for a good cry. Hysterically clinging to mother she had howled something about not wanting to go back to the orphan home, and the whole story had been dragged from her. Father said that I should be spanked, Dru told me. I did not mind frightfully, and was only mildly apprehensive as I walked up to the Cottrells' house with her. Father had come over to fetch me and was waiting. I never had been spanked, but Dru and Ronald had, and relinquishing for a moment her superior position as the bearer of bad tidings, she assured me generously that it really did not hurt much.

Then I thought sadly that I had better take this opportunity of telling father about the negligent killing of my grandfather and so get it all over at once: if Margaret had not been able to keep her secret I doubted that I could keep mine much longer. The prospect of explaining this nightmare business now thoroughly frightened me. I thought of Time – the sure passing of Time was my ally now, for once. Time was bound to go on, to get me through this. Good old Time. But father grimly dismissed the grandfather affair as a red-herring of no importance when I tried to explain it, which was an enormous, startling relief to me. He said he was going to spank me for what I had done deliberately to Margaret. With a pleasantly lightened heart I pointed out that he could, of course, if he liked, but that it would be an awful waste of time for both of us.

Characteristically, father was so tickled by what seemed to me this self-evident statement that he grinned broadly: and I grinned back, and was then let off altogether.

I had a delightful evening. Having been fetched from the Cottrells' in disgrace I could not very well be sent back, so until bedtime I sat and listened to father's exciting talk with the Italians. By and by he was induced with difficulty to spin the best yarn about his wild days in Chile – the

31

one about the rebel-fellow that ended ' "Everything in my poor house," he said "is yours, señor!" And blast the swine, it was literally true too.'

I loved that one; I was always a little afraid, when father modestly laughed off demands for the tale, that he really would not tell it this time. It did not strike me till long afterwards that as he practically always obliged in the end, he required to be pressed just a little too hard.

CHAPTER II

THE BURROW

'Panem et circenses,' observed our other neighbour, Mr.
Quest, who might as well have said it in English, or better
still, said something within my comprehension, since he was
presumably talking to me: no one else was in sight when he
dropped his children at the Cottrells' door with an air of
thankful disembarrassment. 'Or as you will unfortunately
learn to say, ' "Pahnem et kir-ken-says," That's all they
think of, our respective families, isn't it? Food and entertainment. Well, they're right, no doubt, they're right.'

I said yes, I supposed so, and rapidly sidled away, suggesting that he would like to see Mr. or Mrs. Cottrell: but he
said no to this, and drove on towards the London road in
his glossy car.

Basil and Stella Quest were joining us and the Cottrells
for my birthday treat which we had all been planning for
weeks, a trip to Littlehampton in two of our boats. Eleventh
birthdays were considered important in our family: a sort of
half-way mark between nothing and twenty-one: one chose the
treat oneself. In their time Dru and Ronald, both winter
babies, had voted respectively for a pantomime in London
and an all night punt-gunning expedition with father. That
superlatively uncomfortable sport being at its best in the hardest
weather, Ronald's choice had been much admired by us all.
Secretly yearning for another pantomime I was sorry that my
birthday fell at the end of May, for this impelled me to do
the Rush thing too and ask for a sailing trip. It was the time
of the year I most enjoyed at Pin Mill because the bird tides

33

had just set in, and I could go nesting along the shore with Ted, Sootie Mawley's son and my great friend; but father's approval was everything, and so I had dutifully worked myself into a state of excitement about my chosen treat.

Basil and Stella edged past the pile of old sandshoes and goloshes which I had been turning over on the Cottrells' doorstep, and sat docilely on their little suit-cases in the hall. Mr. Quest had been told to bring them to the Cottrells' house at ten if he wanted them to come with us: he always seemed glad to be rid of this stolid pair; but, even so, it was now nearly eleven. And yet the Cottrells were nothing like ready, to father's annoyance. Mr. Quest, the wealthiest man in the neighbourhood, never asked any of us to his house (a slight for which we were really thankful, finding him a terrifying person) but he traded on the good nature of both families by sending his own children to join us whenever, by the defection of servants or tutors, he would otherwise have had to endure their company, which he disliked. In comparison with the bumptiously clever Cottrells, Stella and Basil Quest, in their decorous dullness, seemed more attractive than they really were, so that we did not mind: at least we had all the local lowbrow interests in common with them. 'Mental squalor' was the description grandly given by Lester Cottrell to our conversation about boats and village happenings: it was one of his parents' favourite expressions.

A promising clinking and thumps of packing still came from the kitchen, where the leisurely Mrs. Cottrell was putting up boat provisions: mother was helping with occasional exhortations to hurry. The Rushes were habitually a little before time and the Cottrells unpunctual, and as both knew the other's peculiarity, neither family's protests ever had any effect on what Mr. Cottrell called 'our relative tempo'.

'What's panem and that got to do with Littlehampton?'
I asked, returning to my job of trying to find a left-foot
golosh in the pile that I had dragged out of a dark cupboard
under the stairs. The Cottrells' house was nearer the Hard
than ours, and we often threw our sailing things in here
when we stopped to see them on the way home. A fine
assortment of worn-out shoes belonging to both families
had accumulated with years.

'Oh, that's just something that father says,' Stella told
me in an indulgent voice, by way of full explanation.

'Father says,' she began again in a moment. She had
gathered that he was a highly intellectual person and, as
such, someone to show off about; but the purport of the
remarks she repeated, out of a perfect parrot-memory for
phrases, she rarely seemed to understand in full. Probably
she never realized how passionately bored her peculiar
father became if he had to endure her society: probably,
too, he never knew how much she retained of the remarks
which he let fall in these moments of desperation. 'Father
says it's time we went to boarding school. Both of us.
Next term. He says the best nurses – and of course we
always had awfully good ones – he says they always act on the
principle that you shouldn't put ideas into children's heads,
and now public schools must carry on their work. Isn't he
funny?' I agreed that he was, very funny; and felt glad, in
spite of his eminence as a specialist in educational psychology
(whatever that was) and his lovely garden, and the amount
of money spent carelessly on Basil and Stella (' "From
intellectual remorse", he says') that he was not my father.

There did not seem to be a whole pair of my goloshes in
the pile, and a minor tragedy threatened. Father always
went sailing in goloshes, disliking the clamminess of sea
boots; also, I suspect, he fancied the idea of himself as a
hard-bitten adventurer wearing such old-lady-like things.
His troupe copied him as closely as possible, and if I could only

35

find a second odd left foot it would do. As long as I need not go home to fetch another pair I should just have time before we went on board to race over to Sootie Mawley's cottage and get Ted to show me the doe's burrow he had found in the bank behind the Butt & Oyster inn. Because a long-planned day had arrived, and we were really starting quite soon, it had become suddenly urgent that I should see the nest, an essential touch of perfection to add to this rich day. Ted had come up to our house late the previous evening to tell me exactly where it was, but look as I would before breakfast I had not been able to find it; the mother rabbit was hiding it from sharper and more dangerous eyes than mine — those of her mate.

Anxiously I asked Mr. Cottrell, who ran errands for everyone, whether he had seen any more of our goloshes, but he was busy unstrapping packed suit-cases to put in the unnecessary oddments which Marnie kept producing, and replied absently that he had not seen any of our shoes. His house was at the moment so full of Rushes and their kit, and Cottrell preparations, and the Quests and their gear, unobtrusive as they were, that I supposed it was possible for a short-sighted adult to overlook the rash of shoes that was spreading round his doorstep. I was now half in the cupboard, getting down to the last stratum of tattered bits which had not been disturbed for years. Anyway, if he had not yet noticed these it was hopeless to expect him to find more, I thought, and searched more frantically.

Father strolled through the house at intervals, observing with marked calm that it was out of the question to take more than half this luggage – however long did Marnie think we were going for? or else that Ronald, whom he proposed to roast slowly over the Primus, had apparently taken all our South Coast charts ashore and mislaid them. After Ramsgate, said father, he would not be responsible for the lives of the party. And if we did not get a move on in twenty minutes we should have lost the best part of this tide, and might as well put off starting till the next day. This was really unthinkable to me, when the great 29th of May had actually come: surely Time would not allow us to play about with it like that? To-morrow might never arrive.

The Cottrells, most devoted of parents, became uneasy when they heard of the loss of the charts, which father knew by heart in any case. They asked him unseaworthy questions, and Mrs. Cottrell held up her preparations to lounge against the kitchen door and argue in her slow and for once infuriating drawl that we ought to borrow some from other sailing people in the village.

But on this occasion I was glad of the way the Cottrells frittered away the minutes, understanding nothing of tides – One golosh of father's – a torn left one of mine – Ronald's – Dru's – Ronald's – Margaret's – And they had to be the right fit or they would not keep on over sandshoes – 'Oh, please, Mother of God, let me find the other one in time!' 'Father's – MINE – no, *Mother of God*, mine, but with a split in it down the heel, so that it would not hold. Like a dog digging a hole I was now throwing out behind me the last things in the cupboard. Somewhere in the New Testament it said that if you owned Christ before men, He would own you (and presumably answer your prayers, then). And of course, owning His Mother was owning Him. So if you prayed aloud you would be more likely to get what you wanted, because it took courage to do that in the daytime, away from church. Especially in front of ardent unbelievers like the Cottrells. But Mr. Cottrell appeared suitably distrait, at the other end of the hall, tapping the barometer; he was not coming on the trip himself and was disturbed about the charts. He would make a nice inattentive audience. 'Oh, Mother of God, do let me find it,' I implored, just audibly enough for the prayer to be considered 'aloud', I hoped, by the heavenly powers, but sufficiently under my

37

breath for the words to have some chance of not reaching Mr. Cottrell.

Even this had no result. Time, waiting inexorably in the past, where it had accumulated so long that it made me almost giddy to think of it, was stretching out greedily to snatch away from me the precious seconds of the present in which I must find a golosh if I were to see the burrow. Ted had told me that the male rabbit shows his resentment of the young ones which occupy the doe's attention by killing them if possible, so that when she leaves the secret breeding place to which she steals at night to suckle them, she must build afresh an elaborate shield of cut grass and leaves over the entrance. I felt that life would be more or less wasted if I did not see that door to-day.

Dru and Margaret, equally excited – or at least Dru was – dropped on their knees behind me to sort out their goloshes, and anything being catching when we were in such a state, they began chanting, 'Oh, Mother of God!' after me, but not in my circumspect tone. Mother came out of the kitchen. 'Dru! – Margaret!' She was gently disapproving. They were not to say that. (She had not heard me.) 'Mother of God!' repeated Dru stubbornly, worked up to rebellion in a second because excitement had reached the fermenting stage. She and mother stared at one another stormily. Between them already ran a tiny current of ill-feeling: it came to the surface unexpectedly at times, through the affection which they showed one another more freely than was usual among us.

'Say that again and you stay at home!'

I scrambled back from the cupboard. Everything was going to be ruined, the lovely day and the whole trip, and even the idea of the burrow: I was sure the words would come, knowing Dru. But Margaret happened to speak first, 'Well, *I* shall say, "Oh, Hoogie!" instead,' she remarked negligently, turning over the pile to find her property. 'I can call her anything, and she'll know who I mean.' Just the same as saying "Mother of God" . . . Oh, *Hoogie*! Here's one of mine. Oh, Hoogie, where's the other? Here's yours, Lallie, chucked behind the umbrellas. No one can stop that, because if they do I shall just call her something else. She'll still know.'

Mother looked at her, perplexed and angry, and hesitated. Mr. Cottrell said something admiring to mother in French about it. '*You'd* never have thought of that,' said Margaret with faint contempt to Dru, and wandered off with her goloshes in her hand: but the remark might equally well have been meant for mother. There was no air of triumph in her bearing, as there would have been in Dru's or mine if we had carried off the situation like that. But then, neither of us could have done it. Yet Margaret was the one person whose trip would not have been spoilt by Dru's absence. It was by a chance intervention, and the way she had with her, that she had saved the pleasure of the day for the rest of us, particularly for father, who would have been really upset if his favourite daughter had been left behind. Margaret's insolence, kindness, or unkindness at all times appeared so impersonal that it was hard to say how far she was conscious of being insolent, kind or unkind.

'Give you five minutes more, that's all,' said father, strolling through the hall again, and speaking as though the occasion were a trivial one.

'*We're* ready,' said one of the Quests smugly.

'Mummy, did you put in my straw hat?' came Marnie's adenoidal whine from upstairs. 'Oh, mummy, you always say yes. Sure you did? Mum*mee*!'

'Come on, Marnie, you won't be able to wear it anyhow,' shouted Ronald. 'Glass is rising with a north wind; that means more wind.' (This with a mixed imitation of father's sailing omniscience and exaggerated sang-froid in moments of stress.) 'It'll only blow overboard.'

'But, mummy, *which* did you put it in?' The shrill little voice rose to a wail.

'What a flap,' observed Lester Cottrell distastefully to the Quests, his tone dissociating him from any part in this panic of departure. He was also copying father, by whom he always seemed to be strangely fascinated: there could not have been two more dissimilar characters. Lester at thirteen already had a nice sense of words; the use of this piece of sailing slang for a shore scurry was extremely apt. Any small boat mishap, such as running aground, getting 'in irons', or breaking a halyard, is likely to be accompanied by a flogging of canvas: and 'a flap' embraces all these troubles. It was the only nautical term that Lester knew: his progress, on the one or two occasions when we had shamed him into sailing one of our dinghies, had been from flap to flap.

After one languid effort to close his bulging attaché case, he handed the thing to Stella Quest, who was only a month older but motherly by nature, in order that she might wrestle with the clasps for him. Father gave him one glance, and he hurriedly took it back, knelt on it and closed it himself.

Mrs. Cottrell emerged from the kitchen laden with the last batch of pies. Lovely smells wafted from them through the hall. She insisted on showing them for mother's admiration before closing the hamper. Mrs. Cottrell could not be hurried, and was used to disregarding father's ultimatums. With passionate hate I had just finished the job of rounding-up and flinging back into the cupboard the scattered collection of Cottrell shoes and Rush oddments, and was now wrestling with my own attaché case. Bless Margaret for my golosh. The burrow!

'Lovely, Eleanor. Get the boys to take them on board. Arthur says we must *go*, dear.' Between father and Mrs. Cottrell, mother was growing distracted. 'Yes, yes, I'm sure that'll be delicious too. What a wonderful cook you are. Do get your things. We've lost so much tide already.'

'Oh, well,' said Mrs. Cottrell, ambling upstairs, 'you know I always say, damn the sort of undomesticated woman who marries an improvident musician and stays too refined to make a job of it!' It was indeed a favourite theme of hers. She elaborated it with a sentence or two as she went, and even mother looked as if she would like to scream.

'Oh, Lallie,' she said as an afterthought when I was about to slip off unobtrusively, 'Race home, darling, and get a pair of father's goloshes while Mrs. Cottrell's dressing. They're in the sea-chest in his room. You'll have to run all the way, I'm afraid.'

'Oh, Hoogie, Hoogie, Hoogie!' I muttered vindictively as I tore up the road and back, struggling with a hot feeling round my eyes. I did not see the doe's nest in the end, for when we came back from Littlehampton only an ordinary burrow remained; – no wonderful grass door, and no young ones.

CHAPTER III

THE TREAT

As things turned out I might just as well have stopped to see Ted Mawley's find, for contrary to Ronald's knowingness the breeze puffed itself out as the tide slackened. A calm had fallen by the time that we and some of the food had been sorted out on board the *Guadalupe* and *Wanderer*, and father had finally convinced Mrs. Cottrell that quite a number of her bulkier packages must be left behind if we were to have sitting room in the cabins. Very little fair tide remained, and catspaws of air, from varying points of the compass, barely wrinkled the pale surface of the Orwell to a lively, swift-fading blue. Father decided to wait and see in which quarter the wind would settle before letting go of the moorings.

I could not go ashore again because I could not convey to anyone the importance of the burrow, now that the treat might start at any minute if one of these light airs held: it did not occur to me to try. Even if, by some chance, I had made my desire understood by betraying something – one always betrayed something, I felt, when one told older people about anything that mattered – I should have lost the burrow, for some of them would have insisted on coming ashore to see it too. Not Mrs. Cottrell, of course; she was so sensitive towards children's feelings, and so careful to refrain from violating their mental privacy, that one was more conscious of her non-invasion than of my happy-go-lucky parents' occasional trespass. Mrs. Cottrell would have said, with intolerable comprehension, 'No, dear, I'll see it another time, if you'll show me. It must be your very own. You go . . . alone.' And then the burrow would have been simply stuffed with her, for ever. It was at least more my doe's nest if I kept quiet about it, even though I might never see it, than if anyone but Ted saw it with me.

Father busied himself in getting both boats in condition to start at a moment's notice, or as much in condition as our boats could be. They were used all the year round, for he was always buying and selling small craft, and as he could never spare the time or the money to give them a proper fit-out they were in a chronic state of overhaul. At the moment, *Wanderer's* mizen mast was badly sprung and some child was constantly being shouted at not to lean against it or the shrouds; and the *Guadalupe's* topmast backstays wanted replacing.

She was a new racing cruiser which made everyone less water-innocent than the Cottrells gasp at the huge spread of canvas carried on so slim a hull. Father had arranged that the Cottrell children were to travel aboard her, knowing that their mother (in the safe old *Wanderer*) would not be able to judge beforehand from *Guadalupe's* lines what sort of performance this boat could put up in a sea. We had been warned to say nothing to the Cottrells of the terri-fying liveliness of our latest acquisition. As a friend of the family father was always eager to do the pampered Cottrell children good against their parents' will.

I was in *Wanderer*. Her sails flapped, and filling the inter-vals between the grunts of the boom, as it swung over lazily, the reef points kept up a quick, light pattering on the canvas. Most sailing people loathe that sound, connecting it in memory with hours of helpless rolling, becalmed in Channel or north sea swells: but we made a point of liking it, being proud of our hard-won detachment from our stomachs. 'Lord, yes,' father would say to anyone who inquired about any of our worse passages, 'all my troupe were sick as dogs. Doesn't affect them, though. Get used to it, you know.

43

They carry on all right.' And we glowed. Dru positively gloried in cutting to the minimum the necessary pause in her work. As the eldest of us she had had even more experience, and a well-timed turn of her head was all that was now required. I envied her; this was so awfully Rush. I think she enjoyed seasickness as a means of earning father's commendation.

It just crossed my mind to be thankful that here, six miles up the river, we had no swell to contend with, only scorching sun reflected back into our eyes from the smooth, heavy looking water. Except by going below, where it was unbearably stuffy, there was no way of keeping in the shade while the slack sails shifted continually. It is practically always unpleasantly hot in a small boat, on the very rare occasions when it is not uncomfortably cold in the wind from which, like the sun, there is no chance of shelter on deck. Shocked by my own thoughts, I wrenched my mind away from this disloyal reflection on our beloved hobby.

'Oh, Mum*mee!* You haven't put in my blue dress! And I'm too *hot* in this one. I *told* you. . . .' Marnie's voice carried across from the *Guadalupe*.

'. . . But Eleanor, butter is *always* kept in that tin, dipped in sea water occasionally to cool it. . . .'

'It won't, dear. . . . Air and water the same temperature . . . may feel cooler . . . go rancid just as easily . . . bacterial action . . . water. . . .'

'. . . Not *sea* water, Eleanor. . . . Always *has* been kept in that tin. . . .' Like father and Mr. Cottrell, mother and Mrs. Cottrell were inclined to talk down to each other, whenever they disagreed on some point like this, on which each had some reason to feel superior. The Cottrells were scientifically well-informed, as well as artistic, but then mother was a Rush, and as such surely entitled to speak with authority of the benign qualities of the local ocean.

'. . . So I happened to be in that part of Chile when he

44

brought off the raid – Gosh, what a chap he was!' (In his modest recitals father always 'happened' to be in just those places where the revolution, earthquake, epidemic, or other interruption of humdrum life also 'happened' to take place at the same time. It was not until you knew him well that you realized that if Arthur Rush were anywhere within reach of the locality, there was about as much chance in this coincidence as in the 'happening' together of iron and magnet.) 'And the trouble from the first with the punitive expedition we organized – What, Basil? Well, yes, as a matter of fact I was. There didn't happen to be anyone else to take command. – The trouble was that it wasn't clear which side was getting the punishment. – My men got sunstroke in the plains and frost-bite as soon as we got into the mountains, and day after day we never saw the fellows we were after, but they got away with some of our equipment every few hours. – Margaret! let go of that mizen stay: how many more times – ?' The Quest children had never heard the bandit story, though they had asked for it often enough, and I could not hear it too often. They were lucky to-day: one could not generally prise it out of father so soon after a re-telling.

Still, when it was over, time stretched out again rather boringly just when it was not wanted. Excellent time, minutes that I should soon wish, in vain, to slip into some other situation to prolong it, now crawled by unfilled, and I could not do anything about it. Consolingly, three shelduck alighted on the water between us and the shore, planing down over our heads at the extraordinary landing-speed of these birds. Simultaneously, as they whistled by in line, the scarlet legs withdrew from the belly-feathers that had covered all but the curled toes, and stuck out stiffly in front of the hurtling bodies. The birds might have been drilling by numbers, so exactly together were their movements: it always seemed to be a matter of pride with them in this, the mating season, to slacken speed as little as they dared until the last second. Fascinated, I used to watch these showy creatures by the hour as they took off or landed on the water. Now, at the same instant, all the brilliant webbed toes turned upwards and opened widely, to go skithering over the water as the birds braked suddenly, with vertical wings. Even so, the impact of the tough little bodies sent up, as one, three small fountains of spray. Two drakes were courting a female. They settled down close to the *Guadalupe*, wagging their tails and muttering discontentedly as though the rivals were criticizing one another's performance in taking the water. Having had the biological wisdom to develop a flavour like stewed sawdust, which no method of cooking can disguise, this handsome black, white, and orange bird increases yearly on the east coast, where the dull but edible teal and widgeon are dwindling in numbers.

Those three shelduck, with the heron that had drifted delicately from one clump of trees to another on the edge of the marsh the year before, still fly through my memory of those days, with the troubling graciousness of a child's sense of some new quality in familiar things – still cut, in a grey and in a cloudless sky, wider than any skies seem nowadays, the lovely lines along which I hold them transfixed in movement – still may be recalled in clearer detail than the people or the circumstances in which, at the time, I was really more engrossed.

They swam away with a curved arrowhead of ripple spreading out further and further from each breast across the still water, while on the other side of us the surface of the river darkened all at once, and crumpled before a puff of wind from the south-east. The boom swung over again, less lazily, and the reef points stopped tapping.

'Going to hold! Get under way, Ronald,' shouted father to the other boat and went below to start up our auxiliary engine, in order to keep pace with the faster *Guadalupe* under sail alone.

The venerable marine motor, which only father could coax into action, gave what sounded like a series of apologetic coughs and expired with a smothered hiccough. Afterwards it would only hiccough. Then it refused to do that. Father put his head out of the hatch to say, 'Battery's shorted. Damn!' his eyes shining with pleasure. He settled down to the most congenial occupation possible for him as a professional engineer on holiday, tinkering an engine that he was not paid to run. 'Cast off, someone. Lallie, it's your trip, you steer.'

The light breeze hardened. We tacked in the wake of the *Guadalupe*. Instantly time began to tear along, much too fast, because I had just discovered, with a burning curiosity to know why, that there was something delightful about those curving arrowheads of ripple which the wind was rapidly confusing with many others, of uninteresting shape. They mattered in the same incomprehensible way in which a heron's flight had lately begun to matter, and something about Margaret had always mattered, or for as long as I could remember.

I looked at her: she, too, was glancing back, watching the swimming shelduck creasing the water with little forward surges of their puffy breasts, but what she thought about anything I could rarely guess or ask. With a child's anxiety to get everything clear and settled I wondered whether the spreading ripples could have been quite so . . . whatever they were, exciting or touching, but anyway important – if they had not been shaped to those curves but had been only triangular ridges in the water.

'Move, Lallie! I can't get at the sheet. Whatever are you looking at, dear?' Mother asked as I craned my neck round desperately for a second while *Wanderer* gathered way, trying to see the last of the ripples before the wind obliterated

47

them. For the moment I had forgotten the dangerous presence of older people. Returning my attention to the course, I felt myself turning scarlet, because I had been surprised doing something much more seriously private than the things that no one was supposed to see you doing. I was deciding hurriedly that it would probably have mattered just about as much, but in a different way. Time, gathering itself indolently all the morning, had now leapt forward and grabbed the only thing I wanted at the moment.

'Nothing,' I said, turning to give one more glance astern; but trying, too late, to give the glance a casual appearance. It was annoying to have to decide, at random, and in a hurry like this, a problem which I felt was really important.

'Now, Lallie, what is it?' said mother, smiling and Olympian, and positively hateful for the moment.

I knew that the treacherous crimson was spreading round my ears. Oh, Hoogie, *Hoogie*, don't let anyone find out, and laugh! One must not pray to the Holy Virgin against mother, but Hoogie would not matter, and Hoogie would understand.

'What a long way ahead *Guadalupe* is getting!' said Mrs. Cottrell with sudden forced brightness. Intuitively she was trying to trail a red herring for me, I knew, because my face had already given me away. 'Why is she faster than this boat when this boat is so much bigger, Phyllis?'

Evidence of her care never to force the confidence of a child always had the effect of making my thoughts feel miserably naked before her imagination. Echoes from other occasions when Mrs. Cottrell had tiptoed away from the holy ground of my immature mind still rang loudly in my memory. If possible, I grew hotter, resenting her intrusive sympathy more than mother's curiosity.

'Racier build – larger sail area for her size, Eleanor. – Come on Lallie, out with the big secret!'

Why did grown women make such a kindly fuss when one

came in with a skinned knuckle, and then do this sort of thing lightly at other times? What made them resent instinctively the mystery and excitement of this vague something in the mind – the something that the ripple or a flying heron called into being? They tried to prevent one from discovering about it by laughing, or being too understanding, or asking one to run on an errand for them and not waste time, whenever one was getting tinglingly close to it. In their dull kingdom of food and clothes and talk they felt shut out of it, and women more than men did not like to feel that about anything, I knew already. Women were afraid of this unknown spirit, which called through quite ordinary voices, like curlews' over the water at night: it was the thing that took men such as father away from them into wild corners of the world, and could take even children like me out of their reach for a while, though they could bring us back and hurt us for going. Perhaps they half-knew that one day they would not be able to recall us at will.

'Oh, well, then, to balance that, I suppose she draws more water than we do?' (Mrs. Cottrell surreptitiously squeezed my shoulder to show me that I had an ally.)

'Yes, Eleanor; you're getting quite intelligent about sailing! – You know, this queer kid gets the oddest notions in her head –' (Mrs. Cottrell frowned reprovingly at mother for me. Curse her, oh curse her! But mother did not notice.) 'What on earth has she got hold of now? Be a sport and tell a pal, Lallie?'

I thought that in a moment I should have to be rude; often one's only resource in childhood. It would cause a rotten sort of distraction, but at least they would not then get at the ripples, which Mrs. Cottrell had now turned into something about which I was somehow ashamed, instead of just something that I wanted to keep to myself.

'Birds,' said Margaret, turning her indifferent glance from

49

the far-off duck to me, and my heart stood still with fear. 'Lallie doesn't want people to know she's mad about them. She'd like to cry now because those three ducks came down on the water when we were on the mooring and she can't watch them. Thinks they're wonderful. Just shelduck! And herons. Thinks they're all hers!'

Margaret laughed, and mother, too, of course, and asked more questions, and Mrs. Cottrell deliberately asked none, and my whole secret world crashed about me, along with the ruins of that day's hoped-for enjoyment. They made me sound a fool in the hearing of father, whom I loved better than anyone else, and because I was eleven years old that was almost intolerable, but after a time, between them all they somehow made the birds seem silly, too, and that was much worse.

It is hard to guess what sense reveals to people like Margaret things far beyond the compass of their understanding. I had never told her anything that went on in my mind, because she never told me anything. This was the first occasion, as far as I remember, on which she spoilt for me something that I greatly valued, not from malice, but through her own indifference to such things. She was superbly armoured against revenge, caring for no one and nothing herself.

Robust humour was a speciality in our family, and being laughed at was considered a tonic automatically wholesome for anyone at any time, with the exception of God, Who alone was not supposed to be improved by having His corners rubbed off (mother's favourite expression) with this strong mental abrasive: the Old Testament contained too many records of His inability to take a joke in good part; but save on sacred subjects one was always safe in being funny with a Rush; it was part of the home-made tradition.

'Look, Lallie, there's a kittiwake gull – are you going all goosey over it? Why don't you write it a little poem?'

50

And because the day was done for anyway, so that now it wasn't worth while being rude and standing all the fuss that would follow, I grinned and played up to them as the quickest way of getting this wretchedness over.

'It *is* a kittiwake, isn't it? – Of course, you know them all on the wing, don't you?'

Angrily I grinned harder and told them I only knew the ordinary birds, and anyway it was a black-cap, not a kittiwake. Out of the wreck of my joy in birds, which could never be quite the same again now that people knew of it, I saved just this one species, saved it even from Mrs. Cottrell. They could go on being funny or sympathetic if they liked about the kittiwake; I had crept into a small unhappy security inside my own mind, from which I would with less effort smile out on their ignorance that it was a white tern, one of the exquisite little diving birds which fishermen call sea-swallows. But now they could not get at it and make it look as stupid as they could me, for the bird they spoilt with their nonsense did not exist. As if any kittiwake ever bounced off the water in that entrancing way when it dived!

'Well, I'm afraid I'm not much interested in birds,' said Mrs. Cottrell with dogged protectiveness. 'I must say, Phyllis, *Guadalupe* looks a much more dangerous support for my entire offspring now that she's going along leaning over on her side' – very properly mother shot her a horrified look at this description of our finest boat listing in a good breeze – 'than she did at anchor. I suppose she is quite sound, isn't she?'

' "Anchor" – Oh, my God!' Father from below suddenly leapt up into the cockpit. 'Does Ronald know that the new cable's in two parts? – I forgot to shackle it. There's only about six fathoms of loose chain on *Guadalupe*'s anchor. My best, too! The stockless one, Phyl! Does Sootie know? Pull yourselves together, people, and think!'

None of us, of course, had any idea. Father bounded forward and hallooed from the bows after the other boat, but *Guadalupe* was now about half a mile ahead, dead to windward. No one on board could hear. Seeing him shouting, they hallooed back cheerily. The breeze had been hardening all the time; we were both cutting through a jabble of rising sea at a fair speed, but they were much faster than we were without the engine. Mrs. Cottrell, the adoring mother, was probably the only person in Pin Mill who did not know that all the fishermen, uncertain of the pronunciation of the new boat's real name, called her the Gawdelpus because she was much too lean and tender to stand safely the length of mast and the sail area which father had given her.

'Arthur, what will happen? – I don't quite understand – I mean, it doesn't matter, does it?' Mrs. Cottrell was alarmed – 'I mean, the children . . .'

'Eleanor, don't be an ass,' said father in the heat of the moment, dancing grotesquely on deck to attract the attention of the other boat. 'Does it matter? When they bring up they'll chuck the thing over and just stand watching the damn chain run out, and then tinkle-tinkle, splash-splash, good-bye my anchor! And six fathoms of chain.'

'Yes, but it won't – They'll be all right, won't they? If the boat – er – drags, in this wind. . . .?'

'It won't "drag",' said father impatiently, continuing to dance about. 'There won't be an anchor to drag! No kedge on board. They'll probably run her aground in the flap, though. But anyway, it's not the children who'll go overboard. Only the anchor, damn it. Children float.'

Ronald, very pleased with himself for being left in charge of a party with Sootie, got up on deck and danced back, and Marnie, Lester, and Dru performed gnomelike actions in support. They held on. Passing ahead of us, a puff of wind with extra weight in it laid *Guadalupe* over till the lee rail was awash: it took nothing of a breeze to do that. She drew still further away from us.

'Blast! We'll have to chase them. Phyl, get out the topsail.'

'Arthur, you can't chase Gawdelpus in this boat!' mother protested. Catching the nickname that we had kept from her, Mrs. Cottrell asked several questions which no one had time to answer soothingly.

The sail went up in record time. With our increased speed we just held them, but Ronald, thinking that father was making a sporting effort to race him, replied with his big reaching foresail as *Guadalupe* rounded an elbow in the river and the wind came freer. She drew away again; but the wind was gathering weight every minute. It was now stiff enough to be perfect for us and a little too much for the lighter craft. If it hardened any more we might catch her yet, for with that absurd length of mast she would have to heave-to and reef. We chased her hopefully past Bloody Point, through Harwich harbour, and out to the Naze and the open sea, where the wind blowing against the tide was already kicking up short steep waves.

Everyone badly needed a meal by now, but all the cooked food that had not been condemned as surplus by father had been stowed on board *Guadalupe*, and with *Wanderer* as lively as she was at the moment it was asking too much of anyone's stomach to expect primus cookery down below. Father, to whom food never meant much, was not going to sacrifice his anchor to a meal by heaving-to for a while. Once out of the harbour he took the tiller and gave a marvellous display of boat handling, cutting in over the tricky under-water sandbanks that lay shorewards in a way that Ronald and even Sootie dared not do, saving yards here and cheating a current there, taking advantage of every favourable shoot of tide, keeping me or Margaret sounding all the time, and getting the ponderous, long-keeled *Wanderer* round on the other tack with almost the ardour of a racing boat whenever either of us sang out that the bottom was shelving up again to within a foot or so of our keel.

53

'I really think you'd better give up the anchor, dear,' said mother, who was nearly always right and after sixteen years with father had not yet learnt to refrain from advising him at such times. She was envisaging the boat piled up and holed on the chalk-humps with which the sands hereabout are strewn.

We were level with *Guadalupe* but about a mile inshore of her when Ronald, furious at being overhauled by the old *Wanderer*, ran up his flying jib in spite of knowing the dubious condition of the topmast backstays – and undoubtedly in spite of Sootie's protests. Now *Guadalupe's* hull was only visible at intervals because of the pother she made, driven like that through steep water, and she took the lead again. The seas were not yet vicious, but we were all drenched through on board the stout *Wanderer*: it was easy to see that Mrs. Cottrell, growing greener and greener and trying not to gasp when sheets of spray came over, was imagining without difficulty exactly what her children must be suffering in a boat shipping solid water at every plunge.

We held on, using all our resources for speed, but catching up with *Guadalupe* was now no longer father's prime concern. We must be at hand in case of an accident. His silence about Ronald's extraordinary foolhardiness was more eloquent than anything the rest of us said of the grave risk to their masthead. A broken mast, which Ronald was courting, was a really expensive item.

'Arthur, I know I'm being ridiculously maternal,' said Mrs. Cottrell apologetically, 'but it is dangerous, isn't it, when a boat gets dismasted?'

'Oh, only with bad luck,' said father, who could never take seriously the Cottrells' fear of the water. 'One of the big racers lost a hand that way this year, and a French boat – one of the 12-metres – she lost two. But quite often a falling mast doesn't kill anybody. Believe me, I'm with you at the moment in your hope that if either of our sons cop it, it'll be mine, not yours.'

'Arthur, I really don't think . . .' mother began, and then, in her quietest tone, 'Oh, look, what a pity!'

Through the smother of spray round *Guadalupe* we saw a billow of flapping canvas, and the top of the mainsail sagging over into a tangle of broken gear.

'*What* a pity,' said mother again gently. 'How silly of Ronald.'

Even after this we could not get near enough to shout a warning to them about the anchor. *Guadalupe's* mainsail, being a Bermudan, would not come down with the top of the mast broken, and holding almost as much wind as before, continued to drive her faster than *Wanderer*, with Sootie and Ronald doing their best to lash up the hanging masthead and the flapping head of the sail. Clearly they were making for the shelter of the Colne off Brightlingsea. The position at last warranted Mrs. Cottrell's anxiety, for the wind now came in strong squalls and *Guadalupe* was burdened with a heavy press of canvas that could not be lightened. *Wanderer*, too, ought to have shortened sail, but father still held on in case of further trouble aboard the other boat.

Cold, frightfully hungry, and feeling increasingly queasy in consequence, we chased them all the way – a four-hour passage – and watched their mainsail split right across, as father expected, in the troublesome patch of water which seethes round the Bar buoy in the Colne estuary.

Instead of sailing on into the harbour, they brought up, again exactly as father feared, as soon as they were under the shelter of East Mersea shore. Had they gone on into Brightlingsea there was a chance of their picking up a mooring, and so saving the anchor for which we had worked so hard. But when we were still about a quarter of a mile behind them they rounded up nicely into the wind and, in spite of

55

our despairing howls, threw the anchor over and idly stood by watching the first few fathoms of cable run out through the fairlead. At the sight of the loose end of the chain, Dru flung herself gallantly down on it, and was dragged half over the bow, losing bits of skin on the way. Ronald gripped her legs and they hung on grimly, and then, as the remnants of the mainsail could not be brought down in a hurry, though Sootie made a heroic attempt, the torn canvas filled with wind, the *Guadalupe* bowed her broken mast towards us ironically and began to sail herself. The chain was dragged out of their hands, to disappear under water. We anchored at once. They got the boat under control as quickly as the ill-balanced canvas allowed, missed going ashore by what must have been inches, and sailed back towards us. Having seen the figure of her son leaning negligently against the mast throughout the anchoring flap, while Marnie sat in the well and waved to us with equal calm, the relieved Mrs. Cottrell went down below and was sick, before grappling splendidly with the primus stoves to get us all some food.

We on deck made ready to hand over to *Guadalupe* our spare anchor and warp. To do this we needed their dinghy; ours had been left behind to save its drag on *Wanderer's* speed. *Guadalupe* manœuvred to slide by *Wanderer's* stern so that the dinghy tow-rope could be passed to us.

'Way enough! Way ENOUGH, you fools!' shouted father as they tacked up to us, in spite of knowing that one should never interfere with the management of another boat. But the loss of the anchor had disturbed father's confidence in both Ronald and Sootie, and they seemed to be shooting up to us too hard. The dejected Ronald at the tiller looked startled by the command, and Sootie, in the bow, even more so: the boat turned further into the wind, losing all steerage way abreast of us. Then, suddenly, *Guadalupe's* foresail filled, bringing her bow swinging towards us. Nothing that Ronald could do now would turn her back; the tattered mainsail was no match for the foresail and she bore down relentlessly upon *Wanderer*. – 'Enough, ENOUGH!' shouted father again, futilely, as Sootie made frantic efforts to let go the foresail halyard. *Guadalupe's* bowsprit came across us between our shrouds and mast. There was a rending noise as our chain-plates on that side buckled and tore out, and a horrible cracking of the rail of one or both boats as they ground together, fairly ravening for each other's tender topsides.

'What – the hell – think you were doing – Sootie?' father gasped between enormous exertions to part the boats.

'What – you say – "luff" – for, sir?' Sootie gasped reproachfully.

' "Enough" not "luff" – you fool!'

'Yessir.'

'You – didn't!' panted Ronald.

'*I* wondered what you said "luff" for, Daddy,' Margaret remarked dreamily as she stood beside him, taking no part in the mix-up.

'Oh, my God,' said father with an air of wild resignation, letting up the strain he was keeping on the encroaching bowsprit. 'If everyone's gone mad in this boat as well . . . !' He lit a cigarette and sauntered below to help Mrs. Cottrell, a little comforted, no doubt, by the knowledge that no other sailing man in the world could leave the scene of a marine accident like that. The rest of us spent many hours clearing up the wreckage.

'Clean, wholesome fare,' remarked Lester Cottrell, apropos of nothing, half way through the meal which followed. The *Wanderer*, where we had all gathered to eat because *Guadalupe* was dancing around her anchor in the swell, rolled ponderously from side to side, occasionally throwing in a slight pitch. He gazed distastefully at the marvels of food which his mother had produced. 'Excuse me a moment, Mrs. Rush' (Lester's manners were always faultless). He

57

disappeared on deck. Stella Quest was ill in sympathy shortly afterwards, but refused to turn in to her bunk as mother suggested, because of her self-imposed task of helping to look after 'the little ones', as she maddeningly called Margaret and me. All the older people were very hearty, however, during the meal, and throughout the two days we were forced to spend in Brightlingsea, patching up the boats. We dredged at intervals with a grapnel for the anchor and chain, but failed to recover them; and they said it was all great fun, so I obediently supposed it was. Only Lester and Marnie were immune from that kind of suggestion: assured almost sharply by mother that any child must enjoy a lovely exciting sail, Lester said plaintively, 'Yes, but Marnie and I aren't really adapted to childhood,' which earned him another peculiar look from father.

CHAPTER IV

AFTER THE TREAT

FATHER inevitably became very matey indeed with the carpenter who came on board to re-build *Guadalupe's* rail. Looking back, it occurs to me that father must have had an exceptionally strong social sense to get the kick that he obviously did out of friendship with men of a different class.

An interesting little fellow (almost any dull-looking person became miraculously interesting when father drew him out with self-effacing skill) the carpenter had been in Greenland during one of the great fish famines, when three open boats, manned by crews weakened by want of food, forced their way through the seventy miles of ice and wintry seas from Durhapp to Uigilak to bring relief. Father volunteered nothing of his own experiences in Greenland, merely asking a few knowledgeable questions: he was usually too modest to offer his personal account of any incident to which others referred. But somehow a pause occurred in the conversation into which the carpenter dropped the remark, 'You did ought to go there. A grand country, in a way,' much as though the words were being drawn from him by some spiritual magnet.

'Oh, I've been.' Carelessly. Just that; no more.

'Have you now! When was you there?'

'Same year as you. Look here, Harry, what's your boss going to charge me for this rail? I'm pretty broke, you know, through this smash up. New cloths in the mainsail, mast shortened, new shrouds and chain plates, new anchor. Filthy luck, wasn't it?'

'*Where* was you? – Goo' Lord, why . . .'

'Oh, there was a lot of bunk talked about the relief boats. We didn't have anything like such a time as people made out. – Tell him if the bill's small enough I may pay it: if not, I'll go bankrupt and he won't get a penny; there's a good chap.' And that was all. He firmly held the conversation off Greenland after this. So like father. I thrilled with horror and anger when Ronald, sore from the slating he had earned over the dismasting, referred to him a little later as 'our self-conscious buccaneer'. I think Ronald himself was shocked as soon as he had said it. Basil Quest seemed unable to believe his ears. He had developed a boundless admiration for father because of the Greenland business, a full-blooded, embarrassing hero-worship which lasted for years and was of a very different quality from Lester Cottrell's intellectual fancy for him. Lester approved of Ronald's description, and if the three boys had been more of an age – Basil was only eleven while the others were thirteen – his slow wits would probably have prompted threats of violence. My treat was going badly enough without that.

The outward journey, which was to have taken two days, lasted nearly a week. We finished all the ready cooked provisions, and the whole supply of butter went rancid, though it had always kept nicely in its perforated tin until Mrs. Cottrell suggested that the laws of science were against it. Suppressed irritation started between us and the Cottrells; they felt that we ought to have learnt how to preserve butter on board, while we darkly suspected Marnie, who had been told off to dip it, of having taken the scientific view and scamped the job as useless – which, of course, it probably was. Still, butter always had kept. . . .

The trouble nearly came to a head over the saucepan which Mrs. Cottrell condemned as dirty just when mother was about to use it. As cook's assistant for the day, on whom the washing-up devolved, I privately thought it was quite clean enough for boat purposes: the Cottrells were fussy about that sort of thing. Mother thought as I did, but obligingly picked off a tiny piece of dried stuff sticking to the bottom.

'Only a bit of cauliflower-leaf, Eleanor.' (Greenstuff, we knew, was considered particularly wholesome by enlightened people like the Cottrells.)

' "*Only!*" My dear Phyllis, haven't you ever seen decaying vegetable matter under a microscope? Well, if you had . . .!'

There was a surface-friendly battle over the saucepan, in which mother was too kind to use the strongest argument on her side, 'Well, we *always* cook like this and my children are healthier, not to say better looking than yours!' Mrs. Cottrell amiably called her by several rude names that we could not have used, and firmly took over all the cooking for the rest of the trip. It was hardly necessary for her to point out again that she was not one of those women who so annoyed her by marrying unexpected poverty and then failing to become reconciled to it: we were, however, reminded by inference on several occasions during the next few days of her excellence in this respect. It was not till some years later, when I accidentally discovered that Mrs. Cottrell had never been anything but desperately hard up and domesticated, that I really began to like this formerly too flawless woman.

I was sadly conscious that in Pin Mill the bird tides were practically wasting themselves without me. These two days of delay, when we could do nothing but wait about for shipwrights and sail-makers, were infuriating. In the seabirds' breeding season – May to July, later than on land – the tides slacken all round this coast, by what seems like a pure dispensation of a bird-minded Providence, so that the terns, shelducks and many of the gulls can safely raise their beach-coloured families among the litter flung up by the full spring tides. Ted, bother him, must be stealing any number of marches on me by locating the first eggs. My one consolation was that father, tinkering the recalcitrant engine, became lavish with the loveliest stories. I heard for the first time of his idiotic escapade as a young man in Chile, when he was trying to find his way across the Anje mountains on the sort of horse that stops if one holds its head up, and stumbles if one lets it down. He knew only vaguely the whereabouts of the nitrate prospector with whom he meant to join up for a while. (I decided on my own that he was probably going to the man's assistance, but he did not tell us that: father was much freer with accounts of being made ridiculous than with stories in which he could not help figuring as life size, or over. But there were so many of both kinds in his strange store of memories that new ones were always coming to the surface, 'like bubbles in a stagnant pond' as the Quests' extraordinary father once remarked, prompted no doubt by jealousy.) Having swum a ford in a flooded mountain torrent, where he lost the horse because it turned back carrying his clothes and supplies on its back, he arrived half-naked at a dilapidated shanty. Here he took over the effects of a British surveyor who had died some years before. The only wearing apparel not hopelessly damaged by ants was a complete Charterhouse soccer kit, lovingly kept in a zinc trunk – the sort of expected unexpectedness of the wilds. Feeling that in this part of the world the solecism should pass uncondemned, father pressed on in this striking get-up, and reached the man he had come to join after an appalling march in which fever from the immersion was only one of his troubles. It'll be just my luck, he thought, if the fellow turns out to be an Old Carthusian, and resents the rig. Swaying as he stood, on the verge of collapse, he went through an emotional parody of the Dr.-Livingstone-I-presume meeting of white men in isolated places.

'Good God. Rush!' said a cockney voice which relieved him of the Charterhouse apprehension. 'You were at Wanstead Grammar School with me!'

'Yes,' said father, while the ground heaved and receded before his eyes. He had some vague memory of helping to scrag this scion of a socialist family for airing his father's views. 'As a matter of fact . . .'

'Then why that bloody shirt? Eton, or Harrow is it?'

'Charterhouse, I believe,' said father. 'But as . . .'

'Good God. Isn't the old school good enough for you?'

'Yes,' said father, 'and as a matter of fact . . .'

'That's rich, that is! Thought you'd get away with the haw-haw stuff here, did you? . . . Think I'd demean myself wearing a class badge . . . ticks like you who let down the workers . . . bolstering up the capitalist system . . .' and a good deal more father heard just before he became unconscious, and when he came round again he found himself alone, with a small – a very small – store of food. So after a short rest he walked back across the mountains, and crawled weakly to an outpost of civilization in semi-nakedness, for safety's sake, having left the offending shirt on the other side of the ford, which he had re-swum.

Oh, a marvellous man; I could not imagine what Mr. Quest could have meant when he accepted father's invitation to his children for the treat – 'Delighted, Rush. I'm regrettably devoid of the glamour o' far places myself. Pump it into them. Pump it into them. Such a normalizing influence.' There had been something funny about his tone. There always was. Surely even a dank sort of person like Mr. Quest ('dank' was Lester's word for him) who did not care much about his own children, must admire father and enjoy hearing his experiences?

Mrs. Cottrell had another of her delicate moments when we reached Littlehampton at last and she prepared to go ashore to shop. Picking up what she imagined to be mother's shopping list, she took off the table a piece of paper which Marnie had just laid down. Marnie protested crossly that it was her drawing. Without thinking, Mrs. Cottrell glanced at the scrawl and then apologized charmingly for looking at an unfinished sketch without permission. The older Cottrells had the modern parents' conscientiousness in disclaiming rights of discourtesy over their children. Recalling them now, I fancy their disclaimers sounded very much like high-principled wallowings in the joy of self-abasement: at the moment I was stunned with envy of Marnie.

'I was drawing the back of a wave, and you've wah wah wah.' When Marnie was in a bad temper her adenoids became obstructive.

'Darling, I'm sorry. I didn't really look at it. I think I had it upside down.'

'It wasn't nearly done. And now you've gone and spoilt it all.'

'Oh, Marnie, I haven't, have I? I know just how you feel. I loathe people looking at my rough designs. I wouldn't have looked at it without asking you if I'd thought. Honestly I didn't mean to.'

'. . . you've *crumpled* it!' wailed Marnie, who was really longing, I knew of old, for someone to take an interest in her extraordinary drawing. She would thoroughly have enjoyed being the centre of the sort of attention that I had endured over the shelducks, but in this her adoring parents always thwarted her with kindliness and tact. Like a psychological angel, Mrs. Cottrell persisted in not treading where the inrush of fools would have been welcome. She asked diffidently, while helping Marnie to straighten out imaginary creases, to be allowed to see the drawing when it was quite, quite finished, and Marnie nodded sulkily, knowing that it never would be. How could anyone be expected to finish the drawing of a back of a wave when none of the beastly things would keep still enough to be properly studied?

At Littlehampton, as usual in seaside places, there was nothing to do. Perspiring women, tightly encased in black, towed shrilly protesting children along the shadeless promenade, showering them with threats in whose execution the experienced children obviously disbelieved. Over the sands as well, and for several yards out into the sea, brooded that atmosphere of vague maternal menace which is peculiar to English coastal resorts. For want of occupation all the children of the party fell under the spell of a Salvation Army band. We returned to the boats singing 'I'm so H–A–P–P–Y' (*fortissimo*) 'for I'm S–A–V–E–D!' (smug *pianissimo*) to the distress of both the mothers on board. It would be hard to say which of them disliked the hymn more, mother for religious reasons, or Mrs. Cottrell because of the deep Cottrell prejudice against everything of that kind. On the whole we took our religion more lightly than they took their agnosticism. Even the superior Lester could not be weaned from this catchy tune, and such was the religious feeling it engendered that Ronald and Lester were moved to sneak ashore on our last afternoon and cadge a Bible off the delighted leader of the band, in order to study those parts of the Old Testament which had not been thought suitable reading matter for the children of either family. They had always meant to see what was in the Book of Judges to make my mother take the Mawleys' Bible hurriedly out of Marnie's hands one day, when we were all having tea at Sootie's cottage and Marnie, as usual, settled down to read the nearest thing to hand. After surreptitious skimmings of the 19th and 20th chapters on the way home, both came to the same conclusion. Ronald said proudly that the bits not dull were bawdy, this being a new word with him, picked up in his first term at Dartmouth, and therefore to be used whenever possible for a while. Lester pronounced them 'bitchie,' having still more recently acquired the term from an American art critic who had been staying with his parents.

The Cottrells were evidently right in their contention that if introduced to it too early, children were likely to overlook the poetry of the Old Testament. Only the Quests were uninterested: they had had a religious housemaid for years, and brought up by servants, knew all that they wanted of the Bible.

'. . . for I'm S–A–V–E–D!' carolled Dru irrepressibly from *Wanderer* as we approached Ramsgate in the gathering dusk on the first lap of the return journey. I joined in from *Guadalupe*: by letting out our cut down mainsail till it spilled the breeze we were sailing level with them as we reached towards the harbour, where we intended to spend the night. Father shouted at her irritably to go below and read out the harbour directions from *The Pilot's Guide*, partly to stop the hymn, partly to see how Mrs. Cottrell took them, I imagine.

'The leading mark is the green light on the west cliff in one with the green light in the lighthouse,' she must have read (I could not hear her from the other boat, but I still know long passages of that discouraging book by heart). 'As there are no good clearing marks for the west side of the Brake Sand, vessels should not attempt to work through Ramsgate Channel without local knowledge. *During night*, vessels should not attempt to run for Ramsgate, except in the event of extreme necessity.'

As the last light faded from water and sky, father shouted at us from the other boat to follow him in; we dropped behind and he sent someone forward to watch from *Wanderer's* bow for the gleam of water breaking on the shoals near the entrance. Father explained to the anxious Mrs. Cottrell, when the night thickened and no buoys were seen, that with a four-knot tide sluicing across the pier heads we could not sound-in slowly for fear of being swept on to the leeward jetty: it was a case of cracking on all sail and praying, while both boats rushed through the darkness towards what looked at the moment like a blank wall of cliff. Making the harbour was really nothing like as perilous as he allowed

66

it to sound, with some characteristic idea of teaching Mrs. Cottrell not to worry unduly.

And then Mrs. Cottrell, to everyone's astonishment, turned adamant. She was not going to have her maternal heart agonized again on this trip. She said that she did not care what we thought of her nor whose boats these were, we must go on up the coast, all night if necessary: anything rather than attempt this dreadful harbour in these dreadful conditions. A second, and even greater surprise followed: father gave in to her courteously, having done something with his head which Basil tried to convey to me afterwards by reproducing the gesture. But one had to be father to carry off his mannerisms successfully: copied by a boy of eleven that fling-back of the head and air of intense abstraction looked theatrical. Father never did that: not to me, anyway. I could remember, with something like awe, many occasions when I had seen him start listening suddenly, as he must have done at that moment, to something inaudible to other ears. The Cottrell children were travelling in *Guadalupe*, having come on board late that morning, when the slow *Wanderer* had already started. Father merely warned Mrs. Cottrell that if it should come on to blow hard (it was then a trustworthy-looking night, and there seemed no possibility of it) *Guadalupe*, having a partially new mainsail, would not be able to reef: whatever happened she would have to carry on with full canvas, because new cloths must be stretched by many hours of sailing before they can safely be subjected to the uneven strain of setting with a reef down. Was she prepared to accept that?

Yes, she was. Anything. Fierce winds were not an immediate menace, like the black bulk of the cliffs ahead. She was not frightened for herself in *Wanderer*, but she said again, a little hysterically, that she was not going to have her children wrecked in the smaller yacht in order that father might show off his sailing dexterity with this one.

Father signalled to us with a flash lamp to bear away and carry on, and by the time that *Guadalupe* was clear of the foreland we began to think, not yet knowing the situation in the other boat, that for once his sailing sense had deserted him. For how it blew! A few minutes after we had turned away from the harbour a new wind, a patchy little north-easterly, crept off the blackness of the land and playfully pushed *Guadalupe's* lee rail under water as an earnest of what was to come. Marnie got her feet wet and was cross until she became too frightened to be cross. I have never known even a fisherman who could beat father at smelling a wind before it came. How he must have enjoyed himself, in spite of the atmosphere of increasing hostility in his own boat, when it began to howl through the rigging as though summoned by his wish, and howled louder and louder all night.

Even the two Cottrells had to work at intervals, pumping out the water that came solid over *Guadalupe's* low sides to swish about in the bilge, slopping up into the blanket locker and soaking most of the stores. There was no question of sleep for more than a few minutes at a time, towards morning, when we were all tired out. We lost touch with the other boat, and because of Sootie's orders about the accursed new canvas we dared not heave-to, which required reefing in this over-ardent boat.

In desperation we stood boldly but miserably out into the North Sea to get space enough in which to lower all the sails and ride to an improvised sea-anchor, waiting for daylight, while *Guadalupe* alternatively stood on her nose and her counter, throwing in an occasional terrifying lurch and wallow as a sea broke aboard.

Margaret was very much father's child that night. The channel always seems to be crowded with shipping when one is out in a small boat at night, and being run down was our only real danger, as father knew: snugged down to a

68

sea-anchor, *Guadalupe* could ride out a far heavier gale than
this. With pride, with envy perhaps; with some such strong
emotion in any case, I watched her standing under the port
sidelight holding to the shrouds as the boat plunged, with
the red light flickering over her wet face and wild, black,
blowing hair, staring serenely at the dim bulk of an oncom-
ing steamer which was showing us both port and starboard
lights. This meant that the ship was steering straight towards
us, and because of the violence of our motion, our own sidelights kept going out: we were not very visible in this welter
of humped water without our white sails spread to catch
whatever light there was. We should not be the first yacht to
disappear hereabouts without trace if the steamer's look-out
failed to see us. Margaret was not scared. She watched the
approaching vessel with the same far-off air that sometimes
maddened me because it seemed to me that, to look like this,
she must have safe hold of something which I could never
reach. But now it was a comforting thing, that calm expression on the queerly lit face. I was thoroughly scared myself,
and clutching at straws of reassurance I thought – I felt
without thinking rather – that loveliness like hers would be
beyond the reach of danger from such ordinary things as
ships and seas and winds. Surely anything so perfect must
be safe. I was young enough to believe beauty enduring,
and strong.

The ship saw us, in plenty of time really, and altered her
course with a peevish blast from her siren. All night, tankers
and tramps and Dover-bound continental packets passed
uncomfortably close to us. Every hour or so, soaked to the
skin in spite of their oilies, Sootie and Ronald came down
into the cabin for a few minutes' rest out of the wind, but
they could not leave the untrustworthy sidelights for long
and it was essential to keep constant check of our position
by cross-bearings on the North and South Foreland lights:
if this north-easterly veered at all we should be just to wind-

ward of the Goodwin Sands. Ronnie grumbled at father as audibly as he thought safe in Sootie's hearing, expressing the blasphemous conviction that in his efforts to raise a tough family father would do us all in, one of these days. And for once Sootie, who must have heard, did not shut him up loyally.

Father, in the other boat, had just the sort of night he enjoyed, hove-to under three reefs in the lee of the Goodwins, occasionally taking short boards back into shelter when *Wanderer* drifted out towards rough water. He knew that we were safe from anything but bad luck: almost any boat can endure more than her crew: in ninety per cent of yachting accidents it is the human element that gives way; and Sootie and Ronald were hard-boiled enough to remain efficient through any ordinary gale. Mrs. Cottrell, with whom father was still very angry, did not know that: spiritually she must have had a much more wearing night in the steady old *Wanderer* than we did in *Guadalupe*.

Lester distinguished himself. Too shaken to be ill, he sat on the sodden bunk expressionlessly reading aloud, by the light of the wildly swinging lamp, remnants of old issues of the *Times*, which had swilled out of the lockers they had been used to line. This was the occasion on which he sowed his afterwards famous habit of producing solemn extracts from that paper at irrelevant moments, to emphasize his detachment from immediate cares. That night the Letters to the Editor shed on their subjects – bimetallism, Consular pensions or the first recorded appearance of potato blight in Dorset: I have forgotten what most of them were about – an ephemeral charm lacking from them in other circumstances. Their leisurely calm suggested a continuity of life which was very welcome just then. I even found myself trying to discuss them with Lester to make the time pass, while we listened apprehensively with three-quarters of our attention to the chaos outside the cabin. Years later, I came on one of these almost pulped pieces of paper in the pocket of a coat which had by then, in the usual way of family clothes, passed on to Margaret: 'Card Houses: It may interest some of your readers to know that I built a card house 26 storeys high, and have a photograph of it at 25 storeys. It took four packs of cards and was erected on a billiard table – Mrs. Fox, Tonbridge,' followed by 'Convolvulus Hawk Moth: A member of the Woodcote Park Golf Club near here recently found, on fencing near his house, a fine specimen of the Convolvulus Hawk Moth. The appearance of this rare moth so near London must be very exceptional. – Mr. T. Lewis, Wallington.' This still seems to me the right sort of reading matter for gales: it encourages the belief that the importance of anything is a strictly relative matter. Lester and I agreed, for once, that it was difficult to imagine anyone reading it for choice when there was no gale on hand.

The weather stayed filthy all the next day, when we butted and rolled our way across the Thames estuary back to the familiar Suffolk waters.

As the last batch of us went ashore in the bobbing dinghy, mother and Mrs. Cottrell were brighter and more affable than ever, laughing as the spray flipped in. Mother said cheerily to us as we disembarked on the Hard, 'Well, children, that was great fun, wasn't it?' Lester and the Quests agreed, with courteous thanks, that it was. So did I.

I rushed to Ted Mawley for news of the now empty burrow. He told me that the heron's nest which we had been watching had been blown out of the elm on the edge of the Quest's garden and, piled up by the same raging north wind, the previous night's tide had risen far above the ordinary bird-tide level, sweeping the flats right up to the height of winter springtides; it would be useless to look for nests now.

As soon as I heard this news, I was laid low by an agonizing attack of conscience. I had told mother a lie. I was not unnaturally truthful as a rule, but just occasionally the urge to righteousness won, as now, against my reluctance to confess anything to older people and so let them get at my mind. Driven by remorse, I went in search of mother, whom I found lying down with a headache. Feeling almost as bad as I had done about my grandfather's death, I told her without any explanation that I had not enjoyed my treat at all. She sat up and stared at me. 'What did you say, Lallie?' I thought she was going to be cross. I repeated what I had said, awkwardly, wishing that I need not confess. Mother, that pillar of calm strength, burst into tears. It was by far the most harrowing moment of my childhood.

CHAPTER V

SUBSCRIPTIONS

'FROM God's Own Boy Scout Grown Up?' asked Mr. Quest when I handed him a note.

'From father,' I said. I rarely knew what he meant and had learned that it was pleasanter not to try to find out because, when obscure, Mr. Quest was generally being disagreeable.

While he opened and read it I looked surreptitiously round the huge, almost legendary study into which I had never penetrated before, though the Quests had lived within a few hundred yards of our house for over ten years. The War, which broke out a few months after the Littlehampton trip, took Mr. Quest away to prison, and he had not been back very long: his experiences as a seditious lecturer seemed to have made him danker than ever, I thought. 'Wants money for a regatta, does he? More clean, healthy sport. One would hardly think he'd need it so soon after Active Service.'

One of my unhappy blushing fits threatened at once. We were asking for money, and however worthy the cause, anything to do with the need of money was considered indelicate in our family, because we had so little of it ourselves, even less than before the War. Also we were all, including father who joked about it a good deal, slightly sensitive on the subject of father's war. He was so exactly the person one might reasonably expect to be well to the fore in such a period, getting notably killed or decorated, that there was something incongruous in his remaining at the base almost to the end, lent as a bombing instructor to foreign troops, before being knocked out by a bit of British anti-aircraft shell just when he was due to join his battalion in the line. All right for anyone else, but somehow, for Arthur Rush – !

When the regatta was planned, as a suitable celebration of the first summer of peace, everyone on the committee had cried off going to 'River View', the Quests' place, with the note which father sent round the village in order to raise funds. Seeing the addressee personally and waiting for an answer was the only way of forcing contributions, and the prospect of tackling our only rich man in this way was not inviting. Even Basil and Stella, themselves enthusiastic about the regatta, refused to open the subject of a contribution with their father. It was strongly felt by everyone except father that father was the man for the job. But he said at the last minute that one did not speak to pacifists or conchies, one merely kicked their backsides if possible: and as this was obviously not possible while asking for regatta funds, his children had unwillingly drawn lots for the ordeal, and I had lost.

'It's because we haven't been able to have a regatta for such ages,' I explained, 'that he wants to make this one a very special sort of do.'

'Oh, he does, does he? And why should I encourage my expensive view to be spoiled by hordes of repulsive small children propelling egg boxes and tin baths about the river, as they've been doing for days? Presumably that's for – what is it he wants me to endow?' – he consulted the letter – 'The Orwell one-design class.'

'Oh, no,' I said, clutching at a safe point as I twisted a handkerchief into a warm rag behind my back. 'The egg-boxes and all that'll be for the Odd Craft race. The one-designs are – well, they're quite different, Mr. Quest, really they are.' (How did one convey to the unseafaring the social superiority of one-designs over any other kind of dinghy?) 'There won't be anyone smaller than Margaret in the one-designs.'

'Well,' said Mr. Quest, 'I expect that's quite small enough to be repulsive.' He got up from the desk where he was vaguely supposed by the awed village to 'do statistics' even at week-ends, and walked over to the great window, set so as to overlook the longest possible stretch of the lovely estuary and the rolling timbered grounds beyond. The whole house had been built for that window. It was a gay, blustering day, too rough for the makeshift craft of every description that had lately been crawling about the river whenever conditions were not too perilous. There was only one boat in sight, a dinghy with an occupant lying almost horizontally out to windward in an attempt to keep her from shipping water.

'Remarkable,' said Mr. Quest with fascinated distaste. 'What keeps the person in the boat at that angle?'

'Feet under a thwart. And a wishbone tiller.'

'Whenever a particularly fine squall roars up this reach, out of it pops a half-drowned Rush in an inadequate boat, disfiguring the scene with human interest – I suppose that's one of your family?'

I nodded, feeling for once ashamed of Ronald. This interview was turning out worse than I had expected.

'And so strong is the human instinct to enjoy the misfortunes of a fellow-creature that one is forced against one's will to watch in hopes of the worst. – There!' he said, as Ronald's dinghy heeled over and dipped her gunwale alarmingly before righting with a jerk. 'But it never happens. And now your father, fresh from inculcating other blood sports, wants me to help him enjoy a little more vicarious danger.'

I could not blush any harder. But through indignation I became quite articulate for once. Mr. Quest had insisted on showing his obstructive pacifism from the beginning of the War, not only by articles in highbrow papers but in lectures which he delivered locally – a gratuitously brave thing to do in a small country place like Pin Mill, but at sixteen I could not realize this. And now he dared to refer slightingly to father's army record.

'Well, if you think our sailing's silly, I think *your* children look a lot sillier playing cricket-for-two! It'll be rounders next. *Rounders*! –' With furious irrelevance I pointed out of the other window to where Stella and Basil, daily growing more pink-and-white and public-schoolish in their teens, were practising bowling and occasionally rushing about the lawn after the ball. The game of rounders had always been considered by us the epitome of un-Rushly softness.

'Possibly. But then I avoid looking out of that window during their holidays – their far too long holidays.' His tone was surprisingly friendly. I was expecting something crushing. He looked out of that window now, however, standing by me while I wondered desperately how best to extricate myself from this unsuccessful mission. Should I just walk out of the house without another word, or wait for him to say something more in dismissal, or refer to father's note with the formula that I had used elsewhere, 'Well, I'm sure father will quite understand if you don't feel – etc?' His next remark was not helpful. 'Aren't they dreadful!' he said, confidentially, surveying the unconscious players as though they were no concern of his. 'Animal spirits. Youthful ebullience. So right and proper at their ages. One must strive for thoughtless normality – I don't myself, of course, but other people should. Never think, Drusilla, it's a disruptive process. Stick to sailing. Which races are you personally interested in?'

'I'm Lalage, Mr. Quest. It's my sister who's Drusilla: the fat one. My dinghy's in for the Orwell one-designs. I'm just one of a crew for other races – sailing against Basil in the Under-Five-Tons. But the one-designs will be single-handed.' (I was bursting with pride over my first 'class' dinghy, given by father as a sixteenth birthday present. Even Mr. Quest seemed worth telling that I was going to race it alone.)

'Well, here's five pounds for a cup for the one-designs, whatever they are – Don't tell me. The winner's to keep it; I don't want to encourage this business next year. Between you all, you're going to ruin one of my few pleasures, that inhumanly fine view, for several days to come.' He sat down at his desk and opened a notebook as though I were no longer there.

'Oh, but Mr. Quest! Oh, no really – I mean, five pounds! After what I said, and everything –' There was a difficult pause, in which I struggled to find suitable words of thanks. He flicked over page after page of minute handwriting until he found some loose leaves at the end.

'In moments of social embarrassment,' he said, 'consider the ramifications of the figure 2. Very helpful. I jotted some down the other day. (They let one read astronomy and such things in prison: an administrative mistake; it dwarfs one's idea of human time and so lessens the penal effect.) Interesting to notice how often this particular numeral occurs in calculations of inhuman immensity. For instance, there are two million extra-galactic nebulae, each averaging two thousand million suns, careering about outer space. And they also average out at two million light-years apart. Doesn't this put my donation in less overwhelming perspective, somehow? And the radius of an electron is two multiplied by ten to the minus thirteenth centimetres: one might feel that this relegates your view of my children's activities (with which I heartily agree, by the way) to comparative unimportance. Your mind, like theirs, is composed of such things, and as we have noticed, the radius, though interesting, is not impressive. And the age of the earth is computed to be two multiplied by ten to the ninth years, though I can't at the moment see how this bears on the situation, except that perhaps it diminishes us all in our own eyes?'

He took a glance at me but saw, evidently, that I was still overwhelmed by the gift. He rose. 'If only I had been told about the figure 2 in my youth,' he said, putting a hand on my shoulder and gently propelling me across the great room, 'I might have retained some measure of composure through one of my first dinner parties, when I was served with the toughest chop I ever met, before or since. The experience may be of use to you. Some other, more socially accomplished guest got one too, but she gave up the struggle early.' He opened the door with his other hand, but the dry voice did not pause as we started down the long passage. 'She even chaffed her hostess about it, to my speechless envy. Everyone else had chosen another dish. The hostess asked me anxiously if mine were all right. And I lied, because I was seventeen or thereabouts. (Avoid lying, like thought: neither of these things can be done satisfactorily by the young. Animal spirits and the truth for you for several years to come. But not, oh, not in my presence, of course)'— We turned off into another passage leading to a side door, he still behind and I almost an arm's length in front. My speech of thanks was now ready for the first opportunity. There was, however, no interruption in his purposeful monologue.

'Bit by bit,' went on Mr. Quest, 'I forced all the chop into my mouth. But it would go no further. It turned into a leather gag. People spoke to me of this and that, and I nodded or shook my head. I had no idea then that the age of the universe could be expressed as two hundred multiplied by ten to the twelfth years. Or I might have replaced the wodge of meat on my plate with some nonchalance. There's something about those gigantic time figures, made friendly by the two which links them together — Instead, I hit on the plan of pretending to blow my nose, and manipulated the meat into my handkerchief. Afterwards, when we had rejoined the ladies, I forgot and pulled it out. A shower of chewed and fibrous fragments fell about me on the drawing-room carpet, and in the silence which followed no one thought fit to assure me that, beyond all reasonable doubt, the

78

temperature of the annihilation of an atom is two thousand multiplied by ten to the ninth degree (centigrade).' Without letting go of my shoulder he managed to open the awkward door into the garden, which required a jerk at the top and a kick at the bottom to unstick it.

'At this heat the whole scene of my degradation, as well as the mortal onlookers, would be not only changed by the melting process, but utterly non-existent: as if they had never been, that's the point. For my mind, drowning in shame, such a consideration would have been a bigger and better straw to clutch at than the hopes of sudden death in the near future, which naturally filled it. . . .'

(Basil and Stella, who had not seen me arrive, stopped their cricket practice to stare at us as we walked, side by side now, along the garden path, but they came no nearer. I was getting a crick in my neck from looking sideways and upwards at Mr. Quest while he went on talking: but with the five pounds in my pocket it did not seem polite to look away all the time. I wished that it were not such a long garden.)

'. . . for my death, though better than nothing, would leave the surviving witnesses of the incident still able to discuss it, and matter being indestructible at all but theoretical temperatures, somewhere, in some form, the elements of that chop would survive to remind the earth of what had once happened upon it. That heat, however, would destroy even the air displaced by the chop, which would also be properly disintegrated at last – And there are a great many more of these vast facts beginning with two,' he finished briskly, 'which might be steadying to the shy, only I can't remember them just now.'

'But, Mr. Quest, you couldn't ever have been shy!' I gasped when he stopped at last, having conveyed me to the other side of the gate.

'As a boy, agonizingly. I had to make immense efforts to get over it. That's why I can now be unpleasant with less

79

effort than most people. Good-bye, tell your father I hope that the whole lot of you will be drowned in the first lap of your races, before you impinge on my view. Otherwise, against my will, I shall stop my work to watch the egg boxes, in the hope of their foundering. How weak one is!' He shook his head over the frailties of the human mind, and retreated rapidly towards the house, while I went on up the road towards the village in a daze, making for the cross-roads where I could intercept the midday bus to Ipswich.

The conductor, a nephew of Sootie's wife, obligingly changed our library books for us in the town. His girl lived next door to the local Boots', and whenever mother could think of nothing that she wanted to read, or believed that we ought to read, we left the choice to her. If not impeccable, her taste was at least jollier than that of the Cottrells, the only other people we knew who were interested in literature. Until I was eighteen my reading was practically controlled by the busman's girl.

Feet pounded up the road behind me as I chatted with the busman, and Basil and Stella appeared, too eager for information to wait with their customary courtesy until I had finished my conversation with Sootie's nephew-in-law.

'Hello, Charlie – I say, Lallie, what happened with father? Silly time to break in on him.'

'At *twelve* o'clock on a *weekday*!' said Stella in an awestruck tone, as though I had deliberately disturbed God half-way through one of the days of creation.

'Well, he's given five pounds to the regatta all the same – Right-O, Charlie, leave them at Sootie's on Sunday, will you? – for the one-design cup.'

'Golly,' said Basil, too staggered even to wave back at Charlie when the bus drove on. 'Why?'

'I don't know. He was sniffy about our sailing, so I was a whole lot sniffier about your playing cricket. And he said, "Weren't you awful?" and then he gave me the note.'

'He's cracked,' said Basil, resignedly. 'Here've I been waiting nearly half the holidays to tell him I must have his written permission to take riding next term. I mean, if I am to take riding. You see, I asked him before if I could, and he said yes, and now whenever I start explaining about having it in writing, he says that he said yes once, and will I kindly not bother him about that again. And I can't get hold of him to tell him properly' – (I knew Basil's exasperating way of telling anything 'properly'; slowly, confusedly and at unnecessary length, padding out the explanation with 'you sees' and 'sort ofs') 'because he's always in London, or dashing off to ask council-school children whether they think of jam when he says "bread" at them, or something.'

'That's his Work,' interrupted Stella, as if I did not know. 'You can't do educational psychology without hundreds of statistics like that. It takes hours and hours, but they let him do it in school hours, because it's so useful. Not to the children, of course, but the authorities. Shows them things about the brain. He says he sent us to Eton and Sherborne because there we'd be safe from other educational experts.'

'And when he is here, you see,' went on Basil, who was used to disregarding Stella, 'he won't be interrupted by us. But you just stroll in at the silliest time, and get five pounds. It isn't fair. *Cracked!*'

'Oh, Basil, he's not cracked,' said Stella indulgently. 'You know it's just his way, because he is so frightfully clever, really.' Stella, at seventeen, was already developing a 'men-are-just-big-babies' manner which charmed many people and made her, as far as I was concerned, an impossible companion: she could be relied on to point out the obvious, save when she did not see it herself. I wondered whether she could be at all like her mother, whose early death, it was understood, had soured Mr. Quest ten years ago. It was hard to imagine anyone being soured for so long

81

by the death of somebody like Stella. Now she said, uneces-
sarily, 'You know father hates attempts to draw him into
social life here, Lallie. You mustn't take anything he said
seriously. He says he has to be ruder and ruder to all you
people to keep any peace at all to work in. He says small
country places are heaps worse than London for not leaving
a person a minute to themselves, because if once you get
embroiled in local affairs, he says . . .'

'Well, Lallie knows what he says,' Basil interrupted
impatiently. 'He's just been saying it to her, hasn't he?'

Stella smiled indulgently at him, leaving her mouth open
for a few seconds when the smile was over, which gave it a
fatuously lingering end. Expressions habitually took just
too long to wear off her face, which made every member of
the Rush family, save mother, long to shout at her, in the
hope of startling another look into its place. Surely the
mythically lovable Mrs. Quest could not have had this
trait? The touching rumour of Mr. Quest's undying regret
for her had much to do with the village's persistence, despite
every discouragement, in courting his participation in local
affairs: nothing he could say would permanently alienate
anyone who regarded him as a romantically bereaved figure.
(A second, and even more potent, reason for trying to include
him in all our activities, of course, was that he was the only
person in the locality with money to spare: but romance
made rebuffs bearable.)

'Still, five pounds!' Basil was saying, and then burst out
with the question which almost everyone in the village
wanted to ask, 'I say, Lallie, is it true that the Cottrells
are only giving ten bob to the prize fund? There's only ten
bob against their name on the list at the Butt & Oyster.'

I nodded. Curse. This was the subject which every
member of our family had been avoiding while canvassing
since the fund was opened. In three days Pin Mill had
already divided into two factions over it. One was indignant

because the Cottrells were not giving anything like as much as we were, and the other was indignant that anyone should expect them to. There had also been at first a tiny party which said it was no business of anyone else's; a surprising attitude in a village, and one that was not likely to survive heated discussion in bar-parlours and sewing meetings. Practically everyone we met had now taken sides.

'Old Chandler says it's a shame,' Basil went on, 'when Mr. Rush is doing all the work, handicapping and all that, and giving cups for two of the events himself, and the Cottrells are lots better off than – I mean, ten bob isn't enough from them. Considering old Cottrell's vice-president of the sailing club, and everything.'

'But he's only vice-president because father asked him to be,' I said. 'After all, the Cottrells don't sail.' We were their staunch champions, but we were already growing tired of defending them from our own supporters. And they and Mr. Quest were probably the only people who were not even aware that there were two excited factions in Pin Mill over the subscription question.

Stella took the pro-Cottrell view – which we took in public though we seethed on the other side in private – that the regatta was father's affair since father suggested it, and it was nice of the Cottrells to contribute at all. After all, she pointed out, even if Mr. Rush were giving two cups, his children were in for all entries and he was doing the handicapping – Basil, violently pro-Rush, interrupted that this was just the point. Mr. Rush was so frightfully fair that his own family was always severely handicapped. (The *non sequitur* of this escaped Basil's notice as it escaped father's: Ronnie and I were the only two who could not always see why father's sense of fair play should make it impossible for us to win anything.) Was Stella suggesting –? Basil grew hot at the thought. Stella was sweetly reasonable with him again, treating him – and eventually me too,

83

when I argued on the Cottrell side – with so much of the air of a mother indulging a couple of fractious children, that it was all I could do to go on agreeing with her.

I started back down the hill towards our house, hoping to shake them off, but Basil, still arguing vehemently in father's favour, came with me, with some vague idea of showing his partisanship by his company I suppose, until we saw Lester Cottrell strolling up the road with two odd-looking guests of his parents. Basil and I gazed round for a way of escape: two of the three seemed to be deep in the sort of Cottrell conversation – very earnest, and requiring explanatory diagrams drawn in the air by Lester's long thin fingers – which we both felt that we should not be able to follow comfortably.

'I'm off,' said Basil, who could not bear the unathletic Lester at any time, and particularly not now.

' "What boots the long laborious Quest?" (Wordsworth. A Literary Jest)' said Lester, watching Basil loping back up the road, harnessing retreat to the improvement of his wind. With no one have I carried on so many imaginary conversations, at night or when out in the dinghy alone, as with Lester Cottrell. I always came off best in them; in reality I could never think of any effective counter-irritant to his superciliousness. But for the moment I felt quite fond of all the Cottrells, because I had been forced to champion them.

Without waiting for the explanation of Basil's disappearance, which he knew in any case, he introduced his friends, a young waxen-faced Frenchman, so slim and limp that he looked as if he had guttered, and an American so strikingly ugly and inarticulate that I supposed he must be very distinguished or he would not have been invited to stay even by the Cottrells (who, living for beauty, seemed to collect the most hideous friends). I had never before chanced to meet an American who was naturally silent; and was moved to make several trivial remarks by curiosity as to what would happen to his mouth when he opened it; it was hard to imagine how two such unlikely halves, once separated, could come together again, but he only grunted something each time, as he had done on introduction, and walked away to the side of the road where he rubbed imaginary dust from his shoes with grass.

'Never mind about Schuster,' said Lester. 'He's conversationally exhausted. Only about an hour ago we got him to agree out loud that Fernan, here, mustn't go about a self-respecting village in this beret. "That's so," he said, and then relapsed.'

'Mais, vois tu . . .' The Frenchman seemed puzzled and aggrieved. (It gave me quite a warm glow of affection to think that Lester could lightly discuss hats, not knowing how feeling ran about that ten-shilling subscription! For once the Cottrells, who looked down on us, were in the ignominious position of protégés.)

'Now, now, Fernan. It's settled. Schuster has *spoken* about it. And besides, you really can't; it's the sort of thing the Prince of Wales wears.' The Frenchman looked still more puzzled, but less aggrieved. 'You'd better get Miss Rush to tell you about the regatta – He's studying *l'esprit sportif britannique*, Lallie, for articles in a French newspaper, and, of course, none of my family can help. You're just the person to supply the information.'

Serve him right if I supplied information on the real question of the regatta, I thought almost lovingly while I gave details about the races, dwelling a little on the one-designs, because it was even worth letting a Cottrell and some foreigners know that I should be single-handed in this race. The Frenchman was so duly impressed that all his English deserted him. 'Et quand il y a du vent? On doit être bien mouillé?'

'Oui et comment!' said Lester with feeling, under the

85

impression that he was making himself intelligble to both his friends by translating the slang of one into the idiom of the other. Since that trip to Littlehampton we had not been quite so friendly with the Cottrells as we had been before: it was curious that this regatta feeling should cement us again. 'So boyish of you!' said Lester with a deprecating shake of the head at the end of my recital. His adjectives were locally famous, and 'boyish' was the favourite at the moment. To-day even Ronald, after arguing on behalf of Lester's family with practically every acquaintance he met, would probably not yearn to do him personal injury if Lester used it in front of him.

'Talking of boys, here's rather a little gem from *The Times* to-day,' said Lester, pulling out the inevitable cutting, and reading to a completely uninterested audience, ' "My boy has just returned to his preparatory school, and I was sitting alone with my Aberdeen terrier. I said to her, 'Where is Grosvenor?' And she at once looked straight at his photograph. She jumped on a chair and, standing on her hind legs, she was just able to reach the photograph. Taking it carefully in her mouth she brought it and laid it at my feet with a glad cry. Mrs. Stevenson, Blenheim Road, W." What could be more endearing in one of our dumb friends than that glad cry?'

'I 'ave a dog 'oo do not like leever sawsage!' said Fernan.

Undamped by the blank reception of his gem, Lester folded it up tenderly and produced another.

I wanted to hurry home to break the news of my five-pound haul, but Lester and his friends turned politely and escorted me, strolling, so that I could not very well dash on ahead. As Lester walked behind with Fernan I was forced on to the unwilling American. Never at ease with strangers, I tried on him every conversational opening that my harassed mind could find: it was socially too much, I felt, that after coping with Mr. Quest who had talked as though he were never going to stop, I should immediately be required to deal with another difficult person who would not talk at all, and yet seemed ill at ease when I fell silent. It was his nerviness that unnerved me. I thought of the figure two, but no comfort came from it, and then clutched thankfully at an idea suggested by Mr. Quest's garden wall, in whose shade we walked for over a quarter of a mile. I gave the American what I hoped at the time was a bright little account of how River View's aggressively concealing wall had nearly made father a friend of Mr. Quest's, when the Quests first settled in Pin Mill, two years after we did. To the fury of my family, as day after day the wall had risen relentlessly at the speed which only wealth commands, it became apparent that this would completely shut out our view of the Orwell river, which had been, until then, as magnificent as the Quests' was designed to be. It was doubtful whether Mr. Quest ever saw the letters of protest written by father and the vicar and one or two other residents. Coldly regretful replies, promising nothing, were received from a secretary in London, and the wall grew steadily to its present eccentric height. When the words 'River View' – offensively appropriate if unoriginal – were cut in bold lettering into the stone pillars of the gateway, father changed the name of our house, formerly 'Marsh End' to 'Wall View' as an angry compliment. He and Ronald were at work on the alteration, painting neat little letters on our dilapidated gate, when the Quests arrived in their big Daimler, and noticed the name. The idea appealed so much to the unaccountable Mr. Quest that he returned mother's call, a courtesy that he extended to no one else. But after that the friendship languished.

My story languished too in that silence: I could not imagine why I had thought for an instant that it might entertain the American, and the American looked as though he were wondering the same thing. He murmured something inaudible, and swallowed tablets out of a bottle.

(Lester told me afterwards that though only twenty-eight he was one of the best known authorities on colloidal chemistry: the need for taking part in ordinary conversation at the Cottrells' meals made them such ordeals for him that he suffered from violent indigestion, and seemed to live chiefly on pepsin in the ten days he spent with them.) I was no longer interested to see how his unlikely mouth opened to admit the tablets; I could not make any more conversation, or bear any more nerve-racking companionship of any kind. I only wanted to get away. Fortunately we were practically at our gate. 'Oh, there's father,' I exclaimed, still brightly, 'Must catch him . . . regatta . . . ask him . . . expect meet again . . .' My voice trailed off as I ran. Safe inside our thick laurel hedge I sat down on a wheelbarrow to compose myself before going in, in order that I might be able to get the full flavour of triumph from my recital of adventure at River View.

'. . . but quite a nice child,' I heard, in Lester's superior tones, as they passed in a minute or so on the other side of the hedge. This no doubt referred to me. ('Child!' – Lester, confound him, was not a full two years older. and 'nice' – After the way I had been condoning that mean ten shillings I should think so! My affection dwindled. It *was* a mean sum.) I wondered what came before the 'but'. Probably 'no brains at all' or something like that, for he went on, 'The whole family is much the same. Lives Dangerously in mental squalor.' And then the silent man actually volunteered a question. 'Are they all,' he asked morosely – damningly – 'so very vivacious?' Hidden as I was, I felt myself beginning to blush again. To this day I find it difficult not to hate very shy people on sight for their unfair, devastating effect on those who are merely rather shy. *'Vivacious'*! To most women few of the sorrows of after life, I suppose, are as devastating, in the first moments of realization, as a social failure at sixteen.

Even when I cooled down, at last, the breaking of my grand financial news turned out to be less sensational than I had hoped; indeed, it was very disappointing. Though no one else had gathered such a windfall in one place, Margaret, who was not even at home to hear of my luck, had collected far more in driblets. Ronald was too full of 'Old Chandler's bloody nerve' to pay much attention to my story. He had just reached the age when a new desire for dignity often coincides awkwardly with another for ebullience in dress. Feeling that such errands were better left to the girls, he had, nevertheless, condescended to canvass our one general shopkeeper for the fund, and had gone to old Chandler's buoyed up by the consciousness of a happy set of silk socks, tie and handkerchief to match. Old Chandler, who had never presumed on his life-long acquaintance with us all, apparently felt that his open championship of the Rush side of the regatta question now entitled him to privileges. He leant across the counter, ignoring several customers of his and friends of ours, to stare open-mouthed at Ronald, whom he had rarely seen before in anything but weather-worn sailing kit. 'Aha, Master Ronald! *Shershee la fem.* That's what I say when young gentlemen doll up of a sudden.' He wagged a knowing finger at the speechless youth. '*Shershee la fem.* Want a shilling or two from me, do you? Well, here's fifteen. I'm not like some people we know of.' And he bestowed the cash, 'as if he were tipping me, the old sod!' Ronald kept repeating furiously. (After this one outburst of mateyness Chandler retired again into his habitual impassivity, and shortly afterwards died of a disease from which he must have known for years that he was suffering, but neither his wife nor the local doctor heard of it until just before the end. Even this remarkable stoicism, however, could not earn Ronald's subsequent forgiveness.)

But it was Dru who really eclipsed me and my five pounds – not only her news but her way of presenting it. The

Ladies' Regatta Committee had approached her with an invitation to 'say a few words' at the dinner which was to be held at the Butt & Oyster at the end of the great day. The formation of a Ladies' Committee was father's idea for roping in small donations from nearly all the married gentry in the neighbourhood: the duties of the committee were not onerous, consisting of buying a ticket for the dinner (2s. 6d.) and giving between five and ten shillings to the prize fund. Dru – a girl of action rather than social poise – would have to say her few words before almost all the people whom we knew intimately. And yet she seemed quite unimpressed by this flattering ordeal.

We said, excitedly, 'Oh, Dru! You couldn't, could you?' And 'D'you think they really meant it? Make a sort of speech! What on earth would you say?' And she replied off-handedly that she had already accepted and would merely pass some remarks about the results of the races. 'Something quite simple,' she added airily.

Admiringly I asked whether she would take the speech with her written down, or learn it off by heart. Such careless self-confidence seemed to me splendid beyond envy.

'Good lord, no,' said Dru. 'I'll think of something during the dinner. Say that everybody did frightfully well, and the best sailor won, and all that.'

During lunch she was so much the modest heroine of the hour that Ronald got little sympathy in his grouse against old Chandler. Father was particularly short with him. 'Time enough to stand on your dignity, me bucco, when you're captain of a man-o'-war and responsible for the discipline of the whole ship!' Several times these holidays he had rubbed into Ronald that a Dartmouth cadet was not a person of outstanding importance.

'A captain isn't responsible for discipline!' Ronald said, pleased to score in return. 'That's the commander's job.'

'Oh, her navigation, then,' father said testily.

'Not responsible for navigation either! That's for the navigation officer.' It was fun to be able to correct father on technical matters connected with the sea.

'What does the captain of a big ship do, then?' Instinctively mother tried to smooth down her men, by introducing a side issue as a toy to distract them, without realizing, I think, that there was anything more than surface friction between them: Ronnie was just being a little trying, and must not be allowed to annoy daddy.

It seemed to work well, for the moment. Ronald gave the brief broad grin which made him exactly like father at times, and said, 'He sits in his gilded cabin, fervently hoping for the best!' We greeted this with laughter, not because it was especially funny but because it was the sort of family idiocy that we were accustomed to and so enjoyed. It was father's sort of joke: he ought to have made it, really. If Ronald had given him time he probably would have said something of the sort, but Ronald was developing a knack of being first with his little witticisms. For the moment father laughed as heartily as the rest of us, but he sobered up sooner, and over the end of the meal hung a slight feeling of restraint that I did not understand, though I was aware of it and worried by it.

It seemed so odd, and such a pity, that those two did not get on nowadays, when they might have had real companionship from one another, as well as they had done until a year or so ago. I did not know when they had begun to grow apart: normally one lives too close, in family life, to notice major things, like changes in relationship, until one has really been aware of them for a long while. But I remembered that as a small boy Ronald had adored father, and father had been openly proud of his son's endurance and habit of knowing, without being told, what needed doing in a boat. It had always been apparent that Ronald was going to be very much like him in feature; father seemed pleased when people spoke of the promised resemblance; presumably, not being a fool, he knew how good-looking he was. And now that the promise was fulfilled physically, Ronald had also taken to making in company the sort of remarks which had always been father's speciality – grave absurdities on serious subjects, and deliberate lapses into bad form, like father's claim to have been the bravest man in the British Army because he had volunteered to teach the Portuguese bombing. Surely that could not be the reason, I thought, for his manifest resentment? But there was nothing else.

Disturbed and restless, I wandered aimlessly about the house and garden afterwards, wondering what I wanted to do. I imagine that a considerable part of any normal adolescence must be spent in searching vainly for means of staving off that boredom which is a child's main stimulus towards development, mental or physical. I tried to talk to Olive, our part-time maid, but she only looked coyer and coyer, giggling occasionally. Coyness was her usual reaction to any remark, on any subject. I tried to stir our huge, indolent cat from its day-dreaming, by making it self-conscious about its position on the silly little stool which Ronald had made for it when it was a kitten. Though it had long outgrown this particular resting place, habit held it there and for the greater part of every day it lay with its fore part on the stool and its after-end overhanging absurdly on to the floor. When I pushed its hind legs on to the stool, the forelegs came off, but even in this new uncomfortable attitude it maintained its soft, savage aloofness until, in the effortless way of a cat, it had made me look the sillier of the two. Then it rose, stretching gloriously, its back a braced arch of sudden muscle, its trembling tail an arch, every finely curved claw visible for a second, but when the jungle had looked briefly out of its eyes, the placid mask was re-assumed and it strolled to the door, where, glancing back at me with contempt, it opened its pink mouth enormously, but was as usual too languid to produce the slightest sound. Obediently I let it out – no one ever disobeyed this spoilt beast's imperious silent mewing, and followed it into the garden, to find father talking across the gate to Mr. Cottrell and the French guest. Pained dignity demanded that, after saying good-afternoon, I should stand by perfectly silent, proving to Fernan at least that my vivacity was not chronic. But while father was present it was hardly noticeable whether anyone else were silent or not: usually there was little spare attention going for anyone else, even when he was not laying himself out to be interesting; and at the moment he was. Throughout the regatta tension, father was as markedly 'bonhomous' (Lester's word) with all the Cottrells as it was possible to be without arousing their surprise. We wanted to make it clear to everyone, especially to that family, that we at least did not care what they gave to the fund.

To Fernan, father, who liked rubbing up his French, was charming but probably misleading about *l'esprit sportif britannique*, but I did not listen very closely after Mr. Cottrell had laughingly explained to the French youth the sort of man that father was, mentioning his wild years in Chile and the Chaco, because even the bandit story sounded strangely flat in French. One of the few lasting results of my education, acquired by intermittent attendance at a day school in Ipswich, is the conviction that anything said or written in a foreign language is innately dull, even when I understand it.

'J'avais doublé les gardes, mais malgré tout, ces voleurs épatants ont parvenus à les pénétrer. Je commandais à mes copains de s'endormir avec leurs fusils enterrés au-dessous de leurs corps, mais ces montagnards ont l'habitude de travailler à deux. L'un chatouillait le dormeur avec une plume, pendant que l'autre balancait une pierre au dessus de sa tête, prêt à lui casser la gueule s'il ouvrait les yeux. Heureusement personne ne s'etait éveillé: on s'etait simple-ment retourner à cause du chatouillement. Et le matin on s'etait rendu compte qu'un autre fusil avait disparu.'

It hardly bore any resemblance, I felt, save in the bare facts, to the original version.

Then Fernan let out that the Cottrells were arranging to give one of their famous parties, on the evening before the regatta, which was now four days ahead. Mr. Cottrell abruptly changed the subject, feeling, I imagined, that considering the close tie of friendship between the two families, it might seem inconsiderate of them to have picked on that evening. It would naturally be a little inconvenient to us, with all the handicapping and organization being left to father, and there was sure to be a last-minute alteration of some kind which would mean extra trouble.

A Cottrell party without the Rushes was unthinkable (unfortunately) I reflected, feeling that now there were two ordeals awaiting me instead of one. Secretly I was dreading the regatta and my single-handed race, for the weather had been growing more boisterous for a week, and showed no signs of changing: while we had had enough experience of highbrow gatherings at the Cottrells to know what fish out of water we were sure to feel among their other friends. A bad time lay ahead: I decided that the only thing I could do to forget this was to watch birds. Yes, that was what I wanted to do. My restlessness evaporated.

A female heron, blind in one eye from a recent fight, had won possession of a particularly fine fishing point about a mile up the river, where the woods swept down to the water and threw a deep shadow over it in the afternoons. Only the excellence of her haunt, which made her invisible to the fish for half the day, had saved her from slow starvation after her sight began to fail. Desperately and pathetically she practised at intervals all day, when fishing was slack, the quickness of her one remaining eye, throwing up and catching a twig in her beak time after time with a persistence

94

that fascinated me, knowing as I did – and as she did too, apparently – that it was only a matter of time before some other hungry fisher discovered that she was maimed by that last fight for possession and might now be driven off successfully, to take her chance where there was no kindly shadow to help her, and only the keen of sight could survive.

One could creep quite close to her on the sightless side. With a sudden lightening of spirit I felt Time, which had been running badly to waste, rushing back to its pleasanter job of fetching good minutes for me instead of carrying them aimlessly away. I had had enough, these last few days, since the regatta subscription was opened, of father showing augmented friendship to Mr. Cottrell. Because really, ten shillings! When, as Basil had almost said, they had much more money than we had! 'Lives Dangerously, in mental squalor' and 'Vivacious!' Not even my championship of them could make me feel kindly towards the family if they were going to inflict an intellectual party on us.

I slipped through the gate hoping to get away unquestioned. Mother called from an upstairs window – Where was I going? – Oh, Sootie's. (This was within the law, and gave away nothing; it was also part of the truth.) Well, all right; but I was to be back for tea! – Oh, no, couldn't I have it with the Mawleys, I pleaded. (We often did, but to-day this would mean that I could miss the meal if I found anything more interesting.) Mother guessed that. No, I was to come back for tea, did I understand?

I promised angrily and went on into the sun-dappled woods, accepting none of their shining green consolation at first because of my preoccupation with the longed-for day when I should be able to walk out of any house at any moment, giving no reason to anyone. Time, though I might not be able to control it satisfactorily even then, would at least be my own tool, with which to fashion a private world unfettered by meals. Like most maternally-minded

95

women, mother was unconcerned about the spiritual welfare of those she loved as long as she could personally ensure that they over-ate several times a day. I thought of an incident described by a naturalist in one of my most cherished books, the record of an adult wasp attendant on a wasp-grub, both of which were kept under observation without food for a period, during which the wasp grew more and more agitated on behalf of its hungry charge. Finally it bit off the grub's hind leg, offering it solicitously to what remained. Just the sort of devoted wasp, I felt, that mother might have been. This disloyal comparison made me feel better: it was a form of revenge; and a glimpse of a green woodpecker at work completed my release from home. — It was true, then, what other observers had said: from about twelve yards away you could not see the beak moving when it tapped, though the ear, for once quicker than the eye, could distinguish the separate strokes. This was something to tell Ted (we were both very earnest in hesitating to accept the word of acknowledged authorities because — glorious occasions — we had twice found them wrong on some minor point connected with the migration of terns).

I meant to fetch Ted on my way to the heron's haunt. Alone in our families, we were interested in the same things: I could admit to Ted that watching birds seemed to me more exciting than sailing; indeed, telling him did not feel like 'admitting' anything as it would have done with anyone else: when we were together it seemed natural to talk as though our discovery that two decadent pairs of black-cap gulls were nesting in our marshes, instead of flying north, was the distinguishing feature of that summer, more important even than the regatta.

We had long ago pooled what small knowledge of birds we had; I did all the reading and he the larger share of the observing, for the Mawleys' cottage was on the edge of the saltings, between the woods and the river, built expressly for the purpose it might have been, where the territory of the land-birds overlapped that of the sea-fowl who disputed the marshy ground with them. I could not compete with Ted in observation, because of that advantage. But, in spite of his superiority I always came back from hours with Ted with a pleasant little sense of self-importance, though the reason for this was silly: he was the only person in Pin Mill who used my beautiful Roman name in full instead of its horrid contraction.

A tree that I had never liked whined, branch fretting on branch, as I passed hurriedly through the familiar wood that lay between our houses. Rare in summer, this boisterous north-easterly breeze, which now like a showman pointed the graces of the supple trees, was the same wind that in the autumn would tear at the leaves when their gay strength was over, relentlessly despoiling the branches. It was as if that particular tree knew it, and had not spirit enough to be arrogant in its brief triumph.

Mrs. Mawley, when I arrived, was standing at her door looking over the wind-darkened river. She told me where Ted was, digging for lug-worms on the shore, and asked me to come back with him to tea later on. This worn, unsmiling woman was much kinder to us than mere policy dictated, for father could afford to pay Sootie so little that Sootie could easily have found a better berth as a yacht-hand for the summer, when fishing was poor. I hated refusing her hospitality, which was of the very best kind that never included apologies if there was not enough butter, nor embarrassed me by giving me more than a fair share of anything there was.

'What are you and Ted so interested in up-river? He said, dinner-time, he guessed you'd be over.'

I told her about the heron.

'Good luck to her,' said Mrs. Mawley, 'but you wouldn't catch me trapesing over mud-flats for that!'

'Oh, it's a nice day for mucking about. Not too hot,' I

said, feeling, as usual with an older person, slightly ashamed of any serious interests I had. It was a mark of Mrs. Mawley's worth that with her one only tried to excuse them, not to deny them.

She did not say anything. Generally when any of the Mawleys were silent it did not matter; one need not trouble to talk: that was one of the excellent things about them, especially Ted. But now something in her quietness made me feel awkward. Staring out over the river, her eyes looked so strained, and as if she were angry with everything, much as I had been angry with everything just now.

A wind-squall passed slowly down the Orwell, and remembering Mr. Quest, I said, nodding towards it, 'Looks fine, doesn't it? Makes the water just behind it almost purple.'

'Oh, Nature!' Mrs. Mawley's hard laugh startled me, it held so much more meaning than I could understand. 'I hate Nature,' and she went back into the cottage, shutting the door.

At intervals, during the afternoon and for years after, came back to me the memory of her face as she stared over that smiling view of small, bright waves and green marsh, towards the woodlands, blue-shadowed by distance, on the farther side of the water; – seeing none of it, and resenting with sudden fierceness something that she could not explain.

Ted did not halloo to me as usual when I appeared. He waited, leaning on his spade, looking puzzled, with his eyes screwed up against the sun, until I was quite close. Then he waved.

'Thought you were Miss Dru!' he said. 'That's her hat' (it was). 'Sun behind you, and the wind got in your dress. Made you look ever so fat!'

I was delighted. The pleasant queerness of such a mistake offset the unpleasant queerness of Mrs. Mawley's outburst. It seemed extraordinary that to another person I – I – could look as solid and complete as anybody else. So solid and complete, indeed, that I could be mistaken for a real four-square human being like Dru. I have always been half-surprised to find that I cast as dense a shadow as anybody; and my back view, seen unexpectedly in some arrangement of mirrors, is invariably startling, because it looks so much like anybody else's back. I wondered if everyone secretly felt as I did in this matter – not as real, to other people, as other people were to me? whether young policemen, for instance, stepping into the road for the first time to control traffic, knew the unreasoning panic that I should feel in their place – 'Surely everybody will guess that there is no one but me inside this uniform, not a real policeman at all, and they just won't stop when I hold out my arm!'

I tried explaining this to Ted, not very successfully; but it did not matter, because the short afternoon turned, after all, into one of those lustrous, immeasurable stretches of childhood's time which almost compensate for the boredom of other periods: hours when each blade of grass shone separately with a rare excellence, and there was a feeling abroad of breath-stopping newness – (that sense of superbly recent creation which earth has a little lost the knack of reproducing for me these last ten years). At such times unimaginably exciting or lovely things might come at any moment, I knew, out of the haze which made the usual call of all horizons more insistent than I could bear with any peace of mind. They did come too; solan-geese driving stoutly northwards in wedge formation – the same curved arrow-head shape that had stirred me years ago – against the wind which still ripped mares' tails and curled pennons of transparent vapour out of the dissolving clouds, though near the ground, like a proper summer afternoon breeze, it had died to nothing more than a soft air. Long skeins of duck crossed the horizon, too, on all sides, making dark smudges on the radiant sky when they wheeled and the thickness of the bodies turned towards us, growing almost invisible when they flew in silhouette, so that each skein looked like a succession of puffs of smoke drifting out over the water towards the sea. For a few seconds a hare, lolloping by, paused close to us without seeing us as we lay in the bushes that overlooked the heron's point – what was a hare doing on the edge of a wood? It moved clumsily, as hares do when at ease, hampered in all slow movements by the ill-balanced length of the hind legs. That anything so awkward-looking could outpace a galloping horse, for a short distance, was difficult to believe while I could examine it closely. Then the great eyes and nervous ears became restless; the hare sensed some alien presence and was off, transformed in an instant by speed to a streak of sinewy grace, a seemly part of this magnificent afternoon. I thought how good and rather improbable a dispensation of Providence it was that things which were specially adequate for some workaday purpose, such as fleetness in an animal, or working to windward in a boat, should have latent in them this stunning quality of loveliness, have it to such a lavish degree that even to eyes untrained by the sea, the under-water lines of an ardent boat are invariably lovelier than those of a craft less ably designed for this one object, which has nothing to do with beauty. How nice of Heaven, I thought warmly, to chuck in such a really unnecessary excellence with all the other benevolences about me at the moment.

And the emaciated heron was there, desperately playing her strange game at intervals. We worked our way closer to her than I had ever been before. Though she struck down into the water several times she caught only one thing, so small that we could not make out what it was, all the long while that we lay in the bushes just behind her. Without turning my head I could see a fleck of sun showing up the whiteness of the skin where Ted's much-darned blue guernsey had torn widely over the shoulder. In strong sunlight there are tiny violet glints in protected flesh, and ordinarily invisible hairs show golden. He moved carefully, silently, when the scorching of this spot on his back made itself felt, and grinned round at me for no reason but that the sense of quiet companionship lay over both our minds like a gentler sunshine.

A squirrel, so young that it still wore grey fur on its over-fat stomach, chattered from a branch above us, and the wary heron rose instantly, with that clean dive forward into space, and swift, unhurried opening of the great wings which surprised me with delight however often I watched these movements. Her flight seemed to add a touch of almost unbearable perfection to the water over which the violet shadow sailed, to the bright, pale sky that received the moment's imprint of all wild loneliness on the wing as this one living thing cried desolately in the warm silence, to the shimmering wall of trees which hid her suddenly as the currents of upper air caught her and swirled her, gleaming white in the sun as she banked, over them and beyond our sight, back into a secret existence of her own that we could not share. I wanted to cry out that I was not prepared for this royal extravagance of one afternoon. Water and sky and trees, these familiar blue and gold and green partners of a well-loved scene, did not need a grey bird's magic to enhance their richness. It was too much. – What queer, glowing discontent such trifles as a heron's flight could let loose in one's mind in the days before it had grown a little inured to joy, the days when despair lurked behind every sunset because of the mingling of a child's greed to treasure its glories for ever, with the adolescent's knowledge that in a few moments nothing would remain of them, nothing at all save a vague and priggish satisfaction in regretting them. The feeling seemed so shamefully inadequate to the dying splendours which might never, one felt, crowd into the sky again in just such profusion, and at sixteen it was not yet tolerable to know oneself unworthy of sunsets and birds.

We both looked round, into the wood, for the cause of the squirrel's scolding. Intent on one thing only – a butterfly resting on the ground, of all unlikely prey – and with no eyes for such irrelevancies as ourselves, a cat crept forward into the low aisle of our view along the ground, between the stems of the bushes; crept and paused, and crept on, thin-flanked, quivering, every limb alive with a separate conscious-ness of its own. Each paw, as it advanced, delicately, examined the loose soil without help from the creature's fixed eyes before pressing softly into it, clinging to the ground when the weight of the body had passed on, loth to break this contact, achieved in difficult silence, for fear of the next. But more alive than in movement among the shadows was the cat possessed by stillness, crouching for seconds at a time in the sun patches that flickered over it, and over stumps of wood and stones no more motionless than this taut and eager body. There should have been something absurd in such caution directed to so small an end, a yellow insect tired out by the morning's wind: instead, the sunlight and the empty wood grew baleful; here, in this creature driven and obsessed by an almost objectless desire (for the butterfly was only incidental to its need: the cat did not want it but only its capture) were all skilled and merciless hunters, and the incongruous quarry was one with all hunted things. The silence turned from an absence of noticeable sound to an expectancy, making audible the con-stant murmur of falling beech-mast and the tiny swish of caught twigs releasing themselves from the wind's interweaving.

By its markings and its size it was our cat, but what continuity of existence was there between this silk-muscled killer and the sleepy pet at home? It paused again, shifting its weight from haunch to haunch, limbering for the spring. I moved to stop it; I thought of moving rather, but Ted was quicker in seizing my arm: and the cat pounced on the bright living flower, a yard or two away from us.

'It's not your butterfly, Miss Lalage!' he said as we scrambled up.

'Of course it isn't anyone's,' I said, feeling wretched as the cat softly rolled the body under its paw and a torn off wing quivered on the ground.

'Well, then. You've no call to interfere.' ('But how un-English!' observed Lester Cottrell when I told him of this remark. 'Was it sentiments such as these that annexed us an Empire?')

Over-fed at home, the cat shook its head distastefully as it started to eat the furry little body, and dropped the pieces from its mouth. Changed back into the animal I knew, it rubbed itself against Ted's legs, mewing soundlessly for a caress, and took it sensually with half-closed eyes, behind which the jungle was hidden once more. But the sunlight and the quietness of the wood did not so soon shed the feeling of savagery which the cat had brought into them, and the carelessness of the river, running by to its chuckling meeting with the North Sea tides, made sadder the know-ledge that something sweet and happy had gone out of existence and it did not matter, not to anyone or anything, not even to the butterfly itself now that it was safely dead. The earth was too rich to feel so tiny a loss: there were plenty more butterflies, particularly that year. And very soon I should forget, as the cat had done already, and there would be nothing left, nothing at all. Trying to get the feeling out of my mind I looked at Ted playing with the cat, and wondered that I had not noticed before how finely the muscles ran in his brown arms, on which the colour faded so abruptly that one could tell that he always rolled the right sleeve higher than the other. I had noticed the lopsidedness of that mark before, but this was the first time, I think, that anything else about him seemed worth observing; the shape of the strongly corded throat was suddenly important too. The world was growing better again: it could afford a few butterflies, even though it could not remake the one that had died.

Along the shore from the Cottrells' came Margaret. Few of her habitual movements were slow, but most of them appeared so to me, because I had watched them all minutely so often, trying to make out why they were so much better, somehow, than anyone else's movements, that to me they seemed very leisurely, like the repetition by another person of words or an air that one knows by heart. So now when she began jumping, with arms outstretched for balance, from one tussock to another on the squelchy edge of the salting, I saw each time before it came the shake of the head, to get the loose hair away from her eyes, with which she settled down again for a few steps into her usual quick walk. That free swinging step gave her an air of moving against a light wind, making the sweet, immature lines of her body discernible in spite of the sloppy old clothes that were our usual wear.

Even to me, not two years older than Margaret, her lovely youth was moving. Margaret went by without seeing us, and the quality of the afternoon fused for me suddenly into her image. Here, though I did not think of it clearly at the time, was beauty almost as fragile, almost as swift-passing too in its way, as the butterfly's; here was the graceful ruthlessness of the thing that had preyed on it, and the heron's disturbing appeal to the imagination. The inviolability of water and woods and sky was hers too, keeping her remote however close one came to her; and she had transcendingly that goodness of human flesh which had lent Ted a moment's surprising unity with everything I loved. Consciously I was aware only that the sight of Margaret passing by, grave and unaware of us, had crowned and summed up all the exciting things of this great afternoon, and I did not mind leaving them now, to obey mother, though the scene was smiling again and the dark cruelty of the cat forgotten.

'Must go now,' I said hurriedly to Ted, and wriggled out of the bushes, calling to her to wait.

CHAPTER VI

THE REGATTA

MARGARET was sometimes unsatisfactory to talk to because one could not tell her about moments of private exaltation like those of to-day, and the feeling she produced made it seem silly to say ordinary things. Now, however, there was my five-pound triumph to discuss, and Dru's forthcoming 'few words', and the menace of the Cottrell party. I gave her a harrowing description of the last function at their house, which had been given during father's embarkation leave in the War. She had been considered too young to go, though the Cottrells had clamoured for the presence of what they called our show-piece; presumably she would have to come to this one. The narration of social horrors lasted all the way home.

Our real, unrecognized grievance against the Cottrells' friends on that occasion was that instead of talking right above our heads, as we had felt that intellectuals should (the conversation would then have been merely dull for us, but not exacting) they had talked of just the sort of subjects that we discussed among ourselves, only in a different way. They had all been bewildering enthusiastic, for instance, about Charlie Chaplin, who was in his hey-day at the time; but they spoke of his innate tragic quality, while we flattened ourselves back in our chairs, hoping not to be asked for our opinions, because until then we had merely thought him very, very funny.

It had been much the same with the topic of babies, on which the devoted Mrs. Cottrell had embarked earnestly with mother, and a timid-looking woman novelist, who seemed to crouch for protection behind her one fierce feature, horizontal front teeth. Mother might well have expected to hold her own here, but the novelist, who seemed to have married a man or two in spite of her teeth, said she had always been too busy to be able to accept the tremendous responsiblity of maternity with a clear conscience –'It's unfair, don't you think, to have children unless you're prepared to recognize that motherhood's a full-time job mentally, even if it isn't physically?'

'Well – I suppose – Do you mean . . .?' Mother, who had found it a full-time job physically, and had never given a thought to its moral responsibilities, was soon out of her depth.

In a breathlessly nervous voice which matched her face, downright and bewildering statements which matched the teeth had come pouring from the writer, with Mrs. Cottrell agreeing earnestly, 'Awfully doubtful ourselves at first if we were fit for parenthood . . . both merely dabbled in psychology, you see . . . discussed it for two years . . . often wonder now . . . decided not more than two, in order to give them all the attention they need. . . .' Then mother was asked by the novelist how many children she had had. Wriggling out of a direct answer, 'I've got four,' she said, slightly grateful for the first time, probably, for the death of two of us in infancy. It did reduce the number to what, in this company, seemed more tolerable proportions. Even so, the mild eyes had looked at her with scared apology while the firm voice, backed up by those teeth, laid down the law, 'Well, *I* should never have felt competent to deal with more than two, and I feel sure no woman who . . .'

'. . . in evening dress, my dear, and there was I in my painting rags, positively festooned with gouts of decaying porridge!' Somebody else's conversation had broken in, and I did not hear the end of mother's thorough pulverization.

One man, a very young soldier from the officers' convalescent home at Ipswich, Gordon somebody, I had felt at first that I might have liked. He had seemed out of place and ill at ease too. When he passed me a plate of Mrs. Cottrell's superb cheese truffles (to think that a woman who could produce such things from war-time ingredients should doubt her fitness for anything!) he had looked at me as if in desperate appeal, but afterwards turned out to be an archæologist, and became so erudite on Roman remains in the locality that I lost heart again. A dreadful party.

However, I told Margaret by way of consolation, the food was marvellous even by Cottrell standards, and one ate nearly all the time.

At intervals, throughout the next few days, various members of the family raked up from their memories of that terrifying party other social embarrassments, presumably to be suffered again, and brought them forth excitedly between speculations about the handicapping: 'Oh, do you think the Cottrells will have the awful woman who asked me . . .' '. . . And d'you remember the person with the beard who was always kissing somebody . . .'

These counter-irritants did little, however, to distract me from worrying about the weather, which remained horribly rough. Morning after morning I woke to hear the same north-easter tearing past my window. It dropped each afternoon at about five, but that was no comfort with the one-design race timed for 2.30. I went about in a state of secret tension. Taking a small open boat single-handed among the white sea-horses that now rode the river would be nerve-racking anyway, but racing under father's eye meant sailing as hard as possible: better drive a boat under water than risk losing speed through caution while he was watching.

A desire to pray for the abatement of the wind grew daily in spite of my struggles against it. Father, of course, would be disgusted if he knew of this temptation, I realized. Long ago, with mother's help, I had fashioned God somewhat in father's image, so that God, too, would almost certainly despise any prayer for calm weather that I was contemptible enough to make to the Virgin, who out of kindness would probably not pass it on. And God, as our priest frequently assured us in sermons, often answered prayers indirectly, not giving people what they asked for, but something that would really be better for them. If I succumbed to my fear, then, and prayed wildly for a gentle breeze, Heaven might rightly feel that what I deserved on Saturday was half a gale: I dared not pray.

But it was not prudence alone which prevented this alleviation of my feelings: pride helped, too, or such remnants of pride as remained to me after realizing that I was afraid of something to which every other Rush looked forward! I had lately caught Doubts from my mother, who shortly after this finally lost her faith and left the Roman Catholic Church; though how or why this great mental upheaval took place in her life at this period none of us ever knew: we saw only the outward symptoms of turmoil and nervous weariness, fuss over trifles, a little less than her usual sweetness, but the inner change remained, even for father, one of the mysteries of family life which are easily disregarded because they evolve so close to the observers. The feeling of tension in her was contagious only for one member of the household, apparently: I was no longer sure that I believed in a God who seemed to have let down someone so kind and gentle, and made her unhappy. If it would be disgusting, anyway, to pray because I was afraid, it would be still more contemptible to pray to a being whose existence I occasionally doubted.

At meal-times for the next few days, as a relaxation from the regatta topic, Dru was constantly threatened by us all with the renewed attentions of the tape-like person whom the

Cottrells had introduced at the last party as 'Bertie-the-sculp'. 'N'tell me,' he had started time after time, and then forgotten what he had wanted to be told. With our old-world taste for simple puns we had christened him Bertie-the-Scalp because he had coiled down his extraordinary, flexible length at the feet of the embarrassed Dru, throwing over his shoulder to her, all the evening, a one-sided discussion of his personality.

He was Dru's one and only admirer, we insisted, taking our cue from mother, who had lately begun to single out Dru – father's favourite – for the lion's share of all the teasing that went on in our household. Besides being the eldest, Dru was the plainest of the family (her excess of puppy-fat saved me from that position) and at eighteen she had none of the crowd of admirers by whom mother had been surrounded at that age. The irritability of a fading beauty at her daughter's failure to repeat her triumphs is as common a thing as jealousy of her success, but so much subtler in its effects that it more often escapes notice. Taking our cue from mother we rubbed in the jest with the tireless-ness of family humour. He, at least, would be sure to come again, we said, not knowing that he had been killed in France. How disappointed he would be to see that she had grown so much fatter! Hearing our table-talk about Dru's figure, any blind person would have gathered that the girl was abnormal. Dru herself came to believe it, I think: it was in these days that she began avoiding the society of young men. Soon mother's gibe – never openly expressed – that her uncourted state was her own fault, became perfectly justified, at least on the surface.

Unconsciously protecting her from mother's friendly-seeming mockery, father drew a red herring of handicap problems across the trail whenever Dru's staunch smile showed signs of weakening. She herself countered the attacks by emphasizing her usual attitude of carelessness towards everything, particularly the ordeal of making a speech. She pooh-poohed still more firmly any suggestion of learning her few words by heart beforehand.

My admiration of her reached great heights in those few days before the regatta. We shared a bedroom, and as I watched her gabbling through her prayers night and morning, I realized with envy that she had no need of belief or disbelief: she never thought about such things. The only difference that the crisis in mother's spiritual life had made to her, apart from the indirect one of becoming the family butt, was that she did not now have to cycle seven miles to Ipswich for Mass on Sundays. Asked if there were a God she would have said, 'Yes, of course,' in surprise. But required to back up her words in any practical way, even to the extent of sixpence of her pocket-money, she would certainly have hesitated, and probably refused. I knew that if she guessed how ardently I longed to pray for a calm day she would have despised me even more than father. The sense of isolation was very depressing.

Indeed, the next four days were far more richly charged, emotionally, than was usual in Pin Mill, what with the forthcoming party, the regatta itself, Dru's speech, my secret religious trouble, and the great Rush-Cottrell subscription question, which came to a head in a public fight outside the Butt & Oyster between Mrs. Mawley's cousin and the local milkman (the Cottrells drank pints more milk a day than we did). Their champion was bloodily disposed of. And then came the handicapping, which father only announced on the day before the notable Saturday. He had refused to give his own family any early information. We found, when we clustered round the notice board with the rest of the village, that father's famous sense of fair play had penalized us to an extent that Ronald, for one, considered out of all proportion to our abilities. He and father had the beginning of a scene about it at lunch, before Dru came in, late, and sat down with an expression of bewilderment on her jolly face. She said nothing for a while.

'Making up your speech!' Margaret accused her.

Dru made a contemptuous noise. 'I've just seen Mrs. Cottrell,' she began uncertainly, and paused. 'She asked me – she asked us to stay to supper after tea on Sunday.'

'Oh! All right.' Father and Ronald seemed about to return to their discussion. Both looked angrier than the situation appeared to warrant: Ronald was rather white, as usual when his temper was getting the better of him.

'She said,' Dru went on, still in the same half-stunned voice, "As I don't suppose I'll see you till then. You'll be so busy over the regatta, won't you?"'

There was a longer hush while the implication of this sank into our minds, and then everyone talked together:

'But the party . . .'

'They aren't expecting . . .'

'We shan't be going . . .'

There was another long pause, in which astonishment turned to resentment, and after that fury raged. Our former dislike of the prospect of their party was nothing to our present bitterness at being left out of it. The Cottrells were giving a party and not asking us! Not including us, rather; for we had imagined that we were on terms which made invitations unnecessary!

From that moment all of us but father, who laughed at us for caring so much, came in openly at least on the Rush side of the regatta-subscription question. Even mother, for once, criticized straightforwardly and not by implication. Would that the Mawley cousin had battered the partisan milkman even more effectively.

Dru and Ronald, feeling that retaliation of some sort was essential, slipped off to Ipswich on their bicycles and procured a set of loathsome postcards from a versatile chemist's shop in the docks. Officially practising for the regatta, they were absent at supper time on the night of the party, when opulent limousines and ramshackle cars in great variety drove up one after the other to the Cottrells' modest gate. It was a party of celebrities, we gathered; and this in no way soothed us. Standing on either side of the Cottrell gate, disguised in filth and rags, Dru and Ronald molested every comer. Their behaviour was extremely un-Rush; but then the situation, they felt, was unparalleled.

'Buy a feelthy peecture, lady?' Dru's grimy hands plucked at the arms that passed. 'For one sheeling I show de shentle-man de twenty-seex poseetions of lof?' Having inevitably picked up a repertoire of such phrases from the continental docks (cruising, as father often said, is a fine clean game that teaches one a lot besides seamanship) Ronald kept recommending the repulsive looking Dru to each male arrival as 'Vair cheap, vair lofing, vair clean!' and pestered them almost to the front door. The pair were bent on show-ing the Cottrells that though we might not talk of such things as a rule, we knew just as much about Life as their beastly friends did, and there was therefore no excuse for our exclusion. Though they could not see the pair from the house, the Cottrells were bound to guess who was responsible for this nuisance. (Really, it was greatly to the credit of that kindly family that neither of our parents, who would have been distressed by the incident, ever heard of it.)

Dame Ethel Smythe (Dru thought; but it may have been Edith Evans, since both were there) gave her a shilling to go away, and she surreptitiously slipped three postcards into the spacious cuff of this lady's coat. Childish and regrettable as the whole business was, it would still interest me to know, if they survived the evening in that hiding place as seems probable, in what company these pictures were subsequently discovered, and how their presence was explained.

Having acquitted themselves with a lewdness unsurpassed by the Cottrells at any time, the representatives of our prudish but outraged family returned home well pleased with themselves, comfortably aware that they had matured, between the younger members of both families at any rate, the long-sown estrangement which had really been growing imperceptibly ever since the unfortunate trip to Little-hampton years ago.

Whole-heartedly approving at the time, I was, all the same, a little worried: being at feud with Marnie and Lester was going to prove boring. I should have been much more worried if I could have foreseen the little ripples of cause and effect spreading out from this affair towards issues affecting all my life. No one, at sixteen, would welcome the idea of a future in any way moulded by the hawking of what the angry vendors called 'feelthy peectures'. At the moment I was chiefly concerned with more immediate troubles: the glass was rising jerkily, which suggested even more wind to-morrow, the great and dreadful day.

Dru's much-abused rotundities, those fruits of a calm, self-confident spirit, took on godly proportions in my eyes as, this night of all nights, she knelt in her straining pyjamas to say her absent-minded prayers, undisturbed by thoughts of to-morrow.

I wrestled against the temptation of prayer for the last time, and won. Conscious of a certain nobility in this victory, I had a faint last hope that God (if any) might reward my abstinence with a suitable day for the regatta, but such subtleties seemed to be above the heavenly mind: Saturday was just like the rest of the week. No worse: I had at least escaped that retribution, but a brute of a day from what I could see of it at about five o'clock in the morning – sun-patched and wildly blowing.

The first and only immediate result of our split with the Cottrells was that the four of us Rush children had constantly to find new excuses for not accompanying mother on to the committee boat, where she wanted to settle down early for the day: as vice-chairman Mr. Cottrell would have to be there, with his family, however superior they might all feel to aquatic sports in which they did not indulge, and meeting them with the necessary public friendliness would be more than we could manage.

Until eleven o'clock, when the racing started and took my mind off my ordeal a little, I ambled about the shore numb with terror, saying like everyone else, 'Topping, isn't it, to get such a bright day? Rotten if it had rained! I'd much rather have too much wind than not enough, wouldn't you?'

Everyone agreed except Ted Mawley, whose firm 'That I wouldn't! Could do with a drop of rain, too, to flatten this jabble!' made me fonder of him than ever. The courage some people had! To say that in father's hearing when really, as a stolid and unimaginative lad, he could not be feeling one-tenth of my hatred for these whooping gusts which were ploughing white tracks through the leaping water!

I was not at hand to wish Dru good luck when she went off for the first big event, the twenty-mile race to the Cork lightship and back, in which she was skippering *Guadalupe*. It would have seemed a useless wish anyway: for luck would not have much showing, we felt: father was handicapping her skill as well as his boat's speed when he arranged that she should get only twenty minutes time allowance from the biggest boat, a racing yacht from Burnham-on-Crouch, fairly bulging with polished brass and paid hands. Several craft easily able to outsail the little *Guadalupe* had arrived from Harwich and Walton for this race, and if Dru had not been his daughter she would have received at least forty minutes. But he knew with pride that he could rely on Dru to put up a first-class struggle to finish fifth or thereabouts.

Just before she started I was forced to hurry back to our house, filled with new forebodings by a sick headache which had suddenly developed. Matters, I found on investigation, were just as I feared. Ill luck, or sheer fright, or the Cottrell upset, or a combination of the three, had added a premature last straw to my load of misery: I had the curse. Like most thin, overgrown girls of that age, I always got it very badly. Standing about for hours in a cold wind, between bouts of violent exertion, was going to be much worse than I had expected; almost beyond endurance, in fact. I suddenly decided that whatever father might think of me, I was not going to do my damnedest in the racing. But the idea of getting out of the whole business because I was unwell did not occur to me: nor would it to any girl in our family, or, I suppose, in any of the hundreds of similar families in England.

I returned to the Hard hot against whatever gods there be, who not content with ignoring unspoken prayers must malevolently confuse this Saturday with next Wednesday. There I found to my surprise that the starting gun for Dru's race had only just gone, though the 'Get Ready' signal had been given before I left the water-side. The Cottrell party had just arrived, late of course, and father, greeting Mr. Cottrell with marked public joviality, had been drawn into eager conversation with their American guest, out of whom not even his hosts had hitherto prised more than two sentences at a time. The talk went on and on – father, the official starter, becoming as usual oblivious of every irrelevant claim upon him in the course of fascinating a stranger.

In view of the high feeling in the village Sootie was not going to let Mr. Cottrell, the other possible starter, fire the ten-minutes gun during father's absence in the Butt & Oyster with the American. Why not? demanded the pro-Cottrells, and our supporters merely reiterated annoyingly that we'd be damned if he should. Public feeling began working up again, between the friends of the milkman and the innumerable Mawley relatives, towards another fight. Sootie maintained our position by saying, untruthfully, that father had all the blank cartridges in his pockets. Unwilling to get under way until the ten-minutes gun went, because there was not much room for large yachts to tack about near the starting-line, the competitors for this race remained at shortened anchor, tossing and rolling horribly. The result of this movement, harder on the stomach than anything a boat can do while cutting through water, was that Dru turned sick a few minutes after the starting gun was fired at last.

This only incapacitated her for a few seconds, but they were crucial ones, in which *Guadalupe* swerved wildly up to windward, menacing the next boat, while Dru at the tiller leant blindly over the lee rail. She was entitled to bluff her rivals out of their course if she could, but unwittingly she now took a risk of fouling the nearest yacht which looked like a certainty to us on shore. To those in the threatened boat, too, a collision must have seemed almost inevitable, for in panic their skipper shoved his helm hard down – too hard – and his boat, the favourite for the race, rushed straight into the wind and hung there with flogging canvas, while Dru regained control of *Guadalupe* and bore away, her bowsprit escaping the other's shrouds by a few inches. The savage wind swooped on the boat that had lost her steerage way and flung her, rail under, back on the former tack. As she paid-off helplessly before she could gather speed again, she butted into the boat that was closely following Dru, putting both parties to the collision out of action: it was a fine mix-up of spars and cross-trees. Though technically within her rights, Dru would not have cut her margin of safety so fine at any other time: as it was, she had rid herself at the start of the two boats who had been considered practically sure of the first and second places.

They passed out of sight behind Collimer Point, Dru a little behind the eighteen-tonner who would probably win now, and level with another boat to whom she was giving a quarter of an hour on time. Though this marvellous accident, which we all cheered wildly, did not really give Dru a proper chance of winning the race, she had at least acquired quite good prospects of being third.

Still, these boats would not be home for at least three hours; and meanwhile there was the Under Five Tons race in which Ronald, in a bold moment on a calm day, had entered his own nailsick craft *Hedgehog*, given to him years ago by father to save the bother of scrapping her. *Hedgehog* was about the only floating object which even father could not sell. There was a family legend, started by father, that whenever one of our linen-backed charts disappeared, the odds were that Ronald had found another spot between wind and water where daylight shone through her hull, and needed something for patching.

'Hullo,' Lester greeted him icily in passing, 'Indulging in any of your merry pranks to-day?'

Ronald did not answer: he was standing by me trying to get father's ear, but father was deep again in conversation with the American chemist, whose brother, it appeared, had been on a scientific expedition up the Amazon many years before, but still vividly remembered meeting father – and no wonder. Listening distractedly, with my eyes on the tumultuous water, I could picture that encounter from what was being said – the once-trim little Amerian steamer stuck in a floating morass of flowering weed, her paint blistered off, her crew appalled by their growing suspicion that the stream up which they had been forcing their way for weeks was only a tributary of the giant river, into which they had turned by error; and the impenetrable wall of tropical forest on either side, broken by no sign of human habitation for hundreds of miles. And then the canoe with the half-naked man in it, skimming through openings in the damnably scented vegetation that blocked their passage: their excited attempts to hail this gold-skinned god in Brazilian-Spanish

117

and the local Indian dialect. And his answering, 'Where are you from? . . . No, this is the Parana . . . you'll have to go back two hundred miles . . . My name's Rush . . . did you hear before you left who won the America Cup last year?'

Genuinely, I knew, the fate of the America Cup contest of the previous year would have been one of father's first interests on meeting white men again after months in the Chaco. But what satisfaction he must have derived, immediately afterwards, from realizing just how odd this interest really was! I could imagine, too, without the American's halting efforts to convey his brother's lasting stupefaction, what father must have looked like in those days. He was still the handsomest man I had met. It was not surprising that hearing the name Rush, and seeing him standing on the sunlit Hard with his light, wild hair ruffled by the wind, the American had known without hesitation that this man with the figure of a boy must be the apparition seen long ago by someone else on the other side of the world.

The firing of the first gun for the five-tonners brought him back to Pin Mill. Ronald got his word in at last.

'I'll have to scratch my old *Pig*,' he said, regretfully, 'she couldn't stand such a bucketing.'

'Too late,' said father curtly. 'First gun's gone. If you wanted to get out of the race you should have given notice before. Off you go.'

Ronald stiffened and the slight change in his face and bearing was reflected in father's.

'It's nothing to do with getting out of the race,' he said hotly, 'I know the state of the hull. So ought you. She'd sink.'

'That's your look-out.' Father was angry, half smiling in a way I had not seen before. He said slowly, dropping the words one or two at a time into a cold pause, 'And personally, I'd rather my family didn't do their funking in public, Ronald.' I do not think the American heard: even if he did, no outsider would have guessed the slow-kindled enmity that flamed up between father and son. The two looked at one another for a few seconds while I dug my nails into my hands, wishing furiously I did not know what: that father had not just this splendid air which always brought me on to his side in any argument; that I did not feel such intense sympathy with Ronald.

He stood quite still for a minute, with the blood draining out of his face, 'All right, I'll go,' he said. Turning he ran down the Hard. Margaret and I, who were to have been his crew, shouted after him; he took no notice, and I at least was relieved. 'You'll come. And you. And you. To bale,' he said high-handedly to three of the village boys of his own age. They had already withdrawn their own boat from the race. He was curiously like father at the moment, though much more vehement than they had ever known father: somehow he made them go with him. All through the race they passed a bucket at top speed from hand to hand – cabin to step, step to well, contents shot overside in one movement, and then back to the cabin, where the water rose in spite of their efforts, rushing in through the rotten hull while Ronald drove her with 'all plain sail' on her. Each of his five competitors (four others had scratched on account of the weather) had three reefs in the mainsail and only a rag of a jib. As she sank lower in the water the over-'tender' *Hedgehog* seemed stiffer. Ronald chanced the water gaining on them too much to be fought back later, and we saw him signal to the balers to come out for a second and get her spinnaker ready as she approached the last buoy, only a length or so ahead of Basil Quest's taut little boat, to which Ronald had to give five minutes on time, through a whim of father's. From here on he had a straight run home.

To the spectators it was the most exciting race of the day. No one who knew the state of the *Hedgehog's* planking expected her to stand, from one minute to the next, the constant burying of her bow by the weight of the canvas to which Ronald clung stubbornly even when, yawing perilously, *Hedgehog* was running goose-winged and by the lee on the last lap.

Father was fairly dancing about the committee boat towards the finish. 'She'll do it – Christ! Did you see her boom lift then? – If he gybes all standing she's a gonner – About three minutes ahead – No, she can't possibly do it now. . . .'

Ronald won, beaching the sinking boat on Cathouse Point before he left her. Father walked over to welcome him, but mother was there first. Ronald looked worn out and still rather pale when he waded ashore. 'Done the old *Pig* in,' he said to her. 'Well, it doesn't matter, she wouldn't have lasted another season anyway.'

'Well done, Ronnie!' father said, standing behind mother. 'Awfully good show.'

'I say, there's at least three inches of mud over some of this shingle, mother,' Ronald said quickly. 'You'll get it over the top of your goloshes. I'll give you a lift across the worst bit, because I'm soaked anyway.' He picked her up in spite of protests, holding her small body like a shield between himself and father, whose congratulations he did not acknowledge.

'Got a welt over the eye from the foresail cringle,' he told her. 'You know how that makes it stream. Could hardly see for weeping on one side.' But there was no mark on his forehead that I could see, and both eyes looked equally shiny beyond the normal, and slightly red, I thought. *Hedgehog* had been his first command, and father his closest friend. I do not know if father realized, as he hurried back to the Hard to resume his duties, that because his son was so like him, he had lost the boy for ever by that one insult, an aspersion, absurdly enough, on the one quality, physical courage, which was really beyond question in both of them.

Taking place in the shallows, through which the competitors could easily swim ashore when necessary, several of the minor races were all the better fun for the roughness of the water. I wondered if Mr. Quest was watching unwillingly. Ronald was surprisingly easily beaten in sculling by Basil Quest, and even by Lester Cottrell in swimming; he seemed to have no heart left. In the 'Pull-devil-pull-baker' event, the soot and flour thrown at one another by the contestants was swept by the wind all over the Committee boat, a pleasing diversion, we felt, the chief sufferers being Mrs. Cottrell, charmingly dressed for the occasion, and Marnie, who had read a book through most of the proceedings so far. After this, they and their party retreated to the shore, and took to wandering about the Hard, which made it impossible for us to avoid them. Smiles of hypocritical sweetness were produced by all save father, who still felt genuinely cordial towards everything Cottrell.

Lester, proving his detachment from the scene, having participated in just that one race, enjoyed a great success among his own family and guests, by quoting aloud from the current issue of his inevitable *Times*. 'Those who believe in the Resurrection can afford to wait,' he culled from the solemnities of the Saturday sermon, and standing by, pretending not to hear, we failed as usual to understand why the Cottrells and their friends rocked with laughter. There was also something about 'loyal convicts' in an account of a recent prison riot, apparently meaning those who had not supported their fellows in cracking warders on the head; and the report of the savage quelling of the mutiny ended with the words 'we hear from a reliable source that there is still some discontent among the convicts', which also seemed to afford them a certain grim pleasure.

Anxiety prevented my attending to any further gems that Lester discovered: the one-designs would start in three-quarters of an hour, and mother and Stella Quest were talking to me with the soothing cheerfulness of the patient's friends, who are not going to undergo the operation themselves, and therefore entertain no doubts as to its happy results.

The Odd Craft race was billed to come first, but there was talk of cancelling it. I ardently hoped that this would not be done, for it would put forward the other races: anything for a few more minutes before I need face this leaping water myself! Obviously most of the floating junk which the village had produced as a joke could not possibly live for a minute in such weather. Margaret, as the youngest entrant, had been allotted the safest if slowest thing available, an eccentric miniature paint-float which father had built as an experiment. Now, to father's annoyance, Margaret was insisting on wallowing over the course on it alone, if necessary, put up to this by Ronald. As a competitor it was her right; by the accepted official ruling, if one entrant was prepared to sail, the race must take place. Father wanted to wash out the whole thing, to prevent the prize that he had given himself going to one of his own family. To my momentary relief and Ronald's vindictive joy, he had to give in, and Margaret steered the ridiculous craft to undisputed victory. From Mr. Quest's point of view this much-discussed event must have been unexpectedly innocuous, for there was no possibility of the paint-float capsizing to distract him from his work.

Father became distrait from the moment he realized that, in spite of his handicapping, his children had already won two of the principal events.

My heart, my head and my stomach all felt unfit to grapple with the situation. With a griping pain making me double up unobtrusively at intervals, I could not get through my share of the sandwiches which mother had put up for lunch, and in order to avoid comment, fed them surreptitiously to the Cottrells' nasty little dog. The Cottrell party amalgamated with us for lunch, at father's hearty suggestion. Besides the two foreign guests of the last few days, they had with them the archæologist whom I had met at the previous party, and a friend of his, a dark woman with a limp who had also stayed on from yesterday's gathering. The latter kindly tried to talk to me, and I answered at random. Another quarter of an hour at most – ten minutes – seven. At intervals I partially emerged from the coma of fear which possessed me, and heard in a dream-like way the lowered voice of Mrs. Cottrell expatiating on Margaret's looks to the pair beside me; or the eager tones of the young Frenchman, asking questions and absorbing sporting information from mother for his newspaper series. Then the squeal of the wind took on a shriller note, and my immediate surroundings faded away while I visualized what might be happening a few minutes hence. I was the only one of our family who was not a good swimmer. Twenty yards was about my limit; after that my strokes got faster and faster and I disappeared below a trail of bubbles: in clothes I was not sure that I could swim at all, and almost certainly not in this sea.

By the time that I was again fully conscious of anything in my surroundings but the look of the water and the vehemence of the squalls, the young Frenchman, entirely charmed by mother, was half-shouting his views on life, love and food up-wind to her, and Mr. Cottrell was giving the two new guests his version of the bandit story, father having self-effacingly refused to oblige.

'. . . in that *quartier*, Madame, there is but one sole restaurant *pour les gourmets*; and in it you shall eat always of one thing, special of the house, *cuisse d'une nymph émue* . . .'

'Rush, here, went back to his tent and found that in spite of his double sentries, this amazing chap had pinched his sleeping bag. There wasn't a sign of the thief. So Rush stood at the door and shouted furiously at the sentries that the fellow must still be in the camp, and when he looked back, damn it if the thief hadn't got clean away with his camp bedstead! . . .'

'Ah, mais n'est ce pas, pour une femme, Madame, c'est une volupté d'obéir?'

(After this, Dru would have a bad time at home for a while, the unexpressed burden of much teasing would be that if mother could still captivate men, at her age, surely Dru at eighteen might be expected to do the same?)

'Odd,' remarked the dark woman confidentially to the archæologist, forgetting how voices carried down-wind, 'the way foreigners never let up on being foreign.' In spite of my preoccupation, this struck me as the most sensible remark I had ever heard from the brainy Cottrells or any of their friends. She and the man I had once liked, Gordon Summers, smiled at one another more than at her words, I thought; and at once they seemed to be isolated together by some emotion that I could not understand; it did not seem to be connected with what she had said. I was not a particularly sensitive person, but acute feeling on my own account for once sharpened my perception beyond the normal, instead of deadening it. Suddenly I envied them, envied them intensely; and not knowing why, supposed that it was because they were not faced with my ordeal.

'*Windflower* or *Semiramis!*' father coolly interrupted Mr. Cottrell's account of his adventures to point out the yacht just coming into view round Collimer Point. The big boats of the first race had now been gone for over three hours; we knew that they must have been getting a tremendous dusting out in the open sea by the Cork light vessel, and when the returning yacht came clear enough of the land to show that it was *Windflower*, we saw, too, that her foresail was in ribbons.

'I'll be glad when Dru gets back,' mother said, un-Rushly. 'You only gave her twenty minutes on *Windflower*, didn't you,

Arthur? Still, I shan't expect *Guadalupe* to show up for another half hour.' Father nodded agreement, but continued to strain his eyes down river.

Lying over at a tremendous angle, the top of another mast appeared behind the elbow of land. Too little of it showed as yet for anything more than a guess at the identity of the boat, but 'Oh, Christ!' said father with foreboding.

No one who had watched his jubilant reception of Ronald's victory, and now observed his face as *Guadalupe* plunged round the bend, would have guessed that Dru was his favourite child, and this staggering victory on her meagre time allowance the fine fruit of all his training. It was a triumph of endurance and daring: Ted's subsequent description of what the crew went through near the Cork was hair-raising.

'We're doing very well, aren't we, sir?' ventured Mrs. Mawley, beaming for once. 'Three races!'

'Yes, aren't we,' said father without enthusiasm. 'Warning gun for the one-designs, Sootie! Go on, Lallie. Good luck!'

(Oh, Holy Mother, please – No, no. It'll be over in half an hour.) With an inarticulate prayer that I should not be reduced to praying, I went down the Hard acknowledging good wishes with a grin because I could not speak, my mouth was too dry. I was facing the prospect of returning (presuming that I did return, which part of my mind refused even to hope, at the moment) to family obloquy. Whatever might be said or thought of me, I knew now that I was going to sail a shamefully careful race. Anything to avoid being capsized. It was bad enough to have to sail at all in my condition: I should have a worse time than usual for several months to come: I must not be immersed altogether in cold water.

'Reef right down, Miss Lalage. It's crool!' was all that Ted was able to make me hear as our boats crossed.

'Damn that, you've *got* to win!' said Ronald, who was rowing me out to my dinghy, too fragile a craft to be allowed to bump about with the others at the end of the Hard. 'This is the only race father couldn't handicap us in, and we've won all the others that matter. Made him look a proper fool. He'll be frightfully sick if you do, and I'll wring your neck if you don't."

It was a minor athletic feat to climb from one boat to another in this weather, and a worse struggle to get the reefs in the sail while the wind tore at the loose canvas, banging the light spars about threateningly. My hands were shaking so much that my sailing self fell into a panic lest the five minutes gun should go before I was anything like ready, and the rest of me hoped it would. The pain of a badly torn finger nail, ripped on the canvas when a gust snatched at the loose sail, only made itself felt long after the race. Water started flipping in over the bow when I crawled forward to sweat up the sail, so that I was forced to bale while still on the mooring. Perhaps the worst moment of the whole race was the one in which I had to let go of the mooring. For an immeasurable space of time the boat hung in the wind, and I watched a heavy squall bearing down on me. Then the crackling sail filled suddenly, terrifyingly: the gunwale dipped so that for a fraction of a second a green wave-edge bulged over it, but had no time to break in before the boat leapt forward, out of its individual menace into that of another wave. After that I had no time to think at all in the battering wind, save of what to do in the immediate present.

I did not know before that race what a good sailor I was, in what father would have called the worst sense. My greatest temptation and danger was to sail the boat too gently, so that in my efforts to keep her as upright as possible I should lose way, leaving her at the mercy of an extra hard puff. I performed cowardly marvels of compromise, judging nicely the varying weight of the squalls, and the breaking point of each successive wave. Gradually every faculty became numb, save this one.

The other five boats left me behind almost at once. I had little attention to spare for them, but out of the tail of an eye I saw the sudden disappearance, in a flurry of wind and water, of the bobbing splodge of red which had been the hull of the Mawleys' boat, showing down to the keel. Soon I passed her, floating full to the gunwale, with Ted's younger brother Ratty clinging to her and waving me on. A fine swimmer, he preferred all the same to stay where he was and watch, until someone from the shore came out to pick him up, rather than get to land by his own efforts through that water.

A woman competitor from Harwich had her boat dismasted on the windward leg of the first round. By the time that the race was half over I was oblivious of the sick wrench in the stomach that had at first come paralysingly whenever I had to stretch back over the windward gunwale for balance. In the wildly unstable world where I existed, second after second without past or future, there was nothing – no pain, no hope of the race ever ending, no conscious fear, even – nothing except my sailing self and this small bucking, fighting craft, that for some forgotten reason must be driven from one point to another despite our three enemies – water in sheets of blinding spray, water in solid, crashing waves, and the screaming air that shifted its direction a trifle from second to second.

On land, a fierce wind sweeps by in separate gusts, with softer intervals between, flowing constantly from one direction. But over water the pulse in the angry air quickens to a relentless fluttering. The invisible hands that batter at one's face and body have an infinite variety of weight and cunning with which to bruise the senses, and the point of attack alters subtly, with each flutter, so that the dazed mind longs for continuity almost as much as for respite, if only of a few seconds' duration; and finds neither.

I would not look ahead more than need be, and in consequence I came up with each buoy a little before I dared let myself expect it.

There were only three of us left in the race by the time that I came to the last leg to windward, the final out-and-back turn before the finishing line. Had there been any way of staging a safe and convincing accident of some kind – the mast or halyard breaking, or the sail splitting – I should have taken it then, for turning dead into the wind again was misery. But I had thought all that out before; there was no disqualification that I could manage less risky than carrying on. From an unreasoning belief in the old wives' idea that one's feet must be kept dry on the first day of a period I still held mine carefully out of the water swilling over the bottom boards. I had been wet to the skin from the beginning of the race, and every cold douche of wave-top that broke in-board drenched me again so thoroughly that I need not have bothered.

I did not follow the other two boats into the shallows, where they were fighting to cheat the adverse tide, when we started the last run home. To do so I should have had to gybe violently and, unwilling to risk that, I stuck to the deep water. They were in another world as far as I was concerned; what did it matter who won? I did not even see them cutting the under-water mudflats finer and finer in their efforts to outsail each other, until eventually both ran aground. They got off again in a minute or so, but meanwhile, keeping my attention strictly to myself, unaware of my isolation, I had passed them and won.

'Well, congratulations, Rush!' said Mr. Cottrell heartily. 'Your children *have* scooped the pool,' and seemed amazed when father turned on him at last and was exceedingly rude about his subscription.

'Ladies and gentlemen, I do hope everybody understands . . .'

Hoisted to her feet by friendly force, Dru stood, terrified, at the top of the Butt & Oyster table, staring fixedly at an envelope on which, during the dinner, she had tried to scrawl something to say. In belated panic she had realized the impossibility of observing brightly and briefly that the best sailors had won.

'I mean, it isn't as if – I mean, father doing the handicapping, and all that . . .'

I gripped the edge of the table hard with my hurt finger, trying not to feel too keenly for her, trying not to see the Cottrells exchanging glances.

'Of course, everybody knows it was perfectly fair, but all the same I do hope everybody understands . . .' She stopped again. I dared not look at her in the long pause. I knew she was gazing hopelessly at the envelope. Then either some vestige of self-possession returned to her or her knees gave way. She sat down, amid applause.

I slipped out of the hot crowded room, which smelt of beer and the smoke from oil lamps. My head was still aching wretchedly from the exertions of the day, and I did not want to remain on the scene of Dru's discomfiture.

In the soft summer dusk in which the squalls had died (*why* could they not have done it earlier!) the water lapped against the yard wall over which I leant. Two other people stood near by, silent, very still, a little apart, looking out over the velvet-black river which was touched in-shore by dancing gold reflections from the lit windows of the inn. They were smoking, and when their cigarette tips glowed I saw that close to me was the dark woman with the limp, Mrs. Macdonald, and beyond her, Gordon Summers, the archæologist. For as long as I was there – ten minutes or so – neither of them spoke: but I did not feel that I was interrupting their companionship.

A curlew passed overhead unseen, calling repeatedly. I wondered if their preoccupation with each other armoured them against the disturbing magic of that wild sound, the feeling it gave one of nearing, for a second, the exciting heart of some dark unhappiness, deeper than anything a human mind could hold for longer than the passing instant of the call. But at the moment they did not seem to be aware of anything outside themselves, even though they did not look at one another. There was something vivid about their quietness. Suddenly, for the second time, I envied them intensely.

Looking back, it seems odd that I should have envied those two, of all people, on the day which ended the least unsatisfactory part of their long, unhappy companionship.

CHAPTER VII

OLIVE AND FATHER

'IF there's one thing I hate,' said father, 'it's unnecessary fresh air.' He gave his hard-case scowl at the assembled Cottrells, who had the passion for draughts common among intellectuals, and enjoyed himself going round their sitting-room shutting all the windows. (The thoughts of everyone present ran at once, I suppose, to the storms he had weathered at sea, and the days of exposure in the Chaco and Green-land, almost unendurably hot and cold, both of which he had enjoyed.)

We all laughed, because like most of father's sayings about himself, it would have been so funny if anyone had believed it; and this lightened the atmosphere of the awkward family conclave which was being held about Olive, whose services economy had forced us to go on sharing with them, in spite of the split. Olive, whose response to the most ordinary remark was still to look arch – who grew flustered if asked a question – whose procedure, when told to fetch anything, was to retire hurriedly to the kitchen from which issued, after a long pause, a slight clink heralding another long silence, but practically never the thing required – who after five years of service remained too shy to speak directly to the males of either family if she could help it – Olive, giggling coyly at her predicament, was swelling up in an unmistakable fashion, and as coyly refusing to father the child on to anyone; so that being an orphan without known relatives, she would shortly be responsible for the sole support of another human being besides herself on a weekly wage of eighteen shillings, and no prospects. Very shortly, indeed; she had got away with her condition for nearly six months, because no one could believe what they noticed.

She had considerably aggravated her offence in our eyes by practically forcing us to parley with the Cottrells about it. Only a week had passed since the regatta.

This was my first contact with the workings of romance, or what ought, I felt, to have been romance. I was aggrieved that it should prove so disappointing from close at hand. I was only too eager to champion lawless splendour in any form, even Olive's if it could house such a thing, but everyone around her was being so kind that there was no call for champions, and no splendour anyway. Romance was not possible in a situation which held none of the germs of tragedy, and in no circumstances could Olive become a tragic figure, not with that fat loose mouth, of which the upper lip was constantly drawn down into a dreadfully roguish smile; not with those bulbous hands and feet. A slightly more than half-witted servant having a baby by an unknown man – really unknown; probably some Ipswich lout whose name she had not learned when she met him casually on her day out, too shy to resist his advances – No, it was utterly undramatic, and merely irritating, because I foresaw that it would mean housework for me. I looked with increasing disapproval on the grotesque mysteries of pregnancy.

Still, it was flattering to be allowed into this conference. Everything had been conscientiously discussed before the Cottrell children at any age, but I felt that my parents' tolerance of my presence here must mean that they considered me grown up at sixteen. It was always a mean satisfaction to me when Margaret was considered too young for something for which I was qualified: it meant that I could enjoy a feeling of being really life-size for once; when we were together she eclipsed me so thoroughly not only in other people's eyes but in my own.

Lester and Marnie were in their element on such a committee. When mother, the ex-Catholic, suggested doubtfully, 'But couldn't something – you know – something be done to – well, I suppose it's too late, though, isn't it?' Marnie briskly reminded us of her self-dedication to medicine by saying, 'Procure an abortion, you mean, Mrs. Rush? I shouldn't think so.' And mother, who could have meant nothing else, disclaimed the idea with hauteur.

'I don't mind asking some people I know,' pursued Marnie, with engaging childish eagerness. 'About drugs, I mean. Anything else too risky, unfortunately – I'd like to help Olive out of this.'

'So disinterested of you, my poppet,' said Lester. 'Remember when you took my clock to bits to get out the alarm that wouldn't stop ringing? As a clock it hasn't been so good since then. I think you'd better let Olive stick to her alarm – "bear those ills we have than fly to others that we know not of" . . .'

'Lester, we're really not concerned with all that!' said father sharply. Lester's literary manners always irritated him. 'The question is, are we going to pay her more between us, and where is the child to go when it's born?' The financial side was uppermost in his mind: I had never known father, incurably unbusinesslike at heart, so full of worldliness: it was as if he felt, strangely enough, that money counted before anything else in such matters.

People showed up in unexpected ways over the Olive business, I thought, not knowing them really well at the time. Cool Mrs. Cottrell saw only the emotional values for once, urging over and over again that Olive must be enabled to keep the child with her if she wanted to. 'It's all she'll have, poor girl,' and to mother's suggestion that it would be better off in some institution, 'Oh, no, no, Phyllis! You see, if the man doesn't show up, it means she's lost him already – never really had him, rather, in any way that matters – and life would be simply unbearable for her unless the child remained. I'm sure it would.'

Mother, surprisingly, was the least sympathetic party to the discussion. A charitable institution was so much the nicest place for the child, from our point of view, that she grew more and more convinced of its niceness all round. 'To Olive's own advantage in the end, Eleanor! Because having an illegitimate baby with her would ruin her chances, don't you see?'

'She hasn't any "chances," poor devil!' said Mr. Cottrell, and so helped his wife to prevail in the end. It was agreed that Olive should have an attic bedroom in the Cottrell house where she could keep the child: both families would contribute to its support, hoping that the churchy section of the village would not find out that, in this case, the wages of sin were to be an additional four shillings a week.

'As busy agnostics we can't afford to do the Christian thing openly in an English village,' said Mrs. Cottrell, light-hearted because she had carried her point. 'It entails too much argument with good people. Raising Olive's wages for having a baby would be called "an incentive to im-morality". So silly, isn't it, when at her age every dam' thing – air and grass and spring and mere existence – is an incentive a whole lot stronger than four bob?'

Mr. Cottrell said very little, much less than anyone else, but watched his wife while she argued Olive's cause. His nice spaniel eyes often held so sad an expression that it did not strike me then that his air of unhappy comprehen-sion meant anything more than the sympathy apparent between the elder Cottrells at all times.

It was a trivial affair, this discussion, only memorable at the time because more important things rarely seemed to happen in Pin Mill. It was quite a long while later that I realized how out of character the four older people had been, according to the natures which I had assigned to them through seeing them daily for many years.

Marnie and Dru and I agreed to do Olive's work between us when she should be laid up in due course. To outdo Marnie, Dru even offered to start helping in our house at once. 'All this chivalry to the fallen!' began Lester. 'So boy . . .' and shut up, seeing father's eyebrows lifting prodigiously. Father's unlikely fascination for Lester had survived Lester's boyhood and the late Rush-Cottrell trouble, remaining undiminished now that this sublime youth had put away childish things and become a semi-serious student of architecture, with a leaning towards extravagant styles. It was the baroque in father's character which appealed to him, he told Basil Quest, who told me. Not understanding the term we were at a loss, as usual, to know whether Lester were being rude or not: neither of us could believe that he properly appreciated father. But in any case father was the one person whose glance could stop Lester in full flight after the perfectly irritating word. The attraction was not mutual. 'Cottrell was once my very good friend,' said father as we walked home. 'And if I hear that son of his saying "So boyish!" again, in a lady-like voice, I'll do him the service of giving Lester a clip on the ear.'

In an expansive moment I broke our new rule of nothing but polite monosyllables in reply to Cottrell greetings, and repeated this saying to Lester when I came on him one day, several months later, blocking the lower end of the Hard with a mass of sketching gear, assembled for the production of one very small and unrecognizable water-colour. Margaret and Dru were with me.

'Off to occupy the deep again? How . . .' Lester began. He seemed taken aback for a few seconds by my warning, and then returned magnificently to form with, 'How – how old-world!' his air of over-studied courtesy belied for once by a grin. To do him justice I doubt that he would have minded much if the clip had ever been administered. I rather wished that we had not quarrelled with the Cottrells; there were points about Lester. But the characteristic inertia of village life, which lets such affairs run on of their own momentum, prevented anyone on either side from making a decisive move for friendship. For several years to come we were not exactly on bad terms with them: we were just not on good ones.

There must have been at least half a dozen sub-feuds existing between various Pin Mill families, because in a small country place, as in home life, sore people are almost invariably forced into fresh contact before the rub of the last contact has had time to heal. Neither we nor the Cottrells could ever go out without seeing at least one of the other camp doing something typical, and therefore irritating.

Margaret, Dru and I went on down the Hard to the dinghy in which Ted Mawley sat waiting for us. One bare brown arm hung over the side, a live cable of fine slack muscle, holding the rocking boat in to the causeway. He stood up to make way for us, still leaning out towards the Hard, effortlessly balancing on the unstable floor of the boat. Ted, whose face was mooney and uninteresting, was the first person to make me aware of the beauty of men's bodies. I had noticed before that father was impressive when I saw him half-stripped sometimes during a cruise; but father being father, I thought that this excellence was part of his peculiar quality – one expected father to look grand at all times because he was Arthur Rush, a grand person to be, and nothing less than fineness would have seemed appropriate: but I had vaguely understood that women were the beautiful sex; it was a small, pleasant shock to realize that this goodliness of Ted's was not a personal peculiarity but something shared by all hard and healthy men. I looked for it after that among other fishermen, and the

136

men who worked the sea-going barges which passed by on their way to Ipswich, and finding it, felt grateful to Ted. Sootie was really rather a splendid looking person, too, I discovered with surprise when we reached his smack, in which we were to go trawling all day – we were being hurried out of the way because Olive was having her baby in our house unexpectedly.

Messy things had happened to her in the middle of a morning's light housework, events which were not due for another six weeks. Dru had been sent running for Mrs. Mawley and Ronald for the doctor, while Olive lay panting on the sofa, giggling between pains at the thought, presumably, of the unheard-of liberty she had taken with the drawing-room carpet: one could never tell, however, what Olive meant by that infuriating coy giggle of hers. She had produced it to acknowledge father's announcement of the increase in her wages, and Mrs. Cottrell's offer of a room in their house where she could keep her child. – One could not even be sure that she was pleased by these arrangements.

I was thinking now, as we trawled slowly down to Harwich, of what Mrs. Mawley had said when she arrived at our house. Trying to sound as unimpressed as though confinements in the drawing-room were part of our daily routine, I had remarked while boiling a kettle for her, 'Olive's unlucky about everything, isn't she? Nearly two months premature.' That sounded, I thought, quite technical and adult.

'Unlucky? What's she got to grumble about?' Mrs. Mawley rounded on me almost fiercely. 'Six weeks less to carry. And nobody nosing out all about her trouble. No man to bother her afterwards. Some people don't know when they're lucky!' And then after a minute she added in the dull, sour voice in which she had once said, 'Oh, Nature! I hate Nature.' – 'I don't see why she shouldn't have to pay for her fun, though, same as other people!'

I should have liked to get Ted alone to ask him what his

mother meant: I could talk over anything with Ted, but somehow not in front of Dru. Though she was the most slangy and out-doorish of us all, there was about her some quality – a kind of spiritual shyness which mother shared – that made it impossible to discuss with her any but the surface aspects of everything. Dru would make (though only in feminine company) quite vulgar jokes about taboo subjects, almost Cottrell jokes; but unlike them she would be embarrassed by any serious reference to the same subjects: all the Englishness of the family was concentrated in Dru. Because it was impossible to ignore what was happening to-day at home, she was saying nervously now, to keep the topic on a light plane, 'Such a weird thing to happen in an ordinary family like ours!'

'Oh, but Dru, ours isn't an ordinary family!' I protested, thinking first of our Rushness and then of the cross-currents that ran under the surface smoothness of our communal life – the growing antagonism between father and Ronald, between mother and Dru, one prompted by resentment of a successor, and the other by the resentment of having none, the queer inverted jealousy of another's failure: and then of my feeling for Margaret, who remained enchanting to me however often, trying to get in touch with that rare something which I believed must lie behind such loveliness, I came up against the blank wall of an alien mind, and drew away baffled and for a little while resentful. No, surely ours could not be an ordinary family.

I did not think that Margaret was listening. She was playing with the wet mesh of the trawl pockets, holding her fingers to the sun to see the scales on them turn iridescent. She said unexpectedly, 'I suppose all families are like ours, really. Not ordinary when you know them.' Where does it come from, this strange, earthy wisdom born sometimes in quite unintelligent people?

On the impulse of the moment, seeing that Dru was forward out of earshot, I turned to Sootie and repeated what Mrs. Mawley had said on the two occasions when she had puzzled me. 'What made her say that, Sootie?' Could the Mawleys be like us, ordinary only on the outside?

He looked at me, startled in a stolid sort of way, and then turned his honest blue fisherman's eyes to the near horizon, where mirage-like the ugly Felixstowe shore floated high and dream-like in the sky. What he said was not helpful. 'Maybe she didn't mean anything. Tired, as likely as not. – Let 'er come round, Miss Margaret, we'll shoot the trawl 'ere.'

There came over me then an intense desire to know more of all the familiar people who filled my days than just their words and gestures, which told so little and held so few surprises – a sudden longing for intimacy not only with their hidden, tantalizing minds, but with the real selves that I guessed at as something lying behind their minds, having an existence separate from their ordinary lives, which mingled with mine. I wanted, as urgently as I had ever wanted anything, to be made free of those lightless, trackless countries to which even the owners had such difficult entry that few ever penetrated there – the places where the seeds of all their thoughts and feelings and wishes lay buried, from which they sprang full-grown into the waiting minds. I wanted to know people. That burning new curiosity consumed the smaller one from which it had risen. I was less anxious now to know what prompted Mrs. Mawley's bitterness, and Sootie's evasion of the explanation because I had realized that it was not only the friendly deck-hand and his wife who were strangers to me, but indeed everyone I knew. I did not yet realize that they must always remain so; I hoped that my old friend-enemy, Time, would make them gradually transparent. Time was so wonderful; surely it was able to do that?

We were allowed to see Olive's baby when we came in: a small thing, as unappetizing and red in the wrong places as Olive herself. But though we thought him a poor result of all that morning's mess we took more apparent notice of him than the mother did. In the following weeks it was hard to interpret that giggle of Olive's which broke out whenever the baby was mentioned – her submissive 'Yes'm' and 'No, miss', and coy silences – as covering either unnatural indifference or deep primitive emotion towards the child, or any intermediate sentiment. How could one guess what she felt? A girl brought up in unthinking respectability, she might be miserably ashamed of that one remarkable lapse and its result: we could not tell. Mother occasionally tried to convey to Olive that this was what she ought to feel, and then, adoring babies herself, she would soon counteract whatever nebulous good she had hoped to accomplish by saying, while she superintended the bath, 'Oh, look, Olive, how sweet; he's blowing bubbles! Aren't you glad it's a boy?'

Olive spent most of her spare time upstairs with him in the Cottrells' house: there was no other personal interest in her life to share her attention. But if anyone came into the room they found her not playing with him as a rule, and never talking to him, but sitting looking at the child expressionlessly. When mother, who was always running in and out on his behalf, protested that she was clothing the baby far too warmly for this soft autumn weather, Olive only smiled deprecatingly and jogged the creature up and down in the traditional manner, which the doctor said was so bad for infants. If she deferred by taking off one of his many wrappings, the garment went on again the next day, though the last part of October, in which he was born, and the whole of November was particularly gentle that year.

Very soon, being strong, she was carrying him out, sometimes through the village to old Chandler's shop on a household errand, but more often to the saltings where she could sit and mend stockings for us unnoticed. I cannot imagine that in a Suffolk village she escaped scathing comments, or looks from the women at least as scathing as the comments they withheld, but we had no means of telling how much she minded, or if at all. Like some woodland creature she would sometimes leave her child in a fold of ground or between the roots of one of the Quests' trees, which fringed the marsh, while she wandered off a little distance.

When he cried she fed him with the unconcern of an animal, glad to ease the nagging weight of milk. Without any sign of joy or resentment, she did whatever was necessary for this small living creature which was almost the only thing in the world entirely her own.

And in a few weeks time she returned from the marsh without him one day, the same nervous giggle interrupting her explanation of how for a little while she had left him – 'such a nice, dry day'm' – on the bank where the Quests' garden bordered the common land, while she ran back to fetch some forgotten socks – 'Master Ronald's blue ones'm.'

'Olive! Where is the child?'

'There'm. Such a nice, warm day for the time of year, I didn't think, like –' She had come to mother, because people automatically did, in times of trouble. She sank down on a chair in our hall and put her face in her hands while her shoulders heaved hysterically. The child must have rolled down the slope, she said. Swathed according to her idea of what was right he made a round enough bundle to roll, but the bank was not very steep: it was a puzzling business. The tide was up and the shallow marsh pools were full. The child, found lying by one of them, had certainly died from drowning. Mr. Quest, on one of his solitary walks, was the unlikely person to discover the thing, while father, following Olive's incoherent directions, was searching the wrong side of the garden: and Mr. Quest was reticent when questioned at the inquest. The coroner elicited nothing from Olive but evidence of her exceptional stupidity;

141

in humanity she could not be censured for carelessness. Why should father or Mr. Quest, the only other people in court who had seen the child within an hour of the alarm, hold up the formalities to point out the curious fact that his clothes seemed to have been dry all the time? After all, it had been such a nice, fine day as Olive said: perhaps the outer ones had had time to dry between the accident and their handling of the body: perhaps the baby had somehow lain so that only the nose and mouth were covered by the water: perhaps there was some other explanation. Nothing was said, for what did any of us know for certain?

Conjecture brought one no nearer to the inscrutable life going on in the dark – deep inside the coyly giggling creature whom we knew as Olive – an inner existence inviolably secret because she herself knew so little of it.

We had no reason for getting rid of her. Sometimes, lying awake in bed – the time when fantastic things seem both most credible and most fantastic – I was amazed that it was not more amazing to be in dull daily contact with a person who had done – perhaps – an almost unthinkable thing under the pressure of some violent emotion which none of us could fathom. An agony of respectability – blind spite against the man responsible – desire that everything should be as it was before – hopelessness for the future of the child, or her own – a concern or hatred fierce beyond our comprehension may have struggled into overwhelming possession of this dim mind, while we saw nothing but the placid exterior, which remained placid. In after-years Olive always giggled with that meaningless coy air when some chance reference put her in mind of her unlikely interlude of maternity. While I lay thinking of her in the mornings she would knock to call me, looking archly round the door, and then it was no longer possible to imagine that there had been anything more than an accident. Also it ceased to matter whether there had been or not: death is not necessarily dramatic, I discovered, however it comes; nor even important. Olive remained obstinately a figure devoid of the makings of tragedy.

It was on other people that the effects were most noticeable: the occurrence seemed to shock them temporarily into a new kind of friendliness. We nearly patched things up with the Cottrells. Mr. Quest turned quite human and offered the loan of his gorgeous car and chauffeur to take Olive into Ipswich for the funeral, because he thought that so many mysterious silver fittings would distract her nicely; and they did. When I brought over mother's note of acceptance he actually gave me a peach and took me to see the kittens which Stella's valuable Persian had just produced in the greenhouse. With a quiet kind of fury he talked all the way down the garden of the toll of Christianity among the working classes: it was mostly above my head; I only gathered that he was very much annoyed with Christ because of the drowning of Olive's baby, and Dean Inge and Mr. Middleton Murry and several other people would shortly be responsible too, if they were not more careful, but I forget how they were implicated. The cat, with the single-minded domesticity of her kind, was busy eating the excrement of her young when we disturbed her. Just what a Cottrell cat might do, I thought. I had not expected such behaviour at the Quests'. I had seen this happen before, but now I did not know what to say: Mr. Quest, however, watched her with sombre satisfaction, '*There's* motherhood for you, Lalage!'

Father was surprisingly upset by the whole business. He took me out in *Guadalupe* on the day of the funeral and, off his guard for a moment, made none of the accepted pretence of believing the child's death accidental; a pretence to which, parent-like, he afterwards returned quite confidently.

'I feel, if only there'd been more money to give the child some chance in life – If we could have offered her more, or

143

promised it later on, so that the outlook wasn't so hopeless . . .'

Not realizing for the moment all that the words implied, he was talking more to himself than to me, I knew; and suddenly, while we lay becalmed off Landguard Point, he began telling me, still with that air of speaking to an equal though his hand was on my shoulder, a story of his younger days which came the more surprisingly from him because he had told so many others in my hearing, and the core of them had always been grotesque exaggeration: obviously he had appreciated himself in them as a fantastic actor, moving against a well-painted background. Now he gave only bare outlines and could not see himself apart from the story, because these far-off days had not faded into the stuff of anecdote but were still real to him. '. . . she was awfully clever at making me want to see her again, when I meant to break with her. I always had an idea that I wasn't the only man she was – kind to, though I wouldn't let myself quite believe it. – I was only a few years older than Ronnie, you see, and at that age these things matter. After all, there was no reason why I should be anything special to her: my boat was only in for three days out of every six weeks, and even when it was I couldn't give her as good a time as other men did: presents and all that. And she'd only her looks to live on, and the clever way she had with them. Women in hot countries flower so early, and then it's all so soon over: you can't blame them. Really it was decent of her to fancy me at all, when I was always so hard up . . .'

(And this was father, this unknown human being talking high-coloured nonsense that was not quite nonsense because it was actually Arthur Rush speaking!) . . . 'She knew I was away exactly six weeks each trip. Sometimes I meant to vary the time, so she shouldn't know, but I didn't. I was proud of the regularity I got out of those incredible engines. Any fool could run an Atlantic liner: it took an engineer to keep such junk working at all . . .'

Yes, that bit was father as I had always known him: but his voice was taken over again by the person I did not know, who said, 'This is a tale no woman will quite understand, Lallie. I stuck to that job because I thought I was doing something no one else could. One thinks that rather easily at the age I was then, but as a matter of fact I was probably right, for once, because the whole trading concern broke up after I left: and good riddance. I think she got out of me pretty well everything her father paid me for running his boat. I can't imagine why, with all those rivets gone, the plates didn't just fall apart and sink under us some quiet night: I suppose the river water was too thick to let them through. Like treacle, almost. The smell of flowers gone rotten with wet takes me right back there for a second or two if I meet it unexpectedly – makes me feel a bit sick, because that smell was always steaming up from the water and it was all so damnable in a way. Nearly every time I started up-river I made up my mind to tell her father, or uncle, or friend or whoever he really was, that he could find some other half-wit to sweat his guts out over those decrepit engines, and tell her to go to hell too. And before I got there I'd stop off at one of the trading ports and buy her whatever I could afford. I didn't give her money if I could help it because – she was generous in a way. There was the fellow supposed to be in charge of the boat: friend of hers. Walked about the deck swaying like a lily, polishing his dirty nails, and never did a hand's turn except in emergencies, and then he was terrific. Sometimes all one trip – generally after she hadn't been kind to me, because she wouldn't be sometimes, several trips running: she wasn't what you'd think – he'd be flaunting a bit of new jewellery, watch or cigarette holder or something. Fairly asking for comment on it. And though there was nothing else to talk about – you can't imagine what it's like being shut up for weeks at a time in a tin box in the tropics, with only one white or whitish man to talk to – I wouldn't dare ask him where it came from or notice it at all, because I suspected that I'd paid for it indirectly, and I didn't want to hear for certain. Well, then I got pera fever. You've heard that bit before about my thinking I'd got to tell God why two tides a day weren't nearly enough in shoal water, and raving for a padre to translate my trading-Spanish into Latin. So I was shipped home, and stayed in England a year that time, and met your mother, and so on, and her family got me a job though they didn't like me. A good job, but too easy, I thought. (Wish I had one like it now: one loses the need to be always cracking nuts which may or may not break one's teeth, but I still had it then.) Phyllis said her family wanted her to spend three months with them in Ireland: hunting season or something . . .' (Father had forgotten me again almost entirely, or he would have said 'your mother'). 'She asked if I'd mind, thinking I would, and I thought I would too, but then I realized there'd be time to get to South America and back, to tie up a lot of loose ends I'd left, before I finished with that part of the world for good. I was keen to find out whether anyone else could run that boat. And, of course, to see *her* too. Nothing more than just see her, of course. I was pretty sure she wouldn't count with me at all, after so long. I just wanted to see her to be sure I was free in my mind. I'd a lot more money than I'd ever had when I was working out there, and I had a wild fancy to buy the old paddle boat and set a steam hammer to work on her engines, because of the trouble they'd cost. But I didn't mean to really, of course. Instead, I looked up the little dago skipper whom I'd always loathed just about as much as he loathed me, and he greeted me like a favourite brother, and we got sentimentally tight together because the old boat *had* been scrapped – the next man couldn't run to time. I didn't mention the girl to him, because I didn't want to hear how well he still knew her. And

I lushed up everyone I'd ever spoken to on the way up river, feeling glad I should never have to see any of them again. And then at the last stopping place I bought absolutely everything there was that I hadn't been able to give her before. I'd always known that I could get her to myself if I could afford to take her right away from the settlement, as I wanted to. But it turned out that the epidemic which nearly got me grew a lot worse after I left. I don't know why I'd never thought of that. About a quarter of the people in that place had been wiped out, and she was one – because money had been so scarce with me in the old days. And after I'd heard that, I chucked the stuff I'd got for her into the stinking river during the night, and I was never so near chucking myself in too.'

Just for a few minutes the veil of relationship lifted between us, through the death of a servant-girl's child, and the person beside me became a man to me, and not only my father, and I could have cried because what he told me was so wretched and improbable and true, and because I could see what for the moment he could not – the lovely young man he had been, and how much he still had in common with that touching fool who would not see a tawdry woman in the colours of her reality. 'She wasn't what you'd think . . . Really it was decent of her . . . Women in hot countries flower so early, and it's all so soon over, you can't blame them. . . .' The illusion lived on, by the strength with which the boy had once clung to it. He said again 'She was awfully clever in her way; but I can't make you understand. I haven't thought of her for years, though,' and then the voice of the stranger died away, for we were drifting towards the breakwater on the ebb. The engine had to be started, and the petrol tank proved to be almost empty, which was Ronald's fault; and while father cursed the absent offender half-heartedly, life turned normal again.

We chugged homewards, passing Sootie and Ted Mawley

to whom father had given the day off. They were spending Sootie's free time in the way common among yacht-hands and fishermen even in winter, sailing for pleasure. Father hailed Sootie autocratically to help him with the engine, which was 'missing', and unloaded me into the Mawleys' dinghy with Ted, eager to be rid of me because of what he had said.

I did not much mind, for once, losing father's company, because mother knew that I had gone out with him and so would not bother about me if I did not come in to lunch: there were always stores aboard our boats. Father and Sootie would be out till dusk fell at about five o'clock: I could have the whole afternoon, then, looking at things with Ted without an anxious sense of the racing of time as it slid by maliciously, faster than usual, trying to outstrip my vigilance and get me into trouble at home.

It was one of the still, sunless winter afternoons that I liked for the feeling of respite they gave from the perpetual warring of sea and land, specially noticeable in this estuary, when the land flings off a mass of salt-loosened earth in every winter gale, to silt up old channels and force the cramped water to assault in fresh places; and the tides worry their way farther and farther under the banks, bringing down great trees to rest on one elbow in the water, so that wherever heavy timber closes in with the shore, squeezing out the marsh, the Orwell is fringed with dying lateral woods of twisted trees, straining their last living branches out of reach of the flood tides into which they subside gradually, as root after root fails them.

Now, outwardly at least, there was peace: cold yellow light spread out from the river like a benison over the fore-shore, saltings and woods, where snags and grass tufts and bare branches stood out quivering clear: and spreading upwards into the darker sky, that dull glow made the water seem the source of all light, and of such colour as remained to us in a world in which even the light-hued sea birds – gulls and terns in great variety – took on a uniform blackness as they drove over, heading inland before the presage of January gales whose warnings we had not yet received.

Ted was important with news, of our private kind. 'There's something you'll like down at Decoy Reach,' he said, and would not tell me what it was. 'And something else in the oak between the yews behind your house – something you missed! Which d'you want to see first?' It was tacitly understood that I would spend the afternoon off the water for choice, though I could not yet admit this to myself.

'I know about the oak. Two families of red bank voles in the roots, and who cares?' They were only the small change of observation; unworthy of our serious attention. Ted should not give himself airs about finding things around our house which I had missed.

'Better'n that.'

'Not in that tree.'

'There is that.'

'There isn't. Ronald got back last night, and he's been up to fix the wireless. There's nothing, or he'd have said.'

'I thought his holidays must have started: the tree looked like a hurricane had struck it. Funny nobody in your family can climb,' said Ted in an irritating way. 'And blind . . .! There's a squirrel asleep in a hole in the second fork.'

'Ted!' A squirrel's drey ranked very high in our personal currency of discovery, in which every find had a comparative value. 'Well, I hope you didn't wake it, getting up to look, because it'll starve for certain if you did!' There was only a likelihood of its doing so, but it was thoroughly annoying of Ted to have this sudden access of capital with which he could more than buy off my recent superiority, founded on a fossil shell. Fine warm days in winter killed off quite enough hibernating squirrels and mice, I thought to excuse my discontent to myself, without a lout of a boy intruding in semi-private trees.

'*I* can climb, Miss Lalage,' he said in retort.

Nothing would now induce me to come and see his squirrel. Not with him. Later I might try to look at it though, as he conveyed, I was such a bad climber that the disturbance I made floundering among the branches, losing my nerve, getting stuck and yelling for Ronald would be enough to wake the most soundly dormant animal.

We headed the boat for Decoy Reach, where the marsh widens as the Orwell merges into Harwich Harbour. Here, in a mile or so of barren ground, lies one of the strange aerial traffic centres chosen by migrating birds, for no apparent reason, as a halting-place where they may snatch a few hours' rest, and such food as can be found before the pitiless urge seizes upon them again. It is as if, over this small area, the air were not charged for them with that impulse to be gone exhaled by all other land which has turned alien to them in due season. I have seen first year birds, strangers, flying steadily into the dead zone of instinct, falter and drop feebly earthwards, as though some great force no longer bore them up: and older birds may remain here for days after their fellows have disappeared, fluttering contentedly within the invisible boundaries, flying as birds do on trivial occasions, with not more than half their full wing-beat, until a stray gust blows them out into air pulsing, perhaps, with a half-forgotten rhythm, and they climb with certainty up the wind, orienting themselves, their wings sweeping full out, eagerly, and in a few seconds are only dwindling points on which human eyes cannot long focus as they sink steadily down the sky, to be lost to sight before they reach the horizon.

There is no shelter in the marsh, nor sufficient insect life to attract them: at all seasons of the year I have found the bodies of travelling birds that had died of weakness and hunger, unable to struggle farther than this place which drew them in some inexplicable way, just as that place in South America had drawn my father, who knew that in reality it held nothing for him. I was thinking of him, as we drifted down, with a little jealousy in my mind for my mother. 'She was awfully clever in her way. . . .' Mother was not. – No, that wasn't true, the two women changed places suddenly in the slight resentment I felt. Mother was alive and the other was dead. The living triumphed over the dead just by possessing their heritage: it was much cleverer to be alive than to be dead. Poor devil of a woman whom a boy had craved, she must have been marvellously alive to hold such power, and lovelier than Margaret, perhaps, and young too, but – 'I haven't thought of her for years.' Truly, she was dead.

So beautiful things were less important than the humdrum associations of every day. That fact fitted uncomfortably well into the new world in which I was being forced to live for increasingly long intervals as I grew older, a world not snugly built for man's benefit by mother's benevolent ex-deity, but produced by chance alone, as far as any save religious people could say, to roll insecurely about a pointless joke of a universe for no one's advantage at all. And religious people had the best of this gigantic jest in heavenly bad taste only because they could not see that the laugh was mainly against them. It would be all right, I thought, if one could go on not seeing the joke right to the end, but I had been increasingly afraid for some time that, like mother, I was not going to be lucky in this way.

Ted suddenly chuckled. 'Aren't you sore because I found the squirrel! What price your fossil now?' And because this was true no longer, and sounded silly, I laughed with him and we were back on our normal plane of friendship.

'Oh, that! I wasn't even thinking of it!' I was struck suddenly with the odd idea that Ted's views on what was really in my thoughts would be saner, and altogether of greater worth, than those of the well-informed Cottrells, who pretended that only Beauty and intellectual interests mattered; or of my family, who thought that if you made outdoor occupations matter enough, you could avoid bothering as to whether anything else mattered at all: or of the distinguished Mr. Quest, who said that nothing mattered, and then showed angry concern for the fate of Olive's baby.

'Go on. I'll bet you were! Looking so solemn.'

'If you'd like to know,' I said, pleasantly conscious that I won on this point, 'I was thinking about God!'

But Ted was not crushed. He showed no sign of surprise or embarrassment. 'What about God?' He pulled up the centre-board and we grounded on the one patch of negotiable mud in the reach.

'Well, anything in all that, do you think?' I asked as casually as possible. I hoped at the moment for the assurance of a world in which everything came right in the end; a world robbed, by the certainty of eternal justice, of that infinite, exquisite sadness which lay close to the surface in tales like father's, and buried deep under Mrs. Chandler's silly self-dramatizing talk of her son killed in France, but was there all the same; as it was, too, a little, in squirrels' deaths on unseasonable fine days, and in the apathy of a pair of swallows sitting miserably hour after hour among the ruins of a late nest which Dru had smashed with a tennis ball: for to animals and birds as well these things would be 'made up' somehow, somewhere, I had half-believed. Pain, though it had not yet come my way, seemed unendurable for others if it was utterly futile, to be redressed only by forgetfulness.

Ted carried on lowering the sail, and squelching and sliding ankle deep in ooze, we began hauling the dinghy out of reach of the returning tide. 'Well, what do you think?' he asked cautiously.

152

I felt – being not yet seventeen – that I abolished the comfortable possibility of God once and for all if I denied His existence. Standing on the edge of the saltings I looked round, to steady myself for the dreadful decision, on the calm, grey-yellow river scene, bounded by familiar hills whose far sides had always held for me the suggestion of every mystery in the world, and by the sea over which the bird-crossed sky fitted very closely that day, pressing us down intimately into the earth that I wanted to keep for ever as my own, not just for a life span. Time would take this away from me, birds and all. Take it eternally. God had been the one idea with which I could offset Time, my shadow, when I became oppressively aware of it. If I gave the answer in my mind, I should not only put a term to my possession of everything that I loved, but deepen almost unendurably the tragedy of all 'old, unhappy far-off things', and of every sorrow yet to be.

'Well, I think it's all rot!' I said, wondering, with a lapse into completely childish panic, whether that rayed finger of sunlight suddenly stabbing through a broken cloud were Heaven's warning to me – just too late; how like celestial methods – not to damn myself for all eternity.

As soon as the words were said (possibly as a reward for one of my very few brave acts) God ceased from troubling me for ever, though He had long been a special problem of mine. This was one of the best moments of my childhood, and one of the last, the sudden entering into a kind of despairing peace that did not pass all understanding.

Ted looked disapproving. It appeared that he thought me too young not to believe in God. I was highly tickled by this; but so, later on, did father, nominally a Catholic and also an agnostic: and so, I gathered from him, would every-one else I knew, with the exception of Mr. Quest and the Cottrells. Mr. Quest would think age immaterial, and from the Cottrells, had we been still intimate, I should have been careful to hide my new freedom, because they would have welcomed me as a sort of convert, and there was something distressingly religious about their unfaith.

'Well, what do you believe, then?' I asked Ted.

'Nothing. But then I'm a good lot older,' and to my surprise it was my turn to disapprove. Relics of my mother's social sense still remained to me: I was not quite sure if it was all right for the lower classes to be without religion. So we went on into the marsh slightly shocked by one another.

'There you are!' he said, and I found that he had built me a hide, of old sailcloth painted and partly covered with mud and marsh weed, which he had dug out of one of the dykes: a noble gift. To flighting birds, human beings were frighteningly conspicuous on this flat, treeless ground, and this was the time of the year when birds never seen at other seasons – snow-bunting, peregrine falcons and great northern divers – broke their southern migration on our marshes for a few days' stay. They took my imagination because of the dreary white land-wastes, the dangers of the bleak miles of thundering grey sea that they must have passed to reach this strange haven.

The hide had spy-holes on three sides. We crawled in as far as its dimensions allowed, and lay happily on our stomachs in a cold stuffiness, wondering why the birds still refused to alight anywhere near us, until we realized that my protruding legs were the trouble. There was no room for them beyond the knee in the hide, however closely we packed ourselves. Ted's legs, in muddy grey thigh boots, were not alarming, but I had on a pair of the scarlet woolly sailing stockings which Olive knitted for us all: they were not even dimmed by dirt, because I had taken them off with my sand-shoes and goloshes to wade ashore. We had a long discussion. There would be protests at home if I slimed them all over thickly enough to hide the colour. Bare legs, pinky-purple with cold, would be almost as alarming, and mud would not stick well enough to skin, though it behaved like

154

glue in thick wool. Eventually Ted went back to the dinghy to fetch a can of paint which he had used on the sailcloth, and we spread the remains of the paint over the backs of my legs, after removing the stockings. It was a great success.

The afternoon was all joy, and memorable besides for half a dozen glimpses of birds which we rarely managed to see, during migration.

One, a great skua, the fierce bird pirate of the north, winging wearily to the south on its long trip from the Icelandic breeding grounds, swooped as though it felt suddenly the attraction of this lodestone of land, alighting within a yard of us. It staggered about, like a man drunk or over-tired, between the thick crusts of Mrs. Mawley's jam sandwiches which we had saved as lures. All its grand eagle arrogance had gone. The last of the crusts stuck in its throat and, choking, it began a grotesque, squawking dance, tearing at its throat with its feet. Down from the sky hurtled a little kittiwake gull, screaming defiance at its now helpless enemy. I saw other small gulls, passing to seaward, veer from their course and race for the land, shrieking as they came. Only a curlew, who had no race-memory of eggs stolen and young killed by the great skua, went on digging for lug worms unconcernedly in its usual haunts, disregarding these loud winter trippers. The lesser gulls gathered in a narrowing circle, watching and waiting in triumph while the skua flapped and retched itself to an exhausted stillness, in which it lay on one side with beak open and neck distended, occasionally struggling convulsively as one of its enemies approached. I did not know what to do; the wildest of all the gulls, the great skua would not let a human being come near enough to help while any of its strength remained: we stayed where we were. A pair of tiny fire-crested wrens dropped out of the grey gloom overhead, folded their wings fussily, chirruped in a tone of authority to the menacing ring of spectators whose clamour had called them to the

155

scene of the accident, and then with heads on one side and an air of professional gravity they peered down the skua's gullet, holding a shrill consultation together. They were so small that the skua considered them negligible. With a flirt of wings, spurs digging into the ground for steadiness, one of the wrens darted its head inside the skua's beak and dragged at the crust. Its assistant seized a corner as the bread came up, and in a second or two the pair were away in the sky, not waiting to note the recovery of their patient, with the crust as payment for the operation. Not another sound made the lesser gulls as they shot up in mingled flight and pursuit, and the skua, after a breathing space, turned savagely on the curlew, the harmless witness of its discomfiture, and would have killed it but that to Ted's very proper indignation I wriggled out and interfered.

We were delighted with this incident; it made us, in our own estimation, real bird-watchers because we had witnessed something which we could hope that no one else had seen.

We ran the dinghy home before a rising south-easter, into the brief glory of a winter sunset that flared through widening wind-rents in the black pall of cloud over Ipswich. Ted's dull face was lit almost to beauty for a few minutes by the radiance reflected up from the water: the thin, hard, boy's body with its supple movements and promise of strength did not need that marvellous light to be wholly admirable. Earth seemed to do very well for itself, I thought, with its chance creations – gulls' wings and sunsets, men's bodies and the flower faces of women. Really it was rather dreadful how little one missed God even so soon after a desertion like mine. Everything suddenly existed for me on its own merits alone, without any other significance, and its merits seemed all the greater for that. 'Oh, brave new world, that has such people in it' – and such things!

We were both so blinded by the brilliance on the water that we could not make out for some time whether the man hallooing and waving on the east shore were signalling to us or not: neither of us recognized the figure, which seemed to be that of a navvy. Eventually, because the wind was easy and nobody else appeared to be taking any notice of his hails, we ran across the half mile or so of water, and not until I was out of the boat, and face to face with him on the broken landing stage there, did I recognize Gordon Summers. In an old trench-coat covered with clay, he looked like something from a war film, being hung about with an entrenching tool, a haversack and other oddments: an extraordinary figure in this scene.

'I'm so sorry,' he said blankly, 'I thought you were some-one I knew!'

'Well, I am.'

He seemed surprised and confused. '. . . awfully sorry, bringing you all this way over. – Foully dirty, I'm afraid – preparing for new diggings at Levington – you know the regrettable Roman preference for clay soil and springs. No, of course, why should you? Thought the two of you were Lester and Marnie Cottrell . . .'

'What, in a sailing boat?'

To hear that I could be mistaken for Marnie was hardly compensation for being called far out of my course, when I was beginning to raven for tea, to manœuvre a dinghy among broken under-water piles for the sake of a comparative stranger. I might not be up to the Rush standard of looks, which was high, but in my modest moments, when I decided that Dru beat me in features in spite of her fat, I never imagined that our worst could be confused with the Cottrell best, and Marnie was not even that.

'Don't they sail? No, I suppose not, really. I ought to have guessed it wasn't.' He grew more and more hot and bothered over his mistake. 'I don't know them very well. They seemed quite keen about a regatta I saw here, so I thought – At least, they said what fun it would have been if everyone concerned had been dead, and they could have come on snapshots of the events in an old family album three hundred years hence. Or something like that: which I gathered was the Cottrell way of showing interest in sport. Was it during the regatta I met you? – So sorry – Awfully rude of me not to remember.'

'No, I just saw you then' (I hoped that he had not watched me winning my ignoble race) 'but you talked to me about Roman remains once at a party at their house, ages ago.'

'Good lord, was it you I talked to like that? I remember I trotted out every fact I knew because I'd just taken up archæology as an antidote to shellshock. Mustn't you have been bored!'

'I was simply terrified.'

'So was I. I thought if I stopped for a minute you might think of some intelligent question about art, and I shouldn't be able to answer. Everyone was talking about art, and you see – I'm so sorry – I mistook you for a Cottrell even then! Frightfully clever family . . .'

'Yes. Did you want a lift across the river?' His apparent embarrassment made me embarrassed.

'It seems rather a shame to expect that, after not remembering – But it really was rather dark – Not then, I mean, but just now, when I mistook you again. Anyway, that was what I was going to ask if you had been the Cottrells. Or rather, if they had been you. Well, thanks, I want to get to Pin Mill.'

I had a feeling that inwardly this shy-seeming man was not really embarrassed at all, and when he signalled a convenient passing boat he had merely reflected that it might possibly contain a Cottrell, since the family lived in the neighbourhood, and if not it would not matter; he would get his ferry, which was all that he cared.

'We're going to Pin Mill. Get in the middle, will you?'

My heart warmed to anyone who had felt like a fish out of water at that party, and warmed still more when he said frankly about it, 'Wasn't it a ghastly evening? All those enlightened elderly women saying earnestly to each other, "No, dear, not *im*moral, just *a*-moral, that's what I call it,"' and then relapsed at once into more explanations and apologies – 'Low of me when really it was kind of them to ask me at all – friend in common – and perhaps you know some of them – keen on that kind of thing yourself?' And still I felt that really he did not care what I thought: he had a most confident smile. I liked him, though he refused to tell me anything about the recent discoveries at Levington, of which rumours had reached even us, saying that I had had quite enough archæology from him. This time I should have enjoyed it.

There did not seem to be anything to talk about as we blew across the darkening water. Ted was never conversationally helpful with strangers: he said 'Yessir', 'Nosir', and 'Mind your head.'

Something in the time and place and the man's constrained silence made me aware of that other occasion when I had seen him with the woman who limped, Mrs. Macdonald. They, too, had been silent, but not, I thought, because they had had nothing to say to one another. I felt now as though I had been spiritually eavesdropping when I stood by them and they did not notice me. With the night-touched water splashing up gently about us, I fancied that he was remembering also.

I tried again to recall Mr. Quest's ramifications of the figure 2 but found that they had escaped me. Thinking how much better the self-possessed Marnie would have done in my place, I volunteered that it had been a good sunset, for something to say in order to break the silence, and immediately regretted the banality.

'Do you mean, good for weather?' Evidently he could not

believe that I considered its appearance worth comment, I thought, with sinking heart.

'No.' (There had been too much gold and green.) 'Just – nice.' Nothing could have sounded lamer.

'A perfectly *marvellous* sunset,' he agreed, his voice growing warm all at once, as though he were greatly impressed by my observation. 'Do you know, as your boat was coming in I was thinking of things to say about it because I felt one daren't admire anything so obvious before a Cottrell. "Pompous", I was going to suggest: Or "a bit perfunctory" perhaps. But as a matter of fact I just thought it good, too!'

We were very pleased with one another for approving wholeheartedly of this ordinary miracle; and thought out, all the way across, new defensive combinations of adjective and noun for use if either of us were ever forced into an artistic social gathering again: all shyness lifted.

'Batty!' observed Ted amiably, 'both of you,' after Gordon Summers had retreated up the dark Hard in a profusion of unnecessary gratitude. 'What's that thing you said lambs were?'

'Don't remember,' I said, hoping to put him off.

' "Redolent".'

'No, that was history,' I told him, with the glumness of one who sees ahead a long post-mortem on an exhumed joke. 'I think lambs were "self-conscious to the point of priggishness" – showing off, you know, when you're watching them.'

'But they don't,' said Ted.

'We thought they did. Only a little,' I said meekly, adding in further propitiation, 'Just sometimes.'

'Well, what's "redolent" mean?'

'Nothing – at least – I can't explain.'

'There you are then!' said Ted triumphantly, 'Batty,' and kindly let me off further explanation by rowing out to lay off the dinghy. I went home.

'Hallo, Mrs. Ted Mawley.' Margaret swivelled half round from the tea-table when I came in. The firelight flickered over the soft face: she looked like an angel. I could feel her amused eyes studying me as I bent down to fondle the cat on the hearth, in order to hide the quick colouring which she knew that I could not control if anything were said to annoy me. A cold breath of apprehension touched and dulled the warm glow inside me left by the afternoon's happiness.

'Don't be silly, darling,' mother said indulgently, 'she's been out with daddy' – None of us but mother still called him that – 'Where is he, Lallie? It's getting so dark; I wish he'd come in.'

The cat that all day long lay dreaming cosily, domestically, on her absurd little stool before the fire, rose stiffly now with her eyes stretching in a tawny stare that did not see me, and the secret jungle life that I had glimpsed once before came back into them, as she mewed soundlessly at the door to be let out, into the bitter, rustling cold of the outside world where she would live that real, inscrutable life of hers until morning transformed her again into the pet we knew. I got up too: stooping and the heat of the fire would account for my flush.

'He wanted Sootie to help him with the engine,' I told mother. 'Feed pipe choked or something. So I went down the marsh.'

'With Ted,' put in Margaret, still with the same indolent smile that was not consciously malicious.

'It was grand along Decoy Reach to-day,' I said quickly, speaking only to mother. 'I've got a hide now, and there was a big skua who got hold of a crust . . .'

'Who built the hide, dear?'

'Well, Ted. Do listen, mother, something so funny happened.' Nowadays, talking to them about birds, though I rarely did it, no longer held for me a sense of violation: they had found out and spoilt my secret so long ago. It was just not enjoyable. But anything was better than this new talk of Ted, who had always been taken for granted as my companion.

'Darling, run up and change your wet stockings before you tell us. I'll make you some cocoa, shall I? You must be cold.'

'No, thanks. And they aren't wet.'

In mother's love for us as her children, we hardly figured as individuals at all; she often called us by the wrong names, and could never remember which of us loathed cocoa.

'Well, I'll get Olive to bring some fresh tea, then. This has been standing rather a long time. And really I think you ought to change.'

'No, mother, do listen. The crust got stuck, and the bird carried on just like Dru when she had whooping cough. And then a pair of fire-crested wrens came down right within a yard of me.'

'Run upstairs first, Lallie,' mother said firmly. 'I'm sure they're wet.'

I knew that I should not her tell any more when I came down: the great gull episode dwindled to the dull proportions of a natural history anecdote: after all, it was not particularly funny, nor even interesting: it never had been.

I do not know what passed between mother and Margaret while I was upstairs, rummaging for a pair of stockings thicker than my ordinary wear because the paint would not scrub off my calves all at once, and it showed through lisle thread. Perhaps nothing more needed to be said to produce that tone of careful casualness in mother's questions when I reappeared.

'Lallie, how big is the tent-thing Ted built you? . . . Just room for one of you at a time?'

The feeling of sick coldness mounted in me as I contemplated the picture that mother saw and yet would not let her mind present to her plainly. She seemed increasingly worried by my answers. Often as I told her fibs in the ordinary way about missed meals, pocketed instead of eaten, and damp clothes that were dry enough in my opinion, I could not wilfully mislead her now; though I knew that in the circumstances lies would bring her nearer to the truth than my telling of it could do. But they would add the last touch of beastliness to the new, revoltingly exciting picture that was building itself in my brain, to take the place of Ted's friendly image.

'But, dear, two hours you say! . . . like that? . . . all the time?'

Uncomfortable for herself, uncomfortable for me, mother spoke as she did from conscientiousness alone: all her instinct was against touching such matters. Another part of her mind was troubled, too, because I was not eating as heartily as usual: unconsciously, I think, she pushed food towards me once or twice.

'Oh, well, if she's fond of the smell of fishermen's jerseys . . .' Margaret said lightly, getting up from tea to settle on the floor by the fire with the pile of rigging screws which father had given her to clean.

And I remembered exactly how we had lain; and where my body had touched his – the young fineness of this had somehow become part of the rising tide of disgust and interest flowing through my mind – and the times when one or both of us shifted to relieve cramp and his head or hand had come in contact with mine. Yes, his jersey, all his clothes smelt of cheap salt-sodden wool and sweat. I knew the smell of old: now I knew too that I had enjoyed it, many times; had turned my head towards him when speaking so that I might get it. A mould of nastiness grew over the bright recollection not only of this day but of many similar hours. The skin of his shoulder, whiter than mine, had little gold hairs and almost-purple lights in it,

I remembered from the summer, hating the memory. Oh, but Ted with his clod face and coarse hands was surely unthinkable in the way in which they were making me think of him! In a way, too, he was my brother, as intimately barred from such relationship in my thoughts as Ronald, I should have supposed: and yet by some horrible contradiction mother must be justified in her growing anxiety: my answers to her questions, and my mind's response to Margaret's suggestions, told me that.

I sat shivering in the warmth, pressing my hands together between my knees. Another minute's indirect questioning from mother raised nervous fury in me, anger directed chiefly against myself because, stronger than the desire never to see or hear of Ted again, was the curiosity to know how he would look to my opened eyes. Angry because I was bitterly ashamed, I wanted passionately for the first time in my life, to have done with our habitual skirting of all unseemliness. I said, choosing words that brought out the nastiness of both our thoughts because, expressed, they became a little less nasty – 'Do you suppose we lie and cuddle? Or he puts his hand up my skirt? Or what do you think?'

'Oh, Lallie, don't, darling . . .!' It was not fair of me, knowing that to mother words could never be a disinfectant. She was pitiful in her distress at having upset me. 'You know it isn't that. Of course it's all right from your point of view. Of course I know that. Only from his – a village boy – such a different home – nearly eighteen, isn't he . . .?'

That was a fresh aspect of the foulness that a joke had called into being between the two of us: did Ted think of me as, from now on, against my will, I should think of him? – sneakingly, with a loathsome quickening of the blood?

Dru and Ronald came in with father. 'Oh, hallo, what's Lallie doing her blush act for now? "*Ted*"? No, Margaret, not really? Oh, how gorgeous!'

164

Obscurely glad, I think, that for once Dru was not the butt of it, father led the good-natured teasing, doing a funny love-scene in which Ted's amorous yearnings were bellowed in broad Suffolk dialect, and my replies called for a shy falsetto of refinement. Mother and I joined fervently in the laughter. (Mother with relief, because laughter was accepted as a first-rate poultice for every inflammation of the mind. She shot me a glance of grateful, almost humble approbation when I suggested another idiocy for the love-scene.) And in laughter dissolved my long, untroubled friendship with Ted; the second thing, very precious to me, that Margaret had spoilt wantonly, carelessly, without hostility.

CHAPTER VIII

TO ANNOY THE COTTRELLS

RELIGION went bad in mother. It was just her luck to lose her faith when her children were growing independent of her and she needed it, after it had coerced her into bearing six children in her early married life, when she would rather have remained father's gay out-of-doors companion – the girl he married and sometimes seemed vaguely disappointed that he had lost, in this devoted nurse to his children. If religion had to leave her stranded sometime, why could it not have done so before, when she would have found compensations? But unlike Mrs. Cottrell, who dressed well, talked well, kept house well and drew well, all with one hand as it were, mother was a bad manager. Mrs. Cottrell might be late for everything social, but she would not be late spiritually, like this.

Long ago, as the social pet, Phyllis Laidler, mother had felt that she was marrying romantically beneath her in taking this penniless young adventurer: father probably thought so too. While she shed lustre on him, or they imagined that she did, both were happy. Father remained contented on the whole, but she was one of the many women who can give more graciously than they can receive. He became 'that interesting man who has been everywhere and done everything', and her position dwindled into merely that of his wife. Socially, even in small country places, interesting men are always more in demand without their wives. By now all the people we knew had forgotten, or else had never known that, as Ronald put it disrespectfully, mother's male relatives habitually died on the best frontiers, with the Eton Boating Song on their lips.

She was worried about Ronald, growing away from her at Dartmouth and off to sea next year; and about Dru, too, because of the girl's wilful unattractiveness. Even so, teasing the good-natured Dru on that score had become one of the family habits that are easier to start than to stop, and in any case, being too gentle to nag, mother needed an outlet for her own uneasiness of mind, so that her concern over the weakening of her relationship with her children did not save Dru from constant mock-sympathetic references to the faithlessness of Basil Quest. (He had once shown a brief flicker of special friendship for her, and so automatically succeeded Bertie-the-sculp in the amorous hagiology that we devised for her at meals.)

Margaret, so spiritually untouchable that no widening of her distance from the family would be noticeable, was the only one over whom, absurdly enough, mother did not seem to be worrying at this time. About me, I knew irritably, she would have prayed with relief if she could in this period. Puzzled and aggrieved, she faced the sad and seemingly inevitable coincidence by which maternal-minded women become obsessed with the importance of their relationship to their children just at the stage when, to the growing children themselves, this relationship has declined into something of less importance than almost anything else in the expanding world at their feet.

Standing on the edge of the wood behind the Quest's house, I saw mother moving uncertainly up the road to the village, looking round often, and loitering at the bend from which she could see the Hard; and I guessed that she wanted me to come into Ipswich with her for Christmas shopping. I walked forward unwillingly into sight, and then, knowing that I was still practically invisible here against the trees unless I moved, I bargained with my conscience, stepped back carefully, and stood stock-still, holding my dress to my sides so that the skirt should not flap in the wind and catch her eye. Unless she called me by name how could I know for certain that my guess was right? And if she called I would answer, I promised. But having no reason to suppose I was anywhere within hearing, she was not likely to call.

The quick resentment of pity, felt for someone who has once seemed strong, was fed by those uncertain movements of hers. Why should I go the long dull bus journey into Ipswich again, when all that was wanted was my company, not my help, though there would be a pretence of that – I should be called the one who remembered best Margaret's size in gloves, and the sort of crystallized fruit that father liked. All our meagre Christmas shopping could have been done in the day spent in Ipswich the previous week, leaving me free now to go over to the Mawleys, as I wanted to do. I had not seen Ted alone since the day of the trouble, over a week ago. Shame had kept me away; curiosity had now grown stronger: I must see how things would be between us to-day. But mother, who made every purchase a small social event in the shop, liked the excuse of a few odds and ends left unbought till the last minute to lunch in the Ipswich A.B.C. for a change. There she could exercise her gifts of persuasion and charm on the hard-worked waitress – 'Would it be a bother if we had custard instead of rice with our stewed plums? I see it says rice on the menu, and of course – Oh, thank you. How kind of you! And not *too* much milk in the coffee?' In another walk of life mother would have been one of the optimists who always ask for a *nice* cup of tea, with some vague belief, perhaps, in the existence of two separate urns kept behind the scenes, for the purpose of differentiating.

Mother so much enjoyed preferential treatment as a tribute to her quality that I felt it mean of me not to make her an audience, so that she might enjoy her small treat to the full, for nothing that happened when she was alone could be of any real pleasure to her. I hesitated, with an impulse to wave and attract her attention. Another part of my mind suggested that this was almost equally a treat for me, an opportunity to put lunch in my pocket or miss it altogether and secure several hours at a stretch with Ted down at the hide, instead of wasting half the time going to and fro in the dinghy between meals. And I disliked the steak-and-kidney-pie smell of the A.B.C. If there was a chance of our going to any other restaurant, I would be kind, I told myself. But the A.B.C. was particularly congenial to her because tipping was forbidden there, so that apart from saving (which was nice, too, because then she could get something sixpence dearer for one of us), the waitress's personal interest and deference could be described as 'conscientiousness'. 'Conscientious' was mother's highest praise for someone of the lower orders. Averse from sweating anyone herself, she dearly loved a self-sweater. It would certainly be the A.B.C. I did not move while she sauntered on until she was hidden from me for a moment or two by a dip in the road. Now for Ted. Or better wait until she had passed the corner where she would reappear. It would be queer – exciting if horrible in a way – to know what it would be like, lying closely with him in the hide, now that my mind was changed to him. (And his to me, perhaps, by the influence of my thoughts?)

The indecision of the little figure on the road, more touching now that I could not see her, and the realization that mother was one of the people who exist solely in their relationship with others, forced me several steps out into the open, in order to make a better bargain with my conscience. But there I 'froze' again. If she glanced up she would see me (I knew that people very seldom look upwards). Because I had always found it difficult to believe in the existence of my back-view, I was in sympathy on just this one point with mother who, if she could not think of herself as the wife of Arthur Rush, the producer of his children and the friend and customer of people in the village, could not realize her own existence at all. Peel away from her all her human relationships and, like an onion and its skins, there would be nothing left of her for her own mind to grasp, no solid core that was unalterably Phyllis Laidler, now called Mrs. Rush for convenience. To make a person like that take her pleasure alone seemed particularly rotten of me.

Just before she reappeared, our local ex-service band of three came into sight, also on their way to catch the Ipswich bus. Seeing one of the gentry they began to play. In a few seconds I saw mother walking much faster than she did usually, which meant that she was not going to give them any pennies to-day and so felt that it would be unfair to walk in time with the music. The humanity of that action suddenly overcame me; I started waving to catch her eye; no one could have made her hear from this distance above the music. She had too long a start for me to catch her up while she quick-marched like that, but if she saw me she would wait and we would go into Ipswich together. She was moving with an air of determination, however: one had to walk very fast indeed to keep out of step with that band, and having taken up this uncomfortably rapid pace, she could not fall back on the slow one that would also have kept her out of step.

'It's all right, she won't see you now!' said a dry voice.

I jumped and looked round. Mr. Quest was not to be seen at first glance. Then I noticed a shoe protruding between some thick gorse and bramble bushes.

'Which of the Rushes are you? I can only see the lower half.'

'Lallie, Mr. Quest.' Reluctantly I came round to face him, aware that the brand of my guilty conscience flamed in my face. Cold as it was that late December day, he was sitting on a mackintosh with a rug round his knees, having brought a pile of books and writing things to this odd hiding place within a hundred yards of his great garden wall. He had one look at my face, and affably refrained from asking for an explanation of my behaviour, which he must have been wondering at for some time.

'My children have invited friends for Christmas,' he said, waving an explanatory hand round his encampment. 'They say they didn't want to "bother" me about it, knowing "how busy" I am, so thinking I was going to be away they didn't tell me. Unfortunately I was moved by the need of peace to come down last night, and there isn't a passable train back to Town till 3.46. The boys call me "sir" in every second sentence, and the girls ogle with an air of humouring the aged, which is even more devastating. The house rings with clean, boisterous mirth. Their conversation seems more penetrating physically than mentally, judged from my study. They tiptoe by the door, knowing that Basil and Stella are unlucky in their surviving parent and courteously wishing to spare them a family scene, and then they explode into giggles and muffled screams as soon as they get past. Don't give away my sanctuary, Lallie.'

I had met this merry horde of visitors, the first that his children had ever had the nerve to invite, at tea at our house on the previous day.

I said I wouldn't. They must be pretty trying to him, I supposed, because apart from his fierce liking for quiet, an atmosphere of gaiety at home would remind him of the days when his adored young wife was alive. His next remark confirmed me in this idea: 'All too reminiscent of a life with which I hoped I had finished for ever.'

'How did you know I was a Rush, Mr. Quest, if you couldn't see who I was?'

'Floral pattern on the dress, even in winter. It is a curious thing,' said Mr. Quest, throwing himself back into a more comfortable position, and I thought, Oh, golly, he's going to talk! An honour, and all that, but what about Ted? Once the taciturn Mr. Quest really got started, there was no knowing when he would stop. However, there was nothing to be done but look attentive and wait for a lull. I had always had a grievance against that dress, a velvet ex-'best' of Dru's, cut down by lovingly incompetent hands which had failed to reconcile its fullnesses to my recesses, so that I had been told to wear it out. I loathed it from now on.

'. . . a curious thing that in families where there are many children – and I am told by Stella, who knows these things, that there were several more of you at one time? – there is also a predilection for decoration in the form of fruit and flowers. A feeling, perhaps, that one can't go wrong if one sticks to nature. Restriction of family and geometrical patterns have some strange affinity for one another. It is quite a good working generalization that if you observe cubes and lozenges on the furnishing fabrics of a strange house, you can depend on finding not more than two children. And there's particularly something about concentric circles – but that would lead us from the point. Where will you find a greater profusion of roses on walls and floors and ornaments than in the cottages of the agricultural labourers of this neighbourhood, which I sometimes have to visit in the course of my work? Or more children, per house? The Cottrells, with their meagre output of two, incline to checks and stripes in clothing, and my own chair-covers, curtains and so on, are either plain or rectilinear in design (actually I prefer plain and often wonder whether the two children I have can really be mine at all). The neo-Georgian tendency is to keep nature in her proper place, outside the home. Note how the Victorians rioted in applied nature. That grand profusion of progeny, occasionally tortured to behave with unnatural decorum, matched the grand profusion of chintz flowers, also tortured into impossible conventional neatness: but what a great display it was all the same! Then we come to less of both among the Edwardians. You, of course, are spiritually Edwardian, or rather your family is, the fine flower of its middle period. The rosebuds on your frock are merely life-sized. If you had been a Victorian they might have been as large as cabbages, and you would have had eight brothers and sisters at least. But nowadays, with the exception of the labouring classes, who are always living twenty to forty years behind the times (see how mealy-mouthed their women have become in the last two decades, while ours have grown freer, just as they retained their innocent Regency bawdiness throughout the Dickens period of upper class delicacy) . . .' The end of this terrific sentence, on which I was rapidly losing grip, was drowned by an amicable roar from his son on the other side of the wall.

'No, I say, Peter, you hound! I must finish three-quarters of an hour on it. I've only done about twenty minutes . . .'

'Look here, old man, you be careful you don't go stale from over-training. I knew a fellow . . .'

And then a girl's voice, 'Oh, but *Basil*, what a *marvellous* machine! I've heard of the things, but I've never *seen* one. It's killingly funny. Does it *really* give you all the movements of rowing? How marvellous. Peter, let me try it, there's a sweet. Gosh, what a fag to move. Didn't know you had to lie so flat on your back. Now am I bending forward far enough? Won't it really go faster? Oh, *that's* the idea, is it? Well, Basil, I think you're *marvellous* doing this for three-quarters of an hour every day! Isn't there a close season for river men?'

Howls of merriment arose. I sympathized, having seen Basil's elaborate rowing-carriage in action, when he worked it jerkily along the roads on summer evenings at a maximum sweat-producing speed of a mile an hour, impervious to ridicule in an athletic cause. But poor Mr. Quest looked gloomier.

'Do – it – with – your – legs – not – your – arms – Beryl.' 'Put – your – back – into – it.' From the increased volume of the shouts of advice, we gathered that the machine had progressed several yards further from the jolly group. 'Sh – sh!' from someone reduced them to giggling.

'It's that carrying "sh-sh" ing which makes my study uninhabitable,' complained Mr. Quest in a whisper. 'One wonders why the human race should have chosen, as a sound enjoining silence, a sibilant, which . . .'

'Now let Basil have it back, Beryl darling,' called Stella in her richly maternal voice. 'He must finish his time before lunch.'

'Lunch!' said Mr. Quest softly. 'I hadn't thought of that. I don't think I can face any more youthful *bonhomie* with civility. And unfortunately, by the strange accident of paternity, these people are my guests, to whom I can't be as rude as to mere fellow residents. A curious social quibble this may seem to you, but still upbringing sticks, you know; it sticks, alas. In some ways you will always be an Edwardian just as I shall always suffer from these outworn Victorian disabilities. That's why I rarely allow anyone whom I may want to hold off afterwards to come inside my house. But I shall be abominably hungry before I get tea on the train. You wouldn't burgle my pantry for me, would you, Lallie? Say half a cold chicken or something like that? For a really large box of chocolates as reward? It's no use my going, I'd be caught, I'm not nippy enough nowadays.'

Normally, because luxuries did not often come our way, my pride would not boggle at tips, in kind or specie. But this was Christmas week, when chocolates must soon be plentiful. Pride won easily from greed. 'No, I won't,' I said with more spirit than usual. 'I've never been invited into your house so I've no idea where the pantry is. I'd only go wrong and meet somebody, and then I'd feel frightful.'

'You could think of the figure 2,' said Mr. Quest almost pleadingly. 'And marron glacés as well as chocolates? It's their continual imitations of people whom I don't know and hope never to meet – It's the daring sallies of the girl Beryl, who has already asked me twice whether she isn't awful (I assumed that this was a rhetorical question. But it isn't one I can bear again).'

'I did try to remember what you said about 2,' I told him, 'at another time when I couldn't think what to say. Quite lately. But it didn't help.' Or had it? I remembered my unexpected success with the sunset and softened a little. The dignified Mr. Quest seemed more of an equal, skulking in the cold because he was afraid of a pack of school and university children. (Basil was still at his public school, but Stella had gone on to Oxford, where she was even safer, no doubt, from educational psychology.) 'Tell you what I will do, though. I'll fetch you something from home. It won't be chicken, of course. I can always get round Olive to give me something to take out if mother isn't there. And father's got a weird man out in *Guadalupe* with him, a Bulgarian who's probably going to buy her, so there's sure to be something extra going, because he keeps people like that to lunch. It's a sort of habit.'

'Heaven reward you, child. And in my small way I'll do what I can, too. It's their untiring sense of humour! But I forgot, your family has an official sense of humour, hasn't it? Like the Cottrells' official sensitiveness towards Art and Such. So perhaps you don't sympathize with me in shrinking from the thought of any more jollity?'

'Oh, Mr. Quest, I do!' I said mournfully, feeling how un-Rush of me it was. I was moved to confidence because his long thin nose looked so blue, and his whole attitude so dejected as he sat up to hug his bony knees under the rug.

175

Liability to cold and hunger were such human traits to find in him. 'You see, my trouble is, I'm the only one in our family who hasn't a sense of humour.'

Mr. Quest let go of his knees, struggled up out of his cocoon of rug and stared at me with astonishment.

'My dear, that is the only original claim that I have ever heard made by a woman. In fact, I doubt that anyone else has ever made it and meant it.'

Equally surprised, I grinned with embarrassment, not being used to praise. This was the second time in a week (and only the third time in my life, incidentally) that I had struck lucky with a simple statement which was somehow better than I knew. 'Well, it's true, I haven't.'

Prolonged squeals of distant laughter, and the sounds of a gay hue and cry and much 'sh-sh'-ing floated from another part of the garden, coming nearer. 'Damn it, she's got my . . .' 'Let go, Beryl, or I'll . . . Ow, you're smothering . . .'

'I've no doubt you're right!' he said with a momentary return to his usual chilling manner. 'The astonishing thing is that you should know it. Let us not bother about food from either house. Help me to carry all this stuff up the road, away from those depressing sounds, to my chauffeur's. We can leave it there and tell him to get the car out as soon as he can, then we'll go and have a rather late lunch at the Falcon in Norwich, which is quite a passable place, and afterwards we'll get your chocolates, because a girl who owns to having no sense of humour deserves all the chocolates she fancies without specifically earning them. When you've dropped me at the station at Ipswich on the way back you can do what you like with the car till you think it's time for Archer to take you home. How will that do?'

'Oh, Mr. Quest – I . . .' (And he called the most famous hotel in East Anglia, a place in which I had never even hoped to eat, 'quite passable'!) 'But will it be all right in this dress?'

176

offence, because we all knew the cause of it, and pitying, forgave.

As my revelation went on, he looked increasingly grim and amazed, and also increasingly something else – an expression that I could not fathom – at learning that his private affairs were frequently discussed by people whom he had persistently snubbed for years. But as he normally looked a bit grim, amazement and the other feeling were probably uppermost in his mind. Guessing this, I did not lie for Stella when he asked if she were the source of information. At first, during this raking over of painful associations, I avoided looking at Mr. Quest as much as possible, but after a time I felt emboldened to suggest, 'Stella says that people who knew Mrs. Quest say she's very like her mother?' If Mr. Quest would insist on hurting himself and putting me through a rather awful catechism I was surely entitled to one small piece of information as compensation: in spite of Stella's sentimental reiterations, I had never been able to believe in the likeness. But Mr. Quest absently corroborated her statement, though whether he meant a similarity of looks or character I did not know. The odd expression deepened; it reminded me a little of the way in which he had regarded the Persian cat while it attended to its young.

'Very interesting,' he said non-committally at last. 'I had no idea that I was such a benefactor to Pin Mill society in the long winter evenings,' and then changed the subject abruptly. It was never re-opened between us, so that I was left alternating, in amazement equal to his, between the belief that something had suddenly happened to my hearing, and the still more impossible one that he had actually said, quite casually, while being very funny about women, '. . . the most god-dam-awful one I ever knew used to say, before we married . . .' No, it must have been something else that sounded like that. At the moment, in any case, I was feeling too oppressed of stomach to care.

He said it would. All the same, I was doubtful on the way, and acutely self-conscious as I followed relays of waiters between tables at which everyone looked fashionable, and no other woman was hatless. But soon after we arrived I forgot all about those misplaced bulges of flowered velvet, because he gave me sherry first, and then wine of some kind, and half way through the meal I found myself volubly telling him – Mr. Quest, the unapproachable! – about mother, and my not wanting to go to Ipswich with her, and how hard it was to make women understand that birds were more interesting than food. Than home-food, I meant, not food like this: encouraged by Mr. Quest I was ordering everything I fancied. I suddenly realized that I had been forgetting all about Ted: mother was not likely to be out to lunch again for a long time: in a way I had wasted the whole day. But it didn't matter just then. Ted could wait. I had a whole lobster. Incredibly friendly as Mr. Quest had turned, I thought better of telling him about Ted and the trouble over the hide.

He agreed that women were on the whole a mistake.

'Of course, not all women,' I said politely, remembering through the sherry and wine the wife whom he had mourned so long.

'As nearly all as makes no matter,' insisted Mr. Quest, and I could not argue with him because what seemed at the moment a full-sized catastrophe had just happened. All my remaining powers of concentration, which were little by this time, were required to grapple with it. My napkin had slipped off my knees and half under the table. Wine, which I had never tried before, save in sips from other people's glasses, had made me clammily hot all over, and my hands were growing too disgustingly sticky to touch anything that Mr. Quest or the waiter might have to handle afterwards. Deciding that in this place I dared not grovel for it myself, I turned to the nearest black-coated figure. 'Pick that up!' I said in a good imitation of father's sailing voice, and pointed commandingly at the napkin, which I could almost have reached without moving from my chair. As far as I could judge in my panic, the words were delivered almost in a shout. Several people near by looked surprised, but not as surprised as the man addressed, who was, Mr. Quest told me afterwards, the *maître d'hôtel*. After a few seconds he bent ponderously and returned the thing to me. Out of the corner of an eye I looked anxiously at Mr. Quest, to discover from his face whether I had done something unpardonable, but found that he was grinning as broadly as some of the waiters. Dear, unbelievable Mr. Quest, it was too bad that his wife should have died, I felt, when he hastily gave me some more wine in case I grew depressed by this blunder.

At increasingly frequent intervals, as my enormous meal went on, I found it impossible to take seriously the fact that I was lunching with Mr. Quest at the Falcon. Fortunately my laughing at such moments did not matter, because he was talking and talking, being very entertaining and no doubt aware of it. He was not likely to expect a woman to laugh in the appropriate places only. Hazily I knew that I ought to listen more carefully, in order to remember afterwards the wittiest conversation that was ever likely to be made to me, but I was too much taken up with a suggestion that he had thrown off at random before he started talking about women, the idea that father and his troupe ought to take up cross-running into Russia while the anti-God going was still good. Gun-running, father had already tried in his early youth; Mr. Quest had heard some of his stories of that; rum-running had become definitely vulgar and *démodé*, but an illicit trade in ikons and crucifixes should yield a fine return of excitement and profit for years. Just the sort of thing that father would love.

I was planning, in a pleasant daze, how we would smuggle

178

the sacred images into the country in bits, and assemble them there, when the recollection of something that Mr. Quest had said a moment or two ago woke me up with a jump, or rather I was startled by a muzzy recollection of what I must have misheard, for I realized at once that he could not have spoken as I fancied.

I thought that I had caught a reference to his wife. No one in Pin Mill had ever heard him mention her, and even Stella, when she remembered, refrained in his presence from saying anything 'mothery' that might lead the conversation to Mrs. Quest's memory, though she frequently told other people with satisfaction that she could remember her gay young mother ('Mutlets' to everyone who knew her) calling her Moon-child – Mr. and Mrs. Quest having got engaged by moonlight. No, he must have said something else.

Wine was mellowing even Mr. Quest: '. . . unreasonable of me, I suppose, to complain that if nine out of ten of the women one meets were men, they'd be considered half-wits.'

'Well, I do think it is a bit unreasonable,' I said, unguardedly, 'when you've been so lucky yourself.'

'Oh, and how have I been lucky?'

'Well – I mean – of course you weren't lucky in one way. Rottenly unlucky. But in another way . . .' I was properly bogged now. 'And I don't mean exactly lucky, because I expect you deserved it, Mr. Quest.'

'Deserved *what?*'

'Well . . .' There was no way out of it now. 'Your wife. Being so sweet and that. Like everyone says.'

'Exactly what,' asked Mr. Quest in his most intimidating voice, 'does "everyone" say on this interesting topic?'

The next few minutes almost spoilt the whole lunch. Twist and wriggle out of his questions as I would, bit by bit he drew from me a complete picture of the romantic figure that he cut in Pin Mill, the great lover whose rudeness in defence of his angry solitude could never give lasting

179

I had a little anxiety while walking out between the ubiquitous tables, because though they seemed considerably closer together than they had been when we came in, my legs and head felt a great deal further apart. However, concentration and sea-balance carried me through nicely: there were some advantages in being a Rush after all. The coldness of the air outside was more trying: I was glad to get into the car, and went to sleep between Norwich and Ipswich, where I felt all right again for a time, and Mr. Quest bought me the biggest box of chocolates I had ever had, but I did not fancy opening it at the moment.

I took it as a matter of course when he said that we must lunch again one day, and saw him into the 3.46 from Ipswich feeling quite an old and intimate friend: so much at ease, in fact, that I had the forethought to borrow a penny from him with a view to being sick in comfort as soon as the train should have gone. By the time that we had reached the station, I was just beginning to long for the opportunity, but about ten minutes before starting time the desire became acute. It did not seem to me the grateful course, however, to indulge myself before he left. Still slightly under the influence of drink, I had more self-possession than usual, or I could not have asked for the coin. He seemed concerned when I explained why I wanted it, and suggested that I should not wait to see him off, but though at times the train waved to and fro a little before my eyes, nothing in my vicinity was yet going up and down; and I remembered father saying that wave-like movements of one's surroundings were the real danger-sign on land   I was obstinately determined to do the right thing in return for all that lovely food. Afraid that I had let the family down a bit by my confidences, I was going to vindicate it in a way that only a Rush could do with safety, by showing off abdominal discipline. We had quite an argument about it.

'But, Mr. Quest, I've had heaps of practice in judging just

how nearly ill I am,' I insisted. 'It's about the only thing I'm truly a Rush in. Thank you so much for everything.' The train gave a slight stagger, but the time was now 3.43. Even a non-Rush might be expected to retain command of his or her stomach for three minutes: it should be child's-play to me.

'Lallie, we must certainly have lunch again soon,' he said warmly. 'I had no idea that such beautiful manners still existed among the young. Thank you for saving me from high spirits. And if you start feeling worse, make a bolt for it, do. I oughtn't to have given you so much wine.'

'It doesn't matter a bit. We're always quite all right again two minutes afterwards, thank you.'

I put out one arm and leant against the open carriage door so that the train and I could rock imperceptibly together if necessary. Mr. Quest, seeing that I was bent on staying, was most helpful and talked all the time, marvellously I expect. Fortunately the train started with superb punctuality; for a moment before it was due out I detected a new near-and-far effect in the slight circular movement of the station clock, but out of bravado I merely sauntered away towards the waiting-room even when the carriage at last began to move, because I could see Mr. Quest hanging out of the window, watching me anxiously. In the end I had to run, but for once I felt triumphantly father's daughter and the equal of Dru as I let myself go and was splendidly sick in seclusion. After the growing tension of waiting, it was almost enjoyable. I knew that I had established my new friendship with Mr. Quest on a basis of mutual respect.

'Levington, please,' I told his chauffeur, having had an idea while recovering in the waiting-room. This would annoy the Cottrells! Since the day when I had sailed their archæologist across the Orwell and enjoyed the meeting, Marnie and Lester had taken to rowing laboriously across at dusk to fetch him themselves, in case one of us might poach him again. The idea that Ted and I could be mistaken for them must have been as objectionable to them as to me.

Gordon Summers, who lived in Norwich, had some elaborate, unpractical and, as I found later, characteristic arrangement for sharing a car with another Norwich man, temporarily working at Nayland on our side of the river. It had a time-table, to which neither of them managed to keep, for meetings at Woolverstone cross-roads. In theory Summers either cadged a lift across the river and walked there, or took the long way round the head of the Orwell by bus, to be picked up by his friend at five o'clock on wet afternoons and six-thirty on fine ones. Actually their views on the weather rarely agreed, and about three times a week, according to Olive, something went wrong with the meeting and Summers returned to the Cottrell house, in a welter of uncalled-for apologies, to accept their proffered supper before going home by bus and train. His job made him a person after their own hearts.

I kept my eyes away from the people in the streets while we crossed the Cornhill in Ipswich. Mother, tired with shopping, would very likely be waiting for a bus there, and if I saw her, conscience would make me stop and pick her up and drive straight home. But we got through safely. Feeling perfectly fit again now, I was charmed by the idea of sweeping up an acquaintance in this gorgeous limousine, thus wiping out the Cottrells' advantage in having a disreputable old car of their own. From the road I recognized Gordon Summers' back as he bent over a trench, out of which men were climbing with the grand ponderous movements of navvies at the end of a day's work. They stacked their picks and came swinging down the road past us; lovely men, bare-armed and earthy. Fancy anyone believing in a God Who made ordinary things so unnecessarily beautiful and then remained coy with proofs of His existence! If I had produced anything as stupendous as a navvy, I thought, waving back to one I knew, I would have finished off the job by seeing that everyone gave Me due credit.

Bent on extracting the last ounce of lordliness from my temporary position, I sent the Quest's sulky chauffeur wading and sloshing through the trampled clay of the neighbouring field to fetch Gordon Summers, who was still messing about in the diggings. Save for the feet, he was quite clean this time. Now that the location of the villa was clear, the heavy work could be done by others. I could not tell why I was disappointed at seeing him look so nice; perhaps because it made a stranger of him again. I decided not to get out of the car to exhibit the wretched velvet dress when he offered, without much eagerness certainly, to show me the corner of a tessellated pavement which had recently been uncovered. No doubt the Cottrells had already seen it and said all the appropriate things.

'Well, not to-day, thanks awfully, because I ought to get home. Would you like a lift to the cross-roads? Or Ipswich? We'll be passing both on the way home. I was just driving by and I thought – er . . .' He did not appear as impressed as I hoped by the gorgeousness of my vehicle, seeming to take my ownership for granted. Later I found that he was not a person to whom property mattered.

'That's very nice of you, but you see the Cottrells generally . . .'

'North-east wind,' I said firmly. 'Dead across the river. Shouldn't think those two could row against it. But just as you like, of course.'

He hesitated. 'Is it blowing hard? We're rather sheltered here, but still it doesn't feel – Rather a shame if they struggled over to fetch me – And goodness knows why they should: frightfully kind of them – and then found I'd gone.'

'It isn't hard enough to stop anyone but a Cottrell,' I admitted. 'But you know how they row. Like digging potatoes.'

He smiled, showing very nice teeth. 'And I suppose that's appalling? Do I get a share of your contempt for owning that to me they look quite competent?'

'Oh, no. But maybe you would if I saw you lending a hand in the boat. Really, it'd be a stiff pull for them to-day, and after all, they know you can get home without them, don't they?' I was afraid that Lester or Marnie might appear at any moment. In that family even Lester could be relied on to face unusual physical exertion in pursuit of a fellow intellectual, such things being uncommon in Pin Mill. 'Tide should be right up by now, too: makes it nearly half a mile further for them to row against the wind. Do you really think it's worth chancing their coming?'

'No, I suppose they won't to-day. After all, there's nothing to make them, except that I've got into a lazy way of counting on them. I certainly don't feel like walking half way to Ipswich in the hope of being overtaken by that erratic local bus.'

'Well, hop in, then,' I said grandly, and carried off the Cottrells' pet.

He was thoroughly nice, I thought: he talked of ordinary things in an ordinary way, which people rarely seemed to do in the families I knew. Usually, if they were not pretending that something mattered to them either more or less than one knew it really did, they pretended it mattered in a different way. But he said he thought that cricket was dull, and Thomas Hardy was dull, and Mrs. Cottrell's cooking was delightful, and so was Mr. Cottrell's music – I disagreed about the music – and he very much wished that he had enough money to go ski-ing in Norway every year, which was his idea of heaven. When I asked him if he liked the pictures in the Cottrell house, which were all modern French and the object of our hearty derision, he said that about a third of them appealed to him considerably but several of the nudes seemed a cheap effort at originality, and I felt sure that unlike the Cottrells (who cherished these for their cleverness) and my family (who hooted at them for the same reason; only we called them 'clever-clever', whatever that meant), and Olive (who would have liked to be shocked but thought that it wasn't her place, so called them 'pretty') and Mr. Quest (who rated them on some elaborately different standard of his own), Gordon Summers felt about them, simply enough, exactly what he said he did. After sixteen years of family life, I found this entirely charming.

I made Archer wait at the cross-roads to see if his car turned up. By this time Archer's back was bristling with criticism of the way in which I was taking advantage of Mr. Quest's car. He, not having been sick, wanted his tea. I did not, in spite of my recovery, and returned meaning glance for meaning glance – conveying, I hoped, that I had frequently seen him taking the Quest maids for jaunts in this car when the family was away, and now it was my turn to lord it in her. When we had waited an hour, Gordon Summers gave it up, and I insisted on his coming back to supper with us. A ship from Chile had come up the Orwell (biggish ships usually lie to the buoys below Pin Mill while unloading, being too deep to reach the docks), and I was fairly certain that father would collect somebody off her for the evening, captain or stoker or what-not (but preferably stoker from his point of view).

We could not offer Gordon Summers the marvellous food that Mrs. Cottrell provided with a flick of the wrist and three disparaging words, but Olive made use of the one accomplishment which she had acquired after years of practice, the knack of turning a limited quantity of tinned salmon into an apparently unlimited quantity of kedgeree with the aid of baking powder and eggs. People did not feel particularly full after several helpings, but they generally believed the evidence of their eyes, which told them that they had eaten so much that they could not possibly be hungry still. There was also, as usual with us when we had guests, much better wine than the food warranted. Father had sold *Guadalupe* to the unwary Bulgarian for nearly half as much again as she was worth, and to celebrate this he brought out some of the best of the drink that had come over from the Continent with us on the last summer trip. Most owners of sea-going yachts smuggle for their own use. Father genially told his guests (also as usual) to help themselves freely because the stuff cost him nothing, disregarding the arduous forty odd hours of cold and wet and seasickness and fatigue that it cost his troupe, who had to bring the boats back by the heroic passage straight across that part of the north sea which lies between the Scheldt and the Suffolk coast, in order to avoid the ports where we might be searched by customs officials.

'I'm really relieved not to have to trade on the Cottrells' kindness again,' Gordon Summers said. 'They must be getting so sick of my turning up saying that I've missed the car.' I did not see why I should undeceive him on this point if they had failed to convince him of his value as snob-fodder. With low pleasure I decided I must see to it to-morrow that Olive let them hear of his dining with us.

It was a nice evening: the Australian mate whom father had collected from the steamer turned out to be an authority on tropical birds. At the beginning of supper I was afraid for a few minutes that Gordon Summers was not going to get on well with father, who said something to the sailor in praise of the Australian troops in France. '. . . Amazing fellows. Could go through any barrage.'

'Only a poor barrage,' said Summers firmly. 'Whatever troops they were. Getting through isn't a question of morale, it's a question of shells per square yard.' Just the sort of remark that father did not care for; he tried to brush it aside, but failed because Summers had a persistently unromantic mind. 'Unfortunately human courage has no power of protecting human flesh from the effects of high explosives,' he said dryly in reply to father's protest. 'Well, you were in France, you must have seen a barrage . . .'

And of course father hadn't; it was most unfortunate. However, the subject was changed and then everything went well; there was a pause into which, with no prompting, Summers dropped a question pulled from him, as it were, by a kind of mental gravitation – that force which father exercised unconsciously. He asked the Australian's opinion about some political upheaval in a part of the world which father knew intimately.

We even got the bandit story by great persistence. Gordon Summers nearly failed to catch the last bus because of it. He had to borrow Ronald's bicycle to get to the main road in time. I think he enjoyed himself. He saw Margaret close to for the first time, that day. He had not noticed her at the regatta. She was then reaching the age that for most girls is the gawkiest of all, fifteen, but somehow Margaret never seemed to go through the usual plain periods.

And I did not see Ted as I had intended; neither that day nor for a long while afterwards, save in the presence of other people. I heard later from his mother that, hurt because I did not seem to appreciate the hide he had made for me, he had waited about for me all day, just as he had done with growing puzzlement throughout the week. Then something must have changed in him. When I wanted him he was not available, day after day. Shortly after Christmas he went down to Harwich for a fortnight to help Sootie's brother on a rush job. I found, when I went alone to Decoy Reach, that he had dismantled the hide. Ted was too humble and too good-natured to be hurt for long: when he came back we might have got together again, but even then I was still ashamed of the sneaking excitement and eagerness about him in my own mind. I had tried to see him several times; I would not try again, I thought; he must

make the first move. And before the trouble mended between us it had become Margaret, a much more daring
sailor than I was, whom he waited upon for choice whenever
he could get out of helping Sootie. It was horrid that Ted
should have a boy's admiration for Margaret, who laughed
at him behind his back; horrid but not surprising: it would
be hard, I thought, for anyone of his age not to feel an
impulse to service before something so lovely and vital.

'I say, what a splendid looking family!' Gordon Summers
said to Dru that first evening with the sudden boldness of the
shy, as she bicycled with him to the Ipswich road in order
to bring back Ronald's machine.

'I know. Marvellous!' she said warmly, for the moment
forgetful of herself as one of us (and forgetful of me too,
I expect) in her pride in mother and father, Margaret and
Ronald. She told us about it when she came back, giggling
though a little shocked by her own unselfconsciousness. It
was not often that one of our family could achieve any degree
of the happy immodesty which enabled Lester Cottrell to
say confidingly, 'I know; that's what I like about myself!'
when people made personal remarks to him.

Telling us of this little *gaffe* was a cleverer move on Dru's
part than I should have expected from her. Temporarily
at least it transferred to Gordon Summers, to whom she was
indifferent, the chief role in the family chaff which had
been reserved for Basil Quest, of whom she was really fond,
though their liking for each other as 'good sorts' had none
of the significance that our jokes pretended to find in it.
(These were generally about cradle-snatching, because Dru
was two years older than Basil.) Useless as the realization
might have been – probably I could have done nothing
to help her, and two people in our family would have been
discomfited instead of one – I am still angry that I did not
see at the time that Dru might have easily cared for Basil
later on, when the discrepancy of age had ceased to matter,

if the subject had been let alone while they were both very young. But a thorough sickening of the idea of Basil as a lover made that impossible for her for ever. Perhaps I could have turned some of this galling chaff aside: it would have been worth trying.

They were very well matched: she was as staunch and nice-minded and athletic as he was, and just as immune from serious intellectual disturbance. It is immaterial, as well as uncertain, whether he would ever have grown more than fond of her, if she had not avoided him for her own sake: loving him she would at least have had something more in her life than her interest in boats and her unshakable affection for mother. Poor Dru.

CHAPTER IX

BUSINESS WITH BOATHOOK

FATHER, with the *Guadalupe* profits burning a hole in his common sense, suddenly decided that Margaret and I were badly educated. We were; and so was Dru, but as she was already nineteen and college was out of the question, there was nothing to be done about her, and father characteristically managed to feel that it did not matter so much. Ronald's education had been the concern of the Lords of the Admiralty since he was thirteen, but for none of the rest of us had attendance at a day-school at Ipswich been allowed to interfere with sailing whenever father wanted a crew. However, it was obvious to everyone but father that a sudden change of heart could not put this right, and personally I thought (and still think) that beyond a smattering of the usual subjects, education in the scholastic sense is a waste of time and money for all but the naturally studious: neither Margaret nor I was interested in knowledge for its own sake.

We quieted him down for a month or two: there were so many important things that should have been done with the money. I became increasingly friendly with Mr. Quest and Gordon Summers at this time, in my efforts not to miss Ted, whom I grudged bitterly to Margaret: bird-watching was nothing like such fun alone: still, it gave me some good hours. Then *Barbara*, *Guadalupe's* cheap successor, was chartered profitably for the whole summer, and on top of that father had a run of luck in his engineering business. Success had always come in streaks for him; everything he touched would inevitably turn out well for a while before a long spell of disappointments: but one could rarely get father to look ahead to the barren period. On the top of his luck, he put one small advertisement of the old-fashioned, disreputable-looking *Wanderer*, which he had been trying to sell for years, into a Belgian yachting paper, and she was bought unseen by a fool who only specified that she must be delivered in Ostend. Margaret and I helped to take her over and were dispatched to a finishing school near Brussels. In our case the finishing process had to be applied to an almost non-existent foundation, but I doubt that this really made any difference to the result.

Life there was quite pleasant; a feeling of suspended animation hung over our trivial days. I should not have minded but for my acute sense of time slipping by inexorably. I did not know what I wanted to do with Time, but it was certainly not playing at music and sketching and the acquisition of foreign languages, for none of which had I any aptitude, nor talking to girls at the romantic age, who bored me unless I did most of the talking, when I bored them.

Only two things mildly enlivened the eighteen months which we spent in being finished. One was that, with the incredible snobbishness rife in such establishments, we came to be looked on almost with awe by the daughters of much wealthier parents (who were at first inclined to comment with veiled unpleasantness on the poverty of our clothes) when it got about that we had come from England to Ostend in a yacht belonging to our father. Later it was learned that we had spent the summer holidays in Holland in another yacht and, as it happened, returned to Ostend in a different one; also his; and finally we expected to be taken home in yet a fourth, his latest purchase, known to us only by Dru's flattering snapshots from home. These were pounced upon as soon as we opened her letters, and shown round almost without our permission. The meanest sailing craft has a way of looking impressive in photographs; size is hard to judge, shoddy paintwork looks brilliant, and clumsy lines rarely appear in silhouette. Taking back the prints from admiring hands, Margaret studied them with a knowledgeable eye, and endorsed my opinion that the new boat was 'our lousiest yet' in such a tone of calm sincerity that from then on the meagreness of our wardrobe was accepted as the endearing English idiosyncracy of the very rich. Towards the end of our time, girls angled for an invitation to come yachting with us, an English yacht being to their imaginations inevitably the most luxurious and expensive form of ocean conveyance. How they would have loathed father's idea of passage-making if we had liked any of them well enough to act on their hints.

The other break in the monotony put an end to our popularity; fortunately it happened just before we left. A nephew of the Italian mistress was invited to stay at the school for a few days. It was understood that he had nominally honourable designs on the plainer of our two dull heiresses, countrywomen of his who had come to shed some of their lire here through the influence of his aunt, a decayed noblewoman, like all Italian mistresses abroad, apparently. As the plainer of the heiresses was not the richer, it is even possible that he honestly liked the girl, but we were all prepared to fall a little in love with him, through idleness, and in most cases would not have been deterred by the fact that he turned out to be as squidgily repulsive as only an undersized Italian can be. A detailed description of the fuss made by the staff before his arrival would sound improbable to anyone not familiar with the spirit of a continental finishing school. All the training was covertly directed to making us marketable to men, but even the usual thin pretence that charm might have some extra-marital value was dropped now that we were faced with what might be regarded as a practical test. We were expected to show some results of the care lavished upon us; we were to be utterly fascinating, short, of course, of getting ourselves into trouble. It had been delicately drummed into us that men preferred women to be bewildering; sometimes indifferent, sometimes coyly attentive; always the adorable mystery. At eighteen (the average age in the school) indifference seemed the more dignified opening strategy, and as it was assumed to be just as likely to lure him to our individual feet as the alternative of subtle flattery, all of us chose it for our preliminary attack, except Margaret and the Italian girl of his supposed choice. Margaret was scornful of the whole competition, and the plain Italian was much too genuinely anxious to plan anything. Dressed with exceptional care the rest of us lurked about the staircase and hall all the afternoon when he was due to arrive, ready to brush past him almost unseeingly; just one brilliant smile and then no second glance. Margaret refused even to change the hideous green dress which mother had sent her. She was so much the youngest girl in the place that no one bothered what she did. While the rest of us were waiting indoors, she strolled through us with that unseeing look of hers, and out into the garden, swinging her old straw hat by its ribbon.

She met him where the drive was hidden by the shrubbery, and we waited an extra quarter of an hour or so, but throughout his visit, which to his fury was cut short by several days, he had no attention to spare for anyone but *l'angelo Inglese*. I think the headmistress was afraid that there might be a real scandal, though Margaret remained only amused by her conquest.

'But what did you do? – You can't talk Italian,' I asked her at night in our room, half-delighted, half-shocked.

'Oh, just let him kiss me and mess about a bit,' she said and laughed. 'He was funny.'

194

Something, probably the choice of words, chilled me. There was an earthiness, a directness and vulgarity about Margaret that one could not help admiring in a way, or I could not, even when it disgusted me a little, as now. Surely to be kissed and – whatever she meant by 'messed about' which I would not let myself quite realize – could not be so casual a first experience as she made out? Perhaps it was not a first experience? – No, it must be, I thought, with Margaret not yet seventeen. At least she was superbly honest, if only because other people's opinions were of less importance to her than the trouble of dissimulation: I knew that the hot-blooded young man, carried away by this willing beauty of hers, had been only 'so funny' in her eyes, nothing more. She could not even take the trouble to answer the letters which he wrote to her afterwards in bad French, leaving them about from pure carelessness where the disappointed Italian girl might read them if she pleased.

But it was as if this conquest fulfilled some need of her body or mind: she blossomed out more richly, though this may have been only the natural course of her development. Certainly even mother, who must once have been lovely herself, seemed astonished by Margaret's looks when we joined her and father and Dru at Ostend.

I was glad to be done with the school, not only because I, as well as Margaret, had been first cut and then cold-shouldered by everyone over the stupid affair of the nephew (in which I could not see how I was implicated), but also because it struck me happily, in the Brussels-Ostend train, that now childhood was over for me; officially over as well as actually so; really it had ended that day when I went to the hide with Ted. Looking back I realized that I had loathed being a child. Occasionally one had marvellous times which might not come again with just that clear high degree of unalloyed delight: but to be spiritually vulnerable, unpractised at hiding one's feelings, and body and soul the property of other people, however kind, was a very unsatisfactory state, I thought. I was surprised that it had not been more unpleasant on the whole.

Because the flat Belgian landscape sliding by the window offered me no distraction to the eye, I went on thinking how queer it was that to the four of us children the same home had always been quite a different place: is it usually like that in families? To Dru, for whom childhood was the most satisfactory period in life, it was the centre of her heart, and would remain so however old she grew: to Ronald it had been the starting point of grand sailing and duck-shooting expeditions with father, until they grew apart when the likeness between them had become remarkable; and now Ronald often spent his leave with friends, to mother's distress. He and father had been nothing to one another since that day at the regatta, though on the surface their attitude to one another had not changed. To me it had been a well-situated, gently-managed prison: but a prison; joy began as soon as I got ticket-of-leave: probably I should go on feeling like that. And to Margaret – what had it been, and what would it be? I had no idea. It was startling to realize that after eighteen months of sharing a room with her I knew her no better than I had done before: that is, hardly at all. But now this inability to get in touch with whatever lay behind her fine, calm mask was not the sharp annoyance to me that it had been in childhood: I was beginning to know that beauty, – all beauty and not only hers – might have no meaning at all, and be precious still, partly for its transience and futility.

Father was having a great time with a Dutchman on a neighbouring *rhineschiff* when Margaret and I arrived at the yacht basin. We had caught an earlier train than the one arranged and were not yet expected. Walking round the quay, I was surprised by the sudden warmth of feeling that glowed in me when I saw him and mother. The basin was too big to shout across: they were in sight but unaware of us for some minutes before we were near enough to hail: somehow their unawareness made the passing emotion stronger. These were my people, to whom I was tied by so much more than blood, by shared experiences, and prejudices, forgotten kindnesses, and jokes: only spiritually was there no contact. At the moment I was as moved by pleasure and affection as though they had been my chosen friends, instead of the two persons in all the world most irrevocably barred from my confidence, by the fact of their relationship, whenever we chanced to speak of anything that really mattered. All strangers were potentially closer to me than either of them, not because they were uncongenial people – fundamentally they were not – but because they were my mother and father, in whose intimate, unknowable lives I had once played so quaint a part. (Is that, too, always the same in ordinary families?) But just for these few minutes they were immensely important to me again.

Mother was sitting on the hatch of the *rhineschiff*, patchily powdered all over with thick white dust, like everything else on board this cement-carrier, loyally trying to get matey with the enormous *schiffrau*, the Dutchman's wife. She was not having quite such a good time as father because her eyes and throat were affected by the clouds of cement that hung in the air for seconds after anything had stirred on deck, and the Dutchwoman's conversation, or as much as they seemed to understand of one another's French, was largely concerned with dental decay. At intervals the *schiffrau* opened a mouth in proportion to her size to give mother a demonstration. No one, except Margaret perhaps, could have helped a spasm of protective love for mother when from the quay we watched her politely peering in, following the direction of a pudgy forefinger. Father, from whom we could have learnt all the more useful European languages without leaving home, was obviously telling the lighterman dirty stories from the way in which the Dutch-man was rocking to and fro at intervals, endangering his mug of beer. They both belonged to the generation which still finds fun in a long preamble about a foreigner, Jew, or newly-married couple, serving to introduce words which most of the succeeding generation can use conversationally, without a titillating sense of naughtiness. (There must be, I suppose, many anecdotal throw-backs among post-war people, but I do not know personally anyone of my own age who is not passionately bored by the smoke-room stories of older people: we do not mind the point but we tire on the way to it.)

Mother answered our hail with enthusiasm, and we went on board into the cement haze. The conversation between father and the Dutchman cleaned up, in respect for our youth and sex. These *rhineschiffs*, extraordinary-looking boats evolved for the needs of inland waterways, are im-mensely long in proportion to their width, sometimes measuring nearly three hundred feet though the beam may not be more than twenty-five. This was a small one or it could not have got into the yacht basin, but even so at either end lived a family which kept to itself, so that whenever we came over to see the bow occupants, in the two days that we spent in Ostend, the stern would only nod to us distantly: we were not their friends. I was told that in some schiffs the bow and stern might not be on speaking terms for days on end, save in the matter of sailing directions, the trouble generally arising from the primitive fuelling arrangements, by which the smoke from forrard smutted the washing hung out aft: or in a following wind it might be vice versa. But such a state of affairs was deplored by the Dutchman: a nice distance should be kept by both families, tolerance observed, and meals occasionally shared on an invitation basis, but no more.

Dru rushed over from our boat, which was even smaller

198

and scabbier than we had expected, and while the Dutch-man hospitably insisted on drawing beer for us all to cele-brate the re-union, she began pouring out the gossip of Pin Mill. It was good to hear all the not intrinsically interesting news of what Mrs. Chandler had said, and Mrs. Mawley replied, and whether the Cottrell dog had had any more skirmishes with our cat, and how relations stood between them and us: did we add a few words to our greeting, or only greet them when we met them alone, and exactly how much more friendly were we in public? Dru had become a great retailer of small tidings; in some ways she was absurdly the premature old maid at twenty – Dru, that devilish sailor and bang-about good sort!

A gleam of sun pierced the heavy sky for a moment, and filtered through our private cloud of cement. The Dutch-man rose hurriedly, took off one of the long hatch-planks, considerably thickening the air as he did so, and disclosed a tiny compartment of the hold. From this he scooped out half a dozen of the most dejected hens I have ever seen. Fortunately for me, my feeling for birds stops short of domestic fowls. Ruffled, cement-filmed, they drooped about the deck in the sun for about two minutes, until the sky clouded over again and the Dutchman shovelled them back. 'They haf goot of a little air,' he said to mother, evidently feeling it necessary to apologize, not for their condition but for their appearance on deck.

Dru took up again her unending story, much of which I knew already through letters, but she enjoyed the retelling. Ted was away, yacht-hand on a south coast boat, but Mr. Quest was back at Pin Mill after a long absence, and had even stopped her and asked after me a few months back. This was flattering, but Dru added dashingly that he seemed sur-prised to hear that I had then been gone well over a year. Marnie Cottrell grew more unbearable at every tea party at which Dru could not avoid meeting her, during the University vacations. She had eagerly discovered decadence at Cambridge, where she was supposed to be doing wonders, and to hear her talk of it, Dru said disgustedly, one would imagine that the sole reason why Cambridge was able to put up some sort of show in the boat-race was because every member of the Oxford crew was riddled with the same vices.

'Oxford won't win next year. They're losing two of their best men,' called father, interrupting his own conversation in Dutch because he had heard the words, 'Cambridge . . . boat-race . . . Oxford,' and still fondly believed that his daughters discussed sporting chances among themselves.

'Yes. And Stella Quest is just as maddening in the sentimental way. But at least she got it in the neck last week from Gordon Summers, of all people! Oh, and then from Mrs. Cottrell, of all other people! My dear, too funny . . .'

Gordon Summers had finished his job at Levington and gone elsewhere long ago, I knew. It seemed that he had reappeared in Pin Mill one day, just before Dru, mother and father started over to fetch us; there was some question of covering in the Levington pavement to preserve it until it could be removed; but his part of the job would only take a week, he would probably be gone again by the time we reached home. Dru's account of his recent behaviour did not tally with my memory of that quiet, straight-thinking young man, entirely self-possessed under his air of shyness. He had gone up to Stella, whom he hardly knew by sight, as she emerged from the Cottrells' house, and demanded, 'Who's staying there? Is it the Macdonalds? Both of them?' without any preliminary how-do-you-do. Stella had seen him loitering about the road, just out of sight of the house, before she went in to see Marnie: it was as if he had been waiting for her or anybody else to come out.

'Yes.'

'Why?'

'Goodness, how do I know!' Stella had said, quite sensibly for her.

'And *then*,' went on Dru, warming to it, 'she said he said . . .'

'Oh, Stella always *says* people *say* . . .' I put in just to show that I was not particularly interested. Actually, I did want to hear about Gordon Summers, and hoped that he would still be about the neighbourhood when we reached Pin Mill, but now that I was among the family again I must remember to put up, almost automatically, these little verbal guards which alone could prevent the fastening of a leech-like joke on some irritating spot. The half-forgotten weariness of this returned to me, slightly dimming my pleasure at being here. 'You know it was always "Father says . . ." and then something rude that she couldn't even see *was* rude! Well, what did he say?'

'Oh, something abrupt about "Her child's ill. I thought she'd be in London." And then Stella went all soupy, like she does when anything can be made pathetic, and told him she'd heard from Marnie it was dead – though of course Marnie knew the treatment that would have saved it! And Stella said, perhaps that was why Mr. Macdonald had brought his wife away into the country. – "To forget" – you know how Stella says things like that!'

I knew, and could imagine that Summers might have found it hard not to laugh, but according to Dru via Stella, he had seemed quite stunned; so that Stella, fancying herself as the little comforter of all the world, had told him archly and circuitously (and quite unnecessarily, I am sure), that poor Mrs. Macdonald looked as though another little baby might one day replace this one. ('So it will all come right in the end!' we guessed that Stella had added with her lingering madonna look, that being a favourite phrase of hers.) Because he did not respond to this bit of news, she must have said something infuriating about the wind being

201

tempered to the shorn lamb, for I gathered that Gordon Summers had laughed at this point, shortly, and then become exceedingly rude in a cold, sarcastic, Mr. Quest-ish way about that smuggest of all the English wish-fulfilment proverbs, 'Had anyone,' he asked nastily, 'ever got the lamb's view on the tempering of the wind? And if not, who was the authority?' Really it was most surprising, from him! Stella, used to somewhat similar outbursts from her father, had taken it better than most people would have done: men were like that, unaccountable big babies, and she liked making allowances for them. Sticking to the practical feminine point of view, she had merely asked Summers whether she should give the Macdonalds any messsage from him if she saw them again: sympathy made so much difference. 'No. For God's sake, no!' Summers had gripped her arm so hard that she complained afterwards that it hurt. If I knew him at all, and particularly her, he must have been longing to shake her. 'Say nothing to them about it. I only – wanted to know.'

But of course Stella, being Stella, had described to everyone she met that day how concerned Mr. Summers had been about Mrs. Macdonald's poor little kiddie. She started the rigmarole in front of some other guests of the Cottrells when she met them without the Macdonalds. At the time, in public, Mrs. Cottrell had merely smothered the words with her own lazy drawl, but later in private she rounded quite energetically on Stella for spreading gossip under sentimental cover. But Stella still being Stella, it was now all over the village that there was at least some scandal where none had been dreamt of before.

Margaret was amused. Perched incongruously on the dirty hatch, too brilliant a bird of passage for this prosaic resting-place, she was nursing one slim ankle across her knee with the limberness that made Dru and even little mother appear solid and ungainly beside her. She looked oracle-wise when she smiled her remote, inward-seeming smile. Out of the far-off world where that smile was born, the serene territory of her mind which I could never explore, came often a jumble of small spiritual vulgarities and sudden gleams of wisdom which seemed equally out of keeping with her appearance: as soon might one expect a flower to be vulgar, or wise. She said now, 'Oh, Stella's got bats in the belfry. And a slate loose. – That was one of the bats getting out!' She laughed at this witticism, and then, rocking herself lightly while her face turned grave and distant again, she said, 'As if anything ever comes right in the end! In the end . . .' (to and fro, to and fro) 'everybody grows old and sick and bored. I suppose things don't matter so much to them then; but that isn't "coming right." And then they die, and it just doesn't matter that they don't, that's all. Silly. There's only now, really.'

Where does such knowledge come from – how do they see things like that, these close-to-earth people who are aware of more than their trivial minds can tell them? Or are their minds not trivial? Something in me leapt at what she said: something tried to deny it: to me it was not natural nor easy to see simple things straightly as she did. By conscious struggle only could I come where instinct led her without effort.

With an increase of interest in Gordon Summers, I wished that we could start home without the inevitable delay for buying wine in small quantities from different shops. I wanted to be back in Pin Mill before he left: otherwise I might not see him again. I had only slight curiosity about the reasons for his remarkable outburst, which I should probably never know, but the outburst itself had taken my imagination. 'The wind is tempered' – certainly this was the religious spirit run riot, it seemed to me, this fatuous example of human ability to believe whatever is most comfortable to believe, for no better reason than that it is comfortable. Such thin, mean lies people told one another, in their desire not to realize in full the blind cruelties which chance threw into the lives of others. – I must see Gordon Summers again: he seemed to be excellently immune from this weakness.

I began buying wine for father that day, against the protests of mother, who wanted to sit cosily on board and talk *à trois* after Margaret's and my long absence. But though I worked up Dru and Margaret to help too, it was over two days before we had all the contraband that father wanted. There seems to be some understanding between the customs officials of England and the nearer continental ports, by which information is sent on ahead of yachts whose crews are observed buying dutiable goods in any quantity. We deduced that some of the storekeepers must also be in league with the officials, to their mutual profit, from the fact that, in other years, several of our friends on reaching English ports had been boarded, searched and heavily fined as a result of buying everything from the same shop. Usually, cruising between Dunkirk and the Hague, we had the chance of buying an insignificant amount of our year's supply in every place we touched. One or two bottles at a time were carried down to the yacht by local errand boys, in baskets laden with loaves and cauliflowers and other stores: but now that everything was to be taken from the one town we had to dawdle over our purchases: a long string of grocery-boys arriving one after the other, however innocent-looking their loads, would be likely to arouse suspicion.

As it was, while I was ashore, casting off the mooring ropes on our last evening in the Basin, a quayside loafer dropped into impudent conversation with me – I was one of the '*jolies matelottes*' from the English yacht? He would give me a job in his boat (with a wink) he would! We sailed this evening? (Knowing that father intended to go out on the night tide I told him, no, to-morrow: we were now only moving into the outer harbour in preparation for a morning start. This he could not check, because the Ostend docks extend for miles, with bays and locks galore: we might pass the night anywhere.) And then we would go all across the North Sea in that little boat? What courage, indeed! To 'Rhumsgit' perhaps? (To Dover, I corrected, because if the weather turned nasty we might have to put into Ramsgate.) Well, he wished us a good voyage, and he shambled off.

This talk may have had no significance at all: such quay-side gallantries were common enough, but something of the kind happened so regularly just when we showed signs of moving, and the casual question about the first port of call was so invariable a feature, that lying on the subject had become second nature to all of us. We never flew our local club burgee in foreign waters, but a plain whimple like those on the Dutch barges: it had the excuse of being more efficient in light airs.

Light airs for once seemed to be coming our way on a passage. We started out into a soft evening breeze. Then fog came and we put back for the night. We started again shortly after dawn. I had told a possible custom-spy the truth by accident, I thought regretfully: it would give the warning time to get across if by any chance official suspicion had fallen upon us. We should be liable to a fine of about fifty pounds (three times the duty) and the confiscation of the liquor if we were caught, but worse still it would stop father's harmless little amusement if we were marked down along both coasts, and every yacht convicted made it more difficult for others to get away with their yearly luxury of cheap drinks for home consumption. (I have never known any yachting folk make a business of it, the carrying is too arduous for the results to be commercially worth while, but most people will cheerfully endure for pleasure more dis-comfort than they would be willing to stand for pay.) We had on board the usual ten bottles of Benedictine and Grand Marnier, and several dozens of table wines, ranging from good claret to vin ordinaire, which I privately thought was not worth the trouble of stowage. But father was like a boy about smuggling, from which he got far more kick than from the drink itself.

When we were a few miles off shore, still within sight of land, the wind failed altogether, and after rolling about sickeningly for some time, waiting for a breeze, we chugged back into the outer harbour: *Thessaly's* auxiliary motor would not work for more than an hour or so at a time without over-heating. Inwardly I grew fretful through the delay, which made me keener to get back to Pin Mill while Gordon Summers was there, just because everything had begun conspiring to prevent it. After making up some of our arrears of sleep, in spite of the alternate howls and moans of a dredger working close by, we left the harbour once more in the evening, and the faint air which had been abeam when we started, turned directly against us before we had reached the spot where we had been becalmed twelve hours before. A two hundred mile tack, against a wind too gentle to do more than just move us through the water, was an uninviting prospect even to father, but I won in the argument as to whether we should turn tail again or not, for the others were half-hearted and by this time, through the opposition of the weather, I was not. Perhaps I really fell in love with Gordon eventually because *Thessaly* was weather-bound in Ostend for twenty-four hours. We held on, pointing far off our course because of the direction and weakness of the wind; and the soft sea-dusk came down, touched with every pale hue like a pearl, and the sky turned inexpressibly tender as the light faded.

The night was lovely, full almost beyond bearing, in a few hours, of moons that shone from the dark-shadowed ripples, reflected from the compass glass and the points of metalwork on hatch and rail and gear, and gleamed dully on dew-wet planking and paint – hundreds of small dancing moons, like lively offspring of the big calm one sailing over us, which brought back a familiar desire first known to me on an afternoon in my childhood, spent with Ted in watching a heron – the longing to cry out that here, after many thin days, was Time grown too rich and generous all at once, and I could not take all it gave. Loveliness that might not come again was passing by me, unapprehended, because my mind could grasp no more.

As I was responsible for our staying at sea, I took the tiller for an indefinite spell: *Thessaly* was light enough to handle alone in this weather, and father turned in with the others, telling me to wake him when I was tired. Being alone, it was a relief not to have to remember any longer to call the stars, which were as grandly multiplied by reflection as the moon, 'them fancy sparklers', because this was not a night when they could be ignored conversationally, even by Rushes, and our brand of inverted sentimentality made it embarrassing to refer to them without facetiousness.

Hours followed – a stretch of them much longer than I realized – of which the essence is incommunicable because they had no reference to common human experience, save that in them for a while I grew reconciled to Margaret's true, hard saying: it did not matter as it had mattered before, and as it would matter again bitterly, that nothing came right in the end, that there was only 'now', if 'now' could be like this, and the queer pain of letting the stars get at one's mind so infinitely worth while for once.

The paling of moon and stars in a paling sky surprised me; surely it could not yet be dawn. But Dru stumbled up, sleepy and solicitous, with thermos-tasting tea, saying that it was past four o'clock; and father was so impressed by my supposed nobility and self-sacrifice in taking the whole night-spell, that I became a little impressed too, and almost forgot that I should have resented an earlier relief.

We had made very little progress during the night, and the tide had sagged us so far to the south-westward that we were in sight of the North Hinder lightship. Because he always enjoyed the idea as well as the neat manœuvre of passing fresh vegetables to the isolated crews of such vessels, father slanted further still out of our course to come alongside her. I stayed up to help until by a series of delicate feats of steering we had taken the men's letters out of a net which they extended to us on a pole, and had filled it with all the lettuce and other perishables that we could spare. Between their regular reliefs, friendly yachts are the only chance which these men have of getting a welcome change of diet and of sending letters to the post. On a passage we usually took extra greenstuff with us in case we had an opportunity to hand it over like this, and I was always impressed by the friendly insistence of the French and Belgian crews that we should take their stamps, even when we were bound back to England, so that if we kept them until we came over again we need not be out of pocket through posting their letters.

One of the men, shouting his thanks, added something that we could not catch in spite of many repetitions. I turned into my bunk for several hours' sleep, leaving the others still arguing as to whether the key words of the sentence had been 'du brouillard' or 'du vent'.

A lightship was close astern when I next put my head through the hatch, not knowing how long I had slept. 'Is that the Galloper?' I asked soggily, thinking that we had made quite good time on the crossing after all.

'It is not,' said father testily. 'It's still that Hinder, blast it. Can't get away from the thing.'

I went back to sleep again and was awakened in the late afternoon by the loud, cow-like mooing of a foghorn. So

208

it had been 'brouillard!' I came up into a white clammy world of swirling mist which lifted at intervals to show us the shadowy North Hinder, from which this deafening, maddening sound came at regular intervals for the next thirty-six hours. Circling round and round her, as close as possible, we dared not relieve our eardrums by distance for fear of losing our position in the fog. Thirty-six hours, and Gordon Summers might never come back to Pin Mill! It aggravated the discomfort a little to know that on the lightship they earned 'hard lying money' for every hour of the foghorn's blaring; all that we got was shortness of temper for everyone because sleep was impossible. After a time, inevitably, it became all my fault because I had insisted on starting without a proper wind.

When the fog lifted at last before a faint northerly air, the tide was foul, dragging us south-west again. By the time that it turned favourable the wind had run round and headed us once more, strengthening as it backed, and long before we came in sight of any of the English coastal marks it was blowing too hard for *Thessaly* to do more than wallow into the weather, making hardly any progress. I began to remember more about Gordon Summers than I was aware of having noticed, as uncomfortable hour succeeded hour and brought us scarcely any nearer home.

'No good. We'll turn and run for Ramsgate,' said father, and refused to give in to me this time, though he seemed gratified to see faint signs of fight, in spite of my increasing seasickness. Usually I was far too keen, for his liking, on making for the nearest shelter whenever a blow threatened. There must have been 'du vent' as well as 'brouillard' in the North Hinder's warning. It blew so that we had several nasty minutes outside the harbour, among the tall green seas that were smashing themselves against the lee pierhead, towards which the sluicing tide carried us helplessly: we were hampered by the unusual pull of the dinghy, underneath which, in a sack made out of the reaching foresail, we were carrying all our bottles.

Packing them for towing like this had been a long and difficult job, made wretched for me by the violent motion of the yacht as we tore down wind (running is much worse than tacking for bad sailors in small boats, because the yacht rolls instead of jerking) but my part of it had been less harrowing than Dru's: she had had to choose her moment as father brought *Thessaly* round into the wind, jump into the wildly bucking dinghy, half full of water as it was, and attach the cumbersome bundle to a line rove through the centre-board case before tipping it over the side, trying not to capsize the dinghy at the same time; and when this was done successfully, she had the still trickier task of choosing her moment to climb perilously aboard again, round the overhanging counter of the yacht.

With the drag astern spoiling the steering, we only missed a collision with the pierhead by a breath-taking shave. Overdoing his air of nonchalance, father knocked out his long-dead pipe on the heel of his golosh as we slid into the calm water of the west gulley; a sign that his nerve, too, was a little shaken. Margaret alone seemed unmoved: I think she enjoyed these moments.

Only an unobtrusive knot of rope showed in a corner of the centre-board case to arouse suspicion as we came in: it was a hundred to one, we had decided outside, against anyone noticing it. But unfortunately, as it was a bright, fierce day – the sort of day that we had had for the regatta – visibility under water, which we had not considered, became startlingly good as soon as we were settled in a sheltered place. Sunrays, probing down crookedly through the comparatively calm surface of the harbour water, picked out the curious white bulge under the dinghy and made it obvious to anyone standing either on our deck or on the quay above us, where the customs men might appear at any moment.

Shift her about as we would, we could not get the dinghy into the shade, and we could not retrieve the bottles in daylight. For what seemed hours, Dru and Margaret and I, dead tired already, took it in turns to keep the water about her keel safely agitated by throwing down from the counter of the yacht a bucket on a line and swilling *Thessaly's* well-washed deck with the water scooped up by this passable but inefficient method. And father, I thought irritably, as the whole scene danced giddily before my seasick eyes, would soon be assuring guests hospitably that his lavishness with drinks cost us next to nothing! I could have hugged the customs men when they appeared at last.

'Nothing on board to declare,' father was telling the literal truth, but my conscience was illogically relieved when the officials frankly disbelieved us and began a thorough search. Evidently news of our purchases had crossed before us.

They found nothing, and were affable in their disappointment, standing chatting on that part of the deck from which the white bulge would be most obvious in unbroken water. Margaret and I swilled vigorously with breaking backs. If they stayed much longer they would think us mad for keeping on with this unnecessary job. Dru, standing in the dinghy itself, with a foot on either thwart, was rocking it as she baled with a teacup, but she was getting out only a thimbleful of water at a time now: the dinghy would soon be bone dry. Finally they handed over our clearance papers and prepared to go back up the ladder. Father over-emphasized his friendliness. They paused, for more chat. 'Give us a shove across to that boat in your dinghy, will you?' said one of them. 'Save us fetching ours.'

Our efforts stopped. Father's smile wavered. The dinghy with that weight under her would move like a battleship: anyone used to boats would realize in an instant what was wrong with her. But there was a grand splash aft; Dru displaced a lot of water when, apparently missing her foot-hold on the thwart, she tipped over the side of the dinghy and fell between it and the yacht.

'Oh, help' . . . bubble bubble . . . 'Oh, help.' Dru, our best swimmer, thrashed about in the water ineffectually.

With a show of panic we bunched together in the stern and impeded the customs men's intelligent efforts to help her. Father, apparently behaving like a fool, cast off the dinghy in his fumbled attempt to bring it alongside. His belt knife clattered on to the stern seat, jerked out, it seemed, by the accidental movement of an arm.

Wild business with the boathook, jabbing at the dinghy which it pushed farther out of reach, covered Dru's actions as she groped over the dinghy's stern for the knife. 'Hold on, hold on,' shouted the little crowd that had collected on the quay above us in a few seconds. (There was enough pother in the water round the dinghy to hide that inexplicable white bulge from them; though probably no one would have noticed it then, even had it been visible.) But Dru, having got the knife, let go of the dinghy and disappeared under water for several seconds: it took some time to get at the cord between the bag and the bottom of the centre-board case. By the time that she reappeared, both customs men had their coats off. Really ashamed because of their kind-ness, I was seriously considering throwing my arms round the nearer one and having hysterics on his shoulder, hoping that someone else would hamper the other man; but it proved to be unnecessary, because Dru rescued herself at this point. Still beating water uselessly with her hands, swimming strongly with her legs, she came alongside with the dinghy painter caught up in her clothing, and she and it were hauled in together. With expressions of genuine relief we lent it, normally light in movement once more, to her would-be saviours, who kept dropping in for more friendly conversation all the time that we remained in Ramsgate.

This made our next three days all the harder, for until we could surreptitiously grapple up our bag of bottles, which had sunk into the mud at the bottom of the deep gulley when the rope was cut, we could not get away from this utterly wretched port, where no fresh drinking water is available for small boats, excessive dues are imposed, and for some obscure reason the authorities do everything possible to discourage visiting yachts, though the harbour does not pay. Its one efficiency is that it is embarrassingly well lit all night. This, and the fact that it never seems to be entirely deserted at any hour, as well as the surprise visits of the kindly revenue couple, almost made us despair of being able to drag the gulley thoroughly enough to recover the cargo: our growing fear, as time crept on and we could not settle down to a long stretch of searching, was that some other boat would come in and moor over the errant bag before we located it.

Eventually we found it when the tides had sucked it almost to the harbour mouth, and got it on board unobserved, intact save for three bottles which may well have been smashed by the keel of the dinghy plunging in the seas outside the entrance as we came in. This successful end to the whole childish business, about which father did not seem in the least uncomfortable, finally discovered to me, in a flash of awed delight, my loathing for small boats and everything connected with sailing; more, that I had unconsciously hated them for years!

I was amazed by the realization. It brought nearly as much upheaval of mind as my former discovery that I must relinquish God and all the heavenly etceteras; but jettisoning my family religion like this was a mental act that required nearly two years more preparation than the other apostasy. With a pleasant, mounting sense of blasphemy, I recalled, one by one, all the occasions which I had believed to be red-letter sailing days, and decided that I had not enjoyed any of them. When, as on the night passage from Ostend or my first single-handed sail in a dinghy, I had had a marvellous time, it had always been for some non-marine reason; stars or a new sense of power.

For a minute or two I wondered nervously, as we ploughed our way up the Edinburgh Channel, whether I should have to tell the others of my change of heart, feeling as disinclined for the confession as I had done when I let go of God. But from the family's point of view this infidelity was much more serious. I decided, as before, to temper the un-Rushly truth with discretion, and merely to refrain, when possible, from telling downright lies. So that when mother said heartily, with *Thessaly* reaching rapidly up the Swin, 'Well, *this* is better than circling round the North Hinder with the foghorn going!' (meaning that we were now having a perfectly lovely time) I agreed equally heartily, meaning that it was rather less unpleasant: we were at least getting somewhere.

All the way across the Thames estuary I felt so exhilarated by my secret freedom from an old servitude of mind, that I hardly minded hearing, when we reached Pin Mill, of Gordon Summers's departure two days before we arrived.

CHAPTER X

THE MAWLEYS

'PORE ole pussycat!' Dru would lapse into baby-talk, with the defensive exaggeration demanded by Rush sentiment, whenever she petted the self-sufficient, dreaming beast which held a secret jungle shut in its brain. 'Poor' and 'pussy' made it seem a sit-by-the-fire creature, wanting her caresses – the cat, that lived instinctively a more satisfying life than Dru would ever know!

'It's only "pore" when you come in because you wake it up,' Margaret told her, but Dru went on offering it her disregarded, belittling blandishments: they were part of her attitude towards the home that she needed to love, and the family that would never quite lend itself to her affections. As sisters Margaret and I must have been most satisfactory to her while we were abroad. 'I wish Lallie could have been home for her birthday . . . Margaret wants some thicker shoes, she says . . . Poor . . . Poor.' Now, even more than mother and father, she was hurt without knowing it by the suspicion that I wanted to get away again, not for the reason that I gave when I suggested looking for a job soon (to help the family finances) but simply because I wanted to get away from the communal life in which she herself longed to find all content.

Since early childhood I had not had all time on my hands at home for long: in the term there had been school, and part of the holidays at least was always spent in cruising.

After three weeks or so of doing nothing, pleasant enough in their way, I had grown restless for want of some excuse to free myself at times from the kindly tyranny of family interest. I had forgotten, or had never before realized, how devastating this could be. 'Going out, darling? . . . Which way? If you see Mrs. Chater, ask her . . .' and then later, 'Oh, so you didn't go by the field after all? . . . Did you see anyone? . . . What did they say?'

It was impossible openly to resent such questions, so light in themselves, so crushing to the spirit in their cumulative weight: their harmlessness was their most depressing quality; it tied my hands in the brief tussle of wills that became inevitable as soon as mother made it clear that she was against my taking a job, for a year or two at any rate. Treated so well, I could offer no convincing reason for wanting to leave the home that to my parents still vaguely represented romance and freedom – the place that father had given up his congenial wandering life to build; the place for which mother had broken away from her own family, so that they might be together there: how could they be expected to see it through my eyes, as the most cramping place on earth, where life was shadowed by the almost continuous probability of meeting Mrs. Chater and being asked what she said?

Mother showed that she was bewildered by my desire, not that she was hurt: but in little ways this too became apparent, and angered me against her, because I had not wanted to hurt her. Father's masculine pride objected to the idea of any of his daughters taking a lowly commercial job, and at present I was not even fitted to be a typist. He considered, like mother – though this was never admitted – that we were all good-looking enough to be certain of marriage, and meanwhile, in order to avoid any appearance of sitting about and waiting for it, we could busy ourselves with his boats, which would incidentally serve to introduce us to a number of fresh young men each season.

Of course, it would have been different had I felt a call

to some special kind of work – This was the burden of Dru's and mother's reproach to me, as 'Using the house as a hotel' was the burden of their occasional reproach to Margaret, who was always out in these days with the new friends that she had made shortly after her return.

She was quite content to live at home, giving nothing, asking nothing, immune from my nervous dislike of loving hands reaching out to fumble idly with one's mind, one's time, one's whole essential being, not from curiosity but for want of anything better to do. 'Note for you from Mrs. Chater, Lallie. Anything interesting ?' – No, of course not: when had she ever anything interesting to say, except perhaps long ago, to Mr. Chater? But even so, the note is mine; to keep to myself if I choose! – 'Oh, just thanks for the flowers, mother, and Betty's in bed with a cold.' – Let me get away from your constraining love, confound you – confound you because I too am fond of you – without asking me for reasons which you know I cannot give: you have sacrificed too much for me, unasked, and now you want your due return.

In very few of the thousands of good homes, from which the children struggle to escape, can the truth ever be told, I suppose, even in the heat of a family row – the unfortunate truth that devotion easily grows unbearable when it is given to the young by those whose own lives are no longer, for some reason, of self-absorbing interest. Mother was like that, and Dru too, absurd as this seemed at her age. Such people crave for companionship, and it is their need which makes willing companionship impossible.

We had no open disagreements. Using her incongruously adroit social manner, mother always managed to get the subject of a job for me safely shelved again almost as soon as I had re-introduced it, in some roundabout way.

What decent argument had I on my side, with the labour market for women so low? If I earned two pounds ten a week in Ipswich, which was all that I could hope for after learning shorthand and typing, almost a third of my salary would go in lunches and fares. The remainder, even if I handed over every penny, would obviously be negligible compared with mother's satisfaction in having all her daughters with her again. – Later, perhaps, she suggested vaguely, and meanwhile some course of study that took up two afternoons a week, say, if boats were not enough. London was out of the question financially as well as spiritually: it would cost the family at least a pound a week more than my salary for me to live there. London, indeed, could not be mentioned: the realization that I wanted to get away as badly as that would have been deeply wounding.

I tried citing Marnie Cottrell and Stella Quest in support of my contention (mainly a conversational one, I tried to convey, with hardly any personal bearing) that nowadays every girl was expected to take up a job whether it was financially worth while or not; but I was unfortunate in my examples. Marnie was considered even by my people to have a real vocation for medicine; partly, perhaps, because her adenoids, which her adoring parents had unaccountably left in, had made her nose so small and her mouth so apt to drop open that no one was likely to want to marry her: Stella ran a chicken farm near Ipswich with several other Sommervillians: it was a show-place of applied science, and cost Mr. Quest some hundreds a year, on top of a huge initial outlay.

For a day or so, feeling at last that I had no right to hurt these sweet people to gratify an adolescent's mania for privacy, I toyed with the idea of a temporary call to zoology. There was a botany and a zoology course starting in the autumn term at the Ipswich Technical Schools, and zoology took the greater number of hours: it would give me almost half the unquestioned leave-of-absence that I might have had from a job.

'Oh, I should take botany if I were you,' said Dru when I mentioned the idea to her while we were dressing one morning. 'It's so much less dull' – 'Dull' had become her description of anything that she connected with sex; gossip was only dull when it was frankly scandalous, and books enjoyed by the Cottrells were generally dull in patches, and any social function like dancing, which brought her into contact with strange men, was emphatically dull, though women's parties were not, or at least not necessarily.

She was partly right, I thought with a leaden mind, suddenly relinquishing my plan. Zoology would be very dull, in my sense of the word, taken as I should have to take it, in snippets, with father's call for a crew coming first whenever a new purchase of his had to be brought round the coast, or a possible buyer wanted a try-out, because it would only be 'Lallie's new fad. Didn't you know she'd gone all brainy?' And if I stuck to my fad I should be aware, during lectures, that at home mother was glancing occasionally at the clock to see how much longer she need wait for my return. If I missed the usual bus home she would grow, not exactly anxious or fretful, but unsettled, feeling at a loose end because I was not there to help in supplying her with the illusion of personal life, which had somehow slipped away from her in the hurry and trouble of so much maternity – I, the child still, her property; someone to chat with; someone to question aimlessly, inoffensively; but always to question. I gave up, finally, not only the idea of the course in Ipswich, but all hope of freeing myself from home in any way. Mother had won: I would not take a job: it could not be worth the price.

Immediately after breakfast I went out, shutting the door on a voice, gently raised, which might or might not have been going to ask me whether I was likely to be passing the post office, because if so . . .

There were still young shelduck about, at the entertaining

stage when they run over the surface of the water, waggling their behinds like fat women chasing a bus: and many summer migrants that would soon be gone: I had not watched them for over two years; it was absurd, I told myself, to feel so dreary: but that did not cure my feeling.

Basil Quest met me. 'Hello to you, Lal-age.' Mispronouncing my name phonetically, without the final syllable, was a perennial joke with him, so old that one need no longer smile at it: it was safely in the category of accepted household humours, like Dru's fatal fascinations or Lester's excerpts from the *Times*, which could dispense with the courtesy of appreciation: they were known to be funny. To my consternation he fell into step beside me, finding nothing to say. Basil, once he had tacked himself on to anyone, was hardly to be detached by kindness: apart from his father, from whom no one expected forbearance under boredom, Margaret was the only person who could rid herself of him whenever she pleased. I was in no mood to prattle for him. We walked in silence.

'What's the news from old Ronald?' he produced at last. I told him some unimportant items from the last letter we had received from Malta, both of us knowing that he did not really want to hear them. He then asked after father's success in putting a new engine into *Thessaly*, in which he was slightly more interested: anything to do with father still had glamour in his eyes; and so we came casually, via Dru's sprained wrist, which had been all right for so long that he had forgotten to ask her about it when he saw her last, to the subject that he had really wanted to broach all along. 'Margaret anywhere about?'

'Yes. Why?'

'Oh, I just thought – d'you know if she's going in to town to-day?' ('Town' meant Ipswich, to us.)

'No. She's playing tennis at the Reddilands either to-day or to-morrow, but I'm not sure which.'

Basil's old liking for the rackety Reddiland brothers, who were almost as devoted to athletics as he was, had been modified in the last few weeks, since they had taken up Margaret.

'Well, you see, I've got to get my brake linings seen to sometime before I go up to Cambridge on Monday, so I'll be tootling in with the car to-day or to-morrow, and I mean, if she'd like a lift. . . .' He maintained a repetitive technical explanation of the function of brake linings, and the state of his own, till I stopped in the road. 'If I were you,' I suggested with the air of one suddenly inspired, ' I'd drop in and ask her now, before she goes out.' Poor Basil, he would get short shrift from Margaret if he could not be useful to her; and if she were going into Ipswich, one of the Reddilands would certainly come tearing round to fetch her himself, in the sort of noisy sporting car that wears an enormous strap round the bonnet: Basil's decorous *coupé* seemed unexciting by comparison.

'Right oh, if you think that's the notion. . . .' Basil looked at me with gratitude and turned back. We should almost certainly have all this conversation over again at lunch, I thought. 'What did he say? – what did I say? – Dru, aren't you jealous?' Weeks, months, years, of this. And some day I should want greedily all time, now running to waste.

Desiring no more chance meetings, I went by devious ways, through woods and fields, to the Mawleys' cottage, hoping that I might find Ted. He had been expected home from Cowes, where his yacht was being laid up, at any time during the last few days, and in spite of not having seen him for a year and a half, I had a pleasant feeling that Ted would not have grown too old for the sort of things that we used to enjoy together. Little shelduck, skittering over the water with that anxious wobble, would be much more consoling to me in my present mood of unhappy resignation if he were there to laugh at them too.

But Ted was still away, I learned. I was too used to Mrs. Mawley's strained manner to give it any consideration when she complained in her dull, bitter voice that he had 'Chosen to stay on, if you please, when 'e could a come home to help 'is dad for a bit! But oh, no . . .'

Sootie chuckled good humouredly. 'Don't blame 'im. Got a girl there, our Ted 'as! Looks quite the smart young lady, don't she? Sort of frenchified, 'e says, from being nurse in a foreign family that's just come over to the Wight for a holiday.' He showed me several snaps of a peculiarly wooden-looking Ted, with his fuzzy hair plastered flat on his forehead, standing or sitting squarely to the camera, beside a dapper little person who seemed perfectly at ease and coy in her attitudes. Ted's expression did not alter in any of the prints except the one in which his arm was round her; and there he managed to look self-conscious as well as wooden. But her face interested me.

'Think she's like anyone?' Sootie enquired diffidently.

'Oh, don't be silly,' said Mrs. Mawley.

'Yes, Sootie, Margaret.' Indeed the face was a vulgarized edition of that exquisite mask which Ted as a boy must have loved even more than I knew for it so to have moulded his young man's taste.

Sootie looked gratified. 'Well, I didn't like to say, but if you think so . . . !'

'Anyways, he can't see much more of her,' said Mrs. Mawley tartly. 'She's going back to France with the family she's in. I don't see 'ow 'e manages to stay on at his own expense when 'e sent back so much of 'is wages regular till 'e took up with 'er. 'E's a good boy to us, reelly, Ted is,' she added fairly, but there was a note of satisfaction in her voice when she reckoned that he would have to come home even before his girl left England, for lack of funds. – 'It takes gentry, of course,' she said sarcastically, jerking her head in what was vaguely the direction of the Cottrells' house, 'to go lovering all over the place, just when they please. *They* can afford it, never mind who's who or what's what – You'll find Ted here, Miss Lallie, same's you're round again in two days, and maybe to-morrow!' Resenting her satisfaction I took no notice of the reference to the supposed goings-on in the Cottrell house – The fruit of Mrs. Chandler's imagination, helped by that of her customers, working on the details supplied by Stella, was a much embroidered story about the two guests, Mrs. Macdonald and Gordon Summers, whose present guilty relationship the Cottrells were said to condone, in spite of their friendship for the husband. The pair were interesting to the village less as immoral individuals, since no one knew much about them personally, than as proof of what many people had always suspected: the Cottrells were artistic; it was understood that such leanings naturally tended towards lax standards of conduct; and they and their friends had been exemplary, as far as anyone knew, for so many years that it was nice to find lower-middle-class folk-lore vindicated once more: so much for Art. The speculations of one handler of the story became automatically, in the way of village gossip, the accredited information of the next. Mrs. Mawley, whose loyalty to us had never forgiven the Cottrells their regatta subscription, firmly believed in a sordid rigmarole of angry husband and child dying from neglect, all connived at by the Cottrells, immoral by proxy.

Sootie took up his cap when I said good-bye. 'Show Miss Lallie that martins' nest,' he mumbled to his wife. 'You know, where the little birds was learning to fly yesterday.' And then eagerly to me, as though to excuse this unusual interest in Ted's and my subject, 'Very pretty, that is! Bit late, isn't it? Will the young ones fly well enough by the time all the swallow things have to go?'

'No,' I said. 'I hate seeing these late broods because of that. They'll start out with the older birds in a week or so, but they won't be able to keep going on the long sea passages.

Thanks awfully, Sootie, but I'd just as soon not see. Ted used to say I was sloppy about this, but little swallows and martins look so really adorable when they're being taught to fly.'

He seemed nonplussed, and then said anxiously, 'Well. there's a hare's form by the side of Weyland's path . . .'

'Course she's seen that!' scoffed Mrs. Mawley. 'Noticed it myself.'

I was just going to say that as a matter of fact I had, (no one passing that way could have missed it) when I realized that for some reason Sootie wanted to come with me; and so professed interest.

He said as soon as we were out of earshot, 'Miss, people can send money anywheres in a hurry, sort of like a telegram, can't they?' And when I assented, 'Mrs. Chandler at the post, she knows me, of course. And she knows the missus. Great one for a talk, too.' He stopped, and I nodded again: Mrs. Chandler still made occasional efforts to impart the Cottrell rumours to me, in spite of my assurance on the day of my arrival that I already knew all the ascertained facts.

'Suppose I sent three pounds to Ted, she'd sure to say something to Mrs. Mawley. Couldn't ask her not to, could I, and you see . . .'

I think that when he set out to ask my help he did not mean to tell me all that now came from him haltingly, in ill-chosen words which stressed the trivial things, understating the real values, so that the story should have been distorted by the clumsy telling into a bucolic tragi-comedy, but instead shone through more movingly than it would have done had Sootie had more time or more skill for choosing phrases.

He had stumbled into the middle of it before he felt that he had made clear enough to me his reason for 'taking a liberty' and asking me to bicycle into Ipswich for him that day – his desire to enable Ted to stay on in Cowes until the

224

girl left ' . . . and maybe give her some present to keep, like I couldn't when it was the same with me. You see, I do know how 'e's feeling, and 'is mother, she don't, quite. Though, of course, you couldn't really say it was the same, being as it was a married woman I went with when I was a lad. And at home, too – Orford, you know, where I come from. Of course, we knew it was wrong all the time, and we didn't want to. Only you can't always help yourself'. And having said so much he did not know how to stop, and so went on with an account of his shipping for two years on foreign freighters, to make it easier to break with this woman of his. It did not occur to Sootie to try to make me understand how deeply he cared for her, nor what love there was on her side: by chance these things came through to me: nor did he say whether there were children to hold her to the husband. What he repeated, as his reason for leaving, was that they knew it was wrong, and through the irrelevant details of places and cargoes and changes of ship I heard in memory the unusual warmth of Mr. Quest's calm, dry voice talking of the toll of Christianity among the working classes. '. . . Only sometimes it didn't seem fair, after we'd acted right, that it didn't get easier for either of us. Same sort of hard feeling about things; you know, things we'd liked when we was together. Jokes, and other couples courting, and anything pretty. Seemed just a waste. She said it was because we'd done wrong before. She used to write to me sometimes, but what's the good of letters, and I couldn't write back because of him. – There's the hare's form, Miss . . .' Sootie walked on, barely indicating it with his hand, at a pace that almost made me run to keep up with him. 'It was a funny thing,' he said, in a voice that denied the words, 'You see, the man she'd married before I came along, 'e 'adn't been bothering 'er for years. Tired of 'er, like, almost as soon as got 'er. Never much of a chap for women. Only while I was away, someone let on to 'im that I was keen on

225

'er, and then 'e took more notice of 'er, like. It made no difference to him that she didn't want him, once 'e knowed some other fellow thought all that of her. See?'

Yes, I saw. And the angry pity that Mr. Quest had felt ran through me in a moment of despairing revolt against things as they were, and the stupid pain that men made for one another, who were already sure enough of pain that was not of human devising.

Sootie told me of his hearing of this new misery from the woman herself, on his first night home, and of his getting half drunk in helpless fury, and picking up with a bright, flighty girl who had always fancied him a little – Mrs. Mawley as she used to be. It was more difficult to picture her in youth than Sootie. They had gone for a walk across the fields and she had teased him, flaunting herself, and he had responded savagely, not really wanting her. She had learnt how little he really cared, by gossip, after the affair had become a habit. 'But what could she do, Miss,' said Sootie, 'with young Ted coming and all, even when she knew I wanted someone else? There were her people pushing us into it. So I was married when Dorrie's husband died, and it would have been all right for us. Only Mrs. Mawley knowing about Dorrie and how I felt, nothing was ever right between 'er and me, either. We moved, of course, soon as we married, and I only been back to Orford once since then – couldn't help it, in the governor's boat. Time we went aground with *Wanderer* at Shingle Street. You was there: do you remember? Well, I saw Dorrie then. Woman in the shop where we had tea. Though I'd hardly a known 'er.' (I had some vague recollection of a faded, untidy woman.) 'So you'll go to Ipswich right away and send this, won't you, miss, if it isn't asking too much?'

'Yes. He'll get it about tea-time, Sootie.'

He gave me three £1 notes and the address. 'It's funny,' he said again dully. 'Dorrie being changed doesn't make much difference to the way I look at things. She's just gone, like being dead. Because in our time she wasn't a bit like what you saw. Always one for a laugh and that. I still think of her when I see things that used to make me want her, only not of her being anywheres. Just gone, but the sort of fret goes on, only now it doesn't mean anything. Funny.'

I ran part of the way home, trying to keep out of my mind Mrs. Mawley's face as it had looked long ago when she said: 'Oh, Nature! I hate Nature.' And 'I don't see why she shouldn't pay, same's others!' Mr. Quest's silent-moving car almost ran me down as I hurried across the road, oblivious of the blind corner. It skidded to a standstill. Archer looked at me malignantly. 'Come into Town with me?' Mr. Quest asked surprisingly.

'Well . . .' It would certainly be nicer than cycling, but I had no money on me for the return bus fare, and I must be back before lunch in order to avoid questions. 'How long are you going to stay there?'

'An hour or so. I've got some business.'

It was now about half-past ten. Yes, that would do. I got in.

Mr. Quest soon seemed to forget my presence in the car. That was usual enough on the rare occasions when he gave me lifts, but I wondered why he had particularly asked for my company on the way to Ipswich if he were going to be busy all the time in checking long lists of figures. In a few minutes I forgot him.

So one could never know people. Time did not help. In spite of what he had told me, the new Sootie whom I had met to-day remained a stranger; a different stranger from the one I had imagined, that was all; like the other father whom I had once glimpsed for a few minutes when we lay becalmed off Landguard Point. Unguessed-at vistas opened suddenly into minds with which, in thoughtless moments, one believed oneself familiar, and revealed very little, really, but that there must be more such unexplored territory, much more, lying still hidden and undiscoverable beyond.

I looked out and did not recognize the road for a second, because it was not what I had expected to see. Then I realized that we were nearing Brambleton ponds.

'I've never known anyone take this way to Ipswich!'

Mr. Quest glanced up inattentively from his paper. 'No,' he said. Then his eyes focused on me and he stared as if I were making vapid conversation. 'An idiotic way,' he commented severely, and relapsed into his study of the relative times taken by children in learning by heart verse that they liked and understood, liked but did not understand, and neither liked nor understood – an idiotic study, I decided, peering surreptitiously at the papers.

I did not like to venture anything else for some time and so returned to my own thoughts. Father could say truly of his old love, 'I haven't thought of her for years.' Somehow, though humanly it was better that way, those words echoed in my mind with a sadness less tolerable, because more universal and hopeless, than Sootie's 'The fret goes on, only now it doesn't mean anything.' In father's mind a passing loveliness had found its natural, dreadful end: it was forgotten.

Troubled, I turned to Mr. Quest, not caring for the moment whether I were snubbed or not. We were nearly at Tolleshurst. 'I say, this simply *can't* be on the way to Ipswich!'

'Well, of course it isn't,' said Mr. Quest, looking at me in a still more deprecating manner. 'Why should it be? I never go through Ipswich on my way to Town.'

' "Town". Oh, but . . .' I was aghast. 'Are you going to London?'

'My good child, I asked you . . .'

'Yes, but I thought you meant "town" – Ipswich.'

' "Town" means London and nothing else to right-minded people. Still, I'm relieved to hear that you were thinking something,' he said. 'I was beginning to fear that you suffered from some obsession about Ipswich.'

From this rather unpromising beginning a splendid day rolled forward on gilded wheels. When I had at last managed to impress him with the necessity of explaining my absence at home – it took considerable argument – we stopped at Ingatestone and with difficulty made Olive understand on the telephone that he had kidnapped me. He wrote out the form for me when I telegraphed the £3 to Ted, asking no questions about it, not from delicacy, which might have restrained Mrs. Cottrell, the only other person I knew who could have kept silence, but because he would not have been particularly interested to hear if I were keeping Ted altogether. (Incredibly lucky Basil and Stella – who had always envied us our family life!)

Then we bought a hat for me because he intended to lunch at the Carlton, and though he did not mind my looking out of place through hatlessness, he gathered that I would rather not, all things being equal. (This was the end, then as now, of my interest in dress – not to appear remarkable.)

What seemed to concern him, when I had managed to convey it, was the atmosphere of spiritual inter-dependency at home which would have been disturbed by my unheralded absence for a meal, surely the normal atmosphere in any household where one member has no interests but the welfare of the others. 'But that must be extremely irksome,' he said with an air of surprise, which suggested to me again that his memories of family life were dimmer than Pin Mill believed. Later he said, 'Come to think of it, I do remember one of my main reasons for moving into the country, in the period when I still had to come up to Town every day – my discovery that a married man's only real privacy is in the train on the way to his work. It's the one place where he can be certain of not being appealed to for an opinion, for more than five minutes at a stretch.' And at lunch he asked suddenly, 'Why don't you get a job?' I had carefully confined myself to one glass of wine on this occasion, but all the same confidences poured out of me then: this unlikely person seemed the right recipient for them, because his interest, very slight anyway, was of an impersonal kind.

At the moment he said nothing much, nor would he talk of anything but pictures while he conducted me on a rapid, exhilarating tour round the National Gallery, to fill in the three-quarters of an hour between the end of his incomprehensible address to a teachers' conference, in a building on the opposite side of Trafalgar Square, and the time when Archer was to pick us up in the car at Charing Cross station. 'Magical obstetrics. – More magical obstetrics,' he observed in his high pitched, carrying whisper before various births of Christ, Visitations of the Virgin, and an accouchement of St. Anne, to the disgruntlement of a couple of earnest middle-aged women who looked like the teachers we had just left. They had already irritated themselves gratuitously by following us about, just within earshot, to hear Mr. Quest's exposition of the badness of nine out of ten of the pictures. In this short visit I learned more that was afterwards of value to me, in deciding what I really liked about art, than I had done in all the reverent hours spent in the Brussells galleries while I was being 'finished'.

We had tea at Witham on the way home, and when we reached River View, a little before supper-time, Mr. Quest took me into his study to give me a glass of sherry. Evian water, ryevita biscuits and cheese were laid out for him on a tray. He did not ask me to share this. 'You can use my garden as a refuge from all that love if you like,' he said, startling me more than he had ever done. 'It won't be as family-proof as a job, because they'll be able to stop your getting here with errands and the like. But once you are here, you'll be undisturbed.'

'Oh, Mr. Quest! Bless your enormous wall, which we

still curse heartily at times!' I said gratefully. 'That's awfully decent of you, when you've got such a mania for seclusion yourself.'

'Not at all.' (It was quite an exchange of courtesies.) 'You are the only woman I've allowed into this place in the last sixteen years who hasn't conveyed, "You ought to have somebody looking after you – horrid cold supper alone in a vast bare room! – you poor, dear man!" – meaning: "Why aren't you supporting one of us on all that money, you selfish brute!" The terrible trade-unionism of women! – Good-night, Lallie. Run away now. I want to read.'

I wandered out into my new, delightful domain. There was a fragile, dreamlike quality in the October dusk now rising from the slopes of the garden which stretched away, mistily, to the dim river; and so many birds joining in the evening chorus that I could not distinguish the separate songs. I had never been alone before in this perfectly tended place, and went softly over the wet lawns, for fear of disturbing something, towards the main gate. There was, for a moment, a dreamlike quality, too, about the figure that came through the gate and walked to meet me, something vaguely familiar in movement or form, perhaps, which reached my memory before my mind, for in the first second of disappointment at finding that someone shared this instant of time with me in the garden, I pretended idly to myself that it might be Gordon Summers, some while before I could really suspect and at last make sure that it was.

'Lallie Rush! *Is* it Lallie Rush? How long is it since I saw you? Well, not since you were a long-legged child, anyway.' We stood and smiled at one another. He looked very tired, more than two years older, and preoccupied: the smile died. 'I wish you hadn't been away a few weeks ago, when I was here last,' he said with abrupt seriousness, as though we were close friends. 'I shouldn't have made such a mess of things if I could have talked to you instead of to some girl

231

called Stella Quest. Is she at home, do you know? I want to see her.'

'No, I don't think she'll be back till the week-end. What do you want with Stella?' The edge to his voice had made it plain that he had not come for the pleasure of seeing her.

'I want to know exactly what she's been saying in this extraordinary village about a friend of mine. And exactly why.'

'Well, I can tell you all that, I think. So it doesn't matter that Stella isn't here.'

'Probably it's just as well,' he said. 'The temptation to wring her neck would be very strong. I'm feeling slightly light-headed from want of sleep; two evenings ago I was working in Skye when I got a letter, and I've been travelling ever since. Let's go down to that bit of wood. There's no point in my seeing the rest of the family.'

We turned away from the drive and walked by the river, among thick trees that stretched out damp-leafed twigs, unseen in this failing light, to pluck our sleeves with cold fingers as we passed. I shivered, because of the half-survival of my childish belief that trees turn sentient in the darkness and hate their conquerors. I would never go among them for choice after the passing of full daylight; but Gordon Summers was too disturbed and too weary to be interrupted by fancies; and we walked there, up and down, for many minutes, while I told him as much as Pin Mill imagined that it knew about his private affairs. I noticed again that he did not seem to have any sense of property, being unaware that he was trespassing; I could only hope that Mr. Quest's reading would prove too absorbing for him to come out.

Summers laughed shortly at the scandal as the village had fashioned it. 'Very funny if it wasn't irritating. I haven't even seen Mrs. Macdonald, except among crowds of people, for oh, over a year or more, though I've known her for five or six. And yet this stupid business starts up now!'

232

'Why does it matter?' There was about us still that curious sense of unreality which comes on summer evenings when the air begins to pulse with the gathering darkness, and distances grow uncertain. No question seemed impertinent.

'To me, personally, it wouldn't matter at all. Nor to her. But – I suppose this really is funny even if it is irritating – it would bother very much a man whom I rather like, Carlisle Macdonald, her husband.' We said nothing for a few steps, and then, 'She's very fond of him. He depends on her a great deal. It's generally supposed that he has an important political career in front of him.' His voice sounded parrot-like, exhausted, as though he were repeating phrases that other people often used, being too tired to think of his own, but he added, more in the way that I remembered as his, 'That is, by people who consider political careers important. I always think this kind of prophecy is like saying of a man, "What a wonderful second footman he'll make if his calves don't slip." However, the Macdonalds don't feel that way about it. And wives still matter politically, if a man's to be offered a comfortable Conservative seat. There mustn't be talk of this kind about them just now. You'd think it would be harmless enough down here, but it's incredible how it spreads. The story has already reached two sets of people who know him. That was what she wrote to me.'

'Look here, sit down,' I said. There was a seat in the open overlooking the river. He looked tired out, and to me the trees were becoming more menacing. The measure of my liking for him was that I had stayed here so long, unprotesting.

'No. Do you mind? If I do I shall drop straight off to sleep, even though this business interests me more than anything else at the moment. Are you tired yourself?'

'No,' I said. 'That's all right, we'll walk,' and forgot that at home supper should have started some time ago.

'How does one stop a village scandal?'

'Well, one can't. At least, you can't. I'll do what I can.

233

And Dru might help. Will you stay in this part of the world for a few days?'

'Yes, I suppose now I'm here I'll stay in Norwich long enough to see how things are at Levington. I'll have to be back in Skye at the end of the week.'

'If you dropped in to a meal with us again once or twice, it'd be all round the place in a flash, of course. And then Dru and I would be more likely to be believed when either of us said, "Oh, nonsense. I know Gordon Summers and" – Esther, isn't her name? – "Esther Macdonald. He and the Macdonalds have been friends for ages. There's nothing in it. Of course he was upset about the child dying." And that would go round, too, though not so fast because not so interesting.'

'Lallie, you're a dear! She'll be very grateful. So shall I.' He put his hands on my shoulders, squeezing them slightly, but I could hardly see his face now because of the trees which emanated each a little darkness of its own, as though impatient for the night that brought them new, baleful life. 'Can I come over to lunch to-morrow? Where shall I find you, so that the Cottrells don't commandeer me on the way to your house. It's no use asking them to help, kind as they are; they're implicated.'

'Here,' I said. 'You can slip in by the side gate, off the main road.' His lack of regard for ownership seemed catching; I wondered too late whether Mr. Quest would mind; and remembering the existence of other people's claims on me, remembered also the family who might still be waiting for supper at home; and so left him hurriedly and ran.

There was too much argument going on in our house for anyone to bother about my lateness, though mother must have seen Mr. Quest's car turn in at the gate a long while ago, and would normally have been moved to ask what had delayed me. Margaret wanted to go with the Reddilands to a moonlight picnic, for which four or five car loads of friends were rallying at Ipswich in about an hour's time; or rather she had announced that she was expecting Tom Reddilands to fetch her shortly, and was now calmly going on with supper, which had at last been started without me. She was taking little part in the heated argument that had sprung up at once between Dru and mother, and disregarded the usual 'Using the house as an hotel' charge. Mother's veto had inevitably drawn Dru into the discussion as Margaret's champion. 'Oh, but darling, why shouldn't she at her age? – Why, that's absurd – Come now, mother, you can't pretend Tom Reddiland's a bad driver, whatever the others may be – Margaret, hasn't he raced at Brooklands three years running without a smash?' They disagreed so easily, those two; and after this, I knew uncomfortably, Dru would be unnecessarily contrite and wretched, and mother more demonstrative for a while than was natural to her.

Mother grew flustered, producing too many different reasons to defend her natural objection to the idea of her baby dashing about the countryside, until the early hours of the morning, with a set of hare-brained young people. Dru demolished them one by one, with little assistance from Margaret; who probably did not care very much whether she went or not. Unless his favourite daughter were getting the worst of it, father never interfered in 'squaw-squabbles', as he called these little scenes between mother and Dru, in order to minimize their significance in his own mind.

'Well, I don't like her going alone. It looks so bad.' Mother returned weakly to the beginning of her argument as a car drew up near the gate.

'*I*'m not going,' said Dru promptly. There would be young men with girls: an atmosphere of 'dullness'. No.

'Come on, then, Lallie. They won't mind one more person. Basil's pushed in, too,' Margaret said, picking up her coat and cramming on one of the ownerless woolly caps that we used for sailing, without even looking in the glass as she passed through the hall.

For me it was a queer end to a queer day, the rowdy, haphazard meal we ate at midnight on Hesson Common, sitting round a bonfire of green wood collected from the bushes by the light of the headlamps, and lit, after many vain efforts, by the sacrifice of most of the spare cans of petrol. These moneyed youngsters were much freer with one another in their manners than the people I was accustomed to, all except Basil Quest, who was invariably conventional. He had got himself invited, for the sake of being with Margaret, by offering to fetch any members of the Scanniland gang who had no cars, and he now looked almost as much of a fish out of water as I felt inwardly, though I tried not to show it: I was at least well practised in playing second-fiddle to Margaret.

She did not say or do much, but the whole life of the party seemed to eddy round her: even the girls paid special attention to her; not, I think, because she was popular but because she was outstandingly lovely, and the behaviour of the men showed that they were continually aware of this: like sheep, the girls followed their lead: 'Margaret darling, promise you'll come on Thursday . . .' 'I say, Margaret, listen. Such a scream . . .'

Afterwards, Basil insisted conscientiously that we could not leave the common until the beaten-out embers of the fire had had time to cool, and people wandered off in twos and threes in the darkness, leaving him to see to his own good work and stamp out any sparks that remained. Disappointed in getting Margaret, whom his brother had claimed, Tom Reddiland took me, fooling with me lightly with his arm round my waist, much as some other couples had done openly by the fire. I was not expecting anything more than that when he pulled me to him suddenly and kissed me. We were still within the range of Basil's voice, talking solemnly to someone about the risk of fire spreading underground. The night, and the strangeness of the place; defiance of the black trees looming over us, and also, for some reason, the ridiculous proximity of Basil, combined to fire me to answer the kiss – my first, incidentally, and as casual as Margaret's had been, though the casualness of that easy initial encounter of hers had slightly shocked me at the time. Now for the moment my own physical response, startling me, shut out all thought: I was stirred beyond anything that I had imagined.

The day had been too full, too varied for once: the relinquishing of my hopes of freedom – Sootie's story – London and the kindliness of Mr. Quest – Gordon Summers.

This impersonal kissing, in the darkness, of a man whom I knew only by sight was the release of a tension of which I had been hardly aware. The man's hold became less half-hearted, and his kisses. His hands fumbled about me, but the few seconds of excitement were over for me. He seemed surprised at my sudden withdrawal, and annoyed when, turning rougher, his mouth met only tight closed lips that jerked away. 'Aren't you a little fish!' he said irritably.

I had an idiotic impulse to apologize for having misled him at first; he could not be expected to know the history of my day; but I controlled this, and we walked back towards the cars.

'Are you younger than Margaret?' he demanded with rising, puzzled annoyance in his tone.

'No. Year and a bit older.'

'*Older.* Good Lord . . .!' And I did not like his laugh.

Some of the party were already sitting in the cars, smoking, when I climbed into Basil's two-seater, in order to avoid further conversation with Tom Reddiland. We waited ten minutes or so for stragglers, while the picnic spirit oozed away into the chilly night. It was difficult to make out, in the darkness, who was there and who was not.

'Well, how many are still missing,' called a girl's voice impatiently. 'Two? I suppose it's Angela and Colin!'

'No. Present and correct.'

'Present but *not* correct,' suggested the recognized wit of the party, and a shriek of laughter greeted him. I decided that if younger than Margaret in some ways, I was at any rate much too old for this party, and always had been.

'Oh, Margaret and somebody, probably!' suggested another girl, and there was a renewed titter.

'No, I'm here,' said Margaret's cool, soft voice.

'Sorry, darling, but one never knows, does one!' I suspected dislike under the good-natured tone. Basil must have longed to murder the speaker, but found nothing to say.

So Margaret did not mind those kisses and fumbling hands – dealt calmly with more of that sort of thing, possibly, than any of the other girls. I guessed that this group of young people was not particularly sophisticated, save in pose. These were post-War conventional girls, of the type that had filled the finishing school: for all their talk, sexual inexperience would be almost invariable among them until they were married or seriously engaged. They were as safely sentimental at heart as their mothers and all the other relatives whom this trivial love-making would have alarmed, unnecessarily, had they known of it, as a symptom of a promiscuity that did not in fact exist.

But Margaret was not sentimental. She would never fall slightly in and out of love, as the others did occasionally, judging by their conversation. 'I say, someone, is it all off between Dill and William the Second?' – 'Lord, yes, didn't you know? Tell you who's got it badly now, though . . .' And instinctively the others resented that unemotional quality which would allow her to take whatever she wanted, if she could ever be made to want anything. My thoughts

of her went no farther than that just then: If ever . . .
Surely not yet . . . she was still like the others in inexperience . . . She must be.

The last couple appeared, blinking and grinning in the
light of the headlamps. There was a final spurt of vitality
in the party, while derisive comments were called on the
state of the girl's hair, and then we drove home, silent and
sleepy, most of us a little cross.

CHAPTER XI

ENOUGH FOR ENCHANTMENT

'Do tell me, what is a flint arrowhead, exactly?' mother asked at lunch.

'A small piece of chipped stone, of uncertain age, found by anyone but me,' Gordon Summers told her with his nice, apologetic smile, so she asked him instead in which period, exactly, he was most interested.

'Exactly', used by mother to any man, was less a demand for precision than a conversational aid, intended to convey her working knowledge of the topic in hand, along with encouragement to him to spread himself upon it, presumably with enjoyment, as she made a charming listener.

But with Gordon Summers this did not work: he disliked explaining anything about his job to people whose interest in it was purely social, and had developed a knack for side-tracking inquiries with a courtesy that often passed for shyness. If pressed, he grew more apologetic, but obdurate. Mother found him charming. She liked the air of deference he adopted towards father, a much older man, whenever they disagreed; and did not notice that he never conceded a point. Even father did not seem to realize, when the guest got up to go, that they had differed on every subject mentioned on which there could possibly be two opinions, but all the same his invitation to come again was not quite as warm as mother's: he remembered the barrage trouble on the previous occasion. Because of that he had kept off the War all through lunch, to my secret relief (the one man, of any class, with whom father found it impossible to hobnob was the savage pacifist with an irrelevant argument of front line experience behind him). Father's patriotism had come undimmed through his bomb-instructing experience: I had a feeling that Gordon Summers's pleasing diffidence would forsake him altogether if any gleams of it in its pre-War effulgence shone out while they were together.

He said to me, after thanking mother for the meal, 'Would you ferry me across to the Levington shore?' and when I set out with him towards the Hard, expressed gratitude and regret for bothering me that were both out of proportion to the small kindness.

I was beginning to know just how little this perturbed manner of his meant, and laughed at him. 'Well, I couldn't get out of doing it even if I wanted to, could I, when you asked like that in front of everyone?'

'I know,' he said composedly.. 'That's why I did it while I was still a guest in the house, and your mother could hear. Otherwise you might have got someone else to take me over. The boat-boy probably. And I thought it would be nice if you came up to Levington. Nice for me,' he put in hurriedly seeing that I was going to protest about the word 'nice', which was becoming a private joke of ours.

He had kept me waiting half the morning in the Quests' garden, having very naturally overslept, after two nights spent, one in crossing from Skye, and the other in driving south. I did not mind the emptiness of these hours; it was the pleasantest waste of time to wander in this unexpected sanctuary, knowing that he would come soon . . . any minute. When he appeared, apparently a martyr to remorse, I assured him politely that it did not matter, and he accepted the assurance much too readily, agreeing with me. 'Awfully nice, really, dawdling about such a lovely place on a gorgeous morning,' and then in answer to my look of mild indignation, amended this lamely. 'Awfully nice for me, I mean, starting for Norwich so late, to know that you were dawdling in such a soothing place – soothing weather, too. If you had to dawdle anywhere, that is.' He smiled a disarming admission that he did not greatly care how long he had kept me waiting.

Mr. Quest, fortunately, did not notice the trespasser.

But we did not go to Levington that afternoon after all. It was a hot climb through the woods that fringed the steep shore, and half way up the hill we sat down to smoke, and stayed there till rooks came cawing back to their usual trees in the evening, reminding me that tea would be over long before I reached home, and I had better concoct some explanation of the hours that had somehow melted away – the dinghy drying out on the shingle or a mislaid rowlock – in order to kill the germs of a new family joke, coupling me with Gordon.

For that would be unbearable now. He had talked not as at lunch, defensively, but with the curiously rare directness and honesty that I had remembered for years, from our first conversation in Mr. Quest's car, on the occasion when I was out to annoy the Cottrells. It was not particularly witty talk, like Mr. Quest's: sometimes it was amusing, because he had an observant mind and an unsparing use of words, but to me the marvel was to be with someone who spoke, with all barriers of pretence down for a friend, without desire for effect of any kind, save that of approaching another mind as closely as possible; and because he talked straightforwardly of simple things, I could too, and that seemed wonderful.

No, there was more in our talk than this. In itself, this almost unhampered contact with another mind, however fine, would not have been enough for enchantment, and enchantment was there, waiting upon us, guiding high white clouds over the sun so that at times a hush fell over the bee-flecked wood, blessing us with silence. And as the clouds sailed on and the hum of insects rose again, enchantment led back to us once more, through the thick, waving leaves and branches that strove to trap them, the shafts of sunlight which played over the man's brown hands and hair and pleasant body, flickering in his eyes so that, rolling over, he lay with his head on his arms, his eyes shut, and I could watch him unobserved. Enchantment painted blue the distant, lengthening shadows on the Quests' lawns, across the water.

This was the immeasurable moment for which all other moments, all other excellent things, were only a lovely preparation: the companionship of Ted, as he lay face down-wards in almost the same position with the sun scorching his shoulder, before the squirrel chattered: hundreds of little moons dancing from black north-sea wave to wave as lightly as the motes of dust swirled in and out of these sunrays; birds' beauty and the colour of forgotten sunsets and every good hour of my life, they were all the fore-shadowing of this 'now' of which Margaret had spoken once with a wisdom beyond her own, the 'now' beyond which nothing exists, nor needs to exist, since 'now' is magni-ficently enough. Time was neither my enemy nor my friend: there was no time, till the rooks came.

I did not want to touch him, nor for him to do anything more than talk, while his delightful voice went on making magic of anything that wandered through his mind; or else to be silent in the long pauses that fell without embarrass-ment between us. It was as if each trivial happening, every breath of wind sweeping through the wood, every bee droning by laden with its heavy autumn cargo, was fixed in an unalterable pattern of perfection, so that, whether we spoke or were quiet, we could not have done better, any more than the wind or the bees. I was blissfully sorry that I could thank no god for the sudden rightness of everything.

But at home, grown wary again, I said of him, 'Nice, only a bit of a bore if he gets on to archæology,' which he had not mentioned. This would keep them from bothering him about it, and inwardly I hugged myself, because if one were forced into lying for safety, as I was too often, it was good to redeem the inherent meanness of a lie by making it of stupendous size and unbelievable audacity for once, – of such offensive contours, indeed, in the sight of all decent spiritual powers that, were there any, they would be forced into instant and annihilating action. 'A bit of a bore' – the owner of that companionable mind and darling smile.

'Oh, I daresay,' said father. 'Specialists usually are on their own subjects,' and went on to talk about boats.

CHAPTER XII

'WHERE THINK'ST THOU...?'

'Has he got any money?' mother asked, in an elaborately off-hand tone.

'No,' I said, answering her real question, not the spoken one: obviously Gordon was not entirely destitute. 'He's got some kind of University research grant, about three hundred a year.'

Mother's interest in him wilted, though I could still ask him to stray meals if I pleased without meeting opposition. We were unusually lucky, as children of a hard-up household, in the freedom with which we could extend hospitality to our personal friends: nowadays Margaret's young men were constantly in and out, which was to my advantage, since I could assume casual interest in several, to guard myself still further from the glut of clean, wholesome fun that would have followed the slightest suspicion of the manner in which my world had been suddenly transfigured. One of the nicest things about father as a father was his firm suppression of mother's 'county' desire to offer people four-course dinners or none at all.

Gordon came in to tea again two days later, and lost his remaining friends at court – Dru, who remembered him kindly for admiring the looks of her beloved family; and father, who had at least been non-committal.

In the course of the meal father made some intimate reference to an Australian gaol: it was succeeded by one of those silences into which, almost inevitably, a guest dropped the question that drew from him, reluctantly, an interesting personal story. But Gordon said nothing, and when

245

the same sort of pause occurred again, started gravely on a remarkable idea of his by which the managers of Royal tours through the Empire could revitalize the popularity of members of our reigning House; – hiring assassins to fire at and miss them, in the way in which he had long suspected Mussolini of hiring his.

'Take Australia, since you mentioned it. Royal tours in Australia are always a bit of a frost. Nasty democratic people, the Australians. Strong anti-English feeling. But if some Australian raised his hand, not in the way of kindness . . .'

'But think of the feelings of the Australians!' said mother, horrified, though not as horrified as if the scheme had been mentioned in connection with other red portions of the map. With no suitable frontiers, Australia had never been a favourite dying ground for her male relatives. Father visibly prepared to take it all as a joke, and then changed his mind. Gordon seemed earnest, and this was not father's brand of permissible bad taste. His reminiscences shelved, he became unusually quiet. Both he and mother were partial to owning Empires vociferously loyal to the Crown.

Gordon apologized profusely to me afterwards. 'Idiotic of me – at his table, too, – ought to have made it clear I was being feebly funny – prone to these lapses into shocking bad taste . . .' and then added in the same breath with his abrupt, staggering frankness, 'when I don't like a man.'

With Dru it was inevitable that he should fall from favour: both of them had deceptive manners, Gordon a coating of social diffidence that wore through unexpectedly, and Dru a hail-fellow-well-met-air which covered a deeper prudishness than he could easily imagine.

He thanked her awkwardly for her help in stopping the tale that Stella had started.

'Oh, that's all right. As a matter of fact I thought of a damn good counter-rumour,' she said, her voice a little too loud as it often was when she talked to a man. 'Hope it doesn't matter, I've said to several people who were talking about the Cottrells that way . . . "Oh, Lord, no; Summers has got a girl of his own in Norwich. We happen to know." Then it struck me that if it's true by any chance, this might be just as awkward as the original story. Have you?'

'No.'

'Oh, well, I suppose you might have. I mean, I thought it was just possible.' When she was ill at ease, Dru always found it difficult to end a conversation and get away, as she wanted to. She would probably go on saying meaningless things like this for some time. She and Margaret and I were walking down with Gordon to the Butt & Oyster yard, where he had left his car, to see him off.

'Thank you for the suggestion that I don't look entirely impotent.' Gordon said, smiling, and Dru turned scarlet.

'Oh, well, I mean – I didn't mean. . . .'

Margaret laughed, and Basil Quest, who must have been loitering by River View gate in the hope of her passing, heard her unmistakable chuckle and strolled out to join us, as if by accident. Presently Mr. Quest appeared. During the diversion caused by introductions, Dru faded away – A remark 'dull' beyond bearing; she would not easily forgive Gordon.

Can't I delay him somehow? Can't I? said something inside me. He may not come again. Why should the enchantment of that afternoon have been shared? I have no reason to suppose that it was. It was enough for me – then – that I felt it myself. (The two intervening days had been an agony of time suspended, lest he should not come back.)

'I met you at a cricket match at Norwich last year,' Gordon said to Basil. Why could they not all go away and leave me with him for these few minutes? I did not want to listen to trivial talk, made to people who did not matter.

'Ah?" said Basil, who did not either. He dragged his eyes away from Margaret and gazed moonily at the interloper.

'Weren't you playing for the Visitors? In fact, you bowled me.'

'Bowled?' echoed Basil. 'For the Visitors? – Oh, yes – rather.'

'It's useless to talk to my son at present,' said Mr. Quest, with a brutality of exasperation that I had not met in him for a long while. 'He's in a state of sexual coma. I have already asked him twice why he particularly wants to borrow my car this evening, his own being out of action, and he is unable to think of a reason.'

'Thought I might feel like a run later on,' muttered Basil with a look of pardonable hatred at his father. The possession of a car was his only hold over Margaret, who frankly tolerated his company for convenience' sake alone, and this was the night of the dance that had been arranged at the Reddilands' picnic.

Through my preoccupation with my own anxiety to keep Gordon a little while longer, somehow, anyhow, I detested Mr. Quest for the moment for that piece of unwarrantable cruelty, and was glad that Dru was not there: she would have been distressed by the remark for its own sake, for Basil's sake, and more than all, perhaps, because Margaret only found it funny that Basil should be publicly discomfited.

Gordon, at twenty-nine, had somewhat forgotten the miseries of being nineteen – he had been in France at that age anyway, so that they had been very different miseries – and he took to Mr. Quest at once. The two started talking of common acquaintances at Oxford, while Gordon stood with one foot on the running-board of his dilapidated car, ready to go.

In a way I did not want this conversation to end: at least it meant that I could look at him and listen, and yet it was maddening that these minutes should be taken up by the peculiarities of unknown dons.

I looked away, digging my nails into my hands. To-morrow, at this hour, he would be well on his way back to Skye. As a casual friend, who had chimed with his mood for one afternoon, I might not even know of it if he ever returned to Levington. After he had gone, time would creep leaden-footed. Time, be kind for once, move gently now when there is purpose in your slowness; stop for a little while, because his voice, and the way in which his eyes wrinkle up when he laughs, have become more important than anything else in the world. And no longer amazed by your sudden richness, I want more delight than you have ever given me – the chance to learn his face and its expressions better than I could while the first enchantment was on me – to learn it so well that I shall be able to see it clearly whether he is with me or not, instead of groping for it in memory as I have done these last two days, losing detail after detail while I groped until I could hardly remember it at all. Time, be kind.

Knowing the foolishness of it, I made my old childish effort of mind to arrest the passing seconds, and in some strange way half succeeded. For a while, through the straining of the will, it was as if something dislocated in my consciousness: I have never come nearer to Brooke's 'I saw the immortal moment stand . . .', nor do I want to, for it was horrible. Timelessly, as I looked back from the river to the other people in the group round the car, I saw Margaret glance from Basil to Gordon; not for once idly, as she looked at most people, but appraisingly; a woman comparing two men who might serve her need. The need was not imperative, being satisfied for the moment; the comparison was instinctive. And of the two men whose desire she held at the moment, Gordon, – older, harder, more experienced – was the better in her eyes. I saw

Margaret's serene loveliness anew, as something that could not have bloomed from soil stinted in any way. Ardour appeased before it was fully awake had left her colder, spiritually, than Dru; Margaret did not want Gordon as much as he wanted her in that moment, when something flamed up between them, but she was experienced with men – I knew that for certain now – and already this looking on men as potential lovers had become a habit. The moment's urgent attraction between them was a normal thing, a trivial occurrence that had amused me before when I had noticed it in gatherings of youngish people, a blaze up of sex in its purest form, undistorted by emotional falsities. There was nothing horrible in it save that to me Gordon was something more than a finely made body; and in these last two days I had learnt that I wanted his body as well as his mind.

Time poured back into the gap that had opened in it. Mr. Quest finished the brilliant parody of High Table conversation which he had been improvising all the time: I found nothing to say: Gordon drove away: Margaret strolled back up the road, with Basil beside her earnestly asking her something: the entire Cottrell family appeared, walking towards us: Mr. Quest said something casually over his shoulder to me and moved too, to avoid meeting them; he could just about reach his garden gate before they did.

I did not hear what he said. Gordon's car was still in sight, nearing the bend that would hide it. It was as if I could not turn my attention away. Mr. Quest repeated his remark or question a little querulously, and I said, 'Oh, yes,' at random. He turned and walked the few steps back to me, staring at me I knew, though I kept my eyes away, on the now empty road behind the advancing Cottrells. He took my elbow in a hard-gripping, bony hand and walked me along, as he had done once when I was a child. And he talked, now as then, continually, purposefully, and of entirely irrelevant matters.

'In the far off days when I was somebody's good-looking nephew, dependent for my expectations on sex-appeal alone, since my manners were never up to much . . .' and went on to tell me the graceless story of his inheritance, from a wealthy aunt, of the money that had set him free from the drudgery of life as a science master in a badly run secondary school at Kingston – 'Where I was remarkably more incompetent than anyone else. One of the worst teachers I have ever known, which is saying a great deal. I started in my present line with a good working knowledge of how one subject, at least, should not be presented to the growing mind. That is, if one really desires the growing mind to absorb any of it. It was probably just as well that no one remembered the facts of science as I produced them.' He barely nodded to the older Cottrells, who would have stopped and spoken to us – to me particularly. I was still a little dazed, beyond intelligent response. His hand kept hold of my elbow unobtrusively, propelling me onwards.

'To think that there are poaching stalwarts who tickle trout to death for a living. What an occupation, year in, year out! I thought my old trout would never die, and I only had about six months of it. She had so many nearer and, in the eyes of the world, more deserving relatives, all tickling in relays, that I could do no more. Fortunately charm won when it did; I had almost decided to let worth and consanguinity triumph, and go on schoolmastering.'

Next to his romantic bereavement, the greatest source of discussion about Mr. Quest in Pin Mill was the origin of his money, of which even Stella seemed to know nothing.

He jerked open River View's gate as he had done before, without a pause in his conversation, but now we went the opposite way, up the path, into the house, along one corridor and then another, I still in front; mute, grateful, and attentive, because I knew that so Time would steady best around me, and the world become bearable again. We sat down in his study, where he poured me out a large dose of sherry.

'The horrible laughter of scientists.' We had slid smoothly from his aunt on to this congenial subject. Mr. Quest was not looking at me, but leaning back in an armchair, talking of the early days when his nerves were happily impervious to this awe-inspiring sound, now resounding in his ageing ears, '. . . the thin cackle of mirthless superiority with which Man, potentially the saddest animal and the only one possessed of humour, recognizes the discrepancy between the range and grasp of the individual human mind, and the futility of its ultimate destiny. Higher mathematics – and the waiting worm. Say forty years of intellectual activity in which to examine inter-stellar space or atomic behaviour – and after that senility, and then nothingness.

'It is one of the blessings of your age, Lallie (your otherwise over-rated age!) that you cannot be intimidated by the laughter of scientists. You know that you are mortal, but only with your head, not deep down in your stomach. You wait.

'What did we care, I and the young men, "beautiful in anger, magnificent in lust" (they were generally other assistant masters) who dallied in company on the river through the long summer evenings – What did we care that the young women of Kingston, with whom we dallied, really consisted on the outside of a chance collection of light-reflecting planes made visible by continuity? Or that inside they were only a system of inefficiently communicating tubes, a disgrace to a Heavenly Plumber: and so were we? These aspects of us, on which science insists, were not self-evident after dusk in the backwaters, and we easily ignored them. – Drink my sherry, too, will you? Your digestion can stand it at this hour: I was forgetting that mine can't.

'Already, in that thoughtless period, physiologists were probably as gruesomely hilarious as I have heard my friend Leonard Hill being since, about transferring the eye of a newt to the stump of its amputated tail, and watching the useless sight-tissue develop, in obedience to tremendous and idiotic laws.' (Mr. Quest, who had started talking only from kindness, was really enjoying himself now.) 'And astronomers rollicked among light-years, those vacuous horrors of time, as heartily as Jeans was doing at the Royal Society last Tuesday. But I knew so little about science in those days that it did not matter to me. (We called it Heat, Light and Sound, and it just included Elementary Electricity, to my discomfort.) I and the lady of the moment could still laugh louder than they did, at least in our own ears.

'But now that my youth is past (thank goodness, on the whole) and I know considerably more about science than I did while I earned a living at it, I cannot stay comfortably unaware, for long at a time, of this brave and barren glee which is echoing louder and louder about the world to-day – the amusement of innumerable scientists, inviting me to share with them their pleasure in the spectacle of Myself, observed from various angles, strutting with careful dignity to no-where at all by the light of dwindling, decaying sun and stars which I once – te, he! ho, ho! – believed to be eternal. (Largely, of course, in order to bolster up my delicious sense of self-importance.)

'And really, you know,' said Mr. Quest confidentially, getting up from his armchair, 'apart from its dismaying aspect, it *is* rather an enjoyable spectacle.'

He looked at me inquiringly, seeming to expect comment, but though feeling already the cheering effects of the sherry, I found nothing to say to this, and walking about the room he went on talking again, dealing now with his difficulties in demonstrating electricity in the class-room.

'Only necessity could make me handle a wire, once

electrically "alive," which had been disconnected, not between me and the source of power (I could understand that), but on the further side, so that if I touched it I should have to do so *between* the break and the battery, dynamo, or what-not. No boy seemed to have any hesitation about it, nor did any, I hope, suspect my reluctance. But what, I asked myself, would tell the electricity that it could not complete the circuit and get at me without running along to the end of the wire – past my hand – to find the break for itself? If it did not do that, how would it know that there was an obstacle to its passage? And the only answer I could give myself, that electricity had never yet behaved like that, seemed unpleasantly irrelevant. It might when I touched it; it very easily might.'

'Oh, Mr. Quest, I'm glad some intelligent person has felt like that,' I said. 'Because father always gets wild with Dru and me when we let him see that we've got that sort of mind.'

Mr. Quest looked relieved that I had come to life again, and accompanied me at once to the door. Incalculable person, who could be so callous sometimes, and so intuitively kind, on other, similar occasions.

If he saw me, he took no notice of me in the garden the next morning. I was thankful to be alone, in the small orchard which I liked because I had his leave to eat the windfalls, and also because the grass was allowed to grow long and unkempt between the fruit trees, so that there were livelier bird and animal doings here than in the formal grounds nearer the house. It was warm for October, save in the wind, and to get out of this I curled down low in the grass.

A hedgehog ambling about, caring for nobody, with its worried air of having mislaid something; and a trio of magpies pretending that none of them was after one special fallen apple, which each coveted from cantankerousness

254

alone, since there were more windfalls than I could eat – these things must hold all my interest again. Gordon had gone: enchantment had waited breathlessly in the wood for me alone.

Try as I would, I could not make them matter at first, and I had a superstitious feeling, in which I consciously disbelieved, that Gordon would not think of me on his journey while my thoughts were with him, and I wanted him to do that. It was a kindred silliness to the feeling which everyone, surely, has had about some long-awaited letter – If only I could once come into the house without thinking of it, the letter might be there.

I thought about Margaret as I had seen her yesterday, with all the urgent, unpleasant curiosity of a virgin outgrowing spiritual virginity. So she knew, better than by sight, men's lean, lovely bodies; knew the touch of demanding hands passing over her small, firm breasts and thighs; did not turn from kisses given 'with inside lip' as some forgotten writer called them, kisses in which the tongue was a symbol and perhaps a delight – I did not really know; I had turned away too soon, myself. That sudden rage of passion which came to men (and to women, too, as fiercely? Again, I did not know): she had known that; and submitting to it, or sharing it, she had been left almost unchanged. It seemed strange to some disgusted, envious part of my mind that she should look so much the same as she had done at school – a girl dreaming with the mists of childhood still about her, not a woman fulfilled – save for that one glance which I had seen answered by Gordon. – No, I must not think of Gordon. But the amusing hedgehog had lumbered off, and the magpies were now amicably eating the apple together. I stretched out at full length in the grass, excusing myself for taking Gordon's exact position in the wood, by keeping my eyes open where his had been shut. With an effort at self-forgetfulness I stared down into the miniature world of beetles and spiders intent on their individual needs, and ants scurrying about in the service of their tribe, until the jointed stems of the grass became great forest trunks, and the crumbs of dry earth, boulders over which the insects clambered in constant peril; the small shining cobwebs of early autumn were spread everywhere to catch them if they blundered in this trackless jungle.

Presently I did forget everything else, for a beast relatively the size of an elephant came cautiously to reconnoitre the ground, and finding no cause for alarm, disappeared to return with her delightful family – five balls of brown fur about the width of a thumb-nail, very young harvest mice who stopped following her to scratch their chins with thread-like pink toes when she was trying her hardest to herd them all together, and scattered to poke their noses into ant-holes and fallen leaves, taking no notice of her shrillings. If I had been the distracted mouse I should have whipped them all with that long and handy tail. Lying very still, I tried to make out what limits there were to the concertina powers of these little round bodies, which would suddenly stretch out to what looked like breaking point, as the forelegs dashed excitedly away from the other pair, till the front end of the mouse was stopped by some passing interest of the head, and the tail caught up. Could they double their length, or more, when they pleased? One of my shoes just grazed the other as I jerked a knee stealthily, trying to dislodge a fly which had found the end of my stocking. The mother 'froze' at the slight sound, squeaking a warning, and for once the young ones obeyed, copying her. In the forest of grass she could see little more than her own length ahead: she ran up a bunch of tough stems, whose tops waved a few inches in front of my chin. They bent under her weight, towards me, so that when she reached the ears of the grass, and sat up to look round, holding on with her hind feet, she gazed into my face from a distance that made me squint uncomfortably in returning the look. She showed no fear; this vast expanse overhead was merely a pink sky to her; she searched round it for something moving and ominous. Unable to keep up the squint, I blinked. Instantly the stillness of horror transfixed the bright wandering eyes and quivering nose; it seemed extraordinary that so tiny a face could find room for so much expression. It was exactly the expression to be expected on the face of a human sentry did he observe a gigantic eye closing and opening again in the heavens. She fell off the grasses with a piercing squeak and chivvied her family away, all shrilling at the top of their powers, all leaving their back legs farther and farther behind as they ran. I sat back on my heels and laughed, and then fervently blessed her for making me forget everything but her small world of panics and domesticity . . . just long enough to let him come. Gordon was crossing one of the near-by lawns, looking for me.

We said the most ordinary things when he sat down beside me: 'I thought you were starting early this morning.' – 'Well, I meant to, but I've put it off till this afternoon. As long as I'm there by Saturday . . .' But I knew then that the enchantment had not been entirely unshared: almost all mine it may have been, but something of it still clung in his memory.

He said in a matter of fact tone, 'I thought I'd like to talk to you again. And it didn't seem much good staying on yesterday in the hopes of it with so many people around. Particularly your far-too-beautiful sister. A most disturbing person.' He smiled, as a man does at an infection that is over, and I minded nothing; no memory, no fear of the future: yesterday and to-morrow were far away, trumpery things to be shared with lesser people: only this new 'now' existed, with Gordon here alone.

I could afford to waste time in talking trivialities, I had grown so rich again in lovely minutes: he need not go for some hours. 'Are you going to see Mrs. Macdonald on your way through London? Because if so, do tell her the latest from Mrs. Chandler. That's the widow at the shop who acts as a sort of rumour-exchange for Pin Mill: she adores Dru, who's had several talks with her on your behalf. She now says that "Spreading a pack of lies, about a nice-spoken gentleman and lady that hardly know one another, is just the sort of thing that a college-bred girl would do. All that education – (sniff) – give her people who haven't got queer fathers, even if they don't go to Oxford and Cambridge. Like father, like child. Thinking himself too good to know anyone, etc." – a rather involved dig at Mr. Quest. The Quests are the black sheep for the moment, instead of the Cottrells. "Makes a nice change, don't it?" as she always says herself when we buy Players instead of Gold Flake or vice versa (there aren't any other kinds of cigarette in the shop) . . .'

I was running on happily because it was so good to be able to watch him under cover of my own talk, knowing exactly now what I wanted of him – mind, body, everything; putting off for sheer sensuous pleasure the instant when I would hear his voice again. 'I think from what I remember of her, Mrs. Macdonald is the sort of person who'd be amused by that.'

'She would.' He played with grass, running the stems between his nice fingers. 'And very relieved. Incidentally, we can neither of us thank you properly – I'm not good at thanking; remember Dru. But I shan't be seeing Esther for – Oh, I don't know how long,' he said in a voice that suddenly changed my mood, because all the lightness had gone out of his.

Grown serious, I asked – knowing again that between us, for the moment, there could be no impertinence in any question – 'Why did you care so much about the child dying?'

He looked at me intently for a few seconds, making up his mind. 'Because I believe it was mine,' he said. 'And because it was three years old, the nicest age for little girls. And also because it was the jolliest child I knew. . . . Oh, well, no; just because it was mine, I suppose; and all that was left of something that Esther and I had shared. I don't suppose it made much difference that I also liked it as a child. It's odd how deep conventional feelings go, even with fairly reasonable people: I had reason to think it was mine, so I cared. And I knew that Esther never would be again, and I also cared about that. I want you to understand, Lallie; the present gossip you've helped to squash *is* unfounded. It's true what I told you, I haven't even seen her alone for goodness knows how long, and it will be only by chance if I ever do again. Neither of us will make the chance. Not knowing you very well when I came down here, after getting her letter, I would have lied about it all, of course, in order to get the talk stopped, if it had been necessary. But it wasn't; I'm not her lover. I haven't been since the child was born. Not, that is, in any way which interests the world. But there was just enough shadow of truth in this talk, from four years ago, to make it dangerous. Damnably unfair, but that doesn't matter. Four years. Time of the regatta; do you remember?'

I saw the two of them, whom I had envied, standing again silent in the darkness leaning over the water-side wall, oblivious to a bird's call, to my presence, to everything but each other. His voice went on, quickening, as though it were a relief to talk and yet he knew that if he did not say what he wanted to tell me without stopping to think, he would not say it at all.

'And then our coming together was a mistake. An unnecessary one. My fault. I'd been in love with her for years. Mentally there'd never been anyone else for me. (And as a matter of fact, mentally it's just the same now that we're friends who can't often meet.) She said the scheming and lying and fear of discovery would spoil everything. We daren't even go away somewhere by ourselves, but had to stay with friends – everything looking respectable. I wouldn't believe she was right, because I wanted her so much; but she was, quite right. It was not worth the price of hating everything but the actual few moments of being together. Each of us had had, for years, nearly all the best that the other could give. Companionship, and affection, and absolute trust, and so on. I don't think she was ever in love with Macdonald; she married him very young, after the death of the man she did care for, because she could do a great deal for Macdonald, and at the time she badly needed that. He was a raw Scot with a good head and terrific ambition, and no social graces whatever, set on suceeding in a profession where social graces help a man up the ladder quicker than anything else; and she has more or less made him. I think if she had once been in love with him, her feelings might have changed to him altogether when we found that we – that . . .' He stopped, questing for words that would convey their feelings to me, and inadvertently found those which would hurt longest in my memory – 'that if we could be silent together, it was worth everyone else's talk,' for this was what I had felt exultantly with him in the wood on the other side of the river. 'I don't know if that means anything to you, but it seems to me the highest plane of friendship.'

'Yes.'

'But she always felt the same, quite coolly: liked him, respected him for his shrewdness and single-mindedness; knew, too, that he would not get so far without her help to cover his deficiencies – to get him considered a rugged character instead of rather a boor. And she wouldn't hurt him more than she could help. I think what was wrong with us,' Gordon said with a wry smile, 'was that we were much too unselfish as lovers, and mildly grateful to existence. I was grateful for being left alive at the end of the War, and she was grateful to Macdonald because through him she had made something of her life, which had looked pretty well smashed up at one time. We were the most considerate couple. Lord, whom didn't we consider; even the servants, yes, particularly the servants! You see, with the tremendous sense of freedom and life that peace brought – for a bit – we both believed that she would be able to come to me openly, decently, soon: he'd be on his own feet and could do without her. That was why we let the child happen. But we'd waited either not long enough or too long, I don't know which. She had to go abroad with him on some political mission. We thought she would tell him when they came back, but she said afterwards she realized that she couldn't leave him then. Professionally, things weren't turning out for him as well as he'd expected. And later, well, the moment had passed, somehow. He'd always kept his side of their agreement, knowing that she was only fond of him. There was her other child – his child – too. Someone else to consider! We'd got in the habit of considering. Or I may have failed her in some way, I don't know. Anyway – one illicit week-end and seven years of friendship, and yet I suppose nine people out of ten would say that the important part of our relationship – the part that really counted – was that week-end, two days of disappointment and pretence! The only pretence there has ever been between us, as far as I know: neither of us had the courage to own, at the time, that it wasn't all we'd hoped. A curious anti-climax. Spiritually we were both tired out, and what our bodies did, which should have seemed marvellous, was only what they had done with other people. – Lallie.'

'Yes?' I was sitting up, turned away so that I could no longer see him, for all this was wretched hearing. Not because of the past: that did not matter; but because of what his voice told me more than his words, the present strength of his feeling for this woman, who held so great a part of what I wanted, his mind.

'Are you wondering why I'm telling you all this?' He pulled me down with a hand on my shoulder, to make me lie so that, propped on one elbow, he could see my face.

'A bit.' It was not true; I was not thinking like that at all. I would not have him guess what I was thinking.

He pushed stray hair away from my eyes with gentle fingers. 'I like you better than anyone else I know, I think. Like you, not love you. And I want to see you again when I come back from Skye: so I thought I'd rather explain something to you myself that you're likely to hear of anyway, and it might possibly hurt you a bit if you heard it from someone else. Puzzle you, anyway. Probably I'm assuming rather a lot in thinking you might be hurt. The hope of another talk, like this, wasn't the only thing that stopped me starting north yesterday. I heard Margaret say at tea that she was going to a dance with some Ipswich people I've known for years. So I rang them up and went too. Because I was in the mood for the small, rather meaningless triumph of cutting out other men for one evening with a very beautiful young woman. And I had that. Margaret is lovely. She's also, I think – I'm sorry she's your sister – a rather worthless human being. This is ungrateful; she gave me a very good evening – because I was a novelty, I suppose. I had the fun of being envied, which everyone enjoys. To my advantage, she behaved damnably to the man who brought her, young Quest, who is in love with her. I was quite ready to get all the satisfaction I could from the fact that making him look a fool for my sake, the whole evening, was her idea of a good joke; but I think her a bitch for it all the same. I suppose most men would react in that way – play up to her ruthlessly at the moment, enjoy Quest's trouble because they'd been through it themselves at his age, and then afterwards resent her part in the old, mean game of calf-baiting.

'I don't quite understand that,' I said. 'At least, not for you . . .'

'No, I was afraid you wouldn't. You must just take it on trust that human nature is like that. I'm now sounding insufferable, but you can get your own back if you want to, because I'm going to lay myself open to an exceedingly unpleasant snub – Lallie, are you surprised that I don't make love to you? It seems to me that at your age, looking as you do at this moment, you've every right to be. And particularly now you know I'm ready to go out of my way for the chance of paying attention to Margaret, whom I don't like as I like you?'

I did not answer, except by saying, 'Oh, Gordon . . .!' stupidly, in appeal. His eyes were on mine, and his face close, between me and the branches of the apple tree overhead. I did not want to say yes, of course I had, and it would have been hard to lie unsuccessfully.

He looked away, frowning with the effort to make clear to me what he meant, or with a kind of nervousness at putting himself so much in someone else's hands: even hands he liked. 'I thought someone would be certain to let you know that Margaret and I were rather noticeably together at that dance.'

'Oh, quite certain,' I said, knowing my family. Obscurely aware that here was a sure source of present discontent, they would feel bound to tell me about it with an idea of saving me from some vague possibility of future unhappiness.

'You seem to me a person that anyone might hurt, rather easily, without intending to. No, that's not what I mean – that *I* might hurt. This is where you can retort crushingly if you want to. Margaret plainly isn't made of the same stuff at all. She had from me the sort of intense casual admiration – very exciting to me at the moment, and gratifying to

263

.her, I suppose – which was exactly what she deserved. But because at the back of my mind there's still Esther, I haven't anything to give you that you deserve. I'm not being un-selfish, about this – I've had enough for good of being the unselfish lover . . .' He laughed in a way that rang in my memory after he had gone, until by recalling it deliberately, even though it hurt, when all dearer tones of his voice had grown blurred by my constant thoughts, I did at last lose the echo of it when I should have been grateful to have kept even that. 'Obviously I should get a good deal of pleasure out of trying to convince you, either by body or mind, that no one else mattered at all for the moment; but I have a feeling that I might possibly succeed – My dear, you're being an angel of forbearance! – And it wouldn't be true; not even for the moment; not in my mind. I would rather have you as you are, as a satisfactory friend. I've already spoilt one lovely friendship.'

'I see,' I said, critically pleased, with one part of me, by the ordinariness of my voice. 'And being kind, you'd be a bit unhappy for me if you thought I was unhappy.'

'. . . Not even as mildly unselfish as that, I'm afraid! People simply aren't, when it comes to love-making. They think of themselves. Or at least all the decenter men I know will admit that they do. I'd be worried on my own account. It would be very disturbing to know that I'd upset someone I was fond of. One is always a little resentful against the person upset for getting in the way to be hurt – why couldn't they be hurt by someone else, and so save one's feelings? But that isn't the main point: what I wanted to make you understand was how much your friendship means. I didn't want you to mind about Margaret and all that. (And you haven't even said "Why should I?", as every other woman I know would have done in your place, bar one.) I like you much too much for the sort of attention that just doesn't mean anything. And can't, unfortunately. You would be a delightful person, too, to be in love with – freckles only on your nose,' he said inconsequently and flicked a very light kiss on the end of it before getting up. 'It's getting cold here. Come and have lunch with me in Ipswich before I go? I don't want to share you with your hospitable family to-day.'

Outside the gate we came on Lester Cottrell.

'Good,' said Gordon when we saw him. 'We'll get him to drop in at your house and say you won't be back for a bit. If we go, your people will kindly try to keep us.'

I was elsewhere in thought, still lying in the orchard grass hearing the wings of joy rustling by me, as unseen sea-birds pass at night, hovering close by, and then sweeping on and away. Did Gordon know, so poor was my pretending, what I already felt for him, and was this why he told me so much, almost in warning, that I might not be hurt more than need be? I was too far off to remember everyday facts – that none of the Cottrells, for instance, had been to our house since a little while after the Olive affair, which had nearly made us friends again.

Lester crossed the road to us with as much alacrity as his languid gait allowed, bent on showing that there was no Cottrell resentment for the Rush lifting of their archæologist.

'You'll be interested – I hope – to hear that the Editor's correspondents have surpassed themselves to-day,' he said, producing the inevitable *Times* cutting. "One need only look through the hymns selected for the Army Prayer Book to realize how few hymns we have which really inspire spiritual activity." From the Rev. Herbert England, The Vicarage, Tisbury. A reflection both striking and accurate, no doubt. And followed by one of those nature phenomena which the readers of this newspaper observe so painstakingly – the description of an unknown bird recently sighted on a heath, together with a list of the species it wasn't, ending with –

listen – "We returned to the place two days later, only to find, however, that the bird had gone." That divine "however"! – By the way, Gordon, I must congratulate you on the finds in Skye: I was reading about them this morning. I'd no idea they were so bonny.'

'Thanks. And I must congratulate you on those dear little hairs on the chest,' said Gordon, who had a prejudice against artistic *négligé* for men, 'I'd no idea they were so bonny either.' Unusual adjectives were another peculiarity with which he had little sympathy.

But nothing perturbed Lester. Obligingly he did up a couple of buttons on his bright blue shirt, which he always wore open as far as possible, and did not look startled, even for a second, by Gordon's unwitting demand that he should break the malevolent neutrality of years by calling on my mother at home.

'Certainly, I'm passing that way in any case, so it's no trouble,' he said with his grave courtesy.

'Nice chap,' said Gordon when he had gone. 'But I can't understand why I like him.'

'Nor can I. Nor can anyone. But everyone does,' I said. 'Except father.'

'Oh well,' said Gordon, who had worked himself into a mood for conveying uncomfortable facts, 'They've got a talent for self-dramatization in common. Only Lester'd be ready to admit his. You couldn't expect them to get on.'

But by lunch he had got over this mood and was charming to me, telling me, as I had not hoped he would, of his present job and its bearing on what was already known or conjectured of the dim early-Bronze age, when man, the most frightened of all earth's creatures, had already begun to distinguish himself from other animals by his valiant dishonesty – that strange thrifty daring which led him, beset by the terrors of the visible world, to try to placate the spirits of his dead, for fear of unseen terrors, by burying with them broken or inferior weapons and crude imitations of the household goods that were their right, in the hope that, with the stupidity of the dead, they would not notice the difference. (The present western religion is the only one which has not assumed that the dead are inevitably more stupid than the living, as well as more vindictive.)

Even though he was going away, and nothing else really mattered, my imagination was gripped by what he told me about the recent discoveries, in Germany, of primitive burials where the feet of the dead had been cut off, to keep the ghosts from climbing out of the graves. He broke off suddenly: 'Lallie, it's nearly three – I'd no idea – I must go. My dear, was I unforgivable this morning?' (Did he know that I loved him?) 'I think I sounded the complete pompous ass.' (All through lunch I had been trying to hold my thoughts away from the full meaning of what he had said, and to listen only to his voice, talking of things long ago, which could not hurt me, but knowledge kept creeping back into possession of my mind, and then I would not hear all he said – Someone else held what I wanted: the little I could have given him, physical love, he did not want, from me, but only good fellowship.) 'People say, don't they, that it's idiotic to wish for life over again, though everyone does it at times, because even if it were possible it would only mean making the same damn silly mistakes the second time . . .'

'D'you think that's true?' I said, for something to hold away from my mind the realization that my respite was nearly over now: he was paying the bill, almost ready to go. 'Don't you think it's chance that makes people do the most important things?' (A silly-seeming remark, but I was thinking of Ronald and Dru hawking those postcards at the Cottrells' gate, years ago, which had led to my friendship with Gordon.)

'Well, I don't know. Anyway, I seem to be getting in one life – marvellous luck, really – two chances of something very valuable in the way of companionship. And as it's the same life I don't have to be exactly the same kind of fool. Only another kind!' he said smiling and stood up.

He drove me home. 'When will you be here again, Gordon, do you think?' I had put off asking this, because I was afraid that I could not put it casually enough, but now that we were actually saying good-bye I must risk how it sounded: I must know.

'I can't say. It's impossible to tell beforehand when a job like this will be finished. Depends on the weather up there, and how nearly right I've been in my forecasts, and a lot of other things like the supply of local labour. Then I'm going to Spain as soon as I'm through with this, or before if winter shuts down early up north and the man already working in Spain finds anything else that looks important. And I don't know how long I'll be there. But after that I'll have ten days at home before going on to something else. It may be in five weeks, or months. Anyway, I'll ring you up from Norwich.'

'All right.' I would not wait this time to see him go, but swung our gate behind me hurriedly, and was in the house before I heard his car starting again. I came into the sitting room in time for the tail of the bandit story: the peace interview – ' "Everything in my poor house is yours, señor!" And blast the swine' – Father was telling it to an appreciative audience of a man to whom he hoped to sell Ronald's old one-design dinghy and – to my dull amazement – Lester Cottrell, who had so flustered mother by wandering into the hall, unannounced, in the manner of bygone years, that without meaning to do so she had asked him to stay to lunch in my place. Lester, savouring this situation, had accepted, and the breach between the two families quietly closed, still without any open reference being made to its several causes. (I wondered whether I was now glad or sorry that it had indirectly brought me Gordon.)

268

Father was in great form, having forgotten that the stranger had only come to buy a racing dinghy. The Australian gaol yarn was arduously dragged out of him, and Lester, though he must have heard it before, stayed on to tea. On the pretext of looking up, for our prospective customer, the best roads back to Sedbury, I got out a motoring map of southern England and pored over alternative routes to the north . . .

> 'Oh, Charmian,
> Where think'st thou he is now? Stands he? or sits he?
> Or does he walk? Or is he on his horse –
> Oh, happy horse to bear the weight of Antony!
> Do bravely, horse. . . .'

I decided that the battered Morris should average twenty-seven miles an hour, very good going on a long run, which meant that he would probably sleep at Nottingham or Lincoln.

CHAPTER XIII

ESTHER MACDONALD

In hours spent wandering about in the marshes I could still reach complete self-forgetfulness and be happy, absorbed in the excitement of winter migrations: but otherwise the days seemed over-full of Time that scarcely moved, Time was pressed slowly past me by the weight of heavy hours piled up behind the present empty one, and no longer drawn onwards by the eagerness of minutes ahead, impatient for possession of the present – 'Mrs. Chater . . .' – 'Did you go the field way after all?' – 'Marnie says, will you and Dru . . .'

Birds, besides their ordinary interest for me, now had a secondary value: they became a protection against Marnie, who took me up with the fervour of reaction, for want of better occupation. Some minor throat trouble, due, probably, to those lovingly ignored adenoids and tonsils, was keeping her away from Cambridge for a term. She was run down, and a specialist had forbidden intensive study for a while. She fastened upon me as a creature of weak good-nature who could be made to give her the outlet she needed – gloomy conversation about herself. Fortunately she was shortsighted enough to find boring beyond endurance, even for the sake of my company, the one or two hours which I made her spend in the marshes, peering at distant specks on the horizon. I insisted that we should observe from places ankle-deep in cold ooze, while regretfully agreeing with her that this was hardly the sort of open air morning prescribed by her specialist.

'You know, Lallie, everyone will say the usual things about us for being so much alone together in odd places! Especially at our ages,' she said, her eyes shining with satisfaction like a child's.

I knew by now what 'the usual thing' meant in Marnie's talk. 'No, they won't,' I assured her unkindly, observing a soggier patch of marsh and squelching towards it. 'Hold on to your gum-boots, or they'll be sucked off here.'

'Oh, but they will. Round about six, fifteen and twenty are the recognized "homo" ages in women – in men, of course, they come about two years later . . .'

'Well, but nobody knows that in Pin Mill. Except probably Mr. Quest, and he wouldn't care anyway.'

'They mayn't know about it medically, but they feel it just the same, if they've got any tendencies that way. So they naturally suspect other people. Really, you know, there's *more* vice of all sorts,' said Marnie, with her rather engaging enthusiasm 'among primitive living people than there is in towns, where choice is less restricted. After all, it's a question of opportunity, isn't it? – Look here, this ground's getting softer and softer. Couldn't we go farther that way, where it's firmer?'

'No. Sorry. I was over there yesterday. There must be an up-eddy of air from those trees. The birds go over high. They should be lower here.'

'Well, take the incest figures,' said Marnie, gallantly ploughing her way after me. 'East Anglia's very high. Scattered population and low standards of living. So you can't say they're ignorant about abnormalities in sex – Give me a pull, my boot's stuck – And there must be lots of cases we don't hear of . . .'

'Keep still. Never mind your boot. Keep *still*. That's a diver I don't know. Fishing this way against the tide. I think it's – No, it isn't . . .'

But when I was satisfied about the bird, Marnie, having

kept a bored silence, started again with her favourite kind
of opening, 'The odd thing about me is that as a "pic" type
I should be so purely "hetero" in spite of lack of opportunity . . .'

Brought up, with the greatest care, to see life steadily and
see it whole, or as nearly as possible, she was much more
honest about herself than Dru. She wanted a love affair,
and spoke of it with uncomfortable courage – uncomfortable, because the listener could do so little for her: Marnie
was far too intelligent in her own way to be taken in by
reassurances that she was not as unprepossessing as she
thought. But her clear-seeing did not seem to make her any
happier. Marnie's parents had long and passionately held
the view, widespread among their friends, that the sexual
problems of women could be solved by extending to them
the freedom previously enjoyed by men alone. In their
ideal state there would be, it was assumed, no more thwarted
instincts and their attendant ills. It did not occur to them
that in any such Utopia, with the enjoyment of beautiful
women no longer restricted, the plain girl, to whom promiscuity may at present give some chance of satisfaction,
would have no hope of attracting any amorous attention
at all. In particular, they failed to realize that no amount
of the freedom of mind which they had laboriously implanted
in Marnie was ever going to help the poor girl to live a
normal sex life while the slightest freedom of choice remained to men. In a world of Margarets, Marnie would
find herself more hopelessly handicapped in that way than
she would have been in an Early Victorian household,
where goodness or money or birth might possibly have
offset that loud breathing and porridge-like complexion.

The point at which her surprising honesty broke down,
as it was bound to do somewhere, was that she bitterly
blamed her parents, because to save themselves pain and
anxiety they had managed not to recognize the need of an

early operation on her adenoids and tonsils. No one had the heart to tell her that even had the shape of her nose and mouth been greatly improved, it would have made little difference to the possessor of such hair and eyes.

She was funny, and tragic, and because I did not want to be moved to pity for someone whom I admired in one particular – her comparative lack of self-delusion – I avoided her when I could. The marshes were safe enough from her when one was actually there, and so was Mr. Quest's garden, but on the occasions when she went up to London for treatment by a specialist, it was difficult to get out of her invitations to accompany her in the car, for she knew that I had nothing else to do. It is impossible, in a small country place, to lie successfully about social engagements, and her desire for an audience to whom she could exhibit her mind was strong enough to make her over-ride without mercy any obvious pretences I put up.

She and Lester had a mania for advanced art shows, being at the intellectual stage when any nude is better than no nude, and since Marnie, as a future doctor, could not evince interest in realistic portrayals of flesh, we confined our picture-gazing to the private views of the Cottrells' wilder artist friends. There seemed, however, an extraordinary supply of these, coinciding with the days on which I could not get out of being driven to London by her. I yearned sometimes, while trying to make something of the exhibits, for the astringent company of Mr. Quest. The sole pleasure I derived from these shows was the memory of a woman saying nervously to the artist in front of a design of intertwining limbs 'So so – *relevant*, isn't it?' 'Relevant' would have done for one of the defensive adjectives that Gordon and I had thought of while I sailed him across the Orwell, years ago.

'Let's drop in to see the Macdonalds,' Marnie said carelessly after one of these exhibitions. 'They live near here.'

'Oh, no!'

'Why not? They're great friends of ours – stayed with us – asked me to come along when I was next in London.'..

What excuse could I give? There was none. Somehow I had overlooked this possibility.

I was in a cold sweat of nervous dislike while we waited for Mrs. Macdonald in the drawing-room. But when I really met her – we had only exchanged a few words at the regatta, and then my attention had been elsewhere – I saw unwillingly what Gordon saw: an enthralling person; someone alive and generous-minded who existed not in reference to anyone or anything, but as a complete individual. Something she said of Gordon applied to herself more than to anyone else I knew, even Gordon: she said, as if it were a very rare compliment, 'One of the people who make up their own remarks.' One could not imagine this quick, eager intelligence accepting anything ready-made.

It was Marnie who had brought Gordon's name into the conversation: I did not know whether she did it because she half guessed what those two had been to one another, or because she knew that he was now my friend, and she was pricked by the vague jealousy of a woman at a disadvantage – jealousy of both of us. She told Esther Macdonald, with a pretence of laughter, that I was Gordon's chief attraction in Suffolk now that the Levington pavement had gone. If she expected to discountenance that gay, secure creature, even a little, she failed: at once Esther, who had been merely amusing her guests with an account of former election experiences, became frankly and personally interested in me; and I knew, somehow, that the interest was genuine: kindly deep down, not only on the surface. She was glad that Gordon had found a friend whom she too seemed to think nice. Marnie was left to talk to Macdonald, a man well-informed, I gathered, on every subject which did not interest me personally.

The little limp that Esther had got from a hunting accident seemed unimportant at last. I had thought fiercely, day after day, these last few weeks, How can he love, even mentally, anyone with such a serious bodily defect? How could he ever have loved her physically? But now it seemed entirely unimportant – the right sort of limp if one had to have something of the kind. I found that I could actually think, in her presence, not of Gordon, nor of her with Gordon, but of her alone, or rather of her in this household, which had for me so strange an atmosphere.

This delightful woman, with her handsome, slow, shrewd husband, and their children, one a baby only a few weeks old – they made up another usual-seeming family. But behind what the world saw, lay reserves and secrets that remained secrets in essence, even when one knew the facts. Having seen her, and talked to her with the easy feeling that Gordon had first given me – of all barriers laid down for a friend – I was no nearer to the hidden woman who had gone to Gordon and then borne his child in such retreat and turmoil of spirit. Did even Esther know, in the intimacy of their scarcely-interrupted life together, how much her husband suspected or cared about the dead child? Yes, spiritually, if not in actual circumstances, they were quite an ordinary family.

'Isn't she *splendid?* So soon after the tragedy. (You heard about the dear little girl – ?) Such a *wonderful* mother, I always say,' cooed an elderly canvasser when Marnie and I were left alone with her for a few minutes after tea, because of the sudden piercing howls of the baby upstairs.

('Of course, the canvasser-person is obviously in love with Macdonald, and loathes Esther, but doesn't know it,' Marnie began about this colourless creature on the way home. 'She thinks it's Esther she admires. It's curious, this fetish-transference in unsatisfied women. Though of course the odd thing, in my case . . .')

Before we left, Esther said to me 'Will you come again any time you can?'

'I'd like to,' I said, and was surprised to realize that I meant it.

'Well, Lallie had better come here while I'm having my throat painted next Tuesday.' Marnie loved arranging things for people. 'I'll motor her up. Then we could go on to Andrew's show. You come too, Esther.'

'No.'

'Oh, but he's *good*. Such tremendous energy . . .'

'Five years ago,' said Esther with the kind of firmness that I lacked and envied, 'he painted a charwoman with a much-lain-on air and called it "Madonna". That was his last inspiration.' We did not go to this or any other show of Andrew's work.

I had tea with Esther alone that day and, after an hour or so in her company, was suddenly struck with inward amusement at the absorption with which Gordon's old love and I, having found common ground, were discussing the peculiarity of a snail. It was the most endearing thing about Esther that she could turn her mind to any topic at an instant's notice, talking of it with such seriousness that listeners found themselves taking its importance for granted. She was always full of something, and at the moment it was *Succinea Putris*, the snail that eats, without killing by digestion, the eggs of a fluke which must live every second generation as a parasite in birds. We had started with birds and branched off to the fascinating *Succinea*, and Esther told me about it as though its fate were of far greater moment to her than that of her husband's candidature, which would be decided shortly. As the only living thing which strives to get its young eaten, this fluke creeps through the body of its snail-victim, becoming so closely a part of the host that dissection cannot separate the fibres of the two creatures, and finally distends the snail's horns so that the unlucky

Succinea cannot withdraw them when menaced by a bird. This menace is brilliantly increased by the fluke, which colours the horns, its egg-sacks, with vermilion tips on a green and white stalk – 'What are you laughing at?' Esther asked. (I did not know that my face had moved.) 'I think stunned admiration is the only suitable tribute – oh, well, yes, I suppose it *is* funny that you and I should fraternize – sororize, or whatever the word should be – over *Succinea* with Gordon as a sort of living ghost between us.' It was the only reference she made to the real basis of our friendship, and coming casually like that it staggered me: I had grown unused to such matter-of-fact frankness since Gordon left. She admitted so much, and assumed so much, by those words; an unexpected sharing of secrets. Did I give away my feelings, when his name was mentioned? Had he written to her of how much I knew of the past? She did not tell me, but went on, earnestly, 'But you must listen about this snail-fluke partnership. Just think of the odds against the survival of the fluke's eggs. The horns get snapped off, and if they're eaten by a full-grown bird the eggs die. But there's that one in a hundred chance that they get fed to a nestling, whose digestive juices aren't strong enough to kill them. Then there's a race between the strengthening of the young bird's gastric juices and the development of the flukes. If the eggs win, the second generation of flukes develop in the bird, and the eggs pass out in the droppings, for *Succinea* to start her part of the cycle again. (I feel that the snail must always be a female, somehow – that long, absurd, highly-coloured martyrdom!) Well, think of the odds against the leaf on which the droppings fall being eaten by the only possible victim. Anything else, any other species of snail, even, and they die. But along comes *Succinea* once in a million times. And you know, I do feel that of all the creatures I've ever heard of, a full-grown fluke, thinking back along its ancestry, has the best reason for believing in the care of a benevolent

God. But not, of course, *Succinea*, who has always to be growing new and appetizing horns – Oh, bother, that ring will be my husband's devoted canvasser again, calling for more leaflets. She's sure to stay, too. And I spent so long this morning trying to make sure that she had everything she wanted for the day, so that we shouldn't have anyone else here. It seems impossible ever to be alone in this house! This woman is so dull, and so valuable; she actually canvasses for pleasure. Entertain her for a few minutes while I go up and yearn over the cot to encourage the nurse at feeding time. (My chief occupation is keeping people keen on the jobs I ought to do myself and don't like.) Get her some tea.'

'Impossible to be alone in this house.' How she, to whom candour was natural, must have fretted sometimes against the constant necessity to act, entailed by the presence of other people. Surely there must have been days, shortly after Gordon's child was born and she gave him up, incomprehensibly, when it became very nearly intolerable.

As if this were the house of a friend of long standing, I ordered fresh tea from the maid, and pressed the visitor to make up her mind (she hardly seemed to have one) whether she preferred Indian or China, and then acted as deputy hostess while Esther was upstairs. Gordon's former love – no, his present love, who still kept lightly and carelessly all that I wanted – It seemed hardly possible that, while I talked to the unpaid political tout who had made herself a Cause out of Party intrigue, I was eagerly looking forward to the re-appearance of that charming, limping figure.

For small-talk I asked the visitor if she had met Marnie's family. (I was expecting to be fetched in their car.) The woman did not seem to gather that Marnie was a friend of mine, not only of Esther's.

'Oh yes, of course. You see, I'm such an old friend of the Macdonalds. She'll be the daughter, no doubt, of the Mrs.

Cottrell with whom Mrs. Macdonald's best friend -- such a sweet woman -- shared a flat for a bit before she married. Before dear Mrs. Macdonald married, I mean. Mrs. Cottrell, of course, was married, and so was Mrs. Macdonald's friend. . . .' Here followed a long and pointless anecdote about the unknown friend: how could Esther go on with this existence, living day after day among uncongenial people, when she must have kept some feeling for Gordon -- how much I did not know -- and knew that he still cared for her? . . . 'Mrs. Macdonald was a Sieveking, you know. A Surrey family. But Mrs. Cottrell was, I think, a Londoner. No, I'm wrong. . . .'

'You can't be meaning Marnie's mother, Mrs. Cottrell of Pin Mill, because her husband's alive now, so if she was already married then, she wouldn't have been sharing with another woman, would she?' (Charming person whom I had expected to loathe, come down and make human intercourse mean something again: in your house these pointless questions sound even more futile than they do at home.)

'Oh, but she was. It was when she left her husband.'

'She left . . .? Mrs. Cottrell?'

'Oh, *nicely* you know. I mean -- I've always been so close to the Macdonalds, ever since Carlyle said -- of course I don't call him Carlyle in public: "Our Member" ha! ha! So absurd, isn't it, when we've been such pals for years? He said, "I've got a surprise for you, Bertha" (that's my name) and introduced his fiancée: so I know all about their friends. There wasn't another man, or anything like that. She just wanted to leave him and earn her own living. Such an artistic woman -- those wonderful wall papers. . . .'

'Are you talking of Mrs. Cottrell?' Esther asked as she came in.

'Yes, I was just telling Miss -- er -- that there wasn't anything *unpleasant* in her leaving her husband. And perhaps it was just as well she couldn't make enough to live on, though personally I loved her designs, because then she *had* to go back to him, and I hear. . . .'

'Oh, don't! You make her sound like a whore,' said Esther angrily. 'She went back because of the children. And it wasn't "just as well". It was damnable.' There was more heat than the situation demanded. She, too, had gone back, and rebuilt a life that she had thought ended. I knew more of her then – as much, perhaps, as I could ever know of another person – from the sound of that 'It was damnable'. Conversation had certainly acquired meaning again. The visitor sat seething for a few minutes, replying to my questions about the forthcoming election in monosyllables, and then got up to go.

'I say, haven't you made an enemy of your devoted canvasser?'

'Not more than before.' Esther was undisturbed on that score. 'She never could bear me anyway. And you know, it really pays a candidate's wife to be at loggerheads with all the best female supporters. Then they work much harder on their own for "that poor man". An appeal to their protective instincts. This is Carlyle's fourth election, counting "bye's", and really I think he's won them all so far largely because the women turned maternal and combative for him, seeing how badly I let him down. She'll just go and kiss a lot more babies in the constituency, thinking "For *him*!" – Hullo, Marnie.'

Reaction set in after I reached home. This was a woman whom I should have loved to have as a friend, with no ghost between us. But away from her, the ghost grew stronger. In her presence I could think how delightful she was: out of it, only that she was the person for whom Gordon cared.

I must do something – anything – or I shall forget that I liked her, and something nice will have gone, I told myself, wandering aimlessly about the house. Finding no other distraction I sat down and wrote a letter to the *Times*, describing with heavy playfulness the extraction of the crust from the skua-gull's throat by the fire-crested wren, modelling the style on Lester's 'gems'.

Ronald's unexpected return on long leave put it more or less out of my mind for two days, and I was surprised when Lester showed it to me in the *Points from Letters* column. My surprise was nothing to my family's. I had not realized their respect for print of any kind. Publication raised the gull-and-crust story from something so dull that they would not listen when I tried to relate it personally, into a matter for modest boasting when mother went out to tea in the neighbourhood: 'Did you see my daughter's letter in the *Times*? . . . Oh, the bird-watcher one. . . . Such an extraordinary incident, wasn't it? . . . Always been her hobby . . . Only brains in the family, I'm afraid!' (Self-deprecating Rushness set in here.) 'Don't know where she gets them!' (Until this happened Ronald had always been the brains of the family, and was again as soon as the excitement had subsided.)

Though almost equally impressed, he took it in a different way. 'I hope to God no one in the ship thinks it's me. They know I come from Pin Mill. You won't be doing this often, will you?'

'Oh, I don't suppose so,' I said airily, knowing that I had nothing else to write to the *Times* about, but unwilling to relinquish any of my new prestige.

'Well, for goodness' sake put "Lalage" in full. Then I can say it's only an aunt, or something. Otherwise you'll get me routed out every time I go below and the first lieutenant spots a couple of arse-up ducks in the harbour – his compliments to Mr. Rush, and wouldn't he like to come and observe them from a southerly aspect?'

Dru was immensely proud, though her pride had to take the form of belittling the supposed achievement: one of her family doing something in a London newspaper! Betty

281

Chater asked me to sign her autograph album. Margaret, when forced to take notice of the letter at last, thought the fuss very silly, and I was curiously disappointed, while agreeing with her. Lester's comments were more subtly condemning, in the form of over-courteous congratulations. I wriggled under them but found no adequate reply.

Ronald's experience with Lester this leave was rather like mine with Marnie: in the first flush of family reunion Lester sought him out constantly. Still, fixed hours in an architect's office in Ipswich prevented Lester from being so overwhelming in his friendship. Finding nothing to do in Pin Mill, Ronald unwisely agreed to a week-end walking tour round Wendover and Tring where the Cottrells had friends. After years of disdain for all forms of hearty exercise, Lester was now in the throes of the Stevenson-Borrow revival of tramping among intellectual young men: Nature was to be rescued from the moron classes. He and Ronald arranged to sleep soft in private houses, proving their open-roadhood by day, when they planned to cover incredible distances.

Mother was sorry to see him go, even from Friday to Monday out of a three weeks' stay. She did not know that Ronald was only with us so long because of the falling through of an invitation, and loved having her two handsome men about her, with friends commenting again on the likeness. For the first time for years they were getting on excellently.

The failure of the tramp, on account of rain and lost bearings, sleet, blisters and finally snow, brought Ronald home on Sunday afternoon, furious, steaming, and with a sore throat, into the middle of a tea-party of local residents thrilled by the stories of the two tremendous Swedish sailors whom father had fetched off a Russian timber-ship in the river: father was capping most of their yarns. The tale of the Charterhouse soccer kit was held up by Ronald's entrance but father welcomed him genially, giving up the best place

282

by the fire: at Ronald's age he would not have got tonsilitis from exposure: a well-disposing reflection. 'What luck?'

'Bloody awful,' mouthed Ronald silently, and winced as he swallowed hot tea. His voice came back unexpectedly in a hoarse undertone, 'Christ – that ass Lester!'

'Ronald!' protested mother, who really liked to hear nice men swear: it was male of them, and the maler a nice man was, the nicer. The lower classes were different; she had not been enjoying the conversation of the sailors: 'Damn' said by a man who spat into the fire was nasty language.

People demanded the end of the soccer kit story, but father postponed it to hear Ronald's disgusted account of Lester parading through the rain with his artistic shirt still open to the waist, foretasting lyrically, much as Ronald himself talked about beer, the pleasures of a glass of milk at the next village. Probably their conversation was equally insincere; both were conventional, but Lester's was the newer convention. What each enjoyed was not so much his chosen beverage as the picture of himself consuming it beneath the blackened beams of fire-lit bar-parlours, listening to the heavy speech of wise and weathered yokels.

The guffaws of the yokels over the milk was music in Lester's ears, but not in Ronald's. And Ronald, after drinking much more beer than he wanted (he went off it for several days afterwards in consequence) had caught this appalling cold while Lester had stayed infuriatingly fit. Ronald had finished with Lester.

'. . . Bellocing about the shires, looking like a nursing father!' he said, inspired to eloquence by his annoyance. The phrase had an immense success. 'Oh, lovely!' said everyone, and repeated it admiringly; all but the two sailors to whom it meant nothing, and father, who became bored with the soccer kit story and finished it lamely.

'Bellocing about the shires, looking . . .' That was not only his sort of joke – unexpected flamboyance – it was just

283

a little wittier than anything he ever managed. People hung on Ronald's grimacing whispers as he went on, in spite of the pain, making a very funny story out of his misfortunes on the road . . . The interesting fellow. . . .

Father went out to answer the telephone at once when it rang, instead of waiting for one of us to go. He came back looking mystified. 'Quest has asked himself to supper!' he said.

'*Mr.* Quest?' 'Good heavens!' 'Oh, no, Arthur,' said mother, 'It must be Basil, home for the week-end.'

I was sure that it was not Basil, because he had written to me from Cambridge on the Saturday, arranging to motor over the following week. Besides, no one could confuse his beefy voice with his father's thin, precise tones.

'Family likenesses come out on the 'phone when they don't anywhere else,' suggested a visitor.

'Oh, Betty, those two just haven't *anything* in common,' said Dru quickly: she saw no charms in Mr. Quest.

'After living opposite a man's garden wall for fifteen years, I ought to know who he is when he says who he is, oughtn't I?' father asked testily. 'Basil would hardly address me as "Rush". At least I hope not: one never knows nowadays.'

'Perhaps he thought you were Ronnie – he may have heard about the leave,' said mother, who had the unneighbourliness of Mr. Quest too firmly fixed in mind to relinquish the pleasing idea that Basil was willing to motor fifty miles on a snowy afternoon for the chance of seeing her son.

The identity of the guest had not been settled by the time that Margaret and I left for a cinema party in Ipswich – a film had been 'shot' locally, in which two of father's boats figured accidentally, to our great excitement. Mother and Olive were performing wonders in the kitchen: there would be tinned salmon puff again, in case the unbelievable

had happened, and it was really Mr. Quest. Basil would
only get cold mutton.

I was sorry to be out of the way, but not even the hope of
assisting at a local miracle would make me miss this evening
with Margaret and the Reddiland group. I was with
Margaret as much as possible in these days, watching her
more intently than usual, not only now for the disturbing
joy of her beauty. I wanted to notice minutely everything
about her, both when she was alone with us and when she
was with men, particularly with men. I would see as clearly
as possible – perhaps it was not possible to see at all ? –
what look, or movement, or expression of hers carried the
quality which made her different from me –that quality
which had nothing to do with her loveliness, but told men
like Gordon that here was casual pleasure for the taking,
an hour's amusement and the satisfaction of sexual vanity,
if nothing more, with no aftermath of pain. Margaret did
not seem to break hearts very thoroughly, though she took
them easily enough: even Basil Quest, shocked into surprising clear-sightedness by her behaviour at the dance to
which Gordon had gone, seemed to be recovering from his
infatuation more rapidly than was to be expected at his
age. But then his infatuation was really with the whole
Rush family. He had briefly tried Dru, and then turned
more ardently to Margaret as an object for admiration.
He was now taking the one remaining chance of expressing
by proxy his hero-worship of father. I received pages of
athletic news from him nearly every week, and letter-writing
to Basil was purgatory. His style had progressed little
beyond the formulas of his schoolboy letters to mother,
father's first deputy in his affections. Then it had been,
'Last Saturday our first eleven played their second eleven.
We won, three goals to two. It is raining to-day. My nose
bled in chapel. Next Saturday our second eleven . . .'
Now it was, 'My sticky finish . . . getting my hands away . . .

Sometimes wonder if I went into training too soon this year.
. . . Rather worried about my left.' Presumably these were in
some sort love-letters, unlikely as it seemed; one could not
imagine why Basil wrote them if they were not. Once, in
the bravado of self-victory, he added a postscript: 'Give my
love to Margaret.' The scars must be healing nicely.

Even Tom Reddiland, who was supposed to be wildly in
love with her, and was to be found hanging about our house
at all hours, did not appear to mind, this evening, that she
gave most of her attention to his younger brother Sandy.
Perhaps it was because she gave so little of it to anyone,
really, and gave that to the first-comer – Not a woman
to arouse jealousy as easily as she aroused desire. Narrowly
I observed them together: was it that remote half-smile,
turning to something more personal as she laughed at a joke
of his? – That lazy reserve of body, which made her put out
an arm only, not follow the movement with her shoulders as
the other, livelier girls did, when coats were handed along
the line of places in the cinema? — The way her eyes had of
resting, neither interested nor abashed, on any other eyes
that caressed her? – Her eyes, which seemed when they
looked full at you to be seeing something else, an unimportant
yet rather pleasant thing that was nothing to do with you,
existing only in her mind: so that you could not really make
her see you when you wanted to, but only on the rare
occasions when she wanted to look at you. – Was it here, the
thing I longed to understand?

Tom Reddiland was twenty-six, and would be very well
off indeed when his uncle died: already he had more money
at his disposal than any young man we knew. It was thought
that he would marry Margaret: by their special friends
they were already treated in a subtly different way from the
other recognized couples in that crowd, who might pair off
differently at any time: it seemed that this was a serious
affair. But when Dru, giggling because of the rumour's

'dullness' repeated to Margaret some gossip about an engagement, Margaret said casually, 'Oh, and to Uncle Tom Cobley an' all, I suppose!' and then laughed in the way that always shocked me.

How well did he know her? Was he the only one? My thoughts fretted on this as they had done in the orchard. I was tormented by uneasy curiosity in those days. His hands – his kisses – What was possession to her; fierce joy, or little beyond the fulfilment of a physical need, which alone had importance in her mind, so that the man was scarcely more than the means of ending desire, a bearer of peace?

At long intervals, through an exceptionally bad film, came flashes of a quality which made the rest seem more tawdry in comparison, just as Margaret's rare, high wisdom made her witticisms so unbearable – a glimpse of men in a shipbuilders' foundry, gnomes handling molten metal with grand dexterity, used only as a background to some emotional imbecility; and the lean, eager lines of our boats butting through a head sea off Harwich, as they raced (father in a wild mood was aboard one, and Dru had charge of the other) across the bows of the tug which was officially in the picture. And then my thoughts were freed from Margaret for a new bondage, Gordon's. All things lovely and exciting were Gordon to me at this period; for a long while there had been no meaning but Gordon in far horizons and a heron's flight and the gracious bowing of branches in the wind that stripped the garden; now he was one with these small accidents of beauty, surprising me in the midst of futility. I could not escape anywhere from the want of him, save briefly, by an effort of will, down on the marshes. And then sometimes he came unfairly, in a sudden thinning of clouds on a wet day, in the smell of the earth after rain, when I was not armoured against the realization of desire.

The others were whispering and laughing round me,

making fun of the film, poor even from their point of view. The need to be a social success, for once, rescued me from present loneliness. I must exert myself if I were to live down the new highbrow reputation I had acquired, a reputation appalling in this set – that of a girl who wrote nature notes for the *Times*. Horses and dogs were proper interests, according to their standards; even rabbits, I discovered, were permissible; one girl, whom Tom was making much of, bred Angoras for profit without apparently losing her lowbrow status, but for some reason birds were definitely 'brainy'. Ordinarily I knew that when Margaret was about I was bound to be a social failure, especially among such people, and I did not mind more than a little: this evening it mattered. I wanted, if I could not be like her, at least to be accepted by the people who accepted her. I was surprised by my success, heartened and yet made self-contemptuous by hearing my voice saying things which they thought funny – thin sallies about the film, and when it was over, a dissertation on its sickly moral in the manner of a comic curate, followed by a summary of the plot in rhyme, which caught on at once:

> It was rush-hour in the brothel,
> (Woman's work is Never Done:
> Pray that Providence's wrath'll
> Make men pay for All Their Fun)

Some strain of jealousy in me was eased by the proof that I could, if necessary, be as brightly silly as they were: sillier. Somehow it was necessary, just then, for my self-esteem. They were generous in their efforts to make up for having thought me what I really was, the unattractive sister, whom they must sometimes tolerate, lest Margaret should not be allowed to come. I went home with my head a little turned by my first taste of general popularity, knowing that when at leisure I had time to remember all I had said – and all the things I really liked about which I had been funny for lack of other topics – the taste would be stale and rather nauseating.

It was so, but I had other things to think of the next morning, so that this particular shame of adolescence passed lightly – The visitor had been Mr. Quest himself. Making no excuses for previous unfriendliness, he had come straight to the point: a Swiss educational expert, who worked in Basle and Edinburgh, wanted an English-speaking secretary. General intelligence was the main qualification – one of those vague qualifications which make a post difficult to fill. Feeling that it was useless to apply to an agency, he had sent a flowery cable for advice to his esteemed colleague in England. Moved by the inclusion, at threepence a word, of assurances of distinguished sentiments, and a reply form prepaid for thirty-six words, Mr. Quest proposed to be help-ful at once. As I had spent eighteen months in Brussels, presumably I wrote and spoke French with some fluency: should he recommend me or a woman he knew in London for the job? He had only stayed about half-an-hour after supper, being particularly busy, but to my surprise I found that he had completely conquered my parents. Basle and Edinburgh! It would be like living in another world: and a world of intellectual activity into which none of us had ever dreamed of penetrating. The salary Mr. Quest thought far too small: paid in francs it would come to just under four pounds a week: but that was nearly double what I could expect to earn in Ipswich. It seemed excellent to us. And while in Basle, the secretary was to live with the family, pleasant acquaintances of Mr. Quest's. Escape! My first feeling was one of slight sickness. Escape, with no battle, no hurting of feelings! It need not matter to me any longer what Mrs. Chater said: in Edinburgh one would not hear; in Basle one could not be questioned about it, aimlessly, tenderly, inexorably.

'Of course it need only be a temporary arrangement,' said mother. 'I mean, if you found you didn't like living so far away . . .' I had merely to agree.

'I wasn't too keen about the idea to Mr. Quest,' she added. 'After all, as I told him, you have your hobby and just now, when you're beginning to make something of it. . . .'

'Oh, mother, you didn't show him that cutting!' I said nervously.

'He'd seen it himself. And as I told him, we'd been reading only the other day of that girl in Norfolk who watches birds half the year and has a wonderful job as a curator in a museum, for the rest of the time: six hundred pounds a year. You said yourself it was the nicest job you ever heard of. Still of course . . . educational psychology. . . .' (It would be very pleasant, apparently, to talk of 'My daughter, the one who is secretary to such a brilliant man – most interesting job – lucky we sent her to school abroad . . .') 'You'd better go over and see Mr. Quest now, dear, he'll tell you all about it. He was so sorry you weren't in last night.'

No, I did not want to hear any more details of a way of escape that had come too late. I realized that it was too late while mother was talking. Perhaps in a few days now, as it was over five weeks since he left, or in a few months, Gordon would reappear for little more than a week, and then go off again on his wanderings. We were not on terms which made it possible for me to say, 'You must let me know a long time before you come, weeks before if possible, so that by some means I can arrange to be with you!' He had not even asked me to write to him, and had sent no word himself: he wanted nothing from me, save occasional companionship. But that I could not give if I went away now; now, when things were transitional between us, or so I believed at times, and at times dared not even hope.

I walked unannounced into Mr. Quest's study. He was

at work and did not look up for more than a second when I said abruptly, 'I can't take that job.'

'No? Well, it doesn't matter: there's another woman who'll do. I only thought of you because you wanted to get away. All that love . . . That's why I talked round your people.'

'Thank you, Mr. Quest. I mean, thank you very much indeed. It was awfully good of you. I'm sorry. I did want to – I do want to – you see . . .'

Mr. Quest slowly swivelled round in his chair and looked at me. 'I think,' he said, 'that you are about to tell me what you had much better not. You'll only regret it. Go away instead. I am in the middle of something interesting, and it doesn't in the least matter to me whether you take the job or not. To-morrow, however, we will go and have an ideally indigestible meal at the Falcon, and talk of something else. I shall then have been working at stress almost continuously for a week. On top of a period of this kind, lobster thermidor always brings on a sort of gastric aphasia. Or indeed, anything but the plainest food. I can do nothing afterwards but sit sleepily reading newspapers by the fire, while the attacking juices skirmish round the lump of intractable fare. We will have lobster thermidor. Write to the Falcon to-night in my name, ordering it for 1.15, will you? This is the pleasantest way of ensuring myself a holiday when a fit of energy outlives its use. I shall only work badly if I keep at it to-morrow. But I will to-day. Run along.'

He murmured something as I went – 'What? I didn't hear.'

'Bortch,' he said, 'And bortch, tell them: with the cream separately.'

I also put in tangerine ice-soufflé on my own, because we had had it the first time I lunched there with him and I had been unable to appreciate it, coming at the end of that meal. I did not see why I should not have some of the lesser blessings in life – Gordon would think that attitude funny.

To-day of all days. Gordon, Gordon, Gordon! – even when I tried deliberately to think of trivial things that left no room for him, he crept like this into my mind. I could not keep to myself the feeble private jokes which everyone tries to enjoy alone, at times, in order to make some days bearable. In the quiet of my own room, after I had explained to my disappointed family that psychology was not in my line and bird-watching was, I put my head down on the table, careless of smudging the postcard about the tangerine soufflé, and cried because Gordon's image was not fair, like Gordon himself. Gordon – real Gordon in Skye, or Spain perhaps by now – would not hurt anyone in little ways if he could help it, but the special Gordon in my thoughts did: wanting nothing, taking everything, Basle – Edinburgh – escape – even to the passing interest of a grand meal with Mr. Quest. Nothing was free of him: to-day not even birds.

I took a dinghy down river and across to Decoy Point. Very little was moving: it was soft weather for the end of the year, so that the winter migrants had not been driven inland on their way south. I saw them drifting like the shadows of clouds, far out over the quiet sea beyond the harbour entrance; and could not even guess at their kind by watching to see whether they hung low over the water, making a scalloped fringe to the sky by their sweeping flight, or came straight and high in small formations, or straggled up and down the wind in great formless companies – for claiming all my attention came the image of Gordon, saying: It was not for my sake that you made this stupid sacrifice, I did not want it. It is your choice alone if you let all your days slide by as empty as this one.

I went home and spent the afternoon in arguing with my family, who were all for my accepting the secretarial job by now; and the evening in concocting something much more striking than the gull-and-crust story for the *Morning Post*.

This was published on the day following my enormous lunch with Mr. Quest.

True to his prophecy, he spent the morrow of the meal in a state of lethargy, bordering on nervous exhaustion, sitting in a dressing-gown by the fire reading newspapers. He gave me the cutting when I went over in the afternoon to inquire about the progress of the lobster thermidor, of which we had both eaten hugely: but it had no after-effects on me. 'It feels about half-way down, now. A large hard ball, perhaps half an inch smaller in circumference than it was at this hour yesterday. Doing nicely. This,' he said, tapping the printed letter, 'is a very sound idea, Lalage,' and he returned to his busman's holiday, reading for pleasure the notes on Handling the Child Mind in the women's pages of the *Daily Mail*. Whether or not he realized that my note described a wholly imaginary incident, I could not be certain. At lunch the previous day we had avoided all personal topics: but on the way home in the car he said: 'I'm afraid you may have trouble with your people, now that they've come round to the idea of your getting a job right away from Pin Mill. I should fall back on Nature, hard, if I were you.'

CHAPTER XIV

EXPEDIENCIES

TEN days later, when mother grew worried again because I had thrown away a marvellous chance, as it seemed to her, I supplied another gem for Lester's collection of cuttings from the *Times*. This sort of thing is easy for anyone with the smallest specialized knowledge of wild life; I knew just enough to keep on the plausible side of improbability, sprinkling in a few facts to carry conviction. If I wrote of the remarkable death of a hen-harrier, a local bird with the characteristic of turning on its back to fight, which had rammed its beak through the breast of one of the clay decoy widgeon used in the winter by punt-gunners, and drowned before it could extricate itself, I could not be required to prove my statement by producing another bird suicide in similar conditions in front of witnesses. But to amuse myself I avoided making any false statements, even though they could not be checked. I merely asked, Would your readers be interested to hear that, etc.? Well, would they? I could not imagine it myself; considering that for the sake of publication I always gave the stories an offensively humanized 'Mr-and-Mrs.-Bird' atmosphere; but apparently they were. Throughout the winter and early spring I did not write one letter about 'our feathered friends' which was not published. Mother and Dru were gratified by the number of snippets from various papers sent to us by relatives and friends in their letters. (We only took the *Daily Sketch* ourselves.)

Apparently they did not realize that as letters to the editor were not paid contributions, their appearance in print implied no particular standard of merit.

'But darling, why didn't you ever tell us you'd seen this adder and cormorant fighting on the sea-wall?' said mother, 'It must have been exciting!' This was one of my freer fancies, which Mrs. Chater had saved me the trouble of showing to mother myself.

'Well, I did try about the skua-gull with the crust. . . .' She seemed a little abashed, and I was sorry.

These letters quieted mother's uneasy new feeling (at least as far as I was concerned) that perhaps after all her girls ought to 'do something', like other post-War women. Everything that I had once argued for in vain, day after day, Mr. Quest had brusquely accomplished in half an hour's talk over Sunday supper. It was annoying, now that I wanted to stay at home, to hear frequent discussion of the sort of jobs which my parents would like to see me filling.

Dru was exempt from this moral pressure for the moment; she could not be spared from the boats, particularly now that I had slacked off sailing almost entirely. (After one very mild threat of appendix trouble in the summer – it was probably wind – I had managed to make our amiable doctor agree that seasickness might bring it on again.) I could parade my hobby which, it was assumed, would no doubt lead to a distinguished six hundred a year post in due course. But Margaret was not so protected. She was talked at a good deal on this subject for a while. 'Using the house as an hotel' gave place to 'Surely you want to do something more than idle about in other people's cars?' when anything happened to harrass mother unduly. Margaret settled this in her own way, though her choice of this moment for her escape from home was probably a coincidence: she was not easily moved by talk. She came in one day with her feet muddy to the ankle, and sat tugging off her slippery goloshes in the hall.

'Wherever have you been, darling? Through the fields?'

'To Chandler's. The short way. I wanted to send a telegram.' Questioning left no marks on this serene, alien spirit.

'Oh, dear, in this weather! Why the hurry?'

'Couldn't get Sandy on the 'phone about this afternoon. The Reddilands' line is out of order.' Margaret was bending forward limberly from the chair to wipe mud off her fingers on the hall mat. Her voice came muffled so that we missed one or two of the next words '. . . about meeting . . . engaged.'

'Sandy is? How jolly.' Mother was always pleased by engagements. 'To anyone we know?'

Margaret sat up, her face faintly flushed for a second by the stooping position, surprising me afresh with her loveliness. The colour faded to her ordinary pallor. 'I'm engaged to him,' she said. 'He wants us to get married rather soon because he's going out to the Madras branch of the firm . . .'

So she was taking the younger; not the brother to whom the bulk of the money would come in due course. But why had she chosen Sandy, less good-looking, less wild and amusing, less a little everything than Tom?

In spite of the sharp eyes focused on him by everyone in the neighbourhood in the days that followed, no one could make out what Tom himself felt about the engagement, the announcement of which surprised us all. There may have been more in the young man than I suspected, and he was an accomplished actor, for he seemed geniality itself, fooling with Margaret about his broken heart, and making the running with the girl I had noticed that evening in the cinema as the object of his temporary attention. Was he generously trying to stop the local gossip that his brother had taken her from him without his suspecting what was going on, or had he found in time that what he had already had from Margaret was all that he wanted of her?

But still, from Margaret's point of view, why Sandy, even if she were disappointed over Tom? At her age she could well afford to wait. Pique, perhaps? Possibly she really loved Sandy, but that was an explanation which did not naturally occur to me when thinking of Margaret; and yet I knew that one of the things which no one could ever tell for certain about another person was the point where genuine feeling would over-ride all self-interest. She called him darling, seemed contented when she was with him: but then she had always worn that look of secret content in her eyes. Most of her talk was of India ('Fancy me with a lot of native servants!') or of the arrangements for the wedding.

These must be hurried on if she was to go out with him when he took up his new post in the Reddiland's family business, and as both families professed themselves delighted by the engagement there was no reason for delay, absurdly young as Margaret was then – only nineteen. But one could not think of her as in any way immature.

There was no doubt that Sandy was in love with her – had been from the beginning, people said now, and agonizingly jealous of his brother. 'Damned if I'd go out to India and leave something like that behind!' said Sandy's uncle to father when they were discussing the financial settlement. 'Shouldn't expect to find her free in six months' time! Loveliest girl I've seen for years.' All the Reddilands seemed to think so. They wanted a big London wedding to show her off and a reception from their town house, but again, to my puzzlement, Margaret said she preferred the idea of Ipswich, where all her friends could come to see her married. Was this pride, because father could not afford to do his share on a grand scale, or genuine simplicity? I could not discover. But any wish she expressed was law; Ipswich it must be. However, the Reddilands were not to be baulked of their display. Sandy might not be the heir, but he was a son of the

only county family in those parts whose fortune had survived the war: the biggest Catholic church available, five
bridesmaids in dresses from Bond Street, the historic County
Hall for the reception since their house was some way out
of the town – if Margaret really wanted simplicity she was
not going to get it.

Time passed in a rush of ordering and organizing, which
consoled mother a little for the prospect of losing her
youngest child almost without warning. For the first time
since her own marriage she could enjoy an orgy of buying
the best, regardless of price: Sandy, who had fifteen hundred
a year apart from his handsome salary, had sensibly insisted
on paying for the trousseau, in which mother took more
apparent interest than Margaret.

I was glad of the occupation of packing quantities of
china and household silver in crates for safe transit – 'One
simply can't trust shops,' said mother, with an inherited
experience of going out to every part of the Empire. It made
the days slip by, and for once I felt that every hour passed
was something gained. It was early March, and Gordon
had been gone for nearly five months. Any day now. Any
day, as I had felt for the last six weeks. But surely each day
made it more likely that the 'phone would ring, and for
once it would not be Sandy asking for Margaret; nor Basil
Quest ringing up sheepishly from Cambridge to say that his
colleg ight had started 10-18-35½, against the wind, and six
had stopped shooting his slide. He just thought father might
like to hear – er . . . Poor lad, he had to tell somebody and
one could not imagine this sort of message being received in
his own home with the courtesy, bored but invariable,
which it was sure to get in ours, unless Margaret answered
the 'phone.

My dishonest softness in pretending an interest in the
progress of the Caius crew encouraged Basil to make a
nuisance of himself. I had always envied the foresight

with which people like Margaret avoided my initial mistake of seeming over-sympathetic with everyone; and so also avoided the horrible moments when I had to hurt people unnecessarily by telling the truth much too late. At this period, Stella was offended with me because she had just discovered my lack of enthusiasm for chickens, which I had dissembled for years; and Marnie was annoyed because, my nerves taut with waiting, I had suddenly burst out one day, 'Oh, shut up about yourself for a bit!' and Lester now knew that I did not see the fun of half his newspaper 'gems' and presumably despised me for having laughed when he first read them.

Sooner or later there was bound to come an hour when Basil's assumption of my affection would grow intolerable. Like a fool I had let him kiss me, the Sunday that he had arranged to drive over from Cambridge for the day. It was so soon after I had refused the Basle and Edinburgh job that I had not the heart to keep up the flow of light chatter which was the only means of keeping Basil's endearments in check. I was growing surprisingly good at turning this on, as from a tap. At his suggestion we had gone out in my dinghy, because from the first I had not sufficient energy to exert my will against his, and the wind, blowing his clothes tight against his magnificent body, made him unexpectedly attractive. He was always impervious to cold, and went sailing even in March with his sleeves rolled away from massive arms. I rather enjoyed his love-making on this occasion, though casual kissing could not stir me now as it had done once, but at least I could shut my eyes and half pretend for a few seconds. Thereafter Basil began a horrifying monologue, rambling through repeated assurances that a girl must not think a decent sort of fellow would ever think less of her for allowing him to kiss her, though some sort of cad might . . .

'Oh no, surely, Basil, not in these days.'

But at the moment Basil was not in these days but well back in the Romance ages – A decent sort of fellow would only think it absolutely grand of her and put her on a higher sort of pedestal than ever. So that a girl need not feel . . .

'A girl wouldn't – doesn't – I don't.'

'Oh, that's all right then,' said Basil happily, and prepared to go on kissing me indefinitely.

Made irritable by the difficulty of successful pretence, I won peace for the moment by temporizing feebly. All the same, I said, to do much of 'that sort of thing' was a mistake unless people really cared for each other. Why, I could not think; but the remark served for that day. It gave Basil's mind, which worked like the Mills of God, something to turn over, and back in Cambridge he turned it over to some purpose in the intervals of rowing practice. All that was required, he concluded, was to convince me of the reality of his esteem. A costly two-seater made little of the fifty miles between Cambridge and Pin Mill, and as a third-year man he had exeat privileges; at every meeting I was driven from one untenable moral position to another in my efforts to disguise my growing distaste for the thought of his kisses. Basil had a gift of relentless logic which only rudeness could combat.

No one but myself, I felt, would have lost ground so rapidly as to be in a position, by the middle of the following vacation, when Basil could and did take it for granted that now only the finest ethical scruples restrained me from becoming his mistress. For these scruples he revered me increasingly while attempting to persuade me of their unreasonableness. 'But, Lallie, I've often heard you say . . .' and 'Well, if you think that, I don't see how you can . . .' Somehow, with more than my usual skill, I had at least managed to convey that while I clung to them, any active love-making from him would be an unfair temptation to me, obscuring the moral issue. He was much too nice to try and take advantage of this. In some ways Basil was a dear creature, which made my skips from precarious foothold to foothold down the steep slopes of courtesy more alarming, now that I could at last see clearly the edge of the waiting precipice. It was coming very close. Almost anyone else would have realized its presence before venturing on the slopes at all.

The end of the vacation would see Margaret married. 'Such mind as my son possesses,' Mr. Quest observed to me one day, 'seems to be deranged by the imminence of his loss. Yesterday I was discussing with him the possibility of enlarging the garage in order to take in Stella's confounded truck, and he said "Yes, that's first rate. And suppose Lallie ever wants a car of her own, could we find room for it next to yours?" Are we to infer from this that he has matrimonial designs for you and me?'

I was glad that for once Mr. Quest's sharp eyes had failed him. He had formerly observed that his son was in love with Margaret, and as there had been no perceptible interval of recovery in Basil's state of sexual coma, he assumed that the cause was still Margaret. I laughed as heartily as I could manage, feeling ashamed of my part in this stupid business.

But as a counter-irritant it may have been of some value. Like packing and labelling frantically for Margaret, it prevented time from hanging as heavily as it would have done otherwise. About half way through March, I think it was, my brittle faith in Time gave way. It had so little to sustain it. The full five months had now gone, and Gordon had not come. I was gradually overwhelmed by a doubt that grew to certainty in my mind. The days that passed were not bringing him nearer, but instead carrying me farther and farther from the time, already past, when he had returned to Norwich and thought, perhaps, of seeing me, but other things, more interesting, had distracted him from his first intention. Perhaps the intention had never been very strong; and only my hope had made of it a promise.

I could not rest once the idea that he had already come and gone again from Norwich took hold of me. There was no one of whom I could safely inquire. Had his people been on the telephone I would have risked asking them about his return, speaking as a stranger and giving no name: but the four Summers in the Norwich directory were no relations of his, I found, when I was driven to trying them all. There was Esther Macdonald – it was odd that she of all people, the woman he loved, was my first thought – but she was away for a week, I learnt, when casually I suggested to Marnie that we might go and see her. And in that week, because I was already upset by the doubt, came the moment when Marnie irritated me beyond bearing and I was thoroughly unkind at last, breaking our renewed friendship.

After the Macdonalds were presumably back, I could not ask the incensed Marnie to drive me to London. I could not write to Esther, asking her for news – what could I say? It would be practically impossible in a note, written on some other pretext, to make the inquiry sound casual enough to satisfy my pride, and even if I did it would probably be treated as casual inquiries are in letters; ignored. Then I could not ask again. There was no excuse for taking a train to London by myself, now, when mother and Margaret were planning all their shopping in as few visits as possible, to save father some of the inevitable expenses of the marriage.

Eventually, desperate, I went to Mr. Quest. 'Are you motoring up to London soon?'

'No. Too cold at this time of the year. I prefer the train.'

'Well . . .'

'Well, what?' Mr. Quest looked at me chillingly. I had struck a bad morning. Stella and her three jolly partners had been staying for the week-end, and had exasperated Mr. Quest into a general dislike of all young people.

'Will you, please? Because I want to go, very badly, and unless I can say you asked me to come in the car, I've no excuse to give them at home.'

'No, I will not,' said Mr. Quest. 'You have got a nerve, young woman!'

I went away disconsolately and then came back, when he had resumed work. 'Toss you best out of three,' I suggested boldly. 'And if I win, will you make Archer take me? I can pretend it was your invitation.'

'Certainly not. Why should I? In any case you ought to know by now my distaste for sporting offers. Go away, and put the mat up against the outside of the door when you shut it. I've told the servants twice about that draught, but no one in this house does any work except myself . . .'

'And you only do it for fun. I don't suppose your work is of the least value to anyone but yourself.' It was easy, and pleasant for a change, to be strong-minded with someone whose feelings could not possibly be hurt.

'I dare say you're right,' said Mr. Quest, weighing my opinion seriously. 'I'm not sure. There are some results – still we won't go into this now. The justification is that, as you say, I do get fun out of it. You are at the moment preventing this innocent amusement: will you kindly . . .'

'Mr. Quest, I must get to London . . .'

'Not in my car.'

I retreated across the room, my footsteps echoing on the parquet floor in the middle, muffled by the mat near the door, which I opened, and then closed again as an after-thought, so that Mr. Quest thought I had gone. He had resettled himself in his chair and picked up his pen before I spoke again. 'The trouble is, I can't ask father for the money to go by train, because I don't want to tell him the reason.'

Mr. Quest fairly spun round. 'And to think I used to

believe, in my pacific way,' he said, 'that assaults on young girls by elderly men were necessarily of a sexual nature. Justifiable homicide . . .'

'It'll cost about a pound. Have you got a pound on you?'

'As it happens,' he said, stunned to mildness by my persistence, 'I haven't. Not that I should lend it to you if I had. Lallie, get . . .'

'Well, then, write me a cheque that I can get changed at one of the shops in Ipswich where you have an account.'

'I – I really don't know which they are,' he said.

I rang the bell and the parlour maid told me the name of the Quests' grocer.

'Lallie, is it by any chance with you that Basil is in love, instead of Margaret?' he asked with seeming irrelevance while the servant was coming. He was looking at me as though he had never seen me before. 'Something in his last letter, coupled with that remark about the garage, and your astonishing impertinence . . .'

'Well —'

'Are you going to trade on his infatuation to get yourself comfortably settled for life?'

'That's no business of yours.'

'Yes, it is. I shall undoubtedly have to support him indefinitely as his own brains won't: and also his family. After being bullied in an unprecedented manner I consider it is now my turn. Are you?'

'He isn't really in love with me. He's in love with the whole Rush family. Because it's so much nicer than his own. Anyway, I shan't marry him.'

'Thank God,' said Mr. Quest with simple piety. 'I should greatly dislike having you as a daughter-in-law. Shall I make it two pounds?'

I nodded, and thanked him ungraciously when the servant had gone. ('And get something done about that draught!' he shouted irascibly after her.)

304

'I shan't pay it back, you know,' I said. 'You've been so unpleasant about it, I feel I've earned it.'

To my surprise, as I turned to go at last, Mr. Quest slapped my behind hard, with the utmost friendliness.

With an extra pound in hand I could risk not finding Esther at home when I called. But remembering the day on which her nurse went out for the afternoon, I was lucky the first time, so that with the rest of the money Margaret received a better wedding present than she could have expected from me.

Most of the way up in the train I was rehearsing methods of leading conversation to the point where I could drop in my question, almost unnoticed; but I forgot them all when I was talking to Esther. It seemed unnecessary to pretend anything with her. I asked her directly whether she knew if he had come back to Norwich or not since I last saw her: it was such a long time, and I had not heard from him at all.

Her face became troubled. 'I don't know for certain. Some weeks ago I had a letter posted in England saying that he was going abroad again. It looks as if he had been back. But I didn't notice where the letter came from, and there was no address. There usually isn't; you see, he sometimes writes to me, but I – don't write to him.' (The queer calm that came into my mind then, when I knew that almost certainly he had come and gone again without trying to see me, gave me leisure to wonder idly whether this arrangement, this not writing to him, was a promise made to Macdonald or an agreement with herself alone; but I thought, from the look of her at the moment, that it was not for choice that she had given this undertaking.) 'And of course it's so – dull, writing when you don't get answers, that I can't expect to hear from him often. I wish I could tell you definitely, my dear!'

From the table which she was laying for the elder child's

tea she came over to me suddenly and took my face between her hands, kissing it. 'You're lucky!' she said urgently. 'Remember that, whatever happens. If things don't turn out the way you want, you won't have to look back and know that you lost because you wanted to keep too much – wanted everything at once – didn't know what to give up. You're free. I would like you to get everything you hope for, but if you don't, it won't be your fault, for trying to keep more than you have any right to. That will be something to remember.'

She went out quickly and brought in the children, and we played with them until it was time for me to go, Esther laughing and gay again, telling me undignified stories of the election, which Macdonald had won.

'Oh, Nature! I hate Nature.' Walking home in the early darkness from the cross-roads where the Ipswich bus had left me, I remembered again the peculiar, acid tone of Mrs. Mawley's voice. I could understand that now. The stars were out, brilliantly clear above the ground-mist rising from the warming earth, and the soft air felt alive and troubled with the first stirring of spring. Small things, newly awakened, rustled in ditches and bushes as I passed. When the winter breaks, the country is a bad place in which to be unhappy.

It was not only Nature that I could have hated sometimes, in those days, but Margaret. Seeing her with Sandy became a bitterness to be avoided whenever possible.

CHAPTER XV

THE FAMILY'S CANDIDATE

'Did Basil find you? I told him where I thought you'd be!' said mother when I came in from the marshes, where I had been lying flat for hours, ignoring the wetness of the ground, in order not to be observed myself while observing. Father, in the midst of the spring fit-out, his busiest selling season, grumbled that Basil was the only person who gave him a hand nowadays. 'Damned nice chap. And the muscle on him! – Oh, Lallie, he asked me to tell you he'd be round this afternoon. I said you'd be painting *Seamew* on the Hard.'

'Oh, all right.' I could have snapped at them both.

This was the day before Margaret's wedding. Everything had been done: idleness hung heavily on us all after days of bustle. I had volunteered to do the hull of one of the boats in order to fill in unoccupied hours, in which otherwise I should think rancorously of Margaret, who would soon be out of my life now – Margaret who seemed to have everything that she desired. I did not want leisure in which to envy her with the resentment that had been growing in me. Why should she have everything? When she had gone I should be able to bear her good fortune in a less mean spirit.

Now I was sorry that I had offered to do this painting job. There would be no getting rid of Basil all the afternoon on the Hard. Still, he would be just as much of a bore wherever I was; the marshes palled when one dared not stand up on their clear, flat expanses for fear of that cheerful hallooing in the distance. Now that he was down from Cambridge, Mr. Quest's garden, safe refuge from most things that I wanted to avoid, had become worse than useless as a hiding-place. Basil was at his most argumentative in gardens, where there were places to sit, and I could be pinned down by politeness and forced to listen. Painting a hull, I could at least move about when my mental agility failed. I was tired out physically and mentally; I did not even know whether I should be glad or sorry when the wedding was over. After it, time would stretch out unmarked by any event on which I could fix my mind, telling myself that it was to this I was looking forward, even though I knew, really, that it was not, and I still waited hopelessly for something which would not happen now: Gordon had returned from Spain weeks ago, and had gone again: he had not come. He had not come: I must remember that, with my heart as well as my brain. After Margaret had gone, time would drag on with no purpose in view for me save the dreary one of its own passing, which must surely make things better at last, though it did not seem to have helped much in these six months.

Basil was more persistent than usual that day, perhaps unconsciously fortified by the friendliness of my people, who had been awakened – rather late, in the manner of English families – to the advantage of moneyed alliances for their daughters by the generosity of the Reddiland family. Two of father's bigger boats had already been sold this season through introductions from Sandy's uncle.

It was a pity that they had not thought Basil's fancy for Dru worthy of anything more than a laboured joke; it was almost more of a pity, I thought unfairly, being biased by a headache towards self-condolence, that he was now accepted so obviously as the family's candidate for me. Mother had asked me to bring him in to a late tea when it grew too dark to go on painting.

'. . . Because if a fellow's got the least respect for a girl – a fellow that isn't a complete swine, that is . . . .'

Ted Mawley went by and grinned at us with mistaken sympathy.

'. . . Regards it as something pretty sacred. I mean, quite different from any other affairs he may have had. . . . '

I was suddenly nauseated by the nobility of Basil's sentiments, at variance with his natural human behaviour, the more so because I realized that Basil had persuaded himself of the honesty of these sentiments. He would not consider respectable his desire to have a healthy female of his own age unless it were swathed in coverings of pretence. As neither of us would be twenty-one till June, and he was still entirely dependent on Mr. Quest, he felt that a formal engagement need not be discussed just yet, but meanwhile . . .

'You see, it isn't as if we didn't feel rather differently about each other from the way we feel about everyone else.'

When had I allowed this to be assumed, I wondered wearily? But no doubt I had, in an attempt to hold off without violence some other advance. The dizzy drop over the precipice, on to the wounding rocks of truth, was imminent now.

'Oughtn't you to put on the anti-fouling a bit thicker?'

Probably I was slapping it about carelessly, scamping some places: throbbing over one eye was the kind of ache which makes one keep one's eyebrows up till the skin on the forehead feels stiff in its creases, to lift the dull weight of the pain off the eye itself – the usual form taken by my rare but awful headaches. The sun reflected brightly from the wet mud-flats on either side of the Hard, making it worse; it was a wasted day, glorious with spring.

'Look here, considering that I've put on a great deal more anti-fouling in my life than you have! Gallons more. Quarts more.'

'Oh Lallie, aren't you a darling ass when you get huffy,' he said indulgently, sounding like Stella. 'Quarts aren't bigger than gallons. Afraid that rather spoils the ticking-off! Never mind, stop work a second.'

He manœuvred me into the corner between the rudder and the hull, where there was a painting trestle to sit on. His voice went droning on: 'Always thought it was so marvellous of you to think . . . And then you know you said . . . Only I don't see why, if you feel that . . . Fellow who didn't look up to women generally would be pretty low . . . Girl who really trusted a man . . . That is, if he wasn't . . . .'

I could not edge farther along the hull, as I seemed to have been doing nervously all the afternoon: he was blocking the way of escape with his body, lavishly displayed in shorts and loose shirt. I resented the excellence of it because it was not the one I wanted. He stood propped against the boat; under his outstretched arm I saw, as a tiny dot on the farther shore, a man on the broken landing-stage where I had taken off Gordon. It was not Gordon. It should have been. For a long while I strained hurting eyes over the bright water until I was sure that the lovely improbability had not happened; and then Basil's voice came to me as though it had been moo-ing on for hours: 'What would you say if I told you that you'd made me think better of all women, somehow?'

I told him in the only adequate word. 'And now,' I said, 'I'm going in.'

'Lallie!'

'Well, you asked me. Move.'

'You don't understand what you said.'

'Oh yes, I do. I was afraid you wouldn't. Talking too much to take it in.'

'In that case,' said Basil with dignity, 'there is no more to be said.' If he had laughed, or threatened to rub my nose in the anti-fouling, I might just possibly have given in to him that day; I was so tired of waiting for nothing, and it would have seemed so unimportant.

As it was, feeling silly, both of us walked up the Hard trying to ignore one another. Our old cat flashed across the top of the Hard, pursued by the Cottrells' fat dog. The chase, almost a daily occurrence, ended in the way in which it always ended, convulsing Basil and me with laughter whenever we saw it happen. The cat stopped suddenly, prepared to give battle, and the dog, unable to check itself, jumped over the crouching beast, as high as possible, and rushed on, barking vaguely into the air in an effort to persuade the onlookers that it had not been made ridiculous, but was enjoying a friendly race with the cat, which the cat had unsportingly abandoned.

I stole a look at Basil: not a muscle moved, so that I too preserved whatever dignity I had, and at Margaret's wedding the next day we bowed to one another with extreme stiffness.

CHAPTER XVI

NIGHT SAILING

THE sight of Basil's face was the one thing which helped me through the wedding. I kept telling myself how funny it looked . . . stuffed owl . . . funny . . . very funny. He was one of the ushers, and as a bridesmaid, sent on ahead of Margaret to the church in a last-minute panic, I had heartening glimpses of him, bending with splendid solemnity over people whom he knew quite well, asking whether they were friends of the bride or bridegroom. A little while ago I should have been disturbed at having hurt him; but being in love is a hardening process: I was merely glad of something ludicrous on which to fix my thoughts: I must remember how funny he looked when Margaret arrived, glorious in her wedding dress.

I had not foreseen the overwhelming emotion which came to me in the church: I could not even tell of what it was compounded: savage jealousy, yes; but of Margaret, because she was fortunate, or of Sandy, because he would have for himself this loveliness which had been a bewilderment and joy and exasperation to me from childhood? And sorrow for losing Margaret; and awe before familiar beauty made manifest anew: and the relief of finding a conventional outlet for my own distress, which had nothing to do with Margaret: all these, probably, were in my feeling for her; human relationships are too complex to be known in full. I was aware only that I could hardly bear to look at her, radiant in white, lovelier than I could remember seeing her before, save perhaps in that one moment which had remained stamped in my memory: when as a child she stood under the lamp in *Guadalupe's* rigging, with her wild dark hair blown away from her wet face, staring unafraid at the onrushing steamer. That recollection of her came back to me with others, many of them like chance-found photographs of unimportant occasions, more moving because they had been long forgotten.

Basil's solemnity over his duties – I must keep my mind on that. It was absurd to be so deeply stirred when Margaret herself remained cool and sensible. While we were waiting for her in the porch she called Dru and me across to the car to borrow two shilling pieces ('or halfpennies will do,' she said, giggling, 'I shan't be able to give them back!') because the white satin garters were too slack for her slim legs; and kneeling on either side of her to keep out the stares of the crowd we twisted the coins into the tops of her stockings with insincere hilarity, making a roll that would hold over the knee.

It was about seven when we got back from the reception: mother, much too bright to seem natural, had insisted on staying on, after the departure of Margaret and Sandy, until almost all the guests had gone. She must have shrunk from the thought of seeing our house empty of Margaret's things at last, and littered with the refuse of packing.

The effects of the champagne had worn off: the feeling of idleness and depression on the day before the wedding was nothing to the reaction which followed immediately after it. Before we reached the house father had a characteristic inspiration. 'Come on. We'll all go night fishing. Sootie left his trawl in *Sesame*. There's plenty of our sailing kit spread about the boats. We'll collect it and change on board.'

'Oh, I say, this is my number one shore suit!' protested Ronald, who had managed to get forty-eight hours leave from Chatham.

313

'Well, this is the only top-hat I've ever had, or mean to have,' said father, and we scattered among the yachts, standing in the rocking dinghies in our wedding finery, sculling gingerly to avoid sitting down, in a boat-to-boat search for old sweaters and skirts and trousers. Dru, as was to be expected of her, damaged her filmy dress in climbing aboard; but the evening and the first part of the night were amusing, instead of turning into a wallow of ill-suppressed sentiment at home. We had good luck with the trawl, and had a huge feed at midnight, off the Naze, of new-caught dabs, which are marvellous boiled at once in salt-water, but become utterly tasteless if cooked that way even a few hours later.

We had to reef as soon as we were out of the shelter of Harwich breakwater, because mother would not risk heavy water on the unsound deck, lest it should seep through a 'crawled' seam and get at the lockers where our best clothes were stowed, wrapped up in spare jibs. For a moment a passage of arms between father and Ronald seemed certain: all our shortening sail had to be done in the laborious old-fashioned way, because no patent roller-reefing-gear was ever allowed in father's boats: he grew almost incoherent with disgust at any suggestion of its utility. 'Not seamanlike . . . don't see fishermen using it . . . Good Lord, they know, don't they? Gear gives way . . . breaks the boom in a real blow – lets you down properly. Serves you damn-well right for laziness . . .' As most of his boats were recklessly over-canvassed, an unexpected blow was liable to dismast them, so that roller-reefing would have made no difference beyond saving us a good deal of sweat and bother. Ronald ventured to point this out, at last, and mother and Dru and I waited apprehensively for the outburst. But father said disarmingly that perhaps he was a bit of a crank about sailing-boats; still, his experience of them was slightly more variegated than that of a sub-lieutenant in a destroyer, and then lapsed into a pained and puzzled silence, looking as though Ronald had attempted to stab him in the back.

'By the way, I forgot, swain of yours rang up when you'd gone on to the church,' he said, talking to me to break the ponderous silence. 'Dammit, as soon as one's children can blow their own noses they start collecting followers! He'll be round to-morrow afternoon, if you'll be in. I told him I thought so. Said to tell you he was sorry about something: I didn't hear; Margaret and Dru were bullying me about the time.'

'Oh, no,' I said in dismay, 'I'm going to be out.' Really, if Basil were intending to apologize to me for my having been rude to him, as I guessed, I should have gained nothing by hurting his feelings.

The others turned drowsy round about three o'clock, fishing became a bore, and as the wind failed towards dawn we hove-to, waiting for the tide to take us up-river.

Unable to sleep, I sat listening to the voices in the rigging, which cannot often be heard by day. They come only in calms, from the direction of the mast – sounds like the soft murmur of several human voices talking, a few short sentences at a time, not whispering, but as if they spoke in a natural tone a very long way away. Holding my breath, I have almost caught words when sailing single-handed, several miles from shore and out of sight of any other boat. I do not know if these sound-mirages can be explained by the faint creaking of the leather on the gaff-jaws, inaudible at other times, or are the magnification, through the hollow sounding-box of the hull, of the noise of currents moving against the keel, but air-borne or water-borne, they creep through the boat, bringing with them a sense of companionship. When I was particularly lonely they were comforting to me. Gordon's voice . . .

'Father! It was Basil on the phone, I suppose? Father!'

'Er?' He could be practically half-asleep and remain efficient at the tiller.

'On the phone to-day. Basil, was it?'

'No. Try and remember there are other people in the world!' Father was approvingly facetious. 'That other fellow. Forgotten his name. Came over once or twice last summer. Archæologist, with rather odd views. You remember.'

'Yes. I remember.'

2

'It's good to see you.'

'It's lovely to see you, Gordon.'

'Shall we go over to Levington? Cross to that shore, anyway. That was a gorgeous wood . . . I only had twenty-four hours in England, between Spain and Germany, instead of ten days as I expected. So I couldn't get over to see you . . . Oxford, with the official report . . . Sorry . . .'

It was so simple, in explanation: it had been so heart-breaking in fact. I had thought of the possibility of his time being limited, and rejected it, because it was comforting and I was in love.

'Doesn't matter.' What did matter now, except that his voice, which I had tried in vain to remember, sounded like this, and there were innumerable small things about him which I had not even known that I had forgotten? I talked fast and inconsequentially of everything that occurred to me, otherwise I could not have kept sober in the heady air of enchantment that had come back to the river and hills and woods. Gordon said, 'Lallie, you've altered somehow?'

He was right, I knew. In love one grows not only harder but older very quickly in some ways. For so many months, now, I had watched Margaret, noting, remembering her ways, her looks, everything that she did or said: not in order to copy her, exactly, since this was impossible for me, but to understand that manner of hers, which told people so much. On so many occasions, too, I had been forced to use speech as a defence, a disguise for my thoughts: these things must have affected me. Probably I was not more like Margaret, but I was changed from the Lallie he had known in the autumn.

Later, he said: 'As a matter of strict truth I wasn't altogether sorry that I couldn't come and see you two months ago. I was rather uncertain about a lot of things in my own mind, then. Last time we talked, I may have sounded like Galahad, but I was feeling much nearer Lancelot in his Guinevere moments – "Oh, to hell with my shining knighthood, here's something worth while." I had an idea that I mightn't cut quite so fine a figure in my own eyes after another meeting. In fact I knew I shouldn't, so I felt rather pleased with myself for not being able to manage it. Splendid fellow, I thought, starting for Germany. Of all the bloody fools, I said on the boat, but then it was too late to turn back, and take another day in England, as I probably could have done with a certain amount of trouble. Now, well, various things have sorted themselves out in my mind. I feel a lot less ponderous altogether. If a donkey wanders down a dull path bordered with delectable fields, ought he to keep a mild eye from lifting over the nicest gates because of what happened when he tried to kick down the first locked one? Just the sort of thing that only a donkey would do. Why on earth should I have assumed that my ineffable worth and charm . . .!'

He kissed me, not lightly and absurdly as in the garden, and enchantment no longer hung about us, impalpable, waiting: enchantment was made tangible, came royally into instant possession of everything that it had only

317

enhanced before: the texture of his skin, feeling rougher than mine when I moved my cheek against his: his hair, that I had so much wanted to have under my hands: his mouth, different from my imagining of it in desired kisses; harder, more contenting. Enchantment was no longer a quality added to these things, it was the stuff of these things. I touched nothing else.

Surprised, 'You've grown up in these six months,' he said, 'or were you always deceptive-looking? Anyhow, it's a pity donkeys can't kick themselves – no, you *have* changed in some way.' He leant against one of the trees, linking his hands behind me, so that partly resting against him I had to lean back to be able to see his face.

'Yes,' I said, steadying my voice to casualness, 'after all, six months . . .'

'And some men aren't such fools as others? Is that it? I should have foreseen that, I suppose.'

He looked away, frowning, and in a little while I grew afraid, more frightened physically than I had ever been.

'Well, why should you mind, Gordon? As long as it isn't your responsibility – you more or less said that yourself.'

He let go of me, and moved away a few steps, to pick up the old raincoat that he had thrown on the ground, and felt slowly through the pockets, without thinking, for the cigarettes whose absence we had already discovered. Coming back to me, he smiled at this forgetfulness.

'Listen, Lallie. Be kind. Remember you're with a man who's already broken one resolve about you – a damned silly one, but that's nothing to do with it – and if you remind me of what I said, naturally you make me want to break the only one I have left – not to let myself go entirely when making love to you. So be kind.'

'All right,' I said, 'just as you like.'

His face flushed at my tone, became less friendly. 'Do you mean – You can't. My dear, I've no business to be jealous

318

about this, but with you I am, stupid as it seems. – How much has any man had from you?'

'Six months is a long time . . .'

'Tell me! Is there any one? More than one? Are you like Margaret?'

'Yes.'

He laughed, with the wryness of his laughter at himself in the garden. 'Lord, what a fool you must have thought me. Were you laughing at me all the time? Are you now?'

Presently I was in his arms, that were no longer gentle, and he was bending over me, and the wood changed as trees change at night, and became dark with fear, outside my closed eyelids.

Inevitably, rough because he believed me, he hurt me badly. Expecting it, still I could not bear the searing pain without showing it. Afterwards, crying helplessly in his arms, I saw his face looking grave and, I thought, angry.

'Lallie, why did you lie to me like that?'

I could not answer at the moment.

He did not say anything for a while. 'My dear, is it possible – Lallie, do you love me?'

There did not seem any use in lying now. I kissed the fingers that stroked my face, and tried after a time to tell him what the last months had meant to me.

'Will you marry me? Not because of what's happened but because of a hundred other things. Because I think we might be happy together: and I would like to marry you. Will you?'

'I expect so,' I said. 'To-morrow I know I'll be wild to. Only just at present I'm not feeling very enthusiastic about anything.'

He found my handkerchief for me, and we sat for a long while on a fallen tree, with an arm round each other, not talking much, and presently all the birds in the wood began to sing, one by one. They sang enormously, and the

319

wind became a perfectly marvellous wind, and the sun shone so that the motes dancing in its rays were particularly excellent motes.

'Oh, sweetheart,' he said, 'I've just realized that this is the loveliest thing that has ever happened to me. I'm sorry you can't feel that too just yet.'

He decided for me gaily that eventually I should become bored by his love-making, which seemed to me at the moment the most blissful physical state to which I could reasonably look forward.

We wandered down the hill eventually, in the late evening, drunk with new happiness, having indifferently watched two lanterns moving about the shore below us for some while before we realized that they must be carried by my father and Sootie, come over to see if any accident had happened to the dinghy.

'I was just beginning to wonder,' said Gordon, before starting off to pacify my aggrieved parent, 'whether I could decently mention that I was hungry.'

CHAPTER XVII

THE THIRD TIME

WE were married early in the summer, after an engagement almost as brief as Margaret's, because Gordon grew resentful of the slight ill-feeling which he sensed among my people and wanted to get me away for both our sakes. They had set their hopes on Basil Quest and, with the exception of Ronald, did not much like Gordon. That barrage incident rankled unconsciously with father: and even when he might have forgotten it, Gordon managed by ill-luck to stumble against more of what Lester called the rococo flying-buttresses of the baroque mind: then there were sparks.

Trained by the Reddilands to expect punctiliousness in marriage matters, father wrote to Gordon when we had been engaged about six weeks, requesting with almost insulting politeness, 'an hour of your time, very fully occupied just now no doubt, in which to discuss the monetary position.' Gordon was working hard at Durham, and could only dash over for half a day at week-ends. 'How on earth,' he wrote to me in cheerful irritation, 'does he expect me to spin out for an hour the statement that I have three hundred a year, on which I intend to keep his daughter in extreme squalor? Especially as all your people know that already, judging from their attitude.'

However, out of consideration for me, he managed a thoroughly submissive talk, which father appreciated; and by this means got his own way: we were married the next week at nine in the morning, in the Ipswich Registrar's office: a wedding as different from Margaret's as could be imagined. To neither of us was the ceremony in itself of any importance: we had been happy lovers now for some time: all that we wanted was to get away from the restrictions of not being married, the pretence and separation it entailed. Being together had become more and more satisfactory after the first torment of physical excitement was over. The actual procedure at the registrar's seemed like a trifling intrusion of other people's interests into an enthralling personal conversation which he and I had been enjoying before, and would enjoy even more when there were no interruptions.

'The promised squalor starts immediately,' said Gordon as we came out of the office. 'Will you slip across to a grocer's and get half a pound of coarse oatmeal while I strap the luggage on the car? I had a minor smash, skidding on my way here this morning, and there's a leak in the radiator. We'll fill it with a layer of porridge. I've done that before in emergencies: it works quite well. The best use for porridge. At least it'll get us away.'

There was, I suppose, a certain amount of squalor in our first year and a half, spent in a variety of lodgings; anything to be near his work. A miner's cottage in Wales, where I did part of the cooking; two farmhouses, which I particularly liked; a barn, once, while the weather was fine; a crofter's lodge in which we had unexpectedly to act as an armed picket in an outbreak of sheep-maiming, and then two months in the house of a rich American who bullied his angry gardeners, generously placed at Gordon's disposal, into digging trenches across part of a marvellous old lawn in the hope of finding something that might keep us there longer. We had a feeling that he would be quite capable of salting the ground with prehistoric pottery, in the manner of the famous Glozel frauds, in order to ensure our company, and practically stole away from his kindness by night in the end, to spend some while camping out in the car, in acute discomfort. The only room available within a mile of the new diggings was one which we should have had to share at night with two small children: Gordon and I were not going to be driven, by the lack of privacy, into making love out of doors by day; we had had enough of this during the engagement. Idyllic possibly for the man, it is comparatively unsatisfactory for all but the most determinedly romantic woman; insects, fir-cones, hummocks in the ground being always discovered too late; so we made do to sleep in the Morris by turning round the front seats and filling the hole between them and the back seat with suit-cases. (We grew scrubbier-looking daily because washing and shaving required so much organization. Mother and Dru took the opportunity of our being in the next county to drive over in Lester Cottrell's car, and went home again feeling still more certain, we feared, that I had thrown myself away.)

But life in the hard-up Rush household had been only just above the line between respectability and squalor; I did not mind crossing over at times. I liked cooking odd meals over primus stoves, at which I had become expert in father's boats, and not bothering at all about clothes; and even if I had not, Gordon's companionship would have made these things tremendously worth while. It was as if, in these days, we went on indefinitely with that communion, that old conversation, partly of the senses, partly of the spirit, which we had started the day that enchantment first blew through the wood on the Levington shore, on a wind laden with bees and sun-motes. I did not reach the state of indifference that he had promised me, in which I was to be only bored by his love-making; he had been extraordinarily forbearing and kind to me in the early days, when the distaste and pain, and the shock of hating his possession of me, were still fresh in my memory: a month or more passed before suddenly, overwhelmingly, I had pleasure from it, and cried again in his arms. And now there was so much glory in the world when we made love to each other that I could not say what part of this joy was the body's alone, and what was the mind's. Sometimes the senses answering, sometimes the spirit: only for him, certainly the body more than the mind. He was utterly satisfying to me in every way, but I knew that I held chiefly his physical allegiance. Great affection there was between us, and sometimes more than that, but there were reservations, and I knew them, and did not grieve overmuch, as a rule, about what I could not have; for already I had so much. He liked me as a companion and was passionately attracted to me as a woman. To be often sad, because there were flaws in the excellence of love, would have seemed as absurd to me, now, as to discount all the riches of high summer in the old days at home because of those late broods of swallows and martins that could never reach maturity. We were immensely happy.

I was certain that he would not say now, as he had once during the engagement, 'You know how little I have to give,' because of unforgettable moments which we had shared; moments that left me for ever in his debt in a way, since he could make joy more complete for me than I could ever do for him – lovely moments of tenderness; of good talk so free, for once, of the difficulty of crossing the gap of individuality that it was as if our minds had fused; of jolly downright vulgarity, sometimes, when we were both in a robust mood, though that mood could turn very easily to tenderness; and (for me alone, perhaps, since I think that this is peculiar to the woman) moments of intensest fondness immediately after physical satisfaction, when I was grateful to him for having so much pleasure from me; and moments of excitement and elation and disappointment connected with his work; moments when the shadow between us, my knowledge that I was not really the woman his heart wanted, whatever his senses said, lifted entirely, and the grand feeling of recent creation came back to the world.

For my sake, though I was well content to have no settled

home, he put in for a better-paid lecturing job that would keep us in London, and gave up field archæology in the second year of marriage.

We took a mews flat in Pimlico, consisting of three rooms so remarkably small that we could not get, into the sitting-room, a table large enough to accommodate more than two extra people with any kind of comfort: but by shutting it up and carrying it into the bedroom we managed, on occasions, to squeeze in a fair number of friends after dinner for coffee, and gave parties much nicer than I had ever imagined any social gathering could be. Gordon had delightful friends, odd dons, and other archæologists, and people with the initiative to do unexpected things, from a girl journalist secretly paid by several film firms to write disparaging articles about their most expensive stars, in order to keep down salaries, to a research man who prolonged the life of three flatworms for eleven times the normal span by amputating selected portions at intervals, and wore the air of a bereaved lover when he told us at last that they had died, through the carelessness of his assistant. Mr. Quest came once or twice, bringing, unexplained, a dignified grey-haired woman with traces of considerable beauty in her face, whom he introduced briefly as Ann, and seemed to have known for a great number of years.

But more often than anyone else, after the first six months of London life, we had Esther Macdonald coming in for an hour or so in the evening, because her town house was full of dreary people whom she was expected to entertain and longed to escape. She was asked first of all on my suggestion, in one of the hours – rare as they were, they were devastating when they came – in which I could no longer feel resigned to being Gordon's lover and chosen companion, not his beloved. It seemed to me that it would be easier to bear seeing them together as they were now, two mature people whose lives had diverged, giving to each interests which the other could not share, than to be conscious of her with the wretchedness of my present mood, as someone enshrined for ever by him in a past beyond my reach.

'After all, Gordon, you've been married some time,' I said, 'and people know that we get on awfully well together. Whatever Macdonald knows, and you aren't sure that he knows anything, I don't see that he can very much mind her coming to see us both, nowadays. If I ask her. Shall I?'

'Oh, Lallie! Darling—' he put his arms round me, and soon the hold changed to a caress – my small triumph, and Time's, over Esther and all human love denied, I thought at that instant. But I knew, later, when I saw her in the rooms I shared intimately with Gordon, that I was powerless against her; there could be no triumph; anything that I had not won already I could never win; I was so much the better-looking, and Gordon was aware of this, and it made no difference at all to his feeling for her; why should it, when that feeling had always been of the mind more than of the body? I had not thought before of her looks and mine, compared feature by feature like this: the bitterest minute of that day's unhappiness was reached with the realization that when I won on my own ground, the victory was un-important, and I could not meet her on hers. I was like the knight in an old nursery story, who saw his sword, his only weapon, turning to dust in his hands, useless against a magic greater than his strength.

But I had been right: it was better for me in this mood to see them together, people of to-day, for whom the old agonies had passed and only the ache of memory remained. Gordon was happy in the reunion, answering Esther's invincible, absurd gaiety with his own, and presently the grey cloud lifted from me. It was a good evening after all. Two other friends came in, and she had on them, and on me, her peculiar effect of lifting people to her own level of intelligence for the time being; even drawing me out, though I was not good in conversation as a rule, to make a really funny story of my imaginative bird letters in the newspapers and their successful effect on my family. (Since getting engaged to Gordon I had not written any more, though they had been appearing with increasing frequency up to that day – another reason for the Rush feeling that I had wasted myself. My help in Gordon's lectures, being obscure to the public, was not considered a good enough use for my journalistic talents.)

When the other couple said good night, long after Esther had hurried off regretfully to a formal late reception, Gordon and I stood at the top of our stairs, listening to their feet clattering down flight after flight into silence. He reached out for my hand, shutting the door on the outer darkness: 'They go, and we stay; isn't that perfect!' and that particular evening, it did seem so. But not always. On some evenings, when Gordon was busy preparing lectures for which I had already given all the help I could, Esther came in to talk to me only, knowing that I should be at a loose end. Usually I was glad, liking her more and more, and knowing, too, that she was genuinely fond of me: but there were times when, if Gordon were finding concentration difficult, we would sit silent together for a long while, reading, and these were the moments in which, if I were unlucky, the dark cloud of which I was ashamed, because jealousy is so mean an emotion, would very occasionally creep back into my mind. Hers was not a disturbing presence, vital though she was; Gordon got into the habit of working comfortably while she was with us, liking her to be there, not only for the prospect of amusing talk when he should have finished his notes, but because of some pleasant feeling that her nearness gave him in these days, now that the fret and distress of the past had ebbed, like a spent tide, into some remote part of his mind where only dreams and recollections remained, and he was as secure from its old surging strength as anyone can be from the recurring floods of memory.

I knew, in bad hours, a subtle, dreary jealousy of the silence that stretched on between them if I went out for a few minutes on some household job. It would not be broken: nothing would alter save that it would become in some strange way, I felt, a better silence because of my absence. But the nights gave back to me the warm, living assurance of his body sleeping by me in the darkness, dear flesh that would turn friendlily to me on waking; and then nothing mattered; there could be no jealousy left in me, save of the kind that we both knew and laughed at together – light-hearted resentment of any slightest scar on the other person's body, of which the bearer could remember no cause. It seemed to each of us preposterous, in moods when the spirit was only an attendant on the flesh, that this adored beautiful thing, this shared temple to no god, the other lover's body, should have suffered any experience that could mark it permanently, even in a trivial way, which must remain its own secret for ever. A small cut by the corner of his mouth I loved and would not have wished away; it was so intimately part of his face when I recalled his appearance, detail by detail, during brief absences, and he could tell me exactly the circumstances of its getting; but for a much bigger one on his forearm he could not account, though it must have been painful enough to take all his attention at some moment in his life, and this long pucker in the brown skin I used to hurt a little when I could, to punish it for holding a secret from me, pinching or biting it, or scratching at it gently, to his amusement and occasional violent protest. I had no griefs that could live until the morning.

A week seemed to me, in prospect, a long time to give up to other people when mother wrote in great excitement that Margaret was coming home in a month's time, and hoped that I would meet her at Southampton: if I took the car I

328

could drive her straight to Pin Mill, staying there with the family for that period. But Gordon had been putting off for months an essential visit to Oxford, where he would stay in college and I could not be with him; when the time came our absences fitted well.

I had not seen Margaret since her wedding. Sandy had come home on a business trip once in the hot weather, but she had been having too good a time in the hills to accompany him; she lived a strange life, for a girl brought up in the needy Rush household, as a society beauty with everything that money could give her. Once, a year ago, there had been some scandal, connected not with her but with Sandy, of which rumours had come to us; but it had been hushed up. Her letters were like herself, they told nothing that anyone really wanted to know; not even conveying whether she was happy or not.

Waiting for her on the quay I had a curious moment of panic, lest she should not be as lovely as I remembered, for then something would have gone out of my life. But she took my breath away when she appeared. She was twenty-two now: India and those two and a half years had given her between them a finish, a completeness both in looks and manner that made me almost shy with her for the first few days in Pin Mill; she seemed too brilliant a creature to be treated familiarly.

I was a little dazed by her. Dru was too, though with her this embarrassment found an outlet in slangier, louder talk than usual, and mild back-slapping.

Wanting to be happy among so many acquaintances of childhood, I would not let myself think of what Dru's life must be like when there was no special excitement, like this family gathering, to enliven it; she protested often, though no one said anything to the contrary, that there was never time for all that she wanted to do. Nothing had changed for her in these last years: her days were still given to boats and tennis and small local activities ('Mother, where've you put those rose-cuttings for Mrs. Chater? Well, why did you move them? I wish you'd leave my things alone!') but there was beginning to be a certain forced heartiness about her; and she bickered much more often with mother.

It was fun to talk again to Ted, married now to a Harwich girl (had he ever seen again his first love, who was so like Margaret, I wondered), and to the elder Mawleys and the Cottrells. Mrs. Cottrell seemed as perfect as ever in her long-sustained role of utterly devoted wife and mother: seeing her, and knowing how she had once struggled to get away, I felt again, with slight personal distress at the thought of Gordon, my childish resentment at the discovery that one could never really know people. Was she contented, now that dreams were dead? Was he?

I was more excited at the thought of seeing him again, after a week's separation, than I had been by the anticipation of meeting Margaret. She came up to London with me for shopping when I left Pin Mill, accepting my invitation to stay for a day or two.

As I hoped, he was in when we arrived, having got back from Oxford an hour earlier in order to be there to welcome me. We were still unable to kiss before a third person.

He greeted Margaret friendlily. I was conscious of the difference between us, I, tired and dishevelled after the long drive in the shaky little car, and she radiant, and with that fine, hard, new polish about her which made even her present untidiness seem too perfect to be uncalculated – but he did not appear to be. 'Lord, what a beautiful family I've married!' he said. 'Staggering when one sees it in bulk,' and fussed over getting us both some tea.

I went into the bedroom to take off my things.

They had not moved when I came back. Margaret was in our worn armchair, and he was bending over the gas-ring by the fire, but they were tense and still – unnaturally stilled for me by the sudden stopping of Time as I stood in the doorway – and looking at one another with the expression I knew, having seen it once before.

Even this she must have, in all but fact at least. Even this. Gordon was fond of me: actually nothing would happen. For me, Time would start again, sooner or later, would fling tortured seconds into the gulf that had opened in it once more, would flow on and obliterate it at last. One day I should find that I could not remember just how they had looked. Only a tie of allegiance had broken. Even this she must have: all I really had. Even this.

Time. Time was starting now slowly, agonizingly, gathering way. Time, flow on.

VIRAGO MODERN CLASSICS

The first Virago Modern Classic, *Frost in May* by Antonia White, was published in 1978. It launched a list dedicated to the celebration of women writers and to the rediscovery and reprinting of their works. Its aim was, and is, to demonstrate the existence of a female tradition in fiction which is both enriching and enjoyable. The Leavisite notion of the 'Great Tradition', and the narrow, academic definition of a 'classic', has meant the neglect of a large number of interesting secondary works of fiction. In calling the series 'Modern Classics' we do not necessarily mean 'great' — although this is often the case. Published with new critical and biographical introductions, books are chosen for many reasons: sometimes for their importance in literary history; sometimes because they illuminate particular aspects of womens' lives, both personal and public. They may be classics of comedy or storytelling; their interest can be historical, feminist, political or literary.

Initially the Virago Modern Classics concentrated on English novels and short stories published in the early decades of this century. As the series has grown it has broadened to include works of fiction from different centuries, different countries, cultures and literary traditions. In 1984 the Victorian Classics were launched; there are separate lists of Irish, Scottish, European, American, Australian and other English speaking countries; there are books written by Black women, by Catholic and Jewish women, and a few relevant novels by men. There is, too, a companion series of Non-Fiction Classics constituting biography, autobiography, travel, journalism, essays, poetry, letters and diaries.

By the end of 1986 over 250 titles will have been published in these two series, many of which have been suggested by our readers.